TALES, POEMS, AND OTHER WRITINGS

HERMAN MELVILLE

TALES, POEMS, AND OTHER WRITINGS

Edited, with an Introduction and Notes,

by John Bryant

THE MODERN LIBRARY

NEW YORK

2001 Modern Library Edition
Introduction, notes, and fluid text editions of *Typee,* "Camoëns," "Art,"
and "Ur–*Billy Budd*" copyright 2001 by John Bryant

LIBRARY OF CONGRESS CATALOGING-IN-PUBLICATION DATA

Melville, Herman, 1819-1891.
[Selections. 2001]
Tales, poems, and other writings / Herman Melville ; edited,
with an introduction and notes by John Bryant.— 1st ed.
p.   cm.
ISBN 0-679-64105-X (alk. paper)
I. Bryant, John, 1949- II. Title.

PS2382 .B79 2001
813'.3--dc21   2001031580

Modern Library website address: www.modernlibrary.com

Printed in the United States of America on acid-free paper

2 4 6 8 9 7 5 3 1

HERMAN MELVILLE

Herman Melville was born on August 1, 1819, in New York City; his father was a prosperous importer, his mother the daughter of Peter Gansevoort, a military hero of the American Revolution. Bankruptcy forced the family to relocate to Albany, and in 1831, when Melville was twelve, his father died. The young man worked successively as a bank clerk, farmer, and bookkeeper before trying his hand as a teacher in Pitts-field, Massachusetts. In 1839 he signed as a crew member on the trading ship *St. Lawrence,* sailing to Liverpool and back. Soon after his return he toured the Midwest, and in 1841 set sail for the South Pacific aboard the whaling ship *Acushnet.*

In the Marquesas, Melville jumped ship and spent a month in the Taipi valley on the island of Nuku Hiva. Brought to Tahiti by an Aus-tralian whaler, Melville was taken ashore as a mutineer but escaped. In Honolulu, he enlisted in the U.S. Navy and sailed on the frigate *United States* to Boston, where he was discharged in 1844. Back home he quickly transformed his Pacific adventures into several somewhat fictionalized travel books. *Typee* (1846) became an instant success, and was immedi-ately followed by *Omoo.* In 1847 Melville married Elizabeth Shaw, the daughter of the Massachusetts Chief Justice. They moved to Manhattan, where Melville wrote *Mardi* (1849), *Redburn* (1849), and *White-Jacket* (1850). Invigorated by a trip to England and the Continent, he began

Moby-Dick. During this time, he and his growing family moved to Arrowhead, a farm in Pittsfield, where he met Nathaniel Hawthorne whose friendship and conversation inspired Melville as he completed his masterpiece, *Moby-Dick* (1851), which received only mixed reviews.

Melville's next novel, *Pierre* (1852), fared even worse. Seeking the steady cash of magazine writing, he turned out over a dozen tales and sketches, including such classics as "Bartleby" and "Benito Cereno," both of which appeared in his collection *The Piazza Tales* (1856). At this time Melville also published his Revolutionary War novel *Israel Potter* (1855) and the dark comedy *The Confidence-Man* (1857). Mentally exhausted, he embarked on a tour of the Mediterranean and the Holy Land financed by his father-in-law. The journey supplied Melville with numerous inspirations for future writing. Upon his return to America he lectured for three years and turned almost exclusively to poetry; however, in 1860, his first collection of poems failed to attract a publisher.

During the Civil War, Melville returned to New York City where, in 1866, he published a series of war poems entitled *Battle-Pieces and Aspects of the War*. That same year, he received an appointment as deputy inspector of customs at the port of New York, a job he was to hold for the next twenty years. In 1867, tensions between Melville and his wife nearly resulted in a marital separation, and later that year their son Malcolm died from a self-inflicted gunshot wound. As a customs inspector, Melville focused his literary energies on poetry, including *Clarel*, an epic based on his impressions of the Holy Land and consumed with the problem of religious doubt; it was published, in 1876, at his uncle's expense, but made little impression on the public. After his retirement he published two small volumes of poetry: *John Marr* (1888) on the sea, and *Timoleon* (1891) on art, politics, and sexuality. At his death on September 28, 1891, Melville left several uncompleted projects: the prose & poem sketches called *The Burgundy Club*, a book of poems entitled *Weeds and Wildings* (including his sensual Rose Poems), and the novella *Billy Budd*, all of which remained unpublished until 1924.

To Melville's Readers

"all over the world, … hand in hand, and one shock of recognition runs
the whole circle round"

Acknowledgments

Much of Melville's writings remain to be discovered, and this has been true since the 1920s when, subsequent to the actual discovery of *Billy Budd* in manuscript, readers soon began figuratively to re-discover *Moby-Dick* and the rest of Melville's earlier work. Over the decades, compilations of Melville's writings have emerged reflecting new waves of re-discovery as one generation of scholars and readers pass "their" Melville on to the next. While the compilation before you attempts a more comprehensive spread of Melville's tales, poems, and other writings, it is no different from its predecessors as a reflection of a generation. Even so, there are as many similarities as departures in this compilation as in those that preceded it, a condition which is, I hope, a testament to generational consanguinity as well as growth. Thus, I want to acknowledge the editors before me—Willard Thorp, Jay Leyda, Richard Chase, Hennig Cohen, and Warner Berthoff—whose successive and quite varied compilations reveal a sagacity of selectivity I can only hope to emulate. All readers of Melville owe a tremendous debt of gratitude to Harrison Hayford, Hershel Parker, and G. Thomas Tanselle, who, as editors of *The Writings of Herman Melville,* have supplied us with a remarkable set of reliable Melville texts, by which I mean the very words Melville intended us to have, to the degree that research can determine his final intentions. Getting Melville's words in a reliable form is no easy task; it requires the dedication of a lifetime, but more: as a humanist Hayford in particular has set a standard of excellence in scholarship, critical insight, and generosity for generations of students to come.

Tales, Poems, and Other Writings was first conceived almost a decade ago, and it has evolved in shape and size through various versions, shrinking and growing for one reason or another. Numerous colleagues in the community of Melville scholars have lent suggestions, with an eye on strengthening the volume's responsiveness to the needs and interests of the larger community of readers everywhere. Each has helped equally and invaluably; they are Dennis Berthold, Edgar A. Dryden, Wyn Kelley, Robert S. Levine, Robert Milder, Steven Olsen-Smith, Samuel Otter, Elizabeth Renker, Douglas Robillard, Robert C. Ryan, Elizabeth Schultz, Christopher Sten, Robert K. Wallace, and John Wenke. To several good friends dragooned into service, I am deeply indebted: they are Eliza Bryant, Emma Bryant, Ann Gilmartin, and Lauren Novack. Finally, I want to thank my editors, Will Murphy and MJ Devaney, as well as Joseph Sora and Vincent La Scala, whose probity, bright insight, and enthusiasm have contributed immeasurably to both the content and texture of this volume.

But this book and all my endeavor is for Virginia Blanford, my Fayaway and my Rose.

> They marvel and marvel how came you so bright,
> Whence the splendor, the joyance—
> Florid revel of joyance,
> The Cypress in sight!

CONTENTS

PART FIVE. *FROM* BATTLE-PIECES

PART SIX. *FROM* CLAREL: A POEM AND PILGRIMAGE
IN THE HOLY LAND

PART SEVEN. PROSE & POEM: *JOHN MARR,* AND OTHERS

PART EIGHT. BILLY BUDD

PART NINE. *FROM* TIMOLEON, ETC.

PART TEN. *FROM* WEEDS AND WILDINGS, CHIEFLY:

WITH A ROSE OR TWO

Herman Melville: A Writer in Process

John Bryant

Melville could not keep from writing. He was not compulsive about it; he did not have to do it every waking hour or even every day. Nor was he a spontaneous writer, who never had a block and could let it all just flow. Writing did not come easily, but he had to do it.

Often, Melville wrote to find out what he wanted to write about. He wrote in order to "unfold," as though the leaves he scrawled upon were the blank fabric of his being. Although he is known for only a few works with stirring plots—a famous whale hunt; the hanging of a sailor—he preferred not to entangle himself in the intricacies of plotting. He wrote about people. More precisely, he liked to create characters and situate them in front of great imponderables: Tommo "baffled" by the "savage mind," or a Wall Street lawyer trying to get Bartleby to work, or the marooned widow Hunilla gazing at the sea. So much of Melville's creative genius lies in his careful building of character and landscape into something so daringly symbolic that dialog seems to exist only to tease us: "I would prefer not to," repeats Bartleby; "The negro," whispers Benito Cereno. And then silence.

Melville wrote about certain districts of the mind: faith and doubt; beauty, sex, and art. And about certain problems: politics and poverty, war and race. He also wrote about consciousness itself, and then, too, nothingness; hence he wrote of the sea. Transcendence was the driving problem: getting beyond the nothingness, if you could; sustaining a "vacant unconscious reverie" for more than just a moment; or living without ever achieving that Zen-like moment, half-knowing that transcendence can never be, and yet forced by faith-inducing imperatives of mind always to anticipate it. For Melville, "Faith, like a jackal, feeds among the tombs," so that death nourishes life, and all is one. Or so says Ishmael, one of Melville's many voices struggling with the problem of transcendence, faith, and death. For Melville himself, writing was a process that put him somewhere else; it afforded him a certain "repose of If" as he contemplated the possibility or hope of some "spirit above the dust." Writing was Melville's transcendence.

This collection of tales, poems, and other writings is designed to give readers access to Melville's writing process, and to provide a new sense of Melville as a "writer in process," one who revised his words ceaselessly and in the course of living revised himself repeatedly. The volume is also designed to acquaint readers with several "new Melvilles," and to do so by showing a progression of Melville's self-revisions, from adolescence to old age. It offers excerpts from *Typee* and *Clarel*, but otherwise the selections are individual short works complete and self-contained, ranging from Melville's first short story to various poems and prose pieces, found in manuscript and not published until after his death. Rather than providing only the most familiar tales and poems, we also offer representative selections—all that is familiar and some that is not—to show the growth of an artist and the range of his experimentation.

Tales, Poems, and Other Writings includes some experiments of its own. Some of the least familiar pieces collected here derive from Melville's later years, after he left the profession of writing for money and let his writing take its own course. Such virtually unknown works as his Burgundy Club sketches, "Rammon," and "Under the Rose" combine prose and poetry in remarkably different ways but were left in manuscript at Melville's death and, until now, have appeared in print rarely, and only then in partial form or in highly limited academic formats. These works, reproduced here in reliable and readable transcriptions, are given their rightful position in the chronology of Melville's work. A little-known fact is that Melville compiled a volume of poetry in 1860 but, failing to secure a publisher, filed the poems away, revising them over the years, publishing some in one slim volume of poetry or another, leaving the rest among his miscellaneous papers. These miscellaneous poems have appeared in print, but never as works derived from the ill-fated 1860 volume. Here we offer a specific selection of these poems to give readers some sense of Melville's early poetic talent.

Yet another experiment in this collection provides readers a unique opportunity to witness Melville in the act of revision. Melville played with words until they took a form he liked—and then he tinkered again. He would yield up his work to the printer but revise yet again even in page proofs. In many cases these tinkerings are just that—tinkerings—but often Melville's revisions reveal distinct periods of rethinking. Thus, in manuscript we may find several distinct versions of a piece of writing, each of which is quite different from the final print version. Any "fluid text" that exists like this in multiple versions can give us tremendous insight into the writer's creative process and how a piece of writing evolves. *Melville's Tales, Poems, and Other Writings* offers four such fluid texts—Chapter 14 of *Typee*, the poems "Camoëns" and "Art," and the earliest known version of *Billy Budd*.

Many people know Melville because they know *Moby-Dick*, or know *of* it. But there are other Melvilles, rarely witnessed by critics and general readers. To be sure, *Moby-Dick* is a classic, and yet Melville also wrote on a smaller scale. This collection shows Melville pitching himself to an aesthetics of the small: short stories, but also short poems, short shocks of recognition delivered in short tetrameter lines. Melville as poet is the least familiar of the new Melvilles before us, and yet writing poetry was a reigning obsession throughout his life.

Melville rarely told the same tale twice or in the same form; he had to innovate. He played with genre. He experimented repeatedly in travel books and short stories and in intriguing, paired sketches (or "diptychs") both picturesque and dramatic; he experimented in what Hawthorne called "romance" (*Moby-Dick*) and what the French called the *"roman"* (*Pierre*). As a fiction writer Melville exercised his talents in prose to such a level of intensity that he needed poetry to rein himself in. In his early romance *Mardi* (1849), he had inserted poems within his prose; in *Moby-Dick* (1851) he had written prose like poetry. But by 1860 he was ready to embark upon his most radical self-revision: He dropped fiction and became a poet, giving us verse narratives of war, elegies to seamen, odes to sharks and art, "harmless" little ditties on flowers and chipmunks, but also America's longest epic, *Clarel*. Even as he grew with his poetry, he found that the process of writing poems required certain prose interventions.

Thus, he gained new insight into the value of prose and, more important, the possibility of combining prose and poem. A poem, for instance, might sprout a prose note to frame the poem, or it might grow into a character sketch as with "John Marr" or an innovative rewriting of another writer's classic as in "Rip Van Winkle's Lilac." And before Melville died, one such "prose & poem" work grew to the size of a novella: *Billy Budd*.

Because Melville was a writer such as this, he was finally not a very successful author. Like the most successful authors of his time—Bayard Taylor, Longfellow, Stowe, N. P. Willis, and Fanny Fern—he played the author's game as well as he could. But unlike theirs, his publications simply failed to sell. To Hawthorne he wrote: "What I feel most moved to write, that is banned," by which he meant: "it will not pay. Yet, altogether, write the *other* way I cannot." Writing the "*other* way," with sentimental effects and easy resolutions, all for popular consumption, seemed a physical impossibility for him. Not only could he not keep himself from writing, but his writing always made him dive, and make you dive sometimes beyond the depths you think you know. Often you find yourself, mute and baffled, treading at the deep end facing an unexpected problem—a scrivener who prefers not to work; a virgin factory girl making paper packets for a gentleman's seeds; boys chatting and laughing as they march into battle; a slave who will not speak; a captain who kills a handsome sailor; an astronomer seeking to transcend her sex—and the problem yields no resolution. Readers do not always cotton to this. So Melville was not a successful author. Still, he was a writer.

Quitting the authoring profession allowed Melville to become the writer he needed to be. The Melville we like to think we know is the author who wrote America's greatest novel, and was rejected by America for the effort. This portrait of the artist as Failed Author is a fair depiction, but it is only one snapshot of the writer in process. There is the experimenter ceaselessly revising; the reviewer, the letter writer, and lecturer; there is the writer of tales, of sketches, of poems, and of the prose & poem concoctions. The full range of his accomplishment can be seen only when we allow ourselves to read him as he grew from one experiment to the next, from prose to poetry and back. It is time to see this artist for all that he was.

STARTING OUT

At twenty, Herman Melville was itching to write, or travel. He did both. Born in 1819 on Manhattan's Battery overlooking the bay, he had spent his first eleven years learning what boys learn and expecting great things. But his father, Allan Melvill, a respected but uncautious importer of French fineries, had done what fathers sometimes do. With too much debt and his credit gone, he failed; and in 1830 the family moved to Albany, closer to mother Maria Gansevoort's home. Great things would have to wait.

In less than two years, Allan was dead from a brain fever that had left him raving. Fatherless at twelve, but never without caring relatives, Herman entered adolescence, a quiet boy but resourceful enough to convert the sadness of his loss into something, he knew not what. He did what he could for his widowed mother and seven siblings to help keep the family solvent. He went to school, clerked a bit, and joined Albany's Young Men's Association. By 1837, Herman had landed the thankless job of schoolteacher in the Pittsfield woods, tutoring boys his own age and taller, but also finding time (as he told his uncle Peter Gansevoort) to "improve [himself] by occasional writing & reading." These were practices he would follow for the rest of his life, although with no apparent effect on his spelling.

His family having relocated in the nearby town of Lansingburg, New York, Melville made his presence known in the local papers. He wrote letters to the editor, and under the pseudonym "L.A.V." made his literary debut with two "Fragments from a Writing Desk," the second of which is collected here. Locked within the obsessive mind of a nameless first-person speaker and building through romantic settings and gothic absurdities to a shocking conclusion, Melville's adolescent tale is undeniably indebted to Poe, but within its clamorous prose are certain mute silences within nature that would recur in later writings and give his work its distinctive feel.

Despite this promising debut, the young man's more pressing itch at twenty was to travel. Signing aboard the merchant ship *St. Lawrence,* he sailed to Liverpool. Home in four months and still penniless, he toured the Western Reserve on a jaunt to Galena, Illinois, and back via the Mississippi and Ohio Rivers, to visit his beloved uncle Thomas, who like

Herman's deceased father had experienced financial "difficulties" in the turbulent economy of the early republic. Then on January 3, 1841, he shipped again, this time on the whaler *Acushnet* bound for the South Pacific. Denied the kind of schooling his contemporaries Emerson, Dana, Hawthorne, and Longfellow received, Melville understood that his own education was about to begin. As he would later have Ishmael proudly proclaim: "a whale-ship was my Yale College and my Harvard."

This is not to say he enrolled long enough in whaling school to receive a degree. Jumping ship on the Marquesan island of Nuku Hiva, he spent a month with the Taipi natives in the remote valley of Taipivai. Making his escape, he landed aboard an Australian whaler but refused to work and was imprisoned in Tahiti. After his release and some beachcombing, he shipped off again to Hawaii, where he joined the U.S. Navy and returned home an able-bodied sailor on the frigate *United States*. He now had plenty of stories to tell, not the gothic fantasies of his adolescence but strange and stirring tales of a young man at sea, and the itch was on him to write.

Returning home in the festive fall of 1844, Herman was primed to join the family's center stage along with his brothers Gansevoort and Allan, whose respective careers in politics and law were already well launched. On board ship, he had rehearsed anecdotes of his adventures for shipmates during long watches at sea. Now, in parlors back home, he regaled friends and relatives with the same stories, refining the language for both ladies and gentlemen, who in turn encouraged him to write it all down.

By January 1845, Melville was settled back in lower Manhattan, scene of his nativity, composing a first draft of *Typee*. It was to be a genuine rebirth. Or so he told Hawthorne six years later: "Until I was twenty-five, I had no development at all. From my twenty-fifth year I date my life. Three weeks have scarcely passed, at any time between then and now, that I have not unfolded within myself. But I feel that I am now come to the inmost leaf of the bulb, and that shortly the flower must fall to the mould." Despite the exhaustion this confession reveals—Melville was finishing *Moby-Dick* at the time—we cannot fail to hear Melville's wonderment, pleasure, gratitude for his writing ability and for the very act of writing itself, which allowed him to "unfold."

What were Melville's "unfoldings" as he wrote *Typee?* Most certainly, he was learning the language and how to make a sentence unfold. But he was also learning that, in making his language accurately reflect the remembered facts of his island experiences, he was converting memory into fictions that were new revelations about emotions he had only half understood. Through writing, he was understanding more. He found himself not simply rendering the people and sites he had encountered, but creating characters and scenes which now seemed to exude revelations about primal island life, western imperialism and Christianity, and his own evolving sexuality.

These unfoldings are best seen in Melville's manuscript revisions to his first draft of *Typee*, placed here alongside the printed version of one chapter from Melville's final printed text. We find the writer revising the word "savage" to "native" or "islander" to modulate his own initial cultural bias toward the "Typiis." We find him deleting gloomy psychologizings about his friend Toby but also sentimentally expanding upon Fayaway. We find him censoring himself, by toning down scenes relating the full-body massage he received from native women, certain allusions to famous lovers, and the sexualized lighting of a fire by his male servant. He even revises a smutty little joke on why there are no "vestals" in Typee.

In his Preface to *Typee*, Melville announces he will render for "fire-side people" those "strange and romantic" elements of island life that are in fact "as common-place as a jacket out at elbows." However, to do this, Melville had to keep the strange from going too deep and the romantic from becoming too hot. In this regard, *Typee* is something of an "arrested romance" for the story it cannot tell but only implies. Melville's first "unfolding," then, was a lesson in crafting his voice, and in skirting the truth.

MANAGING THE UNMANAGEABLE

In the next seven years Melville published seven books in rapid succession, an unparalleled rate of productivity, all prose fictions of one sort or another. Writing, not whaling, became his college. Emboldened by the success of *Typee*—it would remain his top-selling book—Melville looked for new ways to convey truths, not skirt them. If he could not speak directly, then he would dramatize the light and dark moods one feels while pursuing, confronting, or inhabiting a truth. Some truths, like the silences of nature, God, and man, cannot be put into words; they can only be experienced. Thus, Melville came to see that fiction works best when it forces us into a reading experience that is commensurate with the experience we have in facing unspeakable truths. Fiction must do more than "tell" or even "show," but like "religion, it should present another world, and yet one to which we feel the tie" (*The Confidence-Man*). Thus, "the Great Art of Telling the Truth" (as he put it in his review essay entitled "Hawthorne and His Mosses") required indirection. From *Typee* on, none of Melville's writings was quite like the one that came before it, or the one to come next.

Even the lowly *Omoo* (1847), which continues Tommo's adventures as a comic mutineer and beachcomber in Tahiti, exceeds *Typee* as a bluff, nose-thumbing picaresque rather than a baffled personal narrative. Accused by critics of passing off fictions as narratives of fact, Melville set out to show readers what a true romance might be. The result was *Mardi* (1849), a dive into metaphysics and mixed-genre fiction-writing that brought him recognition as a "prose poet," if little else. A gothic quest after light and dark ladies set in an allegorical archipelago of Pacific islands, this "romance" baffled critics and worried the family, enough so that he assured his British publisher, Richard Bentley, that his next book, *Redburn*, would have "no metaphysics" and be "nothing but cakes & ale." But he also acknowledged that "scribblers" such as he "always have a certain something unmanageable in us, that bids us do this or that, and be done it must—hit or miss." Melville's father-in-law of two years, Judge Lemuel Shaw, was no doubt anxious for his daughter's well-being in the hands of a "scribbler." But young Melville would set him at ease. With admitted "egotism," he proclaimed he could and would write *Redburn* and yet a second, *White-Jacket*, as *"jobs"* for money, but he also stated that it was his "earnest desire to write those sort of books which are said to 'fail.' " How could Judge Shaw not be reassured?

Happily, neither book failed, nor, in fact, were they mere "jobs." *Redburn* (1849), based on the trip to Liverpool on the *St. Lawrence*, follows the growth of a young lad fallen on hard times who slowly awakens to the realities of poverty and death, as well as the ugliness and beauty of masculinity. It is the closest thing he wrote to a true *bildungsroman* and also shows Melville's expertise in modulating his young narrator's voice from puerility and callowness to maturity. For *White-Jacket* (1850), Melville drew upon his two years in the Navy to come up with yet another completely different kind of fiction, one that anatomizes life aboard a man-of-war, turning it into a microcosm of the interior and social life of man. Melville's innovation was the jacket, an experiment in symbolism, innovative not so much for the vestment—that idea he borrowed from Carlyle—but for the color, a blankness that would engulf his next book.

In 1850 Melville returned from a well-deserved trip to London and the Continent, where he met publishers, artists, and writers; saw castles, paintings, and plays. In rooms, on coaches, in ships, he continued to read: Jonson, Shakespeare, Milton, Goethe, Coleridge, and Emerson, but also the likes of moody Robert Burton, Thomas Browne, Rousseau, and De-Quincy, as well as both Shelleys. Having now sold his two "jobs," he was ready to romance again, and the one maritime experience he had not written up was his whaling years. The idea, he told Bentley, would be to do "a romance of adventure, founded upon certain wild legends in the Southern Sperm Whale fisheries," but to a literary confrère like Richard Henry Dana, Jr., who knew about taking on the "unmanageable," he confided that it would be "a strange sort of a book." Not strange like *Typee* or, God forbid, *Mardi*. "Poetry" would run through this one "as hard as sap from a frozen maple," and it would be "ungainly as the gambols of the whales themselves." Yet despite the "fancy" of it, the book would also "give the truth." It would be *Moby-Dick*.

And what was the truth of this book? Banal thematics of good versus evil, or man against God, or faith and doubt, or slavery and freedom, or capital and labor, or black and white might establish certain parameters for this novel's meaning, but they hardly suffice to explain how the language works on you, or how that working upon you is finally what *Moby-Dick* is about. "Sometimes I think there's naught beyond," Ahab admits in a famous aside, and then quickly suppresses the thought. He will invent a rational but evil God, and call it Moby Dick, so that he may strike through the false white mask of his own imagining in order to kill that god, and in all this manly action he unconsciously works to forget his fear of Nothingness, and that there may be no God. Or, if there is a god, then God hardly matters. For man and God are in the same fix, Ahab avers. Neither can solve an important riddle. Both are beings; and both have Being. Each exists, and yet what is existence itself? What is Being? Is it "Me, God, Nature"? These are merely manifestations of Being. Where is the essence, the *ontos*, the Ens that suffuses them all? What is this "ungraspable phantom of life"? "It is this *Being* of the matter," Melville told Hawthorne; "there lies the knot with which we choke ourselves."

Ahab's "ontological heroics" make perfect sense. His self-destructive rage does not. Ishmael's response is different: "Nothing exists in itself."

From this simple axiom, he builds a world of language, and more language. The language does not deny the phantom of life, or will it away, or prettify it. Ishmael "essays" the problem of Being; he "tries it out" in words. He soars like a "Catskill eagle" and hits the dead-end nihility of whiteness itself. Ultimately—or is it just luck?—his poeticizing allows him "the pondering repose of If," like Keats's negative capability, which Ahab can articulate but cannot sustain. Ishmael cannot answer Who am I, or What is God, or What is Being. But his ability to sing out the questions excels Ahab's rage, even Queequeg's quiet mysticism.

Ishmael's song embraces and fills a world both tragic and comic. Like Mahler, he fills the hall with tune upon tune: rich, melodic, and rhythmic yet weirdly arrhythmic, like a whale giving birth, like the pattern and chaos of nature itself. And, like a Mahler symphony, *Moby-Dick* must be "unmanageable," hard as sap in winter, "ungainly" as the thing it tries to grasp so that our reading of this bold nervous lofty language becomes an experience as unstable as Ahab's mind but also as transcendent as Ishmael's line.

Moby-Dick is a pretty good book, but no one got it. (Mixed reviews. Dwindling sales.) Melville went on to something else. *Pierre* (1852), by any standard of measure the greatest departure from any of his previous fictions, is set first in the Berkshire countryside and then in New York City; its only glimpse of the sea is from the docks. Its conflicts are domestic, not naval; its characters moody, transcendental artists, not whalers; its third- (not first-) person narrator, who is given to excessive rants, is neurotic, not redemptive; its imagery riverine and winding, not cetological or white; and its language is highly experimental. Experimental by far. Most readers agreed with one critic who flatly declared it "a bad book!"

Moby-Dick and *Pierre* had taken Melville's talent beyond the last unfolding to the inmost leaf of the bulb of metaphysics and depth psychology. He was exhausted, but only with writing novels. He turned to writing shorter works.

TELLING TALES

Pierre had been an angry affair, a sea dragon or "Kraken," as he called it. It mixes anxieties about his family (a domineering mother and revered but tainted father), tensions over love and writing, and contempt for the world of publishing that had ignored his greatest work. The age of Freud would have to come before readers would fully grasp the meaning of the anger and depressions in this domestic drama. All that readers in 1852 could comprehend was that they found Melville's transcendental language and bohemian morality repulsive. Together both *Moby-Dick* and *Pierre* were evidence that Melville had degenerated from his usual geniality to a dangerously morbid ambiguity. Melville could not fail to get the message; sales were at a new low. He needed to recuperate.

Writing for the magazines was the cure. It allowed him to regain his audience, control his erratic narrative voice and excessive diving, and enhance his cash flow. The timing for Melville could not have been better. From the 1830s on, the numbers of magazines had grown, and so had circulation. Poe and Hawthorne had made their reputations writing for comparatively small journals. Now, in the 1850s, newer, larger, and illustrated magazines found their ways into more homes and railway cars than ever. Moreover, the newest of periodicals, like *Harper's New Monthly* and especially *Putnam's Monthly*, paid top dollar for well-known writers. Melville contributed to both, receiving a steady income for his efforts and a wider circulation for his writing than he had ever had before.

Of the two magazines, *Putnam's* was the more adventurous. Edited by Melville's friend Charles F. Briggs, it featured American writers and offered the "acutest observations." *Harper's* (edited by another Melville associate, the liberal-minded George W. Curtis) stressed "the lessons of morality and virtue" to be found in more sentimental writing. Together these editorial policies provided a perfect balance of aesthetic expectations for Melville at this unstable time: something genial, something sharp. To what degree the writer tailored his tales to fit these editorial policies is a matter of speculation, but his general success in getting his work accepted by both indicates his ability to meet their restrictions and also curb his former excesses. Not surprisingly, in this recuperative period, Melville fell back upon familiar settings for his short fiction: the sea, the city, the farm. But he also experimented with narrative voice: he began to venture, more carefully than he had with *Pierre*, into third-person narration and to make his fictional speakers less and less reliable. In doing so, Melville was able to address everyday matters such as domesticity, race, class, and the world of work with carefully modulated ironies so that the brightness of sentiment and geniality would be made to reveal its darker edges: deception, sexuality, alienation, and poverty. By combining these bright and dark features Melville developed a picturesque style of his own that in one way seems to affirm our sense of life, and then again subvert it.

Melville's first instinct was to write a book-length adventure set at sea and focusing on "Tortoise hunting." For some reason, the idea never caught on with publishers; and, it appears, Melville was "prevented" from completing the book. ("The Isle of the Cross" may have been another ill-fated project, or an alternative title for the tortoise book.) In any event, some hint of the work appears in "The Encantadas," a set of ten sketches (including one on tortoises), which appeared in three installments in *Putnam's*. The title refers to the dry and barren Galápagos Islands, which despite the romantic Spanish name are far from enchanting. The sketches depict the forbidding terrain and its unlikely inhabitants, some desperately comic in their despotism and larceny, but others, such as Hunilla, the Chola widow, tragically ruined first by loss and isolation and then by depravity. Hunilla, her husband, and her brother have been left on a desolate island to hunt tortoise oil, but their ship does not return, and both men are drowned attempting to escape. The young widow waits for deliverance but is ignored by passing ships, and, it is darkly hinted, is sexually abused by whaling men who land and leave. "The Chola Widow" is an ignored gem for its spare narration, feminist focus, and complex position on faith. Is Hunilla's silence emblematic of her faith, or of mere endurance? We see her at the end, like Mary, riding an ass and staring at the shape of a cross formed in the foldings of the ass's shoulders. This image made one reader (no less than James Russell Lowell) weep, and its sentimentality cannot be denied. But did that reader notice Melville's earlier dig at God: "Ah, Heaven, when man thus keeps his faith, wilt thou be faithless who created the faithful one?" Melville was learning to combine subversion and sentiment.

But Melville was eager to avoid the alien venue of the sea. At a crucial turning point in *Moby-Dick*, Ishmael separates himself from Ahab's ocean quest and places his expectations for "attainable felicity" not in the intellect but in domesticity: "the wife, the heart, the bed, the table, the saddle, the fire-side, the country" (ch. 94). Much of the shorter fiction, including such later tales as "I and My Chimney" and "The Piazza," transplants Ishmael into this quieter setting. "Cock-A-Doodle-Doo!" is set in the verdant Berkshires, a greener picturesque than any of the Encantadas, but no less complicated in its playing upon the sentimental expectations of readers. Here, a jauntily dyspeptic narrator takes time from his reading and busy avoidance of paying his bills to track down a rooster whose glorious crowing drives away his melancholy. Merrymusk, the owner and a poverty-stricken sawyer, will not sell the rooster because it gives optimism to his dying wife and children. With the tale's references to locomotives marring the countryside and "chanticleer" waking the neighbors, the tale anticipates happier transcendental images in Thoreau's *Walden*, which was published the following year, but the death of the sawyer, his family, and the rooster leave us with a complicated sense of the brave futility of human existence. The Merrymusks have little choice but to endure, and the narrator, now jolted out of his self-involved indifference, ends the tale by adopting the rooster's "cock-a-doodle-doo," whose crow is typographically rendered as a string of "—oo's," cryptically emblematic of the vacuity of optimism. Again, sentimental tears for sentimental readers are undercut by a sly irony.

But Melville's most memorable tale leaves sentiment behind almost entirely. "Bartleby" begins in a confident, comic mood. It promises to be a study of that odd sort of office worker, the scrivener (copyist), who like the title character is a bit eccentric. Bartleby arrives with no apparent past and no interest in the future; he works palely, mechanically, and efficiently, which is a substantial improvement over his two officemates, Turkey and Nippers, whose temperaments and incompetence make their total effort worth the work of one. Nevertheless, it is a "good, natural arrangement" for the employer, an "eminently *safe*" business lawyer who avoids courts and conflict. The humor grows when Bartleby suddenly states he "would prefer not to" work anymore. But as Bartleby's "passive resistance" grows, it threatens to destroy the office structure. Good manager that he is, the Lawyer attempts to accommodate Bartleby, but his accommodations are merely a low-level humanism designed to facilitate the paperwork of society. Even so, the Lawyer becomes strangely drawn to Bartleby's alienated condition, all the more so as the scrivener becomes increasingly suicidal. As the tale unfolds, the reader's involvement becomes equally split between the mystery of Bartleby's identity and the growth of the Lawyer's consciousness.

Melville works hard to ensure that we are never too sentimentally attached to Bartleby; he is from the beginning far more infuriating than pathetic. Nor is he a self-conscious, heroic system-smasher. His rebellion seems "merely" self-destructive. And it is this "mere-ness" of his self-destruction that both infuriates and appeals. Life is an imperative, not a preference. What makes Bartleby want to die? Humans are programmed to live. How dare he prefer to turn the program off. And yet what is the logic of this program, and who the programmer? Bartleby's self-destruction is a "sane madness." Our anger at Bartleby is that in seeing no sense in the program and preferring to opt out, he leaves us behind with the mere-ness of our own absurdity. And this revelation is unbearable; hence our anger at Bartleby.

Exacerbating our antisentimental response is the rhetoric of Bartleby's "I would prefer not to." The statement is not a refusal. It is a speech act requiring a reaction. By stating his negative preference, he puts the burden on the Lawyer, and us, to respond. And yet there is no response. The Lawyer's final appeal to Bartleby is "will you go home with me now?" But this ultimate Christian charity to share his private self serves no purpose. The Lawyer's frustration is what gives the story its famous doubleness. "Bartleby" is not about Bartleby alone; it is about the Lawyer's growing awareness of the infuriating emptiness of the human condition, an emptiness he has allowed himself to ignore, or rather fill with paperwork—until now. How much has the Lawyer grown? He has deepened his emotions from "a not-unpleasing sadness" to "an overpowering stinging melancholy." For him, Bartleby is no longer an eccentric but a "dead letter," a failed communication, misdirected, lost, destroyed: he is humanity. But is the Lawyer's concluding equation—"Ah Bartleby! Ah humanity!"—just another easy formula whose derivation he does not comprehend?

We are left, then, with two tales in one—Bartleby's and the Lawyer's—and Melville's narrative technique makes this happen. Previously, Melville's most successful first-person narrator had been Ishmael, an unstable fellow with a very stable voice, one that is comic and yet wondrous wise. The first-person Lawyer, however, is not so reliable. Imagine Ishmael telling Bartleby's story. To be sure, he would be no less baffled than the Lawyer, but he would probe more deeply, philosophizing and poeticizing, perhaps even sentimentalizing the scrivener, and that would have been the problem. The Lawyer's detachment from Bartleby, his intellectual shortcoming, has an important effect upon the reader. Because we cannot rely upon him to articulate Bartleby, we are made conscious of his inadequacy and then of our own inability to articulate the problem. We become more active participants in the fiction.

Melville experimented further with unreliable narration. He made successive narrators increasingly dim-witted. And instead of compressing two tales—the Lawyer's and the scrivener's—into one, he created the double tale, or "diptych," which pairs up contrasting scenes from the narrator's life, and concludes with both narrator and reader wondering what the contrast means. In "The Two Temples," for instance, New York's new Grace Church, with its lofty spire and elite congregation, is (to the democracy's discredit) contrasted with London's "temple," a theater, which embraces all folk. *Putnam's* would have appreciated the political critique, but declined to print the two sketches for fear of offending "church readers," or what Melville sarcastically referred to as "the tender consciences of the public," and the diptych was not published until 1924.

But the acceptance of another diptych demonstrated something Melville had learned as early as *Typee:* readers are far more "tender" about religion than about sex. In "The Paradise of Bachelors," our narrator first enjoys a sumptuous dinner with male friends in London's Temple Bar; in the companion piece "The Tartarus of Maids," he then travels a snowy route to a New England paper mill whose maiden laborers are heartlessly entangled in the factory's cruel mechanism. The contrast here is not simply between luxury and poverty, England and America, but also male freedom and female servitude. On the one hand, men deploy their feasting and merriment like a jolly military engagement, indifferent to the cold realities around them, for this indifference is the privilege of their sex. The virginal girls (based on the female factory workers of Lowell, Massachusetts) are symbolically chained to machinery that operates, suspiciously, like the female reproductive system. When we learn that our bachelor narrator comes to the factory for paper to make envelopes for the seeds he sells, we soon enough discover a carefully concealed critique of the politics of sexuality, all of which the narrator misses as he rides off with his phallic black horse.

The risk in making a narrator so unreliable that he cannot see the very story he is telling is that the reader might miss it, too. Indeed, Melville was learning to create fictions that were quiet provocations, like any of a number of Hawthorne's sly picturesques that "give us a ray of his light for every shade of his dark" and which are, moreover, "calculated to deceive ... the superficial skimmer of pages." With *Pierre*, readers could hardly miss the provocations. The narrator of that novel exposed the naïveté of sentiment and the vacuity of morality with no holds barred, and the results were disastrous. Melville toned down the assault on readers, somewhat, in his conventional Revolutionary War narrative, *Israel Potter* (1855), serialized in *Putnam's*. But with the periodical fiction, Melville took his less confrontational strategy in new directions. With "Bartleby" and the diptychs, he recovered and transformed his first-person voice. With "Benito Cereno," he would recuperate the third-person narrative voice he had allowed to get so much out of hand in *Pierre*.

In this, his most complex tale, Amasa Delano, an American sea captain, lends aid to a becalmed slave ship, the *San Dominick,* captained by the Spaniard Benito Cereno. Always at the Spaniard's side is Babo, a servant slave. Unbeknownst to Delano, and to the reader, is that Babo has masterminded a slave revolt, and to prevent capture, he and his followers are playacting their former slave roles, and forcing Cereno to enact his role as master. Just to keep the actors focused, Babo has arranged for the still-gory skeleton of Aranda, the ship's owner, to hang concealed in shrouds from the ship's prow. Delano is a genial man, smart enough to sense that something is amiss, but not smart enough to untie the knot that one knowing sailor symbolically tosses him. The problem, however, is not his lack of intelligence, but the shape of his mind, which can process reality only through the sieve of a culturally conditioned benevolent racism. He condescendingly admires the black race not for its humanity (or ability to revolt) but for its servility. He distrusts the Spanish slavers because of their cruel reputation. In the end, Delano is conned by his most cherished stereotypes.

Delano is ill equipped to solve the mystery on board the *San Dominick,* and, like the Lawyer in "Bartleby," would be a prime candidate for the role of first-person narrator. But the problem with unreliable first-person speakers is that they too easily announce their limitations. (Recall any of a number of Poe's speakers: "They call me mad and yet I tell you I am not!") Melville needed a less conspicuous form of unreliability. His innovation in "Benito Cereno" is to tell this story in the third person, but with a twist. He adopts the voice of an omniscient and supposedly objective speaker, but limits his reporting almost exclusively to Delano's skewed point of view. Thus, this speaker relates only what Delano sees and thinks. Being the trusting readers that we are, we presume that Melville's more knowing speaker will inform us of Delano's false impressions. And yet, this speaker makes no judgments and relates Delano's fatally racist presumptions as fact. In this way, Melville effectively deceives the white readers of *Putnam's Monthly* into adopting Delano's erroneous thinking. The reader, too, is conned. Thus, the denouement is as shocking to us as it is to Delano, and the story's final effect is to force readers to retrace their own racism to discover how, as a condition of mind, it distorts our vision. Like Benito Cereno at the end, we are prepared to be haunted by "the negro."

In his last novel, *The Confidence-Man* (1857), Melville pushed his strategy of ironic indirection in a third-person voice to its extreme. This dark comedy set on a Mississippi riverboat parades before us a series of con men and victims, and Melville's distant narrator gives us no access to the springs and motives of the characters in the play. By mid-novel, with the entrance of one of Melville's more baffling figures, the cosmopolitan Frank Goodman, readers are left to their own wits to make out the knaves and fools. Geniality and deception merge, and the narrative itself becomes an experience of doubt.

Melville's recuperative experimentation with short fiction had not only helped him restore his tragicomic sensibility and expand his narrative skills, it had also introduced him to the possibilities of detaching himself from his characters and readers. It gave him distance. Art need not be self-exposure; it could be an object, a pulse of thought and feeling independent of any speaker or personality. Although he had transformed himself from a romantic stylist to a virtual modernist, and done so through prose fiction alone, he was ready for something new.

MELVILLE AS POET

In 1856, Melville set out on another well-deserved vacation. He had written nine novels and eighteen tales. His collection of *Putnam's* pieces, *The Piazza Tales* (1856), was well received but did not sell. He had worked his New England farm and fathered four children. But his profit was a sinking reputation and growing debt. Mentally drained, he sailed for the Mediterranean to tour the Holy Land, Greece, and Italy. Reports in the local papers stated that by Jerusalem his health had been restored. He returned in 1857 with a journal full of fresh images. He also returned a poet.

The received wisdom is that Melville was a masterful prose writer who turned, cold turkey, to poetry; but this is only partially true. Melville had already versified with incidental ditties in *Mardi;* and in *Moby-Dick* he had created a prose line that critics had called poetic, but such poeticizing had always been contained within the financially safe confines of prose. And wisely so, for then as now, poetry on its own is that land from whose bourn no traveler, not even a Longfellow or Browning, returns with much cash. But with Irving, Dana, and Hawthorne as prose stylists for models, and with the likes of Dickens abroad and Fanny Fern at home as competitors in the prose marketplace, Melville's major achievement in prose had been to write brilliant fictions that brilliantly failed. He was now ready for a major revision of himself. Rarely do we find writers abandoning one genre for another, and succeeding in the perilous transition. Thomas Hardy, perhaps; but not Henry James, who returned to novels after the failure of his dramas. Most professional writers stick to their fields. Melville had moved from novels to tales and back, but did not have the hubris to expect great success in becoming a poet; thus, he kept the news of this metamorphosis to himself, and became a lecturer.

He started off in 1857 with something of keen interest to himself, a presentation on "Statues in Rome," which allowed him to pull together thoughts he had jotted down in his Mediterranean journal about the struggle of the artist to compress expressions of faith and doubt into stone, like the famous sculpture of Laocoön. Audiences were polite but expected more than religion and aesthetics from "the man who lived among the cannibals." The next year he added "The South Seas" to his repertoire, and then a lecture on "Travel," but the engagements dwindled. Melville traveled from Montreal to Charleston and from Boston to the Mississippi, but never made the main circuit. Among friends an affable raconteur, who could rattle off ribald tales in the parlor room, Melville failed to excite audiences when reading from a script and forced to relive a persona long gone. His heart was not in repetition and public speaking. It was in making poems and, proto-modernist that he was, it was in making them new.

But at first, his poems were not at all like the stony objects he lectured about. That would come later. They were instead pastoral, often bumptious, even profane poems. Some were transcendental, like the Wordsworthian "Pontoosuce," reminiscent of the Berkshire woods. Others, like the satiric "Madam Mirror" and outrageous "The New Ancient of Days, or The Man of the Cave of Engihoul" were caustic yet hearty. Still more, like the deceptively simple "Fruit and Flower Painter," or "Immolated" and both poems named "Camoens," were on a subject about which Melville had from the beginning been obsessed: art and the creative process.

By 1860 Melville was ready to announce to the world his new profession. He assembled a collection, entitled simply *Poems by Herman Melville*. He told his brother Allan that "of all human events" the publication of one's first volume of verses "is the most insignificant." But this was just grandstanding. The prospective poet was already envisioning more volumes of verse to come. But he was anxious all the same, and he dealt with his anxiety by leaving town. He shipped out with his other brother, Tom, for a cruise around the world in Captain Tom's ship, *The Meteor*, and left instructions with his wife, Lizzie, Allan, and Evert Duyckinck for the production of his book of poems. When he reached San Francisco, bad news awaited: no publisher wanted it. He cut short the circumnavigation and returned home. The book never materialized. Even so, the poet continued to read, study his craft, and write.

Melville left no table of contents for this book, and one might fear from the message in "Immolated" that he burned the poems. He did, in fact, sell off his "doggeral" for scrap in 1862. But chances are he saved the better works, for numerous poems published in later collections, and several more left in manuscript, seem to date from this period. Of course, being the inveterate reviser that he was, Melville tinkered with his 1860 poems over the years, so that those that do survive in manuscript resemble ancient churches with ever-expanding floor plans. Nevertheless, one can sift through Melville's miscellaneous papers and gather up certain of these poems to provide some sense of what the 1860 volume might have contained. Some of the manuscript poems, for instance, are written in blue ink on distinctive yellow paper and clearly predate other manuscripts, although by how much we cannot tell. The sampling of these "yellow paper poems" offered in this volume gives us an inkling of Melville's poetic skill as he embarked upon his new career. Two of the poems—"Camoens (Before)" and "Camoens (After)"—are so heavily revised that by displaying them in their successive versions, we also gain a clearer sense of how Melville developed, through revision, as a poet in later years.

BREAKDOWN: MELVILLE AND THE WAR

Melville's wife had come into some money, and for a while, the family's finances seemed stable. The country, however, was not. Lincoln's election triggered events that would split the nation in two. Politically, the liberal-minded Melville had been affiliated, as were most in his family, with Jacksonian Democratic politics, but by the Civil War the ensuing shifts in party lines made it morally grievous for one disposed to the freedom and equality of man to support the southern-based Democratic party. And yet no evidence exists for Melville's formal registration with any party, Democratic or the newly formed Republican. Melville was not an abolitionist if abolition meant the dissolution of the Union, although he supported emancipation when it finally occurred, and whether he voted for Lincoln or not, we do not know, but he was happy to shake the hand of "Old Abe" on a trip to Washington in hopes of securing a consulship in the Lincoln administration. As with earlier attempts to gain a government job, no position was offered. Melville returned home, and followed the war primarily from his armchair. In 1862, the family left Arrowhead for a residence in Pittsfield, and a year later he traded homes with his brother Allan, relocating in the vicinity of Manhattan's Gramercy Park.

Too old to enlist, Melville nevertheless experienced something few if any American writers of his caliber and day had managed. In April of 1864, he visited the front in Virginia, where General Grant was conducting the Wilderness Campaign, and rode along with a detail as it scouted for Mosby's guerrillas. The brief encounter with war was uneventful, but Melville returned with vivid impressions. Even so, he wrote only a handful of poems during the war. He was searching for new voices that would of necessity rise above his former pose of geniality and address the unfolding tragedy. With the fall of Richmond, he gathered up his thoughts and *The Rebellion Record* (a compendium of various official and literary writings), and began in earnest to write a book of poems about the war.

Melville's primary goal was to establish a national voice, one that could speak for the nation's ideals but also for its people, one that was "righteous" in the sense of its firm commitment to freedom and peace, but one that honored courage and valor in the field. Of necessity it would be conciliatory, and, as Melville explained in his book's prose "Supplement," it would have to teach through "terror and pity" that moderation is not only a true form of patriotism, but also good poetry. Thus, *Battle-Pieces* would contain naturalistic, "undeceiving" depictions of the fighting (poems as hard and unsparing as the armaments the title implies). But as its fully extended title, *And Aspects of the War,* suggests, the book would also offer varying points of view (poems in voices of both North and South).

According to Robert Penn Warren, Melville "was a mystic who hated mysticism." Which is to say, he knew of the existence of higher truths and knew they could conflict; thus, he was dubious of any transcendent "One." Often, as in "Shiloh" and "Malvern Hill," Melville simply lets the presence of swallows or elms in a battlefield "voice" the power of nature over the human carnage. Unlike Whitman, whose ritualistic incantatory lines made him the more successful national poet, Melville's approach is dramatic: he crafts poems that inhabit opposing sides. In "The Conflict of Convictions," he employs Miltonic gestures (Satan, Michael) and an oddly flippant, mordant chorus ("Ha ha, the rust on the Iron Dome") to project bravery and righteousness but also stress the failure of the "Founders' dream" and the looming "shadow" of the war's resultant unwanted empire. But beyond it all, God (with his "Middle way") and death ("with silent negative") outmatch the vain strife. The concluding poem, "America," ends with similar but more hopeful images of the Capitol's Iron Dome and of the republic poised with "Law on her brow" but ominously, too, with "empire in her eyes." There is a cautious expectancy, but if we have experienced Melville's battle-pieces, and endured the terror and pity of their dramatized conflicts, we may acquire the sensitivity to move the republic back to the "Founders' dream" and away from empire.

Among these poems are unforgettable images of young men heading off to the First Battle of Manassas as if in anticipation of berry-picking on a summer's day, "Chatting left and laughing right" ("The March into Virginia"), unaware of their certain death, thoughtless of a second Manassas. Why do young men fight, "one for Right, and one for Wrong"? The answer is a simple picture of fertility and fate: "Each grape to his cluster clung" ("On the Slain Collegians"). In "Malvern Hill" the voice of a southern victor somberly weighs the cost of victory—"But ah, the sod what thousands meet!"—and is met in turn with nature's chilling reply (again a fated fertility): *"Leaves must be green in Spring."* More voices emerge in the ambitious "Armies of the Wilderness" with its dramatic rendering of fresh battle on an old battlefield—"the rusted gun, / Green

shoes full of bones, the mouldering coat, / And cuddled-up skeleton"—
and its devastating choral rejoinders: "So strange seems mirth in a
camp / So like a white tent to a shroud."

The requirements of crafting his multivalent national voice gave
Melville the further impetus to bury his personality (which flowered so
wondrously in Ishmael) within the formal strictures of verse itself. Poetry
was a way to "annul" himself (as he would later put it in "Buddha") and
let a given subject find its shape on its own terms, like a sculpture emerging out of stone. As with his tales, he found himself once again writing
small. No more the mighty line of prose: Melville compressed thought
and action into a four-beat line that at times forces a twisting of syntax,
even the dropping of definite articles, so that the words laid out in a deceptively familiar ballad structure take on an alien aspect: rough and
ragged, with "entangled rhyme" purposefully designed, as Melville put it
in "Armies of the Wilderness," to hint at "the maze of war." Melville was
using form not only to convey a sentiment but to mimic a congruent pattern of thought. In "A Utilitarian's View of the Monitor's Fight," Melville
weighs the consequences of the mechanization of warfare: warriors are
"but operatives," passion is replaced by "calculations of caloric," war is
less human, and yet it is made "Less grand than Peace." But to deliver this
analysis of machinery, Melville announces in the opening lines that his
verse will be "More ponderous than nimble," and fulfills the promise with
heavily enjambed lines and only one rhyme per stanza. The poem becomes the pounding machine it represents.

Battle-Pieces and Aspects of the War (1866) did not sell. Readers ready to
reconstruct America, and with a vengeance, had little patience with what
one critic called Melville's "treasonable" plea for understanding, charity,
civil rights for Southerners white and black alike, and reconciliation.
They had even less patience for his unfamiliar poetic style. What did not
sound to them like James Russell Lowell's "Commemoration Ode," or
Henry Howard Brownell's stirring *War-Lyrics* (also 1866), or Longfellow's
sentimental gallop-a-trot, or Whittier's serviceable "Snow-Bound," or
even Poe or Whitman's radical rhythms, they heard as "uncouth," "spasmodic," "epileptic," "odd, inelegant, obscure." His verse had an "astonishing crudity and formlessness." Melville had the audacity to rhyme "law,"
"war," and "no more" with "Shenandoah" in his opening piece "The Portent." Or was it ineptitude? Reviewers of the day repeatedly cited the

off-rhymes as an offense to poetic technique. Today, of course, "The Portent" is considered one of Melville's best poems precisely because of the subtle linkages implied in the off-rhyming.

He did have some sympathetic readers. The critic for the New York *Herald* somehow saw the modernity of Melville's rugged poems as "not inappropriately rugged enough" given the "rough time" the country had just endured. The New York *Round Table* called *Battle-Pieces* "original." Granted, but even Melville's most thoughtful reader, the thirty-year-old William Dean Howells, remarked that one of the "negative virtues of originality" evident in Melville's poems is that when they should be shedding "words and blood," they shed "but words alone."

Melville was crushed by the reviews. His efforts to make his versification new were chalked up to ineptitude. His mission to establish himself as a voice for the republic, and as a healer, was aborted. In December 1866, he gave up his aspiration to become a recognized poet and accepted a patronage job in the U.S. Customs House, a post that gave him an office and required him to supervise the inspection of imports. The steady income did not stabilize his emotional state.

Melville's midlife crisis was at full gale. We can imagine moody seclusions, sudden outbursts, and drinking. (The unlikely charge of wife-beating is a recent speculation.) What is not imagined is that in May 1867, tensions had grown to such an extent that Elizabeth Melville sought out the counsel of her Unitarian minister, Henry Whitney Bellows, hoping that he would assist her in a separation from her husband. Some sense of Lizzie's desperation and yet decorum can be gathered from the fact that she hoped Bellows would orchestrate a kidnapping of herself from the house so that sensible men would be seen intervening on her behalf and she could not be accused of abandoning her husband of twenty years. Lizzie's half-brother, Samuel Shaw, sagely advised against abduction, suggesting rather that she make one of her customary visits to Boston and simply not return. Things calmed down, as they can in a family, and Lizzie informed Bellows of her decision to stick it out. But that fall came the worst: their first child, Malcolm, now nineteen, locked himself in his room and put a bullet in his head.

No full record exists of how Melville and Lizzie survived this tragedy. For the most part, they kept to each other. Perhaps Malcolm might live in their renewed embrace. But they also kept apart. Lizzie's "rose fever"—

allergies—gave her a good excuse to seek fresher air at various resorts and thus absent herself from time to time from the demands of her always demanding husband. Melville had his writing, which was his own form of isolation and release.

CLAREL AND REDEMPTION

How Melville confronted and contained his loss can be gathered only from the writings and rewritings of his later years. Few address the matter of Malcolm directly. Melville's revisions of certain poems first written during the lad's boyhood at Arrowhead reveal intriguing patterns of remorse, exposure, and denial. "The Chipmunk," originally about the quick coming and going of that woodland creature, becomes later on, in revision, a poem about "Baby" who "startled / By some inkling Touching Earth" did "flit" away. "Monody," a yellow-paper poem generally thought to be occasioned by Hawthorne's death in 1864, may originally have been composed much earlier about any estranged friend, male or female, and then revised with a new second stanza and new woodland imagery similar to that found in "Chipmunk" (including a flitting snow-bird) to suggest Malcolm. But in "The Little Good Fellows" depicting a "self-slayer sad" who is mourned by forest animals, Melville revises the sibilant phrase to "unfriended man" (borrowed from John Webster), as if to remove the thought of youthful suicide. Hints of Malcolm emerge in *Clarel* (1876). But not until his final years was Melville ready to write out the pain of Malcolm in *Billy Budd,* the story of a bookish, too-rational, and yet fatherly captain who knowingly executes an innocent young man. Billy Budd, the Baby, was Herman's self-slaying boy.

Around 1870, Melville picked up a modern reprint of an eighteenth-century classic, Thomas Warton's *History of English Poetry.* Melville's annotations clearly indicate that he read the lengthy work closely. He was recuperating again, studying his craft and its practitioners. He was also preparing himself for his next project, bigger than anything he had ever attempted before, and longer in the making. The project was *Clarel: A Poem and Pilgrimage in the Holy Land.* Based on his trip in 1857 to the Holy Land, and published in 1876 with financial help from his dying uncle Peter Gansevoort, it was what he later called "a metrical affair ... eminently adapted for unpopularity." Indeed, success in the literary marketplace was hardly the point of this two-volume poem of over eighteen thousand lines. Longer than *Paradise Lost,* Melville's modern epic was adapted to work out certain intellectual and emotional problems brewing since *Moby-Dick* and the death of his son.

Like Ishmael, Melville was both believer and doubter. As Hawthorne put it, "He can neither believe, nor be comfortable in his unbelief." Thus, he was restless, and always questioning. *Clarel* is about a questioner: a divinity student—young like Malcolm, and plagued by doubt like Herman—coming to Jerusalem in hopes of regaining his faith. The young man Clarel (rhymes with "barrel") falls in love and proposes to Ruth, the daughter of Zionists, who must go into seclusion when her father is murdered. During that time, Clarel sets out with a host of American and European tourists, religionists, merchants, and wanderers on the well-worn circuit to the river Jordan, the Dead Sea, Bethlehem, and back to Jerusalem. On the way, he engages in or witnesses conversations touching upon the day's crises in religion, science, and politics. Chief among Clarel's fellow travelers is the thoughtful and reclusive Vine, reminiscent of Hawthorne, who resists fellowship, including Clarel's intellectual and homosocial advances. At a late turning point in the poem, Clarel learns from a handsome and melodious "Prodigal," to whom he is also attracted, that he must cease wasting his time doubting and simply love. Rushing back to Jerusalem, however, he discovers the grieving Ruth is dead.

It may be that Melville put more of himself than Malcolm into the character of Clarel, but what all three share is the masculine gender. The father's loss of a boy and the fictional boy's losses—Vine, the Prodigal, Ruth—revolve within the mystery of Malcolm's suicide: a young man succumbing to the pain of doubt and the ambivalences of adolescent sexuality. Perhaps Clarel's survival is Melville's wish for Malcolm. Those who love *Clarel*—and that number is growing—know that the cantos excerpted here constitute the slimmest of samples from this massive work, but the issues of masculine sexuality and doubt found here are a touchstone for some of Melville's finest works to come.

PROSE & POEM: FROM *JOHN MARR* TO *BILLY BUDD*

Melville continued until his retirement in 1885 with "the job," inspecting imports as they were carried up the Hudson, marveling at where those ships had been, and reflecting on his earlier days at sea. His most ambitious publications all but forgotten, he wrote now without the burden of a professional or national agenda, and without the anxiety of having to anticipate failure in the marketplace. He was, like his reclusive and unknown contemporary Emily Dickinson, a poet about whom the greater public asked, "Who?"

This does not mean that Melville stopped thinking about making books. He wrote new poems, tinkered with the old, and like Dickinson with her fascicles, relentlessly rearranged them in various clusters, renaming the clusters as he proceeded, revising and retitling the poems as he rearranged them. Moreover, some poems grew in startling ways. He now found himself putting poems and prose together.

The concept of integrating prose and poetry was not entirely new. One of his earlier creative instincts, as is evident in *Mardi,* had been to insert whimsical ditties throughout the prose narration, like the occasional songs in Shakespeare's comedies. But now, he found that he could not write a poem without its beckoning him to provide a prose setting for it, not so much as an introduction or supplemental essay as in *Battle-Pieces,* but as a bit of narration whose culmination could be expressed only through a poem. Melville gave no name to this innovative mixture—the familiar expression "prose poem" misses the point—and for lack of a better term we may call these concoctions "prose & poem" pieces, an ugly expression but odd enough to give us pause. For here, before Pound or William Carlos Williams or today's LANGUAGE poets, Melville offers a modernist collage of genres, too seamless to truly prefigure postmodern fragmentation, but nevertheless a fascinating advance upon Sidney's *Arcadia* or Browning's too-prosy dramatic monologues. In most cases, the manuscripts reveal that Melville began with the poem, then added a prose note, and then, over time, revised the poem and expanded the note, until a finished product emerged. With this creative process in mind, we see the writer composing polyphonically, with prose rhythms catching hold of his mind at one time and poetic melodies happening the next. However, from the reader's experience of the final work, we hear the genial but often convoluted prose voice exhausting character, conflict, setting, and symbol so that they can no longer convey meaning; the voice must let loose in poem. And yet the poem does not fully redeem the exhaustion; it flies up but is always and forever only suggestive. The final effect is a synergistic juxtaposition of languages, but there is no real resolution, only voices voicing.

Melville published only two of his prose & poem pieces, both in *John*

Marr and Other Sailors (1888), a collection of several character studies and narratives along with a dozen or so shorter poems. The title work, "John Marr," is a prose self-portrait leading to a poetic invocation of the dead. The old salt Marr, now a lonely pioneer amid the "blank stillness" of the oceanic prairie, seeks "verbal communion" with his shipmates and poetically invokes their combined presence as a broken raft: "Twined we were, entwined, then riven." Melville's present prose sterility contrasts with the poem's broken past fellowship, and together the two bespeak the writer's alienated condition. Following the elegiac dramatic monologues in *John Marr* are, in stark contrast, such poems of shipwreck as "The Aeolian Harp" and "The Berg" as well as short imagistic poems of the sea and its ominous denizens. Of these, "The Maldive Shark" is unforgettable, but more innovative are the often forgotten concluding "Pebbles," seven epigrams, deceptive bits of flotsam, culminating in the line "Healed of my hurt, I laud the inhuman Sea." The sea, like his writing, was an alien thing into which Melville plunged his pain, and continually found redemption.

Among the poems of *John Marr* is "The Enviable Isles," which carries with it the parenthetical comment that it derives "from 'Rammon.' " In an earlier manuscript incarnation, this sonnet-like work was attached to a prose study of a young son of Solomon named Rammon. Intrigued by Buddha's "transcendental teaching[s] alike unprovable and irrefutable," Rammon meets a seemingly shallow merchant who, in response to Rammon's wonderment over "the cessation of being," offers the aforementioned poem, "The Enviable Isles." The sonnet is not so much a consolation as a crystallization of the condition of consciousness, caught "on the marge" (one of Melville's favorite shoreline words) between awareness and nothingness. Although Melville did not include the prose portion of "Rammon" in *John Marr,* we offer the entire prose & poem work here, with both portions reunited, to demonstrate a heretofore unexamined prose context for one of Melville's finest poems.

One other prose & poem work, virtually ignored until now, is "Under the Rose," which Melville may have written to accompany his better-known (but still underappreciated) Rose Poems. This comic piece, reproduced here from manuscript, is all prose except for a devastating little poem at the end, which undercuts the materialist pretensions found in the prose. But Melville's most ambitious prose & poem project was a book-length collection entitled *The Burgundy Club,* which includes character sketches of an unnamed editor and two gentlemen, the Marquis de

Grandvin and Jack Gentian, whose respective tales, "At the Hostelry" and "Naples in the Time of Bomba," follow in verse. Melville may have conceived this book as early as 1859, when he was assembling his ill-fated unpublished volume of poems, and he seems to have revised it considerably from the mid-1870s on. The prose sections introducing the editor and Grandvin are reminiscent of the jaunty bachelorism of the earlier tales but stress, with good enough humor, the writer's alienation from the literary marketplace. The accompanying poem, "At the Hostelry," is a remarkable treatise on the picturesque. Melville's awareness of painting, sculpture, and the fine arts is evident in his earliest writings, but his life as a collector of prints and engravings probably gained momentum during his 1849–1850 trip to Europe, where he may have purchased artworks. During his later years Melville expanded his collection of reproductions to upwards of three hundred items, the full catalog of which has only recently been reconstructed. "At the Hostelry," one of several poetic ruminations on art and aesthetics, is Melville's fullest rendition of his ongoing study of European painting, featuring the views and styles of thirty different artists, many of whose engravings Melville collected, and his own personal definition of the picturesque, the culmination of his individualized thinking on the concept begun as early as the "Hawthorne and His Mosses" essay.

But the most familiar prose & poem piece is *Billy Budd*. For many, the novella is their first exposure to Melville. Not discovered until 1919, nor published until 1924, it is a strikingly modern work about an innocent sailor, falsely accused of mutiny, who kills his accuser and is condemned by an otherwise benevolent captain to die. As in *The Confidence-Man*, the narrator is both detached and equivocal, leaving readers rudderless in a sea of entanglements that make the process of judgment seem futile. Melville did not live to put a final polish on the work, and the difficulty of its language may be attributed to its incompleteness. And yet the roughgoing narration seems intended, for, as the narrator concludes, "truth uncompromisingly told will always have its ragged edges." As a consequence, critics have fiercely debated whether Melville would have us see Billy's death as an acceptance of an absurd world or as an ironic, fistshaking rebellion against authority. The debates swirling around the novella have kept it a primary text of modernism to the present day, and the source of various adaptations in drama, opera, and film.

Few are acquainted with the remarkable genesis of *Billy Budd*. We know it primarily as a prose fiction that happens to conclude with an odd poem entitled "Billy in the Darbies," odd because it depicts Billy as less innocent than the young sailor we find in the novella. This seems to be a purposeful "ragged edge" ending that casts doubt on the events previously told in prose. But, whether intended or not, the provocative disparity between the prose and poem Billys derives from the way Melville composed both parts.

Melville originally intended his novella to be a prose & poem work for inclusion in *John Marr*. This "Ur–*Billy Budd*" consisted of a version of "Billy in the Darbies" preceded by a prose introduction of about one paragraph only. Fragments of this early prose & poem version exist in four manuscript leaves, and these fragments (transcribed in this volume) provide enough text to give us some idea of Billy as a far more canny character, both politically and sexually, than we have previously known.

At some point in the creative process, Melville began to expand the little prose headnote to his poem, first to include Billy's false accuser, Claggart. At this stage Melville remakes Billy entirely: he is no longer the conspirator of the original poem but a loyal and fatally naïve "Handsome Sailor," whose repressed anger erupts out of his stammer to kill his accuser. Claggart's hatred for Billy is as deeply textured as our critical imagination can make it. Melville tempts interpretation by associating Claggart with the Pauline phrase "mystery of iniquity," and by implying that Claggart's envy is rooted in a denial of his attraction to the young sailor's beauty. In this regard *Billy Budd* is Melville's final and most devastating commentary on the dynamics of masculine sexuality, one that can be found in *Clarel*, "The Paradise of Bachelors," *Moby-Dick*, and *Pierre*, and as far back as *Typee*.

But the genesis of *Billy Budd* continued beyond Claggart to include Vere, the captain who becomes Billy's judge, jury, and executioner. In this stage of development, the tragedy of beauty and iniquity grows to include the tragedy of rationality. The bookish Vere cannot humanize his misplaced reverence for "forms, measured forms," and his drumhead trial leads him relentlessly to kill, in the name of law and duty, the very beauty and innocence Claggart's self-loathing aimed to destroy. Out of a short little prose & poem piece, Melville had crafted an exquisitely painful tragedy of Sophoclean proportions.

What inspired Melville to expand the "Billy in the Darbies" prose & poem piece into the novella we know today as *Billy Budd*? Perhaps a desire to dramatize the tensions of mutiny and betrayal was the trigger. Although set during the early Napoleonic Wars, well before Melville's own life at sea, both poem and novella are linked to a mutinous episode that touched Melville personally. Back in 1842 an admired cousin had served aboard the U.S. frigate *Somers,* a training vessel and scene of an infamous alleged mutiny that resulted in the drumhead trial and unnecessary hanging of three recruits, one the son of a government official. Melville's cousin Guert Gansevoort, who had served on the ship, had been exonerated of any wrongdoing in the affair. Over forty years later, in 1888 and 1889, magazine accounts retelling the *Somers* affair may have triggered Melville's memory of cousin Guert's experience and inspired him to expand his text. Or perhaps there is a closer family link, through Malcolm. Long since dead by his own hand and the victim of anger and grief only a father might have caused, or felt he had caused, Malcolm may be the source of a Billy whom Melville was trying to understand. Fathers can kill their sons for the sake of authority; and even they need some release.

TIMOLEON AND THE ROSE

In his final years of retirement, Melville fell prey to increasing periods of incapacity due to the heart disease that eventually claimed his life in the fall of 1891. He preserved his anonymity but haunted libraries and shops that sold books and prints. He would take his granddaughter Eleanor on the horse-drawn trolley to Central Park and watch her climb the rocks and listen to the flapping of her skirts. In his book-lined study bedroom, he kept several stacks of papers, each one a book he was compiling. By 1890, he had the satisfaction of knowing that his moribund reputation was experiencing a small resurrection. For some time, individuals on both sides of the Atlantic had sustained happy recollections of Melville's work, ranking him with Whitman and Thoreau. Slowly, and largely at first through word of mouth, a renewed appreciation of Melville had begun to grow. He was admired by the pre-Raphaelite William Morris, the sexologist Havelock Ellis, and the social critic H. S. Salt. Fellow "writers of the deep," like Robert Louis Stevenson and W. Russell Clark, championed Melville repeatedly. So did a young Canadian professor, Archibald MacMechan, who later helped to spark interest in Melville at Harvard and Columbia.

In the early 1880s, Melville had been asked to join New York's Authors' Club, but he had become shy of large gatherings, perhaps, or seemed to relish being the "outcast" (as one late admirer, the poet James Buchanan, called him), and he declined the invitation. Perhaps, too, he relished the "annulment" of self that comes with being a true writer, as opposed to the puffing of one's personality that comes with the status of being an "author." To Hawthorne in 1856, Melville had admitted contemplating "annihilating" himself, not committing suicide but simply getting out of the writing profession so that the writing process could follow its own path. Back then, he chose poetry over professional "annihilation." And only when the events of 1867 forced him to quit being an Author was he able to become a Writer, to absorb himself into something other than himself. The freedom of anonymity allowed him more fully to inhabit the language, a thing we all inherit but only a few reshape.

Scholars, critics, and fellow writers began to seek him out. The literary critic E. C. Stedman anthologized some of Melville's poems in 1889. But, not surprisingly, most of these new enthusiasts were thrilled by the Author Melville had once been and unaware of the Writer he currently was. They liked *Typee* and *Omoo* but did not inquire about the stacks of papers on his desk. In 1890, the young British editor Edward Garnett drafted a letter on behalf of his publisher, T. Fisher Unwin, asking Melville if he would "recast" *Redburn* as a "personal adventure" or write "your final reminiscences." The aging Melville must have savored that word "final."

Melville had two books of poetry in the works, each building upon a personal past to achieve contact with a deeper redemptive Past of art and culture. Most of the poems in *Timoleon, Etc.* are drawn from Melville's 1857 tour of Italy, Greece, and the Holy Land, and some, like the yellow-paper poem "Monody," may have been first composed as early as 1860. The "*Etc.*" in the title is misleading; this is not a random selection of poems but an excursion through Mediterranean scenes in lyrics expressing a blending of sensibilities both ancient and modern, concerning art, architecture, politics, and sex.

Melville's interest in classical culture was of long standing. Soon after his Mediterranean tour and back at Arrowhead, he regaled two students on a visit from nearby Williams College about "the ancient dignity of Homeric times." By the late 1860s he was reading Matthew Arnold and sharpening his sense of the Hellenic and Hebraic. *Clarel* was not only a stunning immersion in the content of these two cultural ideas; it was also a rigorous honing of the prosodic skills so savagely impugned by critics of

Battle-Pieces. The result was a classical spareness to his four-beat versification. He developed a line that was short and hard, seemingly unpolished,
in places and then suddenly unexpectedly smooth, like a fractured river
stone, like the long writhing figure emerging from marble in Michelangelo's last unfinished work, like the fragment of a Grecian ruin. In *Timoleon,* Melville blends this hard classic style with modern perspectives. In
the remarkable poem "The Parthenon," he telescopes our vision of the
classic structure from a distant view seen by modern tourists down to and
back in time to the placement of the final stone, thus marking the moment of "Art's meridian." A similar compression of past and present occurs in "Syra," in which a current Greek marketplace stands as a lively
but somber recollection of a lost era. The subtle dissociations in these
poems are, however, only symptomatic of deeper fusions.

In "After the Pleasure Party," Melville assumes the voice of a female
astronomer who, having been slighted by a male lover, seeks to "remake"
her sexuality in Sapphic terms, or don a "veil" of Christian virginity, or
adopt the pose of the "armed virgin" Athena. Evoking the Platonic notion
that nature creates each person as half a soul in search of his or her perfect other half, Melville proclaims sex a "Cosmic jest or Anarch blunder,"
and warns against any attempt to transcend this condition, even through
art. But Melville does not dismiss the ability of both sexuality and art to
allow unmatched halves to "meet and mate," a phrase echoed directly in
his most famous poem, "Art." Here, in "truncated sonnet" form, the poet
crystallizes the artistic fusion of "unlike things" in the sexually suggestive
image of Jacob's struggle with the angel. The manuscript for this powerful poem is heavily revised and shows us how Melville reshaped it in at
least six successive versions (each transcribed in this volume). Thus, "Art"
is not only a poem about the creative process; it is, in manuscript, a
demonstration of that process. It was also the last statement on the subject
he would ever see in print. Three months after the publication of *Timoleon,* Melville was dead.

But even up to his final days, Melville was tinkering with another book
of poems. Dedicated to Lizzie, *Weeds and Wildings Chiefly, With a Rose or
Two* contains poems that hark back to the personal past Melville had
shared with her at Arrowhead; it also contains more sensual poems about
roses written to capture the artful Past of the Troubadours. Melville's
Rose Poems are hot and intense scenes of courtship figured in the emblem of the rose, which in due course becomes the vehicle that trans-

forms the sensuality of lovemaking as found in "Amoroso" into the spiritual transcendence of "Rose Window." Throughout these nine poems is an ongoing debate between the powerful materiality of the rose's bloom and the spiritual essence of its attar. These neglected love poems—redolent of medievalism and prefiguring Lawrence—are perhaps the most astonishing achievement of Melville's final days.

The centerpiece of *Weeds and Wildings* is the audacious "Rip Van Winkle's Lilac," a prose & poem rewriting of Irving's classic. Before taking his fabled nap, Melville's Rip has planted a sprig of lilac, which in the intervening years has grown in size and beauty to attract an artist of the picturesque. One is tempted to see the painter—supremely patient with a puritanical critic who interrupts him and careful to "tone down the green" in his work—as Melville's self-portrait. But Rip, too, is another version of Melville, who, after a long sleep, awakens in his final years to see his work spreading throughout the countryside. Melville's reputation, after a long dormancy, was beginning to flower.

A NEW MELVILLE

But Melville's death in 1891 doused the renewing interest in him, and the revival of 1890 did not ignite. In 1919, Raymond Weaver learned of the box into which the Melville family had placed Melville's papers. This time something clicked, and before the end of the following decade *Billy Budd* was transcribed (although inaccurately), Melville's works were published in a standard (although British) edition, and John Barrymore had made two film versions of *Moby-Dick* (silent and sound).

The Melville revival begun in the 1920s has continued unabated to the present day. But in reality only a portion of Melville has been revived. Readers know *Moby-Dick,* and *Typee* has had a respectable resurrection in recent years, but *Redburn, Pierre,* and *The Confidence-Man* still suffer neglect. Readers know "Bartleby," and "Benito Cereno" now grows in popularity, as does "The Tartarus of Maids," but "The Chola Widow" was recently removed from a new edition of a major literary anthology. Readers know *Billy Budd* but nothing of the other prose & poem pieces. And despite attempts by such admirers as Robert Penn Warren to inspire interest in the poetry, Melville's reputation as a poet is only beginning to kindle.

There are many "new" Melville works waiting to be read in this volume, each seeking readers to make them happen. And there is a new Melville waiting to make your acquaintance. He is not the Author who failed in the marketplace, but the Writer who never stopped writing, and never stopped growing. Having just published *Moby-Dick,* Melville wrote to Hawthorne that he was already on to his new Kraken of a novel, *Pierre.* And jokingly he complained of the growth. Indeed, he had been growing even as he had been writing the letter he had just written, and if Hawthorne were to write him back, he would be addressing a different person, "for the very fingers that now guide this pen," he explained, "are not precisely the same that just took it up and put it on this paper." Putting pen to paper, that process changes you. And "Lord," he asked, "when shall we be done changing?" For Melville, the changing never stopped.

A NOTE ON THE TEXT

This volume draws its texts of Melville's tales, poems, letters, reviews, and lectures from the now-standard Northwestern-Newberry edition of *The Writings of Herman Melville* (NN). Still in preparation are the final two volumes of this series featuring the poetry Melville published during his lifetime and the poetry and prose he left in manuscript at his death. Although unpublished, the NN texts for Melville's published poetry (in *Battle-Pieces*, *John Marr*, and *Timoleon*) have been established and made available to the Modern Library for this volume. The texts for the manuscript materials are not yet fully established. However, reliable editions of *Billy Budd* (Chicago, 1962), *The Burgundy Club*, "Rammon," and *Weeds and Wildings* prepared by NN editors or their associates do exist, and these texts have been adopted here. The fluid text editions of *Typee*, "Camoëns," "Art," and the "Ur–*Billy Budd*," as well as the poems in Part Four and the prose piece "Under the Rose" in Part Seven were prepared by the editor of this volume on the basis of direct inspection of manuscripts located at the New York Public Library and Houghton Library, Harvard University. For further details on these and other textual matters, see the annotations at the end of this volume.

TALES, POEMS, AND OTHER WRITINGS

PART ONE
STARTING OUT

Apart from the death of his father, the most significant event in Melville's formative years was his experience at sea. Raised as a gentleman but deprived of a gentleman's income, he signed aboard the whaler *Acushnet*, in January 1841, to make some cash but mostly to see "the watery part of the world," its seedy ports of call and Edenic islands. His four years at sea—two on various whalers and two in the U.S. Navy—deepened the young man's consciousness. He witnessed new worlds: Pacific imperialism, naval authority, the working life of seamen, and the hidden, primal life of both the islanders and the creatures of the sea. But none of this changed Melville more than the experience of writing it all down. As he later told Hawthorne, he wrote so that he might "unfold" within himself, to find the meaning of things, and to announce it. Two of Melville's earliest compositions demonstrate the unfolding.

"Fragments from a Writing Desk, No. 2" first appeared in May 1839 in Melville's local paper, the *Democratic Press and Lansingburgh Advertiser*. Published under the pseudonym "L.A.V.," it is an adolescent yet artful homage to Poe, dark lady and all, but its serio-comic gothicism and images of silence hint at something deeper. Four years at sea would bring that out.

Melville published *Typee* in 1846, soon after his return from the Pacific. Based on his month-long "residence" with the natives of the Taipi valley in the Marquesan island of Nuku Hiva, its goal was to "speak the unvarnished truth" about Western imperialism and missionaries as well as Polynesian customs: taboo, tattoo, and cannibalism; their sexuality; but also Melville's own sexual growth. But to speak *this* kind of "unvarnished truth" required some varnish after all, and a good deal of self-censorship. Melville toned down much of his political, emotional, and sexual musings for the published version of *Typee*, but these myriad revisions are preserved in his working draft manuscript. The version of the sensual Chapter 14 from *Typee* offered here showcases Melville's more significant revisions. Reading them beside Melville's final text gives us a glimpse at Melville's creative process and his remarkable unfolding as a young man and writer, after his return from the sea.

Fragments from a Writing Desk, No. 2

"Confusion seize the Greek!" exclaimed I, as wrathfully rising from my chair, I flung my ancient Lexicon across the room, and seizing my hat and cane, and throwing on my cloak, I sallied out into the clear air of heaven. The bracing coolness of an April evening calmed my aching temples, and I slowly wended my way to the river side. I had promenaded the bank for about half an hour, when flinging myself upon the grassy turf, I was soon lost in revery, and up to the lips in sentiment.

I had not lain more than five minutes, when a figure effectually concealed in the ample folds of a cloak, glided past me, and hastily dropping something at my feet, disappeared behind the angle of an adjoining house, ere I could recover from my astonishment at so singular an occurrence.—"Certes!" cried I, springing up, "here is a spice of the marvelous!" and stooping down, I picked up an elegant little, rose-coloured, lavender-scented billet-doux, and hurriedly breaking the seal (a heart, transfixed with an arrow) I read by the light of the moon, the following:

"Gentle Sir—

If my fancy has painted you in genuine colours, you will on the receipt of this, incontinently follow the bearer where she will lead you.

INAMORATA."

"The deuce I will!" exclaimed I,—"But soft!"—And I reperused this singular document, turned over the billet in my fingers, and examined the hand-writing; which was femininely delicate, and I could have sworn was a woman's. Is it possible, thought I, that the days of romance are revived?—No, "The days of chivalry are over!" says Burke.

As I made this reflection, I looked up, and beheld the same figure which had handed me this questionable missive, beckoning me forward. I started towards her; but, as I approached, she receded from me, and fled swiftly along the margin of the river at a pace, which, encumbered as I was with my heavy cloak and boots, I was unable to follow; and which filled me with sundry misgivings, as to the nature of the being, who could travel with such amazing celerity. At last perfectly breathless, I fell into a walk; which, my mysterious fugitive perceiving, she likewise lessened her pace, so as to keep herself still in sight, although at too great a distance to permit me to address her.

Having recovered from my fatigue and regained my breath: I loosened the clasp of my cloak, and inwardly resolving that I would come at the bottom of the mystery, I desperately flung the mantle from my shoulders, and dashing my beaver to the ground, gave chase in good earnest to the tantalizing stranger. No sooner did I from my extravagant actions announce my intention to overtake her, than with a light laugh of derision, she sprang forward at a rate, which in attempting to outstrip, soon left me far in the rear, heartily disconcerted and crest-fallen, and inly cursing the ignus fatuus, that danced so provokingly before me.

At length, like every one else, learning wisdom from experience; I thought my policy lay in silently following the footsteps of my eccentric guide, and quietly waiting the denouement of this extraordinary adventure. So soon as I relaxed my speed, and gave evidence of having renounced my more summary mode of procedure; the stranger, regulating her movements by mine, proceeded at a pace which preserved between us a uniform distance, ever and anon, looking back like a wary general to see if I were again inclined to try the mettle of her limbs.

After pursuing our way in this monotonous style for some time; I observed that my conductress rather abated in her precautions, and had not for the last ten or fifteen minutes taken her periodical survey over her shoulder; whereat, plucking up my spirits, which I can assure you courteous reader, had fallen considerably below zero by the ill-success of my previous efforts,—I again rushed madly forward at the summit of my speed, and having advanced ten or twelve rods unperceived, was flattering myself that I should this time make good my purpose; when, turning suddenly round, as though reminded of her late omission, and descrying me plunging ahead like an infuriated steed, she gave a slightly audible scream of surprise, and once more fled, as though helped forward by invisible wings.

This last failure was too much. I stopped short, and stamping the ground in ungovernable rage, gave vent to my chagrin in a volley of exclamations: in which, perhaps, if narrowly inspected, might have been detected two or three expressions which savored somewhat of the jolly days of the jolly cavaliers. But if a man was ever excusable for swearing; surely, the circumstances of the case were palliative of the crime. What! to be thwarted by a woman? Peradventure, baffled by a girl? Confusion! It was too bad! To be outgeneraled, routed, defeated, by a mere rib of the earth? It was not to be borne! I thought I should never survive the inexpressible mortification of the moment; and in the heighth of my despair, I bethought me of putting a romantic end to my existence upon the very spot which had witnessed my discomfiture.

But when the first transports of my wrath had passed away, and perceiving that the waters of the river, instead of presenting an unruffled calm, as they are wont to do on so interesting an occasion, were discomposed and turbid; and remembering, that beside this, I had no other means of accomplishing my heroic purpose, except the vulgar and inelegant one, of braining myself against the stone wall which traversed the road; I sensibly determined after taking into consideration the aforementioned particulars, together with the fact that I had an unfinished game of chess to win, on which depended no inconsiderable wager, that to commit suicide under such circumstances would be highly inexpedient, and probably be attended with many inconveniencies.—During the time I had consumed in arriving at this most wise and discreet conclusion, my mind had time to recover its former tone, and had become comparatively calm and collected; and I saw my folly in endeavoring to trifle with one, apparently so mysterious and inexplicable.

I now resolved, that whatever might betide, I would patiently await the issue of the affair: and advancing forward in the direction of my guide, who all this time had maintained her ground, stedfastly watching my actions,—we both simultaneously strode forward, and were soon on the same footing as before.

We walked on at an increased pace, and were just passed the suburbs of the town, when my conductress plunging into a neighboring grove, pursued her way with augmented speed, till we arrived at a spot, whose singular and grotesque beauty, even amidst the agitating occurrences of the evening I could not refrain from observing. A circular space of about a dozen acres in extent had been cleared in the very heart of the grove: leaving, however, two parallel rows of lofty trees, which at the distance of about twenty paces, and intersected in the centre by two similar ranges, traversed the whole diameter of the circle. These noble plants shooting their enormous trunks to an amazing heighth, bore their verdant honors far aloft, throwing their gigantic limbs abroad and embracing each other with their rugged arms. This fanciful union of their sturdy boughs formed a magnificent arch, whose grand proportions, swelling upward in proud preeminence, presented to the eye a vaulted roof, which to my perturbed imagination at the time, seemed to have canopied the triumphal feasts of the sylvan god.—This singular prospect burst upon me in all its beauty, as we emerged from the surrounding thicket, and I had unconsciously lingered on the borders of the wood, the better to enjoy so unrivalled a view; when as my eye was following the dusky outline of the grove, I caught the diminutive figure of my guide, who standing at the entrance of the arched-way I have been endeavoring to describe, was making the most extravagant gestures of impatience at my delay.—Reminded at once of the situation, which put me for a time under the control of this capricious mortal, I replied to her summons by immediately throwing myself forward, and we soon entered the Atlantean arbor, in whose umbrageous shades we were completely hid.

Lost in conjecture, during the whole of this eccentric ramble, as to its probable termination—the sombre gloom of these ancestral trees, gave a darkning hue to my imaginings, and I began to repent the inconsiderate haste which had hurried me on, in an expedition, so peculiar and suspicious. In spite of all my efforts to exclude them, the fictions of the nursery poured in upon my recollection, and I felt with Bob Acres in the "Rivals," that "my valor was certainly going." Once, I am almost ashamed to own it to thee, gentle reader, my mind was so haunted with ghostly images, that in an agony of apprehension, I was about to turn and flee, and had actually made some preliminary movements to that effect, when my hand, accidentally straying into my bosom, griped the billet, whose romantic summons had caused this nocturnal adventure. I felt my soul regain her fortitude, and smiling at the absurd conceits which infested my brain, I once more stalked proudly forward, under the overhanging branches of these ancient trees.

Emergent from the shades of this romantic region, we soon beheld an edifice, which seated on a gentle eminence, and embowered amidst surrounding trees, bore the appearance of a country villa; although its plain exterior showed none of those fantastic devices which usually adorn the elegant chateaux. My conductress as we neared this unpretending mansion seemed to redouble her precautions, and although she evinced no positive alarm, yet her quick and startled glances bespoke no small degree of apprehension. Motioning me to conceal myself behind an adjacent tree, she approached the house with rapid but cautious steps; my eyes followed her until she disappeared behind the shadow of the garden wall, and I remained waiting her reappearance with the utmost anxiety.—An interval of several moments had elapsed, when I descried her, swinging open a small postern, and beckoning me to advance. I obeyed the summons, and was soon by her side, not a little amazed at the complacency, which after what had transpired, brooked my immediate vicinity. Dissembling my astonishment, however, and rallying all my powers, I followed with noiseless strides the footsteps of my guide, fully persuaded that this mysterious affair was now about to be brought to an eclaircissement.

The appearance of this spacious habitation was any thing but inviting; it seemed to have been built with a jealous eye to concealment; and its few, but well-defended windows were sufficiently high from the ground, as effectually to baffle the prying curiosity of the inquisitive stranger. Not a single light shone from the narrow casement; but all was harsh, gloomy and forbidding. As my imagination, ever alert on such an occasion, was busily occupied in assigning some fearful motive for such unusual precautions; my leader suddenly halted beneath a lofty window, and making a low call, I perceived slowly descending therefrom, a thick silken chord, attached to an ample basket, which was silently deposited at our feet. Amazed at this apparition, I was about soliciting an explanation: when laying her fingers impressively upon her lips, and placing herself in the basket, my guide motioned me to seat myself beside her. I obeyed; but not without considerable trepidation: and in obedience to the same low call which had procured its descent our curious vehicle, with sundry creakings, rose in air.

To attempt an analysis of my feelings at this moment were impossible. The solemnity of the hour—the romantic nature of my present situation—the singularity of my whole adventure—the profound stillness which prevailed—the solitude of the place, were enough of themselves to strike a panic into the stoutest heart, and to unsettle the strongest nerves. But when to these, was added the thought,—that at the dead of night, and in the company of a being so perfectly inexplicable, I was effecting a clandestine entrance into so remarkable an abode: the kind and sympathising reader will not wonder, when I wished myself safely bestowed in my own snug quarters in ———— street.

Such were the reflections which passed through my mind, during our aerial voyage, throughout which my guide maintained the most rigid silence, only broken at intervals by the occasional creakings of our machine, as it rubbed against the side of the house in its ascent. No sooner had we gained the window, than two brawny arms were extended circling me in their embrace, and ere I was aware of the change of locality, I found myself standing upright in an apartment, dimly illuminated by a solitary taper. My fellow voyager was quickly beside me, and again enjoining silence with her finger, she seized the lamp and bidding me follow, conducted me through a long corridor, till we reached a low door concealed behind some old tapestry, which opening to the touch, disclosed a spectacle as beautiful and enchanting as any described in the Arabian Nights.

The apartment we now entered, was filled up in a style of Eastern splendor, and its atmosphere was redolent of the most delicious perfumes. The walls were hung round with the most elegant draperies, waving in graceful folds, on which were delineated scenes of Arcadian beauty. The floor was covered with a carpet of the finest texture, in which were wrought with exquisite skill, the most striking events in ancient mythology. Attached to the wall by chords composed of alternate threads of crimson silk and gold, were several magnificent pictures illustrative of the loves of Jupiter and Semele,—Psyche before the tribunal of Venus, and a variety of other scenes, limned all with felicitous grace. Disposed around the room, were luxurious couches, covered with the finest damask, on which were likewise executed after the Italian fashion the early fables of Greece and Rome. Tripods, designed to represent the Graces bearing aloft vases, richly chiseled in the classic taste, were distributed in the angles of the room, and exhaled an intoxicating fragrance.

Chandeliers of the most fanciful description, suspended from the lofty ceiling by rods of silver, shed over this voluptuous scene a soft and tempered light, and imparted to the whole, that dreamy beauty, which must be seen in order to be duly appreciated. Mirrors of unusual magnitude, multiplying in all directions the gorgeous objects, deceived the eye by their reflections, and mocked the vision with long perspective.

But overwhelming as was the display of opulence, it yielded in attraction to the being for whom all this splendour glistened; and the grandeur of the room served only to show to advantage the matchless beauty of its inmate. These superb decorations, though lavished in boundless profusion, were the mere accessories of a creature, whose loveliness was of that spiritual cast that depended upon no adventitious aid, and which as no obscurity could diminish, so, no art could heighten.

When I first obtained a glimpse of this lovely being, she lay reclining upon an ottoman; in one hand holding a lute, and with the other lost in the profusion of her silken tresses, she supported her head.—I could not refrain from recalling the passionate exclamation of Romeo:

> "See how she leans her cheek upon her hand;
> Oh! that I were a glove upon that hand,
> That I might kiss that cheek!"

She was habited in a flowing robe of the purest white, and her hair, escaping from the fillet of roses which had bound it, spread its negligent graces over neck and bosom and shoulder, as though unwilling to reveal the extent of such transcendant charms.—Her zone was of pink satin, on which were broidered figures of Cupid in the act of drawing his bow; while the ample folds of her Turkish sleeve were gathered at the wrist by a bracelet of immense rubies, each of which represented a heart pierced thro' by a golden shaft. Her fingers were decorated with a variety of rings, which as she waved her hand to me as I entered, darted forth a thousand coruscations, and gleamed their brilliant splendors to the sight. Peeping from beneath the envious skirts of her mantle, and almost buried in the downy quishion on which it reposed, lay revealed the prettiest little foot you can imagine; cased in a satin slipper, which clung to the fairy-like member by means of a diamond clasp.

As I entered the apartment, her eyes were downcast, and the expression of her face was mournfully interesting; she had apparently been lost in some melancholy revery. Upon my entrance, however, her countenance brightened, as with a queenly wave of the hand, she motioned my conductress from the room, and left me standing, mute, admiring and bewildered in her presence.

For a moment my brain spun round, and I had not at command a single one of my faculties. Recovering my self possession however, and with that, my good-breeding, I advanced en cavalier, and gracefully sinking on one knee, I bowed my head and exclaimed—"Here do I prostrate myself, thou sweet Divinity, and kneel at the shrine of thy peerless charms!"—I hesitated,—blushed, looked up, and beheld bent upon me a pair of Andalusian eyes, whose melting earnestness of expression pierced me to the soul, and I felt my heart dissolving away like ice before the equinoctial heats.

Alas! For all the vows of eternal constancy I had sworn to another!— The silken threads were snapped asunder; the golden chords had parted! A new dominion was creeping o'er my soul, and I fell, bound at the feet of my fair enchantress. A moment of unutterable interest passed, while I met the gaze of this glorious being with a look as ardent, as burning, as steadfast as her own.—But it was not in mortal woman to stand the glance of an eye which had never quailed before a foe; and whose fierce lightnings were now playing in the wild expression of a love, that rent my bosom like a whirlwind, and tore up my past attachments as though they were but of the growth of yesterday.—The long dark lashes fell! smothered were the fires, whose brightness had kindled my soul in flames! I seized the passive hand, I lifted it to my lips and covered it with burning kisses! "Fair mortal!" I exclaimed, "I feel my passion is requited: but, seal it with thy own sweet voice, or I shall expire in uncertainty!"

Those lustrous orbs again opened on me all their fires; and maddened at her silence, I caught her in my arms, and imprinting one long, long kiss upon her hot and glowing lips, I cried "Speak! Tell me, thou cruel! Does thy heart send forth vital fluid like my own? Am I loved,—even wildly, madly as I love?" She was silent; gracious God! what horrible apprehension crossed my soul?—Frantic with the thought, I held her from me, and

looking in her face, I met the same impassioned gaze; her lips moved—
my senses ached with the intensity with which I listened,—all was still,—
they uttered no sound; I flung her from me, even though she clung to my
vesture, and with a wild cry of agony I burst from the apartment!—She
was dumb! Great God, she was dumb! DUMB AND DEAF!

L. A. V.
1839

VERSIONS OF *TYPEE*

Typee exists in manuscript and in at least two print versions, each of which varies significantly from the other. The manuscript records Melville's first transcription of his island experiences as well as several stages of revision in the form of insertions and deletions. The first British edition reveals that Melville made further additions and subtractions to his book. Stern rebukes from the American religious press concerning Melville's attacks on missionaries motivated Melville's American publisher, John Wiley, to expurgate *Typee* for Americans. Melville's British publisher, John Murray, refused to alter his version of the book. Thus, up until the 1930s *Typee* was reprinted in two different versions, one on each side of the Atlantic. The manuscript version—a three-chapter fragment—was discovered in 1983.

The following "fluid text" version of *Typee*'s Chapter 14 integrates this evidence of manuscript and print revision onto the page so that readers may gain more access to Melville as a writer in process. The British version of Chapter 14 is here reprinted in full with selected manuscript revisions inserted in brackets or boxes.

Small revisions of a word or two in the manuscript appear in brackets in the text; an arrow [→] points to the following revised word or words in italics. Larger revisions appear in boxes following a revised passage. Brief revision narratives explaining both small and large revisions are located in the Notes.

TYPEE,
CHAPTER 14

In the course of a few days Toby had recovered from the effects of his adventure with the Happar warriors; the wound on his head rapidly healing under the vegetable treatment of the good Tinor. Less fortunate than my companion, however, I still continued to languish under a complaint the origin and nature of which were still a mystery. Cut off as I was from all intercourse with the civilized world, and feeling the inefficiency of anything the natives could do to relieve me; knowing too, that so long as I remained in my present condition, it would be impossible for me to leave the valley, whatever opportunity might present itself; and apprehensive that ere long we might be exposed to some caprice on the part of the [natives→ savages→] *islanders*, I now gave up all hopes of recovery, and became a prey to the most gloomy thoughts. A deep dejection fell upon me, which neither the friendly remonstrances of my companion, the devoted attentions of Kory-Kory, nor all the soothing influences of Fayaway could remove.

One morning as I lay on the mats in the house, plunged in melancholy reverie, and regardless of everything around me, Toby, who had left me about an hour, returned in haste, and with great glee told me to cheer up and be of good heart; for he believed, from what was going on among the natives, that there were boats approaching the bay.

These tidings operated upon me like magic. The hour of our deliverance was at hand, and starting up, I was soon convinced that something unusual was about to occur. The word "botee! botee!" was vociferated in all directions; and shouts were heard in the distance, at first feebly and faintly; but growing louder and nearer at each successive repetition, until they were caught up by a fellow in a cocoa-nut tree a few yards off, who sounding them in turn, they were reiterated from a neighboring grove, and so died away gradually from point to point, as the intelligence penetrated into the farthest recesses of the valley. This was the vocal telegraph of the islanders; by means of which condensed items of information could be carried in a very few minutes from the sea to their remotest habitation, a distance of at least eight or nine miles. On the present occasion it was in active opera-tion; one piece of information following another with inconceivable rapidity.§

---

§   *Melville deleted the following paragraph from manuscript:*
These sounds at first scarcely audible & advancing progressively from the water's edge swelling higher & higher as they approached their maximum at the place where I stood, & then sweeping still on & sinking away by an inverse gradation untill they became lost again to the ear, suggested to me the idea of an enormous gamut whose notes were sounded by some musical giant. —

The greatest commotion now appeared to prevail. At every fresh item of intelligence the natives betrayed the liveliest interest, and redoubled the energy with which they employed themselves in collecting fruit to sell to the expected visitors. Some were tearing off the husks from cocoa-nuts; some perched in the trees were throwing down bread-fruit to their companions, who gathered them into heaps as they fell; while others were plying their fingers rapidly in weaving leafen baskets in which to carry the fruit.

There were other matters too going on at the same time. Here you would see a stout warrior polishing his spear with a bit of old tappa, or adjusting the folds of the girdle about his waist; and there you might descry a young damsel decorating herself with flowers, as if having in her eye some maidenly conquest; while, as in all cases of hurry and confusion in every part of the world, a number of individuals kept hurrying to and fro, with amazing vigour and perseverance, doing nothing themselves, and hindering others.

Never before had we seen the islanders in such a state of bustle and excitement; and the scene furnished abundant evidence of the fact—that it was only at long intervals any such events occur.

When I thought of the length of time that might intervene before a similar chance of escape would be presented, I bitterly lamented that I had not the power of availing myself effectually of the present opportunity.

From all that we could gather, it appeared that the natives were fearful of arriving too late upon the beach, unless they made extraordinary exertions. Sick and lame as I was, I would have started with Toby at once, had not Kory-Kory not only refused to carry me, but manifested the most invincible repugnance to our leaving the neighbourhood of the house. The rest of the savages were equally opposed to our wishes, and seemed grieved and astonished at the earnestness of my solicitations. I clearly perceived that while my attendant avoided all appearance of constraining my movements, he was nevertheless determined to thwart my wish. He seemed to me on this particular occasion, as well as often afterwards, to be executing the orders of some other person with regard to me, though at the same time feeling towards me the most lively affection.

Toby, who had made up his mind to accompany the islanders if possible, as soon as they were in readiness to depart, and who for that reason had refrained from showing the same anxiety that I had done, now represented to me that it was idle for me to entertain the hope of reaching the beach in time to profit by any opportunity that might then be presented.

"Do you not see," said he, "the savages themselves are fearful of being too late, and I should hurry forward myself at once did I not think that if I showed too much eagerness I should destroy all our hopes of reaping any benefit from this fortunate event. If you will only endeavour to appear tranquil or unconcerned, you will quiet their suspicions, and I have no doubt they will then let me go with them to the beach, supposing that I merely go out of curiosity. Should I succeed in getting down to the boats, I will make known the condition in which I have left you, and measures may then be taken to secure our escape."

In the expediency of this I could not but acquiesce; and as the natives had now completed their preparations, I watched with the liveliest interest the reception that Toby's application might meet with. As soon as they understood from my companion that I intended to remain, they appeared to make no objection to his proposition, and even hailed it with pleasure. Their singular conduct on this occasion not a little puzzled me at the time, and imparted to subsequent events an additional mystery.

The islanders were now to be seen hurrying along the path which led to the sea. I shook Toby warmly by the hand, and gave him my Payta hat to shield his wounded head from the sun, as he had lost his own. He cordially returned the pressure of my hand, and solemnly promising to return as soon as the boats should leave the shore, sprang from my side, and the next minute disappeared in a turn of the grove.

In spite of the unpleasant reflections that crowded upon my mind, I could not but be entertained by the novel and animated sight which now met my view. One after another the natives crowded along the narrow path, laden with every variety of fruit. Here, you might have seen one, who, after ineffectually endeavouring to persuade a surly porker to be conducted in leading strings, was obliged at last to seize the perverse animal in his arms, and carry him struggling against his naked breast, and squealing without intermission. There went two, who at a little distance might have been taken for the Hebrew spies, on their return to Moses with the goodly bunch of grapes. One trotted before the other at a distance of a couple of yards, while between them, from a pole resting on their shoulders, was suspended a huge cluster of banannas, which swayed to and fro with the rocking gait at which they proceeded. Here ran another, perspiring with his exertions, and bearing before him a quantity of cocoa-nuts, who, fearful of being too late, heeded not the fruit that dropped from his basket, and appeared solely intent upon reaching his destination, careless how many of his cocoa-nuts kept company with him.

In a short time the last straggler was seen hurrying on his way, and the faint shouts of those in advance died insensibly upon the ear. Our part of the valley now appeared nearly deserted by its inhabitants, Kory-Kory, his aged father, and a few decrepid old people being all that were left.

Towards sunset the islanders in small parties began to return from the beach, and among them, as they drew near to the house, I sought to descry the form of my companion. But one after another they passed the dwelling, and I caught no glimpse of him. Supposing, however, that he would soon appear with some of the members of the household, I quieted my apprehensions, and waited patiently to see him advancing in company with the beautiful [Faaua →] *Fayaway.* At last, I perceived Tinor coming forward, followed by the girls and young men who usually resided in the house of Marheyo; but with them came not my comrade, and, filled with a thousand alarms, I eagerly sought to discover the cause of his delay.

My earnest questions appeared to embarrass the natives greatly. All their accounts were contradictory: one giving me to understand that Toby would be with me in a very short time; another that he did not know where he was; while a third, violently inveighing against him, assured me that he had stolen away, and would never come back. It appeared to me, at the time, that in making these various statements they endeavoured to conceal from me some terrible disaster, lest the knowledge of it should overpower me.

Fearful lest some fatal calamity had overtaken him, I sought out young Fayaway, and endeavoured to learn from her, if possible, the truth.

This gentle being had early attracted my regard, not only from her extraordinary beauty, but from the attractive cast of her countenance, singularly expressive of intelligence and humanity. Of all the natives she alone seemed to appreciate the effect which the peculiarity of the circumstances in which we were placed had produced upon the minds of my companion and myself. In addressing me—especially when I lay reclining upon the mats suffering from pain—there was a tenderness in her manner which it was impossible to misunderstand or resist.§

---

§ *Melville inserted the following paragraph in manuscript:*
Whenever she entered the house, the expression of her face indicated the liveliest sympathy for me; and moving towards the place where I lay, with one arm slightly elevated in a gesture of pity, and her large glistening eyes gazing intently into mine, she would murmur plaintively, "Awha! awha! Tommo," and seat herself mournfully beside me.

Her manner convinced me that she deeply compassionated my situation, as being removed from my country and friends, and placed beyond the reach of all relief. Indeed, at times I was almost led to believe that her [gentle bosom →] *mind* was swayed by [thoughts & feelings →] *gentle impulses* hardly to be anticipated from one in her condition; that she appeared to be conscious there were ties rudely severed, which had once bound us to our homes; that there were sisters and brothers anxiously looking forward to our return, who were, perhaps, never more to behold us.

In this amiable light did Fayaway appear in my eyes; and reposing full confidence in her candour and intelligence, I now had recourse to her, in the midst of my alarm, with regard to my companion.

My questions evidently distressed her. She looked round from one to another of the byestanders, as if hardly knowing what answer to give me. At last, yielding to my importunities, she overcame her scruples, and gave me to understand that Toby had gone away with the boats which had visited the bay, but had promised to return at the expiration of three days. At first I accused him of perfidiously deserting me; but as I grew more composed, I upbraided myself for imputing so cowardly an action to him, and tranquillized myself with the belief that he had availed himself of the opportunity to go round to Nukuheva, in order to make some arrangement by which I could be removed from the valley. At any rate, thought I, he will return with the medicines I require, and then, as soon as I recover, there will be no difficulty in the way of our departure.

Consoling myself with these reflections, I lay down that night in a happier frame of mind than I had done for some time. The next day passed without any allusion to Toby on the part of the natives, who seemed desirous of avoiding all reference to the subject. This raised some apprehensions in my breast; but when night came, I congratulated myself that the second day had now gone by, and that on the morrow Toby would again be with me. But the morrow came and went, and my companion did not appear. Ah! thought I, he reckons three days from the morning of his departure,—to-morrow he will arrive. But that weary day also closed upon me, without his return. Even yet I would not despair; I thought that something detained him—that he was waiting for the sailing of a boat, at Nukuheva, and that in a day or two at farthest I should see him again. *But day after day of renewed disappointment passed by; at last hope deserted me, and I fell a victim to despair.*§

---

§ In manuscript, Melville originally wrote the preceding passage as follows: But day after day sped by & with that hope deferred which maketh the heart sicken I clung to the beleif that he could not have abandoned me. At last Hope itself deserted me & I fell a victim to the most picquant despair.

Yes, thought I, gloomily, he has secured his own escape, and cares not what calamity may befall his unfortunate comrade. Fool that I was, to suppose that any one would willingly encounter the perils of this valley, after having once got beyond its limits! He has gone, and has left me to combat alone all the dangers by which I am surrounded. Thus would I sometimes seek to derive a desperate consolation from dwelling upon the perfidy of Toby: *whilst at other times I sunk under the bitter remorse which I felt as having by my own imprudence brought upon myself the fate which I was sure awaited me.*§

> § *In manuscript, Melville originally wrote the preceding passage as follows:*
> But with the inconstancy of a desponding mind that speculates in the dark as to the causes that have produced the misery under which it languishes, I would often experience the most bitter remorse after indulging in these reflections & again & again would seek to peirce the mystery that hung over the sudden disappearance of my companion.

At other times I thought that perhaps after all these treacherous savages have made away with him, and thence the confusion into which they were thrown by my questions, and their contradictory answers, *or he might be a captive* [*In manuscript Melville originally wrote this passage as follows:* It may be indeed that he whom I just cursed in the bitterness of my heart is at this moment a captive] in some other part of the valley; or, more dreadful still, might have met with that fate at which my very soul shuddered. But all these speculations were vain; no tidings of Toby ever reached me; he had gone never to return.

The conduct of the [savages →] *islanders* appeared inexplicable. All reference to my lost comrade was carefully evaded, and if at any time they were forced to make some reply to my frequent inquiries on the subject, they would uniformly denounce him as an ungrateful runaway, who had deserted his friend, and taken himself off to that vile and detestable place Nukuheva.

But whatever might have been his fate, now that he was gone, the [islanders → savages →] *natives* multiplied their acts of kindness and attention towards myself, treating me with a degree of deference which could hardly have been surpassed had I been some celestial visitant. Kory-Kory never for one moment left my side, unless it were to execute my wishes.

The faithful fellow, twice every day, in the cool of the morning and in the evening, insisted upon carrying me to the stream, and bathing me in its refreshing water.§

§ *Melville deleted the following passage at this point:*
Oftentimes when borne on his back through the shady paths of the valley my sadness was pleasurably diverted by calling to mind the picture of "Little Henry & his bearer" which usualy decorates the title page of that pleasing & popular religious tract.

Frequently in the afternoon he would carry me to a particular part of the stream, where the beauty of the scene produced a soothing influence upon my mind. At this place the waters flowed between grassy banks, planted with enormous bread-fruit trees, whose vast branches interlacing overhead, formed a leafy canopy; near the stream were several smooth black rocks. One of these, projecting several feet above the surface of the water, had upon its summit a shallow cavity, which, filled with freshly-gathered leaves, formed a delightful couch.

Here I often lay for hours, covered with a gauze-like veil of tappa, while Fayaway, seated beside me, and holding in her hand a fan woven from the leaflets of a young cocoa-nut bough, brushed aside the insects that occasionally lighted on my face, and Kory-Kory, with a view of chasing away my melancholy, performed a thousand antics in the water before us.

As my eye wandered along this romantic stream, it would fall upon the half-immersed figure of a beautiful girl, standing in the transparent water, and catching in a little net a species of diminutive shell-fish, of which these people are extravagantly fond. Sometimes a chattering group would be seated upon the edge of a low rock in the midst of the brook, busily engaged in thinning and polishing the shells of cocoa-nuts, by rubbing them briskly with a small stone in the water, an operation which soon converts them into a light and elegant drinking vessel, somewhat resembling goblets made of tortoiseshell.

But the tranquillizing influences of beautiful scenery, and the exhibition of human life under so novel and charming an aspect, were not my only sources of consolation.

Every evening the girls of the house gathered about me on the mats, and after chasing away Kory-Kory from my side—who, nevertheless, retired only to a little distance and watched their proceedings with the most jealous attention—would anoint my whole body with a fragrant oil, squeezed from a yellow root, previously pounded between a couple of stones, and which in their language is denominated "aka." And most refreshing and agreeable are the juices of the "aka," when applied to one's limbs by the soft palms of sweet nymphs, whose bright eyes are beaming upon you *with kindness; and I used to hail with delight the daily recurrence of this luxurious operation, in which I forgot all my troubles, and buried for the time every feeling of sorrow.*§

§ *In manuscript, Melville originally wrote the preceding passage as follows:*
with delight & who rise will, one another In the order of their attentions.—I used to hail with transport the daily recurrence of this luxurious operation in which I forgot all my troubles & buried for the time every feeling of sorrow or of care. With Macheath in the opera I could have sung "Thus I lay like a Turk with my doxies around." Never certainly was effeminate ottoman in the innermost shrine of his serglio attended by lovlier houries with more excess of devotion.—Sardanapalus might have experienced such sensations—but I dout whether any of the Sultans ever did.

Sometimes in the cool of the evening my devoted servitor would lead me out upon the pi-pi in front of the house, and seating me near its edge, protect my body from the annoyances of the insects which occasionally hovered in the air, by wrapping me round with a large roll of tappa. He then bustled about, and employed himself at least twenty minutes in adjusting everything to secure my personal comfort.

Having perfected his arrangements, he would get my pipe, and, lighting it, would hand it to me. Often he was obliged to strike a light for the occasion, and as the mode he adopted was entirely different from what I had ever seen or heard of before, I will describe it.

A straight, dry, and partly decayed stick of the Habiscus, about six feet in length, and half as many inches in diameter, with a smaller bit of wood not more than a foot long, and scarcely an inch wide, is as invariably to be met with in every house in Typee as a box of lucifer matches in the corner of a kitchen cupboard at home.§

§ *Melville deleted the following paragraph at this point:*
Having said thus much in brief introduction, I here take Kori Kori by the hand &

introducing him to the reader I have no doubt but that the former is perfectly willing to go through the Promethean operation for his particular gratification.

The [savage →] *islander,* placing the larger stick obliquely against some object, with one end elevated at an angle of forty-five degrees, mounts astride of it like an urchin about to gallop off upon a cane, and then grasping the smaller one firmly in both hands, he rubs its pointed end slowly up and down the extent of a few inches on the principal stick, until at last he makes a narrow groove in the wood, with an abrupt termination at the point furthest from him, where all the dusty particles which the friction creates are accumulated in a little heap.

[Like a locomotive on the start →] *At first* Kory-Kory goes to work quite leisurely, but gradually quickens his pace, and waxing warm in the employment, drives the stick furiously along the smoking channel, plying his hands to and fro with amazing rapidity, the perspiration starting from every pore. As he [attains his climax →] *approaches the climax of his effort,* he pants and grasps for breath, and his eyes almost start from their sockets with the violence of his exertions. This is the critical stage of the operation; all his previous labours are vain if he cannot sustain the rapidity of the movement until the reluctant spark is produced. Suddenly he stops, becomes perfectly motionless. His hands still retain their hold of the smaller stick, which is pressed convulsively against the further end of the channel among the fine powder there accumulated, as if he had just pierced through and through some little viper that was wriggling and struggling to escape from his clutches. The next moment a delicate wreath of smoke curls spirally into the air, the heap of dusty particles glows with fire, and Kory-Kory almost breathless, dismounts from his steed.

This operation appeared to me to be the most laborious species of work performed in Typee; and had I possessed a sufficient intimacy with the language to have conveyed my ideas upon the subject, I should certainly have suggested to the most influential of the natives the expediency of establishing a college of vestals to be centrally located in the valley, for the purpose of keeping alive the indispensable article of fire; so as to supersede the necessity of such a vast outlay of strength and good temper, as were usually squandered on these occasions. *There might, however, be special difficulties in carrying this plan into execution.*§

§ *In manuscript, Melville originally wrote the preceding passage as follows:*
One difficulty however would present itself in the way of this benevolent enterprise which as it might be considered in the light of a slanderous aspersion on the fair fame of the gentle damsels of the vale I courtiously beg to be excused from more distinctly pointing out.

What a striking evidence does this operation furnish of the wide difference between the extreme of savage and civilized life. A gentleman of Typee can bring up a numerous family of children and give them all a highly respectable cannibal education, with infinitely less toil and anxiety than he expends in the simple process of striking a light; whilst a poor European artisan, who through the instrumentality of a lucifer performs the same operation in one second, is put to his wit's end to provide for his starving offspring that food which the children of a Polynesian father, without troubling their parent, pluck from the branches of every tree around them.§

§ *Melville deleted the following concluding paragraph:*
This single practical illustration is, I insist upon it, worth volumes of learned disquisitions on the nature & theory of the respective pretensions of the various forms of social life & I accordingly commend it to the consideration of all the political economists & public spirited Philosophers who are engaged in putting to rights this most imperfectly constituted planet of ours.

1845, 1846

PART TWO
THE ART OF TELLING THE TRUTH

Typee secured Melville's reputation as an "uncommon common sailor" with an irreverent voice. In five years, he published five more books, none quite like the other. Drawing upon his experiences as a whaling man (*Omoo*, 1847; *Mardi*, 1849; *Moby-Dick*, 1851) and naval recruit in the South Pacific (*White-Jacket*, 1850), and as a boy sailor on a merchant ship to Liverpool (*Redburn*, 1849), he experimented not only with genre—travelogue, romance, allegory, and novel—but also with "the great Art of Telling the Truth."

The truths he felt ranged from "one delirious throb at the center of the All" (*Redburn*) to a sense of nothingness in the "colorless, all-color of atheism" (*Moby-Dick*). Like Ishmael, Melville was both believer and doubter—and thus restless. But how do you make narratives out of the restless questioning after ungraspable truths? As Melville put it in his 1850 review of "Hawthorne and His Mosses," truth, like a "scared white doe," leaps off when you see it, and the only way to convey it is "covertly, and by snatches." For fiction to be true, it must work through indirection and symbol, through the tearing off of masks hiding the "sane madness of vital truth." To manage the incumbent "shock of recognition," such probing requires "a great intellect in repose" that can contain the light and dark hemispheres of the soul and thus make fiction an "ever-moving dawn."

Melville's letters ruminate on truth and writing. Encouraging his British publisher John Murray to accept the expurgations of *Typee,* he argues against his own digressions and for "the *intrinsick merit of the narrative alone.*" In three letters to his friend at the *Literary World,* Evert Duyckinck, he defends Emerson, transplants Shakespeare into a democracy, ponders madness, complains of never finishing anything, and wishes he could just "scrape [books] off the brain." The letters to Nathaniel Hawthorne, full of "NO! in thunder," speak of his "unfolding," constant "changing," and longing for "the calm, the coolness, the silent grass-growing mood" of composition. To Hawthorne's wife, Sophia, Melville acknowledges an unintended "subtile significance" in *Moby-Dick* and projects future writings.

LETTERS

FROM LETTER TO JOHN MURRAY
15 JULY 1846 • NEW YORK

New York July 15th 1846

Mr John Murray,

Dear Sir—The decease of my brother Mr Gansevoort Melville leaving me without any correspondant in London thro' whom to communicate with you, I waive cerimony & address you at once by letter.—My object in so doing, is to inform you of certain matters connected with "Typee" which you ought to be made acquainted with, & to allude briefly to one or two other subjects.

In the first place I have to inform you that "Toby" who figures in my narrative has come to life—tho' I had long supposed him to be dead. I send you by this steamer several papers (N.Y. Courier & Enquirer, N.Y. Morning News, & Albany Argus) containing allusions to him. Toby's appearance has produced quite a lively sensation here—and "Truth is stranger than Fiction" is in every body's mouth.—In Buffalo where he "turned up" the public curiosity was so great that "Toby" was induced to gratify it by publishing the draught of a letter which he had originally sent to me. This is not the letter however, which appears in the papers I send you.—I was sorry for this on some accounts, but it could not be helped. However the impression which Toby's letter has produced is this—ie—that every thing about it bears the impress of truth.—Indeed, the whole Typee adventure is now regarded as a sort of Romance of Real

Life.—You would be greatly diverted to read some of the comments of our Western Editors and log-cabin critics.——But to the point.—I am now preparing a short Sequel to Typee containing a simple account of Toby's escape from the valley as related to me by himself. This Sequel will be bound up with all subsequent editions of the book here.—The curiosity of all readers has been awakened as to what became of him—& now that he has appeared & his story is so interesting, it naturally belongs to the narrative that a sequel like this should be supplied. At any rate the public are apprised of Toby's resurrection & are looking for it.—Besides, it is so strange, & withal so convincing a proof of the truth of my narrative *as I sent it to London* that it can not be gainsaid.——

Were it not for the long delay it would occasion, I should take no steps towards the publication of any Sequel until I had sent the M.S.S. to you. But as matters are, this can not be done—for there is a present demand for the book which the publishers can not supply—a new edition is in preperation—& after what has happened, this can not come out very well without the story of Toby.—Still, if you publish the Sequel (which as a matter of course I suppose you will) no one will interfere with the publication, since it will be quite brief (perhaps not exceeding eight or ten pages) & depends altogether upon the narrative which precedes it.— Besides, I shall take care that you receive a copy of it by the earliest possible oportunity.

——I have just said that a new edition of the book was forthcoming— This new edition will be a Revised one, and I can not but think that the measure will prove a judicious one.—The revision will only extend to the exclusion of those parts not naturally connected with the narrative and some slight purifications of style. I am pursuaded that the interest of the book almost wholly consists in the *intrinsick merit of the narrative alone*—& that other portions, however interesting they may be in themselves, only serve to impede the story. The book is certainly calculated for popular reading, or for none at all.—If the first, why then, all passages which are calculated to offend the tastes, or offer violance to the feelings of any large class of readers are certainly objectionable.—Proceeding on this principle then, I have rejected every thing, in revising the book, which refers to the missionaries. Such passages are altogether foreign to the adventure, & altho' they may possess a temporary interest *now,* to some, yet so far as the wide & permanent popularity of the work is conserned, their exclusion will certainly be beneficial, for to that end, the less the book has to carry along with it the better.—Certain "sea-freedoms" also have been modifyed in the expression—but nothing has been done to effect the general character & style of the book—the narrative parts are untouched—In short—in revising the work, I have merely removed passages which leave no gap, & the removal of which imparts a unity to the book which it wanted before.—The reasons which will be given to the public for this step are set forth in the enclosed paper—Something like this will be published in the shape of a "Preface to the Revised Edition." . . .

—As for the matter of the revised edition—if you publish one from the copy I shall send to you, I leave it to yourself to decide, whether I should be considered as entitled to any thing on account of it.—But however that part of the matter may appear to you—I earnestly trust that you will issue a Revised Edition. Depend upon it Sir, that it will be policy so to do. Nor have I decided upon this revision without much reflection and seeking the advice of persons every way qualifyed to give it, & who have done so in a spirit of candor. . . .

I have another work now nearly completed which I am anxious to submit to you before presenting it to any other publishing house. It embraces adventures in the South Seas (of a totally different character from "Typee") and includes an eventful cruise in an English Colonial Whaleman (A Sydney Ship) and a comical residence on the island of Tahiti. The time is about four months, but I & my narrative are both on the move during that short period. This new book begins exactly where Typee leaves off—but has no further connection with my first work.—Permit me here to assure Mr Murray that my new M.S.S. will be in a rather better state for the press than the M.S.S. handed to him by my brother. A little experience in this art of book-craft has done wonders.

—Will you be so good as to give me your views about this proposed publication (it will be ready the latter part of the fall—*autumn* I beleive it is with you) as early as possible.

—Mr Murray must pardon the evident haste in which this long letter has been written—it was unavoidable.—With much respect & esteem, Dear Sir, Beleive me

Very Truly Yours
Herman Melville

To Evert A. Duyckinck
3 March 1849 • Boston

Mount Vernon Street
Saturday, 3d

Nay, I do not oscillate in Emerson's rainbow, but prefer rather to hang myself in mine own halter than swing in any other man's swing. Yet I think Emerson is more than a brilliant fellow. Be his stuff begged, borrowed, or stolen, or of his own domestic manufacture he is an uncommon man. Swear he is a humbug—then is he no common humbug. Lay it down that had not Sir Thomas Browne lived, Emerson would not have mystified—I will answer, that had not Old Zack's father begot him, Old Zack would never have been the hero of Palo Alto. The truth is that we are all sons, grandsons, or nephews or great-nephews of those who go before us. No one is his own sire.—I was very agreeably disappointed in Mr Emerson. I had heard of him as full of transcendentalisms, myths & oracular gibberish; I had only glanced at a book of his once in Putnam's store—that was all I knew of him, till I heard him lecture.—To my surprise, I found him quite intelligible, tho' to say truth, they told me that that night he was unusually plain.——Now, there is a something about every man elevated above mediocrity, which is, for the most part, instinctively perceptible. This I see in Mr Emerson. And, frankly, for the sake of the argument, let us call him a fool;—then had I rather be a fool than a wise man.—I love all men who *dive*. Any fish can swim near the surface, but it takes a great whale to go down stairs five miles or more; & if he don't attain the bottom, why, all the lead in Galena can't fashion the plummet that will. I'm not talking of Mr Emerson now—but of the whole corps of thought-divers, that have been diving & coming up again with blood-shot eyes since the world began.

I could readily see in Emerson, notwithstanding his merit, a gaping flaw. It was, the insinuation, that had he lived in those days when the world was made, he might have offered some valuable suggestions. These men are all cracked right across the brow. And never will the pullers-down be able to cope with the builders-up. And this pulling down is easy enough—a keg of powder blew up Brock's Monument—but the man who applied the match, could not, alone, build such a pile to save his soul from the shark-maw of the Devil. But enough of this Plato who talks thro' his nose. To one of your habits of thought, I confess that in my last, I seemed, but only *seemed* irreverent. And do not think, my boy, that because I, impulsively broke forth in jubillations over Shakspeare, that, therefore, I am of the number of the *snobs* who burn their tuns of rancid fat at his shrine. No, I would stand afar off & alone, & burn some pure Palm oil, the product of some overtopping trunk.

—I would to God Shakspeare had lived later, & promenaded in Broadway. Not that I might have had the pleasure of leaving my card for him at the Astor, or made merry with him over a bowl of the fine Duyckinck punch; but that the muzzle which all men wore on their souls in the Elizebethan day, might not have intercepted Shakspere's full articulations For I hold it a verity, that even Shakspeare, was not a frank man to the uttermost. And, indeed, who in this intolerant Universe is, or can be? But the Declaration of Independence makes a difference.—There, I have driven my horse so hard that I have made my inn before sundown. I was going to say something more—It was this.—You complain that Emerson tho' a denizen of the land of gingerbread, is above munching a plain cake in company of jolly fellows, & swiging off his ale like you & me. Ah, my dear sir, that's his misfortune, not his fault. His belly, sir, is in his chest, & his brains descend down into his neck, & offer an obstacle to a draught of ale or a mouthful of cake. But here I am. Good bye—

H. M.

To Evert A. Duyckinck
5 April 1849 • Boston

Boston April 5th 1849

Dear Duyckinck—Thank you for your note, & the paper which came duly to hand. By the way, that "Smoking Spiritualised" is not bad. Doubtless it has improved by age. The quaint old lines lie in coils like a sailor's pigtail in its keg.

—Ah this sovereign virtue of age—how can we living men attain unto it. We may spice up our dishes with all the condiments of the Spice Islands & Moluccas, & our dishes may be all venison & wild boar—yet how the deuce can we make them a century or two old?—My Dear Sir, the two great things yet to be discovered are these—The Art of rejuvenating old age in men, & oldageifying youth in books.—Who in the name of the trunk-makers would think of reading *Old* Burton were his book published for the first to day?—All ambitious authors should have ghosts capable of revisiting the world, to snuff up the steam of adulation, which begins to rise straightway as the Sexton throws his last shovelfull on him.—Down goes his body & up flies his name.

Poor Hoffman—I remember the shock I had when I first saw the mention of his madness.—But he was just the man to go mad—imaginative, voluptuously inclined, poor, unemployed, in the race of life distanced by his inferiors, unmarried,—without a port or haven in the universe to make. His present misfortune—rather blessing—is but the sequel to a long experience of morbid habits of thought.——This going mad of a friend or acquaintance comes straight home to every man who feels his soul in him,—which but few men do. For in all of us lodges the same fuel to light the same fire. And he who has never felt, momentarily, what madness is has but a mouthful of brains. What sort of sensation permanent madness is may be very well imagined—just as we imagine how we felt when we were infants, tho' we can not recall it. In both conditions we are irresponsible & riot like gods without fear of fate.—It is the climax of a mad night of revelry when the blood has been transmuted into brandy.—But if we prate much of this thing we shall be illustrating our own propositions.—

I am glad you like that affair of mine. But it seems so long now since I wrote it, & my mood has so changed, that I dread to look into it, & have purposely abstained from so doing since I thanked God it was off my hands.—Would that a man could do something & then say—It is finished.—not that one thing only, but all others—that he has reached his uttermost, & can never exceed it. But live & push—tho' we put one leg forward ten miles—its no reason the other must lag behind—no, *that* must again distance the other—& so we go till we get the cramp & die.— I bought a set of Bayle's Dictionary the other day, & on my return to New York intend to lay the great old folios side by side & go to sleep on them thro' the summer, with the Phaedon in one hand & Tom Brown in the other.—Good bye I'm called.—I shall be in New York next week—early part.

H Melville

From LETTER TO EVERT A. DUYCKINCK
13 DECEMBER 1850 • PITTSFIELD

Friday Evening
Pittsfield.

My Dear Duyckinck,

. . . I have a sort of sea-feeling here in the country, now that the ground is all covered with snow. I look out of my window in the morning when I rise as I would out of a port-hole of a ship in the Atlantic. My room seems a ship's cabin; & at nights when I wake up & hear the wind shrieking, I almost fancy there is too much sail on the house, & I had better go on the roof & rig in the chimney.

Do you want to know how I pass my time?—I rise at eight—thereabouts—& go to my barn—say good-morning to the horse, & give him his breakfast. (It goes to my heart to give him a cold one, but it can't be helped) Then, pay a visit to my cow—cut up a pumpkin or two for her, & stand by to see her eat it—for it's a pleasant sight to see a cow move her jaws—she does it so mildly & with such a sanctity——My own breakfast over, I go to my workroom & light my fire—then spread my M.S.S on the table—take one business squint at it, & fall to with a will. At 2½ P.M. I hear a preconcerted knock at my door, which (by request) continues till I rise & go to the door, which serves to wean me effectively from my writing, however interested I may be. My friends the horse & cow now demand their dinner—& I go & give it them. My own dinner over, I rig my sleigh & with my mother or sisters start off for the village—& if it be a Literary World day, great is the satisfaction thereof.—My evenings I spend in a sort of mesmeric state in my room—not being able to read—only now & then skimming over some large-printed book.—Can you send me about fifty fast-writing youths, with an easy style & not averse to polishing their labors? If you can, I wish you would, because since I have been here I have planned about that number of future works & cant find enough time to think about them separately.—But I dont know but a book in a man's brain is better off than a book bound in calf—at any rate it is safer from criticism. And taking a book off the brain, is akin to the ticklish & dangerous business of taking an old painting off a panel—you have to scrape off the whole brain in order to get at it with due safety—

& even then, the painting may not be worth the trouble.——I meant to have left more room for something else besides my own concerns. But I cant help it.—I see Adler is at work—or has already achieved a German translation. I am glad to hear it. Remember me to him.

—In the country here, I begin to appreciate the Literary World. I read it as a sort of private letter from you to me.

Remember me to your brother. My respects to Mrs Duyckinck & all your family. The "sad" young lady desires her regards.

H Melville.

Mrs Melville with Malcolm is in Boston—or that lady would send her particular regards.

TO NATHANIEL HAWTHORNE
[16 APRIL?] 1851 • PITTSFIELD

Pittsfield, Wednesday morning.

My dear Hawthorne,—Concerning the young gentleman's shoes, I desire to say that a pair to fit him, of the desired pattern, cannot be had in all Pittsfield,—a fact which sadly impairs that metropolitan pride I formerly took in the capital of Berkshire. Henceforth Pittsfield must hide its head. However, if a pair of *bootees* will at all answer, Pittsfield will be very happy to provide them. Pray mention all this to Mrs. Hawthorne, and command me.

"The House of the Seven Gables: A Romance. By Nathaniel Hawthorne. One vol. 16mo, pp. 344." The contents of this book do not belie its rich, clustering, romantic title. With great enjoyment we spent almost an hour in each separate gable. This book is like a fine old chamber, abundantly, but still judiciously, furnished with precisely that sort of furniture best fitted to furnish it. There are rich hangings, wherein are braided scenes from tragedies! There is old china with rare devices, set out on the carved buffet; there are long and indolent lounges to throw yourself upon; there is an admirable sideboard, plentifully stored with good viands; there is a smell as of old wine in the pantry; and finally, in one corner, there is a dark little black-letter volume in golden clasps, entitled "Hawthorne: A Problem." It has delighted us; it has piqued a re-perusal; it has robbed us of a day, and made us a present of a whole year of thoughtfulness; it has bred great exhilaration and exultation with the remembrance that the architect of the Gables resides only six miles off, and not three thousand miles away, in England, say. We think the book, for pleasantness of running interest, surpasses the other works of the author. The curtains are more drawn; the sun comes in more; genialities peep out more. Were we to particularize what has most struck us in the deeper passages, we would point out the scene where Clifford, for a moment, would fain throw himself forth from the window to join the procession; or the scene where the Judge is left seated in his ancestral chair. Clifford is full of an awful truth throughout. He is conceived in the finest, truest spirit. He is no caricature. He is Clifford. And here we would say that, did circumstances permit, we should like nothing better than to devote an elaborate and careful paper to the full consideration and analysis of the purport and significance of what so strongly characterizes all of this author's writings. There is a certain tragic phase of humanity which, in our opinion, was never more powerfully embodied than by Hawthorne. We mean the tragicalness of human thought in its own unbiassed, native, and profounder workings. We think that into no recorded mind has the intense feeling of the visable truth ever entered more deeply than into this man's. By visable truth, we mean the apprehension of the absolute condition of present things as they strike the eye of the man who fears them not, though they do their worst to him,—the man who, like Russia or the British Empire, declares himself a sovereign nature (in himself) amid the powers of heaven, hell, and earth. He may perish; but so long as he exists he insists upon treating with all Powers upon an equal basis. If any of those other Powers choose to withhold certain secrets, let them; that does not impair my sovereignty in myself; that does not make me tributary. And perhaps, after all, there is *no* secret. We incline to think that the Problem of the Universe is like the Freemason's mighty secret, so terrible to all children. It turns out, at last, to consist in a triangle, a mallet, and an apron,—nothing more! We incline to think that God cannot explain His own secrets, and that He would like a little information upon certain points Himself. We mortals astonish Him as much as He us. But it is this *Being* of the matter; there lies the knot with which we choke ourselves. As soon as you say *Me,* a *God,* a *Nature,* so soon you jump off from your stool and hang from the beam. Yes, that word is the hangman. Take God out of the dictionary, and you would have Him in the street.

There is the grand truth about Nathaniel Hawthorne. He says NO! in thunder; but the Devil himself cannot make him say *yes*. For all men who say *yes*, lie; and all men who say *no*,—why, they are in the happy condition of judicious, unincumbered travellers in Europe; they cross the frontiers into Eternity with nothing but a carpet-bag,—that is to say, the Ego. Whereas those *yes*-gentry, they travel with heaps of baggage, and, damn them! they will never get through the Custom House. What's the reason, Mr. Hawthorne, that in the last stages of metaphysics a fellow always falls to *swearing* so? I could rip an hour. You see, I began with a little criticism extracted for your benefit from the "Pittsfield Secret Review," and here I have landed in Africa.

Walk down one of these mornings and see me. No nonsense; come. Remember me to Mrs. Hawthorne and the children.

H. Melville.

P.S. The marriage of Phoebe with the daguerreotypist is a fine stroke, because of his turning out to be a *Maule*. If you pass Hepzibah's cent-shop, buy me a Jim Crow (fresh) and send it to me by Ned Higgins.

To Nathaniel Hawthorne
[1 June?] 1851 • Pittsfield

My dear Hawthorne,—I should have been rumbling down to you in my pine-board chariot a long time ago, were it not that for some weeks past I have been more busy than you can well imagine,—out of doors,— building and patching and tinkering away in all directions. Besides, I had my crops to get in,—corn and potatoes (I hope to show you some famous ones by and by),—and many other things to attend to, all accumulating upon this one particular season. I work myself; and at night my bodily sensations are akin to those I have so often felt before, when a hired man, doing my day's work from sun to sun. But I mean to continue visiting you until you tell me that my visits are both supererogatory and superfluous. With no son of man do I stand upon any etiquette or ceremony, except the Christian ones of charity and honesty. I am told, my fellow-man, that there is an aristocracy of the brain. Some men have boldly advocated and asserted it. Schiller seems to have done so, though I don't know much about him. At any rate, it is true that there have been those who, while earnest in behalf of political equality, still accept the intellectual estates. And I can well perceive, I think, how a man of superior mind can, by its intense cultivation, bring himself, as it were, into a certain spontaneous aristocracy of feeling,—exceedingly nice and fastidious,—similar to that which, in an English Howard, conveys a torpedo-fish thrill at the slightest contact with a social plebeian. So, when you see or hear of my ruthless democracy on all sides, you may possibly feel a touch of a shrink, or something of that sort. It is but nature to be shy of a mortal who boldly declares that a thief in jail is as honorable a personage as Gen. George Washington. This is ludicrous. But Truth is the silliest thing under the sun. Try to get a living by the Truth—and go to the Soup Societies. Heavens! Let any clergyman try to preach the Truth from its very strong-hold, the pulpit, and they would ride him out of his church on his own pulpit bannister. It can hardly be doubted that all Reformers are bottomed upon the truth, more or less; and to the world at large are not reformers almost universally laughing-stocks? Why so? Truth is ridiculous to men. Thus easily in my room here do I, conceited and garrulous, reverse the test of my Lord Shaftesbury.

It seems an inconsistency to assert unconditional democracy in all things, and yet confess a dislike to all mankind—in the mass. But not so.—But it's an endless sermon,—no more of it. I began by saying that the reason I have not been to Lenox is this,—in the evening I feel completely done up, as the phrase is, and incapable of the long jolting to get to your house and back. In a week or so, I go to New York, to bury myself in a third-story room, and work and slave on my "Whale" while it is driving through the press. *That* is the only way I can finish it now,—I am so pulled hither and thither by circumstances. The calm, the coolness, the silent grass-growing mood in which a man *ought* always to compose,—that, I fear, can seldom be mine. Dollars damn me; and the malicious Devil is forever grinning in upon me, holding the door ajar. My dear Sir, a presentiment is on me,—I shall at last be worn out and perish, like an old nutmeg-grater, grated to pieces by the constant attrition of the wood, that is, the nutmeg. What I feel most moved to write, that is banned,—it will not pay. Yet, altogether, write the *other* way I cannot. So the product is a final hash, and all my books are botches. I'm rather sore, perhaps, in this letter; but see my hand!—four blisters on this palm, made by hoes and hammers within the last few days. It is a rainy morning; so I am indoors, and all work suspended. I feel cheerfully disposed, and therefore I write a little bluely. Would the Gin were here! If ever, my dear Hawthorne, in the eternal times that are to come, you and I shall sit down in Paradise, in some little shady corner by ourselves; and if we shall by any means be able to smuggle a basket of champagne there (I won't believe in a Temperance Heaven), and if we shall then cross our celestial legs in the celestial grass that is forever tropical, and strike our glasses and our heads together, till both musically ring in concert,—then, O my dear fellow-mortal, how shall we pleasantly discourse of all the things manifold which now so distress us,—when all the earth shall be but a reminiscence, yea, its final dissolution an antiquity. Then shall songs be composed as when wars are over; humorous, comic songs,—"Oh, when I lived in that queer little hole called the world," or, "Oh, when I toiled and sweated below," or, "Oh, when I knocked and was knocked in the fight"—yes, let us look forward to such things. Let us swear that, though now we sweat, yet it is because of the dry heat which is indispensable to the nourishment of the vine which is to bear the grapes that are to give us the champagne hereafter.

But I was talking about the "Whale." As the fishermen say, "he's in his flurry" when I left him some three weeks ago. I'm going to take him by his jaw, however, before long, and finish him up in some fashion or other. What's the use of elaborating what, in its very essence, is so short-lived as a modern book? Though I wrote the Gospels in this century, I should die in the gutter.—I talk all about myself, and this is selfishness and egotism. Granted. But how help it? I am writing to you; I know little about you, but something about myself. So I write about myself,—at least, to you. Don't trouble yourself, though, about writing; and don't trouble yourself about visiting; and when you *do* visit, don't trouble yourself about talking. I will do all the writing and visiting and talking myself.—By the way, in the last "Dollar Magazine" I read "The Unpardonable Sin." He was a sad fellow, that Ethan Brand. I have no doubt you are by this time responsible for many a shake and tremor of the tribe of "general readers." It is a frightful poetical creed that the cultivation of the brain eats out the heart. But it's my *prose* opinion that in most cases, in those men who have fine brains and work them well, the heart extends down to hams. And though you smoke them with the fire of tribulation, yet, like veritable hams, the head only gives the richer and the better flavor. I stand for the heart. To the dogs with the head! I had rather be a fool with a heart, than Jupiter Olympus with his head. The reason the mass of men fear God, and *at bottom dislike* Him, is because they rather distrust His heart, and fancy Him all brain like a watch. (You perceive I employ a capital initial in the pronoun referring to the Deity; don't you think there is a slight dash of flunkeyism in that usage?) Another thing. I was in New York for four-and-twenty hours the other day, and saw a portrait of N. H. And I have seen and heard many flattering (in a publisher's point of view) allusions to the "Seven Gables." And I have seen "Tales," and "A New Volume" announced, by N. H. So upon the whole, I say to myself, this N. H. is in the ascendant. My dear Sir, they begin to patronize. All Fame is patronage. Let me be infamous: there is no patronage in *that*. What "reputation" H. M. has is horrible. Think of it! To go down to posterity is bad enough, any way; but to go down as a "man who lived among the cannibals"! When I speak of posterity, in reference to myself, I only mean the babies who will probably be born in the moment immediately ensuing upon my giving up the ghost. I shall go down to some of them, in all likelihood. "Typee" will be given to them, perhaps, with their gingerbread. I have come to regard this matter of Fame as the most transparent of all vanities. I read Solomon more and more, and every time see deeper and deeper and unspeakable meanings in him. I did not think of Fame, a year ago, as I do now. My development has been all within a few years past. I am like one of those seeds taken out of the Egyptian Pyramids, which, after being three thousand years a seed and nothing but a seed, being planted in English soil, it developed itself, grew to greenness, and then fell to mould. So I. Until I was twenty-five, I had no development at all. From my twenty-fifth year I date my life. Three weeks have scarcely passed, at any time between then and now, that I have not unfolded within myself. But I feel that I am now come to the inmost leaf of the bulb, and that shortly the flower must fall to the mould. It seems to me now that Solomon was the truest man who ever spoke, and yet that he a little *managed* the truth with a view to popular conservatism; or else there have been many corruptions and interpolations of the text—In reading some of Goethe's sayings, so worshipped by his votaries, I came across this, *"Live in the all."* That is to say, your separate identity is but a wretched one,—good; but get out of yourself, spread and expand yourself, and bring to yourself the tinglings of life that are felt in the flowers and the woods, that are felt in the planets Saturn and Venus, and the Fixed Stars. What nonsense! Here is a fellow with a raging toothache. "My dear boy," Goethe says to him, "you are sorely afflicted with that tooth; but you must *live in the all,* and then you will be happy!" As with all great genius, there is an immense deal of flummery in Goethe, and in proportion to my own contact with him, a monstrous deal of it in me.

H. Melville.

P.S. "Amen!" saith Hawthorne.

N.B. This "all" feeling, though, there is some truth in. You must often have felt it, lying on the grass on a warm summer's day. Your legs seem to send out shoots into the earth. Your hair feels like leaves upon your head. This is the *all* feeling. But what plays the mischief with the truth is that men will insist upon the universal application of a temporary feeling or opinion.

P.S. You must not fail to admire my discretion in paying the postage on this letter.

To Nathaniel Hawthorne
[17?] November 1851 • Pittsfield

Pittsfield, Monday afternoon.

My dear Hawthorne: People think that if a man has undergone any hardship, he should have a reward; but for my part, if I have done the hardest possible day's work, and then come to sit down in a corner and eat my supper comfortably—why, then I don't think I deserve any reward for my hard day's work—for am I not now at peace? Is not my supper good? My peace and my supper are my reward, my dear Hawthorne. So your joy-giving and exultation-breeding letter is not my reward for my ditcher's work with that book, but is the good goddess's bonus over and above what was stipulated for—for not one man in five cycles, who is wise, will expect appreciative recognition from his fellows, or any one of them. Appreciation! Recognition! Is Jove appreciated? Why, ever since Adam, who has got to the meaning of his great allegory—the world? Then we pigmies must be content to have our paper allegories but ill comprehended. I say your appreciation is my glorious gratuity. In my proud, humble way,—a shepherd-king,—I was lord of a little vale in the solitary Crimea; but you have now given me the crown of India. But on trying it on my head, I found it fell down on my ears, notwithstanding their asinine length—for it 's only such ears that sustain such crowns.

Your letter was handed me last night on the road going to Mr. Morewood's, and I read it there. Had I been at home, I would have sat down at once and answered it. In me divine magnanimities are spontaneous and instantaneous—catch them while you can. The world goes round, and the other side comes up. So now I can't write what I felt. But I felt pantheistic then—your heart beat in my ribs and mine in yours, and both in God's. A sense of unspeakable security is in me this moment, on account of your having understood the book. I have written a wicked book, and feel spotless as the lamb. Ineffable socialities are in me. I would sit down and dine with you and all the gods in old Rome's Pantheon. It is a strange feeling—no hopefulness is in it, no despair. Content—that is it; and irresponsibility; but without licentious inclination. I speak now of my profoundest sense of being, not of an incidental feeling.

Whence come you, Hawthorne? By what right do you drink from my flagon of life? And when I put it to my lips—lo, they are yours and not mine. I feel that the Godhead is broken up like the bread at the Supper, and that we are the pieces. Hence this infinite fraternity of feeling. Now, sympathizing with the paper, my angel turns over another page. You did not care a penny for the book. But, now and then as you read, you understood the pervading thought that impelled the book—and that you praised. Was it not so? You were archangel enough to despise the imperfect body, and embrace the soul. Once you hugged the ugly Socrates because you saw the flame in the mouth, and heard the rushing of the demon,—the familiar,—and recognized the sound; for you have heard it in your own solitudes.

My dear Hawthorne, the atmospheric skepticisms steal into me now, and make me doubtful of my sanity in writing you thus. But, believe me, I am not mad, most noble Festus! But truth is ever incoherent, and when the big hearts strike together, the concussion is a little stunning. Farewell. Don't write a word about the book. That would be robbing me of my miserly delight. I am heartily sorry I ever wrote anything about you—it was paltry. Lord, when shall we be done growing? As long as we have anything more to do, we have done nothing. So, now, let us add Moby Dick to our blessing, and step from that. Leviathan is not the biggest fish;—I have heard of Krakens.

This is a long letter, but you are not at all bound to answer it. Possibly, if you do answer it, and direct it to Herman Melville, you will missend it—for the very fingers that now guide this pen are not precisely the same that just took it up and put it on this paper. Lord, when shall we be done changing? Ah! it's a long stage, and no inn in sight, and night coming, and the body cold. But with you for a passenger, I am content and can be happy. I shall leave the world, I feel, with more satisfaction for having come to know you. Knowing you persuades me more than the Bible of our immortality.

What a pity, that, for your plain, bluff letter, you should get such gibberish! Mention me to Mrs. Hawthorne and to the children, and so, goodby to you, with my blessing.

Herman.

I can't stop yet. If the world was entirely made up of Magians, I 'll tell you what I should do. I should have a paper-mill established at one end of the house, and so have an endless riband of foolscap rolling in upon my desk; and upon that endless riband I should write a thousand— a million—billion thoughts, all under the form of a letter to you. The divine magnet is in you, and my magnet responds. Which is the biggest? A foolish question—they are *One*.

H.

Don't think that by writing me a letter, you shall always be bored with an immediate reply to it—and so keep both of us delving over a writing-desk eternally. No such thing! I sha'n't always answer your letters, and you may do just as you please.

TO SOPHIA PEABODY HAWTHORNE
8 JANUARY 1852 • NEW YORK

New York Jan: 8th 1852

My Dear Mrs Hawthorne

I have hunted up the finest Bath I could find, gilt-edged and stamped, whereon to inscribe my humble acknowledgment of your highly flattering letter of the 29th Dec:——It really amazed me that you should find any satisfaction in that book. It is true that some *men* have said they were pleased with it, but you are the only *woman*—for as a general thing, women have small taste for the sea. But, then, since you, with your spiritualizing nature, see more things than other people, and by the same process, refine all you see, so that they are not the same things that other people see, but things which while you think you but humbly discover them, you do in fact create them for yourself——therefore, upon the whole, I do not so much marvel at your expressions concerning Moby Dick. At any rate, your allusion for example to the "Spirit Spout first showed to me that there was a subtle significance in that thing—but I did not, in that case, *mean* it. I had some vague idea while writing it, that the whole book was susceptible of an allegoric construction, & also that *parts* of it were—but the speciality of many of the particular subordinate allegories, were first revealed to me, after reading Mr Hawthorne's letter, which, without citing any particular examples, yet intimated the part-&-parcel allegoricalness of the whole.——But, My Dear Lady, I shall not again send you a bowl of salt water. The next chalice I shall commend, will be a rural bowl of milk.

And now, how are you in West Newton? Are all domestic affairs regulated? Is Miss Una content? And Master Julian satisfied with the landscape in general? And does Mr Hawthorne continue his series of calls upon all his neighbors within a radius of ten miles? Shall I send him ten packs of visiting cards? And a box of kid gloves? and the latest style of Parisian handkerchief?—He goes into society too much altogether—seven evenings out, a week, should content any reasonable man.

Now, Madam, had you not said anything about Moby Dick, & had Mr Hawthorne been equally silent, then had I said perhaps, something to both of you about another Wonder-(-full) Book. But as it is, I must be silent. How is it, that while all of us human beings are so entirely disembarrased in censuring a person; that so soon as we would praise, then we begin to feel awkward? I never blush after denouncing a man; but I grow scarlet, after eulogizing him. And yet this is all wrong; and yet we can't help it; and so we see how true was that musical sentence of the poet when he sang—

"We can't help ourselves"

For tho' we know what we ought to be; & what it would be very sweet & beautiful to be; yet we can't be it. That is most sad, too. Life is a long Dardenelles, My Dear Madam, the shores whereof are bright with flowers, which we want to pluck, but the bank is too high; & so we float on & on, hoping to come to a landing-place at last—but swoop! we launch into the great sea! Yet the geographers say, even then we must not despair, because across the great sea, however desolate & vacant it may look, lie all Persia & the delicious lands roundabout Damascus.

So wishing you a pleasant voyage at last to that sweet & far countree—

Beleive Me
Earnestly Thine—
Herman Melville

I forgot to say, that your letter was sent to me from Pittsfield—which delayed it.

My sister Augusta begs me to send her sincerest regards both to you & Mr Hawthorne.

Hawthorne and His Mosses

By a Virginian Spending July in Vermont

A papered chamber in a fine old farm-house—a mile from any other dwelling, and dipped to the eaves in foliage—surrounded by mountains, old woods, and Indian ponds,—this, surely, is the place to write of Hawthorne. Some charm is in this northern air, for love and duty seem both impelling to the task. A man of a deep and noble nature has seized me in this seclusion. His wild, witch voice rings through me; or, in softer cadences, I seem to hear it in the songs of the hill-side birds, that sing in the larch trees at my window.

Would that all excellent books were foundlings, without father or mother, that so it might be, we could glorify them, without including their ostensible authors. Nor would any true man take exception to this;—least of all, he who writes,—"When the Artist rises high enough to achieve the Beautiful, the symbol by which he makes it perceptible to mortal senses becomes of little value in his eyes, while his spirit possesses itself in the enjoyment of the reality."

But more than this. I know not what would be the right name to put on the title-page of an excellent book, but this I feel, that the names of all fine authors are fictitious ones, far more so than that of Junius,—simply standing, as they do, for the mystical, ever-eluding Spirit of all Beauty, which ubiquitously possesses men of genius. Purely imaginative as this fancy may appear, it nevertheless seems to receive some warranty from the fact, that on a personal interview no great author has ever come up to the idea of his reader. But that dust of which our bodies are composed, how can it fitly express the nobler intelligences among us? With reverence be it spoken, that not even in the case of one deemed more than man, not even in our Saviour, did his visible frame betoken anything of the augustness of the nature within. Else, how could those Jewish eyewitnesses fail to see heaven in his glance.

It is curious, how a man may travel along a country road, and yet miss the grandest, or sweetest of prospects, by reason of an intervening hedge, so like all other hedges, as in no way to hint of the wide landscape beyond. So has it been with me concerning the enchanting landscape in the soul of this Hawthorne, this most excellent Man of Mosses. His "Old Manse" has been written now four years, but I never read it till a day or two since. I had seen it in the book-stores—heard of it often—even had it recommended to me by a tasteful friend, as a rare, quiet book, perhaps too deserving of popularity to be popular. But there are so many books called "excellent", and so much unpopular merit, that amid the thick stir of other things, the hint of my tasteful friend was disregarded; and for four years the Mosses on the old Manse never refreshed me with their perennial green. It may be, however, that all this while, the book, like wine, was only improving in flavor and body. At any rate, it so chanced that this long procrastination eventuated in a happy result. At breakfast the other day, a mountain girl, a cousin of mine, who for the last two weeks has every morning helped me to strawberries and raspberries,—which, like the roses and pearls in the fairy-tale, seemed to fall into the saucer from those strawberry-beds her cheeks,—this delightful creature, this charming Cherry says to me—"I see you spend your mornings in the hay-mow; and yesterday I found there 'Dwight's Travels in New England'. Now I have something far better than that,—something more congenial to our summer on these hills. Take these raspberries, and then I will give you some moss."—"Moss!" said I.—"Yes, and you must take it to the barn with you, and good-bye to 'Dwight' ".

With that she left me, and soon returned with a volume, verdantly bound, and garnished with a curious frontispiece in green,—nothing less, than a fragment of real moss cunningly pressed to a fly-leaf.—"Why this," said I spilling my raspberries, "this is the 'Mosses from an Old Manse' ". "Yes" said cousin Cherry "yes, it is that flowery Hawthorne."—

"Hawthorne and Mosses" said I "no more: it is morning: it is July in the country: and I am off for the barn".

Stretched on that new mown clover, the hill-side breeze blowing over me through the wide barn door, and soothed by the hum of the bees in the meadows around, how magically stole over me this Mossy Man! and how amply, how bountifully, did he redeem that delicious promise to his guests in the Old Manse, of whom it is written—"Others could give them pleasure, or amusement, or instruction—these could be picked up anywhere—but it was for me to give them rest. Rest, in a life of trouble! What better could be done for weary and world-worn spirits? what better could be done for anybody, who came within our magic circle, than to throw the spell of a magic spirit over him?"—So all that day, half-buried in the new clover, I watched this Hawthorne's "Assyrian dawn, and Paphian sunset and moonrise, from the summit of our Eastern Hill."

The soft ravishments of the man spun me round about in a web of dreams, and when the book was closed, when the spell was over, this wizard "dismissed me with but misty reminiscences, as if I had been dreaming of him".

What a mild moonlight of contemplative humor bathes that Old Manse!— the rich and rare distilment of a spicy and slowly-oozing heart. No rollicking rudeness, no gross fun fed on fat dinners, and bred in the lees of wine,—but a humor so spiritually gentle, so high, so deep, and yet so richly relishable, that it were hardly inappropriate in an angel. It is the very religion of mirth; for nothing so human but it may be advanced to that. The orchard of the Old Manse seems the visible type of the fine mind that has described it. Those twisted, and contorted old trees, "that stretch out their crooked branches, and take such hold of the imagination, that we remember them as humorists, and odd-fellows." And then, as surrounded by these grotesque forms, and hushed in the noon-day repose of this Hawthorne's spell, how aptly might the still fall of his ruddy thoughts into your soul be symbolized by "the thump of a great apple, in the stillest afternoon, falling without a breath of wind, from the mere necessity of perfect ripeness"! For no less ripe than ruddy are the apples of the thoughts and fancies in this sweet Man of Mosses.

"Buds and Bird-voices"—What a delicious thing is that!—"Will the world ever be so decayed, that Spring may not renew its greenness?"—And the "Fire-Worship". Was ever the hearth so glorified into an altar before? The mere title of that piece is better than any common work in fifty folio volumes. How exquisite is this:—"Nor did it lessen the charm of his soft, familiar courtesy and helpfulness, that the mighty spirit, were opportunity offered him, would run riot through the peaceful house, wrap its inmates in his terrible embrace, and leave nothing of them save their whitened bones. This possibility of mad destruction only made his domestic kindness the more beautiful and touching. It was so sweet of him, being endowed with such power, to dwell, day after day, and one long, lonesome night after another, on the dusky hearth, only now and then betraying his wild nature, by thrusting his red tongue out of the chimney-top! True, he had done much mischief in the world, and was pretty certain to do more, but his warm heart atoned for all. He was kindly to the race of man."

But he has still other apples, not quite so ruddy, though full as ripe;—apples, that have been left to wither on the tree, after the pleasant autumn gathering is past. The sketch of "The Old Apple Dealer" is conceived in the subtlest spirit of sadness; he whose "subdued and nerveless boyhood prefigured his abortive prime, which, likewise, contained within itself the prophecy and image of his lean and torpid age". Such touches as are in this piece can not proceed from any common heart. They argue such a depth of tenderness, such a boundless sympathy with all forms of being, such an omnipresent love, that we must needs say, that this Hawthorne is here almost alone in his generation,—at least, in the artistic manifestation of these things. Still more. Such touches as these,—and many, very many similar ones, all through his chapters—furnish clews, whereby we enter a little way into the intricate, profound heart where they originated. And we see, that suffering, some time or other and in some shape or other,—this only can enable any man to depict it in others. All over him, Hawthorne's melancholy rests like an Indian Summer, which though bathing a whole country in one softness, still reveals the distinctive hue of every towering hill, and each far-winding vale.

But it is the least part of genius that attracts admiration. Where Hawthorne is known, he seems to be deemed a pleasant writer, with a pleasant style,—a sequestered, harmless man, from whom any deep and weighty thing would hardly be anticipated:—a man who means no meanings. But there is no man, in whom humor and love, like mountain peaks, soar to such a rapt height, as to receive the irradiations of the upper skies;—there is no man in whom humor and love are developed in that high form called genius; no such man can exist without also possessing, as the indispensable complement of these, a great, deep intellect, which drops down into the universe like a plummet. Or, love and humor are only the eyes, through which such an intellect views this world. The great beauty in such a mind is but the product of its strength. What, to all readers, can be more charming than the piece entitled "Monsieur du Miroir"; and to a reader at all capable of fully fathoming it, what, at the same time, can possess more mystical depth of meaning?—Yes, there he sits, and looks at me,—this "shape of mystery", this "identical Monsieur du Miroir".—"Methinks I should tremble now, were his wizard power of gliding through all impediments in search of me, to place him suddenly before my eyes".

How profound, nay appalling, is the moral evolved by the "Earth's Holocaust"; where—beginning with the hollow follies and affectations of the world,—all vanities and empty theories and forms, are, one after another, and by an admirably graduated, growing comprehensiveness, thrown into the allegorical fire, till, at length, nothing is left but the all-engendering heart of man; which remaining still unconsumed, the great conflagration is nought.

Of a piece with this, is the "Intelligence Office", a wondrous symbolizing of the secret workings in men's souls. There are other sketches, still more charged with ponderous import.

"The Christmas Banquet", and "The Bosom Serpent" would be fine subjects for a curious and elaborate analysis, touching the conjectural parts of the mind that produced them. For spite of all the Indian-summer sunlight on the hither side of Hawthorne's soul, the other side—like the dark half of the physical sphere—is shrouded in a blackness, ten times black. But this darkness but gives more effect to the ever-moving dawn, that forever advances through it, and circumnavigates his world. Whether Hawthorne has simply availed himself of this mystical blackness as a means to the wondrous effects he makes it to produce in his lights and shades; or whether there really lurks in him, perhaps unknown to himself, a touch of Puritanic gloom,—this, I cannot altogether tell. Certain it is, however, that this great power of blackness in him derives its force from its appeals to that Calvinistic sense of Innate Depravity and Original Sin, from whose visitations, in some shape or other, no deeply thinking mind is always and wholly free. For, in certain moods, no man can weigh this world, without throwing in something, somehow like Original Sin, to strike the uneven balance. At all events, perhaps no writer has ever wielded this terrific thought with greater terror than this same harmless Hawthorne. Still more: this black conceit pervades him, through and through. You may be witched by his sunlight,—transported by the bright gildings in the skies he builds over you;—but there is the blackness of darkness beyond; and even his bright gildings but fringe, and play upon the edges of thunder-clouds.—In one word, the world is mistaken in this Nathaniel Hawthorne. He himself must often have smiled at its absurd misconception of him. He is immeasurably deeper than the plummet of the mere critic. For it is not the brain that can test such a man; it is only the heart. You cannot come to know greatness by inspecting it; there is no glimpse to be caught of it, except by intuition; you need not ring it, you but touch it, and you find it is gold.

Now it is that blackness in Hawthorne, of which I have spoken, that so fixes and fascinates me. It may be, nevertheless, that it is too largely developed in him. Perhaps he does not give us a ray of his light for every shade of his dark. But however this may be, this blackness it is that furnishes the infinite obscure of his back-ground,—that back-ground, against which Shakespeare plays his grandest conceits, the things that have made for Shakespeare his loftiest, but most circumscribed renown, as the profoundest of thinkers. For by philosophers Shakespeare is not adored as the great man of tragedy and comedy.—"Off with his head! so much for Buckingham!" this sort of rant, interlined by another hand, brings down the house,—those mistaken souls, who dream of Shakespeare as a mere man of Richard-the-Third humps, and Macbeth daggers. But it is those deep far-away things in him; those occasional flashings-forth of the intuitive Truth in him; those short, quick probings at the very axis of reality;—these are the things that make Shakespeare, Shakespeare. Through the mouths of the dark characters of Hamlet, Timon, Lear, and Iago, he craftily says, or sometimes insinuates the things, which we feel to be so terrifically true, that it were all but madness for any good man, in his own proper character, to utter, or even hint of them. Tormented into desperation, Lear the frantic King tears off the mask, and speaks the sane madness of vital truth. But, as I before said, it is the least part of genius that attracts admiration. And so, much of the blind, unbridled admiration that has been heaped upon Shakespeare, has been lavished upon the least part of him. And few of his endless commentators and critics seem to have remembered, or even perceived, that the immediate products of a great mind are not so great, as that undeveloped, (and sometimes undevelopable) yet dimly-discernable greatness, to which these immediate products are but the infallible indices. In Shakespeare's tomb lies infinitely more than Shakespeare ever wrote. And if I magnify Shakespeare, it is not so much for what he did do, as for what he did not do, or refrained from doing. For in this world of lies, Truth is forced to fly like a scared white doe in the woodlands; and only by cunning glimpses will she reveal herself, as in Shakespeare and other masters of the great Art of Telling the Truth,—even though it be covertly, and by snatches.

But if this view of the all-popular Shakespeare be seldom taken by his readers, and if very few who extol him, have ever read him deeply, or, perhaps, only have seen him on the tricky stage, (which alone made, and is still making him his mere mob renown)—if few men have time, or patience, or palate, for the spiritual truth as it is in that great genius;—it is, then, no matter of surprise that in a contemporaneous age, Nathaniel Hawthorne is a man, as yet, almost utterly mistaken among men. Here and there, in some quiet arm-chair in the noisy town, or some deep nook among the noiseless mountains, he may be appreciated for something of what he is. But unlike Shakespeare, who was forced to the contrary course by circumstances, Hawthorne (either from simple disinclination, or else from inaptitude) refrains from all the popularizing noise and show of broad farce, and blood-besmeared tragedy; content with the still, rich utterances of a great intellect in repose, and which sends few thoughts into circulation, except they be arterialized at his large warm lungs, and expanded in his honest heart.

Nor need you fix upon that blackness in him, if it suit you not. Nor, indeed, will all readers discern it, for it is, mostly, insinuated to those who may best understand it, and account for it; it is not obtruded upon every one alike.

Some may start to read of Shakespeare and Hawthorne on the same page. They may say, that if an illustration were needed, a lesser light might have sufficed to elucidate this Hawthorne, this small man of yesterday. But I am not, willingly, one of those, who, as touching Shakespeare at least, exemplify the maxim of Rochefoucault, that "we exalt the reputation of some, in order to depress that of others";—who, to teach all noble-souled aspirants that there is no hope for them, pronounce Shakespeare absolutely unapproachable. But Shakespeare has been approached. There are minds that have gone as far as Shakespeare into the universe. And hardly a mortal man, who, at some time or other, has not felt as great thoughts in him as any you will find in Hamlet. We must not inferentially malign mankind for the sake of any one man, whoever he may be. This is too cheap a purchase of contentment for conscious mediocrity to make. Besides, this absolute and unconditional adoration of Shakespeare has grown to be a part of our Anglo Saxon superstitions. The Thirty Nine articles are now Forty. Intolerance has come to exist in this matter. You must believe in Shakespeare's unapproachability, or quit the country. But what sort of a belief is this for an American, a man who is bound to carry republican progressiveness into Literature, as well as into Life? Believe me, my friends, that Shakespeares are this day being born on the banks of the Ohio. And the day will come, when you shall say who reads a book by an Englishman that is a modern? The great mistake seems to be, that even with those Americans who look forward to the coming of a great literary genius among us, they somehow fancy he will come in the costume of Queen Elizabeth's day,—be a writer of dramas founded upon old English history, or the tales of Boccaccio. Whereas, great geniuses are parts of the times; they themselves are the times; and possess a correspondent coloring. It is of a piece with the Jews, who while their Shiloh was meekly walking in their streets, were still praying for his magnificent coming; looking for him in a chariot, who was already among them on an ass. Nor must we forget, that, in his own life-time, Shakespeare was not Shakespeare, but only Master William Shakespeare of the shrewd, thriving, business firm of Condell, Shakespeare & Co., proprietors of the Globe Theatre in London; and by a courtly author, of the name of Greene, was hooted at, as an "upstart crow" beautified "with other birds' feathers". For, mark it well, imitation is often the first charge brought against real originality. Why this is so, there is not space to set forth here. You must have plenty of sea-room to tell the Truth in; especially, when it seems to have an aspect of newness, as America did in 1492, though it was then just as old, and perhaps older than Asia, only those sagacious philosophers, the common sailors, had never seen it before; swearing it was all water and moonshine there.

Now, I do not say that Nathaniel of Salem is a greater than William of Avon, or as great. But the difference between the two men is by no means immeasurable. Not a very great deal more, and Nathaniel were verily William.

This, too, I mean, that if Shakespeare has not been equalled, he is sure to be surpassed, and surpassed by an American born now or yet to be born. For it will never do for us who in most other things out-do as well as out-brag the world, it will not do for us to fold our hands and say, In the highest department advance there is none. Nor will it at all do to say, that the world is getting grey and grizzled now, and has lost that fresh charm which she wore of old, and by virtue of which the great poets of past times made themselves what we esteem them to be. Not so. The world is as young today, as when it was created; and this Vermont morning dew is as wet to my feet, as Eden's dew to Adam's. Nor has Nature been all over ransacked by our progenitors, so that no new charms and mysteries remain for this latter generation to find. Far from it. The trillionth part has not yet been said; and all that has been said, but multiplies the avenues to what remains to be said. It is not so much paucity, as superabundance of material that seems to incapacitate modern authors.

Let America then prize and cherish her writers; yea, let her glorify them. They are not so many in number, as to exhaust her good-will. And while she has good kith and kin of her own, to take to her bosom, let her not lavish her embraces upon the household of an alien. For believe it or not England, after all, is, in many things, an alien to us. China has more bowels of real love for us than she. But even were there no Hawthorne, no Emerson, no Whittier, no Irving, no Bryant, no Dana, no Cooper, no Willis (not the author of the "Dashes", but the author of the "Belfry Pigeon")—were there none of these, and others of like calibre among us, nevertheless, let America first praise mediocrity even, in her own children, before she praises (for everywhere, merit demands acknowledgment from every one) the best excellence in the children of any other land. Let her own authors, I say, have the priority of appreciation. I was much pleased with a hot-headed Carolina cousin of mine, who once said,—"If there were no other American to stand by, in Literature,—why, then, I would stand by Pop Emmons and his 'Fredoniad,' and till a better epic came along, swear it was not very far behind the Iliad." Take away the words, and in spirit he was sound.

Not that American genius needs patronage in order to expand. For that explosive sort of stuff will expand though screwed up in a vice, and burst it, though it were triple steel. It is for the nation's sake, and not for her authors' sake, that I would have America be heedful of the increasing greatness among her writers. For how great the shame, if other nations should be before her, in crowning her heroes of the pen. But this is almost the case now. American authors have received more just and discriminating praise (however loftily and ridiculously given, in certain cases) even from some Englishmen, than from their own countrymen. There are hardly five critics in America; and several of them are asleep. As for patronage, it is the American author who now patronizes his country, and not his country him. And if at times some among them appeal to the people for more recognition, it is not always with selfish motives, but patriotic ones.

It is true, that but few of them as yet have evinced that decided originality which merits great praise. But that graceful writer, who perhaps of all Americans has received the most plaudits from his own country for his productions,—that very popular and amiable writer, however good, and self-reliant in many things, perhaps owes his chief reputation to the self-acknowledged imitation of a foreign model, and to the studied avoidance of all topics but smooth ones. But it is better to fail in originality, than to succeed in imitation. He who has never failed somewhere, that man can not be great. Failure is the true test of greatness. And if it be said, that continual success is a proof that a man wisely knows his powers,—it is only to be added, that, in that case, he knows them to be small. Let us believe it, then, once for all, that there is no hope for us in these smooth pleasing writers that know their powers. Without malice, but to speak the plain fact, they but furnish an appendix to Goldsmith, and other English authors. And we want no American Goldsmiths; nay, we want no American Miltons. It were the vilest thing you could say of a true American author, that he were an American Tompkins. Call him an American, and have done; for you can not say a nobler thing of him.—But it is not meant that all American writers should studiously cleave to nationality in their writings; only this, no American writer should write like an Englishman, or a Frenchman; let him write like a man, for then he will be sure to write like an American. Let us away with this Bostonian leaven of literary flunkeyism towards England. If either must play the flunkey in this thing, let England do it, not us. And the time is not far off when circumstances may force her to it. While we are rapidly preparing for that political supremacy among the nations, which prophetically awaits us at the close of the present century; in a literary point of view, we are deplorably unprepared for it; and we seem studious to remain so. Hitherto, reasons might have existed why this should be; but no good reason exists now. And all that is requisite to amendment in this matter, is simply this: that, while freely acknowledging all excellence, everywhere, we should refrain from unduly lauding foreign writers and, at the same time, duly recognize the meritorious writers that are our own;—those writers, who breathe that unshackled, democratic spirit of Christianity in all things, which now takes the practical lead in this world, though at the same time led by ourselves—us Americans. Let us boldly contemn all imitation, though it comes to us graceful and fragrant as the morning; and foster all originality, though, at first, it be crabbed and ugly as our own pine knots. And if any of our authors fail, or seem to fail, then, in the words of my enthusiastic Carolina cousin, let us clap him on the shoulder, and back him against all Europe for his second round. The truth is, that in our point of view, this matter of a national literature has come to such a pass with us, that in some sense we must turn bullies, else the day is lost, or superiority so far beyond us, that we can hardly say it will ever be ours.

And now, my countrymen, as an excellent author, of your own flesh and blood,—an unimitating, and, perhaps, in his way, an inimitable man—whom better can I commend to you, in the first place, than Nathaniel Hawthorne. He is one of the new, and far better generation of your writers. The smell of your beeches and hemlocks is upon him; your own broad prairies are in his soul; and if you travel away inland into his deep and noble nature, you will hear the far roar of his Niagara. Give not over to future generations the glad duty of acknowledging him for what he is. Take that joy to your self, in your own generation; and so shall he feel those grateful impulses in him, that may possibly prompt him to the full flower of some still greater achievement in your eyes. And by confessing him, you thereby confess others; you brace the whole brotherhood. For genius, all over the world, stands hand in hand, and one shock of recognition runs the whole circle round.

In treating of Hawthorne, or rather of Hawthorne in his writings (for I never saw the man; and in the chances of a quiet plantation life, remote from his haunts, perhaps never shall) in treating of his works, I say, I have thus far omitted all mention of his "Twice Told Tales," and "Scarlet Letter." Both are excellent; but full of such manifold, strange and diffusive beauties, that time would all but fail me, to point the half of them out. But there are things in those two books, which, had they been written in England a century ago, Nathaniel Hawthorne had utterly displaced many of the bright names we now revere on authority. But I am content to leave

Hawthorne to himself, and to the infallible finding of posterity; and however great may be the praise I have bestowed upon him, I feel, that in so doing, I have more served and honored myself, than him. For, at bottom, great excellence is praise enough to itself; but the feeling of a sincere and appreciative love and admiration towards it, this is relieved by utterance; and warm, honest praise ever leaves a pleasant flavor in the mouth; and it is an honorable thing to confess to what is honorable in others.

But I cannot leave my subject yet. No man can read a fine author, and relish him to his very bones, while he reads, without subsequently fancying to himself some ideal image of the man and his mind. And if you rightly look for it, you will almost always find that the author himself has somewhere furnished you with his own picture.—For poets (whether in prose or verse), being painters of Nature, are like their brethren of the pencil, the true portrait-painters, who, in the multitude of likenesses to be sketched, do not invariably omit their own; and in all high instances, they paint them without any vanity, though, at times, with a lurking something, that would take several pages to properly define.

I submit it, then, to those best acquainted with the man personally, whether the following is not Nathaniel Hawthorne;—and to himself, whether something involved in it does not express the temper of his mind,—that lasting temper of all true, candid men—a seeker, not a finder yet:—

> "A man now entered, in neglected attire, with the aspect of a thinker, but somewhat too rough-hewn and brawny for a scholar. His face was full of sturdy vigor, with some finer and keener attribute beneath; though harsh at first, it was tempered with the glow of a large, warm heart, which had force enough to heat his powerful intellect through and through. He advanced to the Intelligencer, and looked at him with a glance of such stern sincerity, that perhaps few secrets were beyond its scope.
>
> " 'I seek for Truth', said he."

* * * * *

Twenty four hours have elapsed since writing the foregoing. I have just returned from the hay mow, charged more and more with love and admiration of Hawthorne. For I have just been gleaning through the Mosses, picking up many things here and there that had previously escaped me. And I found that but to glean after this man, is better than to be in at the harvest of others. To be frank (though, perhaps, rather foolish) notwithstanding what I wrote yesterday of these Mosses, I had not then culled them all; but had, nevertheless, been sufficiently sensible of the subtle essence, in them, as to write as I did. To what infinite height of loving wonder and admiration I may yet be borne, when by repeatedly banquetting on these Mosses, I shall have thoroughly incorporated their whole stuff into my being,—that, I can not tell. But already I feel that this Hawthorne has dropped germinous seeds into my soul. He expands and deepens down, the more I contemplate him; and further, and further, shoots his strong New-England roots into the hot soil of my Southern soul.

By careful reference to the "Table of Contents", I now find, that I have gone through all the sketches; but that when I yesterday wrote, I had not at all read two particular pieces, to which I now desire to call special attention,—"A Select Party", and "Young Goodman Brown". Here, be it said to all those whom this poor fugitive scrawl of mine may tempt to the perusal of the "Mosses," that they must on no account suffer themselves to be trifled with, disappointed, or deceived by the triviality of many of the titles to these Sketches. For in more than one instance, the title utterly belies the piece. It is as if rustic demijohns containing the very best and costliest of Falernian and Tokay, were labelled "Cider", "Perry," and "Elderberry wine". The truth seems to be, that like many other geniuses, this Man of Mosses takes great delight in hoodwinking the world,—at least, with respect to himself. Personally, I doubt not, that he rather prefers to be generally esteemed but a so-so sort of author; being willing to reserve the thorough and acute appreciation of what he is, to that party most qualified to judge—that is, to himself. Besides, at the bottom of their natures, men like Hawthorne, in many things, deem the plaudits of the public such strong presumptive evidence of mediocrity in the object of them, that it would in some degree render them doubtful of their own powers, did they hear much and vociferous braying concerning them in the public pastures. True, I have been braying myself (if you please to be witty enough, to have it so) but then I claim to be the first that has so brayed in this particular matter; and therefore, while pleading guilty to the charge still claim all the merit due to originality.

But with whatever motive, playful or profound, Nathaniel Hawthorne has chosen to entitle his pieces in the manner he has, it is certain, that some of them are directly calculated to deceive—egregiously deceive, the superficial skimmer of pages. To be downright and candid once more, let me cheerfully say, that two of these titles did dolefully dupe no less an eagle-eyed reader than myself; and that, too, after I had been impressed with a sense of the great depth and breadth of this American man. "Who in the name of thunder" (as the country-people say in this neighborhood) "who in the name of thunder", would anticipate any marvel in a piece entitled "Young Goodman Brown"? You would of course suppose that it was a simple little tale, intended as a supplement to "Goody Two Shoes". Whereas, it is deep as Dante; nor can you finish it, without addressing the author in his own words—"It is yours to penetrate, in every bosom, the deep mystery of sin." And with Young Goodman, too, in allegorical pursuit of his Puritan wife, you cry out in your anguish,—

" 'Faith!' shouted Goodman Brown, in a voice of agony and desperation; and the echoes of the forest mocked him, crying—'Faith! Faith!' as if bewildered wretches were seeking her all through the wilderness."

Now this same piece, entitled "Young Goodman Brown", is one of the two that I had not all read yesterday; and I allude to it now, because it is, in itself, such a strong positive illustration of that blackness in Hawthorne, which I had assumed from the mere occasional shadows of it, as revealed in several of the other sketches. But had I previously perused "Young Goodman Brown", I should have been at no pains to draw the conclusion, which I came to, at a time, when I was ignorant that the book contained one such direct and unqualified manifestation of it.

The other piece of the two referred to, is entitled "A Select Party", which, in my first simplicity upon originally taking hold of the book, I fancied must treat of some pumpkin-pie party in Old Salem, or some chowder party on Cape Cod. Whereas, by all the gods of Peedee! it is the sweetest and sublimest thing that has been written since Spencer wrote. Nay, there is nothing in Spencer that surpasses it, perhaps, nothing that equals it. And the test is this: read any canto in "The Faery Queen", and then read "A Select Party", and decide which pleases you the most,—that is, if you are qualified to judge. Do not be frightened at this; for when Spencer was alive, he was thought of very much as Hawthorne is now,—was generally accounted just such a "gentle" harmless man. It may be, that to common eyes, the sublimity of Hawthorne seems lost in his sweetness,—as perhaps in this same "Select Party" of his; for whom, he has builded so august a dome of sunset clouds, and served them on richer plate, than Belshazzar's when he banquetted his lords in Babylon.

But my chief business now, is to point out a particular page in this piece, having reference to an honored guest, who under the name of "The Master Genius" but in the guise of "a young man of poor attire, with no insignia of rank or acknowledged eminence," is introduced to the Man of Fancy, who is the giver of the feast. Now the page having reference to this "Master Genius", so happily expresses much of what I yesterday wrote, touching the coming of the literary Shiloh of America, that I cannot but be charmed by the coincidence; especially, when it shows such a parity of ideas, at least in this one point, between a man like Hawthorne and a man like me.

And here, let me throw out another conceit of mine touching this American Shiloh, or "Master Genius", as Hawthorne calls him. May it not be, that this commanding mind has not been, is not, and never will be, individually developed in any one man? And would it, indeed, appear so unreasonable to suppose, that this great fullness and overflowing may be, or may be destined to be, shared by a plurality of men of genius? Surely, to take the very greatest example on record, Shakespeare cannot be regarded as in himself the concretion of all the genius of his time; nor as so immeasurably beyond Marlow, Webster, Ford, Beaumont, Jonson, that those great men can be said to share none of his power? For one, I conceive that there were dramatists in Elizabeth's day, between whom and Shakespeare the distance was by no means great. Let anyone, hitherto little acquainted with those neglected old authors, for the first time read them thoroughly, or even read Charles Lamb's Specimens of them, and he will be amazed at the wondrous ability of those Anaks of men, and shocked at this renewed example of the fact, that Fortune has more to do with fame than merit,—though, without merit, lasting fame there can be none.

Nevertheless, it would argue too illy of my country were this maxim to hold good concerning Nathaniel Hawthorne, a man, who already, in some few minds, has shed "such a light, as never illuminates the earth, save when a great heart burns as the household fire of a grand intellect."

The words are his,—in the "Select Party"; and they are a magnificent setting to a coincident sentiment of my own, but ramblingly expressed yesterday, in reference to himself. Gainsay it who will, as I now write, I am Posterity speaking by proxy—and after times will make it more than good, when I declare—that the American, who up to the present day, has evinced, in Literature, the largest brain with the largest heart, that man is Nathaniel Hawthorne. Moreover, that whatever Nathaniel Hawthorne may hereafter write, "The Mosses from an Old Manse" will be ultimately accounted his masterpiece. For there is a sure, though a secret sign in some works which prove the culmination of the powers (only the developable ones, however) that produced them. But I am by no means desirous of the glory of a prophet. I pray Heaven that Hawthorne may *yet* prove me an impostor in this prediction. Especially, as I somehow cling to the strange fancy, that, in all men, hiddenly reside certain wondrous, occult properties—as in some plants and minerals—which by some happy but very rare accident (as bronze was discovered by the melting of the iron and brass in the burning of Corinth) may chance to be called forth here on earth; not entirely waiting for their better discovery in the more congenial, blessed atmosphere of heaven.

Once more—for it is hard to be finite upon an infinite subject, and all subjects are infinite. By some people, this entire scrawl of mine may be esteemed altogether unnecessary, inasmuch, "as years ago" (they may say) "we found out the rich and rare stuff in this Hawthorne, whom you now parade forth, as if only *yourself* were the discoverer of this Portuguese diamond in our Literature."—But even granting all this; and adding to it, the assumption that the books of Hawthorne have sold by the five-thousand,—what does that signify?—They should be sold by the hundred-thousand; and read by the million; and admired by every one who is capable of admiration.

1850

PART THREE
TALES AND SKETCHES

Melville's seventh novel, *Pierre* (1852), is a bracing experiment in psychoanalysis, incest, third-person narration, and language. It was, of course, an unqualified failure. Anxious to repair a faltering reputation, Melville turned to the magazines and produced eighteen tales and sketches.

This period of writing, from 1853 to 1856, was recuperative. Forsaking the excesses of *Pierre*, Melville returned to first-person narration, but in an ironic vein. Rather than resurrect the voice of Ishmael—tragic, comic, poetic, wise—he experimented with a series of unperceptive speakers groping toward awareness, whose failure to *see* becomes the ironic point of the tale. Thus, in "Bartleby," about a scrivener who "prefers not" to work, or in "The Tartarus of Maids," about virginal "wage slaves" in a paper mill, we grow beyond the narrator but are no more certain of the social or psychological causes of the alienation depicted. Melville did not wholly abandon sincere narration, as is evident in "The Chola Widow" (concerning rape), the serialized novel *Israel Potter* (1855), his Hawthornean pastiche "The Bell-Tower," and "The 'Gees" (concerning racism). But in "Benito Cereno," the ironies of a speaker, who reports events through the flawed consciousness of an American who unknowingly stumbles upon a slave revolt, force readers to re-inspect politics and race. Melville was honing his rhetoric of deceit for his last novel, *The Confidence-Man* (1857).

In a painterly style that gave a new psychological dimension to the picturesque, Melville offered self-portraits of eccentric "isolatoes" ("Cock-A-Doodle-Doo!" "I and My Chimney," "The Piazza"). But his singular innovation was the diptych ("The Two Temples" and "The Paradise of Bachelors and the Tartarus of Maids"), which pairs up two sketches of seemingly unrelated venues to challenge the reader to draw conclusions best left unwritten.

Melville published in two monthly magazines, *Harper's* and *Putnam's*, both newly dedicated to bringing American writers to the fore, and collected all but two of his *Putnam's* tales in *The Piazza Tales* (1856), which, despite critical acclaim, sold poorly. Even so, Melville's experiment in short fiction paid his bills, and also rejuvenated and refocused his talent.

Bartleby, the Scrivener

A Story of Wall-Street

I am a rather elderly man. The nature of my avocations for the last thirty years has brought me into more than ordinary contact with what would seem an interesting and somewhat singular set of men, of whom as yet nothing that I know of has ever been written:—I mean the law-copyists or scriveners. I have known very many of them, professionally and privately, and if I pleased, could relate divers histories, at which good-natured gentlemen might smile, and sentimental souls might weep. But I waive the biographies of all other scriveners for a few passages in the life of Bartleby, who was a scrivener the strangest I ever saw or heard of. While of other law-copyists I might write the complete life, of Bartleby nothing of that sort can be done. I believe that no materials exist for a full and satisfactory biography of this man. It is an irreparable loss to literature. Bartleby was one of those beings of whom nothing is ascertainable, except from the original sources, and in his case those are very small. What my own astonished eyes saw of Bartleby, *that* is all I know of him, except, indeed, one vague report which will appear in the sequel.

Ere introducing the scrivener, as he first appeared to me, it is fit I make some mention of myself, my *employés*, my business, my chambers, and general surroundings; because some such description is indispensable to an adequate understanding of the chief character about to be presented.

Imprimis: I am a man who, from his youth upwards, has been filled with a profound conviction that the easiest way of life is the best. Hence, though I belong to a profession proverbially energetic and nervous, even to turbulence, at times, yet nothing of that sort have I ever suffered to invade my peace. I am one of those unambitious lawyers who never addresses a jury, or in any way draws down public applause; but in the cool tranquillity of a snug retreat, do a snug business among rich men's bonds and mortgages and title-deeds. All who know me, consider me an eminently *safe* man. The late John Jacob Astor, a personage little given to poetic enthusiasm, had no hesitation in pronouncing my first grand point to be prudence; my next, method. I do not speak it in vanity, but simply record the fact, that I was not unemployed in my profession by the late John Jacob Astor; a name which, I admit, I love to repeat, for it hath a rounded and orbicular sound to it, and rings like unto bullion. I will freely add, that I was not insensible to the late John Jacob Astor's good opinion.

Some time prior to the period at which this little history begins, my avocations had been largely increased. The good old office, now extinct in the State of New-York, of a Master in Chancery, had been conferred upon me. It was not a very arduous office, but very pleasantly remunerative. I seldom lose my temper; much more seldom indulge in dangerous indignation at wrongs and outrages; but I must be permitted to be rash here and declare, that I consider the sudden and violent abrogation of the office of Master in Chancery, by the new Constitution, as a—premature act; inasmuch as I had counted upon a life-lease of the profits, whereas I only received those of a few short years. But this is by the way.

My chambers were up stairs at No. — Wall-street. At one end they looked upon the white wall of the interior of a spacious sky-light shaft, penetrating the building from top to bottom. This view might have been considered rather tame than otherwise, deficient in what landscape painters call "life." But if so, the view from the other end of my chambers offered, at least, a contrast, if nothing more. In that direction my windows commanded an unobstructed view of a lofty brick wall, black by age and everlasting shade; which wall required no spy-glass to bring out its lurking beauties, but for the benefit of all near-sighted spectators, was pushed up to within ten feet of my window panes. Owing to the great height of the surrounding buildings, and my chambers being on the second floor, the interval between this wall and mine not a little resembled a huge square cistern.

At the period just preceding the advent of Bartleby, I had two persons as copyists in my employment, and a promising lad as an office-boy. First, Turkey; second, Nippers; third, Ginger Nut. These may seem names, the like of which are not usually found in the Directory. In truth they were nicknames, mutually conferred upon each other by my three clerks, and were deemed expressive of their respective persons or characters. Turkey was a short, pursy Englishman of about my own age, that is, somewhere not far from sixty. In the morning, one might say, his face was of a fine florid hue, but after twelve o'clock, meridian—his dinner hour—it blazed like a grate full of Christmas coals; and continued blazing—but, as it were, with a gradual wane—till 6 o'clock, P.M. or thereabouts, after which I saw no more of the proprietor of the face, which gaining its meridian with the sun, seemed to set with it, to rise, culminate, and decline the following day, with the like regularity and undiminished glory. There are many singular coincidences I have known in the course of my life, not the least among which was the fact, that exactly when Turkey displayed his fullest beams from his red and radiant countenance, just then, too, at that critical moment, began the daily period when I considered his business capacities as seriously disturbed for the remainder of the twenty-four hours. Not that he was absolutely idle, or averse to business then; far from it. The difficulty was, he was apt to be altogether too energetic. There was a strange, inflamed, flurried, flighty recklessness of activity about him. He would be incautious in dipping his pen into his inkstand. All his blots upon my documents, were dropped there after twelve o'clock, meridian. Indeed, not only would he be reckless and sadly given to making blots in the afternoon, but some days he went further, and was rather noisy. At such times, too, his face flamed with augmented blazonry, as if cannel coal had been heaped on anthracite. He made an unpleasant racket with his chair; spilled his sandbox; in mending his pens, impatiently split them all to pieces, and threw them on the floor in a sudden passion; stood up and leaned over his table, boxing his papers about in a most indecorous manner, very sad to behold in an elderly man like him. Nevertheless, as he was in many ways a most valuable person to me, and all the time before twelve o'clock, meridian, was the quickest, steadiest creature too, accomplishing a great deal of work in a style not easy to be matched—for these reasons, I was willing to overlook his eccentricities, though indeed, occasionally, I remonstrated with him. I did this very gently, however, because, though the civilest, nay, the blandest and most reverential of men in the morning, yet in the afternoon he was disposed, upon provocation, to be slightly rash with his tongue, in fact, insolent. Now, valuing his morning services as I did, and resolved not to lose them; yet, at the same time made uncomfortable by his inflamed ways after twelve o'clock; and being a man of peace, unwilling by my admonitions to call forth unseemly retorts from him; I took upon me, one Saturday noon (he was always worse on Saturdays), to hint to him, very kindly, that perhaps now that he was growing old, it might be well to abridge his labors; in short, he need not come to my chambers after twelve o'clock, but, dinner over, had best go home to his lodgings and rest himself till tea-time. But no; he insisted upon his afternoon devotions. His countenance became intolerably fervid, as he oratorically assured me—gesticulating with a long ruler at the other end of the room—that if his services in the morning were useful, how indispensable, then, in the afternoon?

"With submission, sir," said Turkey on this occasion, "I consider myself your right-hand man. In the morning I but marshal and deploy my columns; but in the afternoon I put myself at their head, and gallantly charge the foe, thus!"—and he made a violent thrust with the ruler.

"But the blots, Turkey," intimated I.

"True,—but, with submission, sir, behold these hairs! I am getting old. Surely, sir, a blot or two of a warm afternoon is not to be severely urged against gray hairs. Old age—even if it blot the page—is honorable. With submission, sir, we *both* are getting old."

This appeal to my fellow-feeling was hardly to be resisted. At all events, I saw that go he would not. So I made up my mind to let him stay, resolving, nevertheless, to see to it, that during the afternoon he had to do with my less important papers.

Nippers, the second on my list, was a whiskered, sallow, and, upon the whole, rather piratical-looking young man of about five and twenty. I always deemed him the victim of two evil powers—ambition and indigestion. The ambition was evinced by a certain impatience of the duties of a mere copyist, an unwarrantable usurpation of strictly professional affairs, such as the original drawing up of legal documents. The indigestion seemed betokened in an occasional nervous testiness and grinning irritability, causing the teeth to audibly grind together over mistakes committed in copying; unnecessary maledictions, hissed, rather than spoken, in the heat of business; and especially by a continual discontent with the height of the table where he worked. Though of a very ingenious mechanical turn, Nippers could never get this table to suit him. He put chips under it, blocks of various sorts, bits of pasteboard, and at last went so far as to attempt an exquisite adjustment by final pieces of folded blotting-paper. But no invention would answer. If, for the sake of easing his back, he brought the table lid at a sharp angle well up towards his chin, and wrote there like a man using the steep roof of a Dutch house for his desk:—then he declared that it stopped the circulation in his arms. If now he lowered the table to his waistbands, and stooped over it in writing, then there was a sore aching in his back. In short, the truth of the matter was, Nippers knew not what he wanted. Or, if he wanted any thing, it was to be rid of a scrivener's table altogether. Among the manifestations of his diseased ambition was a fondness he had for receiving visits from certain ambiguous-looking fellows in seedy coats, whom he called his clients. Indeed I was aware that not only was he, at times, considerable of a ward-politician, but he occasionally did a little business at the Justices' courts, and was not unknown on the steps of the Tombs. I have good reason to believe, however, that one individual who called upon him at my chambers, and who, with a grand air, he insisted was his client, was no other than a dun, and the alleged title-deed, a bill. But with all his failings, and the annoyances he caused me, Nippers, like his compatriot Turkey, was a very useful man to me; wrote a neat, swift hand; and, when he chose, was not deficient in a gentlemanly sort of deportment. Added to this, he always dressed in a gentlemanly sort of way; and so, incidentally, reflected credit upon my chambers. Whereas with respect to Turkey, I had much ado to keep him from being a reproach to me. His clothes were apt to look oily and smell of eating-houses. He wore his pantaloons very loose and baggy in summer. His coats were execrable; his hat not to be handled. But while the hat was a thing of indifference to me, inasmuch as his natural civility and deference, as a dependent Englishman, always led him to doff it the moment he entered the room, yet his coat was another matter. Concerning his coats, I reasoned with him; but with no effect. The truth was, I suppose, that a man with so small an income, could not afford to sport such a lustrous face and a lustrous coat at one and the same time. As Nippers once observed, Turkey's money went chiefly for red ink. One winter day I presented Turkey with a highly-respectable looking coat of my own, a padded gray coat, of a most comfortable warmth, and which buttoned straight up from the knee to the neck. I thought Turkey would appreciate the favor, and abate his rashness and obstreperousness of afternoons. But no. I verily believe that buttoning himself up in so downy and blanket-like a coat had a pernicious effect upon him; upon the same principle that too much oats are bad for horses. In fact, precisely as a rash, restive horse is said to feel his oats, so Turkey felt his coat. It made him insolent. He was a man whom prosperity harmed.

Though concerning the self-indulgent habits of Turkey I had my own private surmises, yet touching Nippers I was well persuaded that whatever might be his faults in other respects, he was, at least, a temperate young man. But indeed, nature herself seemed to have been his vintner, and at his birth charged him so thoroughly with an irritable, brandy-like disposition, that all subsequent potations were needless. When I consider how, amid the stillness of my chambers, Nippers would sometimes impatiently rise from his seat, and stooping over his table, spread his arms wide apart, seize the whole desk, and move it, and jerk it, with a grim, grinding motion on the floor, as if the table were a perverse voluntary agent, intent on thwarting and vexing him; I plainly perceive that for Nippers, brandy and water were altogether superfluous.

It was fortunate for me that, owing to its peculiar cause—indigestion—the irritability and consequent nervousness of Nippers, were mainly observable in the morning, while in the afternoon he was comparatively mild. So that Turkey's paroxysms only coming on about twelve o'clock, I never had to do with their eccentricities at one time. Their fits relieved each other like guards. When Nippers' was on, Turkey's was off; and *vice versa*. This was a good natural arrangement under the circumstances.

Ginger Nut, the third on my list, was a lad some twelve years old. His father was a carman, ambitious of seeing his son on the bench instead of a cart, before he died. So he sent him to my office as student at law, errand boy, and cleaner and sweeper, at the rate of one dollar a week. He had a little desk to himself, but he did not use it much. Upon inspection, the drawer exhibited a great array of the shells of various sorts of nuts. Indeed, to this quick-witted youth the whole noble science of the law was contained in a nut-shell. Not the least among the employments of Ginger Nut, as well as one which he discharged with the most alacrity, was his duty as cake and apple purveyor for Turkey and Nippers. Copying law papers being proverbially a dry, husky sort of business, my two scriveners were fain to moisten their mouths very often with Spitzenbergs to be had at the numerous stalls nigh the Custom House and Post Office. Also, they sent Ginger Nut very frequently for that peculiar cake—small, flat, round, and very spicy—after which he had been named by them. Of a cold morning when business was but dull, Turkey would gobble up scores of these cakes, as if they were mere wafers—indeed they sell them at the rate of six or eight for a penny—the scrape of his pen blending with the crunching of the crisp particles in his mouth. Of all the fiery afternoon blunders and flurried rashnesses of Turkey, was his once moistening a ginger-cake between his lips, and clapping it on to a mortgage for a seal. I came within an ace of dismissing him then. But he mollified me by making an oriental bow, and saying—"With submission, sir, it was generous of me to find you in stationery on my own account."

Now my original business—that of a conveyancer and title hunter, and drawer-up of recondite documents of all sorts was considerably increased by receiving the master's office. There was now great work for scriveners. Not only must I push the clerks already with me, but I must have additional help. In answer to my advertisement, a motionless young man one morning, stood upon my office threshold, the door being open, for it was summer. I can see that figure now—pallidly neat, pitiably respectable, incurably forlorn! It was Bartleby.

After a few words touching his qualifications, I engaged him, glad to have among my corps of copyists a man of so singularly sedate an aspect, which I thought might operate beneficially upon the flighty temper of Turkey, and the fiery one of Nippers.

I should have stated before that ground glass folding-doors divided my premises into two parts, one of which was occupied by my scriveners, the other by myself. According to my humor I threw open these doors, or closed them. I resolved to assign Bartleby a corner by the folding-doors, but on my side of them, so as to have this quiet man within easy call, in case any trifling thing was to be done. I placed his desk close up to a small side-window in that part of the room, a window which originally had afforded a lateral view of certain grimy back-yards and bricks, but which, owing to subsequent erections, commanded at present no view at all, though it gave some light. Within three feet of the panes was a wall, and the light came down from far above, between two lofty buildings, as from a very small opening in a dome. Still further to a satisfactory arrangement, I procured a high green folding screen, which might entirely isolate Bartleby from my sight, though not remove him from my voice. And thus, in a manner, privacy and society were conjoined.

At first Bartleby did an extraordinary quantity of writing. As if long famishing for something to copy, he seemed to gorge himself on my documents. There was no pause for digestion. He ran a day and night line, copying by sun-light and by candle-light. I should have been quite delighted with his application, had he been cheerfully industrious. But he wrote on silently, palely, mechanically.

It is, of course, an indispensable part of a scrivener's business to verify the accuracy of his copy, word by word. Where there are two or more scriveners in an office, they assist each other in this examination, one reading from the copy, the other holding the original. It is a very dull, wearisome, and lethargic affair. I can readily imagine that to some sanguine temperaments it would be altogether intolerable. For example, I cannot credit that the mettlesome poet Byron would have contentedly sat down with Bartleby to examine a law document of, say five hundred pages, closely written in a crimpy hand.

Now and then, in the haste of business, it had been my habit to assist in comparing some brief document myself, calling Turkey or Nippers for this purpose. One object I had in placing Bartleby so handy to me behind the screen, was to avail myself of his services on such trivial occasions. It was on the third day, I think, of his being with me, and before any necessity had arisen for having his own writing examined, that, being much hurried to complete a small affair I had in hand, I abruptly called to Bartleby. In my haste and natural expectancy of instant compliance, I sat with my head bent over the original on my desk, and my right hand sideways, and somewhat nervously extended with the copy, so that immediately upon emerging from his retreat, Bartleby might snatch it and proceed to business without the least delay.

In this very attitude did I sit when I called to him, rapidly stating what it was I wanted him to do—namely, to examine a small paper with me. Imagine my surprise, nay, my consternation, when without moving from his privacy, Bartleby in a singularly mild, firm voice, replied, "I would prefer not to."

I sat awhile in perfect silence, rallying my stunned faculties. Immediately it occurred to me that my ears had deceived me, or Bartleby had entirely misunderstood my meaning. I repeated my request in the clearest tone I could assume. But in quite as clear a one came the previous reply, "I would prefer not to."

"Prefer not to," echoed I, rising in high excitement, and crossing the room with a stride. "What do you mean? Are you moon-struck? I want you to help me compare this sheet here—take it," and I thrust it towards him.

"I would prefer not to," said he.

I looked at him steadfastly. His face was leanly composed; his gray eye dimly calm. Not a wrinkle of agitation rippled him. Had there been the least uneasiness, anger, impatience or impertinence in his manner; in other words, had there been any thing ordinarily human about him, doubtless I should have violently dismissed him from the premises. But as it was, I should have as soon thought of turning my pale plaster-of-paris bust of Cicero out of doors. I stood gazing at him awhile, as he went on with his own writing, and then reseated myself at my desk. This is very strange, thought I. What had one best do? But my business hurried me. I concluded to forget the matter for the present, reserving it for my future leisure. So calling Nippers from the other room, the paper was speedily examined.

A few days after this, Bartleby concluded four lengthy documents, being quadruplicates of a week's testimony taken before me in my High Court of Chancery. It became necessary to examine them. It was an important suit, and great accuracy was imperative. Having all things arranged I called Turkey, Nippers and Ginger Nut from the next room, meaning to place the four copies in the hands of my four clerks, while I should read from the original. Accordingly Turkey, Nippers and Ginger Nut had taken their seats in a row, each with his document in hand, when I called to Bartleby to join this interesting group.

"Bartleby! quick, I am waiting."

I heard a slow scrape of his chair legs on the uncarpeted floor, and soon he appeared standing at the entrance of his hermitage.

"What is wanted?" said he mildly.

"The copies, the copies," said I hurriedly. "We are going to examine them. There"—and I held towards him the fourth quadruplicate.

"I would prefer not to," he said, and gently disappeared behind the screen.

For a few moments I was turned into a pillar of salt, standing at the head of my seated column of clerks. Recovering myself, I advanced towards the screen, and demanded the reason for such extraordinary conduct.

"*Why* do you refuse?"

"I would prefer not to."

With any other man I should have flown outright into a dreadful passion, scorned all further words, and thrust him ignominiously from my presence. But there was something about Bartleby that not only strangely disarmed me, but in a wonderful manner touched and disconcerted me. I began to reason with him.

"These are your own copies we are about to examine. It is labor saving to you, because one examination will answer for your four papers. It is common usage. Every copyist is bound to help examine his copy. Is it not so? Will you not speak? Answer!"

"I prefer not to," he replied in a flute-like tone. It seemed to me that while I had been addressing him, he carefully revolved every statement that I made; fully comprehended the meaning; could not gainsay the irresistible conclusion; but, at the same time, some paramount consideration prevailed with him to reply as he did.

"You are decided, then, not to comply with my request—a request made according to common usage and common sense?"

He briefly gave me to understand that on that point my judgment was sound. Yes: his decision was irreversible.

It is not seldom the case that when a man is browbeaten in some unprecedented and violently unreasonable way, he begins to stagger in his own plainest faith. He begins, as it were, vaguely to surmise that, wonderful as it may be, all the justice and all the reason is on the other side. Accordingly, if any disinterested persons are present, he turns to them for some reinforcement for his own faltering mind.

"Turkey," said I, "what do you think of this? Am I not right?"

"With submission, sir," said Turkey, with his blandest tone, "I think that you are."

"Nippers," said I, "what do *you* think of it?"

"I think I should kick him out of the office."

(The reader of nice perceptions will here perceive that, it being morning, Turkey's answer is couched in polite and tranquil terms, but Nippers replies in ill-tempered ones. Or, to repeat a previous sentence, Nippers's ugly mood was on duty, and Turkey's off.)

"Ginger Nut," said I, willing to enlist the smallest suffrage in my behalf, "what do *you* think of it?"

"I think, sir, he's a little *luny*," replied Ginger Nut, with a grin.

"You hear what they say," said I, turning towards the screen, "come forth and do your duty."

But he vouchsafed no reply. I pondered a moment in sore perplexity. But once more business hurried me. I determined again to postpone the consideration of this dilemma to my future leisure. With a little trouble we made out to examine the papers without Bartleby, though at every page or two, Turkey deferentially dropped his opinion that this proceeding was quite out of the common; while Nippers, twitching in his chair with a dyspeptic nervousness, ground out between his set teeth occasional hissing maledictions against the stubborn oaf behind the screen. And for his (Nippers's) part, this was the first and the last time he would do another man's business without pay.

Meanwhile Bartleby sat in his hermitage, oblivious to every thing but his own peculiar business there.

Some days passed, the scrivener being employed upon another lengthy work. His late remarkable conduct led me to regard his ways narrowly. I observed that he never went to dinner; indeed that he never went any where. As yet I had never of my personal knowledge known him to be outside of my office. He was a perpetual sentry in the corner. At about eleven o'clock though, in the morning, I noticed that Ginger Nut would advance toward the opening in Bartleby's screen, as if silently beckoned thither by a gesture invisible to me where I sat. The boy would then leave the office jingling a few pence, and reappear with a handful of ginger-nuts which he delivered in the hermitage, receiving two of the cakes for his trouble.

He lives, then, on ginger-nuts, thought I; never eats a dinner, properly speaking; he must be a vegetarian then; but no; he never eats even vegetables, he eats nothing but ginger-nuts. My mind then ran on in reveries concerning the probable effects upon the human constitution of living entirely on ginger-nuts. Ginger-nuts are so called because they contain ginger as one of their peculiar constituents, and the final flavoring one. Now what was ginger? A hot, spicy thing. Was Bartleby hot and spicy? Not at all. Ginger, then, had no effect upon Bartleby. Probably he preferred it should have none.

Nothing so aggravates an earnest person as a passive resistance. If the individual so resisted be of a not inhumane temper, and the resisting one perfectly harmless in his passivity; then, in the better moods of the former, he will endeavor charitably to construe to his imagination what proves impossible to be solved by his judgment. Even so, for the most part, I regarded Bartleby and his ways. Poor fellow! thought I, he means no mischief; it is plain he intends no insolence; his aspect sufficiently evinces that his eccentricities are involuntary. He is useful to me. I can get along with him. If I turn him away, the chances are he will fall in with some less indulgent employer, and then he will be rudely treated, and perhaps driven forth miserably to starve. Yes. Here I can cheaply purchase a delicious self-approval. To befriend Bartleby; to humor him in his strange wilfulness, will cost me little or nothing, while I lay up in my soul what will eventually prove a sweet morsel for my conscience. But this mood was not invariable with me. The passiveness of Bartleby sometimes irritated me. I felt strangely goaded on to encounter him in new opposition, to elicit some angry spark from him answerable to my own. But indeed I might as well have essayed to strike fire with my knuckles against a bit of Windsor soap. But one afternoon the evil impulse in me mastered me, and the following little scene ensued:

"Bartleby," said I, "when those papers are all copied, I will compare them with you."

"I would prefer not to."

"How? Surely you do not mean to persist in that mulish vagary?"

No answer.

I threw open the folding-doors near by, and turning upon Turkey and Nippers, exclaimed:

"Bartleby a second time says, he won't examine his papers. What do you think of it, Turkey?"

It was afternoon, be it remembered. Turkey sat glowing like a brass boiler, his bald head steaming, his hands reeling among his blotted papers.

"Think of it?" roared Turkey; "I think I'll just step behind his screen, and black his eyes for him!"

So saying, Turkey rose to his feet and threw his arms into a pugilistic position. He was hurrying away to make good his promise, when I detained him, alarmed at the effect of incautiously rousing Turkey's combativeness after dinner.

"Sit down, Turkey," said I, "and hear what Nippers has to say. What do you think of it, Nippers? Would I not be justified in immediately dismissing Bartleby?"

"Excuse me, that is for you to decide, sir. I think his conduct quite unusual, and indeed unjust, as regards Turkey and myself. But it may only be a passing whim."

"Ah," exclaimed I, "you have strangely changed your mind then—you speak very gently of him now."

"All beer," cried Turkey; "gentleness is effects of beer—Nippers and I dined together to-day. You see how gentle *I* am, sir. Shall I go and black his eyes?"

"You refer to Bartleby, I suppose. No, not to-day, Turkey," I replied; "pray, put up your fists."

I closed the doors, and again advanced towards Bartleby. I felt additional incentives tempting me to my fate. I burned to be rebelled against again. I remembered that Bartleby never left the office.

"Bartleby," said I, "Ginger Nut is away; just step round to the Post Office, won't you? (it was but a three minutes walk,) and see if there is any thing for me."

"I would prefer not to."

"You *will* not?"

"I *prefer* not."

I staggered to my desk, and sat there in a deep study. My blind inveteracy returned. Was there any other thing in which I could procure myself to be ignominiously repulsed by this lean, penniless wight?—my hired clerk? What added thing is there, perfectly reasonable, that he will be sure to refuse to do?

"Bartleby!"

No answer.

"Bartleby," in a louder tone.

No answer.

"Bartleby," I roared.

Like a very ghost, agreeably to the laws of magical invocation, at the third summons, he appeared at the entrance of his hermitage.

"Go to the next room, and tell Nippers to come to me."

"I prefer not to," he respectfully and slowly said, and mildly disappeared.

"Very good, Bartleby," said I, in a quiet sort of serenely severe self-possessed tone, intimating the unalterable purpose of some terrible retribution very close at hand. At the moment I half intended something of the kind. But upon the whole, as it was drawing towards my dinner-hour, I thought it best to put on my hat and walk home for the day, suffering much from perplexity and distress of mind.

Shall I acknowledge it? The conclusion of this whole business was, that it soon became a fixed fact of my chambers, that a pale young scrivener, by the name of Bartleby, had a desk there; that he copied for me at the usual rate of four cents a folio (one hundred words); but he was permanently exempt from examining the work done by him, that duty being transferred to Turkey and Nippers, out of compliment doubtless to their superior acuteness; moreover, said Bartleby was never on any account to be dispatched on the most trivial errand of any sort; and that even if entreated to take upon him such a matter, it was generally understood that he would prefer not to—in other words, that he would refuse pointblank.

As days passed on, I became considerably reconciled to Bartleby. His steadiness, his freedom from all dissipation, his incessant industry (except when he chose to throw himself into a standing revery behind his screen), his great stillness, his unalterableness of demeanor under all circumstances, made him a valuable acquisition. One prime thing was this,—*he was always there;*—first in the morning, continually through the day, and the last at night. I had a singular confidence in his honesty. I felt my most precious papers perfectly safe in his hands. Sometimes to be sure I could not, for the very soul of me, avoid falling into sudden spasmodic passions with him. For it was exceeding difficult to bear in mind all the time those strange peculiarities, privileges, and unheard of exemptions, forming the tacit stipulations on Bartleby's part under which he remained in my office. Now and then, in the eagerness of dispatching pressing business, I would inadvertently summon Bartleby, in a short, rapid tone, to put his finger, say, on the incipient tie of a bit of red tape with which I was about compressing some papers. Of course, from behind the screen the usual answer, "I prefer not to," was sure to come; and then, how could a human creature with the common infirmities of our nature, refrain from bitterly exclaiming upon such perverseness—such unreasonableness. However, every added repulse of this sort which I received only tended to lessen the probability of my repeating the inadvertence.

Here it must be said, that according to the custom of most legal gentlemen occupying chambers in densely-populated law buildings, there were several keys to my door. One was kept by a woman residing in the attic, which person weekly scrubbed and daily swept and dusted my apartments. Another was kept by Turkey for convenience sake. The third I sometimes carried in my own pocket. The fourth I knew not who had.

Now, one Sunday morning I happened to go to Trinity Church, to hear a celebrated preacher, and finding myself rather early on the ground, I thought I would walk round to my chambers for a while. Luckily I had my key with me; but upon applying it to the lock, I found it resisted by something inserted from the inside. Quite surprised, I called out; when to my consternation a key was turned from within; and thrusting his lean visage at me, and holding the door ajar, the apparition of Bartleby appeared, in his shirt sleeves, and otherwise in a strangely tattered dishabille, saying quietly that he was sorry, but he was deeply engaged just then, and—preferred not admitting me at present. In a brief word or two, he moreover added, that perhaps I had better walk round the block two or three times, and by that time he would probably have concluded his affairs.

Now, the utterly unsurmised appearance of Bartleby, tenanting my law-chambers of a Sunday morning, with his cadaverously gentlemanly *nonchalance*, yet withal firm and self-possessed, had such a strange effect upon me, that incontinently I slunk away from my own door, and did as desired. But not without sundry twinges of impotent rebellion against the mild effrontery of this unaccountable scrivener. Indeed, it was his wonderful mildness chiefly, which not only disarmed me, but unmanned me, as it were. For I consider that one, for the time, is a sort of unmanned when he tranquilly permits his hired clerk to dictate to him, and order him away from his own premises. Furthermore, I was full of uneasiness as to what Bartleby could possibly be doing in my office in his shirt sleeves, and in an otherwise dismantled condition of a Sunday morning. Was any thing amiss going on? Nay, that was out of the question. It was not to be thought of for a moment that Bartleby was an immoral person. But what could he be doing there?—copying? Nay again, whatever might be his eccentricities, Bartleby was an eminently decorous person. He would be the last man to sit down to his desk in any state approaching to nudity. Besides, it was Sunday; and there was something about Bartleby that forbade the supposition that he would by any secular occupation violate the proprieties of the day.

Nevertheless, my mind was not pacified; and full of a restless curiosity, at last I returned to the door. Without hindrance I inserted my key, opened it, and entered. Bartleby was not to be seen. I looked round anxiously, peeped behind his screen; but it was very plain that he was gone. Upon more closely examining the place, I surmised that for an indefinite period Bartleby must have ate, dressed, and slept in my office, and that too without plate, mirror, or bed. The cushioned seat of a ricketty old sofa in one corner bore the faint impress of a lean, reclining form. Rolled away under his desk, I found a blanket; under the empty grate, a blacking box and brush; on a chair, a tin basin, with soap and a ragged towel; in a newspaper a few crumbs of ginger-nuts and a morsel of cheese. Yes, thought I, it is evident enough that Bartleby has been making his home here, keeping bachelor's hall all by himself. Immediately then the thought came sweeping across me, What miserable friendlessness and loneliness are here revealed! His poverty is great; but his solitude, how horrible! Think of it. Of a Sunday, Wall-street is deserted as Petra; and every night of every day it is an emptiness. This building too, which of week-days hums with industry and life, at nightfall echoes with sheer vacancy, and all through Sunday is forlorn. And here Bartleby makes his home; sole spectator of a solitude which he has seen all populous—a sort of innocent and transformed Marius brooding among the ruins of Carthage!

For the first time in my life a feeling of overpowering stinging melancholy seized me. Before, I had never experienced aught but a not-unpleasing sadness. The bond of a common humanity now drew me irresistibly to gloom. A fraternal melancholy! For both I and Bartleby were sons of Adam. I remembered the bright silks and sparkling faces I had seen that day, in gala trim, swan-like sailing down the Mississippi of Broadway; and I contrasted them with the pallid copyist, and thought to myself, Ah, happiness courts the light, so we deem the world is gay; but misery hides aloof, so we deem that misery there is none. These sad fancyings—chimeras, doubtless, of a sick and silly brain—led on to other and more special thoughts, concerning the eccentricities of Bartleby. Presentiments of strange discoveries hovered round me. The scrivener's pale form appeared to me laid out, among uncaring strangers, in its shivering winding sheet.

Suddenly I was attracted by Bartleby's closed desk, the key in open sight left in the lock.

I mean no mischief, seek the gratification of no heartless curiosity, thought I; besides, the desk is mine, and its contents too, so I will make bold to look within. Every thing was methodically arranged, the papers smoothly placed. The pigeon holes were deep, and removing the files of documents, I groped into their recesses. Presently I felt something there, and dragged it out. It was an old bandanna handkerchief, heavy and knotted. I opened it, and saw it was a savings' bank.

I now recalled all the quiet mysteries which I had noted in the man. I remembered that he never spoke but to answer; that though at intervals he had considerable time to himself, yet I had never seen him reading—no, not even a newspaper; that for long periods he would stand looking out, at his pale window behind the screen, upon the dead brick wall; I was quite sure he never visited any refectory or eating house; while his pale face clearly indicated that he never drank beer like Turkey, or tea and coffee even, like other men; that he never went any where in particular that I could learn; never went out for a walk, unless indeed that was the case at present; that he had declined telling who he was, or whence he came, or whether he had any relatives in the world; that though so thin and pale, he never complained of ill health. And more than all, I remembered a certain unconscious air of pallid—how shall I call it?—of pallid haughtiness, say, or rather an austere reserve about him, which had positively awed me into my tame compliance with his eccentricities, when I had feared to ask him to do the slightest incidental thing for me, even though I might know, from his long-continued motionlessness, that behind his screen he must be standing in one of those dead-wall reveries of his.

Revolving all these things, and coupling them with the recently discovered fact that he made my office his constant abiding place and home, and not forgetful of his morbid moodiness; revolving all these things, a prudential feeling began to steal over me. My first emotions had been those of pure melancholy and sincerest pity; but just in proportion as the forlornness of Bartleby grew and grew to my imagination, did that same melancholy merge into fear, that pity into repulsion. So true it is, and so terrible too, that up to a certain point the thought or sight of misery enlists our best affections; but, in certain special cases, beyond that point it does not. They err who would assert that invariably this is owing to the inherent selfishness of the human heart. It rather proceeds from a certain hopelessness of remedying excessive and organic ill. To a sensitive being, pity is not seldom pain. And when at last it is perceived that such pity cannot lead to effectual succor, common sense bids the soul be rid of it. What I saw that morning persuaded me that the scrivener was the victim of innate and incurable disorder. I might give alms to his body; but his body did not pain him; it was his soul that suffered, and his soul I could not reach.

I did not accomplish the purpose of going to Trinity Church that morning. Somehow, the things I had seen disqualified me for the time from church-going. I walked homeward, thinking what I would do with Bartleby. Finally, I resolved upon this;—I would put certain calm questions to him the next morning, touching his history, &c., and if he declined to answer them openly and unreservedly (and I supposed he would prefer not), then to give him a twenty dollar bill over and above whatever I might owe him, and tell him his services were no longer required; but that if in any other way I could assist him, I would be happy to do so, especially if he desired to return to his native place, wherever that might be, I would willingly help to defray the expenses. Moreover, if, after reaching home, he found himself at any time in want of aid, a letter from him would be sure of a reply.

The next morning came.

"Bartleby," said I, gently calling to him behind his screen.

No reply.

"Bartleby," said I, in a still gentler tone, "come here; I am not going to ask you to do any thing you would prefer not to do—I simply wish to speak to you."

Upon this he noiselessly slid into view.

"Will you tell me, Bartleby, where you were born?"

"I would prefer not to."

"Will you tell me *any thing* about yourself?"

"I would prefer not to."

"But what reasonable objection can you have to speak to me? I feel friendly towards you."

He did not look at me while I spoke, but kept his glance fixed upon my bust of Cicero, which as I then sat, was directly behind me, some six inches above my head.

"What is your answer, Bartleby?" said I, after waiting a considerable time for a reply, during which his countenance remained immovable, only there was the faintest conceivable tremor of the white attenuated mouth.

"At present I prefer to give no answer," he said, and retired into his hermitage.

It was rather weak in me I confess, but his manner on this occasion nettled me. Not only did there seem to lurk in it a certain calm disdain, but his perverseness seemed ungrateful, considering the undeniable good usage and indulgence he had received from me.

Again I sat ruminating what I should do. Mortified as I was at his behavior, and resolved as I had been to dismiss him when I entered my office, nevertheless I strangely felt something superstitious knocking at my heart, and forbidding me to carry out my purpose, and denouncing me for a villain if I dared to breathe one bitter word against this forlornest of mankind. At last, familiarly drawing my chair behind his screen, I sat down and said: "Bartleby, never mind then about revealing your history; but let me entreat you, as a friend, to comply as far as may be with the usages of this office. Say now you will help to examine papers to-morrow or next day: in short, say now that in a day or two you will begin to be a little reasonable:—say so, Bartleby."

"At present I would prefer not to be a little reasonable," was his mildly cadaverous reply.

Just then the folding-doors opened, and Nippers approached. He seemed suffering from an unusually bad night's rest, induced by severer indigestion than common. He overheard those final words of Bartleby.

"*Prefer not*, eh?" gritted Nippers—"I'd *prefer* him, if I were you, sir," addressing me—"I'd *prefer* him; I'd give him preferences, the stubborn mule! What is it, sir, pray, that he *prefers* not to do now?"

Bartleby moved not a limb.

"Mr. Nippers," said I, "I'd prefer that you would withdraw for the present."

Somehow, of late I had got into the way of involuntarily using this word "prefer" upon all sorts of not exactly suitable occasions. And I trembled to think that my contact with the scrivener had already and seriously affected me in a mental way. And what further and deeper aberration might it not yet produce? This apprehension had not been without efficacy in determining me to summary measures.

As Nippers, looking very sour and sulky, was departing, Turkey blandly and deferentially approached.

"With submission, sir," said he, "yesterday I was thinking about Bartleby here, and I think that if he would but prefer to take a quart of good ale every day, it would do much towards mending him, and enabling him to assist in examining his papers."

"So you have got the word too," said I, slightly excited.

"With submission, what word, sir," asked Turkey, respectfully crowding himself into the contracted space behind the screen, and by so doing, making me jostle the scrivener. "What word, sir?"

"I would prefer to be left alone here," said Bartleby, as if offended at being mobbed in his privacy.

"*That's* the word, Turkey," said I—"*that's* it."

"Oh, *prefer?* oh yes—queer word. I never use it myself. But, sir, as I was saying, if he would but prefer—"

"Turkey," interrupted I, "you will please withdraw."

"Oh certainly, sir, if you prefer that I should."

As he opened the folding-doors to retire, Nippers at his desk caught a glimpse of me, and asked whether I would prefer to have a certain paper copied on blue paper or white. He did not in the least roguishly accent the word prefer. It was plain that it involuntarily rolled from his tongue. I thought to myself, surely I must get rid of a demented man, who already has in some degree turned the tongues, if not the heads of myself and clerks. But I thought it prudent not to break the dismission at once.

The next day I noticed that Bartleby did nothing but stand at his window in his dead-wall revery. Upon asking him why he did not write, he said that he had decided upon doing no more writing.

"Why, how now? what next?" exclaimed I, "do no more writing?"

"No more."

"And what is the reason?"

"Do you not see the reason for yourself," he indifferently replied.

I looked steadfastly at him, and perceived that his eyes looked dull and glazed. Instantly it occurred to me, that his unexampled diligence in copying by his dim window for the first few weeks of his stay with me might have temporarily impaired his vision.

I was touched. I said something in condolence with him. I hinted that of course he did wisely in abstaining from writing for a while; and urged him to embrace that opportunity of taking wholesome exercise in the open air. This, however, he did not do. A few days after this, my other clerks being absent, and being in a great hurry to dispatch certain letters by the mail, I thought that, having nothing else earthly to do, Bartleby would surely be less inflexible than usual, and carry these letters to the post-office. But he blankly declined. So, much to my inconvenience, I went myself.

Still added days went by. Whether Bartleby's eyes improved or not, I could not say. To all appearance, I thought they did. But when I asked him if they did, he vouchsafed no answer. At all events, he would do no copying. At last, in reply to my urgings, he informed me that he had permanently given up copying.

"What!" exclaimed I; "suppose your eyes should get entirely well—better than ever before—would you not copy then?"

"I have given up copying," he answered, and slid aside.

He remained as ever, a fixture in my chamber. Nay—if that were possible—he became still more of a fixture than before. What was to be done? He would do nothing in the office: why should he stay there? In plain fact, he had now become a millstone to me, not only useless as a necklace, but afflictive to bear. Yet I was sorry for him. I speak less than truth when I say that, on his own account, he occasioned me uneasiness. If he would but have named a single relative or friend, I would instantly have written, and urged their taking the poor fellow away to some convenient retreat. But he seemed alone, absolutely alone in the universe. A bit of wreck in the mid Atlantic. At length, necessities connected with my business tyrannized over all other considerations. Decently as I could, I told Bartleby that in six days' time he must unconditionally leave the office. I warned him to take measures, in the interval, for procuring some other abode. I offered to assist him in this endeavor, if he himself would but take the first step towards a removal. "And when you finally quit me, Bartleby," added I, "I shall see that you go not away entirely unprovided. Six days from this hour, remember."

At the expiration of that period, I peeped behind the screen, and lo! Bartleby was there.

I buttoned up my coat, balanced myself; advanced slowly towards him, touched his shoulder, and said, "The time has come; you must quit this place; I am sorry for you; here is money; but you must go."

"I would prefer not," he replied, with his back still towards me.

"You *must*."

He remained silent.

Now I had an unbounded confidence in this man's common honesty. He had frequently restored to me sixpences and shillings carelessly dropped upon the floor, for I am apt to be very reckless in such shirt-button affairs. The proceeding then which followed will not be deemed extraordinary.

"Bartleby," said I, "I owe you twelve dollars on account; here are thirty-two; the odd twenty are yours.—Will you take it?" and I handed the bills towards him.

But he made no motion.

"I will leave them here then," putting them under a weight on the table. Then taking my hat and cane and going to the door I tranquilly turned and added—"After you have removed your things from these offices, Bartleby, you will of course lock the door—since every one is now gone for the day but you—and if you please, slip your key underneath the mat, so that I may have it in the morning. I shall not see you again; so good-bye to you. If hereafter in your new place of abode I can be of any service to you, do not fail to advise me by letter. Good-bye, Bartleby, and fare you well."

But he answered not a word; like the last column of some ruined temple, he remained standing mute and solitary in the middle of the otherwise deserted room.

As I walked home in a pensive mood, my vanity got the better of my pity. I could not but highly plume myself on my masterly management in getting rid of Bartleby. Masterly I call it, and such it must appear to any dispassionate thinker. The beauty of my procedure seemed to consist in its perfect quietness. There was no vulgar bullying, no bravado of any sort, no choleric hectoring, and striding to and fro across the apartment, jerking out vehement commands for Bartleby to bundle himself off with his beggarly traps. Nothing of the kind. Without loudly bidding Bartleby depart—as an inferior genius might have done—I *assumed* the ground that depart he must; and upon that assumption built all I had to say. The more I thought over my procedure, the more I was charmed with it. Nevertheless, next morning, upon awakening, I had my doubts,—I had somehow slept off the fumes of vanity. One of the coolest and wisest hours a man has, is just after he awakes in the morning. My procedure seemed as sagacious as ever,—but only in theory. How it would prove in practice—there was the rub. It was truly a beautiful thought to have assumed Bartleby's departure; but, after all, that assumption was simply my own, and none of Bartleby's. The great point was, not whether I had assumed that he would quit me, but whether he would prefer so to do. He was more a man of preferences than assumptions.

After breakfast, I walked down town, arguing the probabilities *pro* and *con*. One moment I thought it would prove a miserable failure, and Bartleby would be found all alive at my office as usual; the next moment it seemed certain that I should find his chair empty. And so I kept veering about. At the corner of Broadway and Canal-street, I saw quite an excited group of people standing in earnest conversation.

"I'll take odds he doesn't," said a voice as I passed.

"Doesn't go?—done!" said I, "put up your money."

I was instinctively putting my hand in my pocket to produce my own, when I remembered that this was an election day. The words I had overheard bore no reference to Bartleby, but to the success or non-success of some candidate for the mayoralty. In my intent frame of mind, I had, as it were, imagined that all Broadway shared in my excitement, and were debating the same question with me. I passed on, very thankful that the uproar of the street screened my momentary absent-mindedness.

As I had intended, I was earlier than usual at my office door. I stood listening for a moment. All was still. He must be gone. I tried the knob. The door was locked. Yes, my procedure had worked to a charm; he indeed must be vanished. Yet a certain melancholy mixed with this: I was almost sorry for my brilliant success. I was fumbling under the door mat for the key, which Bartleby was to have left there for me, when accidentally my knee knocked against a panel, producing a summoning sound, and in response a voice came to me from within—"Not yet; I am occupied."

It was Bartleby.

I was thunderstruck. For an instant I stood like the man who, pipe in mouth, was killed one cloudless afternoon long ago in Virginia, by summer lightning; at his own warm open window he was killed, and remained leaning out there upon the dreamy afternoon, till some one touched him, when he fell.

"Not gone!" I murmured at last. But again obeying that wondrous ascendancy which the inscrutable scrivener had over me, and from which ascendancy, for all my chafing, I could not completely escape, I slowly went down stairs and out into the street, and while walking round the block, considered what I should next do in this unheard-of perplexity. Turn the man out by an actual thrusting I could not; to drive him away by calling him hard names would not do; calling in the police was an unpleasant idea; and yet, permit him to enjoy his cadaverous triumph over me,—this too I could not think of. What was to be done? or, if nothing could be done, was there any thing further that I could *assume* in the matter? Yes, as before I had prospectively assumed that Bartleby would depart, so now I might retrospectively assume that departed he was. In the legitimate carrying out of this assumption, I might enter my office in a great hurry, and pretending not to see Bartleby at all, walk straight against him as if he were air. Such a proceeding would in a singular degree have the appearance of a home-thrust. It was hardly possible that Bartleby could withstand such an application of the doctrine of assumptions. But upon second thoughts the success of the plan seemed rather dubious. I resolved to argue the matter over with him again.

"Bartleby," said I, entering the office, with a quietly severe expression, "I am seriously displeased. I am pained, Bartleby. I had thought better of you. I had imagined you of such a gentlemanly organization, that in any delicate dilemma a slight hint would suffice—in short, an assumption. But it appears I am deceived. Why," I added, unaffectedly starting, "you have not even touched that money yet," pointing to it, just where I had left it the evening previous.

He answered nothing.

"Will you, or will you not, quit me?" I now demanded in a sudden passion, advancing close to him.

"I would prefer *not* to quit you," he replied, gently emphasizing the *not*.

"What earthly right have you to stay here? Do you pay any rent? Do you pay my taxes? Or is this property yours?"

He answered nothing.

"Are you ready to go on and write now? Are your eyes recovered? Could you copy a small paper for me this morning? or help examine a few lines? or step round to the post-office? In a word, will you do any thing at all, to give a coloring to your refusal to depart the premises?"

He silently retired into his hermitage.

I was now in such a state of nervous resentment that I thought it but prudent to check myself at present from further demonstrations. Bartleby and I were alone. I remembered the tragedy of the unfortunate Adams and the still more unfortunate Colt in the solitary office of the latter; and how poor Colt, being dreadfully incensed by Adams, and imprudently permitting himself to get wildly excited, was at unawares hurried into his fatal act—an act which certainly no man could possibly deplore more than the actor himself. Often it had occurred to me in my ponderings upon the subject, that had that altercation taken place in the public street, or at a private residence, it would not have terminated as it did. It was the circumstance of being alone in a solitary office, up stairs, of a building entirely unhallowed by humanizing domestic associations—an uncarpeted office, doubtless, of a dusty, haggard sort of appearance;—this it must have been, which greatly helped to enhance the irritable desperation of the hapless Colt.

But when this old Adam of resentment rose in me and tempted me concerning Bartleby, I grappled him and threw him. How? Why, simply by recalling the divine injunction: "A new commandment give I unto you, that ye love one another." Yes, this it was that saved me. Aside from higher considerations, charity often operates as a vastly wise and prudent principle—a great safeguard to its possessor. Men have committed murder for jealousy's sake, and anger's sake, and hatred's sake, and selfishness' sake, and spiritual pride's sake; but no man that ever I heard of, ever committed a diabolical murder for sweet charity's sake. Mere self-interest, then, if no better motive can be enlisted, should, especially with high-tempered men, prompt all beings to charity and philanthropy. At any rate, upon the occasion in question, I strove to drown my exasperated feelings towards the scrivener by benevolently construing his conduct. Poor fellow, poor fellow! thought I, he don't mean any thing; and besides, he has seen hard times, and ought to be indulged.

I endeavored also immediately to occupy myself, and at the same time to comfort my despondency. I tried to fancy that in the course of the morning, at such time as might prove agreeable to him, Bartleby, of his own free accord, would emerge from his hermitage, and take up some decided line of march in the direction of the door. But no. Half-past twelve o'clock came; Turkey began to glow in the face, overturn his inkstand, and become generally obstreperous; Nippers abated down into quietude and courtesy; Ginger Nut munched his noon apple; and Bartleby remained standing at his window in one of his profoundest dead-wall reveries. Will it be credited? Ought I to acknowledge it? That afternoon I left the office without saying one further word to him.

Some days now passed, during which, at leisure intervals I looked a little into "Edwards on the Will," and "Priestley on Necessity." Under the circumstances, those books induced a salutary feeling. Gradually I slid into the persuasion that these troubles of mine touching the scrivener, had been all predestinated from eternity, and Bartleby was billeted upon me for some mysterious purpose of an all-wise Providence, which it was not for a mere mortal like me to fathom. Yes, Bartleby, stay there behind your screen, thought I; I shall persecute you no more; you are harmless and noiseless as any of these old chairs; in short, I never feel so private as when I know you are here. At last I see it, I feel it; I penetrate to the predestinated purpose of my life. I am content. Others may have loftier parts to enact; but my mission in this world, Bartleby, is to furnish you with office-room for such period as you may see fit to remain.

I believe that this wise and blessed frame of mind would have continued with me, had it not been for the unsolicited and uncharitable remarks obtruded upon me by my professional friends who visited the rooms. But thus it often is, that the constant friction of illiberal minds wears out at last the best resolves of the more generous. Though to be sure, when I reflected upon it, it was not strange that people entering my office should be struck by the peculiar aspect of the unaccountable Bartleby, and so be tempted to throw out some sinister observations concerning him. Sometimes an attorney having business with me, and calling at my office, and finding no one but the scrivener there, would undertake to obtain some sort of precise information from him touching my whereabouts; but without heeding his idle talk, Bartleby would remain standing immovable in the middle of the room. So after contemplating him in that position for a time, the attorney would depart, no wiser than he came.

Also, when a Reference was going on, and the room full of lawyers and witnesses and business was driving fast; some deeply occupied legal gentleman present, seeing Bartleby wholly unemployed, would request him to run round to his (the legal gentleman's) office and fetch some papers for him. Thereupon, Bartleby would tranquilly decline, and yet remain idle as before. Then the lawyer would give a great stare, and turn to me. And what could I say? At last I was made aware that all through the circle of my professional acquaintance, a whisper of wonder was running round, having reference to the strange creature I kept at my office. This worried me very much. And as the idea came upon me of his possibly turning out a long-lived man, and keep occupying my chambers, and denying my authority; and perplexing my visitors; and scandalizing my professional reputation; and casting a general gloom over the premises; keeping soul and body together to the last upon his savings (for doubtless he spent but half a dime a day), and in the end perhaps outlive me, and claim possession of my office by right of his perpetual occupancy: as all these dark anticipations crowded upon me more and more, and my friends continually intruded their relentless remarks upon the apparition in my room; a great change was wrought in me. I resolved to gather all my faculties together, and for ever rid me of this intolerable incubus.

Ere revolving any complicated project, however, adapted to this end, I first simply suggested to Bartleby the propriety of his permanent departure. In a calm and serious tone, I commended the idea to his careful and mature consideration. But having taken three days to meditate upon it, he apprised me that his original determination remained the same; in short, that he still preferred to abide with me.

What shall I do? I now said to myself, buttoning up my coat to the last button. What shall I do? what ought I to do? what does conscience say I *should* do with this man, or rather ghost? Rid myself of him, I must; go, he shall. But how? You will not thrust him, the poor, pale, passive mortal,—you will not thrust such a helpless creature out of your door? you will not dishonor yourself by such cruelty? No, I will not, I cannot do that. Rather would I let him live and die here, and then mason up his remains in the wall. What then will you do? For all your coaxing, he will not budge. Bribes he leaves under your own paper-weight on your table; in short, it is quite plain that he prefers to cling to you.

Then something severe, something unusual must be done. What! surely you will not have him collared by a constable, and commit his innocent pallor to the common jail? And upon what ground could you procure such a thing to be done?—a vagrant, is he? What! he a vagrant, a wanderer, who refuses to budge? It is because he will *not* be a vagrant, then, that you seek to count him *as* a vagrant. That is too absurd. No visible means of support: there I have him. Wrong again: for indubitably he *does* support himself, and that is the only unanswerable proof that any man can show of his possessing the means so to do. No more then. Since he will not quit me, I must quit him. I will change my offices; I will move elsewhere; and give him fair notice, that if I find him on my new premises I will then proceed against him as a common trespasser.

Acting accordingly, next day I thus addressed him: "I find these chambers too far from the City Hall; the air is unwholesome. In a word, I propose to remove my offices next week, and shall no longer require your services. I tell you this now, in order that you may seek another place."

He made no reply, and nothing more was said.

On the appointed day I engaged carts and men, proceeded to my chambers, and having but little furniture, every thing was removed in a few hours. Throughout, the scrivener remained standing behind the screen, which I directed to be removed the last thing. It was withdrawn; and being folded up like a huge folio, left him the motionless occupant of a naked room. I stood in the entry watching him a moment, while something from within me upbraided me.

I re-entered, with my hand in my pocket—and—and my heart in my mouth.

"Good-bye, Bartleby; I am going—good-bye, and God some way bless you; and take that," slipping something in his hand. But it dropped upon the floor, and then,—strange to say—I tore myself from him whom I had so longed to be rid of.

Established in my new quarters, for a day or two I kept the door locked, and started at every footfall in the passages. When I returned to my rooms after any little absence, I would pause at the threshold for an instant, and attentively listen, ere applying my key. But these fears were needless. Bartleby never came nigh me.

I thought all was going well, when a perturbed looking stranger visited me, inquiring whether I was the person who had recently occupied rooms at No. — Wall-street.

Full of forebodings, I replied that I was.

"Then sir," said the stranger, who proved a lawyer, "you are responsible for the man you left there. He refuses to do any copying; he refuses to do any thing; he says he prefers not to; and he refuses to quit the premises."

"I am very sorry, sir," said I, with assumed tranquillity, but an inward tremor, "but, really, the man you allude to is nothing to me—he is no relation or apprentice of mine, that you should hold me responsible for him."

"In mercy's name, who is he?"

"I certainly cannot inform you. I know nothing about him. Formerly I employed him as a copyist; but he has done nothing for me now for some time past."

"I shall settle him then,—good morning, sir."

Several days passed, and I heard nothing more; and though I often felt a charitable prompting to call at the place and see poor Bartleby, yet a certain squeamishness of I know not what withheld me.

All is over with him, by this time, thought I at last, when through another week no further intelligence reached me. But coming to my room the day after, I found several persons waiting at my door in a high state of nervous excitement.

"That's the man—here he comes," cried the foremost one, whom I recognized as the lawyer who had previously called upon me alone.

"You must take him away, sir, at once," cried a portly person among them, advancing upon me, and whom I knew to be the landlord of No. — Wall-street. "These gentlemen, my tenants, cannot stand it any longer; Mr. B——" pointing to the lawyer, "has turned him out of his room, and he now persists in haunting the building generally, sitting upon the banisters of the stairs by day, and sleeping in the entry by night. Every body is concerned; clients are leaving the offices; some fears are entertained of a mob; something you must do, and that without delay."

Aghast at this torrent, I fell back before it, and would fain have locked myself in my new quarters. In vain I persisted that Bartleby was nothing to me—no more than to any one else. In vain:—I was the last person known to have any thing to do with him, and they held me to the terrible account. Fearful then of being exposed in the papers (as one person present obscurely threatened) I considered the matter, and at length said, that if the lawyer would give me a confidential interview with the scrivener, in his (the lawyer's) own room, I would that afternoon strive my best to rid them of the nuisance they complained of.

Going up stairs to my old haunt, there was Bartleby silently sitting upon the banister at the landing.

"What are you doing here, Bartleby?" said I.

"Sitting upon the banister," he mildly replied.

I motioned him into the lawyer's room, who then left us.

"Bartleby," said I, "are you aware that you are the cause of great tribulation to me, by persisting in occupying the entry after being dismissed from the office?"

No answer.

"Now one of two things must take place. Either you must do something, or something must be done to you. Now what sort of business would you like to engage in? Would you like to re-engage in copying for some one?"

"No; I would prefer not to make any change."

"Would you like a clerkship in a dry-goods store?"

"There is too much confinement about that. No, I would not like a clerkship; but I am not particular."

"Too much confinement," I cried, "why you keep yourself confined all the time!"

"I would prefer not to take a clerkship," he rejoined, as if to settle that little item at once.

"How would a bar-tender's business suit you? There is no trying of the eyesight in that."

"I would not like it at all; though, as I said before, I am not particular."

His unwonted wordiness inspirited me. I returned to the charge.

"Well then, would you like to travel through the country collecting bills for the merchants? That would improve your health."

"No, I would prefer to be doing something else."

"How then would going as a companion to Europe, to entertain some young gentleman with your conversation,—how would that suit you?"

"Not at all. It does not strike me that there is any thing definite about that. I like to be stationary. But I am not particular."

"Stationary you shall be then," I cried, now losing all patience, and for the first time in all my exasperating connection with him fairly flying into a passion. "If you do not go away from these premises before night, I shall feel bound—indeed I *am* bound—to—to—to quit the premises myself!" I rather absurdly concluded, knowing not with what possible threat to try to frighten his immobility into compliance. Despairing of all further efforts, I was precipitately leaving him, when a final thought occurred to me—one which had not been wholly unindulged before.

"Bartleby," said I, in the kindest tone I could assume under such exciting circumstances, "will you go home with me now—not to my office, but my dwelling—and remain there till we can conclude upon some convenient arrangement for you at our leisure? Come, let us start now, right away."

"No: at present I would prefer not to make any change at all."

I answered nothing; but effectually dodging every one by the suddenness and rapidity of my flight, rushed from the building, ran up Wall-street towards Broadway, and jumping into the first omnibus was soon removed from pursuit. As soon as tranquillity returned I distinctly perceived that I had now done all that I possibly could, both in respect to the demands of the landlord and his tenants, and with regard to my own desire and sense of duty, to benefit Bartleby, and shield him from rude persecution. I now strove to be entirely care-free and quiescent; and my conscience justified me in the attempt; though indeed it was not so successful as I could have wished. So fearful was I of being again hunted out by the incensed landlord and his exasperated tenants, that, surrendering my business to Nippers, for a few days I drove about the upper part of the town and through the suburbs, in my rockaway; crossed over to Jersey City and Hoboken, and paid fugitive visits to Manhattanville and Astoria. In fact I almost lived in my rockaway for the time.

When again I entered my office, lo, a note from the landlord lay upon the desk. I opened it with trembling hands. It informed me that the writer had sent to the police, and had Bartleby removed to the Tombs as a vagrant. Moreover, since I knew more about him than any one else, he wished me to appear at that place, and make a suitable statement of the facts. These tidings had a conflicting effect upon me. At first I was indignant; but at last almost approved. The landlord's energetic, summary disposition, had led him to adopt a procedure which I do not think I would have decided upon myself; and yet as a last resort, under such peculiar circumstances, it seemed the only plan.

As I afterwards learned, the poor scrivener, when told that he must be conducted to the Tombs, offered not the slightest obstacle, but in his pale unmoving way, silently acquiesced.

Some of the compassionate and curious bystanders joined the party; and headed by one of the constables arm in arm with Bartleby, the silent procession filed its way through all the noise, and heat, and joy of the roaring thoroughfares at noon.

The same day I received the note I went to the Tombs, or to speak more properly, the Halls of Justice. Seeking the right officer, I stated the purpose of my call, and was informed that the individual I described was indeed within. I then assured the functionary that Bartleby was a perfectly honest man, and greatly to be compassionated, however unaccountably eccentric. I narrated all I knew, and closed by suggesting the idea of letting him remain in as indulgent confinement as possible till something less harsh might be done—though indeed I hardly knew what. At all events, if nothing else could be decided upon, the alms-house must receive him. I then begged to have an interview.

Being under no disgraceful charge, and quite serene and harmless in all his ways, they had permitted him freely to wander about the prison, and especially in the inclosed grass-platted yards thereof. And so I found him there, standing all alone in the quietest of the yards, his face towards a high wall, while all around, from the narrow slits of the jail windows, I thought I saw peering out upon him the eyes of murderers and thieves.

"Bartleby!"

"I know you," he said, without looking round,—"and I want nothing to say to you."

"It was not I that brought you here, Bartleby," said I, keenly pained at his implied suspicion. "And to you, this should not be so vile a place. Nothing reproachful attaches to you by being here. And see, it is not so sad a place as one might think. Look, there is the sky, and here is the grass."

"I know where I am," he replied, but would say nothing more, and so I left him.

As I entered the corridor again, a broad meat-like man, in an apron, accosted me, and jerking his thumb over his shoulder said—"Is that your friend?"

"Yes."

"Does he want to starve? If he does, let him live on the prison fare, that's all."

"Who are you?" asked I, not knowing what to make of such an unofficially speaking person in such a place.

"I am the grub-man. Such gentlemen as have friends here, hire me to provide them with something good to eat."

"Is this so?" said I, turning to the turnkey.

He said it was.

"Well then," said I, slipping some silver into the grub-man's hands (for so they called him). "I want you to give particular attention to my friend there; let him have the best dinner you can get. And you must be as polite to him as possible."

"Introduce me, will you?" said the grub-man, looking at me with an expression which seemed to say he was all impatience for an opportunity to give a specimen of his breeding.

Thinking it would prove of benefit to the scrivener, I acquiesced; and asking the grub-man his name, went up with him to Bartleby.

"Bartleby, this is Mr. Cutlets; you will find him very useful to you."

"Your sarvant, sir, your sarvant," said the grub-man, making a low salutation behind his apron. "Hope you find it pleasant here, sir; nice grounds—cool apartments, sir—hope you'll stay with us some time—try to make it agreeable. May Mrs. Cutlets and I have the pleasure of your company to dinner, sir, in Mrs. Cutlets' private room?"

"I prefer not to dine to-day," said Bartleby, turning away. "It would disagree with me; I am unused to dinners." So saying he slowly moved to the other side of the inclosure, and took up a position fronting the dead-wall.

"How's this?" said the grub-man, addressing me with a stare of astonishment. "He's odd, aint he?"

"I think he is a little deranged," said I, sadly.

"Deranged? deranged is it? Well now, upon my word, I thought that friend of yourn was a gentleman forger; they are always pale and genteel-like, them forgers. I can't help pity 'em—can't help it, sir. Did you know Monroe Edwards?" he added touchingly, and paused. Then, laying his hand pityingly on my shoulder, sighed, "he died of consumption at Sing-Sing. So you weren't acquainted with Monroe?"

"No, I was never socially acquainted with any forgers. But I cannot stop longer. Look to my friend yonder. You will not lose by it. I will see you again."

Some few days after this, I again obtained admission to the Tombs, and went through the corridors in quest of Bartleby; but without finding him.

"I saw him coming from his cell not long ago," said a turnkey, "may be he's gone to loiter in the yards."

So I went in that direction.

"Are you looking for the silent man?" said another turnkey passing me. "Yonder he lies—sleeping in the yard there. 'Tis not twenty minutes since I saw him lie down."

The yard was entirely quiet. It was not accessible to the common prisoners. The surrounding walls, of amazing thickness, kept off all sounds behind them. The Egyptian character of the masonry weighed upon me with its gloom. But a soft imprisoned turf grew under foot. The heart of the eternal pyramids, it seemed, wherein, by some strange magic, through the clefts, grass-seed, dropped by birds, had sprung.

Strangely huddled at the base of the wall, his knees drawn up, and lying on his side, his head touching the cold stones, I saw the wasted Bartleby. But nothing stirred. I paused; then went close up to him; stooped over, and saw that his dim eyes were open; otherwise he seemed

profoundly sleeping. Something prompted me to touch him. I felt his
hand, when a tingling shiver ran up my arm and down my spine to my
feet.

The round face of the grub-man peered upon me now. "His dinner is
ready. Won't he dine to-day, either? Or does he live without dining?"

"Lives without dining," said I, and closed the eyes.

"Eh!—He's asleep, aint he?"

"With kings and counsellors," murmured I.

*   *   *   *   *

There would seem little need for proceeding further in this history.
Imagination will readily supply the meagre recital of poor Bartleby's interment. But ere parting with the reader, let me say, that if this little narrative has sufficiently interested him, to awaken curiosity as to who
Bartleby was, and what manner of life he led prior to the present narrator's making his acquaintance, I can only reply, that in such curiosity I
fully share, but am wholly unable to gratify it. Yet here I hardly know
whether I should divulge one little item of rumor, which came to my ear
a few months after the scrivener's decease. Upon what basis it rested, I
could never ascertain; and hence, how true it is I cannot now tell. But
inasmuch as this vague report has not been without a certain strange suggestive interest to me, however sad, it may prove the same with some others; and so I will briefly mention it. The report was this: that Bartleby had
been a subordinate clerk in the Dead Letter Office at Washington, from
which he had been suddenly removed by a change in the administration.
When I think over this rumor, hardly can I express the emotions which
seize me. Dead letters! does it not sound like dead men? Conceive a man
by nature and misfortune prone to a pallid hopelessness, can any business
seem more fitted to heighten it than that of continually handling these
dead letters, and assorting them for the flames? For by the cart-load they
are annually burned. Sometimes from out the folded paper the pale clerk
takes a ring:—the finger it was meant for, perhaps, moulders in the grave;
a bank-note sent in swiftest charity:—he whom it would relieve, nor eats
nor hungers any more; pardon for those who died despairing; hope for
those who died unhoping; good tidings for those who died stifled by un-
relieved calamities. On errands of life, these letters speed to death.

Ah Bartleby! Ah humanity!

1853

Cock-A-Doodle-Doo!

Or, The Crowing of the Noble Cock Beneventano

In all parts of the world many high-spirited revolts from rascally despotisms had of late been knocked on the head; many dreadful casualties, by locomotive and steamer, had likewise knocked hundreds of high-spirited travelers on the head (I lost a dear friend in one of them); my own private affairs were also full of despotisms, casualties, and knockings on the head, when early one morning in Spring, being too full of hypoes to sleep, I sallied out to walk on my hill-side pasture.

It was a cool and misty, damp, disagreeable air. The country looked underdone, its raw juices squirting out all round. I buttoned out this squitchy air as well as I could with my lean, double-breasted dress-coat—my over-coat being so long-skirted I only used it in my wagon—and spitefully thrusting my crab-stick into the oozy sod, bent my blue form to the steep ascent of the hill. This toiling posture brought my head pretty well earthward, as if I were in the act of butting it against the world. I marked the fact, but only grinned at it with a ghastly grin.

All round me were tokens of a divided empire. The old grass and the new grass were striving together. In the low wet swales the verdure peeped out in vivid green; beyond, on the mountains, lay light patches of snow, strangely relieved against their russet sides; all the humped hills looked like brindled kine in the shivers. The woods were strewn with dry dead boughs, snapped off by the riotous winds of March, while the young trees skirting the woods were just beginning to show the first yellowish tinge of the nascent spray.

I sat down for a moment on a great rotting log nigh the top of the hill, my back to a heavy grove, my face presented toward a wide sweeping circuit of mountains enclosing a rolling, diversified country. Along the base of one long range of heights ran a lagging, fever-and-agueish river, over which was a duplicate stream of dripping mist, exactly corresponding in every meander with its parent water below. Low down, here and there, shreds of vapor listlessly wandered in the air, like abandoned or helmless nations or ships—or very soaky towels hung on criss-cross clothes-lines to dry. Afar, over a distant village lying in a bay of the plain formed by the mountains, there rested a great flat canopy of haze, like a pall. It was the condensed smoke of the chimneys, with the condensed, exhaled breath of the villagers, prevented from dispersion by the imprisoning hills. It was too heavy and lifeless to mount of itself; so there it lay, between the village and the sky, doubtless hiding many a man with the mumps, and many a queasy child.

My eye ranged over the capacious rolling country, and over the mountains, and over the village, and over a farm-house here and there, and over woods, groves, streams, rocks, fells—and I thought to myself, what a slight mark, after all, does man make on this huge great earth. Yet the earth makes a mark on him. What a horrid accident was that on the Ohio, where my good friend and thirty other good fellows were sloped into eternity at the bidding of a thick-headed engineer, who knew not a valve from a flue. And that crash on the railroad just over yon mountains there, where two infatuate trains ran pell-mell into each other, and climbed and clawed each other's backs; and one locomotive was found fairly shelled, like a chick, inside of a passenger car in the antagonist train; and near a score of noble hearts, a bride and her groom, and an innocent little infant, were all disembarked into the grim hulk of Charon, who ferried them over, all baggageless, to some clinkered iron-foundry country or other. Yet what's the use of complaining? What justice of the peace will right this matter? Yea, what's the use of bothering the very heavens about it? Don't the heavens themselves ordain these things—else they could not happen?

A miserable world! Who would take the trouble to make a fortune in it, when he knows not how long he can keep it, for the thousand villains and asses who have the management of railroads and steamboats, and innumerable other vital things in the world. If they would make me Dictator in North America a while, I'd string them up! and hang, draw, and quarter; fry, roast, and boil; stew, grill, and devil them, like so many turkey-legs—the rascally numskulls of stokers; I'd set them to stokering in Tartarus—I would.

Great improvements of the age! What! to call the facilitation of death and murder an improvement! Who wants to travel so fast? My grandfather did not, and he was no fool. Hark! here comes that old dragon again—that gigantic gad-fly of a Moloch—snort! puff! scream!—here he comes straight-bent through these vernal woods, like the Asiatic cholera cantering on a camel. Stand aside! here he comes, the chartered murderer! the death monopolizer! judge, jury, and hangman all together, whose victims die always without benefit of clergy. For two hundred and fifty miles that iron fiend goes yelling through the land, crying "More! more! more!" Would fifty conspiring mountains would fall atop of him! And, while they were about it, would they would also fall atop of that smaller dunning fiend, my creditor, who frightens the life out of me more than any loco-motive—a lantern-jawed rascal, who seems to run on a railroad track too, and duns me even on Sunday, all the way to church and back, and comes and sits in the same pew with me, and pretending to be polite and hand me the prayer-book opened at the proper place, pokes his pesky bill under my nose in the very midst of my devotions, and so shoves himself between me and salvation; for how can one keep his temper on such occasions?

I can't pay this horrid man; and yet they say money was never so plentiful—a drug in the market; but blame me if I can get any of the drug, though there never was a sick man more in need of that particular sort of medicine. It's a lie; money ain't plenty—feel of my pocket. Ha! here's a powder I was going to send to the sick baby in yonder hovel, where the Irish ditcher lives. That baby has the scarlet fever. They say the measles are rife in the country too, and the varioloid, and the chicken-pox, and it's bad for teething children. And after all, I suppose many of the poor little ones, after going through all this trouble, snap off short; and so they had the measles, mumps, croup, scarlet-fever, chicken-pox, cholera-morbus, summer-complaint, and all else, in vain! Ah! there's that twinge of the rheumatics in my right shoulder. I got it one night on the North River, when, in a crowded boat, I gave up my berth to a sick lady, and staid on deck till morning in drizzling weather. There's the thanks one gets for charity! Twinge! Shoot away, ye rheumatics! Ye couldn't lay on worse if I were some villain who had murdered the lady instead of befriending her. Dyspepsia too—I am troubled with that.

Hallo! here come the calves, the two-year-olds, just turned out of the barn into the pasture, after six months of cold victuals. What a miserable-looking set, to be sure! A breaking up of a hard winter, that's certain: sharp bones sticking out like elbows; all quilted with a strange stuff dried on their flanks like layers of pancakes. Hair worn quite off too, here and there; and where it ain't pancaked, or worn off, looks like the rubbed sides of mangy old hair-trunks. In fact, they are not six two-year-olds, but six abominable old hair-trunks wandering about here in this pasture.

Hark! By Jove, what's that? See! the very hair-trunks prick their ears at it, and stand and gaze away down into the rolling country yonder. Hark again! How clear! how musical! how prolonged! What a triumphant thanksgiving of a cock-crow! *"Glory be to God in the highest!"* It says those very words as plain as ever cock did in this world. Why, why, I begin to feel a little in sorts again. It ain't so very misty, after all. The sun yonder is beginning to show himself: I feel warmer.

Hark! There again! Did ever such a blessed cock-crow so ring out over the earth before! Clear, shrill, full of pluck, full of fire, full of fun, full of glee. It plainly says—*"Never say die!"* My friends, it is extraordinary is it not?

Unwittingly, I found that I had been addressing the two-year-olds—the calves—in my enthusiasm; which shows how one's true nature will betray itself at times in the most unconscious way. For what a very two-year-old, and calf, I had been to fall into the sulks, on a hill-top too, when a cock down in the lowlands there, without discourse of reason, and quite penniless in the world, and with death hanging over him at any moment from his hungry master, sends up a cry like a very laureate celebrating the glorious victory of New Orleans.

Hark! there it goes again! My friends, that must be a Shanghai; no domestic-born cock could crow in such prodigious exulting strains. Plainly, my friends, a Shanghai of the Emperor of China's breed.

But my friends the hair-trunks, fairly alarmed at last by such clamorously-victorious tones, were now scampering off, with their tails flirting in the air, and capering with their legs in clumsy enough sort of style, sufficiently evincing that they had not freely flourished them for the six months last past.

Hark! there again! Whose cock is that? Who in this region can afford to buy such an extraordinary Shanghai? Bless me—it makes my blood bound—I feel wild. What? jumping on this rotten old log here, to flap my elbows and crow too? And just now in the doleful dumps. And all this from the simple crow of a cock. Marvelous cock! But soft—this fellow now crows most lustily; but it's only morning; let's see how he'll crow about noon, and toward night-fall. Come to think of it, cocks crow mostly in the beginning of the day. Their pluck ain't lasting, after all. Yes, yes; even cocks have to succumb to the universal spell of tribulation: jubilant in the beginning, but down in the mouth at the end.

> .... "Of fine mornings,
> We fine lusty cocks begin our crows in gladness,
> But when eve does come we don't crow quite so much,
> For then cometh despondency and madness."

The poet had this very Shanghai in his mind when he wrote that. But stop. There he rings out again, ten times richer, fuller, longer, more obstreperously exulting than before! Why this is equal to hearing the great bell of St. Paul's rung at a coronation! In fact, that bell ought to be taken down, and this Shanghai put in its place. Such a crow would jollify all London, from Mile End (which is no end) to Primrose Hill (where there ain't any primroses), and scatter the fog.

Well, I have an appetite for my breakfast this morning, if I have not had it for a week before. I meant to have only tea and toast; but I'll have coffee and eggs—no, brown-stout and a beef-steak. I want something hearty. Ah, here comes the down-train: white cars, flashing through the trees like a vein of silver. How cheerfully the steam-pipe chirps! Gay are the passengers. There waves a handkerchief—going down to the city to eat oysters, and see their friends, and drop in at the circus. Look at the mist yonder; what soft curls and undulations round the hills, and the sun weaving his rays among them. See the azure smoke of the village, like the azure tester over a bridal-bed. How bright the country looks there where the river overflowed the meadows. The old grass has to knock under to the new. Well, I feel the better for this walk. Home now, and walk into that steak and crack that bottle of brown-stout; and by the time that's drank— a quart of stout—by that time, I shall feel about as stout as Samson. Come to think of it, that dun may call, though. I'll just visit the woods and cut a club. I'll club him, by Jove, if he duns me this day.

Hark! there goes Shanghai again. Shanghai says, "Bravo!" Shanghai says, "Club him!"

Oh, brave cock!

I felt in rare spirits the whole morning. The dun called about eleven. I had the boy Jake send the dun up. I was reading Tristram Shandy, and could not go down under the circumstances. The lean rascal (a lean farmer, too—think of that!) entered, and found me seated in an armchair, with my feet on the table, and the second bottle of brown-stout handy, and the book under eye.

"Sit down," said I; "I'll finish this chapter, and then attend to you. Fine morning. Ha! ha!—this is a fine joke about my Uncle Toby and the Widow Wadman! Ha! ha! ha! let me read this to you."

"I have no time; I've got my noon *chores* to do."

"To the deuce with your *chores*!" said I. "Don't drop your old tobacco about here, or I'll turn you out."

"Sir!"

"Let me read you this about the Widow Wadman. 'Said the Widow Wadman—'"

"There's my bill, sir."

"Very good. Just twist it up, will you;—it's about my smoking-time; and hand a coal, will you, from the hearth yonder!"

"My bill, sir!" said the rascal, turning pale with rage and amazement at my unwonted air (formerly I had always dodged him with a pale face), but too prudent as yet to betray the extremity of his astonishment. "My bill, sir!"—and he stiffly poked it at me.

"My friend," said I, "what a charming morning! How sweet the country looks! Pray, did you hear that extraordinary cock-crow this morning? Take a glass of my stout!"

"*Yours?* First pay your debts before you offer folks *your* stout!"

"You think, then, that, properly speaking, I have no *stout*," said I, deliberately rising. "I'll undeceive you. I'll show you stout of a superior brand to Barclay and Perkins."

Without more ado, I seized that insolent dun by the slack of his coat—(and, being a lean, shad-bellied wretch, there was plenty of slack to it)—I seized him that way, tied him with a sailor-knot, and, thrusting his bill between his teeth, introduced him to the open country lying round about my place of abode.

"Jake," said I, "you'll find a sack of blue-nosed potatoes lying under the shed. Drag it here, and pelt this pauper away: he's been begging pence of me, and I know he can work, but he's lazy. Pelt him away, Jake!"

Bless my stars, what a crow! Shanghai sent up such a perfect pæan and *laudamus*—such a trumpet-blast of triumph, that my soul fairly snorted in me. Duns!—I could have fought an army of them! Plainly, Shanghai was of the opinion that duns only came into the world to be kicked, hanged, bruised, battered, choked, walloped, hammered, drowned, clubbed!

Returning in-doors, when the exultation of my victory over the dun had a little subsided, I fell to musing over the mysterious Shanghai. I had no idea I would hear him so nigh my house. I wondered from what rich gentleman's yard he crowed. Nor had he cut short his crows so easily as I had supposed he would. This Shanghai crowed till mid-day, at least. Would he keep a-crowing all day? I resolved to learn. Again I ascended the hill. The whole country was now bathed in a rejoicing sunlight. The warm verdure was bursting all round me. Teams were a-field. Birds, newly arrived from the South, were blithely singing in the air. Even the crows cawed with a certain unction, and seemed a shade or two less black than usual.

Hark! there goes the cock! How shall I describe the crow of the Shanghai at noon-tide? His sun-rise crow was a whisper to it. It was the loudest, longest, and most strangely-musical crow that ever amazed mortal man. I had heard plenty of cock-crows before, and many fine ones;—but this one! so smooth and flute-like in its very clamor—so self-possessed in its very rapture of exultation—so vast, mounting, swelling, soaring, as if spurted out from a golden throat, thrown far back. Nor did it sound like the foolish, vain-glorious crow of some young sophomorean cock, who knew not the world, and was beginning life in audacious gay spirits, because in wretched ignorance of what might be to come. It was the crow of a cock who crowed not without advice; the crow of a cock who knew a thing or two; the crow of a cock who had fought the world and got the better of it, and was now resolved to crow, though the earth should heave and the heavens should fall. It was a wise crow; an invincible crow; a philosophic crow; a crow of all crows.

I returned home once more full of reinvigorated spirits, with a daunt-less sort of feeling. I thought over my debts and other troubles, and over the unlucky risings of the poor oppressed *peoples* abroad, and over the railroad and steamboat accidents, and over even the loss of my dear friend, with a calm, good-natured rapture of defiance, which astounded myself. I felt as though I could meet Death, and invite him to dinner, and toast the Catacombs with him, in pure overflow of self-reliance and a sense of universal security.

Toward evening I went up to the hill once more to find whether, indeed, the glorious cock would prove game even from the rising of the sun unto the going down thereof. Talk of Vespers or Curfew!—the evening crow of the cock went out of his mighty throat all over the land and inhabited it, like Xerxes from the East with his double-winged host. It was miraculous. Bless me, what a crow! The cock went game to roost that night, depend upon it, victorious over the entire day, and bequeathing the echoes of his thousand crows to night.

After an unwontedly sound, refreshing sleep I rose early, feeling like a carriage-spring—light—elliptical—airy—buoyant as sturgeon-nose— and, like a foot-ball, bounded up the hill. Hark! Shanghai was up before me. The early bird that caught the worm—crowing like a bugle worked by an engine—lusty, loud, all jubilation. From the scattered farm-houses a multitude of other cocks were crowing, and replying to each other's crows. But they were as flageolets to a trombone. Shanghai would suddenly break in, and overwhelm all their crows with his one domineering blast. He seemed to have nothing to do with any other concern. He replied to no other crow, but crowed solely by himself, on his own account, in solitary scorn and independence.

Oh, brave cock!—oh, noble Shanghai!—oh, bird rightly offered up by the invincible Socrates, in testimony of his final victory over life.

As I live, thought I, this blessed day will I go and seek out the Shanghai, and buy him, if I have to clap another mortgage on my land.

I listened attentively now, striving to mark from what direction the crow came. But it so charged and replenished, and made bountiful and overflowing all the air, that it was impossible to say from what precise point the exultation came. All that I could decide upon was this: the crow came from out of the East, and not from out of the West. I then considered with myself how far a cock-crow might be heard. In this still country, shut in, too, by mountains, sounds were audible at great distances. Besides, the undulations of the land, the abuttings of the mountains into the rolling hill and valley below, produced strange echoes, and reverberations, and multiplications, and accumulations of resonance, very remarkable to hear, and very puzzling to think of. Where lurked this valiant Shanghai—this bird of cheerful Socrates—the game-fowl Greek who died unappalled? Where lurked he? Oh, noble cock, where are you? Crow once more, my Bantam! my princely, my imperial Shanghai! my bird of the Emperor of China! Brother of the Sun! Cousin of great Jove! where are you?—one crow more, and tell me your master!

Hark! like a full orchestra of the cocks of all nations, forth burst the crow. But where from? There it is; but where? There was no telling, further than it came from out the East.

After breakfast I took my stick and sallied down the road. There were many gentlemen's seats dotting the neighboring country, and I made no doubt that some of these opulent gentlemen had invested a hundred dollar bill in some royal Shanghai recently imported in the ship Trade Wind, or the ship White Squall, or the ship Sovereign of the Seas, for it must needs have been a brave ship with a brave name which bore the fortunes of so brave a cock. I resolved to walk the entire country, and find this noble foreigner out; but thought it would not be amiss to inquire on the way at the humblest homesteads, whether, peradventure, they had heard of a lately-imported Shanghai belonging to any of the gentlemen settlers from the city; for it was plain that no poor farmer, no poor man of any sort, could own such an Oriental trophy— such a Great Bell of St. Paul's swung in a cock's throat.

I met an old man, plowing, in a field nigh the road-side fence.

"My friend, have you heard an extraordinary cock-crow of late?"

"Well, well," he drawled, "I don't know—the Widow Crowfoot has a cock—and Squire Squaretoes has a cock—and I have a cock, and they all crow. But I don't know of any on 'em with 'strordinary crows."

"Good-morning to you," said I, shortly; "it's plain that you have not heard the crow of the Emperor of China's chanticleer."

Presently I met another old man mending a tumble-down old rail-fence. The rails were rotten, and at every move of the old man's hand they crumbled into yellow ochre. He had much better let the fence alone, or else get him new rails. And here I must say, that one cause of the sad fact why idiocy more prevails among farmers than any other class of people, is owing to their undertaking the mending of rotten rail-fences in warm, relaxing spring weather. The enterprise is a hopeless one. It is a laborious one; it is a bootless one. It is an enterprise to make the heart break. Vast pains squandered upon a vanity. For how can one make rotten rail-fences stand up on their rotten pins? By what magic put pith into sticks which have lain freezing and baking through sixty consecutive winters and summers? This it is, this wretched endeavor to mend rotten rail-fences with their own rotten rails, which drives many farmers into the asylum.

On the face of the old man in question incipient idiocy was plainly marked. For, about sixty rods before him extended one of the most unhappy and desponding broken-hearted Virginia rail-fences I ever saw in my life. While in a field behind, were a set of young steers, possessed as by devils, continually butting at this forlorn old fence, and breaking through it here and there, causing the old man to drop his work and chase them back within bounds. He would chase them with a piece of rail huge as Goliath's beam, but as light as cork. At the first flourish, it crumbled into powder.

"My friend," said I, addressing this woeful mortal, "have you heard an extraordinary cock-crow of late?"

I might as well have asked him if he had heard the death-tick. He stared at me with a long, bewildered, doleful, and unutterable stare, and without reply resumed his unhappy labors.

What a fool, thought I, to have asked such an uncheerful and uncheerable creature about a cheerful cock!

I walked on. I had now descended the high land where my house stood, and being in a low tract could not hear the crow of the Shanghai, which doubtless overshot me there. Besides, the Shanghai might be at lunch of corn and oats, or taking a nap, and so interrupted his jubilations for a while.

At length, I encountered riding along the road, a portly gentleman—nay, a *pursy* one—of great wealth, who had recently purchased him some noble acres, and built him a noble mansion, with a goodly fowl-house attached, the fame whereof spread through all that country. Thought I, Here now is the owner of the Shanghai.

"Sir," said I, "excuse me, but I am a countryman of yours, and would ask, if so be you own any Shanghais?"

"Oh, yes; I have ten Shanghais."

"Ten!" exclaimed I, in wonder; "and do they all crow?"

"Most lustily; every soul of them; I wouldn't own a cock that wouldn't crow."

"Will you turn back, and show me those Shanghais?"

"With pleasure: I am proud of them. They cost me, in the lump, six hundred dollars."

As I walked by the side of his horse, I was thinking to myself whether possibly I had not mistaken the harmoniously combined crowings of ten Shanghais in a squad, for the supernatural crow of a single Shanghai by himself.

"Sir," said I, "is there one of your Shanghais which far exceeds all the others in the lustiness, musicalness, and inspiring effects of his crow?"

"They crow pretty much alike, I believe," he courteously replied; "I really don't know that I could tell their crow apart."

I began to think that after all my noble chanticleer might not be in the possession of this wealthy gentleman. However, we went into his fowl-yard, and I saw his Shanghais. Let me say that hitherto I had never clapped eye on this species of imported fowl. I had heard what enormous prices were paid for them, and also that they were of an enormous size, and had somehow fancied they must be of a beauty and brilliancy proportioned both to size and price. What was my surprise, then, to see ten carrot-colored monsters, without the smallest pretension to effulgence of plumage. Immediately, I determined that my royal cock was neither among these, nor could possibly be a Shanghai at all; if these gigantic gallows-bird fowl were fair specimens of the true Shanghai.

I walked all day, dining and resting at a farm-house, inspecting various fowl-yards, interrogating various owners of fowls, hearkening to various crows, but discovered not the mysterious chanticleer. Indeed, I had wandered so far and deviously, that I could not hear his crow. I began to suspect that this cock was a mere visitor in the country, who had taken his departure by the eleven o'clock train for the South, and was now crowing and jubilating somewhere on the verdant banks of Long Island Sound.

But next morning, again I heard the inspiring blast, again felt my blood bound in me, again felt superior to all the ills of life, again felt like turning my dun out of doors. But displeased with the reception given him at his last visit, the dun staid away. Doubtless being in a huff; silly fellow that he was to take a harmless joke in earnest.

Several days passed, during which I made sundry excursions in the regions roundabout, but in vain sought the cock. Still, I heard him from the hill, and sometimes from the house, and sometimes in the stillness of the night. If at times I would relapse into my doleful dumps, straightway at the sound of the exultant and defiant crow, my soul, too, would turn chanticleer, and clap her wings, and throw back her throat, and breathe forth a cheerful challenge to all the world of woes.

At last, after some weeks I was necessitated to clap another mortgage on my estate, in order to pay certain debts, and among others the one I owed the dun, who of late had commenced a civil-process against me. The way the process was served was a most insulting one. In a private room I had been enjoying myself in the village-tavern over a bottle of Philadelphia porter, and some Herkimer cheese, and a roll, and having apprised the landlord, who was a friend of mine, that I would settle with him when I received my next remittances, stepped to the peg where I had hung my hat in the bar-room, to get a choice cigar I had left in the hall, when lo! I found the civil-process enveloping the cigar. When I unrolled the cigar, I unrolled the civil-process, and the constable standing by rolled out, with a thick tongue, "Take notice!" and added, in a whisper, "Put that in your pipe and smoke it!"

I turned short round upon the gentlemen then and there present in that bar-room. Said I, "Gentlemen, is this an honorable—nay, is this a lawful way of serving a civil-process? Behold!"

One and all they were of opinion, that it was a highly inelegant act in the constable to take advantage of a gentleman's lunching on cheese and porter, to be so uncivil as to slip a civil-process into his hat. It was ungenerous; it was cruel; for the sudden shock of the thing coming instanter upon the lunch, would impair the proper digestion of the cheese, which is proverbially not so easy of digestion as *blanc-mange*.

Arrived home, I read the process, and felt a twinge of melancholy. Hard world! hard world! Here I am, as good a fellow as ever lived—hospitable—open-hearted—generous to a fault: and the Fates forbid that I should possess the fortune to bless the country with my bounteousness. Nay, while many a stingy curmudgeon rolls in idle gold, I, heart of nobleness as I am, I have civil-processes served on me! I bowed my head, and felt forlorn—unjustly used—abused—unappreciated—in short, miserable.

Hark! like a clarion! yea, like a jolly bolt of thunder with bells to it—came the all-glorious and defiant crow! Ye gods, how it set me up again! Right on my pins! Yea, verily on stilts!

Oh, noble cock!

Plain as cock could speak, it said, "Let the world and all aboard of it go to pot. Do you be jolly, and never say die. What's the world compared to you? What is it, any how, but a lump of loam? Do you be jolly!"

Oh, noble cock!

"But my dear and glorious cock," mused I, upon second thought, "one can't so easily send this world to pot; one can't so easily be jolly with civil processes in his hat or hand."

Hark! the crow again. Plain as cock could speak, it said: "Hang the process, and hang the fellow that sent it! If you have not land or cash, go and thrash the fellow, and tell him you never mean to pay him. Be jolly!"

Now this was the way—through the imperative intimations of the cock—that I came to clap the added mortgage on my estate; paid all my debts by fusing them into this one added bond and mortgage. Thus made at ease again, I renewed my search for the noble cock. But in vain, though I heard him every day. I began to think there was some sort of deception in this mysterious thing; some wonderful ventriloquist prowled around my barns, or in my cellar, or on my roof, and was minded to be gayly mischievous. But no—what ventriloquist could so crow with such an heroic and celestial crow?

At last, one morning there came to me a certain singular man, who had sawed and split my wood in March—some five-and-thirty cords of it—and now he came for his pay. He was a singular man, I say. He was tall and spare, with a long saddish face, yet somehow a latently joyous eye, which offered the strangest contrast. His air seemed staid, but undepressed. He wore a long, gray, shabby coat, and a big battered hat. This man had sawed my wood at so much a cord. He would stand and saw all day long in a driving snow-storm, and never wink at it. He never spoke unless spoken to. He only sawed. Saw, saw, saw—snow, snow, snow. The saw and the snow went together like two natural things. The first day this man came, he brought his dinner with him, and volunteered to eat it sitting on his buck in the snow-storm. From my window, where I was reading Burton's Anatomy of Melancholy, I saw him in the act. I burst out of doors bareheaded. "Good heavens!" cried I; "what are you doing? Come in. *This* your dinner!"

He had a hunk of stale bread and another hunk of salt beef, wrapped in a wet newspaper, and washed his morsels down by melting a handful of fresh snow in his mouth. I took this rash man indoors, planted him by the fire, gave him a dish of hot pork and beans, and a mug of cider.

"Now," said I, "don't you bring any of your damp dinners here. You work by the job, to be sure; but I'll dine you for all that."

He expressed his acknowledgments in a calm, proud, but not ungrateful way, and dispatched his meal with satisfaction to himself, and me also. It afforded me pleasure to perceive that he quaffed down his mug of cider like a man. I honored him. When I addressed him in the way of business at his buck, I did so in a guardedly respectful and deferential manner. Interested in his singular aspect, struck by his wondrous intensity of application at his saw—a most wearisome and disgustful occupation to most people—I often sought to gather from him who he was, what sort of a life he led, where he was born, and so on. But he was mum. He came to saw my wood, and eat my dinners—if I chose to offer them—but not to gabble. At first, I somewhat resented his sullen silence under the circumstances. But better considering it, I honored him the more. I increased the respectfulness and deferentialness of my address toward him. I concluded within myself that this man had experienced hard times; that he had had many sore rubs in the world; that he was of a solemn disposition; that he was of the mind of Solomon; that he lived calmly, decorously, temperately; and though a very poor man, was, nevertheless, a highly respectable one. At times I imagined that he might even be an elder or deacon of some small country church. I thought it would not be a bad plan to run this excellent man for President of the United States. He would prove a great reformer of abuses.

His name was Merrymusk. I had often thought how jolly a name for so unjolly a wight. I inquired of people whether they knew Merrymusk. But it was some time before I learned much about him. He was by birth a Marylander, it appeared, who had long lived in the country round about; a wandering man; until within some ten years ago, a thriftless man, though perfectly innocent of crime; a man who would work hard a month with surprising soberness, and then spend all his wages in one riotous night. In youth he had been a sailor, and run away from his ship at Batavia, where he caught the fever, and came nigh dying. But he rallied, re-shipped, landed home, found all his friends dead, and struck for the Northern interior, where he had since tarried. Nine years back he had married a wife, and now had four children. His wife was become a perfect invalid; one child had the white-swelling, and the rest were rickety. He and his family lived in a shanty on a lonely barren patch nigh the railroad-track, where it passed close to the base of a mountain. He had bought a fine cow to have plenty of wholesome milk for his children; but the cow died during an accouchement, and he could not afford to buy another. Still, his family never suffered for lack of food. He worked hard and brought it to them.

Now, as I said before, having long previously sawed my wood, this Merrymusk came for his pay.

"My friend," said I, "do you know of any gentleman hereabouts who owns an extraordinary cock?"

The twinkle glittered quite plain in the wood-sawyer's eye.

"I know of no *gentleman*," he replied, "who has what might well be called an extraordinary cock."

Oh, thought I, this Merrymusk is not the man to enlighten me. I am afraid I shall never discover this extraordinary cock.

Not having the full change to pay Merrymusk, I gave him his due, as nigh as I could make it, and told him that in a day or two I would take a walk and visit his place, and hand him the remainder. Accordingly one fine morning I sallied forth upon the errand. I had much ado finding the best road to the shanty. No one seemed to know where it was exactly. It lay in a very lonely part of the country, a densely-wooded mountain on one side (which I call October Mountain, on account of its bannered aspect in that month), and a thicketed swamp on the other, the railroad cutting the swamp. Straight as a die the railroad cut it; many times a day tantalizing the wretched shanty with the sight of all the beauty, rank, fashion, health, trunks, silver and gold, dry-goods and groceries, brides and grooms, happy wives and husbands, flying by the lonely door—no time to stop—flash! here they are—and there they go!—out of sight at both ends—as if that part of the world were only made to fly over, and not to settle upon. And this was about all the shanty saw of what people call "life."

Though puzzled somewhat, yet I knew the general direction where the shanty lay, and on I trudged. As I advanced, I was surprised to hear the mysterious cock-crow with more and more distinctness. Is it possible, thought I, that any gentleman owning a Shanghai can dwell in such a lonesome, dreary region? Louder and louder, nigher and nigher, sounded the glorious and defiant clarion. Though somehow I may be out of the track to my wood-sawyer's, I said to myself, yet, thank heaven, I seem to be on the way toward that extraordinary cock. I was delighted with this auspicious accident. On I journeyed; while at intervals the crow sounded most invitingly, and jocundly, and superbly; and the last crow was ever nigher than the former one. At last, emerging from a thicket of alders, straight before me I saw the most resplendent creature that ever blessed the sight of man.

A cock, more like a golden eagle than a cock. A cock, more like a Field-Marshal than a cock. A cock, more like Lord Nelson with all his glittering arms on, standing on the Vanguard's quarter-deck going into battle, than a cock. A cock, more like the Emperor Charlemagne in his robes at Aix la Chapelle, than a cock.

Such a cock!

He was of a haughty size, stood haughtily on his haughty legs. His colors were red, gold, and white. The red was on his crest alone, which was a mighty and symmetric crest, like unto Hector's helmet, as delineated on antique shields. His plumage was snowy, traced with gold. He walked in front of the shanty, like a peer of the realm; his crest lifted, his chest heaved out, his embroidered trappings flashing in the light. His pace was wonderful. He looked like some noble foreigner. He looked like some Oriental king in some magnificent Italian Opera.

Merrymusk advanced from the door.

"Pray is not that the Signor Beneventano?"

"Sir?"

"That's the cock," said I, a little embarrassed. The truth was, my enthusiasm had betrayed me into a rather silly inadvertence. I had made a somewhat learned sort of allusion in the presence of an unlearned man. Consequently, upon discovering it by his honest stare, I felt foolish; but carried it off by declaring that *this was the cock.*

Now, during the preceding autumn I had been to the city, and had chanced to be present at a performance of the Italian Opera. In that Opera figured in some royal character a certain Signor Beneventano—a man of a tall, imposing person, clad in rich raiment, like to plumage, and with a most remarkable, majestic, scornful stride. The Signor Beneventano seemed on the point of tumbling over backward with exceeding haughtiness. And, for all the world, the proud pace of the cock seemed the very stage-pace of the Signor Beneventano.

Hark! Suddenly the cock paused, lifted his head still higher, ruffled his plumes, seemed inspired, and sent forth a lusty crow. October Mountain echoed it; other mountains sent it back; still others rebounded it; it over-ran the country round. Now I plainly perceived how it was I had chanced to hear the gladdening sound on my distant hill.

"Good Heavens! do you own the cock? Is that cock yours?"

"Is it my cock!" said Merrymusk, looking slyly gleeful out of the corner of his long, solemn face.

"Where did you get it?"

"It chipped the shell here. I raised it."

"You?"

Hark! Another crow. It might have raised the ghosts of all the pines and hemlocks ever cut down in that country. Marvelous cock! Having crowed, he strode on again, surrounded by a bevy of admiring hens.

"What will you take for Signor Beneventano?"

"Sir?"

"That magic cock!—what will you take for him?"

"I won't sell him."

"I will give you fifty dollars."

"Pooh!"

"One hundred!"

"Pish!"

"Five hundred!"

"Bah!"

"And you a poor man?"

"No; don't I own that cock, and haven't I refused five hundred dollars for him?"

"True," said I, in profound thought; "that's a fact. You won't sell him, then?"

"No."

"Will you give him?"

"No."

"Will you *keep* him, then!" I shouted, in a rage.

"Yes."

I stood awhile admiring the cock, and wondering at the man. At last I felt a redoubled admiration of the one, and a redoubled deference for the other.

"Won't you step in?" said Merrymusk.

"But won't the cock be prevailed upon to join us?" said I.

"Yes. Trumpet! hither, boy! hither!"

The cock turned round, and strode up to Merrymusk.

"Come!"

The cock followed us into the shanty.

"Crow!"

The roof jarred.

Oh, noble cock!

I turned in silence upon my entertainer. There he sat on an old battered chest, in his old battered gray coat, with patches at his knees and elbows, and a deplorably bunged hat. I glanced round the room. Bare rafters overhead, but solid junks of jerked beef hanging from them. Earth floor, but a heap of potatoes in one corner, and a sack of Indian meal in another. A blanket was strung across the apartment at the further end, from which came a woman's ailing voice and the voices of ailing children. But somehow in the ailing of these voices there seemed no complaint.

"Mrs. Merrymusk and children?"

"Yes."

I looked at the cock. There he stood majestically in the middle of the room. He looked like a Spanish grandee caught in a shower, and standing under some peasant's shed. There was a strange supernatural look of contrast about him. He irradiated the shanty; he glorified its meanness. He glorified the battered chest, and tattered gray coat, and the bunged hat. He glorified the very voices which came in ailing tones from behind the screen.

"Oh, father," cried a little sickly voice, "let Trumpet sound again."

"Crow," cried Merrymusk.

The cock threw himself into a posture.

The roof jarred.

"Does not this disturb Mrs. Merrymusk and the sick children?"

"Crow again, Trumpet."

The roof jarred.

"It does not disturb them, then?"

"Didn't you hear 'em *ask* for it?"

"How is it, that your sick family like this crowing?" said I. "The cock is a glorious cock, with a glorious voice, but not exactly the sort of thing for a sick chamber, one would suppose. Do they really like it?"

"Don't *you* like it? Don't it do *you* good? Ain't it inspiring? don't it impart pluck? give stuff against despair?"

"All true," said I, removing my hat with profound humility before the brave spirit disguised in the base coat.

"But then," said I still, with some misgivings, "so loud, so wonderfully clamorous a crow, methinks might be amiss to invalids, and retard their convalescence."

"Crow your best now, Trumpet!"

I leaped from my chair. The cock frightened me, like some overpowering angel in the Apocalypse. He seemed crowing over the fall of wicked Babylon, or crowing over the triumph of righteous Joshua in the vale of Ajalon. When I regained my composure somewhat, an inquisitive thought occurred to me. I resolved to gratify it.

"Merrymusk, will you present me to your wife and children?"

"Yes. Wife, the gentleman wants to step in."

"He is very welcome," replied a weak voice.

Going behind the curtain, there lay a wasted, but strangely cheerful human face; and that was pretty much all; the body, hid by the counterpane and an old coat, seemed too shrunken to reveal itself through such impediments. At the bedside, sat a pale girl, ministering. In another bed lay three children, side by side: three more pale faces.

"Oh, father, we don't mislike the gentleman, but let us see Trumpet too."

At a word, the cock strode behind the screen, and perched himself on the children's bed. All their wasted eyes gazed at him with a wild and spiritual delight. They seemed to sun themselves in the radiant plumage of the cock.

"Better than a 'pothecary, eh?" said Merrymusk. "This is Dr. Cock himself."

We retired from the sick ones, and I reseated myself again, lost in thought, over this strange household.

"You seem a glorious independent fellow!" said I.

"And I don't think you a fool, and never did. Sir, you are a trump."

"Is there any hope of your wife's recovery?" said I, modestly seeking to turn the conversation.

"Not the least."

"The children?"

"Very little."

"It must be a doleful life, then, for all concerned. This lonely solitude—this shanty—hard work—hard times."

"Haven't I Trumpet? He's the cheerer. He crows through all; crows at the darkest; 'Glory to God in the highest!' continually he crows it."

"Just the import I first ascribed to his crow, Merrymusk, when first I heard it from my hill. I thought some rich nabob owned some costly Shanghai; little weening any such poor man as you owned this lusty cock of a domestic breed."

"*Poor* man like *me*? Why call *me* poor? Don't the cock *I* own glorify this otherwise inglorious, lean, lantern-jawed land? Didn't *my* cock encourage *you*? And *I* give you all this glorification away gratis. I am a great philanthropist. I am a rich man—a very rich man, and a very happy one. Crow, Trumpet."

The roof jarred.

I returned home in a deep mood. I was not wholly at rest concerning the soundness of Merrymusk's views of things, though full of admiration for him. I was thinking on the matter before my door, when I heard the cock crow again. Enough. Merrymusk is right.

Oh, noble cock! oh, noble man!

I did not see Merrymusk for some weeks after this; but hearing the glorious and rejoicing crow, I supposed that all went as usual with him. My own frame of mind remained a rejoicing one. The cock still inspired me. I saw another mortgage piled on my plantation; but only bought another dozen of stout, and a dozen-dozen of Philadelphia porter. Some of my relatives died; I wore no mourning, but for three days drank stout in preference to porter, stout being of the darker color. I heard the cock crow the instant I received the unwelcome tidings.

"Your health in this stout, oh noble cock!"

I thought I would call on Merrymusk again, not having seen or heard of him for some time now. Approaching the place, there were no signs of motion about the shanty. I felt a strange misgiving. But the cock crew from within doors, and the boding vanished. I knocked at the door. A feeble voice bade me enter. The curtain was no longer drawn; the whole house was a hospital now. Merrymusk lay on a heap of old clothes; wife and children were all in their beds. The cock was perched on an old hogshead hoop, swung from the ridge-pole in the middle of the shanty.

"You are sick, Merrymusk," said I, mournfully.

"No, I am well," he feebly answered.—"Crow, Trumpet."

I shrunk. The strong soul in the feeble body appalled me.

But the cock crew.

The roof jarred.

"How is Mrs. Merrymusk?"

"Well."

"And the children?"

"Well. All well."

The last two words he shouted forth in a kind of wild ecstasy of triumph over ill. It was too much. His head fell back. A white napkin seemed dropped upon his face. Merrymusk was dead.

An awful fear seized me.

But the cock crew.

The cock shook his plumage as if each feather were a banner. The cock hung from the shanty roof as erewhile the trophied flags from the dome of St. Paul's. The cock terrified me with exceeding wonder.

I drew nigh the bedsides of the woman and children. They marked my look of strange affright; they knew what had happened.

"My good man is just dead," breathed the woman lowly. "Tell me true?"

"Dead," said I.

The cock crew.

She fell back, without a sigh, and through long-loving sympathy was dead.

The cock crew.

The cock shook sparkles from his golden plumage. The cock seemed in a rapture of benevolent delight. Leaping from the hoop, he strode up majestically to the pile of old clothes, where the wood-sawyer lay, and planted himself, like an armorial supporter, at his side. Then raised one long, musical, triumphant, and final sort of crow, with throat heaved far back, as if he meant the blast to waft the wood-sawyer's soul sheer up to the seventh heavens. Then he strode, king-like, to the woman's bed. Another upturned and exultant crow, mated to the former.

The pallor of the children was changed to radiance. Their faces shone celestially through grime and dirt. They seemed children of emperors and kings, disguised. The cock sprang upon their bed, shook himself, and crowed, and crowed again, and still and still again. He seemed bent upon crowing the souls of the children out of their wasted bodies. He seemed bent upon rejoining instanter this whole family in the upper air. The children seemed to second his endeavors. Far, deep, intense longings for release transfigured them into spirits before my eyes. I saw angels where they lay.

They were dead.

The cock shook his plumage over them. The cock crew. It was now like a Bravo! like a Hurrah! like a Three-times-three! hip! hip! He strode out of the shanty. I followed. He flew upon the apex of the dwelling, spread wide his wings, sounded one supernatural note, and dropped at my feet.

The cock was dead.

If now you visit that hilly region, you will see, nigh the railroad track, just beneath October Mountain, on the other side of the swamp—there you will see a grave-stone, not with skull and cross-bones, but with a lusty cock in act of crowing, chiseled on it, with the words beneath:

—"Oh! death, where is thy sting?
Oh! grave, where is thy victory?"

The wood-sawyer and his family, with the Signor Beneventano, lie in that spot; and I buried them, and planted the stone, which was a stone made to order; and never since then have I felt the doleful dumps, but under all circumstances crow late and early with a continual crow.

COCK-A-DOODLE-DOO!—oo!—oo!—oo!—oo!

1853

FROM THE ENCANTADAS:
THE CHOLA WIDOW

"At last they in an island did espy
A seemly woman sitting by the shore,
That with great sorrow and sad agony
Seemed some great misfortune to deplore,
And loud to them for succor called evermore."

"Black his eye as the midnight sky,
White his neck as the driven snow,
Red his cheek as the morning light;—
Cold he lies in the ground below.
 My love is dead,
  Gone to his death-bed,
All under the cactus tree."

"Each lonely scene shall thee restore,
For thee the tear be duly shed;
Belov'd till life can charm no more,
And mourned till Pity's self be dead."

Far to the northeast of Charles' Isle, sequestered from the rest, lies Norfolk Isle; and, however insignificant to most voyagers, to me, through sympathy, that lone island has become a spot made sacred by the strongest trials of humanity.

It was my first visit to the Encantadas. Two days had been spent ashore in hunting tortoises. There was not time to capture many; so on the third afternoon we loosed our sails. We were just in the act of getting under way, the uprooted anchor yet suspended and invisibly swaying beneath the wave, as the good ship gradually turned on her heel to leave the isle behind, when the seaman who heaved with me at the windlass paused suddenly, and directed my attention to something moving on the land, not along the beach, but somewhat back, fluttering from a height.

In view of the sequel of this little story, be it here narrated how it came to pass, that an object which partly from its being so small was quite lost to every other man on board, still caught the eye of my handspike companion. The rest of the crew, myself included, merely stood up to our spikes in heaving; whereas, unwontedly exhilarated at every turn of the ponderous windlass, my belted comrade leaped atop of it, with might and main giving a downward, thewey, perpendicular heave, his raised eye bent in cheery animation upon the slowly receding shore. Being high lifted above all others was the reason he perceived the object, otherwise unperceivable: and this elevation of his eye was owing to the elevation of his spirits; and this again—for truth must out—to a dram of Peruvian pisco, in guerdon for some kindness done, secretly administered to him that morning by our mulatto steward. Now, certainly, pisco does a deal of mischief in the world; yet seeing that, in the present case, it was the means, though indirect, of rescuing a human being from the most dreadful fate, must we not also needs admit that sometimes pisco does a deal of good?

Glancing across the water in the direction pointed out, I saw some white thing hanging from an inland rock, perhaps half a mile from the sea.

"It is a bird; a white-winged bird; perhaps a——no; it is——it is a handkerchief!"

"Aye, a handkerchief!" echoed my comrade, and with a louder shout apprised the captain.

Quickly now—like the running out and training of a great gun—the long cabin spy-glass was thrust through the mizzen rigging from the high platform of the poop; whereupon a human figure was plainly seen upon the inland rock, eagerly waving towards us what seemed to be the hand-kerchief.

Our captain was a prompt, good fellow. Dropping the glass, he lustily ran forward, ordering the anchor to be dropped again; hands to stand by a boat, and lower away.

In a half-hour's time the swift boat returned. It went with six and came with seven; and the seventh was a woman.

It is not artistic heartlessness, but I wish I could but draw in crayons; for this woman was a most touching sight; and crayons, tracing softly melancholy lines, would best depict the mournful image of the dark-damasked Chola widow.

Her story was soon told, and though given in her own strange language was as quickly understood, for our captain from long trading on the Chilian coast was well versed in the Spanish. A Chola, or half-breed Indian woman of Payta in Peru, three years gone by, with her young new-wedded husband Felipe, of pure Castilian blood, and her one only Indian brother, Truxill, Hunilla had taken passage on the main in a French whaler, commanded by a joyous man; which vessel, bound to the cruising grounds beyond the Enchanted Isles, proposed passing close by their vicinity. The object of the little party was to procure tortoise oil, a fluid which for its great purity and delicacy is held in high estimation wherever known; and it is well known all along this part of the Pacific coast. With a chest of clothes, tools, cooking utensils, a rude apparatus for trying out the oil, some casks of biscuit, and other things, not omitting two favorite dogs, of which faithful animal all the Cholos are very fond, Hunilla and her companions were safely landed at their chosen place; the Frenchman, according to the contract made ere sailing, engaged to take them off upon returning from a four months' cruise in the westward seas; which interval the three adventurers deemed quite sufficient for their purposes.

On the isle's lone beach they paid him in silver for their passage out, the stranger having declined to carry them at all except upon that condition; though willing to take every means to insure the due fulfilment of his promise. Felipe had striven hard to have this payment put off to the period of the ship's return. But in vain. Still, they thought they had, in another way, ample pledge of the good faith of the Frenchman. It was arranged that the expenses of the passage home should not be payable in silver, but in tortoises; one hundred tortoises ready captured to the returning captain's hand. These the Cholos meant to secure after their own work was done, against the probable time of the Frenchman's coming back; and no doubt in prospect already felt, that in those hundred tortoises—now somewhere ranging the isle's interior—they possessed one hundred hostages. Enough: the vessel sailed; the gazing three on shore answered the loud glee of the singing crew; and ere evening, the French craft was hull down in the distant sea, its masts three faintest lines which quickly faded from Hunilla's eye.

The stranger had given a blithesome promise, and anchored it with oaths; but oaths and anchors equally will drag; nought else abides on fickle earth but unkept promises of joy. Contrary winds from out unstable skies, or contrary moods of his more varying mind, or shipwreck and sudden death in solitary waves; whatever was the cause, the blithe stranger never was seen again.

Yet, however dire a calamity was here in store, misgivings of it ere due time never disturbed the Cholos' busy mind, now all intent upon the toilsome matter which had brought them hither. Nay, by swift doom coming like the thief at night, ere seven weeks went by, two of the little party were removed from all anxieties of land or sea. No more they sought to gaze with feverish fear, or still more feverish hope, beyond the present's horizon line; but into the furthest future their own silent spirits sailed. By persevering labor beneath that burning sun, Felipe and Truxill had brought down to their hut many scores of tortoises, and tried out the oil, when, elated with their good success, and to reward themselves for such hard work, they, too hastily, made a catamaran, or Indian raft, much used on the Spanish main, and merrily started on a fishing trip, just without a long reef with many jagged gaps, running parallel with the shore, about half a mile from it. By some bad tide or hap, or natural negligence of joyfulness (for though they could not be heard, yet by their gestures they seemed singing at the time), forced in deep water against that iron bar, the ill-made catamaran was overset, and came all to pieces; when, dashed by broad-chested swells between their broken logs and the sharp teeth of the reef, both adventurers perished before Hunilla's eyes.

Before Hunilla's eyes they sank. The real woe of this event passed before her sight as some sham tragedy on the stage. She was seated on a rude bower among the withered thickets, crowning a lofty cliff, a little back from the beach. The thickets were so disposed, that in looking upon the sea at large she peered out from among the branches as from the lattice of a high balcony. But upon the day we speak of here, the better to watch the adventure of those two hearts she loved, Hunilla had withdrawn the branches to one side, and held them so. They formed an oval frame, through which the bluely boundless sea rolled like a painted one. And there, the invisible painter painted to her view the wave-tossed and disjointed raft, its once level logs slantingly upheaved, as raking masts, and the four struggling arms undistinguishable among them; and then all subsided into smooth-flowing creamy waters, slowly drifting the splintered wreck; while first and last, no sound of any sort was heard. Death in a silent picture; a dream of the eye; such vanishing shapes as the mirage shows.

So instant was the scene, so trance-like its mild pictorial effect, so distant from her blasted bower and her common sense of things, that Hunilla gazed and gazed, nor raised a finger or a wail. But as good to sit thus dumb, in stupor staring on that dumb show, for all that otherwise might be done. With half a mile of sea between, how could her two enchanted arms aid those four fated ones? The distance long, the time one sand. After the lightning is beheld, what fool shall stay the thunderbolt? Felipe's body was washed ashore, but Truxill's never came; only his gay, braided hat of golden straw—that same sunflower thing he waved to her, pushing from the strand—and now, to the last gallant, it still saluted her. But Felipe's body floated to the marge, with one arm encirclingly outstretched. Lock-jawed in grim death, the lover-husband, softly clasped his bride, true to her even in death's dream. Ah, Heaven, when man thus keeps his faith, wilt thou be faithless who created the faithful one? But they cannot break faith who never plighted it.

It needs not to be said what nameless misery now wrapped the lonely widow. In telling her own story she passed this almost entirely over, simply recounting the event. Construe the comment of her features, as you might; from her mere words little would you have weened that Hunilla was herself the heroine of her tale. But not thus did she defraud us of our tears. All hearts bled that grief could be so brave.

She but showed us her soul's lid, and the strange ciphers thereon engraved; all within, with pride's timidity, was withheld. Yet was there one exception. Holding out her small olive hand before our captain, she said in mild and slowest Spanish, "Señor, I buried him;" then paused, struggled as against the writhed coilings of a snake, and cringing suddenly, leaped up, repeating in impassioned pain, "I buried him, my life, my soul!"

Doubtless it was by half-unconscious, automatic motions of her hands, that this heavy-hearted one performed the final offices for Felipe, and planted a rude cross of withered sticks—no green ones might be had—at the head of that lonely grave, where rested now in lasting uncomplaint and quiet haven he whom untranquil seas had overthrown.

But some dull sense of another body that should be interred, of another cross that should hallow another grave—unmade as yet;—some dull anxiety and pain touching her undiscovered brother now haunted the oppressed Hunilla. Her hands fresh from the burial earth, she slowly went back to the beach, with unshaped purposes wandered there, her spellbound eye bent upon the incessant waves. But they bore nothing to her but a dirge, which maddened her to think that murderers should mourn. As time went by, and these things came less dreamily to her mind, the strong persuasions of her Romish faith, which sets peculiar store by consecrated urns, prompted her to resume in waking earnest that pious search which had but been begun as in somnambulism. Day after day, week after week, she trod the cindery beach, till at length a double motive edged every eager glance. With equal longing she now looked for the living and the dead; the brother and the captain; alike vanished, never to return. Little accurate note of time had Hunilla taken under such emotions as were hers, and little, outside herself, served for calendar or dial. As to poor Crusoe in the self-same sea, no saint's bell pealed forth the lapse of week or month; each day went by unchallenged; no chanticleer announced those sultry dawns, no lowing herds those poisonous nights. All wonted and steadily recurring sounds, human, or humanized by sweet fellowship with man, but one stirred that torrid trance,—the cry of dogs; save which nought but the rolling sea invaded it, an all pervading monotone; and to the widow that was the least loved voice she could have heard.

No wonder that as her thoughts now wandered to the unreturning ship, and were beaten back again, the hope against hope so struggled in her soul, that at length she desperately said, "Not yet, not yet; my foolish heart runs on too fast." So she forced patience for some further weeks. But to those whom earth's sure indraft draws, patience or impatience is still the same.

Hunilla now sought to settle precisely in her mind, to an hour, how long it was since the ship had sailed; and then, with the same precision, how long a space remained to pass. But this proved impossible. What present day or month it was she could not say. Time was her labyrinth, in which Hunilla was entirely lost.

And now follows——

Against my own purposes a pause descends upon me here. One knows not whether nature doth not impose some secrecy upon him who has been privy to certain things. At least, it is to be doubted whether it be good to blazon such. If some books are deemed most baneful and their sale forbid, how then with deadlier facts, not dreams of doting men? Those whom books will hurt will not be proof against events. Events, not books, should be forbid. But in all things man sows upon the wind, which bloweth just there whither it listeth; for ill or good man cannot know. Often ill comes from the good, as good from ill.

When Hunilla——

Dire sight it is to see some silken beast long dally with a golden lizard ere she devour. More terrible, to see how feline Fate will sometimes dally with a human soul, and by a nameless magic make it repulse a sane despair with a hope which is but mad. Unwittingly I imp this cat-like thing, sporting with the heart of him who reads; for if he feel not, he reads in vain.

——"The ship sails this day, to-day," at last said Hunilla to herself; "this gives me certain time to stand on; without certainty I go mad. In loose ignorance I have hoped and hoped; now in firm knowledge I will but wait. Now I live and no longer perish in bewilderings. Holy Virgin, aid me! Thou wilt waft back the ship. Oh, past length of weary weeks—all to be dragged over—to buy the certainty of to-day, I freely give ye, though I tear ye from me!"

As mariners tossed in tempest on some desolate ledge patch them a boat out of the remnants of their vessel's wreck, and launch it in the self-same waves, see here Hunilla, this lone shipwrecked soul, out of treachery invoking trust. Humanity, thou strong thing, I worship thee, not in the laurelled victor, but in this vanquished one.

Truly Hunilla leaned upon a reed, a real one; no metaphor; a real Eastern reed. A piece of hollow cane, drifted from unknown isles, and found upon the beach, its once jagged ends rubbed smoothly even as by sand-paper; its golden glazing gone. Long ground between the sea and land, upper and nether stone, the unvarnished substance was filed bare, and wore another polish now, one with itself, the polish of its agony. Circular lines at intervals cut all round this surface, divided it into six panels of unequal length. In the first were scored the days, each tenth one marked by a longer and deeper notch; the second was scored for the number of sea-fowl eggs for sustenance, picked out from the rocky nests; the third, how many fish had been caught from the shore; the fourth, how many small tortoises found inland; the fifth, how many days of sun; the sixth, of clouds; which last, of the two, was the greater one. Long night of busy numbering, misery's mathematics, to weary her too-wakeful soul to sleep; yet sleep for that was none.

The panel of the days was deeply worn, the long tenth notches half effaced, as alphabets of the blind. Ten thousand times the longing widow had traced her finger over the bamboo; dull flute, which played on, gave no sound; as if counting birds flown by in air, would hasten tortoises creeping through the woods.

After the one hundred and eightieth day no further mark was seen; that last one was the faintest, as the first the deepest.

"There were more days," said our Captain; "many, many more; why did you not go on and notch them too, Hunilla?"

"Señor, ask me not."

"And meantime, did no other vessel pass the isle?"

"Nay, Señor;—but——"

"You do not speak; but *what*, Hunilla?"

"Ask me not, Señor."

"You saw ships pass, far away; you waved to them; they passed on;—was that it, Hunilla?"

"Señor, be it as you say."

Braced against her woe, Hunilla would not, durst not trust the weakness of her tongue. Then when our Captain asked whether any whale-boats had——

But no, I will not file this thing complete for scoffing souls to quote, and call it firm proof upon their side. The half shall here remain untold. Those two unnamed events which befell Hunilla on this isle, let them abide between her and her God. In nature, as in law, it may be libellous to speak some truths.

Still, how it was that although our vessel had lain three days anchored nigh the isle, its one human tenant should not have discovered us till just upon the point of sailing, never to revisit so lone and far a spot; this needs explaining ere the sequel come.

The place where the French captain had landed the little party was on the farther and opposite end of the isle. There too it was that they had afterwards built their hut. Nor did the widow in her solitude desert the spot where her loved ones had dwelt with her, and where the dearest of the twain now slept his last long sleep, and all her plaints awaked him not, and he of husbands the most faithful during life.

Now, high broken land rises between the opposite extremities of the isle. A ship anchored at one side is invisible from the other. Neither is the isle so small, but a considerable company might wander for days through the wilderness of one side, and never be seen, or their halloos heard, by any stranger holding aloof on the other. Hence Hunilla, who naturally associated the possible coming of ships with her own part of the isle, might to the end have remained quite ignorant of the presence of our vessel, were it not for a mysterious presentiment, borne to her, so our mariners averred, by this isle's enchanted air. Nor did the widow's answer undo the thought.

"How did you come to cross the isle this morning then, Hunilla?" said our Captain.

"Señor, something came flitting by me. It touched my cheek, my heart, Señor."

"What do you say, Hunilla?"

"I have said, Señor; something came through the air."

It was a narrow chance. For when in crossing the isle Hunilla gained the high land in the centre, she must then for the first have perceived our masts, and also marked that their sails were being loosed, perhaps even heard the echoing chorus of the windlass song. The strange ship was about to sail, and she behind. With all haste she now descends the height on the hither side, but soon loses sight of the ship among the sunken jungles at the mountain's base. She struggles on through the withered branches, which seek at every step to bar her path, till she comes to the isolated rock, still some way from the water. This she climbs, to reassure herself. The ship is still in plainest sight. But now worn out with over tension, Hunilla all but faints; she fears to step down from her giddy perch;

she is feign to pause, there where she is, and as a last resort catches the turban from her head, unfurls and waves it over the jungles towards us.

During the telling of her story the mariners formed a voiceless circle round Hunilla and the Captain; and when at length the word was given to man the fastest boat, and pull round to the isle's thither side, to bring away Hunilla's chest and the tortoise-oil; such alacrity of both cheery and sad obedience seldom before was seen. Little ado was made. Already the anchor had been recommitted to the bottom, and the ship swung calmly to it.

But Hunilla insisted upon accompanying the boat as indispensable pilot to her hidden hut. So being refreshed with the best the steward could supply, she started with us. Nor did ever any wife of the most famous admiral in her husband's barge receive more silent reverence of respect, than poor Hunilla from this boat's crew.

Rounding many a vitreous cape and bluff, in two hours' time we shot inside the fatal reef; wound into a secret cove, looked up along a green many-gabled lava wall, and saw the island's solitary dwelling.

It hung upon an impending cliff, sheltered on two sides by tangled thickets, and half-screened from view in front by juttings of the rude stairway, which climbed the precipice from the sea. Built of canes, it was thatched with long, mildewed grass. It seemed an abandoned hay-rick whose haymakers were now no more. The roof inclined but one way; the eaves coming to within two feet of the ground. And here was a simple apparatus to collect the dews, or rather doubly-distilled and finest winnowed rains, which, in mercy or in mockery, the night-skies sometimes drop upon these blighted Encantadas. All along beneath the eaves, a spotted sheet, quite weather-stained, was spread, pinned to short, upright stakes, set in the shallow sand. A small clinker, thrown into the cloth, weighed its middle down, thereby straining all moisture into a calabash placed below. This vessel supplied each drop of water ever drunk upon the isle by the Cholos. Hunilla told us the calabash would sometimes, but not often, be half filled over-night. It held six quarts, perhaps. "But," said she, "we were used to thirst. At sandy Payta, where I live, no shower from heaven ever fell; all the water there is brought on mules from the inland vales."

Tied among the thickets were some twenty moaning tortoises, supplying Hunilla's lonely larder; while hundreds of vast tableted black bucklers, like displaced, shattered tomb-stones of dark slate, were also scattered round. These were the skeleton backs of those great tortoises from which Felipe and Truxill had made their precious oil. Several large calabashes and two goodly kegs were filled with it. In a pot near by were the caked crusts of a quantity which had been permitted to evaporate. "They meant to have strained it off next day," said Hunilla, as she turned aside.

I forgot to mention the most singular sight of all, though the first that greeted us after landing.

Some ten small, soft-haired, ringleted dogs, of a beautiful breed, peculiar to Peru, set up a concert of glad welcomings when we gained the beach, which was responded to by Hunilla. Some of these dogs had, since her widowhood, been born upon the isle, the progeny of the two brought from Payta. Owing to the jagged steeps and pitfalls, tortuous thickets, sunken clefts and perilous intricacies of all sorts in the interior; Hunilla, admonished by the loss of one favorite among them, never allowed these delicate creatures to follow her in her occasional birds'-nests climbs and other wanderings; so that, through long habituation, they offered not to follow, when that morning she crossed the land; and her own soul was then too full of other things to heed their lingering behind. Yet, all along she had so clung to them, that, besides what moisture they lapped up at early daybreak from the small scoop-holes among the adjacent rocks, she had shared the dew of her calabash among them; never laying by any considerable store against those prolonged and utter droughts, which in some disastrous seasons warp these isles.

Having pointed out, at our desire, what few things she would like transported to the ship—her chest, the oil, not omitting the live tortoises which she intended for a grateful present to our Captain—we immediately set to work, carrying them to the boat down the long, sloping stair of deeply-shadowed rock. While my comrades were thus employed, I looked, and Hunilla had disappeared.

It was not curiosity alone, but, it seems to me, something different mingled with it, which prompted me to drop my tortoise, and once more gaze slowly around. I remembered the husband buried by Hunilla's hands. A narrow pathway led into a dense part of the thickets. Following it through many mazes, I came out upon a small, round, open space, deeply chambered there.

The mound rose in the middle; a bare heap of finest sand, like that unverdured heap found at the bottom of an hour-glass run out. At its head stood the cross of withered sticks; the dry, peeled bark still fraying from it; its transverse limb tied up with rope, and forlornly adroop in the silent air.

Hunilla was partly prostrate upon the grave; her dark head bowed, and lost in her long, loosened Indian hair; her hands extended to the cross-foot, with a little brass crucifix clasped between; a crucifix worn feature-less, like an ancient graven knocker long plied in vain. She did not see me, and I made no noise, but slid aside, and left the spot.

A few moments ere all was ready for our going, she reappeared among us. I looked into her eyes, but saw no tear. There was something which seemed strangely haughty in her air, and yet it was the air of woe. A Span-ish and an Indian grief, which would not visibly lament. Pride's height in vain abased to proneness on the rack; nature's pride subduing nature's torture.

Like pages the small and silken dogs surrounded her, as she slowly de-scended towards the beach. She caught the two most eager creatures in her arms:—"Mia Teeta! Mia Tomoteeta!" and fondling them, inquired how many could we take on board.

The mate commanded the boat's crew; not a hard-hearted man, but his way of life had been such that in most things, even in the smallest, simple utility was his leading motive.

"We cannot take them all, Hunilla; our supplies are short; the winds are unreliable; we may be a good many days going to Tombez. So take those you have, Hunilla; but no more."

She was in the boat; the oarsmen too were seated; all save one, who stood ready to push off and then spring himself. With the sagacity of their race, the dogs now seemed aware that they were in the very instant of being deserted upon a barren strand. The gunwales of the boat were high; its prow—presented inland—was lifted; so owing to the water, which they seemed instinctively to shun, the dogs could not well leap into the little craft. But their busy paws hard scraped the prow, as it had been some farmer's door shutting them out from shelter in a winter storm. A clam-orous agony of alarm. They did not howl, or whine; they all but spoke.

"Push off! Give way!" cried the mate. The boat gave one heavy drag and lurch, and next moment shot swiftly from the beach, turned on her heel, and sped. The dogs ran howling along the water's marge; now paus-ing to gaze at the flying boat, then motioning as if to leap in chase, but mysteriously withheld themselves; and again ran howling along the beach. Had they been human beings hardly would they have more vividly inspired the sense of desolation. The oars were plied as confederate feathers of two wings. No one spoke. I looked back upon the beach, and then upon Hunilla, but her face was set in a stern dusky calm. The dogs crouching in her lap vainly licked her rigid hands. She never looked behind her; but sat motionless, till we turned a promontory of the coast and lost all sights and sounds astern. She seemed as one, who having experienced the sharpest of mortal pangs, was henceforth content to have all lesser heart-strings riven, one by one. To Hunilla, pain seemed so necessary, that pain in other beings, though by love and sympathy made her own, was unrepiningly to be borne. A heart of yearning in a frame of steel. A heart of earthly yearning, frozen by the frost which falleth from the sky.

The sequel is soon told. After a long passage, vexed by calms and baffling winds, we made the little port of Tombez in Peru, there to recruit the ship. Payta was not very distant. Our captain sold the tortoise oil to a Tombez merchant; and adding to the silver a contribution from all hands, gave it to our silent passenger, who knew not what the mariners had done.

The last seen of lone Hunilla she was passing into Payta town, riding upon a small gray ass; and before her on the ass's shoulders, she eyed the jointed workings of the beast's armorial cross.

1854

THE TWO TEMPLES

Dedicated to Sheridan Knowles

TEMPLE FIRST

"This is too bad," said I, "here have I tramped this blessed Sunday morning, all the way from the Battery, three long miles, for this express purpose, prayer-book under arm; here I am, I say, and, after all, I can't get in.

"Too bad. And how disdainful the great, fat-paunched, beadle-faced man looked, when in answer to my humble petition, he said they had no galleries. Just the same as if he'd said, they did n't entertain poor folks. But I'll wager something that had my new coat been done last night, as the false tailor promised, and had I, arrayed therein this bright morning, tickled the fat-paunched, beadle-faced man's palm with a bank-note, then, gallery or no gallery, I would have had a fine seat in this marble-buttressed, stained-glassed, spic-and-span new temple.

"Well, here I am in the porch, very politely bowed out of the nave. I suppose I'm excommunicated; excluded, anyway.—That's a noble string of flashing carriages drawn up along the curb; those champing horses too have a haughty curve to their foam-flaked necks. Property of those 'miserable sinners' inside, I presume. I dont a bit wonder they unreservedly confess to such misery as *that.*—See the gold hat-bands too, and other gorgeous trimmings, on those glossy groups of low-voiced gossippers near by. If I were in England now, I should think those chaps a company of royal dukes, right honorable barons &c. As it is, though, I guess they are only lackeys.—By the way, here I dodge about, as if I wanted to get into their aristocratic circle. In fact, it looks a sort of lackeyish to be idly standing outside a fine temple, cooling your heels, during service.—I had best move back to the Battery again, peeping into my prayer-book as I go.—But hold; dont I see a small door? Just in there, to one side, if I dont mistake, is a very low and very narrow vaulted door. None seem to go that way. Ten to one, that identical door leads up into the tower. And now that I think of it, there is usually in these splendid, new-fashioned Gothic Temples, a curious little window high over the orchestra and everything else, away up among the gilded clouds of the ceiling's frescoes; and that little window, seems to me, if one could but get there, ought to command a glorious bird's-eye view of the entire field of operations below.—I guess I'll try it. No one in the porch now. The beadle faced man is smoothing down some ladies' cushions, far up the broad aisle, I dare say. Softly now. If the small door ain't locked, I shall have stolen a march upon the beadle-faced man, and secured a humble seat in the sanctuary, in spite of him. — Good! Thanks for this! The door is not locked. Bell-ringer forgot to lock it, no doubt. Now, like any felt-footed grimalkin, up I steal among the leads."

Ascending some fifty stone steps along a very narrow curving stairway, I found myself on a blank platform forming the second story of the huge square tower.

I seemed inside some magic-lantern. On three sides, three gigantic Gothic windows of richly dyed glass, filled the otherwise meagre place with all sorts of sun-rises and sun-sets, lunar and solar rainbows, falling stars, and other flaming fire-works and pyrotechnics. But after all, it was but a gorgeous dungeon; for I could n't look out, any more than if I had been the occupant of a basement cell in "the Tombs." With some pains, and care not to do any serious harm, I contrived to scratch a minute opening in a great purple star forming the center of the chief compartment of the middle window; when peeping through, as through goggles, I ducked my head in dismay. The beadle-faced man, with no hat on his head, was just in act of driving three ragged little boys into the middle of the street; and how could I help trembling at the apprehension of his discovering a rebellious caitiff like me peering down on him from the tower? For in stealing up here, I had set at nought his high authority. He whom he thought effectually ejected, had burglariously returned. For a moment I was almost ready to bide my chance, and get to the side walk again with all dispatch. But another Jacob's ladder of lofty steps,—wooden ones, this time—allured me to another and still higher flight,—in sole hopes of gaining that one secret window where I might, at distance, take part in the proceedings.

Presently I noticed something which owing to the first marvellous effulgence of the place, had remained unseen till now. Two strong ropes, dropping through holes in the rude ceiling high overhead, fell a sheer length of sixty feet, right through the center of the space, and dropped in coils upon the floor of the huge magic-lantern. Bell-ropes these, thought I, and quaked. For if the beadle-faced man should learn that a grimalkin was somewhere prowling about the edifice, how easy for him to ring the alarm. Hark!—ah, that's only the organ—yes—it's the "Venite, exultemus Domine". Though an insider in one respect, yet am I but an outsider in another. But for all that, I will not be defrauded of my natural rights. Uncovering my head, and taking out my book, I stood erect, midway up the tall Jacob's ladder, as if standing among the congregation; and in spirit, if not in place, participated in those devout exultings. That over, I continued my upward path; and after crossing sundry minor platforms and irregular landings, all the while on a general ascent, at last I was delighted by catching sight of a small round window in the otherwise dead-wall side of the tower, where the tower attached itself to the main building. In front of the window was a rude narrow gallery, used as a bridge to cross from the lower stairs on one side to the upper stairs on the opposite.

As I drew nigh the spot, I well knew from the added clearness with which the sound of worship came to me, that the window did indeed look down upon the entire interior. But I was hardly prepared to find that no pane of glass, stained or unstained, was to stand between me and the far-under aisles and altar. For the purpose of ventilation, doubtless, the opening had been left unsupplied with sash of any sort. But a sheet of fine-woven, gauzy wire-work was in place of that. When, all eagerness, and open book in hand, I first advanced to stand before the window, I involuntarily shrank, as from before the mouth of a furnace, upon suddenly feeling a forceful puff of strange, heated air, blown, as by a blacksmith's bellows, full into my face and lungs. Yes, thought I, this window is doubtless for ventilation. Nor is it quite so comfortable as I fancied it might be. But beggars must not be choosers. The furnace which makes the people below there feel so snug and cosy in their padded pews, is to me, who stand here upon the naked gallery, cause of grievous trouble. Besides, though my face is scorched, my back is frozen. But I wont complain.

Thanks for this much, any way,—that by hollowing one hand to my ear, and standing a little sideways out of the more violent rush of the torrid current, I can at least hear the priest sufficiently to make my responses in the proper place. Little dream the good congregation away down there, that they have a faithful clerk away up here. Here too is a fitter place for sincere devotions, where, though I see, I remain unseen. Depend upon it, no Pharisee would have my pew. I like it, and admire it too, because it is so very high. Height, somehow, hath devotion in it. The archangelic anthems are raised in a lofty place. All the good shall go to such an one. Yes, Heaven is high.

As thus I mused, the glorious organ burst, like an earthquake, almost beneath my feet; and I heard the invoking cry—"Govern them and *lift* them up forever!" Then down I gazed upon the standing human mass, far, far below, whose heads, gleaming in the many-colored window-stains, showed like beds of spangled pebbles flashing in a Cuban sun. So at least, I knew they needs would look, if but the wire-woven screen were drawn aside. That wire-woven screen had the effect of casting crape upon all I saw. Only by making allowances for the crape, could I gain a right idea of the scene disclosed.

Surprising, most surprising, too, it was. As said before, the window was a circular one; the part of the tower where I stood was dusky-dark; its height above the congregation-floor could not have been less than ninety or a hundred feet; the whole interior temple was lit by nought but glass dimmed, yet glorified with all imaginable rich and russet hues; the approach to my strange look-out, through perfect solitude, and along rude and dusty ways, enhanced the theatric wonder of the populous spectacle of this sumptuous sanctuary. Book in hand, responses on my tongue, standing in the very posture of devotion, I could not rid my soul of the intrusive thought, that, through some necromancer's glass, I looked down upon some sly enchanter's show.

At length the lessons being read, the chants chanted, the white-robed priest, a noble looking man, with a form like the incomparable Talma's, gave out from the reading-desk the hymn before the sermon, and then through a side door vanished from the scene. In good time I saw the same Talma-like and noble-looking man re-appear through the same side door, his white apparel wholly changed for black.

By the melodious tone and persuasive gesture of the speaker, and the all-approving attention of the throng, I knew the sermon must be eloquent, and well adapted to an opulent auditory; but owing to the priest's changed position from the reading-desk, to the pulpit, I could not so distinctly hear him now as in the previous rites. The text however,— repeated at the outset, and often after quoted,—I could not but plainly catch:—"Ye are the salt of the earth."

At length the benediction was pronounced over the mass of low-inclining foreheads; hushed silence, intense motionlessness followed for a moment, as if the congregation were one of buried, not of living men; when, suddenly, miraculously, like the general rising at the Resurrection, the whole host came to their feet, amid a simultaneous roll, like a great drum-beat from the enrapturing, overpowering organ. Then, in three freshets,—all gay sprightly nods and becks—the gilded brooks poured down the gilded aisles.

Time for me too to go, thought I, as snatching one last look upon the imposing scene, I clasped my book and put it in my pocket. The best thing I can do just now, is to slide out unperceived amid the general crowd. Hurrying down the great length of ladder, I soon found myself at the base of the last stone step of the final flight; but started aghast—the door was locked! The bell-ringer, or more probably that forever-prying suspicious-looking beadle-faced man has done this. He would not let me in at all at first, and now, with the greatest inconsistency, he will not let me out. But what is to be done? Shall I knock on the door? That will never do. It will only frighten the crowd streaming by, and no one can adequately respond to my summons, except the beadle-faced man; and if he see me, he will recognise me, and perhaps roundly rate me—poor, humble worshiper— before the entire public. No, I wont knock. But what then?

Long time I thought, and thought, till at last all was hushed again. Presently a clicking sound admonished me that the church was being closed. In sudden desperation, I gave a rap on the door. But too late. It was not heard. I was left alone and solitary in a temple which but a moment before was more populous than many villages.

A strange trepidation of gloom and loneliness gradually stole over me. Hardly conscious of what I did, I reascended the stone steps; higher and higher still, and only paused, when once more I felt the hot-air blast from the wire-woven screen. Snatching another peep down into the vast arena, I started at its hushed desertness. The long ranges of grouped columns down the nave, and clusterings of them into copses about the corners of the transept; together with the subdued, dim-streaming light from the autumnal glasses; all assumed a secluded and deep-wooded air. I seemed gazing from Pisgah into the forests of old Canaan. A Puseyitish painting of a Madonna and child, adorning a lower window, seemed showing to me the sole tenants of this painted wilderness—the true Hagar and her Ishmael.—

With added trepidation I stole softly back to the magic-lantern platform; and revived myself a little by peeping through the scratch, upon the unstained light of open day.—But what is to be done, thought I, again.

I descended to the door; listened there; heard nothing. A third time climbing the stone steps, once more I stood in the magic-lantern, while the full nature of the more than awkwardness of my position came over me.

The first persons who will reënter the temple, mused I, will doubtless be the beadle-faced man, and the bell-ringer. And the first man to come up here, where I am, will be the latter. Now what will be his natural impressions upon first descrying an unknown prowler here? Rather disadvantageous to said prowler's moral character. Explanations will be vain. Circumstances are against me. True, I may hide, till he retires again. But how do I know, that he will then leave the door unlocked? Besides, in a position of affairs like this, it is generally best, I think, to anticipate discovery, and by magnanimously announcing yourself, forestall an inglorious detection. But how announce myself? Already have I knocked, and no response. That moment, my eye, impatiently ranging roundabout, fell upon the bell-ropes. They suggested the usual signal made at dwelling-houses to convey tidings of a stranger's presence. But I was not an outside caller; alas, I was an inside prowler.—But one little touch of that bell-rope, would be sure to bring relief. I have an appointment at three o'clock. The beadle-faced man must naturally reside very close by the church. He well knows the peculiar ring of his own bell. The slightest possible hum would bring him flying to the rescue. Shall I, or shall I not?—But I may alarm the neighborhood. Oh no; the merest tingle, not by any means a loud vociferous peal. Shall I? Better voluntarily bring the beadle-faced man to me, than be involuntarily dragged out from this most suspicious hiding-place. I have to face him, first or last. Better now than later.—Shall I?—

No more. Creeping to the rope, I gave it a cautious twitch. No sound. A little less warily. All was dumb. Still more strongly. Horrors! my hands, instinctively clapped to my ears, only served to condense the appalling din. Some undreamed-of mechanism seemed to have been touched. The bell must have thrice revolved on its thunderous axis, multiplying the astounding reverberation.

My business is effectually done, this time, thought I, all in a tremble. Nothing will serve me now but the reckless confidence of innocence reduced to desperation.

In less than five minutes, I heard a running noise beneath me; the lock of the door clicked, and up rushed the beadle-faced man, the perspiration starting from his cheeks.

"You! Is it *you?* The man I turned away this very morning, skulking here? *You* dare to touch that bell? Scoundrel!"

And ere I could defend myself, seizing me irresistably in his powerful grasp, he tore me along by the collar, and dragging me down the stairs, thrust me into the arms of three policemen, who, attracted by the sudden toll of the bell, had gathered curiously about the porch.

All remonstrances were vain. The beadle-faced man was bigoted against me. Represented as a lawless violator, and a remorseless disturber of the Sunday peace, I was conducted to the Halls of Justice. Next morning, my rather gentlemany appearance procured me a private hearing from the judge. But the beadle-faced man must have made a Sunday night call on him. Spite of my coolest explanations, the circumstances of the case were deemed so exceedingly suspicious, that only after paying a round fine, and receiving a stinging reprimand, was I permitted to go at large, and pardoned for having humbly indulged myself in the luxury of public worship.

TEMPLE SECOND

A stranger in London on Saturday night, and without a copper! What hospitalities may such an one expect? What shall I do with myself this weary night? My landlady wont receive me in her parlor. I owe her money. She looks like flint on me. So in this monstrous rabblement must I crawl about till, say ten o'clock, and then slink home to my unlighted bed.

The case was this: The week following my inglorious expulsion from the transatlantic temple, I had packed up my trunks and damaged character, and repaired to the fraternal, loving town of Philadelphia. There chance threw into my way an interesting young orphan lady and her aunt-duenna; the lady rich as Cleopatra, but not as beautiful; the duenna lovely as Charmian, but not so young. For the lady's health, prolonged travel had been prescribed. Maternally connected in old England, the lady chose London for her primal port. But ere securing their passage, the two were looking round for some young physician, whose disengagement from pressing business, might induce him to accept, on a moderate salary, the post of private Esculapius and knightly companion to the otherwise unprotected fair. The more necessary was this, as not only the voyage to England was intended, but an extensive European tour, to follow.

Enough. I came; I saw; I was made the happy man. We sailed. We landed on the other side; when after two weeks of agonized attendance on the vacillations of the lady, I was very cavalierly dismissed, on the score, that the lady's maternal relations had persuaded her to try, through the winter, the salubrious climate of the foggy Isle of Wight, in preference to the fabulous blue atmosphere of the Ionian Isles. So much for national prejudice.

Nota Bene.—The lady was in a sad decline.—

Having ere sailing been obliged to anticipate nearly a quarter's pay to foot my outfit bills, I was dismally cut adrift in Fleet Street without a solitary shilling. By disposing, at certain pawnbrokers, of some of my less indispensable apparel, I had managed to stave off the more slaughterous onsets of my landlady, while diligently looking about for any business that might providentially appear.

So on I drifted amid those indescribable crowds which every seventh night pour and roar through each main artery and block the bye-veins of great London, the Leviathan. Saturday Night it was; and the markets and the shops, and every stall and counter were crushed with the one unceasing tide. A whole Sunday's victualling for three millions of human bodies, was going on. Few of them equally hungry with my own, as through my spent lassitude, the unscrupulous human whirlpools eddied me aside at corners, as any straw is eddied in the Norway Maelstrom. What dire suckings into oblivion must such swirling billows know. Better perish mid myriad sharks in mid Atlantic, than die a penniless stranger in Babylonian London. Forlorn, outcast, without a friend, I staggered on through three millions of my own human kind. The fiendish gas-lights shooting their Tartarean rays across the muddy sticky streets, lit up the pitiless and pitiable scene.

Well, well, if this were but Sunday now, I might conciliate some kind female pew-opener, and rest me in some inn-like chapel, upon some stranger's outside bench. But it is Saturday night. The end of the weary week, and all but the end of weary me.

Disentangling myself at last from those skeins of Pandemonian lanes which snarl one part of the metropolis between Fleet street and Holborn, I found myself at last in a wide and far less noisy street, a short and shopless one, leading up from the Strand, and terminating at its junction with a crosswise avenue. The comparative quietude of the place was inexpressively soothing. It was like emerging upon the green enclosure surrounding some Cathedral church, where sanctity makes all things still. Two lofty brilliant lights attracted me in this tranquil street. Thinking it might prove some moral or religious meeting, I hurried towards the spot; but was surprised to see two tall placards announcing the appearance that night, of the stately Macready in the part of Cardinal Richelieu. Very few loiterers hung about the place, the hour being rather late, and the playbill hawkers mostly departed, or keeping entirely quiet. This theatre indeed, as I afterwards discovered, was not only one of the best in point of acting, but likewise one of the most decorous in its general management, inside and out. In truth the whole neighborhood, as it seemed to me— issuing from the jam and uproar of those turbulent tides against which, or borne on irresistibly by which, I had so long been swimming—the whole neighborhood, I say, of this pleasing street seemed in good keeping with the character imputed to its theatre.

Glad to find one blessed oasis of tranquility, I stood leaning against a column of the porch, and striving to lose my sadness in running over one of the huge placards. No one molested me. A tattered little girl, to be sure, approached, with a hand-bill extended, but marking me more narrowly, retreated; her strange skill in physiognomy at once enabling her to determine that I was penniless. As I read, and read—for the placard, of enormous dimensions, contained minute particulars of each successive scene in the enacted play—gradually a strong desire to witness this celebrated Macready in this his celebrated part stole over me. By one act, I might rest my jaded limbs, and more than jaded spirits. Where else could I go for rest, unless I crawled into my cold and lonely bed far up in an attic of Craven Street, looking down upon the muddy Phlegethon of the Thames. Besides, what I wanted was not merely rest, but cheer; the making one of many pleased and pleasing human faces; the getting into a genial humane assembly of my kind; such as, at its best and highest, is to be found in the unified multitude of a devout congregation. But no such assemblies were accessible that night, even if my unbefriended and rather shabby air would overcome the scruples of those fastidious gentry with red gowns and long gilded staves, who guard the portals of the first-class London tabernacles from all profanation of a poor forlorn and fainting wanderer like me. Not inns, but ecclesiastical hotels, where the pews are the rented chambers.

No use to ponder, thought I, at last; it is Saturday night, not Sunday; and so, a Theatre only can receive me. So powerfully in the end did the longing to get into the edifice come over me, that I almost began to think of pawning my overcoat for admittance. But from this last infatuation I was providentially with-held by a sudden cheery summons, in a voice un mistakably benevolent. I turned, and saw a man who seemed to be some sort of a working-man.

"Take it," said he, holding a plain red ticket towards me, full in the gas-light. "You want to go in; I know you do. Take it. I am suddenly called home. There—hope you'll enjoy yourself. Good-bye."

Blankly, and mechanically, I had suffered the ticket to be thrust into my hand, and now stood quite astonished, bewildered, and for the time, ashamed. The plain fact was, I had received charity; and for the first time in my life. Often in the course of my strange wanderings I had needed charity, but never had asked it, and certainly never, ere this blessed night, had been offered it. And a stranger; and in the very maw of the roaring London too! Next moment my sense of foolish shame departed, and I felt a queer feeling in my left eye, which, as sometimes is the case with people, was the weaker one; probably from being on the same side with the heart.

I glanced round eagerly. But the kind giver was no longer in sight. I looked upon the ticket. I understood. It was one of those checks given to persons inside a theatre when for any cause they desire to step out a moment. Its presentation ensures unquestioned readmittance.

Shall I use it? mused I.—What? It's charity.—But if it be gloriously right to do a charitable deed, can it be ingloriously wrong to receive its benefit?—No one knows you; go boldly in.—Charity.—Why these un-vanquishable scruples? All your life, nought but charity sustains you, and all others in the world. Maternal charity nursed you as a babe; paternal charity fed you as a child; friendly charity got you your profession; and to the charity of every man you meet this night in London, are you indebted for your unattempted life. Any knife, any hand of all the millions of knives and hands in London, has you this night at its mercy. You, and all mortals, live but by sufferance of your charitable kind; charitable by omission, not performance.—Stush for your self-upbraidings, and pitiful, poor, shabby pride, you friendless man without a purse.—Go in.

Debate was over. Marking the direction from which the stranger had accosted me, I stepped that way; and soon saw a low-vaulted, inferior-looking door on one side of the edifice. Entering, I wandered on and up, and up and on again, through various doubling stairs and wedge-like, ill-lit passages, whose bare boards much reminded me of my ascent of the Gothic tower on the ocean's far other side. At last I gained a lofty platform, and saw a fixed human countenance facing me from a mysterious window of a sort of sentry-box or closet. Like some saint in a shrine, the countenance was illuminated by two smoky candles. I divined the man. I exhibited my diploma, and he nodded me to a little door beyond; while a sudden burst of orchestral music, admonished me I was now very near my destination, and also revived the memory of the organ-anthems I had heard while on the ladder of the tower at home.

Next moment, the wire-woven gauzy screen of the ventilating window in that same tower, seemed enchantedly reproduced before me. The same hot blast of stifling air once more rushed into my lungs. From the same dizzy altitude, through the same fine-spun, vapory crapey air; far, far down upon just such a packed mass of silent human beings; listening to just such grand harmonies; I stood within the topmost gallery of the temple. But hardly alone and silently as before. This time I had company. Not of the first circles, and certainly not of the dress-circle; but most acceptable, right welcome, cheery company, to otherwise uncompanioned me. Quiet, well-pleased working men, and their glad wives and sisters, with here and there an aproned urchin, with all-absorbed, bright face, vermillioned by the excitement and the heated air, hovering like a painted cherub over the vast human firmament below. The height of the gallery was in truth appalling. The rail was low. I thought of deep-sea-leads, and the mariner in the vessel's chains, drawing up the line, with his long-drawn musical accompaniment. And like beds of glittering coral, through the deep sea of azure smoke, there, far down, I saw the jewelled necks and white sparkling arms of crowds of ladies in the semicirque. But, in the interval of two acts, again the orchestra was heard; some inspiring national anthem now was played. As the volumed sound came undulating up, and broke in showery spray and foam of melody against our gallery rail, my head involuntarily was bowed, my hand instinctively sought my pocket. Only by a second thought, did I check my momentary lunacy and remind myself that this time I had no small morocco book with me, and that this was not the house of prayer.

Quickly was my wandering mind—preternaturally affected by the sudden translation from the desolate street, to this bewildering and blazing spectacle—arrested in its wanderings, by feeling at my elbow a meaning nudge; when turning suddenly, I saw a sort of coffee-pot, and pewter mug hospitably presented to me by a ragged, but good-natured looking boy.

"Thank you", said I, "I wont take any coffee, I guess."

"Coffee?—I guess?—Aint you a Yankee?"

"Aye, boy; true blue."

"Well dad's gone to Yankee-land, a seekin' of his fortin'; so take a penny mug of ale, do Yankee, for poor dad's sake."

Out from the tilted coffee-pot-looking can, came a coffee-colored stream, and a small mug of humming ale was in my hand.

"I dont want it, boy. The fact is, my boy, I have no penny by me. I happened to leave my purse at my lodgings."

"Never do you mind, Yankee; drink to honest dad."

"With all my heart, you generous boy; here's immortal life to him!"

He stared at my strange burst, smiled merrily, and left me, offering his coffee-pot in all directions, and not in vain.

'Tis not always poverty to be poor, mused I; one may fare well without a penny. A ragged boy may be a prince-like benefactor.

Because that unpurchased penny-worth of ale revived my drooping spirits strangely. Stuff was in that barley-malt; a most sweet bitterness in those blessed hops. God bless the glorious boy!

The more I looked about me in this lofty gallery, the more was I delighted with its occupants. It was not spacious. It was, if anything, rather contracted, being the very cheapest portion of the house, where very limited attendance was expected; embracing merely the very crown of the topmost semicircle; and so, commanding, with a sovereign outlook, and imperial downlook, the whole theatre, with the expanded stage directly opposite, though some hundred feet below. As at the tower, peeping into the transatlantic temple, so stood I here, at the very main-mast-head of all the interior edifice.

Such was the decorum of this special theatre, that nothing objectionable was admitted within its walls. With an unhurt eye of perfect love, I sat serenely in the gallery, gazing upon the pleasing scene, around me and below. Neither did it abate from my satisfaction, to remember, that Mr Macready, the chief actor of the night, was an amiable gentleman, combining the finest qualities of social and Christian respectability, with the highest excellence in his particular profession; for which last he had conscientiously done much, in many ways, to refine, elevate, and chasten.

But now the curtain rises, and the robed Cardinal advances. How marvellous this personal resemblance! He looks every inch to be the self-same, stately priest I saw irradiated by the glow-worm dies of the pictured windows from my high tower-pew. And shining as he does, in the rosy reflexes of these stained walls and gorgeous galleries, the mimic priest down there; he too seems lit by Gothic blazonings.—Hark! The same measured, courtly, noble tone. See! the same imposing attitude. Excellent actor is this Richelieu!

He disappears behind the scenes. He slips, no doubt, into the Green Room. He reappears somewhat changed in his habilaments. Do I dream, or is it genuine memory that recalls some similar thing seen through the woven wires?

The curtain falls. Starting to their feet, the enraptured thousands sound their responses, deafeningly; unmistakably sincere. Right from the undoubted heart. I have no duplicate in my memory of this. In earnestness of response, this second temple stands unmatched. And hath mere mimicry done this? What is it then to act a part?

But now the music surges up again, and borne by that rolling billow, I, and all the gladdened crowd, are harmoniously attended to the street.

I went home to my lonely lodging, and slept not much that night, for thinking of the First Temple and the Second Temple; and how that, a stranger in a strange land, I found sterling charity in the one; and at home, in my own land, was thrust out from the other.

1856

The Paradise of Bachelors and the Tartarus of Maids

I. The Paradise of Bachelors

It lies not far from Temple-Bar.

Going to it, by the usual way, is like stealing from a heated plain into some cool, deep glen, shady among harboring hills.

Sick with the din and soiled with the mud of Fleet Street—where the Benedick tradesmen are hurrying by, with ledger-lines ruled along their brows, thinking upon rise of bread and fall of babies— you adroitly turn a mystic corner—not a street—glide down a dim, monastic way, flanked by dark, sedate, and solemn piles, and still wending on, give the whole care-worn world the slip, and, disentangled, stand beneath the quiet cloisters of the Paradise of Bachelors.

Sweet are the oases in Sahara; charming the isle-groves of August prairies; delectable pure faith amidst a thousand perfidies: but sweeter, still more charming, most delectable, the dreamy Paradise of Bachelors, found in the stony heart of stunning London.

In mild meditation pace the cloisters; take your pleasure, sip your leisure, in the garden waterward; go linger in the ancient library; go worship in the sculptured chapel: but little have you seen, just nothing do you know, not the sweet kernel have you tasted, till you dine among the banded Bachelors, and see their convivial eyes and glasses sparkle. Not dine in bustling commons, during term-time, in the hall; but tranquilly, by private hint, at a private table; some fine Templar's hospitably invited guest.

Templar? That's a romantic name. Let me see. Brian de Bois Guilbert was a Templar, I believe. Do we understand you to insinuate that those famous Templars still survive in modern London? May the ring of their armed heels be heard, and the rattle of their shields, as in mailed prayer the monk-knights kneel before the consecrated Host? Surely a monk-knight were a curious sight picking his way along the Strand, his gleaming corselet and snowy surcoat spattered by an omnibus. Long-bearded, too, according to his order's rule; his face fuzzy as a pard's; how would the grim ghost look among the crop-haired, close-shaven citizens? We know indeed—sad history recounts it—that a moral blight tainted at last this sacred Brotherhood. Though no sworded foe might outskill them in the fence, yet the worm of luxury crawled beneath their guard, gnawing the core of knightly troth, nibbling the monastic vow, till at last the monk's austerity relaxed to wassailing, and the sworn knights-bachelors grew to be but hypocrites and rakes.

But for all this, quite unprepared were we to learn that Knights-Templars (if at all in being) were so entirely secularized as to be reduced from carving out immortal fame in glorious battling for the Holy Land, to the carving of roast-mutton at a dinner-board. Like Anacreon, do these degenerate Templars now think it sweeter far to fall in banquet than in war? Or, indeed, how can there be any survival of that famous order? Templars in modern London! Templars in their red-cross mantles smoking cigars at the Divan! Templars crowded in a railway train, till, stacked with steel helmet, spear, and shield, the whole train looks like one elongated locomotive!

No. The genuine Templar is long since departed. Go view the wondrous tombs in the Temple Church; see there the rigidly-haughty forms stretched out, with crossed arms upon their stilly hearts, in everlasting and undreaming rest. Like the years before the flood, the bold Knights-Templars are no more. Nevertheless, the name remains, and the nominal society, and the ancient grounds, and some of the ancient edifices. But the iron heel is changed to a boot of patent-leather; the long two-handed sword to a one-handed quill; the monk-giver of gratuitous ghostly counsel now counsels for a fee; the defender of the sarcophagus (if in good practice with his weapon) now has more than one case to defend; the vowed opener and clearer of all highways leading to the Holy Sepulchre, now has it in particular charge to check, to clog, to hinder, and embarrass all the courts and avenues of Law; the knight-combatant of the Saracen, breasting spear-points at Acre, now fights law-points in Westminster Hall. The helmet is a wig. Struck by Time's enchanter's wand, the Templar is to-day a Lawyer.

But, like many others tumbled from proud glory's height—like the apple, hard on the bough but mellow on the ground—the Templar's fall has but made him all the finer fellow.

I dare say those old warrior-priests were but gruff and grouty at the best; cased in Birmingham hardware, how could their crimped arms give yours or mine a hearty shake? Their proud, ambitious, monkish souls clasped shut, like horn-book missals; their very faces clapped in bomb-shells; what sort of genial men were these? But best of comrades, most affable of hosts, capital diner is the modern Templar. His wit and wine are both of sparkling brands.

The church and cloisters, courts and vaults, lanes and passages, banquet-halls, refectories, libraries, terraces, gardens, broad walks, domicils, and dessert-rooms, covering a very large space of ground, and all grouped in central neighborhood, and quite sequestered from the old city's surrounding din; and every thing about the place being kept in most bachelor-like particularity, no part of London offers to a quiet wight so agreeable a refuge.

The Temple is, indeed, a city by itself. A city with all the best appurtenances, as the above enumeration shows. A city with a park to it, and flower-beds, and a river-side—the Thames flowing by as openly, in one part, as by Eden's primal garden flowed the mild Euphrates. In what is now the Temple Garden the old Crusaders used to exercise their steeds and lances; the modern Templars now lounge on the benches beneath the trees, and, switching their patent-leather boots, in gay discourse exercise at repartee.

Long lines of stately portraits in the banquet-halls, show what great men of mark—famous nobles, judges, and Lord Chancellors—have in their time been Templars. But all Templars are not known to universal fame; though, if the having warm hearts and warmer welcomes, full minds and fuller cellars, and giving good advice and glorious dinners, spiced with rare divertisements of fun and fancy, merit immortal mention, set down, ye muses, the names of R. F. C. and his imperial brother.

Though to be a Templar, in the one true sense, you must needs be a lawyer, or a student at the law, and be ceremoniously enrolled as member of the order, yet as many such, though Templars, do not reside within the

Temple's precincts, though they may have their offices there, just so, on the other hand, there are many residents of the hoary old domicils who are not admitted Templars. If being, say, a lounging gentleman and bachelor, or a quiet, unmarried, literary man, charmed with the soft seclusion of the spot, you much desire to pitch your shady tent among the rest in this serene encampment, then you must make some special friend among the order, and procure him to rent, in his name but at your charge, whatever vacant chamber you may find to suit.

Thus, I suppose, did Dr. Johnson, that nominal Benedick and widower but virtual bachelor, when for a space he resided here. So, too, did that undoubted bachelor and rare good soul, Charles Lamb. And hundreds more, of sterling spirits, Brethren of the Order of Celibacy, from time to time have dined, and slept, and tabernacled here. Indeed, the place is all a honeycomb of offices and domicils. Like any cheese, it is quite perforated through and through in all directions with the snug cells of bachelors. Dear, delightful spot! Ah! when I bethink me of the sweet hours there passed, enjoying such genial hospitalities beneath those time-honored roofs, my heart only finds due utterance through poetry; and, with a sigh, I softly sing, "Carry me back to old Virginny!"

Such then, at large, is the Paradise of Bachelors. And such I found it one pleasant afternoon in the smiling month of May, when, sallying from my hotel in Trafalgar Square, I went to keep my dinner-appointment with that fine Barrister, Bachelor, and Bencher, R. F. C. (he *is* the first and second, and *should be* the third; I hereby nominate him), whose card I kept fast pinched between my gloved forefinger and thumb, and every now and then snatched still another look at the pleasant address inscribed beneath the name, "No. —, Elm Court, Temple."

At the core he was a right bluff, care-free, right comfortable, and most companionable Englishman. If on a first acquaintance he seemed reserved, quite icy in his air—patience; this Champagne will thaw. And if it never do, better frozen Champagne than liquid vinegar.

There were nine gentlemen, all bachelors, at the dinner. One was from "No. —, King's Bench Walk, Temple;" a second, third, and fourth, and fifth, from various courts or passages christened with some similarly rich resounding syllables. It was indeed a sort of Senate of the Bachelors, sent to this dinner from widely-scattered districts, to represent the general celibacy of the Temple. Nay it was, by representation, a Grand Parliament of the best Bachelors in universal London; several of those present being from distant quarters of the town, noted immemorial seats of lawyers and unmarried men—Lincoln's Inn, Furnival's Inn; and one gentleman, upon whom I looked with a sort of collateral awe, hailed from the spot where Lord Verulam once abode a bachelor—Gray's Inn.

The apartment was well up toward heaven. I know not how many strange old stairs I climbed to get to it. But a good dinner, with famous company, should be well earned. No doubt our host had his dining-room so high with a view to secure the prior exercise necessary to the due relishing and digesting of it.

The furniture was wonderfully unpretending, old, and snug. No new shining mahogany, sticky with undried varnish; no uncomfortably luxurious ottomans, and sofas too fine to use, vexed you in this sedate apartment. It is a thing which every sensible American should learn from every sensible Englishman, that glare and glitter, gimcracks and gewgaws, are not indispensable to domestic solacement. The American Benedick snatches, down-town, a tough chop in a gilded show-box; the English bachelor leisurely dines at home on that incomparable South Down of his, off a plain deal board.

The ceiling of the room was low. Who wants to dine under the dome of St. Peter's? High ceilings! If that is your demand, and the higher the better, and you be so very tall, then go dine out with the topping giraffe in the open air.

In good time the nine gentlemen sat down to nine covers, and soon were fairly under way.

If I remember right, ox-tail soup inaugurated the affair. Of a rich russet hue, its agreeable flavor dissipated my first confounding of its main ingredient with teamster's gads and the raw-hides of ushers. (By way of interlude, we here drank a little claret.) Neptune's was the next tribute rendered—turbot coming second; snow-white, flaky, and just gelatinous enough, not too turtleish in its unctuousness.

(At this point we refreshed ourselves with a glass of sherry.) After these light skirmishers had vanished, the heavy artillery of the feast marched in, led by that well-known English generalissimo, roast beef. For aids-de-camp we had a saddle of mutton, a fat turkey, a chicken-pie, and endless other savory things; while for avant-couriers came nine silver flagons of humming ale. This heavy ordnance having departed on the track of the light skirmishers, a picked brigade of game-fowl encamped upon the board, their camp-fires lit by the ruddiest of decanters.

Tarts and puddings followed, with innumerable niceties; then cheese and crackers. (By way of ceremony, simply, only to keep up good old fashions, we here each drank a glass of good old port.)

The cloth was now removed; and like Blucher's army coming in at the death on the field of Waterloo, in marched a fresh detachment of bottles, dusty with their hurried march.

All these manœuvrings of the forces were superintended by a surprising old field-marshal (I can not school myself to call him by the inglorious name of waiter), with snowy hair and napkin, and a head like Socrates. Amidst all the hilarity of the feast, intent on important business, he disdained to smile. Venerable man!

I have above endeavored to give some slight schedule of the general plan of operations. But any one knows that a good, genial dinner is a sort of pell-mell, indiscriminate affair, quite baffling to detail in all particulars. Thus, I spoke of taking a glass of claret, and a glass of sherry, and a glass of port, and a mug of ale—all at certain specific periods and times. But those were merely the state bumpers, so to speak. Innumerable impromptu glasses were drained between the periods of those grand imposing ones.

The nine bachelors seemed to have the most tender concern for each other's health. All the time, in flowing wine, they most earnestly expressed their sincerest wishes for the entire well-being and lasting hygiene of the gentlemen on the right and on the left. I noticed that when one of these kind bachelors desired a little more wine (just for his stomach's sake, like Timothy), he would not help himself to it unless some other bachelor would join him. It seemed held something indelicate, selfish, and unfraternal, to be seen taking a lonely, unparticipated glass. Meantime, as the wine ran apace, the spirits of the company grew more and more to perfect genialness and unconstraint. They related all sorts of pleasant stories. Choice experiences in their private lives were now brought out, like choice brands of Moselle or Rhenish, only kept for particular company. One told us how mellowly he lived when a student at Oxford; with various spicy anecdotes of most frank-hearted noble lords, his liberal companions. Another bachelor, a gray-headed man, with a sunny face, who, by his own account, embraced every opportunity of leisure to cross over into the Low Countries, on sudden tours of inspection of the fine old Flemish architecture there—this learned, white-haired, sunny-faced old bachelor, excelled in his descriptions of the elaborate splendors of those old guild-halls, town-halls, and stadthold-houses, to be seen in the land of the ancient Flemings. A third was a great frequenter of the British Museum, and knew all about scores of wonderful antiquities, of Oriental manuscripts, and costly books without a duplicate. A fourth had lately returned from a trip to Old Granada, and, of course, was full of Saracenic scenery. A fifth had a funny case in law to tell. A sixth was erudite in wines. A seventh had a strange characteristic anecdote of the private life of the Iron Duke, never printed, and never before announced in any public or private company. An eighth had lately been amusing his evenings, now and then, with translating a comic poem of Pulci's. He quoted for us the more amusing passages.

And so the evening slipped along, the hours told, not by a water-clock, like King Alfred's, but a wine-chronometer. Meantime the table seemed a sort of Epsom Heath; a regular ring, where the decanters galloped round. For fear one decanter should not with sufficient speed reach his destination, another was sent express after him to hurry him; and then a third to hurry the second; and so on with a fourth and fifth. And throughout all this nothing loud, nothing unmannerly, nothing turbulent. I am quite sure, from the scrupulous gravity and austerity of his air, that had Socrates, the field-marshal, perceived aught of indecorum in the company he served, he would have forthwith departed without giving warning. I afterward learned that, during the repast, an invalid bachelor in an adjoining chamber enjoyed his first sound refreshing slumber in three long, weary weeks.

It was the very perfection of quiet absorption of good living, good drinking, good feeling, and good talk. We were a band of brothers. Comfort—fraternal, household comfort, was the grand trait of the affair. Also, you could plainly see that these easy-hearted men had no wives or children to give an anxious thought. Almost all of them were travelers, too; for bachelors alone can travel freely, and without any twinges of their consciences touching desertion of the fire-side.

The thing called pain, the bugbear styled trouble—those two legends seemed preposterous to their bachelor imaginations. How could men of liberal sense, ripe scholarship in the world, and capacious philosophical and convivial understandings—how could they suffer themselves to be imposed upon by such monkish fables? Pain! Trouble! As well talk of

Catholic miracles. No such thing.—Pass the sherry, Sir.—Pooh, pooh! Can't be!—The port, Sir, if you please. Nonsense; don't tell me so.—The decanter stops with you, Sir, I believe.

And so it went.

Not long after the cloth was drawn our host glanced significantly upon Socrates, who, solemnly stepping to a stand, returned with an immense convolved horn, a regular Jericho horn, mounted with polished silver, and otherwise chased and curiously enriched; not omitting two life-like goat's heads, with four more horns of solid silver, projecting from opposite sides of the mouth of the noble main horn.

Not having heard that our host was a performer on the bugle, I was surprised to see him lift this horn from the table, as if he were about to blow an inspiring blast. But I was relieved from this, and set quite right as touching the purposes of the horn, by his now inserting his thumb and forefinger into its mouth; whereupon a slight aroma was stirred up, and my nostrils were greeted with the smell of some choice Rappee. It was a mull of snuff. It went the rounds. Capital idea this, thought I, of taking snuff about this juncture. This goodly fashion must be introduced among my countrymen at home, further ruminated I.

The remarkable decorum of the nine bachelors—a decorum not to be affected by any quantity of wine—a decorum unassailable by any degree of mirthfulness—this was again set in a forcible light to me, by now observing that, though they took snuff very freely, yet not a man so far violated the proprieties, or so far molested the invalid bachelor in the adjoining room as to indulge himself in a sneeze. The snuff was snuffed silently, as if it had been some fine innoxious powder brushed off the wings of butterflies.

But fine though they be, bachelors' dinners, like bachelors' lives, can not endure forever. The time came for breaking up. One by one the bachelors took their hats, and two by two, and arm-in-arm they descended, still conversing, to the flagging of the court; some going to their neighboring chambers to turn over the Decameron ere retiring for the night; some to smoke a cigar, promenading in the garden on the cool river-side; some to make for the street, call a hack, and be driven snugly to their distant lodgings.

I was the last lingerer.

"Well," said my smiling host, "what do you think of the Temple here, and the sort of life we bachelors make out to live in it?"

"Sir," said I, with a burst of admiring candor—"Sir, this is the very Paradise of Bachelors!"

II. THE TARTARUS OF MAIDS

It lies not far from Woedolor Mountain in New England. Turning to the east, right out from among bright farms and sunny meadows, nodding in early June with odorous grasses, you enter ascendingly among bleak hills. These gradually close in upon a dusky pass, which, from the violent Gulf Stream of air unceasingly driving between its cloven walls of haggard rock, as well as from the tradition of a crazy spinster's hut having long ago stood somewhere hereabouts, is called the Mad Maid's Bellows'-pipe.

Winding along at the bottom of the gorge is a dangerously narrow wheel-road, occupying the bed of a former torrent. Following this road to its highest point, you stand as within a Dantean gateway. From the steepness of the walls here, their strangely ebon hue, and the sudden contraction of the gorge, this particular point is called the Black Notch. The ravine now expandingly descends into a great, purple, hopper-shaped hollow, far sunk among many Plutonian, shaggy-wooded mountains. By the country people this hollow is called the Devil's Dungeon. Sounds of torrents fall on all sides upon the ear. These rapid waters unite at last in one turbid brick-colored stream, boiling through a flume among enormous boulders. They call this strange-colored torrent Blood River. Gaining a dark precipice it wheels suddenly to the west, and makes one maniac spring of sixty feet into the arms of a stunted wood of gray-haired pines, between which it thence eddies on its further way down to the invisible lowlands.

Conspicuously crowning a rocky bluff high to one side, at the cataract's verge, is the ruin of an old saw-mill, built in those primitive times when vast pines and hemlocks superabounded throughout the neighboring region. The black-mossed bulk of those immense, rough-hewn, and spike-knotted logs, here and there tumbled all together, in long abandonment and decay, or left in solitary, perilous projection over the cataract's gloomy brink, impart to this rude wooden ruin not only much of the aspect of one of rough-quarried stone, but also a sort of feudal, Rhineland, and Thurmberg look, derived from the pinnacled wildness of the neighboring scenery.

Not far from the bottom of the Dungeon stands a large white-washed building, relieved, like some great whited sepulchre, against the sullen background of mountain-side firs, and other hardy evergreens, inaccessibly rising in grim terraces for some two thousand feet.

The building is a paper-mill.

Having embarked on a large scale in the seedsman's business (so extensively and broadcast, indeed, that at length my seeds were distributed through all the Eastern and Northern States, and even fell into the far soil of Missouri and the Carolinas), the demand for paper at my place became so great, that the expenditure soon amounted to a most important item in the general account. It need hardly be hinted how paper comes into use with seedsmen, as envelopes. These are mostly made of yellowish paper, folded square; and when filled, are all but flat, and being stamped, and superscribed with the nature of the seeds contained, assume not a little the appearance of business-letters ready for the mail. Of these small envelopes I used an incredible quantity—several hundreds of thousands in a year. For a time I had purchased my paper from the wholesale dealers in a neighboring town. For economy's sake, and partly for the adventure of the trip, I now resolved to cross the mountains, some sixty miles, and order my future paper at the Devil's Dungeon paper-mill.

The sleighing being uncommonly fine toward the end of January, and promising to hold so for no small period, in spite of the bitter cold I started one gray Friday noon in my pung, well fitted with buffalo and wolf robes; and, spending one night on the road, next noon came in sight of Woedolor Mountain.

The far summit fairly smoked with frost; white vapors curled up from its white-wooded top, as from a chimney. The intense congelation made the whole country look like one petrifaction. The steel shoes of my pung craunched and gritted over the vitreous, chippy snow, as if it had been broken glass. The forests here and there skirting the route, feeling the same all-stiffening influence, their inmost fibres penetrated with the cold, strangely groaned—not in the swaying branches merely, but likewise in the vertical trunk—as the fitful gusts remorselessly swept through them. Brittle with excessive frost, many colossal tough-grained maples, snapped in twain like pipe-stems, cumbered the unfeeling earth.

Flaked all over with frozen sweat, white as a milky ram, his nostrils at each breath sending forth two horn-shaped shoots of heated respiration, Black, my good horse, but six years old, started at a sudden turn, where, right across the track—not ten minutes fallen—an old distorted hemlock lay, darkly undulatory as an anaconda.

Gaining the Bellows'-pipe, the violent blast, dead from behind, all but shoved my high-backed pung up-hill. The gust shrieked through the shivered pass, as if laden with lost spirits bound to the unhappy world. Ere gaining the summit, Black, my horse, as if exasperated by the cutting wind, slung out with his strong hind legs, tore the light pung straight up-hill, and sweeping grazingly through the narrow notch, sped downward madly past the ruined saw-mill. Into the Devil's Dungeon horse and cataract rushed together.

With might and main, quitting my seat and robes, and standing backward, with one foot braced against the dash-board, I rasped and churned the bit, and stopped him just in time to avoid collision, at a turn, with the bleak nozzle of a rock, couchant like a lion in the way—a road-side rock.

At first I could not discover the paper-mill.

The whole hollow gleamed with the white, except, here and there, where a pinnacle of granite showed one wind-swept angle bare. The mountains stood pinned in shrouds—a pass of Alpine corpses. Where stands the mill? Suddenly a whirling, humming sound broke upon my ear. I looked, and there, like an arrested avalanche, lay the large white-washed factory. It was subordinately surrounded by a cluster of other and smaller buildings, some of which, from their cheap, blank air, great length, gregarious windows, and comfortless expression, no doubt were boarding-houses of the operatives. A snow-white hamlet amidst the snows. Various rude, irregular squares and courts resulted from the somewhat picturesque clusterings of these buildings, owing to the broken, rocky nature of the ground, which forbade all method in their relative arrangement. Several narrow lanes and alleys, too, partly blocked with snow fallen from the roof, cut up the hamlet in all directions.

When, turning from the traveled highway, jingling with bells of numerous farmers—who, availing themselves of the fine sleighing, were dragging their wood to market—and frequently diversified with swift cutters dashing from inn to inn of the scattered villages—when, I say, turning from that bustling main-road, I by degrees wound into the Mad Maid's Bellows'-pipe, and saw the grim Black Notch beyond, then something latent, as well as something obvious in the time and scene, strangely brought back to my mind my first sight of dark and grimy Temple-Bar.

And when Black, my horse, went darting through the Notch, perilously grazing its rocky wall, I remembered being in a runaway London omnibus, which in much the same sort of style, though by no means at an equal rate, dashed through the ancient arch of Wren. Though the two objects did by no means completely correspond, yet this partial inadequacy but served to tinge the similitude not less with the vividness than the disorder of a dream. So that, when upon reining up at the protruding rock I at last caught sight of the quaint groupings of the factory-buildings, and with the traveled highway and the Notch behind, found myself all alone, silently and privily stealing through deep-cloven passages into this sequestered spot, and saw the long, high-gabled main factory edifice, with a rude tower—for hoisting heavy boxes—at one end, standing among its crowded outbuildings and boarding-houses, as the Temple Church amidst the surrounding offices and dormitories, and when the marvelous retirement of this mysterious mountain nook fastened its whole spell upon me, then, what memory lacked, all tributary imagination furnished, and I said to myself, "This is the very counterpart of the Paradise of Bachelors, but snowed upon, and frost-painted to a sepulchre."

Dismounting, and warily picking my way down the dangerous declivity—horse and man both sliding now and then upon the icy ledges—at length I drove, or the blast drove me, into the largest square, before one side of the main edifice. Piercingly and shrilly the shotted blast blew by the corner; and redly and demoniacally boiled Blood River at one side. A long wood-pile, of many scores of cords, all glittering in mail of crusted ice, stood crosswise in the square. A row of horse-posts, their north sides plastered with adhesive snow, flanked the factory wall. The bleak frost packed and paved the square as with some ringing metal.

The inverted similitude recurred—"The sweet, tranquil Temple garden, with the Thames bordering its green beds," strangely meditated I.

But where are the gay bachelors?

Then, as I and my horse stood shivering in the wind-spray, a girl ran from a neighboring dormitory door, and throwing her thin apron over her bare head, made for the opposite building.

"One moment, my girl; is there no shed hereabouts which I may drive into?"

Pausing, she turned upon me a face pale with work, and blue with cold; an eye supernatural with unrelated misery.

"Nay," faltered I, "I mistook you. Go on; I want nothing."

Leading my horse close to the door from which she had come, I knocked. Another pale, blue girl appeared, shivering in the doorway as, to prevent the blast, she jealously held the door ajar.

"Nay, I mistake again. In God's name shut the door. But hold, is there no man about?"

That moment a dark-complexioned well-wrapped personage passed, making for the factory door, and spying him coming, the girl rapidly closed the other one.

"Is there no horse-shed here, Sir?"

"Yonder, to the wood-shed," he replied, and disappeared inside the factory.

With much ado I managed to wedge in horse and pung between the scattered piles of wood all sawn and split. Then, blanketing my horse, and piling my buffalo on the blanket's top, and tucking in its edges well around the breast-band and breeching, so that the wind might not strip him bare, I tied him fast, and ran lamely for the factory door, stiff with frost, and cumbered with my driver's dread-naught.

Immediately I found myself standing in a spacious place, intolerably lighted by long rows of windows, focusing inward the snowy scene without.

At rows of blank-looking counters sat rows of blank-looking girls, with blank, white folders in their blank hands, all blankly folding blank paper.

In one corner stood some huge frame of ponderous iron, with a vertical thing like a piston periodically rising and falling upon a heavy wooden block. Before it—its tame minister—stood a tall girl, feeding the iron animal with half-quires of rose-hued note paper, which, at every downward dab of the piston-like machine, received in the corner the impress of a wreath of roses. I looked from the rosy paper to the pallid cheek, but said nothing.

Seated before a long apparatus, strung with long, slender strings like any harp, another girl was feeding it with foolscap sheets, which, so soon as they curiously traveled from her on the cords, were withdrawn at the opposite end of the machine by a second girl. They came to the first girl blank; they went to the second girl ruled.

I looked upon the first girl's brow, and saw it was young and fair; I looked upon the second girl's brow, and saw it was ruled and wrinkled. Then, as I still looked, the two—for some small variety to the monotony—

changed places; and where had stood the young, fair brow, now stood the ruled and wrinkled one.

Perched high upon a narrow platform, and still higher upon a high stool crowning it, sat another figure serving some other iron animal; while below the platform sat her mate in some sort of reciprocal attendance.

Not a syllable was breathed. Nothing was heard but the low, steady, overruling hum of the iron animals. The human voice was banished from the spot. Machinery—that vaunted slave of humanity—here stood menially served by human beings, who served mutely and cringingly as the slave serves the Sultan. The girls did not so much seem accessory wheels to the general machinery as mere cogs to the wheels.

All this scene around me was instantaneously taken in at one sweeping glance—even before I had proceeded to unwind the heavy fur tippet from around my neck. But as soon as this fell from me the dark-complexioned man, standing close by, raised a sudden cry, and seizing my arm, dragged me out into the open air, and without pausing for a word instantly caught up some congealed snow and began rubbing both my cheeks.

"Two white spots like the whites of your eyes," he said; "man, your cheeks are frozen."

"That may well be," muttered I; " 'tis some wonder the frost of the Devil's Dungeon strikes in no deeper. Rub away."

Soon a horrible, tearing pain caught at my reviving cheeks. Two gaunt blood-hounds, one on each side, seemed mumbling them. I seemed Actæon.

Presently, when all was over, I re-entered the factory, made known my business, concluded it satisfactorily, and then begged to be conducted throughout the place to view it.

"Cupid is the boy for that," said the dark-complexioned man. "Cupid!" and by this odd fancy-name calling a dimpled, red-cheeked, spirited-looking, forward little fellow, who was rather impudently, I thought, gliding about among the passive-looking girls—like a gold fish through hueless waves—yet doing nothing in particular that I could see, the man bade him lead the stranger through the edifice.

"Come first and see the water-wheel," said this lively lad, with the air of boyishly-brisk importance.

Quitting the folding-room, we crossed some damp, cold boards, and stood beneath a great wet shed, incessantly showering with foam, like the green barnacled bow of some East Indiaman in a gale. Round and round here went the enormous revolutions of the dark colossal water-wheel, grim with its one immutable purpose.

"This sets our whole machinery a-going, Sir; in every part of all these buildings; where the girls work and all."

I looked, and saw that the turbid waters of Blood River had not changed their hue by coming under the use of man.

"You make only blank paper; no printing of any sort, I suppose? All blank paper, don't you?"

"Certainly; what else should a paper-factory make?"

The lad here looked at me as if suspicious of my common-sense.

"Oh, to be sure!" said I, confused and stammering; "it only struck me as so strange that red waters should turn out pale chee—paper, I mean."

He took me up a wet and rickety stair to a great light room, furnished with no visible thing but rude, manger-like receptacles running all round its sides; and up to these mangers, like so many mares haltered to the rack, stood rows of girls. Before each was vertically thrust up a long, glittering scythe, immovably fixed at bottom to the manger-edge. The curve of the scythe, and its having no snath to it, made it look exactly like a sword. To and fro, across the sharp edge, the girls forever dragged long strips of rags, washed white, picked from baskets at one side; thus ripping asunder every seam, and converting the tatters almost into lint. The air swam with the fine, poisonous particles, which from all sides darted, subtilely, as motes in sun-beams, into the lungs.

"This is the rag-room," coughed the boy.

"You find it rather stifling here," coughed I, in answer; "but the girls don't cough."

"Oh, they are used to it."

"Where do you get such hosts of rags?" picking up a handful from a basket.

"Some from the country round about; some from far over sea— Leghorn and London."

" 'Tis not unlikely, then," murmured I, "that among these heaps of rags there may be some old shirts, gathered from the dormitories of the Paradise of Bachelors. But the buttons are all dropped off. Pray, my lad, do you ever find any bachelor's buttons hereabouts?"

"None grow in this part of the country. The Devil's Dungeon is no place for flowers."

"Oh! you mean the *flowers* so called—the Bachelor's Buttons?"

"And was not that what you asked about? Or did you mean the gold bosom-buttons of our boss, Old Bach, as our whispering girls all call him?"

"The man, then, I saw below is a bachelor, is he?"

"Oh, yes, he's a Bach."

"The edges of those swords, they are turned outward from the girls, if I see right; but their rags and fingers fly so, I can not distinctly see."

"Turned outward."

Yes, murmured I to myself; I see it now; turned outward; and each erected sword is so borne, edge-outward, before each girl. If my reading fails me not, just so, of old, condemned state-prisoners went from the hall of judgment to their doom: an officer before, bearing a sword, its edge turned outward, in significance of their fatal sentence. So, through consumptive pallors of this blank, raggy life, go these white girls to death.

"Those scythes look very sharp," again turning toward the boy.

"Yes; they have to keep them so. Look!"

That moment two of the girls, dropping their rags, plied each a whetstone up and down the sword-blade. My unaccustomed blood curdled at the sharp shriek of the tormented steel.

Their own executioners; themselves whetting the very swords that slay them; meditated I.

"What makes those girls so sheet-white, my lad?"

"Why"—with a roguish twinkle, pure ignorant drollery, not knowing heartlessness—"I suppose the handling of such white bits of sheets all the time makes them so sheety."

"Let us leave the rag-room now, my lad."

More tragical and more inscrutably mysterious than any mystic sight, human or machine, throughout the factory, was the strange innocence of cruel-heartedness in this usage-hardened boy.

"And now," said he, cheerily, "I suppose you want to see our great machine, which cost us twelve thousand dollars only last autumn. That's the machine that makes the paper, too. This way, Sir."

Following him, I crossed a large, bespattered place, with two great round vats in it, full of a white, wet, woolly-looking stuff, not unlike the albuminous part of an egg, soft-boiled.

"There," said Cupid, tapping the vats carelessly, "these are the first beginnings of the paper; this white pulp you see. Look how it swims bubbling round and round, moved by the paddle here. From hence it pours from both vats into that one common channel yonder; and so goes, mixed up and leisurely, to the great machine. And now for that."

He led me into a room, stifling with a strange, blood-like, abdominal heat, as if here, true enough, were being finally developed the germinous particles lately seen.

Before me, rolled out like some long Eastern manuscript, lay stretched one continuous length of iron frame-work—multitudinous and mystical, with all sorts of rollers, wheels, and cylinders, in slowly-measured and unceasing motion.

"Here first comes the pulp now," said Cupid, pointing to the nighest end of the machine. "See; first it pours out and spreads itself upon this wide, sloping board; and then—look—slides, thin and quivering, beneath the first roller there. Follow on now, and see it as it slides from under that to the next cylinder. There; see how it has become just a very little less pulpy now. One step more, and it grows still more to some slight consistence. Still another cylinder, and it is so knitted—though as yet mere dragon-fly wing—that it forms an air-bridge here, like a suspended cobweb, between two more separated rollers; and flowing over the last one, and under again, and doubling about there out of sight for a minute among all those mixed cylinders you indistinctly see, it reappears here, looking now at last a little less like pulp and more like paper, but still quite delicate and defective yet awhile. But—a little further onward, Sir, if you please—here now, at this further point, it puts on something of a real look, as if it might turn out to be something you might possibly handle in the end. But it's not yet done, Sir. Good way to travel yet, and plenty more of cylinders must roll it."

"Bless my soul!" said I, amazed at the elongation, interminable convolutions, and deliberate slowness of the machine; "it must take a long time for the pulp to pass from end to end, and come out paper."

"Oh! not so long," smiled the precocious lad, with a superior and patronizing air; "only nine minutes. But look; you may try it for yourself. Have you a bit of paper? Ah! here's a bit on the floor. Now mark that with any word you please, and let me dab it on here, and we'll see how long before it comes out at the other end."

"Well, let me see," said I, taking out my pencil; "come, I'll mark it with your name."

Bidding me take out my watch, Cupid adroitly dropped the inscribed slip on an exposed part of the incipient mass.

Instantly my eye marked the second-hand on my dial-plate.

Slowly I followed the slip, inch by inch; sometimes pausing for full half a minute as it disappeared beneath inscrutable groups of the lower cylinders, but only gradually to emerge again; and so, on, and on, and on—inch by inch; now in open sight, sliding along like a freckle on the quivering sheet; and then again wholly vanished; and so, on, and on, and on—inch by inch; all the time the main sheet growing more and more to final firmness—when, suddenly, I saw a sort of paper-fall, not wholly unlike a water-fall; a scissory sound smote my ear, as of some cord being snapped; and down dropped an unfolded sheet of perfect foolscap, with my "Cupid" half faded out of it, and still moist and warm.

My travels were at an end, for here was the end of the machine.

"Well, how long was it?" said Cupid.

"Nine minutes to a second," replied I, watch in hand.

"I told you so."

For a moment a curious emotion filled me, not wholly unlike that which one might experience at the fulfillment of some mysterious prophecy. But how absurd, thought I again; the thing is a mere machine, the essence of which is unvarying punctuality and precision.

Previously absorbed by the wheels and cylinders, my attention was now directed to a sad-looking woman standing by.

"That is rather an elderly person so silently tending the machine-end here. She would not seem wholly used to it either."

"Oh," knowingly whispered Cupid, through the din, "she only came last week. She was a nurse formerly. But the business is poor in these parts, and she's left it. But look at the paper she is piling there."

"Ay, foolscap," handling the piles of moist, warm sheets, which continually were being delivered into the woman's waiting hands. "Don't you turn out any thing but foolscap at this machine?"

"Oh, sometimes, but not often, we turn out finer work—cream-laid and royal sheets, we call them. But foolscap being in chief demand, we turn out foolscap most."

It was very curious. Looking at that blank paper continually dropping, dropping, dropping, my mind ran on in wonderings of those strange uses to which those thousand sheets eventually would be put. All sorts of writings would be writ on those now vacant things—sermons, lawyers' briefs, physicians' prescriptions, love-letters, marriage certificates, bills of divorce, registers of births, death-warrants, and so on, without end. Then, recurring back to them as they here lay all blank, I could not but bethink me of that celebrated comparison of John Locke, who, in demonstration of his theory that man had no innate ideas, compared the human mind at birth to a sheet of blank paper; something destined to be scribbled on, but what sort of characters no soul might tell.

Pacing slowly to and fro along the involved machine, still humming with its play, I was struck as well by the inevitability as the evolvement-power in all its motions.

"Does that thin cobweb there," said I, pointing to the sheet in its more imperfect stage, "does that never tear or break? It is marvelous fragile, and yet this machine it passes through is so mighty."

"It never is known to tear a hair's point."

"Does it never stop—get clogged?"

"No. It *must* go. The machinery makes it go just *so;* just that very way, and at that very pace you there plainly *see* it go. The pulp can't help going."

Something of awe now stole over me, as I gazed upon this inflexible iron animal. Always, more or less, machinery of this ponderous, elaborate sort strikes, in some moods, strange dread into the human heart, as some living, panting Behemoth might. But what made the thing I saw so specially terrible to me was the metallic necessity, the unbudging fatality which governed it. Though, here and there, I could not follow the thin, gauzy vail of pulp in the course of its more mysterious or entirely invisible advance, yet it was indubitable that, at those points where it eluded me, it still marched on in unvarying docility to the autocratic cunning of the machine. A fascination fastened on me. I stood spell-bound and wandering in my soul. Before my eyes—there, passing in slow procession along the wheeling cylinders, I seemed to see, glued to the pallid incipience of the pulp, the yet more pallid faces of all the pallid girls I had eyed that heavy day. Slowly, mournfully, beseechingly, yet unresistingly, they gleamed along, their agony dimly outlined on the imperfect paper, like the print of the tormented face on the handkerchief of Saint Veronica.

"Halloa! the heat of the room is too much for you," cried Cupid, staring at me.

"No—I am rather chill, if any thing."

"Come out, Sir—out—out," and, with the protecting air of a careful father, the precocious lad hurried me outside.

In a few moments, feeling revived a little, I went into the folding-room—the first room I had entered, and where the desk for transacting business stood, surrounded by the blank counters and blank girls engaged at them.

"Cupid here has led me a strange tour," said I to the dark-complexioned man before mentioned, whom I had ere this discovered not only to be an old bachelor, but also the principal proprietor. "Yours is a most wonderful factory. Your great machine is a miracle of inscrutable intricacy."

"Yes, all our visitors think it so. But we don't have many. We are in a very out-of-the-way corner here. Few inhabitants, too. Most of our girls come from far-off villages."

"The girls," echoed I, glancing round at their silent forms. "Why is it, Sir, that in most factories, female operatives, of whatever age, are indiscriminately called girls, never women?"

"Oh! as to that—why, I suppose, the fact of their being generally unmarried—that's the reason, I should think. But it never struck me before. For our factory here, we will not have married women; they are apt to be off-and-on too much. We want none but steady workers: twelve hours to the day, day after day, through the three hundred and sixty-five days, excepting Sundays, Thanksgiving, and Fast-days. That's our rule. And so, having no married women, what females we have are rightly enough called girls."

"Then these are all maids," said I, while some pained homage to their pale virginity made me involuntarily bow.

"All maids."

Again the strange emotion filled me.

"Your cheeks look whitish yet, Sir," said the man, gazing at me narrowly. "You must be careful going home. Do they pain you at all now? It's a bad sign, if they do."

"No doubt, Sir," answered I, "when once I have got out of the Devil's Dungeon, I shall feel them mending."

"Ah, yes; the winter air in valleys, or gorges, or any sunken place, is far colder and more bitter than elsewhere. You would hardly believe it now, but it is colder here than at the top of Woedolor Mountain."

"I dare say it is, Sir. But time presses me; I must depart."

With that, remuffling myself in dread-naught and tippet, thrusting my hands into my huge seal-skin mittens, I sallied out into the nipping air, and found poor Black, my horse, all cringing and doubled up with the cold.

Soon, wrapped in furs and meditations, I ascended from the Devil's Dungeon.

At the Black Notch I paused, and once more bethought me of Temple-Bar. Then, shooting through the pass, all alone with inscrutable nature, I exclaimed—Oh! Paradise of Bachelors! and oh! Tartarus of Maids!

1855

THE BELL-TOWER

"Like negroes, these powers own man sullenly; mindful of their higher master; while serving, plot revenge."

"The world is apoplectic with high-living of ambition; and apoplexy has its fall."

"Seeking to conquer a larger liberty, man but extends the empire of necessity."

From a Private MS.

In the south of Europe, nigh a once-frescoed capital, now with dank mould cankering its bloom, central in a plain, stands what, at distance, seems the black mossed stump of some immeasurable pine, fallen, in forgotten days, with Anak and the Titan.

As all along where the pine tree falls, its dissolution leaves a mossy mound—last-flung shadow of the perished trunk; never lengthening, never lessening; unsubject to the fleet falsities of the sun; shade immutable and true gauge which cometh by prostration—so westward from what seems the stump, one steadfast spear of lichened ruin veins the plain.

From that tree-top, what birded chimes of silver throats had rung. A stone pine; a metallic aviary in its crown: the Bell-Tower, built by the great mechanician, the unblest foundling, Bannadonna.

Like Babel's, its base was laid in a high hour of renovated earth, following the second deluge, when the waters of the Dark Ages had dried up, and once more the green appeared. No wonder that, after so long and deep submersion, the jubilant expectation of the race should, as with Noah's sons, soar into Shinar aspiration.

In firm resolve, no man in Europe at that period went beyond Bannadonna. Enriched through commerce with the Levant, the state in which he lived voted to have the noblest Bell-Tower in Italy. His repute assigned him to be architect.

Stone by stone, month by month, the tower rose. Higher, higher; snail-like in pace, but torch or rocket in its pride.

After the masons would depart, the builder, standing alone upon its ever-ascending summit, at close of every day saw that he overtopped still higher walls and trees. He would tarry till a late hour there, wrapped in schemes of other and still loftier piles. Those who of saints' days thronged the spot—hanging to the rude poles of scaffolding, like sailors on yards, or bees on boughs, unmindful of lime and dust, and falling chips of stone—their homage not the less inspirited him to self-esteem.

At length the holiday of the Tower came. To the sound of viols, the climax-stone slowly rose in air, and, amid the firing of ordnance, was laid by Bannadonna's hands upon the final course. Then mounting it, he stood erect, alone, with folded arms; gazing upon the white summits of blue inland Alps, and whiter crests of bluer Alps off-shore—sights invisible from the plain. Invisible, too, from thence was that eye he turned below, when, like the cannon booms, came up to him the people's combustions of applause.

That which stirred them so was, seeing with what serenity the builder stood three hundred feet in air, upon an unrailed perch. This none but he durst do. But his periodic standing upon the pile, in each stage of its growth—such discipline had its last result.

Little remained now but the bells. These, in all respects, must correspond with their receptacle.

The minor ones were prosperously cast. A highly enriched one followed, of a singular make, intended for suspension in a manner before unknown. The purpose of this bell, its rotary motion, and connection with the clock-work, also executed at the time, will, in the sequel, receive mention.

In the one erection, bell-tower and clock-tower were united, though, before that period, such structures had commonly been built distinct; as the Campanile and Torre dell' Orologio of St. Mark to this day attest.

But it was upon the great state-bell that the founder lavished his more daring skill. In vain did some of the less elated magistrates here caution him; saying that though truly the tower was Titanic, yet limit should be set to the dependent weight of its swaying masses. But undeterred, he prepared his mammouth mould, dented with mythological devices; kindled his fires of balsamic firs; melted his tin and copper; and throwing in much plate, contributed by the public spirit of the nobles, let loose the tide.

The unleashed metals bayed like hounds. The workmen shrunk. Through their fright, fatal harm to the bell was dreaded. Fearless as Shadrach, Bannadonna, rushing through the glow, smote the chief culprit with his ponderous ladle. From the smitten part, a splinter was dashed into the seething mass, and at once was melted in.

Next day a portion of the work was heedfully uncovered. All seemed right. Upon the third morning, with equal satisfaction, it was bared still lower. At length, like some old Theban king, the whole cooled casting was disinterred. All was fair except in one strange spot. But as he suffered no one to attend him in these inspections, he concealed the blemish by some preparation which none knew better to devise.

The casting of such a mass was deemed no small triumph for the caster; one, too, in which the state might not scorn to share. The homicide was overlooked. By the charitable that deed was but imputed to sudden transports of esthetic passion, not to any flagitious quality. A kick from an Arabian charger: not sign of vice, but blood.

His felony remitted by the judge, absolution given him by the priest, what more could even a sickly conscience have desired!

Honoring the tower and its builder with another holiday, the republic witnessed the hoisting of the bells and clock-work amid shows and pomps superior to the former.

Some months of more than usual solitude on Bannadonna's part ensued. It was not unknown that he was engaged upon something for the belfry, intended to complete it, and surpass all that had gone before. Most people imagined that the design would involve a casting like the bells. But those who thought they had some further insight, would shake their heads, with hints, that not for nothing did the mechanician keep so secret. Meantime, his seclusion failed not to invest his work with more or less of that sort of mystery pertaining to the forbidden.

Ere long he had a heavy object hoisted to the belfry, wrapped in a dark sack or cloak; a procedure sometimes had in the case of an elaborate piece of sculpture, or statue, which, being intended to grace the front of a new edifice, the architect does not desire exposed to critical eyes, till set up, finished, in its appointed place. Such was the impression now. But, as the object rose, a statuary present observed, or thought he did, that it was not entirely rigid, but was, in a manner, pliant. At last, when the hidden thing had attained its final height, and, obscurely seen from below, seemed almost of itself to step into the belfry, as if with little assistance from the crane, a shrewd old blacksmith present ventured the suspicion that it was but a living man. This surmise was thought a foolish one, while the general interest failed not to augment.

Not without demur from Bannadonna, the chief-magistrate of the town, with an associate—both elderly men—followed what seemed the image up the tower. But, arrived at the belfry, they had little recompense. Plausibly entrenching himself behind the conceded mysteries of his art, the mechanician withheld present explanation. The magistrates glanced toward the cloaked object, which, to their surprise, seemed now to have changed its attitude, or else had before been more perplexingly concealed by the violent muffling action of the wind without. It seemed now seated upon some sort of frame, or chair, contained within the domino. They observed that nigh the top, in a sort of square, the web of the cloth, either from accident or design, had its warp partly withdrawn, and the cross-threads plucked out here and there, so as to form a sort of woven grating. Whether it were the low wind or no, stealing through the stone lattice-work, or only their own perturbed imaginations, is uncertain, but they thought they discerned a slight sort of fitful, spring-like motion, in the domino. Nothing, however incidental or insignificant, escaped their uneasy eyes. Among other things, they pried out, in a corner, an earthen cup, partly corroded and partly encrusted, and one whispered to the other, that this cup was just such a one as might, in mockery, be offered to the lips of some brazen statue, or, perhaps, still worse.

But, being questioned, the mechanician said, that the cup was simply used in his founder's business, and described the purpose; in short, a cup to test the condition of metals in fusion. He added, that it had got into the belfry by the merest chance.

Again, and again, they gazed at the domino, as at some suspicious incognito—at a Venetian mask. All sorts of vague apprehensions stirred them. They even dreaded lest, when they should descend, the mechanician, though without a flesh and blood companion, for all that, would not be left alone.

Affecting some merriment at their disquietude, he begged to relieve them, by extending a coarse sheet of workman's canvas between them and the object.

Meantime he sought to interest them in his other work; nor, now that the domino was out of sight, did they long remain insensible to the artistic wonders lying round them; wonders hitherto beheld but in their unfinished state; because, since hoisting the bells, none but the caster had entered within the belfry. It was one trait of his, that, even in details, he would not let another do what he could, without too great loss of time, accomplish for himself. So, for several preceding weeks, whatever hours were unemployed in his secret design, had been devoted to elaborating the figures on the bells.

The clock-bell, in particular, now drew attention. Under a patient chisel, the latent beauty of its enrichments, before obscured by the cloudings incident to casting that beauty in its shyest grace, was now revealed. Round and round the bell, twelve figures of gay girls, garlanded, hand-in-hand, danced in a choral ring—the embodied hours.

"Bannadonna," said the chief, "this bell excels all else. No added touch could here improve. Hark!" hearing a sound, "was that the wind?"

"The wind, Eccellenza," was the light response. "But the figures, they are not yet without their faults. They need some touches yet. When those are given, and the——block yonder," pointing towards the canvas screen, "when Haman there, as I merrily call him,—him? *it*, I mean——when Haman is fixed on this, his lofty tree, then, gentlemen, will I be most happy to receive you here again."

The equivocal reference to the object caused some return of restlessness. However, on their part, the visitors forbore further allusion to it, unwilling, perhaps, to let the foundling see how easily it lay within his plebeian art to stir the placid dignity of nobles.

"Well, Bannadonna," said the chief, "how long ere you are ready to set the clock going, so that the hour shall be sounded? Our interest in you, not less than in the work itself, makes us anxious to be assured of your success. The people, too,—why, they are shouting now. Say the exact hour when you will be ready."

"To-morrow, Eccellenza, if you listen for it,—or should you not, all the same—strange music will be heard. The stroke of one shall be the first from yonder bell," pointing to the bell adorned with girls and garlands, "that stroke shall fall there, where the hand of Una clasps Dua's.

The stroke of one shall sever that loved clasp. To-morrow, then, at one o'clock, as struck here, precisely here," advancing and placing his finger upon the clasp, "the poor mechanic will be most happy once more to give you liege audience, in this his littered shop. Farewell till then, illustrious magnificoes, and hark ye for your vassal's stroke."

His still, Vulcanic face hiding its burning brightness like a forge, he moved with ostentatious deference towards the scuttle, as if so far to escort their exit. But the junior magistrate, a kind hearted man, troubled at what seemed to him a certain sardonical disdain, lurking beneath the foundling's humble mien, and in Christian sympathy more distressed at it on his account than on his own, dimly surmising what might be the final fate of such a cynic solitaire, nor perhaps uninfluenced by the general strangeness of surrounding things, this good magistrate had glanced sadly, sideways from the speaker, and thereupon his foreboding eye had started at the expression of the unchanging face of the Hour Una.

"How is this, Bannadonna?" he lowly asked, "Una looks unlike her sisters."

"In Christ's name, Bannadonna," impulsively broke in the chief, his attention, for the first time, attracted to the figure, by his associate's remark, "Una's face looks just like that of Deborah, the prophetess, as painted by the Florentine, Del Fonca."

"Surely, Bannadonna," lowly resumed the milder magistrate, "you meant the twelve should wear the same jocundly abandoned air. But see, the smile of Una seems but a fatal one. 'Tis different."

While his mild associate was speaking, the chief glanced, inquiringly, from him to the caster, as if anxious to mark how the discrepancy would be accounted for. As the chief stood, his advanced foot was on the scuttle's curb.

Bannadonna spoke.

"Eccellenza, now that, following your keener eye, I glance upon the face of Una, I do, indeed, perceive some little variance. But look all round the bell, and you will find no two faces entirely correspond. Because there is a law in art——but the cold wind is rising more; these lattices are but a poor defense. Suffer me, magnificoes, to conduct you, at least, partly on your way. Those in whose well-being there is a public stake, should be heedfully attended."

"Touching the look of Una, you were saying, Bannadonna, that there was a certain law in art," observed the chief, as the three now descended the stone shaft, "pray, tell me, then———."

"Pardon; another time, Eccellenza;—the tower is damp."

"Nay, I must rest, and hear it now. Here,—here is a wide landing, and through this leeward slit, no wind, but ample light. Tell us of your law; and at large."

"Since, Eccellenza, you insist, know that there is a law in art, which bars the possibility of duplicates. Some years ago, you may remember, I graved a small seal for your republic, bearing, for its chief device, the head of your own ancestor, its illustrious founder. It becoming necessary, for the customs' use, to have innumerable impressions for bales and boxes, I graved an entire plate, containing one hundred of the seals. Now, though, indeed, my object was to have those hundred heads identical, and though, I dare say, people think them so, yet, upon closely scanning an uncut impression from the plate, no two of those five-score faces, side by side, will be found alike. Gravity is the air of all; but, diversified in all. In some, benevolent; in some, ambiguous; in two or three, to a close scrutiny, all but incipiently malign, the variation of less than a hair's breadth in the linear shadings round the mouth sufficing to all this. Now, Eccellenza, transmute that general gravity into joyousness, and subject it to twelve of those variations I have described, and tell me, will you not have my hours here, and Una one of them? But I like———."

"Hark! is that———a footfall above?"

"Mortar, Eccellenza; sometimes it drops to the belfry-floor from the arch where the stone-work was left undressed. I must have it seen to. As I was about to say: for one, I like this law forbidding duplicates. It evokes fine personalities. Yes, Eccellenza, that strange, and—to you—uncertain smile, and those fore-looking eyes of Una, suit Bannadonna very well."

"Hark!—sure we left no soul above?"

"No soul, Eccellenza; rest assured, no *soul.*—Again the mortar."

"It fell not while we were there."

"Ah, in your presence, it better knew its place, Eccellenza," blandly bowed Bannadonna.

"But, Una," said the milder magistrate, "she seemed intently gazing on you; one would have almost sworn that she picked you out from among us three."

"If she did, possibly, it might have been her finer apprehension, Eccellenza."

"How, Bannadonna? I do not understand you."

"No consequence, no consequence, Eccellenza—but the shifted wind is blowing through the slit. Suffer me to escort you on; and then, pardon, but the toiler must to his tools."

"It may be foolish, Signore," said the milder magistrate, as, from the third landing, the two now went down unescorted, "but, somehow, our great mechanician moves me strangely. Why, just now, when he so superciliously replied, his look seemed Sisera's, God's vain foe, in Del Fonca's painting.—And that young, sculptured Deborah, too. Aye, and that——."

"Tush, tush, Signore!" returned the chief. "A passing whim. Deborah?—Where's Jael, pray?"

"Ah," said the other, as they now stepped upon the sod, "Ah, Signore, I see you leave your fears behind you with the chill and gloom; but mine, even in this sunny air, remain. Hark!"

It was a sound from just within the tower door, whence they had emerged. Turning, they saw it closed.

"He has slipped down and barred us out," smiled the chief; "but it is his custom."

Proclamation was now made, that the next day, at one hour after meridian, the clock would strike, and—thanks to the mechanician's powerful art with unusual accompaniments. But what those should be, none as yet could say. The announcement was received with cheers.

By the looser sort, who encamped about the tower all night, lights were seen gleaming through the topmost blind-work, only disappearing with the morning sun. Strange sounds, too, were heard, or were thought to be, by those whom anxious watching might not have left mentally undisturbed, sounds, not only of some ringing implement, but also—so they said—half-suppressed screams and plainings, such as might have issued from some ghostly engine, overplied.

Slowly the day drew on; part of the concourse chasing the weary time with songs and games, till, at last, the great blurred sun rolled, like a football, against the plain.

At noon, the nobility and principal citizens came from the town in cavalcade; a guard of soldiers, also, with music, the more to honor the occasion.

Only one hour more. Impatience grew. Watches were held in hands of feverish men, who stood, now scrutinizing their small dial-plates, and then, with neck thrown back, gazing toward the belfry, as if the eye might foretell that which could only be made sensible to the ear, for, as yet, there was no dial to the tower-clock.

The hour-hands of a thousand watches now verged within a hair's breadth of the figure I. A silence, as of the expectation of some Shiloh, pervaded the swarming plain. Suddenly a dull, mangled sound—naught ringing in it; scarcely audible, indeed, to the outer circles of the people— that dull sound dropped heavily from the belfry. At the same moment, each man stared at his neighbor blankly. All watches were upheld. All hour-hands were at—had passed—the figure I. No bell-stroke from the tower. The multitude became tumultuous.

Waiting a few moments, the chief magistrate, commanding silence, hailed the belfry, to know what thing unforeseen had happened there.

No response.

He hailed again and yet again.

All continued hushed.

By his order the soldiers burst in the tower-door; when, stationing guards to defend it from the now surging mob, the chief, accompanied by his former associate, climbed the winding stairs. Half-way up, they stopped to listen. No sound. Mounting faster, they reached the belfry; but, at the threshold, startled at the spectacle disclosed. A spaniel which, unbeknown to them, had followed them thus far, stood shivering as before some unknown monster in a brake: or, rather, as if it snuffed footsteps leading to some other world.

Bannadonna lay prostrate and bleeding at the base of the bell which was adorned with girls and garlands. He lay at the feet of the hour Una; his head coinciding, in a vertical line, with her left hand, clasped by the hour Dua. With downcast face impending over him, like Jael over nailed Sisera in the tent, was the domino; now no more becloaked.

It had limbs, and seemed clad in a scaly mail, lustrous as a dragon-beetle's. It was manacled, and its clubbed arms were uplifted, as if, with its manacles, once more to smite its already smitten victim. One advanced foot of it was inserted beneath the dead body, as if in the act of spurning it.

Uncertainty falls on what now followed.

It were but natural to suppose that the magistrates would at first shrink from immediate personal contact with what they saw. At the least, for a time, they would stand in involuntary doubt; it may be, in more or less of horrified alarm. Certain it is, that an arquebuss was called for from below.

And some add, that its report, followed by a fierce whiz, as of the sudden snapping of a main-spring, with a steely din, as if a stack of sword blades should be dashed upon a pavement, these blended sounds came ringing to the plain, attracting every eye far upward to the belfry, whence, through the lattice-work, thin wreaths of smoke were curling.

Some averred that it was the spaniel, gone mad by fear, which was shot. This, others denied. True it was, the spaniel never more was seen; and, probably, for some unknown reason, it shared the burial now to be related of the domino. For, whatever the preceding circumstances may have been, the first instinctive panic over, or else all ground of reasonable fear removed, the two magistrates, by themselves, quickly rehooded the figure in the dropped cloak wherein it had been hoisted. The same night, it was secretly lowered to the ground, smuggled to the beach, pulled far out to sea, and sunk. Nor to any after urgency, even in free convivial hours, would the twain ever disclose the full secrets of the belfry.

From the mystery unavoidably investing it, the popular solution of the foundling's fate involved more or less of supernatural agency. But some few less unscientific minds pretended to find little difficulty in otherwise accounting for it. In the chain of circumstantial inferences drawn, there may, or may not, have been some absent or defective links. But, as the explanation in question is the only one which tradition has explicitly preserved, in dearth of better, it will here be given. But, in the first place, it is requisite to present the supposition entertained as to the entire motive and mode, with their origin, of the secret design of Bannadonna; the minds above-mentioned assuming to penetrate as well into his soul as into the event. The disclosure will indirectly involve reference to peculiar matters, none of the clearest, beyond the immediate subject.

At that period, no large bell was made to sound otherwise than as at present, by agitation of a tongue within, by means of ropes, or percussion from without, either from cumbrous machinery, or stalwart watchmen, armed with heavy hammers, stationed in the belfry, or in sentry-boxes on the open roof, according as the bell was sheltered or exposed.

It was from observing these exposed bells, with their watchmen, that the foundling, as was opined, derived the first suggestion of his scheme. Perched on a great mast or spire, the human figure, viewed from below, undergoes such a reduction in its apparent size, as to obliterate its intelligent features. It evinces no personality. Instead of bespeaking volition, its gestures rather resemble the automatic ones of the arms of a telegraph.

Musing, therefore, upon the purely Punchinello aspect of the human figure thus beheld, it had indirectly occurred to Bannadonna to devise some metallic agent, which should strike the hour with its mechanic hand, with even greater precision than the vital one. And, moreover, as the vital watchman on the roof, sallying from his retreat at the given periods, walked to the bell with uplifted mace, to smite it, Bannadonna had resolved that his invention should likewise possess the power of locomotion, and, along with that, the appearance, at least, of intelligence and will.

If the conjectures of those who claimed acquaintance with the intent of Bannadonna be thus far correct, no unenterprising spirit could have been his. But they stopped not here; intimating that though, indeed, his design had, in the first place, been prompted by the sight of the watchman, and confined to the devising of a subtle substitute for him; yet, as is not seldom the case with projectors, by insensible gradations, proceeding from comparatively pigmy aims to Titanic ones, the original scheme had, in its anticipated eventualities, at last, attained to an unheard of degree of daring. He still bent his efforts upon the locomotive figure for the belfry, but only as a partial type of an ulterior creature, a sort of elephantine Helot, adapted to further, in a degree scarcely to be imagined, the universal conveniences and glories of humanity; supplying nothing less than a supplement to the Six Days' Work; stocking the earth with a new serf, more useful than the ox, swifter than the dolphin, stronger than the lion, more cunning than the ape, for industry an ant, more fiery than serpents, and yet, in patience, another ass. All excellences of all God-made creatures, which served man, were here to receive advancement, and then to be combined in one. Talus was to have been the all-accomplished Helot's name. Talus, iron slave to Bannadonna, and, through him, to man.

Here, it might well be thought that, were these last conjectures as to the foundling's secrets not erroneous, then must he have been hopelessly infected with the craziest chimeras of his age; far outgoing Albert Magnus and Cornelius Agrippa. But the contrary was averred. However marvelous his design, however apparently transcending not alone the bounds of human invention, but those of divine creation, yet the proposed means to be employed were alleged to have been confined within the sober forms of sober reason. It was affirmed that, to a degree of more than sceptic scorn, Bannadonna had been without sympathy for any of the vainglorious irrationalities of his time. For example, he had not concluded, with the visionaries among the metaphysicians, that between the finer mechanic forces and the ruder animal vitality, some germ of correspondence might prove discoverable. As little did his scheme partake of the enthusiasm of some natural philosophers, who hoped, by physiological and chemical inductions, to arrive at a knowledge of the source of life, and so qualify themselves to manufacture and improve upon it. Much less had he aught in common with the tribe of alchemists, who sought, by a species of incantations, to evoke some surprising vitality from the laboratory. Neither had he imagined with certain sanguine theosophists, that, by faithful adoration of the Highest, unheard-of powers would be vouchsafed to man. A practical materialist, what Bannadonna had aimed at was to have been reached, not by logic, not by crucible, not by conjuration, not by altars; but by plain vice-bench and hammer. In short, to solve nature, to steal into her, to intrigue beyond her, to procure some one else to bind her to his hand;—these, one and all, had not been his objects; but, asking no favors from any element or any being, of himself, to rival her, outstrip her, and rule her. He stooped to conquer. With him, common sense was theurgy; machinery, miracle; Prometheus, the heroic name for machinist; man, the true God.

Nevertheless, in his initial step, so far as the experimental automaton for the belfry was concerned, he allowed fancy some little play; or, perhaps, what seemed his fancifulness was but his utilitarian ambition collaterally extended. In figure, the creature for the belfry should not be likened after the human pattern, nor any animal one, nor after the ideals, however wild, of ancient fable, but equally in aspect as in organism be an original production; the more terrible to behold, the better.

Such, then, were the suppositions as to the present scheme, and the reserved intent. How, at the very threshold, so unlooked for a catastrophe overturned all, or, rather, what was the conjecture here, is now to be set forth.

It was thought that on the day preceding the fatality, his visitors having left him, Bannadonna had unpacked the belfry image, adjusted it, and placed it in the retreat provided,—a sort of sentry-box in one corner of the belfry; in short, throughout the night, and for some part of the ensuing morning, he had been engaged in arranging every thing connected with the domino: the issuing from the sentry-box each sixty minutes; sliding along a grooved way, like a railway; advancing to the clock-bell, with uplifted manacles; striking it at one of the twelve junctions of the four-and-twenty hands: then wheeling, circling the bell, and retiring to its post, there to bide for another sixty minutes, when the same process was to be repeated; the bell, by a cunning mechanism, meantime turning on its vertical axis, so as to present, to the descending mace, the clasped hands of the next two figures, when it would strike two, three, and so on, to the end. The musical metal in this time-bell being so managed in the fusion, by some art perishing with its originator, that each of the clasps of the four-and-twenty hands should give forth its own peculiar resonance when parted.

But on the magic metal, the magic and metallic stranger never struck but that one stroke, drove but that one nail, severed but that one clasp, by which Bannadonna clung to his ambitious life. For, after winding up the creature in the sentry-box, so that, for the present, skipping the intervening hours, it should not emerge till the hour of one, but should then infallibly emerge, and, after deftly oiling the grooves whereon it was to slide, it was surmised that the mechanician must then have hurried to the bell, to give his final touches to its sculpture. True artist, he here became absorbed; an absorption still further intensified, it may be, by his striving to abate that strange look of Una; which, though, before others, he had treated with such unconcern, might not, in secret, have been without its thorn.

And so, for the interval, he was oblivious of his creature; which, not oblivious of him, and true to its creation, and true to its heedful winding up, left its post precisely at the given moment; along its well-oiled route, slid noiselessly towards its mark; and aiming at the hand of Una, to ring one clangorous note, dully smote the intervening brain of Bannadonna, turned backwards to it; the manacled arms then instantly upspringing to their hovering poise. The falling body clogged the thing's return; so there it stood, still impending over Bannadonna, as if whispering some post-mortem terror. The chisel lay dropped from the hand, but beside the hand; the oil-flask spilled across the iron track.

In his unhappy end, not unmindful of the rare genius of the mechanician, the republic decreed him a stately funeral. It was resolved that the great bell—the one whose casting had been jeopardized through the timidity of the ill-starred workman—should be rung upon the entrance of the bier into the cathedral. The most robust man of the country round was assigned the office of bell-ringer.

But as the pall-bearers entered the cathedral porch, nought but a broken and disastrous sound, like that of some lone Alpine land-slide, fell from the tower upon their ears. And then, all was hushed.

Glancing backwards, they saw the groined belfry crashed sideways in. It afterwards appeared that the powerful peasant who had the bell-rope in charge, wishing to test at once the full glory of the bell, had swayed down upon the rope with one concentrate jerk. The mass of quaking metal, too ponderous for its frame, and strangely feeble somewhere at its top, loosed from its fastening, tore sideways down, and tumbling in one sheer fall, three hundred feet to the soft sward below, buried itself inverted and half out of sight.

Upon its disinterment, the main fracture was found to have started from a small spot in the ear; which, being scraped, revealed a defect, deceptively minute, in the casting; which defect must subsequently have been pasted over with some unknown compound.

The remolten metal soon reässumed its place in the tower's repaired superstructure. For one year the metallic choir of birds sang musically in its belfry-bough-work of sculptured blinds and traceries. But on the first anniversary of the tower's completion—at early dawn, before the concourse had surrounded it—an earthquake came; one loud crash was heard. The stone-pine, with all its bower of songsters, lay overthrown upon the plain.

So the blind slave obeyed its blinder lord; but, in obedience, slew him. So the creator was killed by the creature. So the bell was too heavy for the tower. So that bell's main weakness was where man's blood had flawed it. And so pride went before the fall.*

1855

---

* It was not deemed necessary to adhere to the peculiar notation of Italian time. Adherence to it would have impaired the familiar comprehension of the story. Kindred remarks might be offered touching an anachronism or two that occur.

BENITO CERENO

In the year 1799, Captain Amasa Delano, of Duxbury, in Massachusetts, commanding a large sealer and general trader, lay at anchor, with a valuable cargo, in the harbor of St. Maria—a small, desert, uninhabited island toward the southern extremity of the long coast of Chili. There he had touched for water.

On the second day, not long after dawn, while lying in his berth, his mate came below, informing him that a strange sail was coming into the bay. Ships were then not so plenty in those waters as now. He rose, dressed, and went on deck.

The morning was one peculiar to that coast. Everything was mute and calm; everything gray. The sea, though undulated into long roods of swells, seemed fixed, and was sleeked at the surface like waved lead that has cooled and set in the smelter's mould. The sky seemed a gray surtout. Flights of troubled gray fowl, kith and kin with flights of troubled gray vapors among which they were mixed, skimmed low and fitfully over the waters, as swallows over meadows before storms. Shadows present, foreshadowing deeper shadows to come.

To Captain Delano's surprise, the stranger, viewed through the glass, showed no colors; though to do so upon entering a haven, however uninhabited in its shores, where but a single other ship might be lying, was the custom among peaceful seamen of all nations. Considering the lawlessness and loneliness of the spot, and the sort of stories, at that day, associated with those seas, Captain Delano's surprise might have deepened into some uneasiness had he not been a person of a singularly undistrustful good nature, not liable, except on extraordinary and repeated incentives, and hardly then, to indulge in personal alarms, any way involving the imputation of malign evil in man. Whether, in view of what humanity is capable, such a trait implies, along with a benevolent heart, more than ordinary quickness and accuracy of intellectual perception, may be left to the wise to determine.

But whatever misgivings might have obtruded on first seeing the stranger, would almost, in any seaman's mind, have been dissipated by observing that, the ship, in navigating into the harbor, was drawing too near the land, for her own safety's sake, owing to a sunken reef making out off her bow. This seemed to prove her a stranger, indeed, not only to the sealer, but the island; consequently, she could be no wonted free-booter on that ocean. With no small interest, Captain Delano continued to watch her—a proceeding not much facilitated by the vapors partly mantling the hull, through which the far matin light from her cabin streamed equivocally enough; much like the sun—by this time hemisphered on the rim of the horizon, and apparently, in company with the strange ship, entering the harbor—which, wimpled by the same low, creeping clouds, showed not unlike a Lima intriguante's one sinister eye peering across the Plaza from the Indian loop-hole of her dusk *saya-y-manta*.

It might have been but a deception of the vapors, but, the longer the stranger was watched, the more singular appeared her maneuvers. Ere long it seemed hard to decide whether she meant to come in or no—what she wanted, or what she was about. The wind, which had breezed up a little during the night, was now extremely light and baffling, which the more increased the apparent uncertainty of her movements.

Surmising, at last, that it might be a ship in distress, Captain Delano ordered his whale-boat to be dropped, and, much to the wary opposition of his mate, prepared to board her, and, at the least, pilot her in. On the night previous, a fishing-party of the seamen had gone a long distance to some detached rocks out of sight from the sealer, and, an hour or two before day-break, had returned, having met with no small success. Presuming that the stranger might have been long off soundings, the good captain put several baskets of the fish, for presents, into his boat, and so pulled away. From her continuing too near the sunken reef, deeming her in danger, calling to his men, he made all haste to apprise those on board of their situation. But, some time ere the boat came up, the wind, light though it was, having shifted, had headed the vessel off, as well as partly broken the vapors from about her.

Upon gaining a less remote view, the ship, when made signally visible on the verge of the leaden-hued swells, with the shreds of fog here and there raggedly furring her, appeared like a white-washed monastery after a thunder-storm, seen perched upon some dun cliff among the Pyrenees. But it was no purely fanciful resemblance which now, for a moment, almost led Captain Delano to think that nothing less than a ship-load of monks was before him. Peering over the bulwarks were what really seemed, in the hazy distance, throngs of dark cowls; while, fitfully revealed through the open port-holes, other dark moving figures were dimly descried, as of Black Friars pacing the cloisters.

Upon a still nigher approach, this appearance was modified, and the true character of the vessel was plain—a Spanish merchantman of the first class; carrying negro slaves, amongst other valuable freight, from one colonial port to another. A very large, and, in its time, a very fine vessel, such as in those days were at intervals encountered along that main; sometimes superseded Acapulco treasure-ships, or retired frigates of the Spanish king's navy, which, like superannuated Italian palaces, still, under a decline of masters, preserved signs of former state.

As the whale-boat drew more and more nigh, the cause of the peculiar pipe-clayed aspect of the stranger was seen in the slovenly neglect pervading her. The spars, ropes, and great part of the bulwarks, looked woolly, from long unacquaintance with the scraper, tar, and the brush. Her keel seemed laid, her ribs put together, and she launched, from Ezekiel's Valley of Dry Bones.

In the present business in which she was engaged, the ship's general model and rig appeared to have undergone no material change from their original war-like and Froissart pattern. However, no guns were seen.

The tops were large, and were railed about with what had once been octagonal net-work, all now in sad disrepair. These tops hung overhead like three ruinous aviaries, in one of which was seen perched, on a ratlin, a white noddy, a strange fowl, so called from its lethargic, somnambulistic character, being frequently caught by hand at sea. Battered and mouldy, the castellated forecastle seemed some ancient turret, long ago taken by assault, and then left to decay. Toward the stern, two high-raised quarter galleries—the balustrades here and there covered with dry, tindery sea-moss—opening out from the unoccupied state-cabin, whose dead lights, for all the mild weather, were hermetically closed and calked— these tenantless balconies hung over the sea as if it were the grand Venetian canal. But the principal relic of faded grandeur was the ample oval of the shield-like stern-piece, intricately carved with the arms of Castile and Leon, medallioned about by groups of mythological or symbolical devices; uppermost and central of which was a dark satyr in a mask, holding his foot on the prostrate neck of a writhing figure, likewise masked.

Whether the ship had a figure-head, or only a plain beak, was not quite certain, owing to canvas wrapped about that part, either to protect it while undergoing a re-furbishing, or else decently to hide its decay. Rudely painted or chalked, as in a sailor freak, along the forward side of a sort of pedestal below the canvas, was the sentence, *"Seguid vuestro jefe,"* (follow your leader); while upon the tarnished head-boards, near by, appeared, in stately capitals, once gilt, the ship's name, "SAN DOMINICK," each letter streakingly corroded with tricklings of copper-spike rust; while, like mourning weeds, dark festoons of sea-grass slimily swept to and fro over the name, with every hearse-like roll of the hull.

As at last the boat was hooked from the bow along toward the gangway amidship, its keel, while yet some inches separated from the hull, harshly grated as on a sunken coral reef. It proved a huge bunch of conglobated barnacles adhering below the water to the side like a wen; a token of baffling airs and long calms passed somewhere in those seas.

Climbing the side, the visitor was at once surrounded by a clamorous throng of whites and blacks, but the latter outnumbering the former more than could have been expected, negro transportation-ship as the stranger in port was. But, in one language, and as with one voice, all poured out a common tale of suffering; in which the negresses, of whom there were not a few, exceeded the others in their dolorous vehemence. The scurvy, together with a fever, had swept off a great part of their number, more especially the Spaniards. Off Cape Horn, they had narrowly escaped shipwreck; then, for days together, they had lain tranced without wind; their provisions were low; their water next to none; their lips that moment were baked.

While Captain Delano was thus made the mark of all eager tongues, his one eager glance took in all the faces, with every other object about him.

Always upon first boarding a large and populous ship at sea, especially a foreign one, with a nondescript crew such as Lascars or Manilla men, the impression varies in a peculiar way from that produced by first entering a strange house with strange inmates in a strange land. Both house and ship, the one by its walls and blinds, the other by its high bulwarks like ramparts, hoard from view their interiors till the last moment; but in the case of the ship there is this addition; that the living spectacle it contains, upon its sudden and complete disclosure, has, in contrast with the blank ocean which zones it, something of the effect of enchantment. The ship seems unreal; these strange costumes, gestures, and faces, but a shadowy tableau just emerged from the deep, which directly must receive back what it gave.

Perhaps it was some such influence as above is attempted to be described, which, in Captain Delano's mind, heightened whatever, upon a staid scrutiny, might have seemed unusual; especially the conspicuous figures of four elderly grizzled negroes, their heads like black, doddered willow tops, who, in venerable contrast to the tumult below them, were couched sphynx-like, one on the starboard cat-head, another on the larboard, and the remaining pair face to face on the opposite bulwarks above the main-chains. They each had bits of unstranded old junk in their hands, and, with a sort of stoical self-content, were picking the junk into oakum, a small heap of which lay by their sides. They accompanied the task with a continuous, low, monotonous chant; droning and druling away like so many gray-headed bag-pipers playing a funeral march.

The quarter-deck rose into an ample elevated poop, upon the forward verge of which, lifted, like the oakum-pickers, some eight feet above the general throng, sat along in a row, separated by regular spaces, the cross-legged figures of six other blacks; each with a rusty hatchet in his hand, which, with a bit of brick and a rag, he was engaged like a scullion in scouring; while between each two was a small stack of hatchets, their rusted edges turned forward awaiting a like operation. Though occasionally the four oakum-pickers would briefly address some person or persons in the crowd below, yet the six hatchet-polishers neither spoke to others, nor breathed a whisper among themselves, but sat intent upon their task, except at intervals, when, with the peculiar love in negroes of uniting industry with pastime, two and two they sideways clashed their hatchets together, like cymbals, with a barbarous din. All six, unlike the generality, had the raw aspect of unsophisticated Africans.

But that first comprehensive glance which took in those ten figures, with scores less conspicuous, rested but an instant upon them, as, impatient of the hubbub of voices, the visitor turned in quest of whomsoever it might be that commanded the ship.

But as if not unwilling to let nature make known her own case among his suffering charge, or else in despair of restraining it for the time, the Spanish captain, a gentlemanly, reserved-looking, and rather young man to a stranger's eye, dressed with singular richness, but bearing plain traces of recent sleepless cares and disquietudes, stood passively by, leaning against the main-mast, at one moment casting a dreary, spiritless look upon his excited people, at the next an unhappy glance toward his visitor. By his side stood a black of small stature, in whose rude face, as occasionally, like a shepherd's dog, he mutely turned it up into the Spaniard's, sorrow and affection were equally blended.

Struggling through the throng, the American advanced to the Spaniard, assuring him of his sympathies, and offering to render whatever assistance might be in his power. To which the Spaniard returned, for the present, but grave and ceremonious acknowledgments, his national formality dusked by the saturnine mood of ill health.

But losing no time in mere compliments, Captain Delano returning to the gangway, had his baskets of fish brought up; and as the wind still continued light, so that some hours at least must elapse ere the ship could be brought to the anchorage, he bade his men return to the sealer, and fetch back as much water as the whale-boat could carry, with whatever soft bread the steward might have, all the remaining pumpkins on board, with a box of sugar, and a dozen of his private bottles of cider.

Not many minutes after the boat's pushing off, to the vexation of all, the wind entirely died away, and the tide turning, began drifting back the ship helplessly seaward. But trusting this would not long last, Captain Delano sought with good hopes to cheer up the strangers, feeling no small satisfaction that, with persons in their condition he could—thanks to his frequent voyages along the Spanish main—converse with some freedom in their native tongue.

While left alone with them, he was not long in observing some things tending to heighten his first impressions; but surprise was lost in pity, both for the Spaniards and blacks, alike evidently reduced from scarcity of water and provisions; while long-continued suffering seemed to have brought out the less good-natured qualities of the negroes, besides, at the same time, impairing the Spaniard's authority over them. But, under the circumstances, precisely this condition of things was to have been anticipated. In armies, navies, cities, or families, in nature herself, nothing more relaxes good order than misery. Still, Captain Delano was not without the idea, that had Benito Cereno been a man of greater energy, misrule would hardly have come to the present pass. But the debility, constitutional or induced by the hardships, bodily and mental, of the Spanish captain, was too obvious to be overlooked. A prey to settled dejection, as if long mocked with hope he would not now indulge it, even when it had ceased to be a mock, the prospect of that day or evening at furthest, lying at anchor, with plenty of water for his people, and a brother captain to counsel and befriend, seemed in no perceptible degree to encourage him. His mind appeared unstrung, if not still more seriously affected. Shut up in these oaken walls, chained to one dull round of command, whose unconditionality cloyed him, like some hypochondriac abbot he moved slowly about, at times suddenly pausing, starting, or staring, biting his lip, biting his finger-nail, flushing, paling, twitching his beard, with other symptoms of an absent or moody mind. This distempered spirit was lodged, as before hinted, in as distempered a frame. He was rather tall, but seemed never to have been robust, and now with nervous suffering was almost worn to a skeleton. A tendency to some pulmonary complaint appeared to have been lately confirmed. His voice was like that of one with lungs half gone, hoarsely suppressed, a husky whisper. No wonder that, as in this state he tottered about, his private servant apprehensively followed him. Sometimes the negro gave his master his arm, or took his handkerchief out of his pocket for him; performing these and similar offices with that affectionate zeal which transmutes into something filial or fraternal acts in themselves but menial; and which has gained for the negro the repute of making the most pleasing body servant in the world; one, too, whom a master need be on no stiffly superior terms with, but may treat with familiar trust; less a servant than a devoted companion.

Marking the noisy indocility of the blacks in general, as well as what seemed the sullen inefficiency of the whites, it was not without humane satisfaction that Captain Delano witnessed the steady good conduct of Babo.

But the good conduct of Babo, hardly more than the ill-behavior of others, seemed to withdraw the half-lunatic Don Benito from his cloudy languor. Not that such precisely was the impression made by the Spaniard on the mind of his visitor. The Spaniard's individual unrest was, for the present, but noted as a conspicuous feature in the ship's general affliction. Still, Captain Delano was not a little concerned at what he could not help taking for the time to be Don Benito's unfriendly indifference towards himself. The Spaniard's manner, too, conveyed a sort of sour and gloomy disdain, which he seemed at no pains to disguise. But this the American in charity ascribed to the harassing effects of sickness, since, in former instances, he had noted that there are peculiar natures on whom prolonged physical suffering seems to cancel every social instinct of kindness; as if forced to black bread themselves, they deemed it but equity that each person coming nigh them should, indirectly, by some slight or affront, be made to partake of their fare.

But ere long Captain Delano bethought him that, indulgent as he was at the first, in judging the Spaniard, he might not, after all, have exercised charity enough. At bottom it was Don Benito's reserve which displeased him; but the same reserve was shown towards all but his faithful personal attendant. Even the formal reports which, according to sea-usage, were, at stated times, made to him by some petty underling, either a white, mulatto or black, he hardly had patience enough to listen to, without betraying contemptuous aversion. His manner upon such occasions was, in its degree, not unlike that which might be supposed to have been his imperial countryman's, Charles V., just previous to the anchoritish retirement of that monarch from the throne.

This splenetic disrelish of his place was evinced in almost every function pertaining to it. Proud as he was moody, he condescended to no personal mandate. Whatever special orders were necessary, their delivery was delegated to his body-servant, who in turn transferred them to their ultimate destination, through runners, alert Spanish boys or slave boys, like pages or pilot-fish within easy call continually hovering round Don Benito. So that to have beheld this undemonstrative invalid gliding about, apathetic and mute, no landsman could have dreamed that in him was lodged a dictatorship beyond which, while at sea, there was no earthly appeal.

Thus, the Spaniard, regarded in his reserve, seemed as the involuntary victim of mental disorder. But, in fact, his reserve might, in some degree, have proceeded from design. If so, then here was evinced the unhealthy climax of that icy though conscientious policy, more or less adopted by all commanders of large ships, which, except in signal emergencies, obliterates alike the manifestation of sway with every trace of sociality; transforming the man into a block, or rather into a loaded cannon, which, until there is call for thunder, has nothing to say.

Viewing him in this light, it seemed but a natural token of the perverse habit induced by a long course of such hard self-restraint, that, notwithstanding the present condition of his ship, the Spaniard should still persist in a demeanor, which, however harmless, or, it may be, appropriate, in a well appointed vessel, such as the San Dominick might have been at the outset of the voyage, was anything but judicious now. But the Spaniard perhaps thought that it was with captains as with gods: reserve, under all events, must still be their cue. But more probably this appearance of slumbering dominion might have been but an attempted disguise to conscious imbecility—not deep policy, but shallow device. But be all this as it might, whether Don Benito's manner was designed or not, the more Captain Delano noted its pervading reserve, the less he felt uneasiness at any particular manifestation of that reserve towards himself.

Neither were his thoughts taken up by the captain alone. Wonted to the quiet orderliness of the sealer's comfortable family of a crew, the noisy confusion of the San Dominick's suffering host repeatedly challenged his eye. Some prominent breaches not only of discipline but of decency were observed. These Captain Delano could not but ascribe, in the main, to the absence of those subordinate deck-officers to whom, along with higher duties, is entrusted what may be styled the police department of a populous ship. True, the old oakum-pickers appeared at times to act the part of monitorial constables to their countrymen, the blacks; but though occasionally succeeding in allaying trifling outbreaks now and then between man and man, they could do little or nothing toward establishing general quiet. The San Dominick was in the condition of a transatlantic emigrant ship, among whose multitude of living freight are some individuals, doubtless, as little troublesome as crates and bales; but the friendly remonstrances of such with their ruder companions are of not so much avail as the unfriendly arm of the mate. What the San Dominick wanted was, what the emigrant ship has, stern superior officers. But on these decks not so much as a fourth mate was to be seen.

The visitor's curiosity was roused to learn the particulars of those mishaps which had brought about such absenteeism, with its consequences; because, though deriving some inkling of the voyage from the wails which at the first moment had greeted him, yet of the details no clear understanding had been had. The best account would, doubtless, be given by the captain. Yet at first the visitor was loth to ask it, unwilling to provoke some distant rebuff. But plucking up courage, he at last accosted Don Benito, renewing the expression of his benevolent interest, adding, that did he (Captain Delano) but know the particulars of the ship's misfortunes, he would, perhaps, be better able in the end to relieve them. Would Don Benito favor him with the whole story?

Don Benito faltered; then, like some somnambulist suddenly interfered with, vacantly stared at his visitor, and ended by looking down on the deck. He maintained this posture so long, that Captain Delano, almost equally disconcerted, and involuntarily almost as rude, turned suddenly from him, walking forward to accost one of the Spanish seamen for the desired information. But he had hardly gone five paces, when with a sort of eagerness Don Benito invited him back, regretting his momentary absence of mind, and professing readiness to gratify him.

While most part of the story was being given, the two captains stood on the after part of the main-deck, a privileged spot, no one being near but the servant.

"It is now a hundred and ninety days," began the Spaniard, in his husky whisper, "that this ship, well officered and well manned, with several cabin passengers—some fifty Spaniards in all—sailed from Buenos Ayres bound to Lima, with a general cargo, hardware, Paraguay tea and the like—and," pointing forward, "that parcel of negroes, now not more than a hundred and fifty, as you see, but then numbering over three hundred souls. Off Cape Horn we had heavy gales. In one moment, by night, three of my best officers, with fifteen sailors, were lost, with the main-yard; the spar snapping under them in the slings, as they sought, with heavers, to beat down the icy sail. To lighten the hull, the heavier sacks of mate were thrown into the sea, with most of the water-pipes lashed on deck at the time. And this last necessity it was, combined with the prolonged detentions afterwards experienced, which eventually brought about our chief causes of suffering. When——"

Here there was a sudden fainting attack of his cough, brought on, no doubt, by his mental distress. His servant sustained him, and drawing a cordial from his pocket placed it to his lips. He a little revived. But unwilling to leave him unsupported while yet imperfectly restored, the black with one arm still encircled his master, at the same time keeping his eye fixed on his face, as if to watch for the first sign of complete restoration, or relapse, as the event might prove.

The Spaniard proceeded, but brokenly and obscurely, as one in a dream.

—"Oh, my God! rather than pass through what I have, with joy I would have hailed the most terrible gales; but——"

His cough returned and with increased violence; this subsiding, with reddened lips and closed eyes he fell heavily against his supporter.

"His mind wanders. He was thinking of the plague that followed the gales," plaintively sighed the servant; "my poor, poor master!" wringing one hand, and with the other wiping the mouth. "But be patient, Señor," again turning to Captain Delano, "these fits do not last long; master will soon be himself."

Don Benito reviving, went on; but as this portion of the story was very brokenly delivered, the substance only will here be set down.

It appeared that after the ship had been many days tossed in storms off the Cape, the scurvy broke out, carrying off numbers of the whites and blacks. When at last they had worked round into the Pacific, their spars and sails were so damaged, and so inadequately handled by the surviving mariners, most of whom were become invalids, that, unable to lay her northerly course by the wind, which was powerful, the unmanageable ship for successive days and nights was blown northwestward, where the breeze suddenly deserted her, in unknown waters, to sultry calms. The absence of the water-pipes now proved as fatal to life as before their presence had menaced it. Induced, or at least aggravated, by the more than scanty allowance of water, a malignant fever followed the scurvy; with the excessive heat of the lengthened calm, making such short work of it as to sweep away, as by billows, whole families of the Africans, and a yet larger number, proportionably, of the Spaniards, including, by a luckless fatality, every remaining officer on board. Consequently, in the smart west winds eventually following the calm, the already rent sails having to be simply dropped, not furled, at need, had been gradually reduced to the beggar's rags they were now. To procure substitutes for his lost sailors, as well as supplies of water and sails, the captain at the earliest opportunity had made for Baldivia, the southernmost civilized port of Chili and South America; but upon nearing the coast the thick weather had prevented him from so much as sighting that harbor. Since which period, almost without a crew, and almost without canvas and almost without water, and at intervals giving its added dead to the sea, the San Dominick had been battledored about by contrary winds, inveigled by currents, or grown weedy in calms. Like a man lost in woods, more than once she had doubled upon her own track.

"But throughout these calamities," huskily continued Don Benito, painfully turning in the half embrace of his servant, "I have to thank those negroes you see, who, though to your inexperienced eyes appearing unruly, have, indeed, conducted themselves with less of restlessness than even their owner could have thought possible under such circumstances."

Here he again fell faintly back. Again his mind wandered; but he ral lied, and less obscurely proceeded.

"Yes, their owner was quite right in assuring me that no fetters would be needed with his blacks; so that while, as is wont in this transportation, those negroes have always remained upon deck—not thrust below, as in the Guinea-men—they have, also, from the beginning, been freely permitted to range within given bounds at their pleasure."

Once more the faintness returned—his mind roved—but, recovering, he resumed:

"But it is Babo here to whom, under God, I owe not only my own preservation, but likewise to him, chiefly, the merit is due, of pacifying his more ignorant brethren, when at intervals tempted to murmurings."

"Ah, master," sighed the black, bowing his face, "don't speak of me; Babo is nothing; what Babo has done was but duty."

"Faithful fellow!" cried Capt. Delano. "Don Benito, I envy you such a friend; slave I cannot call him."

As master and man stood before him, the black upholding the white, Captain Delano could not but bethink him of the beauty of that relationship which could present such a spectacle of fidelity on the one hand and confidence on the other. The scene was heightened by the contrast in dress, denoting their relative positions. The Spaniard wore a loose Chili jacket of dark velvet; white small clothes and stockings, with silver buckles at the knee and instep; a high-crowned sombrero, of fine grass; a slender sword, silver mounted, hung from a knot in his sash; the last being an almost invariable adjunct, more for utility than ornament, of a South American gentleman's dress to this hour. Excepting when his occasional nervous contortions brought about disarray, there was a certain precision in his attire, curiously at variance with the unsightly disorder around; especially in the belittered Ghetto, forward of the main-mast, wholly occupied by the blacks.

The servant wore nothing but wide trowsers, apparently, from their coarseness and patches, made out of some old topsail; they were clean, and confined at the waist by a bit of unstranded rope, which, with his composed, deprecatory air at times, made him look something like a begging friar of St. Francis.

However unsuitable for the time and place, at least in the blunt-thinking American's eyes, and however strangely surviving in the midst of all his afflictions, the toilette of Don Benito might not, in fashion at least, have gone beyond the style of the day among South Americans of his class. Though on the present voyage sailing from Buenos Ayres, he had avowed himself a native and resident of Chili, whose inhabitants had not so generally adopted the plain coat and once plebeian pantaloons; but, with a becoming modification, adhered to their provincial costume, picturesque as any in the world. Still, relatively to the pale history of the voyage, and his own pale face, there seemed something so incongruous in the Spaniard's apparel, as almost to suggest the image of an invalid courtier tottering about London streets in the time of the plague.

The portion of the narrative which, perhaps, most excited interest, as well as some surprise, considering the latitudes in question, was the long calms spoken of, and more particularly the ship's so long drifting about. Without communicating the opinion, of course, the American could not but impute at least part of the detentions both to clumsy seamanship and faulty navigation. Eying Don Benito's small, yellow hands, he easily inferred that the young captain had not got into command at the hawse-hole, but the cabin-window; and if so, why wonder at incompetence, in youth, sickness, and gentility united?

But drowning criticism in compassion, after a fresh repetition of his sympathies, Captain Delano having heard out his story, not only engaged, as in the first place, to see Don Benito and his people supplied in their immediate bodily needs, but, also, now further promised to assist him in procuring a large permanent supply of water, as well as some sails and rigging; and, though it would involve no small embarrassment to himself, yet he would spare three of his best seamen for temporary deck officers; so that without delay the ship might proceed to Conception, there fully to refit for Lima, her destined port.

Such generosity was not without its effect, even upon the invalid. His face lighted up; eager and hectic, he met the honest glance of his visitor. With gratitude he seemed overcome.

"This excitement is bad for master," whispered the servant, taking his arm, and with soothing words gently drawing him aside.

When Don Benito returned, the American was pained to observe that his hopefulness, like the sudden kindling in his cheek, was but febrile and transient.

Ere long, with a joyless mien, looking up towards the poop, the host invited his guest to accompany him there, for the benefit of what little breath of wind might be stirring.

As during the telling of the story, Captain Delano had once or twice started at the occasional cymballing of the hatchet-polishers, wondering why such an interruption should be allowed, especially in that part of the ship, and in the ears of an invalid; and moreover, as the hatchets had anything but an attractive look, and the handlers of them still less so, it was, therefore, to tell the truth, not without some lurking reluctance, or even shrinking, it may be, that Captain Delano, with apparent complaisance, acquiesced in his host's invitation. The more so, since with an untimely caprice of punctilio, rendered distressing by his cadaverous aspect, Don Benito, with Castilian bows, solemnly insisted upon his guest's preceding him up the ladder leading to the elevation; where, one on each side of the last step, sat for armorial supporters and sentries two of the ominous file. Gingerly enough stepped good Captain Delano between them, and in the instant of leaving them behind, like one running the gauntlet, he felt an apprehensive twitch in the calves of his legs.

But when, facing about, he saw the whole file, like so many organ-grinders, still stupidly intent on their work, unmindful of everything beside, he could not but smile at his late fidgeting panic.

Presently, while standing with his host, looking forward upon the decks below, he was struck by one of those instances of insubordination previously alluded to. Three black boys, with two Spanish boys, were sitting together on the hatches, scraping a rude wooden platter, in which some scanty mess had recently been cooked. Suddenly, one of the black boys, enraged at a word dropped by one of his white companions, seized a knife, and though called to forbear by one of the oakum-pickers, struck the lad over the head, inflicting a gash from which blood flowed.

In amazement, Captain Delano inquired what this meant. To which the pale Don Benito dully muttered, that it was merely the sport of the lad.

"Pretty serious sport, truly," rejoined Captain Delano. "Had such a thing happened on board the Bachelor's Delight, instant punishment would have followed."

At these words the Spaniard turned upon the American one of his sudden, staring, half-lunatic looks; then relapsing into his torpor, answered, "Doubtless, doubtless, Señor."

Is it, thought Captain Delano, that this hapless man is one of those paper captains I've known, who by policy wink at what by power they cannot put down? I know no sadder sight than a commander who has little of command but the name.

"I should think, Don Benito," he now said, glancing towards the oakum-picker who had sought to interfere with the boys, "that you would find it advantageous to keep all your blacks employed, especially the younger ones, no matter at what useless task, and no matter what happens to the ship. Why, even with my little band, I find such a course indispensable. I once kept a crew on my quarter-deck thrumming mats for my cabin, when, for three days, I had given up my ship—mats, men, and all—for a speedy loss, owing to the violence of a gale, in which we could do nothing but helplessly drive before it."

"Doubtless, doubtless," muttered Don Benito.

"But," continued Captain Delano, again glancing upon the oakum-pickers and then at the hatchet-polishers, near by, "I see you keep some at least of your host employed."

"Yes," was again the vacant response.

"Those old men there, shaking their pows from their pulpits," continued Captain Delano, pointing to the oakum-pickers, "seem to act the part of old dominies to the rest, little heeded as their admonitions are at times. Is this voluntary on their part, Don Benito, or have you appointed them shepherds to your flock of black sheep?"

"What posts they fill, I appointed them," rejoined the Spaniard, in an acrid tone, as if resenting some supposed satiric reflection.

"And these others, these Ashantee conjurors here," continued Captain Delano, rather uneasily eying the brandished steel of the hatchet-polishers, where in spots it had been brought to a shine, "this seems a curious business they are at, Don Benito?"

"In the gales we met," answered the Spaniard, "what of our general cargo was not thrown overboard was much damaged by the brine. Since coming into calm weather, I have had several cases of knives and hatchets daily brought up for overhauling and cleaning."

"A prudent idea, Don Benito. You are part owner of ship and cargo, I presume; but not of the slaves, perhaps?"

"I am owner of all you see," impatiently returned Don Benito, "except the main company of blacks, who belonged to my late friend, Alexandro Aranda."

As he mentioned this name, his air was heart-broken; his knees shook: his servant supported him.

Thinking he divined the cause of such unusual emotion, to confirm his surmise, Captain Delano, after a pause, said, "And may I ask, Don Benito, whether—since awhile ago you spoke of some cabin passengers—the friend, whose loss so afflicts you at the outset of the voyage accompanied his blacks?"

"Yes."

"But died of the fever?"

"Died of the fever. —Oh, could I but——"

Again quivering, the Spaniard paused.

"Pardon me," said Captain Delano lowly, "but I think that, by a sympathetic experience, I conjecture, Don Benito, what it is that gives the keener edge to your grief. It was once my hard fortune to lose at sea a dear friend, my own brother, then supercargo. Assured of the welfare of his spirit, its departure I could have borne like a man; but that honest eye, that honest hand—both of which had so often met mine—and that warm heart; all, all—like scraps to the dogs—to throw all to the sharks! It was then I vowed never to have for fellow-voyager a man I loved, unless, unbeknown to him, I had provided every requisite, in case of a fatality, for embalming his mortal part for interment on shore. Were your friend's remains now on board this ship, Don Benito, not thus strangely would the mention of his name affect you."

"On board this ship?" echoed the Spaniard. Then, with horrified gestures, as directed against some specter, he unconsciously fell into the ready arms of his attendant, who, with a silent appeal toward Captain Delano, seemed beseeching him not again to broach a theme so unspeakably distressing to his master.

This poor fellow now, thought the pained American, is the victim of that sad superstition which associates goblins with the deserted body of man, as ghosts with an abandoned house. How unlike are we made! What to me, in like case, would have been a solemn satisfaction, the bare suggestion, even, terrifies the Spaniard into this trance. Poor Alexandro Aranda! what would you say could you here see your friend—who, on former voyages, when you for months were left behind, has, I dare say, often longed, and longed, for one peep at you—now transported with terror at the least thought of having you anyway nigh him.

At this moment, with a dreary grave-yard toll, betokening a flaw, the ship's forecastle bell, smote by one of the grizzled oakum-pickers, proclaimed ten o'clock through the leaden calm; when Captain Delano's attention was caught by the moving figure of a gigantic black, emerging from the general crowd below, and slowly advancing towards the elevated poop. An iron collar was about his neck, from which depended a chain, thrice wound round his body; the terminating links padlocked together at a broad band of iron, his girdle.

"How like a mute Atufal moves," murmured the servant.

The black mounted the steps of the poop, and, like a brave prisoner, brought up to receive sentence, stood in unquailing muteness before Don Benito, now recovered from his attack.

At the first glimpse of his approach, Don Benito had started, a resentful shadow swept over his face; and, as with the sudden memory of bootless rage, his white lips glued together.

This is some mulish mutineer, thought Captain Delano, surveying, not without a mixture of admiration, the colossal form of the negro.

"See, he waits your question, master," said the servant.

Thus reminded, Don Benito, nervously averting his glance, as if shunning, by anticipation, some rebellious response, in a disconcerted voice, thus spoke:—

"Atufal, will you ask my pardon now?"

The black was silent.

"Again, master," murmured the servant, with bitter upbraiding eying his countryman, "Again, master; he will bend to master yet."

"Answer," said Don Benito, still averting his glance, "say but the one word *pardon*, and your chains shall be off."

Upon this, the black, slowly raising both arms, let them lifelessly fall, his links clanking, his head bowed; as much as to say, "no, I am content."

"Go," said Don Benito, with inkept and unknown emotion.

Deliberately as he had come, the black obeyed.

"Excuse me, Don Benito," said Captain Delano, "but this scene surprises me; what means it, pray?"

"It means that that negro alone, of all the band, has given me peculiar cause of offense. I have put him in chains; I——"

Here he paused; his hand to his head, as if there were a swimming there, or a sudden bewilderment of memory had come over him; but meeting his servant's kindly glance seemed reassured, and proceeded:—

"I could not scourge such a form. But I told him he must ask my pardon. As yet he has not. At my command, every two hours he stands before me."

"And how long has this been?"

"Some sixty days."

"And obedient in all else? And respectful?"

"Yes."

"Upon my conscience, then," exclaimed Captain Delano, impulsively, "he has a royal spirit in him, this fellow."

"He may have some right to it," bitterly returned Don Benito, "he says he was king in his own land."

"Yes," said the servant, entering a word, "those slits in Atufal's ears once held wedges of gold; but poor Babo here, in his own land, was only a poor slave; a black man's slave was Babo, who now is the white's."

Somewhat annoyed by these conversational familiarities, Captain Delano turned curiously upon the attendant, then glanced inquiringly at his master; but, as if long wonted to these little informalities, neither master nor man seemed to understand him.

"What, pray, was Atufal's offense, Don Benito?" asked Captain Delano; "if it was not something very serious, take a fool's advice, and, in view of his general docility, as well as in some natural respect for his spirit, remit him his penalty."

"No, no, master never will do that," here murmured the servant to himself, "proud Atufal must first ask master's pardon. The slave there carries the padlock, but master here carries the key."

His attention thus directed, Captain Delano now noticed for the first time that, suspended by a slender silken cord, from Don Benito's neck hung a key. At once, from the servant's muttered syllables divining the key's purpose, he smiled and said:—"So, Don Benito—padlock and key—significant symbols, truly."

Biting his lip, Don Benito faltered.

Though the remark of Captain Delano, a man of such native simplicity as to be incapable of satire or irony, had been dropped in playful allusion to the Spaniard's singularly evidenced lordship over the black; yet the hypochondriac seemed in some way to have taken it as a malicious reflection upon his confessed inability thus far to break down, at least, on a verbal summons, the entrenched will of the slave. Deploring this supposed misconception, yet despairing of correcting it, Captain Delano shifted the subject; but finding his companion more than ever withdrawn, as if still sourly digesting the lees of the presumed affront above-mentioned, by-and-by Captain Delano likewise became less talkative, oppressed, against his own will, by what seemed the secret vindictiveness of the morbidly sensitive Spaniard. But the good sailor himself, of a quite contrary disposition, refrained, on his part, alike from the appearance as from the feeling of resentment, and if silent, was only so from contagion.

Presently the Spaniard, assisted by his servant, somewhat discourteously crossed over from his guest; a procedure which, sensibly enough, might have been allowed to pass for idle caprice of ill-humor, had not master and man, lingering round the corner of the elevated skylight, began whispering together in low voices. This was unpleasing. And more: the moody air of the Spaniard, which at times had not been without a sort of valetudinarian stateliness, now seemed anything but dignified; while the menial familiarity of the servant lost its original charm of simple-hearted attachment.

In his embarrassment, the visitor turned his face to the other side of the ship. By so doing, his glance accidentally fell on a young Spanish sailor, a coil of rope in his hand, just stepped from the deck to the first round of the mizzen-rigging. Perhaps the man would not have been particularly noticed, were it not that, during his ascent to one of the yards, he, with a sort of covert intentness, kept his eye fixed on Captain Delano, from whom, presently, it passed, as if by a natural sequence, to the two whisperers.

His own attention thus redirected to that quarter, Captain Delano gave a slight start. From something in Don Benito's manner just then, it seemed as if the visitor had, at least partly, been the subject of the withdrawn consultation going on—a conjecture as little agreeable to the guest as it was little flattering to the host.

The singular alternations of courtesy and ill-breeding in the Spanish captain were unaccountable, except on one of two suppositions—innocent lunacy, or wicked imposture.

But the first idea, though it might naturally have occurred to an indifferent observer, and, in some respect, had not hitherto been wholly a stranger to Captain Delano's mind, yet, now that, in an incipient way, he began to regard the stranger's conduct something in the light of an intentional affront, of course the idea of lunacy was virtually vacated. But if not a lunatic, what then? Under the circumstances, would a gentleman, nay, any honest boor, act the part now acted by his host? The man was an impostor. Some low-born adventurer, masquerading as an oceanic grandee; yet so ignorant of the first requisites of mere gentlemanhood as to be betrayed into the present remarkable indecorum. That strange ceremoniousness, too, at other times evinced, seemed not uncharacteristic of one playing a part above his real level. Benito Cereno—Don Benito Cereno—a sounding name. One, too, at that period, not unknown, in the surname, to supercargoes and sea captains trading along the Spanish Main, as belonging to one of the most enterprising and extensive mercantile families in all those provinces; several members of it having titles; a sort of Castilian Rothschild, with a noble brother, or cousin, in every great trading town of South America. The alleged Don Benito was in early manhood, about twenty-nine or thirty. To assume a sort of roving cadetship in the maritime affairs of such a house, what more likely scheme for a young knave of talent and spirit? But the Spaniard was a pale invalid. Never mind. For even to the degree of simulating mortal disease, the craft of some tricksters had been known to attain. To think that, under the aspect of infantile weakness, the most savage energies might be couched—those velvets of the Spaniard but the silky paw to his fangs.

From no train of thought did these fancies come; not from within, but from without; suddenly, too, and in one throng, like hoar frost; yet as soon to vanish as the mild sun of Captain Delano's good-nature regained its meridian.

Glancing over once more towards his host—whose side-face, revealed above the skylight, was now turned towards him—he was struck by the profile, whose clearness of cut was refined by the thinness incident to ill-health, as well as ennobled about the chin by the beard. Away with suspicion. He was a true off-shoot of a true hidalgo Cereno.

Relieved by these and other better thoughts, the visitor, lightly humming a tune, now began indifferently pacing the poop, so as not to betray to Don Benito that he had at all mistrusted incivility, much less duplicity; for such mistrust would yet be proved illusory, and by the event; though, for the present, the circumstance which had provoked that distrust remained unexplained. But when that little mystery should have been cleared up, Captain Delano thought he might extremely regret it, did he allow Don Benito to become aware that he had indulged in ungenerous surmises. In short, to the Spaniard's black-letter text, it was best, for awhile, to leave open margin.

Presently, his pale face twitching and overcast, the Spaniard, still supported by his attendant, moved over towards his guest, when, with even more than his usual embarrassment, and a strange sort of intriguing intonation in his husky whisper, the following conversation began:—

"Señor, may I ask how long you have lain at this isle?"

"Oh, but a day or two, Don Benito."

"And from what port are you last?"

"Canton."

"And there, Señor, you exchanged your seal-skins for teas and silks, I think you said?"

"Yes. Silks, mostly."

"And the balance you took in specie, perhaps?"

Captain Delano, fidgeting a little, answered—

"Yes; some silver; not a very great deal, though."

"Ah—well. May I ask how many men have you, Señor?"

Captain Delano slightly started, but answered—

"About five-and-twenty, all told."

"And at present, Señor, all on board, I suppose?"

"All on board, Don Benito," replied the Captain, now with satisfaction.

"And will be to-night, Señor?"

At this last question, following so many pertinacious ones, for the soul of him Captain Delano could not but look very earnestly at the questioner, who, instead of meeting the glance, with every token of craven discomposure dropped his eyes to the deck; presenting an unworthy contrast to his servant, who, just then, was kneeling at his feet, adjusting a loose shoe-buckle; his disengaged face meantime, with humble curiosity, turned openly up into his master's downcast one.

The Spaniard, still with a guilty shuffle, repeated his question:—

"And—and will be to-night, Señor?"

"Yes, for aught I know," returned Captain Delano,—"but nay," rallying himself into fearless truth, "some of them talked of going off on another fishing party about midnight."

"Your ships generally go—go more or less armed, I believe, Señor?"

"Oh, a six-pounder or two, in case of emergency," was the intrepidly indifferent reply, "with a small stock of muskets, sealing-spears, and cutlasses, you know."

As he thus responded, Captain Delano again glanced at Don Benito, but the latter's eyes were averted; while abruptly and awkwardly shifting the subject, he made some peevish allusion to the calm, and then, without apology, once more, with his attendant, withdrew to the opposite bulwarks, where the whispering was resumed.

At this moment, and ere Captain Delano could cast a cool thought upon what had just passed, the young Spanish sailor before mentioned was seen descending from the rigging. In act of stooping over to spring inboard to the deck, his voluminous, unconfined frock, or shirt, of coarse woollen, much spotted with tar, opened out far down the chest, revealing a soiled under garment of what seemed the finest linen, edged, about the neck, with a narrow blue ribbon, sadly faded and worn. At this moment the young sailor's eye was again fixed on the whisperers, and Captain Delano thought he observed a lurking significance in it, as if silent signs of some Freemason sort had that instant been interchanged.

This once more impelled his own glance in the direction of Don Benito, and, as before, he could not but infer that himself formed the subject of the conference. He paused. The sound of the hatchet-polishing fell on his ears. He cast another swift side-look at the two. They had the air of conspirators. In connection with the late questionings and the incident of the young sailor, these things now begat such return of involuntary suspicion, that the singular guilelessness of the American could not endure it. Plucking up a gay and humorous expression, he crossed over to the two rapidly, saying:—"Ha, Don Benito, your black here seems high in your trust; a sort of privy-counselor, in fact."

Upon this, the servant looked up with a good-natured grin, but the master started as from a venomous bite. It was a moment or two before the Spaniard sufficiently recovered himself to reply; which he did, at last, with cold constraint:—"Yes, Señor, I have trust in Babo."

Here Babo, changing his previous grin of mere animal humor into an intelligent smile, not ungratefully eyed his master.

Finding that the Spaniard now stood silent and reserved, as if involuntarily, or purposely giving hint that his guest's proximity was inconvenient just then, Captain Delano, unwilling to appear uncivil even to incivility itself, made some trivial remark and moved off; again and again turning over in his mind the mysterious demeanor of Don Benito Cereno.

He had descended from the poop, and, wrapped in thought, was passing near a dark hatchway, leading down into the steerage, when, perceiving motion there, he looked to see what moved. The same instant there was a sparkle in the shadowy hatchway, and he saw one of the Spanish sailors prowling there hurriedly placing his hand in the bosom of his frock, as if hiding something. Before the man could have been certain who it was that was passing, he slunk below out of sight. But enough was seen of him to make it sure that he was the same young sailor before noticed in the rigging.

What was that which so sparkled? thought Captain Delano. It was no lamp—no match—no live coal. Could it have been a jewel? But how come sailors with jewels?—or with silk-trimmed under-shirts either? Has he been robbing the trunks of the dead cabin passengers? But if so, he would hardly wear one of the stolen articles on board ship here. Ah, ah—if now that was, indeed, a secret sign I saw passing between this suspicious fellow and his captain awhile since; if I could only be certain that in my uneasiness my senses did not deceive me, then——

Here, passing from one suspicious thing to another, his mind revolved the point of the strange questions put to him concerning his ship.

By a curious coincidence, as each point was recalled, the black wizards of Ashantee would strike up with their hatchets, as in ominous comment on the white stranger's thoughts. Pressed by such enigmas and portents, it would have been almost against nature, had not, even into the least distrustful heart, some ugly misgivings obtruded.

Observing the ship now helplessly fallen into a current, with enchanted sails, drifting with increased rapidity seaward; and noting that, from a lately intercepted projection of the land, the sealer was hidden, the stout mariner began to quake at thoughts which he barely durst confess to himself. Above all, he began to feel a ghostly dread of Don Benito. And yet when he roused himself, dilated his chest, felt himself strong on his legs, and coolly considered it—what did all these phantoms amount to?

Had the Spaniard any sinister scheme, it must have reference not so much to him (Captain Delano) as to his ship (the Bachelor's Delight). Hence the present drifting away of the one ship from the other, instead of favoring any such possible scheme, was, for the time at least, opposed to it. Clearly any suspicion, combining such contradictions, must need be delusive. Beside, was it not absurd to think of a vessel in distress—a vessel by sickness almost dismanned of her crew—a vessel whose inmates were parched for water—was it not a thousand times absurd that such a craft should, at present, be of a piratical character; or her commander, either for himself or those under him, cherish any desire but for speedy relief and refreshment? But then, might not general distress, and thirst in particular, be affected? And might not that same undiminished Spanish crew, alleged to have perished off to a remnant, be at that very moment lurking in the hold? On heart-broken pretense of entreating a cup of cold water, fiends in human form had got into lonely dwellings, nor retired until a dark deed had been done. And among the Malay pirates, it was no unusual thing to lure ships after them into their treacherous harbors, or entice boarders from a declared enemy at sea, by the spectacle of thinly manned or vacant decks, beneath which prowled a hundred spears with yellow arms ready to upthrust them through the mats. Not that Captain Delano had entirely credited such things. He had heard of them—and now, as stories, they recurred. The present destination of the ship was the anchorage. There she would be near his own vessel. Upon gaining that vicinity, might not the San Dominick, like a slumbering volcano, suddenly let loose energies now hid?

He recalled the Spaniard's manner while telling his story. There was a gloomy hesitancy and subterfuge about it. It was just the manner of one making up his tale for evil purposes, as he goes. But if that story was not true, what was the truth? That the ship had unlawfully come into the Spaniard's possession? But in many of its details, especially in reference to the more calamitous parts, such as the fatalities among the seamen, the consequent prolonged beating about, the past sufferings from obstinate calms, and still continued suffering from thirst; in all these points, as well as others, Don Benito's story had been corroborated not only by the wailing ejaculations of the indiscriminate multitude, white and black, but likewise—what seemed impossible to be counterfeit—by the very expression and play of every human feature, which Captain Delano saw. If Don Benito's story was throughout an invention, then every soul on board, down to the youngest negress, was his carefully drilled recruit in the plot: an incredible inference. And yet, if there was ground for mistrusting his veracity, that inference was a legitimate one.

But those questions of the Spaniard. There, indeed, one might pause. Did they not seem put with much the same object with which the burglar or assassin, by day-time, reconnoitres the walls of a house? But, with ill purposes, to solicit such information openly of the chief person endangered, and so, in effect, setting him on his guard; how unlikely a procedure was that? Absurd, then, to suppose that those questions had been prompted by evil designs. Thus, the same conduct, which, in this instance, had raised the alarm, served to dispel it. In short, scarce any suspicion or uneasiness, however apparently reasonable at the time, which was not now, with equal apparent reason, dismissed.

At last he began to laugh at his former forebodings; and laugh at the strange ship for, in its aspect someway siding with them, as it were; and laugh, too, at the odd-looking blacks, particularly those old scissors-grinders, the Ashantees; and those bed-ridden old knitting-women, the oakum-pickers; and almost at the dark Spaniard himself, the central hobgoblin of all.

For the rest, whatever in a serious way seemed enigmatical, was now good-naturedly explained away by the thought that, for the most part, the poor invalid scarcely knew what he was about; either sulking in black vapors, or putting idle questions without sense or object. Evidently, for the present, the man was not fit to be entrusted with the ship. On some benevolent plea withdrawing the command from him, Captain Delano would yet have to send her to Conception, in charge of his second mate, a worthy person and good navigator—a plan not more convenient for the San Dominick than for Don Benito; for, relieved from all anxiety, keeping wholly to his cabin, the sick man, under the good nursing of his servant, would probably, by the end of the passage, be in a measure restored to health, and with that he should also be restored to authority.

Such were the American's thoughts. They were tranquilizing. There was a difference between the idea of Don Benito's darkly pre-ordaining Captain Delano's fate, and Captain Delano's lightly arranging Don Benito's. Nevertheless, it was not without something of relief that the good seaman presently perceived his whale-boat in the distance. Its absence had been prolonged by unexpected detention at the sealer's side, as well as its returning trip lengthened by the continual recession of the goal.

The advancing speck was observed by the blacks. Their shouts attracted the attention of Don Benito, who, with a return of courtesy, approaching Captain Delano, expressed satisfaction at the coming of some supplies, slight and temporary as they must necessarily prove.

Captain Delano responded; but while doing so, his attention was drawn to something passing on the deck below: among the crowd climbing the landward bulwarks, anxiously watching the coming boat, two blacks, to all appearances accidentally incommoded by one of the sailors, flew out against him with horrible curses, which the sailor someway resenting, the two blacks dashed him to the deck and jumped upon him, despite the earnest cries of the oakum-pickers.

"Don Benito," said Captain Delano quickly, "do you see what is going on there? Look!"

But, seized by his cough, the Spaniard staggered, with both hands to his face, on the point of falling. Captain Delano would have supported him, but the servant was more alert, who, with one hand sustaining his master, with the other applied the cordial. Don Benito restored, the black withdrew his support, slipping aside a little, but dutifully remaining within call of a whisper. Such discretion was here evinced as quite wiped away, in the visitor's eyes, any blemish of impropriety which might have attached to the attendant, from the indecorous conferences before mentioned; showing, too, that if the servant were to blame, it might be more the master's fault than his own, since when left to himself he could conduct thus well.

His glance thus called away from the spectacle of disorder to the more pleasing one before him, Captain Delano could not avoid again congratulating his host upon possessing such a servant, who, though perhaps a little too forward now and then, must upon the whole be invaluable to one in the invalid's situation.

"Tell me, Don Benito," he added, with a smile—"I should like to have your man here myself—what will you take for him? Would fifty doubloons be any object?"

"Master wouldn't part with Babo for a thousand doubloons," murmured the black, overhearing the offer, and taking it in earnest, and, with the strange vanity of a faithful slave appreciated by his master, scorning to hear so paltry a valuation put upon him by a stranger. But Don Benito, apparently hardly yet completely restored, and again interrupted by his cough, made but some broken reply.

Soon his physical distress became so great, affecting his mind, too, apparently, that, as if to screen the sad spectacle, the servant gently conducted his master below.

Left to himself, the American, to while away the time till his boat should arrive, would have pleasantly accosted some one of the few Spanish seamen he saw; but recalling something that Don Benito had said touching their ill conduct, he refrained, as a ship-master indisposed to countenance cowardice or unfaithfulness in seamen.

While, with these thoughts, standing with eye directed forward towards that handful of sailors, suddenly he thought that one or two of them returned the glance and with a sort of meaning. He rubbed his eyes, and looked again; but again seemed to see the same thing. Under a new form, but more obscure than any previous one, the old suspicions recurred, but, in the absence of Don Benito, with less of panic than before. Despite the bad account given of the sailors, Captain Delano resolved forthwith to accost one of them. Descending the poop, he made his way through the blacks, his movement drawing a queer cry from the oakum-pickers, prompted by whom, the negroes, twitching each other aside, divided before him; but, as if curious to see what was the object of this deliberate visit to their Ghetto, closing in behind, in tolerable order, followed the white stranger up. His progress thus proclaimed as by mounted kings-at-arms, and escorted as by a Caffre guard of honor, Captain Delano, assuming a good humored, off-handed air, continued to advance; now and then saying a blithe word to the negroes, and his eye curiously surveying the white faces, here and there sparsely mixed in with the blacks, like stray white pawns venturously involved in the ranks of the chess-men opposed.

While thinking which of them to select for his purpose, he chanced to observe a sailor seated on the deck engaged in tarring the strap of a large block, with a circle of blacks squatted round him inquisitively eying the process.

The mean employment of the man was in contrast with something superior in his figure. His hand, black with continually thrusting it into the tar-pot held for him by a negro, seemed not naturally allied to his face, a face which would have been a very fine one but for its haggardness. Whether this haggardness had aught to do with criminality, could not be determined; since, as intense heat and cold, though unlike, produce like sensations, so innocence and guilt, when, through casual association with mental pain, stamping any visible impress, use one seal—a hacked one.

Not again that this reflection occurred to Captain Delano at the time, charitable man as he was. Rather another idea. Because observing so singular a haggardness combined with a dark eye, averted as in trouble and shame, and then again recalling Don Benito's confessed ill opinion of his crew, insensibly he was operated upon by certain general notions, which, while disconnecting pain and abashment from virtue, invariably link them with vice.

If, indeed, there be any wickedness on board this ship, thought Captain Delano, be sure that man there has fouled his hand in it, even as now he fouls it in the pitch. I don't like to accost him. I will speak to this other, this old Jack here on the windlass.

He advanced to an old Barcelona tar, in ragged red breeches and dirty night-cap, cheeks trenched and bronzed, whiskers dense as thorn hedges. Seated between two sleepy-looking Africans, this mariner, like his younger shipmate, was employed upon some rigging—splicing a cable—the sleepy-looking blacks performing the inferior function of holding the outer parts of the ropes for him.

Upon Captain Delano's approach, the man at once hung his head below its previous level; the one necessary for business. It appeared as if he desired to be thought absorbed, with more than common fidelity, in his task. Being addressed, he glanced up, but with what seemed a furtive, diffident air, which sat strangely enough on his weather-beaten visage, much as if a grizzly bear, instead of growling and biting, should simper and cast sheep's eyes. He was asked several questions concerning the voyage, questions purposely referring to several particulars in Don Benito's narrative, not previously corroborated by those impulsive cries greeting the visitor on first coming on board. The questions were briefly answered, confirming all that remained to be confirmed of the story. The negroes about the windlass joined in with the old sailor, but, as they became talkative, he by degrees became mute, and at length quite glum, seemed morosely unwilling to answer more questions, and yet, all the while, this ursine air was somehow mixed with his sheepish one.

Despairing of getting into unembarrassed talk with such a centaur, Captain Delano, after glancing round for a more promising countenance, but seeing none, spoke pleasantly to the blacks to make way for him; and so, amid various grins and grimaces, returned to the poop, feeling a little strange at first, he could hardly tell why, but upon the whole with regained confidence in Benito Cereno.

How plainly, thought he, did that old whiskerando yonder betray a consciousness of ill-desert. No doubt, when he saw me coming, he dreaded lest I, apprised by his Captain of the crew's general misbehavior, came with sharp words for him, and so down with his head. And yet—and yet, now that I think of it, that very old fellow, if I err not, was one of those who seemed so earnestly eying me here awhile since. Ah, these currents spin one's head round almost as much as they do the ship. Ha, there now's a pleasant sort of sunny sight; quite sociable, too.

His attention had been drawn to a slumbering negress, partly disclosed through the lace-work of some rigging, lying, with youthful limbs carelessly disposed, under the lee of the bulwarks, like a doe in the shade of a woodland rock. Sprawling at her lapped breasts was her wide-awake fawn, stark naked, its black little body half lifted from the deck, crosswise with its dam's; its hands, like two paws, clambering upon her; its mouth and nose ineffectually rooting to get at the mark; and meantime giving a vexatious half-grunt, blending with the composed snore of the negress.

The uncommon vigor of the child at length roused the mother. She started up, at distance facing Captain Delano. But as if not at all concerned at the attitude in which she had been caught, delightedly she caught the child up, with maternal transports, covering it with kisses.

There's naked nature, now; pure tenderness and love, thought Captain Delano, well pleased.

This incident prompted him to remark the other negresses more particularly than before. He was gratified with their manners; like most uncivilized women, they seemed at once tender of heart and tough of constitution; equally ready to die for their infants or fight for them. Unsophisticated as leopardesses; loving as doves. Ah! thought Captain Delano, these perhaps are some of the very women whom Mungo Park saw in Africa, and gave such a noble account of.

These natural sights somehow insensibly deepened his confidence and ease. At last he looked to see how his boat was getting on; but it was still pretty remote. He turned to see if Don Benito had returned; but he had not.

To change the scene, as well as to please himself with a leisurely observation of the coming boat, stepping over into the mizzen-chains he

clambered his way into the starboard quarter-gallery; one of those abandoned Venetian-looking water-balconies previously mentioned; retreats
cut off from the deck. As his foot pressed the half-damp, half-dry sea-
mosses matting the place, and a chance phantom cats-paw—an islet of
breeze, unheralded, unfollowed—as this ghostly cats-paw came fanning
his cheek, as his glance fell upon the row of small, round dead-lights, all
closed like coppered eyes of the coffined, and the state-cabin door, once
connecting with the gallery, even as the dead-lights had once looked out
upon it, but now calked fast like a sarcophagus lid, to a purple-black,
tarred-over panel, threshold, and post; and he bethought him of the time,
when that state-cabin and this state-balcony had heard the voices of the
Spanish king's officers, and the forms of the Lima viceroy's daughters had
perhaps leaned where he stood—as these and other images flitted
through his mind, as the cats-paw through the calm, gradually he felt rising a dreamy inquietude, like that of one who alone on the prairie feels
unrest from the repose of the noon.

He leaned against the carved balustrade, again looking off toward his
boat; but found his eye falling upon the ribbon grass, trailing along the
ship's water-line, straight as a border of green box; and parterres of sea-
weed, broad ovals and crescents, floating nigh and far, with what seemed
long formal alleys between, crossing the terraces of swells, and sweeping
round as if leading to the grottoes below. And overhanging all was the
balustrade by his arm, which, partly stained with pitch and partly em-
bossed with moss, seemed the charred ruin of some summer-house in a
grand garden long running to waste.

Trying to break one charm, he was but becharmed anew. Though upon
the wide sea, he seemed in some far inland country; prisoner in some deserted château, left to stare at empty grounds, and peer out at vague
roads, where never wagon or wayfarer passed.

But these enchantments were a little disenchanted as his eye fell on the
corroded main-chains. Of an ancient style, massy and rusty in link,
shackle and bolt, they seemed even more fit for the ship's present business
than the one for which probably she had been built.

Presently he thought something moved nigh the chains. He rubbed his
eyes, and looked hard. Groves of rigging were about the chains; and there,
peering from behind a great stay, like an Indian from behind a hemlock, a
Spanish sailor, a marlingspike in his hand, was seen, who made what
seemed an imperfect gesture towards the balcony, but immediately, as if

alarmed by some advancing step along the deck within, vanished into the recesses of the hempen forest, like a poacher.

What meant this? Something the man had sought to communicate, unbeknown to any one, even to his captain. Did the secret involve aught unfavorable to his captain? Were those previous misgivings of Captain Delano's about to be verified? Or, in his haunted mood at the moment, had some random, unintentional motion of the man, while busy with the stay, as if repairing it, been mistaken for a significant beckoning?

Not unbewildered, again he gazed off for his boat. But it was temporarily hidden by a rocky spur of the isle. As with some eagerness he bent forward, watching for the first shooting view of its beak, the balustrade gave way before him like charcoal. Had he not clutched an outreaching rope he would have fallen into the sea. The crash, though feeble, and the fall, though hollow, of the rotten fragments, must have been overheard. He glanced up. With sober curiosity peering down upon him was one of the old oakum-pickers, slipped from his perch to an outside boom; while below the old negro, and, invisible to him, reconnoitering from a porthole like a fox from the mouth of its den, crouched the Spanish sailor again. From something suddenly suggested by the man's air, the mad idea now darted into Captain Delano's mind, that Don Benito's plea of indisposition, in withdrawing below, was but a pretense: that he was engaged there maturing some plot, of which the sailor, by some means gaining an inkling, had a mind to warn the stranger against; incited, it may be, by gratitude for a kind word on first boarding the ship. Was it from foreseeing some possible interference like this, that Don Benito had, beforehand, given such a bad character of his sailors, while praising the negroes; though, indeed, the former seemed as docile as the latter the contrary? The whites, too, by nature, were the shrewder race. A man with some evil design, would he not be likely to speak well of that stupidity which was blind to his depravity, and malign that intelligence from which it might not be hidden? Not unlikely, perhaps. But if the whites had dark secrets concerning Don Benito, could then Don Benito be any way in complicity with the blacks? But they were too stupid. Besides, who ever heard of a white so far a renegade as to apostatize from his very species almost, by leaguing in against it with negroes? These difficulties recalled former ones. Lost in their mazes, Captain Delano, who had now regained the deck, was uneasily advancing along it, when he observed a new face; an aged sailor seated cross-legged near the main hatchway. His skin was shrunk up with wrinkles like a pelican's empty pouch; his hair frosted; his countenance grave and composed. His hands were full of ropes, which he was working into a large knot. Some blacks were about him obligingly dipping the strands for him, here and there, as the exigencies of the operation demanded.

Captain Delano crossed over to him, and stood in silence surveying the knot; his mind, by a not uncongenial transition, passing from its own entanglements to those of the hemp. For intricacy such a knot he had never seen in an American ship, or indeed any other. The old man looked like an Egyptian priest, making gordian knots for the temple of Ammon. The knot seemed a combination of double-bowline-knot, treble-crown-knot, back-handed-well-knot, knot-in-and out-knot, and jamming-knot.

At last, puzzled to comprehend the meaning of such a knot, Captain Delano addressed the knotter:—

"What are you knotting there, my man?"

"The knot," was the brief reply, without looking up.

"So it seems; but what is it for?"

"For some one else to undo," muttered back the old man, plying his fingers harder than ever, the knot being now nearly completed.

While Captain Delano stood watching him, suddenly the old man threw the knot towards him, saying in broken English,—the first heard in the ship,—something to this effect—"Undo it, cut it, quick." It was said lowly, but with such condensation of rapidity, that the long, slow words in Spanish, which had preceded and followed, almost operated as covers to the brief English between.

For a moment, knot in hand, and knot in head, Captain Delano stood mute; while, without further heeding him, the old man was now intent upon other ropes. Presently there was a slight stir behind Captain Delano. Turning, he saw the chained negro, Atufal, standing quietly there. The next moment the old sailor rose, muttering, and, followed by his subordinate negroes, removed to the forward part of the ship, where in the crowd he disappeared.

An elderly negro, in a clout like an infant's, and with a pepper and salt head, and a kind of attorney air, now approached Captain Delano. In tolerable Spanish, and with a good-natured, knowing wink, he informed him that the old knotter was simple-witted, but harmless; often playing his old tricks. The negro concluded by begging the knot, for of course the stranger would not care to be troubled with it. Unconsciously, it was handed to him. With a sort of congé, the negro received it, and turning his back, ferreted into it like a detective Custom House officer after smuggled laces. Soon, with some African word, equivalent to pshaw, he tossed the knot overboard.

All this is very queer now, thought Captain Delano, with a qualmish sort of emotion; but as one feeling incipient sea-sickness, he strove, by ignoring the symptoms, to get rid of the malady. Once more he looked off for his boat. To his delight, it was now again in view, leaving the rocky spur astern.

The sensation here experienced, after at first relieving his uneasiness, with unforeseen efficacy, soon began to remove it. The less distant sight of that well-known boat—showing it, not as before, half blended with the haze, but with outline defined, so that its individuality, like a man's, was manifest; that boat, Rover by name, which, though now in strange seas, had often pressed the beach of Captain Delano's home, and, brought to its threshold for repairs, had familiarly lain there, as a Newfoundland dog; the sight of that household boat evoked a thousand trustful associations, which, contrasted with previous suspicions, filled him not only with lightsome confidence, but somehow with half humorous self-reproaches at his former lack of it.

"What, I, Amasa Delano—Jack of the Beach, as they called me when a lad—I, Amasa; the same that, duck-satchel in hand, used to paddle along the waterside to the school-house made from the old hulk;—I, little Jack of the Beach, that used to go berrying with cousin Nat and the rest; I to be murdered here at the ends of the earth, on board a haunted pirate-ship by a horrible Spaniard?—Too nonsensical to think of! Who would murder Amasa Delano? His conscience is clean. There is some one above. Fie, fie, Jack of the Beach! you are a child indeed; a child of the second childhood, old boy; you are beginning to dote and drule, I'm afraid."

Light of heart and foot, he stepped aft, and there was met by Don Benito's servant, who, with a pleasing expression, responsive to his own present feelings, informed him that his master had recovered from the effects of his coughing fit, and had just ordered him to go present his compliments to his good guest, Don Amasa, and say that he (Don Benito) would soon have the happiness to rejoin him.

There now, do you mark that? again thought Captain Delano, walking the poop. What a donkey I was. This kind gentleman who here sends me his kind compliments, he, but ten minutes ago, dark-lantern in hand, was dodging round some old grind-stone in the hold, sharpening a hatchet for me, I thought. Well, well; these long calms have a morbid effect on the mind, I've often heard, though I never believed it before. Ha! glancing towards the boat; there's Rover; good dog; a white bone in her mouth. A pretty big bone though, seems to me.—What? Yes, she has fallen afoul of the bubbling tide-rip there. It sets her the other way, too, for the time. Patience.

It was now about noon, though, from the grayness of everything, it seemed to be getting towards dusk.

The calm was confirmed. In the far distance, away from the influence of land, the leaden ocean seemed laid out and leaded up, its course finished, soul gone, defunct. But the current from landward, where the ship was, increased; silently sweeping her further and further towards the tranced waters beyond.

Still, from his knowledge of those latitudes, cherishing hopes of a breeze, and a fair and fresh one, at any moment, Captain Delano, despite present prospects, buoyantly counted upon bringing the San Dominick safely to anchor ere night. The distance swept over was nothing; since, with a good wind, ten minutes' sailing would retrace more than sixty minutes' drifting. Meantime, one moment turning to mark "Rover" fighting the tide-rip, and the next to see Don Benito approaching, he continued walking the poop.

Gradually he felt a vexation arising from the delay of his boat; this soon merged into uneasiness; and at last, his eye falling continually, as from a stage-box into the pit, upon the strange crowd before and below him, and by and by recognising there the face—now composed to indifference—of the Spanish sailor who had seemed to beckon from the main chains, something of his old trepidations returned.

Ah, thought he—gravely enough—this is like the ague: because it went off, it follows not that it won't come back.

Though ashamed of the relapse, he could not altogether subdue it; and so, exerting his good nature to the utmost, insensibly he came to a compromise.

Yes, this is a strange craft; a strange history, too, and strange folks on board. But—nothing more.

By way of keeping his mind out of mischief till the boat should arrive, he tried to occupy it with turning over and over, in a purely speculative sort of way, some lesser peculiarities of the captain and crew. Among others, four curious points recurred.

First, the affair of the Spanish lad assailed with a knife by the slave boy; an act winked at by Don Benito. Second, the tyranny in Don Benito's treatment of Atufal, the black; as if a child should lead a bull of the Nile by the ring in his nose. Third, the trampling of the sailor by the two negroes; a piece of insolence passed over without so much as a reprimand. Fourth, the cringing submission to their master of all the ship's underlings, mostly blacks; as if by the least inadvertence they feared to draw down his despotic displeasure.

Coupling these points, they seemed somewhat contradictory. But what then, thought Captain Delano, glancing towards his now nearing boat,—what then? Why, Don Benito is a very capricious commander. But he is not the first of the sort I have seen; though it's true he rather exceeds any other. But as a nation—continued he in his reveries—these Spaniards are all an odd set; the very word Spaniard has a curious, conspirator, Guy-Fawkish twang to it. And yet, I dare say, Spaniards in the main are as good folks as any in Duxbury, Massachusetts. Ah good! At last "Rover" has come.

As, with its welcome freight, the boat touched the side, the oakum-pickers, with venerable gestures, sought to restrain the blacks, who, at the sight of three gurried water-casks in its bottom, and a pile of wilted pumpkins in its bow, hung over the bulwarks in disorderly raptures.

Don Benito with his servant now appeared; his coming, perhaps, hastened by hearing the noise. Of him Captain Delano sought permission to serve out the water, so that all might share alike, and none injure themselves by unfair excess. But sensible, and, on Don Benito's account, kind as this offer was, it was received with what seemed impatience; as if aware that he lacked energy as a commander, Don Benito, with the true jealousy of weakness, resented as an affront any interference. So, at least, Captain Delano inferred.

In another moment the casks were being hoisted in, when some of the eager negroes accidentally jostled Captain Delano, where he stood by the gangway; so that, unmindful of Don Benito, yielding to the impulse of the moment, with good-natured authority he bade the blacks stand back; to enforce his words making use of a half-mirthful, half-menacing gesture. Instantly the blacks paused, just where they were, each negro and negress suspended in his or her posture, exactly as the word had found them—for a few seconds continuing so—while, as between the responsive posts of a telegraph, an unknown syllable ran from man to man among the perched oakum-pickers. While the visitor's attention was fixed by this scene, suddenly the hatchet-polishers half rose, and a rapid cry came from Don Benito.

Thinking that at the signal of the Spaniard he was about to be massacred, Captain Delano would have sprung for his boat, but paused, as the oakum-pickers, dropping down into the crowd with earnest exclamations, forced every white and every negro back, at the same moment, with gestures friendly and familiar, almost jocose, bidding him, in substance, not be a fool. Simultaneously the hatchet-polishers resumed their seats, quietly as so many tailors, and at once, as if nothing had happened, the work of hoisting in the casks was resumed, whites and blacks singing at the tackle.

Captain Delano glanced towards Don Benito. As he saw his meager form in the act of recovering itself from reclining in the servant's arms, into which the agitated invalid had fallen, he could not but marvel at the panic by which himself had been surprised on the darting supposition that such a commander, who upon a legitimate occasion, so trivial, too, as it now appeared, could lose all self-command, was, with energetic iniquity, going to bring about his murder.

The casks being on deck, Captain Delano was handed a number of jars and cups by one of the steward's aids, who, in the name of his captain, entreated him to do as he had proposed: dole out the water. He complied, with republican impartiality as to this republican element, which always seeks one level, serving the oldest white no better than the youngest black; excepting, indeed, poor Don Benito, whose condition, if not rank, demanded an extra allowance. To him, in the first place, Captain Delano presented a fair pitcher of the fluid; but, thirsting as he was for it, the Spaniard quaffed not a drop until after several grave bows and salutes. A reciprocation of courtesies which the sight-loving Africans hailed with clapping of hands.

Two of the less wilted pumpkins being reserved for the cabin table, the residue were minced up on the spot for the general regalement. But the soft bread, sugar, and bottled cider, Captain Delano would have given the whites alone, and in chief Don Benito; but the latter objected; which disinterestedness, on his part, not a little pleased the American; and so mouthfuls all around were given alike to whites and blacks; excepting one bottle of cider, which Babo insisted upon setting aside for his master.

Here it may be observed that as, on the first visit of the boat, the American had not permitted his men to board the ship, neither did he now; being unwilling to add to the confusion of the decks.

Not uninfluenced by the peculiar good humor at present prevailing, and for the time oblivious of any but benevolent thoughts, Captain Delano, who from recent indications counted upon a breeze within an hour or two at furthest, dispatched the boat back to the sealer with orders for all the hands that could be spared immediately to set about rafting casks to the watering-place and filling them. Likewise he bade word be carried to his chief officer, that if against present expectation the ship was not brought to anchor by sunset, he need be under no concern, for as there was to be a full moon that night, he (Captain Delano) would remain on board ready to play the pilot, come the wind soon or late.

As the two Captains stood together, observing the departing boat—the servant as it happened having just spied a spot on his master's velvet sleeve, and silently engaged rubbing it out—the American expressed his regrets that the San Dominick had no boats; none, at least, but the unseaworthy old hulk of the long-boat, which, warped as a camel's skeleton in the desert, and almost as bleached, lay pot-wise inverted amidships, one side a little tipped, furnishing a subterraneous sort of den for family groups of the blacks, mostly women and small children; who, squatting on old mats below, or perched above in the dark dome, on the elevated seats, were descried, some distance within, like a social circle of bats, sheltering in some friendly cave; at intervals, ebon flights of naked boys and girls, three or four years old, darting in and out of the den's mouth.

"Had you three or four boats now, Don Benito," said Captain Delano, "I think that, by tugging at the oars, your negroes here might help along matters some.—Did you sail from port without boats, Don Benito?"

"They were stove in the gales, Señor."

"That was bad. Many men, too, you lost then. Boats and men.—Those must have been hard gales, Don Benito."

"Past all speech," cringed the Spaniard.

"Tell me, Don Benito," continued his companion with increased interest, "tell me, were these gales immediately off the pitch of Cape Horn?"

"Cape Horn?—who spoke of Cape Horn?"

"Yourself did, when giving me an account of your voyage," answered

Captain Delano with almost equal astonishment at this eating of his own words, even as he ever seemed eating his own heart, on the part of the Spaniard. "You yourself, Don Benito, spoke of Cape Horn," he emphatically repeated.

The Spaniard turned, in a sort of stooping posture, pausing an instant, as one about to make a plunging exchange of elements, as from air to water.

At this moment a messenger-boy, a white, hurried by, in the regular performance of his function carrying the last expired half hour forward to the forecastle, from the cabin time-piece, to have it struck at the ship's large bell.

"Master," said the servant, discontinuing his work on the coat sleeve, and addressing the rapt Spaniard with a sort of timid apprehensiveness, as one charged with a duty, the discharge of which, it was foreseen, would prove irksome to the very person who had imposed it, and for whose benefit it was intended, "master told me never mind where he was, or how engaged, always to remind him, to a minute, when shaving-time comes. Miguel has gone to strike the half-hour afternoon. It is *now*, master. Will master go into the cuddy?"

"Ah—yes," answered the Spaniard, starting, somewhat as from dreams into realities; then turning upon Captain Delano, he said that ere long he would resume the conversation.

"Then if master means to talk more to Don Amasa," said the servant, "why not let Don Amasa sit by master in the cuddy, and master can talk, and Don Amasa can listen, while Babo here lathers and strops."

"Yes," said Captain Delano, not unpleased with this sociable plan, "yes, Don Benito, unless you had rather not, I will go with you."

"Be it so, Señor."

As the three passed aft, the American could not but think it another strange instance of his host's capriciousness, this being shaved with such uncommon punctuality in the middle of the day. But he deemed it more than likely that the servant's anxious fidelity had something to do with the matter; inasmuch as the timely interruption served to rally his master from the mood which had evidently been coming upon him.

The place called the cuddy was a light deck-cabin formed by the poop, a sort of attic to the large cabin below. Part of it had formerly been the quarters of the officers; but since their death all the partitionings had been thrown down, and the whole interior converted into one spacious and airy marine hall; for absence of fine furniture and picturesque disarray, of odd appurtenances, somewhat answering to the wide, cluttered hall of some eccentric bachelor-squire in the country, who hangs his shooting-jacket and tobacco-pouch on deer antlers, and keeps his fishing-rod, tongs, and walking-stick in the same corner.

The similitude was heightened, if not originally suggested, by glimpses of the surrounding sea; since, in one aspect, the country and the ocean seem cousins-german.

The floor of the cuddy was matted. Overhead, four or five old muskets were stuck into horizontal holes along the beams. On one side was a claw-footed old table lashed to the deck; a thumbed missal on it, and over it a small, meager crucifix attached to the bulk-head. Under the table lay a dented cutlass or two, with a hacked harpoon, among some melancholy old rigging, like a heap of poor friar's girdles. There were also two long, sharp-ribbed settees of malacca cane, black with age, and uncomfortable to look at as inquisitors' racks, with a large, misshapen armchair, which, furnished with a rude barber's crutch at the back, working with a screw, seemed some grotesque, middle-age engine of torment. A flag locker was in one corner, open, exposing various colored bunting, some rolled up, others half unrolled, still others tumbled. Opposite was a cumbrous wash-stand, of black mahogany, all of one block, with a pedestal, like a font, and over it a railed shelf, containing combs, brushes, and other implements of the toilet. A torn hammock of stained grass swung near; the sheets tossed, and the pillow wrinkled up like a brow, as if whoever slept here slept but illy, with alternate visitations of sad thoughts and bad dreams.

The further extremity of the cuddy, overhanging the ship's stern, was pierced with three openings, windows or port holes, according as men or cannon might peer, socially or unsocially, out of them. At present neither men nor cannon were seen, though huge ring-bolts and other rusty iron fixtures of the wood-work hinted of twenty-four-pounders.

Glancing towards the hammock as he entered, Captain Delano said, "You sleep here, Don Benito?"

"Yes, Señor, since we got into mild weather."

"This seems a sort of dormitory, sitting-room, sail-loft, chapel, armory, and private closet all together, Don Benito," added Captain Delano, looking round.

"Yes, Señor; events have not been favorable to much order in my arrangements."

Here the servant, napkin on arm, made a motion as if waiting his master's good pleasure. Don Benito signified his readiness, when, seating him in the malacca arm-chair, and for the guest's convenience drawing opposite it one of the settees, the servant commenced operations by throwing back his master's collar and loosening his cravat.

There is something in the negro which, in a peculiar way, fits him for avocations about one's person. Most negroes are natural valets and hairdressers; taking to the comb and brush congenially as to the castinets, and flourishing them apparently with almost equal satisfaction. There is, too, a smooth tact about them in this employment, with a marvelous, noiseless, gliding briskness, not ungraceful in its way, singularly pleasing to behold, and still more so to be the manipulated subject of. And above all is the great gift of good humor. Not the mere grin or laugh is here meant. Those were unsuitable. But a certain easy cheerfulness, harmonious in every glance and gesture; as though God had set the whole negro to some pleasant tune.

When to all this is added the docility arising from the unaspiring contentment of a limited mind, and that susceptibility of blind attachment sometimes inhering in indisputable inferiors, one readily perceives why those hypochondriacs, Johnson and Byron—it may be something like the hypochondriac, Benito Cereno—took to their hearts, almost to the exclusion of the entire white race, their serving men, the negroes, Barber and Fletcher. But if there be that in the negro which exempts him from the inflicted sourness of the morbid or cynical mind, how, in his most prepossessing aspects, must he appear to a benevolent one? When at ease with respect to exterior things, Captain Delano's nature was not only benign, but familiarly and humorously so. At home, he had often taken rare satisfaction in sitting in his door, watching some free man of color at his work or play. If on a voyage he chanced to have a black sailor, invariably he was on chatty, and half-gamesome terms with him. In fact, like most men of a good, blithe heart, Captain Delano took to negroes, not philanthropically, but genially, just as other men to Newfoundland dogs.

Hitherto the circumstances in which he found the San Dominick had repressed the tendency. But in the cuddy, relieved from his former uneasiness, and, for various reasons, more sociably inclined than at any previous period of the day, and seeing the colored servant, napkin on arm, so debonair about his master, in a business so familiar as that of shaving, too, all his old weakness for negroes returned.

Among other things, he was amused with an odd instance of the African love of bright colors and fine shows, in the black's informally taking from the flag-locker a great piece of bunting of all hues, and lavishly tucking it under his master's chin for an apron.

The mode of shaving among the Spaniards is a little different from what it is with other nations. They have a basin, specifically called a barber's basin, which on one side is scooped out, so as accurately to receive the chin, against which it is closely held in lathering; which is done, not with a brush, but with soap dipped in the water of the basin and rubbed on the face.

In the present instance salt-water was used for lack of better; and the parts lathered were only the upper lip, and low down under the throat, all the rest being cultivated beard.

The preliminaries being somewhat novel to Captain Delano, he sat curiously eying them, so that no conversation took place, nor for the present did Don Benito appear disposed to renew any.

Setting down his basin, the negro searched among the razors, as for the sharpest, and having found it, gave it an additional edge by expertly strapping it on the firm, smooth, oily skin of his open palm; he then made a gesture as if to begin, but midway stood suspended for an instant, one hand elevating the razor, the other professionally dabbling among the bubbling suds on the Spaniard's lank neck. Not unaffected by the close sight of the gleaming steel, Don Benito nervously shuddered; his usual ghastliness was heightened by the lather, which lather, again, was intensified in its hue by the contrasting sootiness of the negro's body. Altogether the scene was somewhat peculiar, at least to Captain Delano, nor, as he saw the two thus postured, could he resist the vagary, that in the black he saw a headsman, and in the white, a man at the block. But this was one of those antic conceits, appearing and vanishing in a breath, from which, perhaps, the best regulated mind is not always free.

Meantime the agitation of the Spaniard had a little loosened the bunting from around him, so that one broad fold swept curtain-like over the chair-arm to the floor, revealing, amid a profusion of armorial bars and ground-colors—black, blue, and yellow—a closed castle in a blood-red field diagonal with a lion rampant in a white.

"The castle and the lion," exclaimed Captain Delano—"why, Don Benito, this is the flag of Spain you use here. It's well it's only I, and not the King, that sees this," he added with a smile, "but"—turning towards the black,—"it's all one, I suppose, so the colors be gay;" which playful remark did not fail somewhat to tickle the negro.

"Now, master," he said, readjusting the flag, and pressing the head gently further back into the crotch of the chair; "now master," and the steel glanced nigh the throat.

Again Don Benito faintly shuddered.

"You must not shake so, master.—See, Don Amasa, master always shakes when I shave him. And yet master knows I never yet have drawn blood, though it's true, if master will shake so, I may some of these times. Now master," he continued. "And now, Don Amasa, please go on with your talk about the gale, and all that, master can hear, and between times master can answer."

"Ah yes, these gales," said Captain Delano; "but the more I think of your voyage, Don Benito, the more I wonder, not at the gales, terrible as they must have been, but at the disastrous interval following them. For here, by your account, have you been these two months and more getting from Cape Horn to St. Maria, a distance which I myself, with a good wind, have sailed in a few days. True, you had calms, and long ones, but to be becalmed for two months, that is, at least, unusual. Why, Don Benito, had almost any other gentleman told me such a story, I should have been half disposed to a little incredulity."

Here an involuntary expression came over the Spaniard, similar to that just before on the deck, and whether it was the start he gave, or a sudden gawky roll of the hull in the calm, or a momentary unsteadiness of the servant's hand; however it was, just then the razor drew blood, spots of which stained the creamy lather under the throat; immediately the black barber drew back his steel, and remaining in his professional attitude, back to Captain Delano, and face to Don Benito, held up the trickling razor, saying, with a sort of half humorous sorrow, "See, master,—you shook so—here's Babo's first blood."

No sword drawn before James the First of England, no assassination in that timid King's presence, could have produced a more terrified aspect than was now presented by Don Benito.

Poor fellow, thought Captain Delano, so nervous he can't even bear the sight of barber's blood; and this unstrung, sick man, is it credible that I should have imagined he meant to spill all my blood, who can't endure the sight of one little drop of his own? Surely, Amasa Delano, you have been beside yourself this day. Tell it not when you get home, sappy

Amasa. Well, well, he looks like a murderer, doesn't he? More like as if himself were to be done for. Well, well, this day's experience shall be a good lesson.

Meantime, while these things were running through the honest seaman's mind, the servant had taken the napkin from his arm, and to Don Benito had said—"But answer Don Amasa, please, master, while I wipe this ugly stuff off the razor, and strop it again."

As he said the words, his face was turned half round, so as to be alike visible to the Spaniard and the American, and seemed by its expression to hint, that he was desirous, by getting his master to go on with the conversation, considerately to withdraw his attention from the recent annoying accident. As if glad to snatch the offered relief, Don Benito resumed, rehearsing to Captain Delano, that not only were the calms of unusual duration, but the ship had fallen in with obstinate currents; and other things he added, some of which were but repetitions of former statements, to explain how it came to pass that the passage from Cape Horn to St. Maria had been so exceedingly long, now and then mingling with his words, incidental praises, less qualified than before, to the blacks, for their general good conduct.

These particulars were not given consecutively, the servant, at convenient times, using his razor, and so, between the intervals of shaving, the story and panegyric went on with more than usual huskiness.

To Captain Delano's imagination, now again not wholly at rest, there was something so hollow in the Spaniard's manner, with apparently some reciprocal hollowness in the servant's dusky comment of silence, that the idea flashed across him, that possibly master and man, for some unknown purpose, were acting out, both in word and deed, nay, to the very tremor of Don Benito's limbs, some juggling play before him. Neither did the suspicion of collusion lack apparent support, from the fact of those whispered conferences before mentioned. But then, what could be the object of enacting this play of the barber before him? At last, regarding the notion as a whimsy, insensibly suggested, perhaps, by the theatrical aspect of Don Benito in his harlequin ensign, Captain Delano speedily banished it.

The shaving over, the servant bestirred himself with a small bottle of scented waters, pouring a few drops on the head, and then diligently rubbing; the vehemence of the exercise causing the muscles of his face to twitch rather strangely.

His next operation was with comb, scissors and brush; going round and round, smoothing a curl here, clipping an unruly whisker-hair there, giving a graceful sweep to the temple-lock, with other impromptu touches evincing the hand of a master; while, like any resigned gentleman in barber's hands, Don Benito bore all, much less uneasily, at least, than he had done the razoring; indeed, he sat so pale and rigid now, that the negro seemed a Nubian sculptor finishing off a white statue-head.

All being over at last, the standard of Spain removed, tumbled up, and tossed back into the flag-locker, the negro's warm breath blowing away any stray hair which might have lodged down his master's neck; collar and cravat readjusted; a speck of lint whisked off the velvet lapel; all this being done; backing off a little space, and pausing with an expression of subdued self-complacency, the servant for a moment surveyed his master, as, in toilet at least, the creature of his own tasteful hands.

Captain Delano playfully complimented him upon his achievement; at the same time congratulating Don Benito.

But neither sweet waters, nor shampooing, nor fidelity, nor sociality, delighted the Spaniard. Seeing him relapsing into forbidding gloom, and still remaining seated, Captain Delano, thinking that his presence was undesired just then, withdrew, on pretense of seeing whether, as he had prophecied, any signs of a breeze were visible.

Walking forward to the mainmast, he stood awhile thinking over the scene, and not without some undefined misgivings, when he heard a noise near the cuddy, and turning, saw the negro, his hand to his cheek. Advancing, Captain Delano perceived that the cheek was bleeding. He was about to ask the cause, when the negro's wailing soliloquy enlightened him.

"Ah, when will master get better from his sickness; only the sour heart that sour sickness breeds made him serve Babo so; cutting Babo with the razor, because, only by accident, Babo had given master one little scratch; and for the first time in so many a day, too. Ah, ah, ah," holding his hand to his face.

Is it possible, thought Captain Delano; was it to wreak in private his Spanish spite against this poor friend of his, that Don Benito, by his sullen manner, impelled me to withdraw? Ah, this slavery breeds ugly passions in man.—Poor fellow!

He was about to speak in sympathy to the negro, but with a timid reluctance he now reëntered the cuddy.

Presently master and man came forth; Don Benito leaning on his servant as if nothing had happened.

But a sort of love-quarrel, after all, thought Captain Delano.

He accosted Don Benito, and they slowly walked together. They had gone but a few paces, when the steward—a tall, rajah-looking mulatto, orientally set off with a pagoda turban formed by three or four Madras handkerchiefs wound about his head, tier on tier—approaching with a salaam, announced lunch in the cabin.

On their way thither, the two Captains were preceded by the mulatto, who, turning round as he advanced, with continual smiles and bows, ushered them on, a display of elegance which quite completed the insignificance of the small bare-headed Babo, who, as if not unconscious of inferiority, eyed askance the graceful steward. But in part, Captain Delano imputed his jealous watchfulness to that peculiar feeling which the full-blooded African entertains for the adulterated one. As for the steward, his manner, if not bespeaking much dignity of self-respect, yet evidenced his extreme desire to please; which is doubly meritorious, as at once Christian and Chesterfieldian.

Captain Delano observed with interest that while the complexion of the mulatto was hybrid, his physiognomy was European; classically so.

"Don Benito," whispered he, "I am glad to see this usher-of-the-golden-rod of yours; the sight refutes an ugly remark once made to me by a Barbadoes planter; that when a mulatto has a regular European face, look out for him; he is a devil. But see, your steward here has features more regular than King George's of England; and yet there he nods, and bows, and smiles; a king, indeed—the king of kind hearts and polite fellows. What a pleasant voice he has, too!"

"He has, Señor."

"But, tell me, has he not, so far as you have known him, always proved a good, worthy fellow?" said Captain Delano, pausing, while with a final genuflexion the steward disappeared into the cabin; "come, for the reason just mentioned, I am curious to know."

"Francesco is a good man," a sort of sluggishly responded Don Benito, like a phlegmatic appreciator, who would neither find fault nor flatter.

"Ah, I thought so. For it were strange indeed, and not very creditable to us white-skins, if a little of our blood mixed with the African's, should, far from improving the latter's quality, have the sad effect of pouring vitriolic acid into black broth; improving the hue, perhaps, but not the wholesomeness."

"Doubtless, doubtless, Señor, but"—glancing at Babo—"not to speak of negroes, your planter's remark I have heard applied to the Spanish and Indian intermixtures in our provinces. But I know nothing about the matter," he listlessly added.

And here they entered the cabin.

The lunch was a frugal one. Some of Captain Delano's fresh fish and pumpkins, biscuit and salt beef, the reserved bottle of cider, and the San Dominick's last bottle of Canary.

As they entered, Francesco, with two or three colored aids, was hovering over the table giving the last adjustments. Upon perceiving their master they withdrew, Francesco making a smiling congé, and the Spaniard, without condescending to notice it, fastidiously remarking to his companion that he relished not superfluous attendance.

Without companions, host and guest sat down, like a childless married couple, at opposite ends of the table, Don Benito waving Captain Delano to his place, and, weak as he was, insisting upon that gentleman being seated before himself.

The negro placed a rug under Don Benito's feet, and a cushion behind his back, and then stood behind, not his master's chair, but Captain Delano's. At first, this a little surprised the latter. But it was soon evident that, in taking his position, the black was still true to his master; since by facing him he could the more readily anticipate his slightest want.

"This is an uncommonly intelligent fellow of yours, Don Benito," whispered Captain Delano across the table.

"You say true, Señor."

During the repast, the guest again reverted to parts of Don Benito's story, begging further particulars here and there. He inquired how it was that the scurvy and fever should have committed such wholesale havoc upon the whites, while destroying less than half of the blacks. As if this question reproduced the whole scene of plague before the Spaniard's eyes, miserably reminding him of his solitude in a cabin where before he had had so many friends and officers round him, his hand shook, his face became hueless, broken words escaped; but directly the sane memory of the past seemed replaced by insane terrors of the present. With starting eyes he stared before him at vacancy. For nothing was to be seen but the hand of his servant pushing the Canary over towards him. At length a few sips served partially to restore him. He made random reference to the different constitution of races, enabling one to offer more resistance to certain maladies than another. The thought was new to his companion.

Presently Captain Delano, intending to say something to his host concerning the pecuniary part of the business he had undertaken for him, especially—since he was strictly accountable to his owners—with reference to the new suit of sails, and other things of that sort; and naturally preferring to conduct such affairs in private, was desirous that the servant should withdraw; imagining that Don Benito for a few minutes could dispense with his attendance. He, however, waited awhile; thinking that, as the conversation proceeded, Don Benito, without being prompted, would perceive the propriety of the step.

But it was otherwise. At last catching his host's eye, Captain Delano, with a slight backward gesture of his thumb, whispered, "Don Benito, pardon me, but there is an interference with the full expression of what I have to say to you."

Upon this the Spaniard changed countenance; which was imputed to his resenting the hint, as in some way a reflection upon his servant. After a moment's pause, he assured his guest that the black's remaining with them could be of no disservice; because since losing his officers he had made Babo (whose original office, it now appeared, had been captain of the slaves) not only his constant attendant and companion, but in all things his confidant.

After this, nothing more could be said; though, indeed, Captain Delano could hardly avoid some little tinge of irritation upon being left ungratified in so inconsiderable a wish, by one, too, for whom he intended such solid services. But it is only his querulousness, thought he; and so filling his glass he proceeded to business.

The price of the sails and other matters was fixed upon. But while this was being done, the American observed that, though his original offer of assistance had been hailed with hectic animation, yet now when it was reduced to a business transaction, indifference and apathy were betrayed. Don Benito, in fact, appeared to submit to hearing the details more out of regard to common propriety, than from any impression that weighty benefit to himself and his voyage was involved.

Soon, this manner became still more reserved. The effort was vain to seek to draw him into social talk. Gnawed by his splenetic mood, he sat twitching his beard, while to little purpose the hand of his servant, mute as that on the wall, slowly pushed over the Canary.

Lunch being over, they sat down on the cushioned transom; the servant placing a pillow behind his master. The long continuance of the calm had now affected the atmosphere. Don Benito sighed heavily, as if for breath.

"Why not adjourn to the cuddy," said Captain Delano; "there is more air there." But the host sat silent and motionless.

Meantime his servant knelt before him, with a large fan of feathers. And Francesco coming in on tiptoes, handed the negro a little cup of aromatic waters, with which at intervals he chafed his master's brow; smoothing the hair along the temples as a nurse does a child's. He spoke no word. He only rested his eye on his master's, as if, amid all Don Benito's distress, a little to refresh his spirit by the silent sight of fidelity.

Presently the ship's bell sounded two o'clock; and through the cabin-windows a slight rippling of the sea was discerned; and from the desired direction.

"There," exclaimed Captain Delano, "I told you so, Don Benito, look!"

He had risen to his feet, speaking in a very animated tone, with a view the more to rouse his companion. But though the crimson curtain of the stern-window near him that moment fluttered against his pale cheek, Don Benito seemed to have even less welcome for the breeze than the calm.

Poor fellow, thought Captain Delano, bitter experience has taught him that one ripple does not make a wind, any more than one swallow a summer. But he is mistaken for once. I will get his ship in for him, and prove it.

Briefly alluding to his weak condition, he urged his host to remain quietly where he was, since he (Captain Delano) would with pleasure take upon himself the responsibility of making the best use of the wind.

Upon gaining the deck, Captain Delano started at the unexpected figure of Atufal, monumentally fixed at the threshold, like one of those sculptured porters of black marble guarding the porches of Egyptian tombs.

But this time the start was, perhaps, purely physical. Atufal's presence, singularly attesting docility even in sullenness, was contrasted with that of the hatchet-polishers, who in patience evinced their industry; while both spectacles showed, that lax as Don Benito's general authority might be, still, whenever he chose to exert it, no man so savage or colossal but must, more or less, bow.

Snatching a trumpet which hung from the bulwarks, with a free step Captain Delano advanced to the forward edge of the poop, issuing his orders in his best Spanish. The few sailors and many negroes, all equally pleased, obediently set about heading the ship towards the harbor.

While giving some directions about setting a lower stu'n'-sail, suddenly Captain Delano heard a voice faithfully repeating his orders. Turning, he saw Babo, now for the time acting, under the pilot, his original part of captain of the slaves. This assistance proved valuable. Tattered sails and warped yards were soon brought into some trim. And no brace or halyard was pulled but to the blithe songs of the inspirited negroes.

Good fellows, thought Captain Delano, a little training would make fine sailors of them. Why see, the very women pull and sing too. These must be some of those Ashantee negresses that make such capital soldiers, I've heard. But who's at the helm. I must have a good hand there.

He went to see.

The San Dominick steered with a cumbrous tiller, with large horizontal pullies attached. At each pully-end stood a subordinate black, and between them, at the tiller-head, the responsible post, a Spanish seaman, whose countenance evinced his due share in the general hopefulness and confidence at the coming of the breeze.

He proved the same man who had behaved with so shame-faced an air on the windlass.

"Ah,—it is you, my man," exclaimed Captain Delano—"well, no more sheep's-eyes now;—look straight forward and keep the ship so. Good hand, I trust? And want to get into the harbor, don't you?"

The man assented with an inward chuckle, grasping the tiller-head firmly. Upon this, unperceived by the American, the two blacks eyed the sailor intently.

Finding all right at the helm, the pilot went forward to the forecastle, to see how matters stood there.

The ship now had way enough to breast the current. With the approach of evening, the breeze would be sure to freshen.

Having done all that was needed for the present, Captain Delano, giving his last orders to the sailors, turned aft to report affairs to Don Benito in the cabin; perhaps additionally incited to rejoin him by the hope of snatching a moment's private chat while his servant was engaged upon deck.

From opposite sides, there were, beneath the poop, two approaches to the cabin; one further forward than the other, and consequently communicating with a longer passage. Marking the servant still above, Captain

Delano, taking the nighest entrance—the one last named, and at whose porch Atufal still stood—hurried on his way, till, arrived at the cabin threshold, he paused an instant, a little to recover from his eagerness. Then, with the words of his intended business upon his lips, he entered. As he advanced toward the seated Spaniard, he heard another footstep, keeping time with his. From the opposite door, a salver in hand, the servant was likewise advancing.

"Confound the faithful fellow," thought Captain Delano; "what a vexatious coincidence."

Possibly, the vexation might have been something different, were it not for the brisk confidence inspired by the breeze. But even as it was, he felt a slight twinge, from a sudden indefinite association in his mind of Babo with Atufal.

"Don Benito," said he, "I give you joy; the breeze will hold, and will increase. By the way, your tall man and time-piece, Atufal, stands without. By your order, of course?"

Don Benito recoiled, as if at some bland satirical touch, delivered with such adroit garnish of apparent good-breeding as to present no handle for retort.

He is like one flayed alive, thought Captain Delano; where may one touch him without causing a shrink?

The servant moved before his master, adjusting a cushion; recalled to civility, the Spaniard stiffly replied: "you are right. The slave appears where you saw him, according to my command; which is, that if at the given hour I am below, he must take his stand and abide my coming."

"Ah now, pardon me, but that is treating the poor fellow like an ex-king indeed. Ah, Don Benito," smiling, "for all the license you permit in some things, I fear lest, at bottom, you are a bitter hard master."

Again Don Benito shrank; and this time, as the good sailor thought, from a genuine twinge of his conscience.

Again conversation became constrained. In vain Captain Delano called attention to the now perceptible motion of the keel gently cleaving the sea; with lack-lustre eye, Don Benito returned words few and reserved.

By-and-by, the wind having steadily risen, and still blowing right into the harbor, bore the San Dominick swiftly on. Rounding a point of land, the sealer at distance came into open view.

Meantime Captain Delano had again repaired to the deck, remaining there some time. Having at last altered the ship's course, so as to give the reef a wide berth, he returned for a few moments below.

I will cheer up my poor friend, this time, thought he.

"Better and better, Don Benito," he cried as he blithely reëntered; "there will soon be an end to your cares, at least for awhile. For when, after a long, sad voyage, you know, the anchor drops into the haven, all its vast weight seems lifted from the captain's heart. We are getting on famously, Don Benito. My ship is in sight. Look through this side-light here; there she is; all a-taunt-o! The Bachelor's Delight, my good friend. Ah, how this wind braces one up. Come, you must take a cup of coffee with me this evening. My old steward will give you as fine a cup as ever any sultan tasted. What say you, Don Benito, will you?"

At first, the Spaniard glanced feverishly up, casting a longing look towards the sealer, while with mute concern his servant gazed into his face. Suddenly the old ague of coldness returned, and dropping back to his cushions he was silent.

"You do not answer. Come, all day you have been my host; would you have hospitality all on one side?"

"I cannot go," was the response.

"What? it will not fatigue you. The ships will lie together as near as they can, without swinging foul. It will be little more than stepping from deck to deck; which is but as from room to room. Come, come, you must not refuse me."

"I cannot go," decisively and repulsively repeated Don Benito.

Renouncing all but the last appearance of courtesy, with a sort of cadaverous sullenness, and biting his thin nails to the quick, he glanced, almost glared, at his guest; as if impatient that a stranger's presence should interfere with the full indulgence of his morbid hour. Meantime the sound of the parted waters came more and more gurglingly and merrily in at the windows; as reproaching him for his dark spleen; as telling him that, sulk as he might, and go mad with it, nature cared not a jot; since, whose fault was it, pray?

But the foul mood was now at its depth, as the fair wind at its height.

There was something in the man so far beyond any mere unsociality or sourness previously evinced, that even the forbearing good-nature of his guest could no longer endure it. Wholly at a loss to account for such demeanor, and deeming sickness with eccentricity, however extreme, no adequate excuse, well satisfied, too, that nothing in his own conduct could justify it, Captain Delano's pride began to be roused. Himself became reserved. But all seemed one to the Spaniard. Quitting him, therefore, Captain Delano once more went to the deck.

The ship was now within less than two miles of the sealer. The whale-boat was seen darting over the interval.

To be brief, the two vessels, thanks to the pilot's skill, ere long in neighborly style lay anchored together.

Before returning to his own vessel, Captain Delano had intended communicating to Don Benito the smaller details of the proposed services to be rendered. But, as it was, unwilling anew to subject himself to rebuffs, he resolved, now that he had seen the San Dominick safely moored, immediately to quit her, without further allusion to hospitality or business. Indefinitely postponing his ulterior plans, he would regulate his future actions according to future circumstances. His boat was ready to receive him; but his host still tarried below. Well, thought Captain Delano, if he has little breeding, the more need to show mine. He descended to the cabin to bid a ceremonious, and, it may be, tacitly rebukeful adieu. But to his great satisfaction, Don Benito, as if he began to feel the weight of that treatment with which his slighted guest had, not indecorously, retaliated upon him, now supported by his servant, rose to his feet, and grasping Captain Delano's hand, stood tremulous; too much agitated to speak. But the good augury hence drawn was suddenly dashed, by his resuming all his previous reserve, with augmented gloom, as, with half-averted eyes, he silently reseated himself on his cushions. With a corresponding return of his own chilled feelings, Captain Delano bowed and withdrew.

He was hardly midway in the narrow corridor, dim as a tunnel, leading from the cabin to the stairs, when a sound, as of the tolling for execution in some jail-yard, fell on his ears. It was the echo of the ship's flawed bell, striking the hour, drearily reverberated in this subterranean vault. Instantly, by a fatality not to be withstood, his mind, responsive to the portent, swarmed with superstitious suspicions. He paused. In images far swifter than these sentences, the minutest details of all his former distrusts swept through him.

Hitherto, credulous good-nature had been too ready to furnish excuses for reasonable fears. Why was the Spaniard, so superfluously punctilious at times, now heedless of common propriety in not accompanying to the side his departing guest? Did indisposition forbid? Indisposition had not forbidden more irksome exertion that day. His last equivocal demeanor recurred. He had risen to his feet, grasped his guest's hand, motioned toward his hat; then, in an instant, all was eclipsed in sinister muteness and gloom. Did this imply one brief, repentent relenting at the final moment, from some iniquitous plot, followed by remorseless return to it? His last glance seemed to express a calamitous, yet acquiescent farewell to Captain Delano forever. Why decline the invitation to visit the sealer that evening? Or was the Spaniard less hardened than the Jew, who refrained not from supping at the board of him whom the same night he meant to betray? What imported all those day-long enigmas and contradictions, except they were intended to mystify, preliminary to some stealthy blow? Atufal, the pretended rebel, but punctual shadow, that moment lurked by the threshold without. He seemed a sentry, and more. Who, by his own confession, had stationed him there? Was the negro now lying in wait?

The Spaniard behind—his creature before: to rush from darkness to light was the involuntary choice.

The next moment, with clenched jaw and hand, he passed Atufal, and stood unharmed in the light. As he saw his trim ship lying peacefully at her anchor, and almost within ordinary call; as he saw his household boat, with familiar faces in it, patiently rising and falling on the short waves by the San Dominick's side; and then, glancing about the decks where he stood, saw the oakum-pickers still gravely plying their fingers; and heard the low, buzzing whistle and industrious hum of the hatchet-polishers, still bestirring themselves over their endless occupation; and more than all, as he saw the benign aspect of nature, taking her innocent repose in the evening; the screened sun in the quiet camp of the west shining out like the mild light from Abraham's tent; as charmed eye and ear took in all these, with the chained figure of the black, clenched jaw and hand relaxed. Once again he smiled at the phantoms which had mocked him, and felt something like a tinge of remorse, that, by harboring them even for a moment, he should, by implication, have betrayed an almost atheist doubt of the ever-watchful Providence above.

There was a few minutes' delay, while, in obedience to his orders, the boat was being hooked along to the gangway. During this interval, a sort of saddened satisfaction stole over Captain Delano, at thinking of the kindly offices he had that day discharged for a stranger. Ah, thought he, after good actions one's conscience is never ungrateful, however much so the benefited party may be.

Presently, his foot, in the first act of descent into the boat, pressed the first round of the side-ladder, his face presented inward upon the deck. In the same moment, he heard his name courteously sounded; and, to his pleased surprise, saw Don Benito advancing—an unwonted energy in his air, as if, at the last moment, intent upon making amends for his recent discourtesy. With instinctive good feeling, Captain Delano, withdrawing his foot, turned and reciprocally advanced. As he did so, the Spaniard's nervous eagerness increased, but his vital energy failed; so that, the better to support him, the servant, placing his master's hand on his naked shoulder, and gently holding it there, formed himself into a sort of crutch.

When the two captains met, the Spaniard again fervently took the hand of the American, at the same time casting an earnest glance into his eyes, but, as before, too much overcome to speak.

I have done him wrong, self-reproachfully thought Captain Delano; his apparent coldness has deceived me; in no instance has he meant to offend.

Meantime, as if fearful that the continuance of the scene might too much unstring his master, the servant seemed anxious to terminate it. And so, still presenting himself as a crutch, and walking between the two captains, he advanced with them towards the gangway; while still, as if full of kindly contrition, Don Benito would not let go the hand of Captain Delano, but retained it in his, across the black's body.

Soon they were standing by the side, looking over into the boat, whose crew turned up their curious eyes. Waiting a moment for the Spaniard to relinquish his hold, the now embarrassed Captain Delano lifted his foot, to overstep the threshold of the open gangway; but still Don Benito would not let go his hand. And yet, with an agitated tone, he said, "I can go no further; here I must bid you adieu. Adieu, my dear, dear Don Amasa. Go—go!" suddenly tearing his hand loose, "go, and God guard you better than me, my best friend."

Not unaffected, Captain Delano would now have lingered; but catching the meekly admonitory eye of the servant, with a hasty farewell he descended into his boat, followed by the continual adieus of Don Benito, standing rooted in the gangway.

Seating himself in the stern, Captain Delano, making a last salute, ordered the boat shoved off. The crew had their oars on end. The bowsman pushed the boat a sufficient distance for the oars to be lengthwise dropped. The instant that was done, Don Benito sprang over the bulwarks, falling at the feet of Captain Delano; at the same time, calling towards his ship, but in tones so frenzied, that none in the boat could understand him. But, as if not equally obtuse, three sailors, from three different and distant parts of the ship, splashed into the sea, swimming after their captain, as if intent upon his rescue.

The dismayed officer of the boat eagerly asked what this meant. To which, Captain Delano, turning a disdainful smile upon the unaccountable Spaniard, answered that, for his part, he neither knew nor cared; but it seemed as if Don Benito had taken it into his head to produce the impression among his people that the boat wanted to kidnap him. "Or else— give way for your lives," he wildly added, starting at a clattering hubbub in the ship, above which rang the tocsin of the hatchet-polishers; and seizing Don Benito by the throat he added, "this plotting pirate means murder!" Here, in apparent verification of the words, the servant, a dagger in his hand, was seen on the rail overhead, poised, in the act of leaping, as if with desperate fidelity to befriend his master to the last; while, seemingly to aid the black, the three white sailors were trying to clamber into the hampered bow. Meantime, the whole host of negroes, as if inflamed at the sight of their jeopardized captain, impended in one sooty avalanche over the bulwarks.

All this, with what preceded, and what followed, occurred with such involutions of rapidity, that past, present, and future seemed one.

Seeing the negro coming, Captain Delano had flung the Spaniard aside, almost in the very act of clutching him, and, by the unconscious recoil, shifting his place, with arms thrown up, so promptly grappled the servant in his descent, that with dagger presented at Captain Delano's heart, the black seemed of purpose to have leaped there as to his mark. But the weapon was wrenched away, and the assailant dashed down into the bottom of the boat, which now, with disentangled oars, began to speed through the sea.

At this juncture, the left hand of Captain Delano, on one side, again clutched the half-reclined Don Benito, heedless that he was in a speechless faint, while his right foot, on the other side, ground the prostrate negro; and his right arm pressed for added speed on the after oar, his eye bent forward, encouraging his men to their utmost.

But here, the officer of the boat, who had at last succeeded in beating off the towing sailors, and was now, with face turned aft, assisting the bowsman at his oar, suddenly called to Captain Delano, to see what the black was about; while a Portuguese oarsman shouted to him to give heed to what the Spaniard was saying.

Glancing down at his feet, Captain Delano saw the freed hand of the servant aiming with a second dagger—a small one, before concealed in his wool—with this he was snakishly writhing up from the boat's bottom, at the heart of his master, his countenance lividly vindictive, expressing the centred purpose of his soul; while the Spaniard, half-choked, was vainly shrinking away, with husky words, incoherent to all but the Portuguese.

That moment, across the long-benighted mind of Captain Delano, a flash of revelation swept, illuminating in unanticipated clearness his host's whole mysterious demeanor, with every enigmatic event of the day, as well as the entire past voyage of the San Dominick. He smote Babo's hand down, but his own heart smote him harder. With infinite pity he withdrew his hold from Don Benito. Not Captain Delano, but Don Benito, the black, in leaping into the boat, had intended to stab.

Both the black's hands were held, as, glancing up towards the San Dominick, Captain Delano, now with the scales dropped from his eyes, saw the negroes, not in misrule, not in tumult, not as if frantically concerned for Don Benito, but with mask torn away, flourishing hatchets and knives, in ferocious piratical revolt. Like delirious black dervishes, the six Ashantees danced on the poop. Prevented by their foes from springing into the water, the Spanish boys were hurrying up to the topmost spars, while such of the few Spanish sailors, not already in the sea, less alert, were descried, helplessly mixed in, on deck, with the blacks.

Meantime Captain Delano hailed his own vessel, ordering the ports up, and the guns run out. But by this time the cable of the San Dominick had been cut; and the fag-end, in lashing out, whipped away the canvas shroud about the beak, suddenly revealing, as the bleached hull swung round towards the open ocean, death for the figure-head, in a human skeleton; chalky comment on the chalked words below, *"Follow your leader."*

At the sight, Don Benito, covering his face, wailed out: " 'Tis he, Aranda! my murdered, unburied friend!"

Upon reaching the sealer, calling for ropes, Captain Delano bound the negro, who made no resistance, and had him hoisted to the deck. He would then have assisted the now almost helpless Don Benito up the side;

but Don Benito, wan as he was, refused to move, or be moved, until the negro should have been first put below out of view. When, presently assured that it was done, he no more shrank from the ascent.

The boat was immediately dispatched back to pick up the three swimming sailors. Meantime, the guns were in readiness, though, owing to the San Dominick having glided somewhat astern of the sealer, only the aftermost one could be brought to bear. With this, they fired six times; thinking to cripple the fugitive ship by bringing down her spars. But only a few inconsiderable ropes were shot away. Soon the ship was beyond the gun's range, steering broad out of the bay; the blacks thickly clustering round the bowsprit, one moment with taunting cries towards the whites, the next with upthrown gestures hailing the now dusky moors of ocean—cawing crows escaped from the hand of the fowler.

The first impulse was to slip the cables and give chase. But, upon second thoughts, to pursue with whale-boat and yawl seemed more promising.

Upon inquiring of Don Benito what fire arms they had on board the San Dominick, Captain Delano was answered that they had none that could be used; because, in the earlier stages of the mutiny, a cabin-passenger, since dead, had secretly put out of order the locks of what few muskets there were. But with all his remaining strength, Don Benito entreated the American not to give chase, either with ship or boat; for the negroes had already proved themselves such desperadoes, that, in case of a present assault, nothing but a total massacre of the whites could be looked for. But, regarding this warning as coming from one whose spirit had been crushed by misery, the American did not give up his design.

The boats were got ready and armed. Captain Delano ordered his men into them. He was going himself when Don Benito grasped his arm.

"What! have you saved my life, señor, and are you now going to throw away your own?"

The officers also, for reasons connected with their interests and those of the voyage, and a duty owing to the owners, strongly objected against their commander's going. Weighing their remonstrances a moment, Captain Delano felt bound to remain; appointing his chief mate—an athletic and resolute man, who had been a privateer's-man, and, as his enemies whispered, a pirate—to head the party. The more to encourage the sailors, they were told, that the Spanish captain considered his ship as good as lost; that she and her cargo, including some gold and silver, were worth more than a thousand doubloons. Take her, and no small part should be theirs. The sailors replied with a shout.

The fugitives had now almost gained an offing. It was nearly night; but the moon was rising. After hard, prolonged pulling, the boats came up on the ship's quarters, at a suitable distance laying upon their oars to discharge their muskets. Having no bullets to return, the negroes sent their yells. But, upon the second volley, Indian-like, they hurtled their hatchets. One took off a sailor's fingers. Another struck the whale-boat's bow, cutting off the rope there, and remaining stuck in the gunwale like a woodman's axe. Snatching it, quivering from its lodgment, the mate hurled it back. The returned gauntlet now stuck in the ship's broken quarter-gallery, and so remained.

The negroes giving too hot a reception, the whites kept a more respectful distance. Hovering now just out of reach of the hurtling hatchets, they, with a view to the close encounter which must soon come, sought to decoy the blacks into entirely disarming themselves of their most murderous weapons in a hand-to-hand fight, by foolishly flinging them, as missiles, short of the mark, into the sea. But ere long perceiving the stratagem, the negroes desisted, though not before many of them had to replace their lost hatchets with handspikes; an exchange which, as counted upon, proved in the end favorable to the assailants.

Meantime, with a strong wind, the ship still clove the water; the boats alternately falling behind, and pulling up, to discharge fresh volleys.

The fire was mostly directed towards the stern, since there, chiefly, the negroes, at present, were clustering. But to kill or maim the negroes was not the object. To take them, with the ship, was the object. To do it, the ship must be boarded; which could not be done by boats while she was sailing so fast.

A thought now struck the mate. Observing the Spanish boys still aloft, high as they could get, he called to them to descend to the yards, and cut adrift the sails. It was done. About this time, owing to causes hereafter to be shown, two Spaniards, in the dress of sailors and conspicuously showing themselves, were killed; not by volleys, but by deliberate marksman's shots; while, as it afterwards appeared, by one of the general discharges, Atufal, the black, and the Spaniard at the helm likewise were killed. What now, with the loss of the sails, and loss of leaders, the ship became unmanageable to the negroes.

With creaking masts, she came heavily round to the wind; the prow slowly swinging, into view of the boats, its skeleton gleaming in the horizontal moonlight, and casting a gigantic ribbed shadow upon the water. One extended arm of the ghost seemed beckoning the whites to avenge it.

"Follow your leader!" cried the mate; and, one on each bow, the boats boarded. Sealing-spears and cutlasses crossed hatchets and hand-spikes. Huddled upon the long-boat amidships, the negresses raised a wailing chant, whose chorus was the clash of the steel.

For a time, the attack wavered; the negroes wedging themselves to beat it back; the half-repelled sailors, as yet unable to gain a footing, fighting as troopers in the saddle, one leg sideways flung over the bulwarks, and one without, plying their cutlasses like carters' whips. But in vain. They were almost overborne, when, rallying themselves into a squad as one man, with a huzza, they sprang inboard; where, entangled, they involuntarily separated again. For a few breaths' space, there was a vague, muffled, inner sound, as of submerged sword-fish rushing hither and thither through shoals of black-fish. Soon, in a reunited band, and joined by the Spanish seamen, the whites came to the surface, irresistibly driving the negroes toward the stern. But a barricade of casks and sacks, from side to side, had been thrown up by the mainmast. Here the negroes faced about, and though scorning peace or truce, yet fain would have had a respite. But, without pause, overleaping the barrier, the unflagging sailors again closed. Exhausted, the blacks now fought in despair. Their red tongues lolled, wolf-like, from their black mouths. But the pale sailors' teeth were set; not a word was spoken; and, in five minutes more, the ship was won.

Nearly a score of the negroes were killed. Exclusive of those by the balls, many were mangled; their wounds—mostly inflicted by the long-edged sealing-spears—resembling those shaven ones of the English at Preston Pans, made by the poled scythes of the Highlanders. On the other side, none were killed, though several were wounded; some severely, including the mate. The surviving negroes were temporarily secured, and the ship, towed back into the harbor at midnight, once more lay anchored.

Omitting the incidents and arrangements ensuing, suffice it that, after two days spent in refitting, the two ships sailed in company for Conception, in Chili, and thence for Lima, in Peru; where, before the vice-regal courts, the whole affair, from the beginning, underwent investigation.

Though, midway on the passage, the ill-fated Spaniard, relaxed from constraint, showed some signs of regaining health with free-will; yet, agreeably to his own foreboding, shortly before arriving at Lima, he relapsed, finally becoming so reduced as to be carried ashore in arms. Hearing of his story and plight, one of the many religious institutions of the City of Kings opened an hospitable refuge to him, where both physician and priest were his nurses, and a member of the order volunteered to be his one special guardian and consoler, by night and by day.

The following extracts, translated from one of the official Spanish documents, will it is hoped, shed light on the preceding narrative, as well as, in the first place, reveal the true port of departure and true history of the San Dominick's voyage, down to the time of her touching at the island of St. Maria.

But, ere the extracts come, it may be well to preface them with a remark.

The document selected, from among many others, for partial translation, contains the deposition of Benito Cereno; the first taken in the case. Some disclosures therein were, at the time, held dubious for both learned and natural reasons. The tribunal inclined to the opinion that the deponent, not undisturbed in his mind by recent events, raved of some things which could never have happened. But subsequent depositions of the surviving sailors, bearing out the revelations of their captain in several of the strangest particulars, gave credence to the rest. So that the tribunal, in its final decision, rested its capital sentences upon statements which, had they lacked confirmation, it would have deemed it but duty to reject.

I, DON JOSE DE ABOS AND PADILLA, His Majesty's Notary for the Royal Revenue, and Register of this Province, and Notary Public of the Holy Crusade of this Bishopric, etc.

Do certify and declare, as much as is requisite in law, that, in the criminal cause commenced the twenty-fourth of the month of September, in the year seventeen hundred and ninety-nine, against the negroes of the ship San Dominick, the following declaration before me was made.

Declaration of the first witness, DON BENITO CERENO.

The same day, and month, and year, His Honor, Doctor Juan Martinez de Rozas, Councilor of the Royal Audience of this Kingdom, and learned in the law of this Intendency, ordered the captain of the ship San Dominick, Don Benito Cereno, to appear; which he did in his litter, attended by the monk Infelez; of whom he received the oath, which he took by God, our Lord, and a sign of the Cross; under which he promised to tell the truth of whatever he should know and should be asked;—and being interrogated agreeably to the tenor of the act commencing the process, he said, that on the twentieth of May last, he set sail with his ship from the port of Valparaiso, bound to that of Callao; loaded with the produce of the country beside thirty cases of hardware and one hundred and sixty blacks, of both sexes, mostly belonging to Don Alexandro Aranda, gentleman, of the city of Mendoza; that the crew of the ship consisted of thirty-six men, beside the persons who went as passengers; that the negroes were in part as follows:

[*Here, in the original, follows a list of some fifty names, descriptions, and ages, compiled from certain recovered documents of Aranda's, and also from recollections of the deponent, from which portions only are extracted.*]

—One, from about eighteen to nineteen years, named José, and this was the man that waited upon his master, Don Alexandro, and who speaks well the Spanish, having served him four or five years; * * * a mulatto, named Francesco, the cabin steward, of a good person and voice, having sung in the Valparaiso churches, native of the province of Buenos Ayres, aged about thirty-five years. * * * A smart negro, named Dago, who had been for many years a grave-digger among the Spaniards, aged forty-six years. * * * Four old negroes, born in Africa, from sixty to seventy, but sound, calkers by trade, whose names are as follows:—the first was named Mure, and he was killed (as was also his son named Diamelo); the second, Natu; the third, Yola, likewise killed; the fourth, Ghofan; and six full-grown negroes, aged from thirty to forty-five, all raw, and born among the Ashantees—Matiluqui, Yau, Lecbe, Mapenda, Yambaio, Akim; four of whom were killed; * * * a powerful negro named Atufal, who, being supposed to have been a chief in Africa, his owners set great store by him. * * * And a small negro of Senegal, but some years among the Spaniards, aged about thirty, which negro's name was Babo; * * * that he does not remember the names of the others, but that still expecting the residue of Don Alexandro's papers will be found, will then take due account of them all, and remit to the court; * * * and thirty-nine women and children of all ages.

[*The catalogue over, the deposition goes on:*]

* * * That all the negroes slept upon deck, as is customary in this navigation, and none wore fetters, because the owner, his friend Aranda, told him that they were all tractable; * * * that on the seventh day after leaving port, at three o'clock in the morning, all the Spaniards being asleep except the two officers on the watch, who were the boatswain, Juan Robles, and the carpenter, Juan Bautista Gayete, and the helmsman and his boy, the negroes revolted suddenly, wounded dangerously the boatswain and the carpenter, and successively killed eighteen men of those who were sleeping upon deck, some with hand-spikes and hatchets, and others by throwing them alive overboard, after tying them; that of the Spaniards upon deck, they left about seven, as he thinks, alive and tied, to manoeuvre the ship, and three or four more, who hid themselves, remained also alive. Although in the act of revolt the negroes made themselves masters of the hatchway, six or seven wounded went through it to the cockpit, without any hindrance on their part; that during the act of revolt, the mate and another person, whose name he does not recollect, attempted to come up through the hatchway, but being quickly wounded, they were obliged to return to the cabin; that the deponent resolved at break of day to come up the companion-way, where the negro Babo was, being the ringleader, and Atufal, who assisted him, and having spoken to them, exhorted them to cease committing such atrocities, asking them, at the same time, what they wanted and intended to do, offering, himself, to obey their commands; that, notwithstanding this, they threw, in his presence, three men, alive and tied, overboard; that they told the deponent to come up, and that they would not kill him; which having done, the negro Babo asked him whether there were in those seas any negro countries where they might be carried, and he answered them, No; that the negro Babo afterwards told him to carry them to Senegal, or to the neighboring islands of St. Nicolas; and he answered, that this was impossible, on account of the great distance,

the necessity involved of rounding Cape Horn, the bad condition of the vessel, the want of provisions, sails, and water; but that the negro Babo replied to him he must carry them in any way; that they would do and conform themselves to everything the deponent should require as to eating and drinking; that after a long conference, being absolutely compelled to please them, for they threatened him to kill all the whites if they were not, at all events, carried to Senegal, he told them that what was most wanting for the voyage was water; that they would go near the coast to take it, and thence they would proceed on their course; that the negro Babo agreed to it; and the deponent steered towards the intermediate ports, hoping to meet some Spanish or foreign vessel that would save them; that within ten or eleven days they saw the land, and continued their course by it in the vicinity of Nasca; that the deponent observed that the negroes were now restless and mutinous, because he did not effect the taking in of water, the negro Babo having required, with threats, that it should be done, without fail, the following day; he told him they saw plainly that the coast was steep, and the rivers designated in the maps were not to be found, with other reasons suitable to the circumstances; that the best way would be to go to the island of Santa Maria, where they might water and victual easily, it being a solitary island, as the foreigners did; that the deponent did not go to Pisco, that was near, nor make any other port of the coast, because the negro Babo had intimated to him several times, that he would kill all the whites the very moment he should perceive any city, town, or settlement of any kind on the shores to which they should be carried: that having determined to go to the island of Santa Maria, as the deponent had planned, for the purpose of trying whether, on the passage or near the island itself, they could find any vessel that should favor them, or whether he could escape from it in a boat to the neighboring coast of Arauco; to adopt the necessary means he immediately changed his course, steering for the island; that the negroes Babo and Atufal held daily conferences, in which they discussed what was necessary for their design of returning to Senegal, whether they were to kill all the Spaniards, and particularly the deponent; that eight days after parting from the coast of Nasca, the deponent being on the watch a little after day-break, and soon after the negroes had their meeting, the negro

Babo came to the place where the deponent was, and told him that
he had determined to kill his master, Don Alexandro Aranda, both
because he and his companions could not otherwise be sure of their
liberty, and that, to keep the seamen in subjection, he wanted to
prepare a warning of what road they should be made to take did
they or any of them oppose him; and that, by means of the death of
Don Alexandro, that warning would best be given; but, that what
this last meant, the deponent did not at the time comprehend, nor
could not, further than that the death of Don Alexandro was intended; and moreover, the negro Babo proposed to the deponent to
call the mate Raneds, who was sleeping in the cabin, before the
thing was done, for fear, as the deponent understood it, that the
mate, who was a good navigator, should be killed with Don Alexandro and the rest; that the deponent, who was the friend, from youth,
of Don Alexandro, prayed and conjured, but all was useless; for the
negro Babo answered him that the thing could not be prevented,
and that all the Spaniards risked their death if they should attempt
to frustrate his will in this matter, or any other; that, in this conflict,
the deponent called the mate, Raneds, who was forced to go apart,
and immediately the negro Babo commanded the Ashantee Matiluqui and the Ashantee Leche to go and commit the murder; that
those two went down with hatchets to the berth of Don Alexandro;
that, yet half alive and mangled, they dragged him on deck; that
they were going to throw him overboard in that state, but the negro
Babo stopped them, bidding the murder be completed on the deck
before him, which was done, when, by his orders, the body was carried below, forward; that nothing more was seen of it by the deponent for three days; * * * that Don Alonzo Sidonia, an old man, long
resident at Valparaiso, and lately appointed to a civil office in Peru,
whither he had taken passage, was at the time sleeping in the berth
opposite Don Alexandro's; that, awakening at his cries, surprised by
them, and at the sight of the negroes with their bloody hatchets in
their hands, he threw himself into the sea through a window which
was near him, and was drowned, without it being in the power of
the deponent to assist or take him up; * * * that, a short time after
killing Aranda, they brought upon deck his german-cousin, of middle-age, Don Francisco Masa, of Mendoza, and the young Don
Joaquin, Marques de Arambaolaza, then lately from Spain, with his

Spanish servant Ponce, and the three young clerks of Aranda, José Morairi, Lorenzo Bargas, and Hermenegildo Gandix, all of Cadiz; that Don Joaquin and Hermenegildo Gandix, the negro Babo for purposes hereafter to appear, preserved alive; but Don Francisco Masa, José Morairi, and Lorenzo Bargas, with Ponce the servant, beside the boatswain, Juan Robles, the boatswain's mates, Manuel Viscaya and Roderigo Hurta, and four of the sailors, the negro Babo ordered to be thrown alive into the sea, although they made no resistance, nor begged for anything else but mercy; that the boatswain, Juan Robles, who knew how to swim, kept the longest above water, making acts of contrition, and, in the last words he uttered, charged this deponent to cause mass to be said for his soul to our Lady of Succor; * * * that, during the three days which followed, the deponent, uncertain what fate had befallen the remains of Don Alexandro, frequently asked the negro Babo where they were, and, if still on board, whether they were to be preserved for interment ashore, entreating him so to order it; that the negro Babo answered nothing till the fourth day, when at sunrise, the deponent coming on deck, the negro Babo showed him a skeleton, which had been substituted for the ship's proper figure-head, the image of Christopher Colon, the discoverer of the New World; that the negro Babo asked him whose skeleton that was, and whether, from its whiteness, he should not think it a white's; that, upon his covering his face, the negro Babo, coming close, said words to this effect: "Keep faith with the blacks from here to Senegal, or you shall in spirit, as now in body, follow your leader," pointing to the prow; * * * that the same morning the negro Babo took by succession each Spaniard forward, and asked him whose skeleton that was, and whether, from its whiteness, he should not think it a white's; that each Spaniard covered his face; that then to each the negro Babo repeated the words in the first place said to the deponent; * * * that they (the Spaniards), being then assembled aft, the negro Babo harangued them, saying that he had now done all; that the deponent (as navigator for the negroes) might pursue his course, warning him and all of them that they should, soul and body, go the way of Don Alexandro if he saw them (the Spaniards) speak or plot anything against them (the negroes)— a threat which was repeated every day; that, before the events last mentioned, they had tied the cook to throw him overboard, for it is

not known what thing they heard him speak, but finally the negro
Babo spared his life, at the request of the deponent; that a few days
after, the deponent, endeavoring not to omit any means to preserve
the lives of the remaining whites, spoke to the negroes peace and
tranquillity, and agreed to draw up a paper, signed by the deponent
and the sailors who could write, as also by the negro Babo, for himself and all the blacks, in which the deponent obliged himself to
carry them to Senegal, and they not to kill any more, and he formally to make over to them the ship, with the cargo, with which
they were for that time satisfied and quieted. * * * But the next day,
the more surely to guard against the sailors' escape, the negro Babo
commanded all the boats to be destroyed but the long-boat, which
was unseaworthy, and another, a cutter in good condition, which,
knowing it would yet be wanted for towing the water casks, he had
it lowered down into the hold.

*　　*　　*　　*　　*

[*Various particulars of the prolonged and perplexed navigation ensuing
here follow, with incidents of a calamitous calm, from which portion one passage is extracted, to wit:*]

—That on the fifth day of the calm, all on board suffering much
from the heat, and want of water, and five having died in fits, and
mad, the negroes became irritable, and for a chance gesture, which
they deemed suspicious—though it was harmless— made by the
mate, Raneds, to the deponent, in the act of handing a quadrant,
they killed him; but that for this they afterwards were sorry, the
mate being the only remaining navigator on board, except the deponent.

*　　*　　*　　*　　*

—That omitting other events, which daily happened, and which
can only serve uselessly to recall past misfortunes and conflicts,
after seventy-three days' navigation, reckoned from the time they
sailed from Nasca, during which they navigated under a scanty allowance of water, and were afflicted with the calms before men-

tioned, they at last arrived at the island of Santa Maria, on the seventeenth of the month of August, at about six o'clock in the afternoon, at which hour they cast anchor very near the American ship, Bachelor's Delight, which lay in the same bay, commanded by the generous Captain Amasa Delano; but at six o'clock in the morning, they had already descried the port, and the negroes became uneasy, as soon as at distance they saw the ship, not having expected to see one there; that the negro Babo pacified them, assuring them that no fear need be had; that straightway he ordered the figure on the bow to be covered with canvas, as for repairs, and had the decks a little set in order; that for a time the negro Babo and the negro Atufal conferred; that the negro Atufal was for sailing away, but the negro Babo would not, and, by himself, cast about what to do; that at last he came to the deponent, proposing to him to say and do all that the deponent declares to have said and done to the American captain; * * * * * * that the negro Babo warned him that if he varied in the least, or uttered any word, or gave any look that should give the least intimation of the past events or present state, he would instantly kill him, with all his companions, showing a dagger, which he carried hid, saying something which, as he understood it, meant that that dagger would be alert as his eye; that the negro Babo then announced the plan to all his companions, which pleased them; that he then, the better to disguise the truth, devised many expedients, in some of them uniting deceit and defense; that of this sort was the device of the six Ashantees before named, who were his bravoes; that them he stationed on the break of the poop, as if to clean certain hatchets (in cases, which were part of the cargo), but in reality to use them, and distribute them at need, and at a given word he told them; that, among other devices, was the device of presenting Atufal, his right-hand man, as chained, though in a moment the chains could be dropped; that in every particular he informed the deponent what part he was expected to enact in every device, and what story he was to tell on every occasion, always threatening him with instant death if he varied in the least: that, conscious that many of the negroes would be turbulent, the negro Babo appointed the four aged negroes, who were calkers, to keep what domestic order they could on the decks; that again and again he harangued the Spaniards and his companions, informing them of his intent, and of his devices, and of the invented story that this deponent was to tell, charging them lest any of them varied from that story; that these arrangements were made and matured during the interval of two or three hours, between their first sighting the ship and the arrival on board of Captain Amasa Delano; that this happened about half-past seven o'clock in the morning, Captain Amasa Delano coming in his boat, and all gladly receiving him; that the deponent, as well as he could force himself, acting then the part of principal owner, and a free captain of the ship, told Captain Amasa Delano, when called upon, that he came from Buenos Ayres, bound to Lima, with three hundred negroes; that off Cape Horn, and in a subsequent fever, many negroes had died; that also, by similar casualties, all the sea officers and the greatest part of the crew had died.

*   *   *   *   *

[*And so the deposition goes on, circumstantially recounting the fictitious story dictated to the deponent by Babo, and through the deponent imposed upon Captain Delano; and also recounting the friendly offers of Captain Delano, with other things, but all of which is here omitted. After the fictitious, strange story, etc., the deposition proceeds*]

—that the generous Captain Amasa Delano remained on board all the day, till he left the ship anchored at six o'clock in the evening, deponent speaking to him always of his pretended misfortunes, under the forementioned principles, without having had it in his power to tell a single word, or give him the least hint, that he might know the truth and state of things; because the negro Babo, performing the office of an officious servant with all the appearance of submission of the humble slave, did not leave the deponent one moment; that this was in order to observe the deponent's actions and words, for the negro Babo understands well the Spanish; and besides, there were thereabout some others who were constantly on the watch, and likewise understood the Spanish; * * * that upon one occasion, while deponent was standing on the deck conversing with Amasa Delano, by a secret sign the negro Babo drew him (the deponent) aside, the act appearing as if originating with the deponent; that then, he being drawn aside, the negro Babo proposed to him to gain from Amasa Delano full particulars about his ship, and crew, and arms; that the deponent asked "For what?" that the negro Babo answered he might conceive; that, grieved at the prospect of what might overtake the generous Captain Amasa Delano, the deponent at first refused to ask the desired questions, and used every argument to induce the negro Babo to give up this new design; that the negro Babo showed the point of his dagger; that, after the information had been obtained, the negro Babo again drew him aside, telling him that that very night he (the deponent) would be captain of two ships, instead of one, for that, great part of the American's ship's crew being to be absent fishing, the six Ashantees, without any one else, would easily take it; that at this time he said other things to the same purpose; that no entreaties availed; that, before Amasa Delano's coming on board, no hint had been given touching the capture of the American ship: that to prevent this project the deponent was powerless; * * * —that in some things his memory is confused, he cannot distinctly recall every event; * * * —that as soon as they had cast anchor at six of the clock in the evening, as has before been stated, the American Captain took leave to return to his vessel; that upon a sudden impulse, which the deponent believes to have come from God and his angels, he, after the farewell had been said, followed the generous Captain Amasa Delano as far as the gunwale, where he stayed, under pretense of taking leave, until Amasa Delano should have been seated in his boat; that on shoving off, the deponent sprang from the gunwale into the boat, and fell into it, he knows not how, God guarding him; that—

* * * * *

[*Here, in the original, follows the account of what further happened at the escape, and how the San Dominick was retaken, and of the passage to the coast; including in the recital many expressions of "eternal gratitude" to the "generous Captain Amasa Delano." The deposition then proceeds with recapitulatory remarks, and a partial renumeration of the negroes, making record of their individual part in the past events, with a view to furnishing, according to command of the court, the data whereon to found the criminal sentences to be pronounced. From this portion is the following:*]

—That he believes that all the negroes, though not in the first place knowing to the design of revolt, when it was accomplished, approved it. * * * That the negro, José, eighteen years old, and in the personal service of Don Alexandro, was the one who communicated the information to the negro Babo, about the state of things in the cabin, before the revolt; that this is known, because, in the preceding midnights, he used to come from his berth, which was under his master's, in the cabin, to the deck where the ringleader and his associates were, and had secret conversations with the negro Babo, in which he was several times seen by the mate; that, one night, the mate drove him away twice; * * that this same negro José, was the one who, without being commanded to do so by the negro Babo, as Lecbe and Matiluqui were, stabbed his master, Don Alexandro, after he had been dragged half-lifeless to the deck; * * that the mulatto steward, Francesco, was of the first band of revolters, that he was, in all things, the creature and tool of the negro Babo; that, to make his court, he, just before a repast in the cabin, proposed, to the negro Babo, poisoning a dish for the generous Captain Amasa Delano; this is known and believed, because the negroes have said it; but that the negro Babo, having another design, forbade Francesco; * * that the Ashantee Lecbe was one of the worst of them; for that, on the day the ship was retaken, he assisted in the defense of her, with a hatchet in each hand, with one of which he wounded, in the breast, the chief mate of Amasa Delano, in the first act of boarding; this all knew; that, in sight of the deponent, Lecbe struck, with a hatchet, Don Francisco Masa when, by the negro Babo's orders, he was carrying him to throw him overboard, alive; beside participating in the murder, before mentioned, of Don Alexandro Aranda, and others of the cabin-passengers; that, owing to the fury with which the Ashantees fought in the engagement with the boats, but this Lecbe and Yau survived; that Yau was bad as Lecbe; that Yau was the man who, by Babo's command, willingly prepared the skeleton of Don Alexandro, in a way the negroes afterwards told the deponent, but which he, so long as reason is left him, can never divulge; that Yau and Lecbe were the two who, in a calm by night, riveted the skeleton to the bow; this also the negroes told him; that the negro Babo was he who traced the inscription below it; that the negro Babo was the plotter from first to last; he ordered every murder, and was the helm and keel of the revolt; that Atufal was his lieutenant in all; but Atufal, with his own hand, committed no murder; nor did the negro Babo; * * that Atufal was shot, being killed in the fight with the boats, ere boarding; * * that the negresses, of age, were knowing to the revolt, and testified themselves satisfied at the death of their master, Don Alexandro; that, had the negroes not restrained them, they would have tortured to death, instead of simply killing, the Spaniards slain by command of the negro Babo; that the negresses used their utmost influence to have the deponent made away with; that, in the various acts of murder, they sang songs and danced—not gaily, but solemnly; and before the engagement with the boats, as well as during the action, they sang melancholy songs to the negroes, and that this melancholy tone was more inflaming than a different one would have been, and was so intended; that all this is believed, because the negroes have said it.

—that of the thirty-six men of the crew exclusive of the passengers, (all of whom are now dead), which the deponent had knowledge of, six only remained alive, with four cabin-boys and ship-boys, not included with the crew; * * —that the negroes broke an arm of one of the cabin-boys and gave him strokes with hatchets.

[*Then follow various random disclosures referring to various periods of time. The following are extracted:*]

—That during the presence of Captain Amasa Delano on board, some attempts were made by the sailors, and one by Hermenegildo Gandix, to convey hints to him of the true state of affairs; but that these attempts were ineffectual, owing to fear of incurring death, and furthermore owing to the devices which offered contradictions to the true state of affairs; as well as owing to the generosity and piety of Amasa Delano incapable of sounding such wickedness; * * * that Luys Galgo, a sailor about sixty years of age, and formerly of the king's navy, was one of those who sought to convey tokens to Captain Amasa Delano; but his intent, though undiscovered, being suspected, he was, on a pretense, made to retire out of sight, and at last into the hold, and there was made away with. This the negroes have since said; * * * that one of the ship-boys feeling, from Captain Amasa Delano's presence, some hopes of release, and not having enough prudence, dropped some chance-word respecting his expectations, which being overheard and understood by a slave-boy with whom he was eating at the time, the latter struck him on the head with a knife, inflicting a bad wound, but of which the boy is now healing; that likewise, not long before the ship was brought to anchor, one of the seamen, steering at the time, endangered himself by letting the blacks remark some expression in his countenance, arising from a cause similar to the above; but this sailor, by his heedful after conduct, escaped; * * * that these statements are made to show the court that from the beginning to the end of the revolt, it was impossible for the deponent and his men to act otherwise than they did; * * * —that the third clerk, Hermenegildo Gandix, who before had been forced to live among the seamen, wearing a seaman's habit, and in all respects appearing to be one for the time; he, Gandix, was killed by a musket-ball fired through a mistake from the American boats before boarding; having in his fright run up the mizzen-rigging, calling to the boats—"don't board," lest upon their boarding the negroes should kill him; that this inducing the Americans to believe he some way favored the cause of the negroes, they fired two balls at him, so that he fell wounded from the rigging, and was drowned in the sea; * * * —that the young Don Joaquin, Marques de Arambaolaza, like Hermenegildo Gandix, the third clerk, was degraded to the office and appearance of a common seaman; that upon one occasion when Don Joaquin shrank, the negro Babo commanded the Ashantee Lecbe to take tar and heat it, and pour it upon Don Joaquin's hands; * * * —that Don Joaquin was killed owing to another mistake of the Americans, but one impossible to be avoided, as upon the approach of the boats, Don Joaquin, with a hatchet tied edge out and upright to his hand, was made by the negroes to appear on the bulwarks; whereupon, seen with arms in his hands and in a questionable attitude, he was shot for a renegade seaman; * * * —that on the person of Don Joaquin was found secreted a jewel, which, by papers that were discovered, proved to have been meant for the shrine of our Lady of Mercy in Lima; a votive offering, beforehand prepared and guarded, to attest his gratitude, when he should have landed in Peru, his last destination, for the safe conclusion of his entire voyage from Spain; * * * —that the jewel, with the other effects of the late Don Joaquin, is in the custody of the brethren of the Hospital de Sacerdotes, awaiting the disposition of the honorable court; * * * —that, owing to the condition of the deponent, as well as the haste in which the boats departed for the attack, the Americans were not forewarned that there were, among the apparent crew, a passenger and one of the clerks disguised by the negro Babo; * * * —that, beside the negroes killed in the action, some were killed after the capture and re-anchoring at night, when shackled to the ring-bolts on deck; that these deaths were committed by the sailors, ere they could be prevented. That so soon as informed of it, Captain Amasa Delano used all his authority, and, in particular with his own hand, struck down Martinez Gola, who, having found a razor in the pocket of an old jacket of his, which one of the shackled negroes had on, was aiming it at the negro's throat; that the noble Captain Amasa Delano also wrenched from the hand of Bartholomew Barlo, a dagger secreted at the time of the massacre of the whites, with which he was in the act of stabbing a shackled negro, who, the same day, with another negro, had thrown him down and jumped upon him; * * * —that, for all the events, befalling through so long a time, during which the ship was in the hands of the negro Babo, he cannot here give account; but that, what he has said is the most substantial of what occurs to him at present, and is the truth under the oath which he has taken; which declaration he affirmed and ratified, after hearing it read to him.

He said that he is twenty-nine years of age, and broken in body and mind; that when finally dismissed by the court, he shall not return home to Chili, but betake himself to the monastery on Mount Agonia without; and signed with his honor, and crossed himself, and, for the time, departed as he came, in his litter, with the monk Infelez, to the Hospital de Sacerdotes.   BENITO CERENO.
          DOCTOR ROZAS.

If the Deposition have served as the key to fit into the lock of the complications which precede it, then, as a vault whose door has been flung back, the San Dominick's hull lies open to-day.

Hitherto the nature of this narrative, besides rendering the intricacies in the beginning unavoidable, has more or less required that many things, instead of being set down in the order of occurrence, should be retrospectively, or irregularly given; this last is the case with the following passages, which will conclude the account:

During the long, mild voyage to Lima, there was, as before hinted, a period during which the sufferer a little recovered his health, or, at least in some degree, his tranquillity. Ere the decided relapse which came, the two captains had many cordial conversations—their fraternal unreserve in singular contrast with former withdrawments.

Again and again, it was repeated, how hard it had been to enact the part forced on the Spaniard by Babo.

"Ah, my dear friend," Don Benito once said, "at those very times when you thought me so morose and ungrateful, nay, when, as you now admit, you half thought me plotting your murder, at those very times my heart was frozen; I could not look at you, thinking of what, both on board this ship and your own, hung, from other hands, over my kind benefactor. And as God lives, Don Amasa, I know not whether desire for my own safety alone could have nerved me to that leap into your boat, had it not been for the thought that, did you, unenlightened, return to your ship, you, my best friend, with all who might be with you, stolen upon, that night, in your hammocks, would never in this world have wakened again. Do but think how you walked this deck, how you sat in this cabin, every inch of ground mined into honey-combs under you. Had I dropped the least hint, made the least advance towards an understanding between us, death, explosive death—yours as mine—would have ended the scene."

"True, true," cried Captain Delano, starting, "you have saved my life, Don Benito, more than I yours; saved it, too, against my knowledge and will."

"Nay, my friend," rejoined the Spaniard, courteous even to the point of religion, "God charmed your life, but you saved mine. To think of some things you did—those smilings and chattings, rash pointings and gesturings. For less than these, they slew my mate, Raneds; but you had the Prince of Heaven's safe conduct through all ambuscades."

"Yes, all is owing to Providence, I know; but the temper of my mind that morning was more than commonly pleasant, while the sight of so much suffering, more apparent than real, added to my good nature, compassion, and charity, happily interweaving the three. Had it been otherwise, doubtless, as you hint, some of my interferences might have ended unhappily enough. Besides that, those feelings I spoke of enabled me to get the better of momentary distrust, at times when acuteness might have cost me my life, without saving another's. Only at the end did my suspicions get the better of me, and you know how wide of the mark they then proved."

"Wide, indeed," said Don Benito, sadly; "you were with me all day;

stood with me, sat with me, talked with me, looked at me, ate with me, drank with me; and yet, your last act was to clutch for a monster, not only an innocent man, but the most pitiable of all men. To such degree may malign machinations and deceptions impose. So far may even the best man err, in judging the conduct of one with the recesses of whose condition he is not acquainted. But you were forced to it; and you were in time undeceived. Would that, in both respects, it was so ever, and with all men."

"You generalize, Don Benito; and mournfully enough. But the past is passed; why moralize upon it? Forget it. See, yon bright sun has forgotten it all, and the blue sea, and the blue sky; these have turned over new leaves."

"Because they have no memory," he dejectedly replied; "because they are not human."

"But these mild trades that now fan your cheek, do they not come with a human-like healing to you? Warm friends, steadfast friends are the trades."

"With their steadfastness they but waft me to my tomb, señor," was the foreboding response.

"You are saved," cried Captain Delano, more and more astonished and pained; "you are saved; what has cast such a shadow upon you?"

"The negro."

There was silence, while the moody man sat, slowly and unconsciously gathering his mantle about him, as if it were a pall.

There was no more conversation that day.

But if the Spaniard's melancholy sometimes ended in muteness upon topics like the above, there were others upon which he never spoke at all; on which, indeed, all his old reserves were piled. Pass over the worst, and, only to elucidate, let an item or two of these be cited. The dress so precise and costly, worn by him on the day whose events have been narrated, had not willingly been put on. And that silver-mounted sword, apparent symbol of despotic command, was not, indeed, a sword, but the ghost of one. The scabbard, artificially stiffened, was empty.

As for the black—whose brain, not body, had schemed and led the revolt, with the plot—his slight frame, inadequate to that which it held, had at once yielded to the superior muscular strength of his captor, in the boat. Seeing all was over, he uttered no sound, and could not be forced to. His aspect seemed to say, since I cannot do deeds, I will not speak words. Put in irons in the hold, with the rest, he was carried to Lima. During the passage Don Benito did not visit him. Nor then, nor at any time after, would he look at him. Before the tribunal he refused. When pressed by the judges he fainted. On the testimony of the sailors alone rested the legal identity of Babo.

Some months after, dragged to the gibbet at the tail of a mule, the black met his voiceless end. The body was burned to ashes; but for many days, the head, that hive of subtlety, fixed on a pole in the Plaza, met, unabashed, the gaze of the whites; and across the Plaza looked towards St. Bartholomew's church, in whose vaults slept then, as now, the recovered bones of Aranda; and across the Rimac bridge looked towards the monastery, on Mount Agonia without; where, three months after being dismissed by the court, Benito Cereno, borne on the bier, did, indeed, follow his leader.

1855

THE 'GEES

In relating to my friends various passages of my sea-goings, I have at times had occasion to allude to that singular people the 'Gees, sometimes as casual acquaintances, sometimes as shipmates. Such allusions have been quite natural and easy. For instance, I have said *The two 'Gees,* just as another would say *The two Dutchmen,* or *The two Indians.* In fact, being myself so familiar with 'Gees, it seemed as if all the rest of the world must be. But not so. My auditors have opened their eyes as much as to say, "What under the sun is a 'Gee?" To enlighten them I have repeatedly had to interrupt myself, and not without detriment to my stories. To remedy which inconvenience, a friend hinted the advisability of writing out some account of the 'Gees, and having it published. Such as they are, the following memoranda spring from that happy suggestion:

The word *'Gee* (*g* hard) is an abbreviation, by seamen, of *Portuguee,* the corrupt form of *Portuguese.* As the name is a curtailment, so the race is a residuum. Some three centuries ago certain Portuguese convicts were sent as a colony to Fogo, one of the Cape de Verds, off the northwest coast of Africa, an island previously stocked with an aboriginal race of negroes, ranking pretty high in incivility, but rather low in stature and morals. In course of time, from the amalgamated generation all the likelier sort were drafted off as food for powder, and the ancestors of the since called 'Gees were left as the *caput mortuum,* or melancholy remainder.

Of all men seamen have strong prejudices, particularly in the matter of race. They are bigots here. But when a creature of inferior race lives among them, an inferior tar, there seems no bound to their disdain. Now, as ere long will be hinted, the 'Gee, though of an aquatic nature, does not, as regards higher qualifications, make the best of sailors. In short, by seamen the abbreviation 'Gee was hit upon in pure contumely; the degree of which may be partially inferred from this, that with them the primitive word Portuguee itself is a reproach; so that 'Gee, being a subtle distillation from that word, stands, in point of relative intensity to it, as attar of roses does to rose-water. At times, when some crusty old sea-dog has his spleen more than usually excited against some luckless blunderer of Fogo his shipmate, it is marvelous the prolongation of taunt into which he will spin out the one little exclamatory monosyllable Ge-e-c-e-e!

The Isle of Fogo, that is, "Fire Isle," was so called from its volcano, which, after throwing up an infinite deal of stones and ashes, finally threw up business altogether, from its broadcast bounteousness having become bankrupt. But thanks to the volcano's prodigality in its time, the soil of Fogo is such as may be found of a dusty day on a road newly Macadamized. Cut off from farms and gardens, the staple food of the inhabitants is fish, at catching which they are expert. But none the less do they relish ship-biscuit, which, indeed, by most islanders, barbarous or semi-barbarous, is held a sort of lozenge.

In his best estate the 'Gee is rather small (he admits it), but, with some exceptions, hardy; capable of enduring extreme hard work, hard fare, or hard usage, as the case may be. In fact, upon a scientific view, there would seem a natural adaptability in the 'Gee to hard times generally. A theory not uncorroborated by his experiences; and furthermore, that kindly care of Nature in fitting him for them, something as for his hard rubs with a hardened world Fox the Quaker fitted himself, namely, in a tough leather suit from top to toe. In other words, the 'Gee is by no means of that exquisitely delicate sensibility expressed by the figurative adjective thin-skinned. His physicals and spirituals are in singular contrast. The 'Gee has a great appetite, but little imagination; a large eyeball, but small insight. Biscuit he crunches, but sentiment he eschews.

His complexion is hybrid; his hair ditto; his mouth disproportionally large, as compared with his stomach; his neck short; but his head round, compact, and betokening a solid understanding.

Like the negro, the 'Gee has a peculiar savor, but a different one—a sort of wild, marine, gamy savor, as in the sea-bird called haglet. Like venison, his flesh is firm but lean.

His teeth are what are called butter-teeth, strong, durable, square, and yellow. Among captains at a loss for better discourse during dull, rainy weather in the horse-latitudes, much debate has been had whether his teeth are intended for carnivorous or herbivorous purposes, or both conjoined. But as on his isle the 'Gee eats neither flesh nor grass, this inquiry would seem superfluous.

The native dress of the 'Gee is, like his name, compendious. His head being by nature well thatched, he wears no hat. Wont to wade much in the surf, he wears no shoes. He has a serviceably hard heel, a kick from which is by the judicious held almost as dangerous as one from a wild zebra.

Though for a long time back no stranger to the seafaring people of Portugal, the 'Gee, until a comparatively recent period, remained almost undreamed of by seafaring Americans. It is now some forty years since he first became known to certain masters of our Nantucket ships, who commenced the practice of touching at Fogo, on the outward passage, there to fill up vacancies among their crews arising from the short supply of men at home. By degrees the custom became pretty general, till now the 'Gee is found aboard of almost one whaler out of three. One reason why they are in request is this: An unsophisticated 'Gee coming on board a foreign ship never asks for wages. He comes for biscuit. He does not know what other wages mean, unless cuffs and buffets be wages, of which sort he receives a liberal allowance, paid with great punctuality, besides perquisites of punches thrown in now and then. But for all this, some persons there are, and not unduly biassed by partiality to him either, who still insist that the 'Gee never gets his due.

His docile services being thus cheaply to be had, some captains will go the length of maintaining that 'Gee sailors are preferable, indeed every way, physically and intellectually, superior to American sailors—such captains complaining, and justly, that American sailors, if not decently treated, are apt to give serious trouble.

But even by their most ardent admirers it is not deemed prudent to sail a ship with none but 'Gees, at least if they chance to be all green hands, a green 'Gee being of all green things the greenest. Besides, owing to the clumsiness of their feet ere improved by practice in the rigging, green 'Gees are wont, in no inconsiderable numbers, to fall overboard the first dark, squally night; insomuch that when unreasonable owners insist with a captain against his will upon a green 'Gee crew fore and aft, he will ship twice as many 'Gees as he would have shipped of Americans, so as to provide for all contingencies.

The 'Gees are always ready to be shipped. Any day one may go to their isle, and on the showing of a coin of biscuit over the rail, may load down to the water's edge with them.

But though any number of 'Gees are ever ready to be shipped, still it is by no means well to take them as they come. There is a choice even in 'Gees.

Of course the 'Gee has his private nature as well as his public coat. To know 'Gees—to be a sound judge of 'Gees—one must study them, just as to know and be a judge of horses one must study horses. Simple as for the most part are both horse and 'Gee, in neither case can knowledge of the creature come by intuition. How unwise, then, in those ignorant young captains who, on their first voyage, will go and ship their 'Gees at Fogo without any preparatory information, or even so much as taking convenient advice from a 'Gee jockey. By a 'Gee jockey is meant a man well versed in 'Gees. Many a young captain has been thrown and badly hurt by a 'Gee of his own choosing. For notwithstanding the general docility of the 'Gee when green, it may be otherwise with him when ripe. Discreet captains won't have such a 'Gee. "Away with that ripe 'Gee!" they cry; "that smart 'Gee; that knowing 'Gee! Green 'Gees for me!"

For the benefit of inexperienced captains about to visit Fogo, the following may be given as the best way to test a 'Gee: Get square before him, at, say three paces, so that the eye, like a shot, may rake the 'Gee fore and aft, at one glance taking in his whole make and build—how he looks about the head, whether he carry it well; his ears, are they over-lengthy? How fares it in the withers? His legs, does the 'Gee stand strongly on them? His knees, any Belshazzar symptoms there? How stands it in the region of the brisket? etc., etc.

Thus far for bone and bottom. For the rest, draw close to, and put the centre of the pupil of your eye —put it, as it were, right into the 'Gee's eye; even as an eye-stone, gently, but firmly slip it in there, and then note what speck or beam of viciousness, if any, will be floated out.

All this and much more must be done; and yet after all, the best judge may be deceived. But on no account should the skipper negotiate for his 'Gee with any middle-man, himself a 'Gee. Because such an one must be a knowing 'Gee, who will be sure to advise the green 'Gee what things to hide and what to display, to hit the skipper's fancy; which, of course, the knowing 'Gee supposes to lean toward as much physical and moral excellence as possible. The rashness of trusting to one of these middle-men was forcibly shown in the case of the 'Gee who by his countrymen was recommended to a New Bedford captain as one of the most agile 'Gees in Fogo. There he stood straight and stout, in a flowing pair of man-of-war's-man's trowsers, uncommonly well filled out. True, he did not step around much at the time. But that was diffidence. Good. They shipped him. But at the first taking in of sail the 'Gee hung fire. Come to look, both trowser-legs were full of elephantiasis. It was a long sperm-whaling voyage. Useless as so much lumber, at every port prohibited from being dumped ashore, that elephantine 'Gee, ever crunching biscuit, for three weary years was trundled round the globe.

Grown wise by several similar experiences, old Captain Hosea Kean, of Nantucket, in shipping a 'Gee, at present manages matters thus: He lands at Fogo in the night; by secret means gains information where the likeliest 'Gee wanting to ship lodges; whereupon with a strong party he surprises all the friends and acquaintances of that 'Gee; putting them under guard with pistols at their heads; then creeps cautiously toward the 'Gee, now lying wholly at unawares in his hut, quite relaxed from all possibility of displaying aught deceptive in his appearance. Thus silently, thus suddenly, thus unannounced, Captain Kean bursts upon his 'Gee, so to speak, in the very bosom of his family. By this means, more than once, unexpected revelations have been made. A 'Gee, noised abroad for a Hercules in strength and an Apollo Belvidere for beauty, of a sudden is discovered all in a wretched heap; forlornly adroop as upon crutches, his legs looking as if broken at the cart-wheel. Solitude is the house of candor, according to Captain Kean. In the stall, not the street, he says, resides the real nag.

The innate disdain of regularly bred seamen toward 'Gees receives an added edge from this. The 'Gees undersell them, working for biscuit where the sailors demand dollars. Hence, any thing said by sailors to the prejudice of 'Gees should be received with caution. Especially that jeer of theirs, that the monkey-jacket was originally so called from the circumstance that that rude sort of shaggy garment was first known in Fogo. They often call a monkey-jacket a 'Gee-jacket. However this may be, there is no call to which the 'Gee will with more alacrity respond than the word "Man!"

Is there any hard work to be done, and the 'Gees stand round in sulks? "Here, my men!" cries the mate. How they jump. But ten to one when the work is done, it is plain 'Gee again. "Here, 'Gee! you 'Ge-e-e-e!" In fact, it is not unsurmised, that only when extraordinary stimulus is needed, only when an extra strain is to be got out of them, are these hapless 'Gees ennobled with the human name.

As yet, the intellect of the 'Gee has been little cultivated. No well-attested educational experiment has been tried upon him. It is said, however, that in the last century a young 'Gee was by a visionary Portuguese naval officer sent to Salamanca University. Also, among the Quakers of Nantucket, there has been talk of sending five comely 'Gees, aged sixteen, to Dartmouth College; that venerable institution, as is well known, having been originally founded partly with the object of finishing off wild Indians in the classics and higher mathematics. Two qualities of the 'Gee which, with his docility, may be justly regarded as furnishing a hopeful basis for his intellectual training, are his excellent memory, and still more excellent credulity.

The above account may, perhaps, among the ethnologists, raise some curiosity to see a 'Gee. But to see a 'Gee there is no need to go all the way to Fogo, no more than to see a Chinaman to go all the way to China. 'Gees are occasionally to be encountered in our sea-ports, but more particularly in Nantucket and New Bedford. But these 'Gees are not the 'Gees of Fogo. That is, they are no longer green 'Gees. They are sophisticated 'Gees, and hence liable to be taken for naturalized citizens badly sunburnt. Many a Chinaman, in new coat and pantaloons, his long queue coiled out of sight in one of Genin's hats, has promenaded Broadway, and been taken merely for an eccentric Georgia planter. The same with 'Gees; a stranger need have a sharp eye to know a 'Gee, even if he see him.

Thus much for a general sketchy view of the 'Gee. For further and fuller information apply to any sharp-witted American whaling captain, but more especially to the before-mentioned old Captain Hosea Kean, of Nantucket, whose address at present is "Pacific Ocean."

1856

I AND MY CHIMNEY

I and my chimney, two grey-headed old smokers, reside in the country. We are, I may say, old settlers here; particularly my old chimney, which settles more and more every day.

Though I always say, *I and my chimney,* as Cardinal Wolsey used to say, *I and my King,* yet this egotistic way of speaking, wherein I take precedence of my chimney, is hardly borne out by the facts; in everything, except the above phrase, my chimney taking precedence of me.

Within thirty feet of the turf-sided road, my chimney—a huge, corpulent old Harry VIII. of a chimney—rises full in front of me and all my possessions. Standing well up a hill-side, my chimney, like Lord Rosse's monster telescope, swung vertical to hit the meridian moon, is the first object to greet the approaching traveler's eye, nor is it the last which the sun salutes. My chimney, too, is before me in receiving the first-fruits of the seasons. The snow is on its head ere on my hat; and every spring, as in a hollow beech tree, the first swallows build their nests in it.

But it is within doors that the preëminence of my chimney is most manifest. When in the rear room, set apart for that object, I stand to receive my guests (who, by the way call more, I suspect, to see my chimney than me), I then stand, not so much before, as, strictly speaking, behind my chimney, which is, indeed, the true host. Not that I demur. In the presence of my betters, I hope I know my place.

From this habitual precedence of my chimney over me, some even think that I have got into a sad rearward way altogether; in short, from standing behind my old-fashioned chimney so much, I have got to be quite behind the age too, as well as running behind-hand in everything else. But to tell the truth, I never was a very forward old fellow, nor what my farming neighbors call a forehanded one. Indeed, those rumors about my behindhandedness are so far correct, that I have an odd sauntering way with me sometimes of going about with my hands behind my back. As for my belonging to the rear-guard in general, certain it is, I bring up the rear of my chimney—which, by the way, is this moment before me—and that, too, both in fancy and fact. In brief, my chimney is my superior; my superior by I know not how many heads and shoulders; my superior, too, in that humbly bowing over with shovel and tongs, I much minister to it; yet never does it minister, or incline over to me; but, if any thing, in its settlings, rather leans the other way.

My chimney is grand seignior here—the one great domineering object, not more of the landscape, than of the house; all the rest of which house, in each architectural arrangement, as may shortly appear, is, in the most marked manner, accommodated, not to my wants, but to my chimney's, which, among other things, has the centre of the house to himself, leaving but the odd holes and corners to me.

But I and my chimney must explain; and as we are both rather obese, we may have to expatiate.

In those houses which are strictly double houses—that is, where the hall is in the middle—the fire-places usually are on opposite sides; so that while one member of the household is warming himself at a fire built into a recess of the north wall, say another member, the former's own brother, perhaps, may be holding his feet to the blaze before a hearth in the south wall—the two thus fairly sitting back to back. Is this well? Be it put to any man who has a proper fraternal feeling. Has it not a sort of sulky appearance? But very probably this style of chimney building originated with some architect afflicted with a quarrelsome family.

Then again, almost every modern fire-place has its separate flue—separate throughout, from hearth to chimney-top. At least such an arrangement is deemed desirable. Does not this look egotistical, selfish? But still more, all these separate flues, instead of having independent masonry establishments of their own, or instead of being grouped together in one federal stock in the middle of the house—instead of this, I say, each flue is surreptitiously honeycombed into the walls; so that these last are here and there, or indeed almost anywhere, treacherously hollow, and, in consequence, more or less weak. Of course, the main reason of this style of chimney building is to economize room. In cities, where lots are sold by the inch, small space is to spare for a chimney constructed on magnanimous principles; and, as with most thin men, who are generally tall, so with such houses, what is lacking in breadth must be made up in height. This remark holds true even with regard to many very stylish abodes, built by the most stylish of gentlemen. And yet, when that stylish gentleman, Louis le Grand of France, would build a palace for his lady friend, Madame de Maintenon, he built it but one story high—in fact in the cottage style. But then how uncommonly quadrangular, spacious, and broad—horizontal acres, not vertical ones. Such is the palace, which, in all its one-storied magnificence of Languedoc marble, in the garden of Versailles, still remains to this day. Any man can buy a square foot of land and plant a liberty-pole on it; but it takes a king to set apart whole acres for a grand Trianon.

But nowadays it is different; and furthermore, what originated in a necessity has been mounted into a vaunt. In towns there is large rivalry in building tall houses. If one gentleman builds his house four stories high, and another gentleman comes next door and builds five stories high, then the former, not to be looked down upon that way, immediately sends for his architect and claps a fifth and a sixth story on top of his previous four. And, not till the gentleman has achieved his aspiration, not till he has stolen over the way by twilight and observed how his sixth story soars beyond his neighbor's fifth—not till then does he retire to his rest with satisfaction.

Such folks, it seems to me, need mountains for neighbors, to take this emulous conceit of soaring out of them.

If, considering that mine is a very wide house, and by no means lofty, aught in the above may appear like interested pleading, as if I did but fold myself about in the cloak of a general proposition, cunningly to tickle my individual vanity beneath it, such misconception must vanish upon my frankly conceding, that land adjoining my alder swamp was sold last month for ten dollars an acre, and thought a rash purchase at that; so that for wide houses hereabouts there is plenty of room, and cheap. Indeed so cheap—dirt cheap—is the soil, that our elms thrust out their roots in it, and hang their great boughs over it, in the most lavish and reckless way.

Almost all our crops, too, are sown broadcast, even peas and turnips. A farmer among us, who should go about his twenty-acre field, poking his finger into it here and there, and dropping down a mustard seed, would be thought a penurious, narrow-minded husbandman. The dandelions in the river-meadows, and the forget-me-nots along the mountain roads, you see at once they are put to no economy in space. Some seasons, too, our rye comes up, here and there a spear, sole and single like a church-spire. It doesn't care to crowd itself where it knows there is such a deal of room. The world is wide, the world is all before us, says the rye. Weeds, too, it is amazing how they spread. No such thing as arresting them—some of our pastures being a sort of Alsatia for the weeds. As for the grass, every spring it is like Kossuth's rising of what he calls the peoples. Mountains, too, a regular camp-meeting of them. For the same reason, the same all-sufficiency of room, our shadows march and countermarch, going through their various drills and masterly evolutions, like the old imperial guard on the Champs de Mars. As for the hills, especially where the roads cross them, the supervisors of our various towns have given notice to all concerned, that they can come and dig them down and cart them off, and never a cent to pay, no more than for the privilege of picking blackberries. The stranger who is buried here, what liberal-hearted landed proprietor among us grudges him his six feet of rocky pasture?

Nevertheless, cheap, after all, as our land is, and much as it is trodden under foot, I, for one, am proud of it for what it bears; and chiefly for its three great lions—the Great Oak, Ogg Mountain, and my chimney.

Most houses, here, are but one and a half stories high; few exceed two. That in which I and my chimney dwell, is in width nearly twice its height, from sill to eaves—which accounts for the magnitude of its main content—besides, showing that in this house, as in this country at large, there is abundance of space, and to spare, for both of us.

The frame of the old house is of wood—which but the more sets forth the solidity of the chimney, which is of brick. And as the great wrought nails, binding the clapboards, are unknown in these degenerate days, so are the huge bricks in the chimney walls. The architect of the chimney must have had the pyramid of Cheops before him; for, after that famous structure, it seems modeled, only its rate of decrease towards the summit is considerably less, and it is truncated. From the exact middle of the mansion it soars from the cellar, right up through each successive floor, till, four feet square, it breaks water from the ridge-pole of the roof, like an anvil-headed whale, through the crest of a billow. Most people, though, liken it, in that part, to a razeed observatory, masoned up.

The reason for its peculiar appearance above the roof touches upon rather delicate ground. How shall I reveal that, forasmuch as many years ago the original gable roof of the old house had become very leaky, a temporary proprietor hired a band of woodmen, with their huge, cross-cut saws, and went to sawing the old gable roof clean off. Off it went, with all its birds' nests, and dormer windows. It was replaced with a modern roof, more fit for a railway wood-house than an old country gentleman's abode. This operation—razeeing the structure some fifteen feet—was, in effect upon the chimney, something like the falling of the great spring tides. It left uncommon low water all about the chimney—to abate which appearance, the same person now proceeds to slice fifteen feet off the chimney itself, actually beheading my royal old chimney—a regicidal act, which, were it not for the palliating fact, that he was a poulterer by trade, and, therefore, hardened to such neck-wringings, should send that former proprietor down to posterity in the same cart with Cromwell.

Owing to its pyramidal shape, the reduction of the chimney inordinately widened its razeed summit. Inordinately, I say, but only in the estimation of such as have no eye to the picturesque. What care I, if, unaware that my chimney, as a free citizen of this free land, stands upon an independent basis of its own, people passing it, wonder how such a brick-kiln, as they call it, is supported upon mere joists and rafters? What care I? I will give a traveler a cup of switchel, if he want it; but am I bound to supply him with a sweet taste? Men of cultivated minds see, in my old house and chimney, a goodly old elephant-and-castle.

All feeling hearts will sympathize with me in what I am now about to add. The surgical operation, above referred to, necessarily brought into the open air a part of the chimney previously under cover, and intended to remain so, and, therefore, not built of what are called weather-bricks. In consequence, the chimney, though of a vigorous constitution, suffered not a little, from so naked an exposure; and, unable to acclimate itself, ere long began to fail—showing blotchy symptoms akin to those in measles. Whereupon travelers, passing my way, would wag their heads, laughing: "See that wax nose—how it melts off!" But what cared I? The same travelers would travel across the sea to view Kenilworth peeling away, and for a very good reason: that of all artists of the picturesque, decay wears the palm—I would say, the ivy. In fact, I've often thought that the proper place for my old chimney is ivied old England.

In vain my wife—with what probable ulterior intent will, ere long, appear—solemnly warned me, that unless something were done, and speedily, we should be burnt to the ground, owing to the holes crumbling through the aforesaid blotchy parts, where the chimney joined the roof. "Wife," said I, "far better that my house should burn down, than that my chimney should be pulled down, though but a few feet. They call it a wax nose; very good; not for me to tweak the nose of my superior." But at last the man who has a mortgage on the house dropped me a note, reminding me that, if my chimney was allowed to stand in that invalid condition, my policy of insurance would be void. This was a sort of hint not to be neglected. All the world over, the picturesque yields to the pocketesque. The mortgagor cared not, but the mortgagee did.

So another operation was performed. The wax nose was taken off, and a new one fitted on. Unfortunately for the expression—being put up by a squint-eyed mason, who, at the time, had a bad stitch in the same side—the new nose stands a little awry, in the same direction.

Of one thing, however, I am proud. The horizontal dimensions of the new part are unreduced.

Large as the chimney appears upon the roof, that is nothing to its spaciousness below. At its base in the cellar, it is precisely twelve feet square; and hence covers precisely one hundred and forty-four superficial feet. What an appropriation of terra firma for a chimney, and what a huge load for this earth! In fact, it was only because I and my chimney formed no part of his ancient burden, that that stout peddler, Atlas of old, was enabled to stand up so bravely under his pack. The dimensions given may, perhaps, seem fabulous. But, like those stones at Gilgal, which Joshua set up for a memorial of having passed over Jordan, does not my chimney remain, even unto this day?

Very often I go down into my cellar, and attentively survey that vast square of masonry. I stand long, and ponder over, and wonder at it. It has a druidical look, away down in the umbrageous cellar there, whose numerous vaulted passages, and far glens of gloom, resemble the dark, damp depths of primeval woods. So strongly did this conceit steal over me, so deeply was I penetrated with wonder at the chimney, that one day—when I was a little out of my mind, I now think—getting a spade from the garden, I set to work, digging round the foundation, especially at the corners thereof, obscurely prompted by dreams of striking upon some old, earthen-worn memorial of that by-gone day, when, into all this gloom, the light of heaven entered, as the masons laid the foundation-stones, peradventure sweltering under an August sun, or pelted by a March storm. Plying my blunted spade, how vexed was I by that ungracious interruption of a neighbor, who, calling to see me upon some business, and being informed that I was below, said I need not be troubled to come up, but he would go down to me; and so, without ceremony, and without my having been forewarned, suddenly discovered me, digging in my cellar.

"Gold digging, sir?"

"Nay, sir," answered I, starting, "I was merely—ahem!—merely—I say I was merely digging—round my chimney."

"Ah, loosening the soil, to make it grow. Your chimney, sir, you regard as too small, I suppose; needing further development, especially at the top?"

"Sir!" said I, throwing down the spade, "do not be personal. I and my chimney—"

"Personal?"

"Sir, I look upon this chimney less as a pile of masonry than as a personage. It is the king of the house. I am but a suffered and inferior subject."

In fact, I would permit no gibes to be cast at either myself or my chimney; and never again did my visitor refer to it in my hearing, without coupling some compliment with the mention. It well deserves a respectful consideration. There it stands, solitary and alone—not a council of ten flues, but, like his sacred majesty of Russia, a unit of an autocrat.

Even to me, its dimensions, at times, seem incredible. It does not look so big—no, not even in the cellar. By the mere eye, its magnitude can be but imperfectly comprehended, because only one side can be received at one time; and said side can only present twelve feet, linear measure. But then, each other side also is twelve feet long; and the whole obviously forms a square; and twelve times twelve is one hundred and forty-four. And so, an adequate conception of the magnitude of this chimney is only to be got at by a sort of process in the higher mathematics, by a method somewhat akin to those whereby the surprising distances of fixed stars are computed.

It need hardly be said, that the walls of my house are entirely free from fire-places. These all congregate in the middle—in the one grand central chimney, upon all four sides of which are hearths—two tiers of hearths— so that when, in the various chambers, my family and guests are warming themselves of a cold winter's night, just before retiring, then, though at the time they may not be thinking so, all their faces mutually look towards each other, yea, all their feet point to one centre; and, when they go to sleep in their beds, they all sleep round one warm chimney, like so many Iroquois Indians, in the woods, round their one heap of embers. And just as the Indians' fire serves, not only to keep them comfortable, but also to keep off wolves, and other savage monsters, so my chimney, by its obvious smoke at top, keeps off prowling burglars from the towns—for what burglar or murderer would dare break into an abode from whose chimney issues such a continual smoke—betokening that if the inmates are not stirring, at least fires are, and in case of an alarm, candles may readily be lighted, to say nothing of muskets.

But stately as is the chimney—yea, grand high altar as it is, right worthy for the celebration of high mass before the Pope of Rome, and all his cardinals—yet what is there perfect in this world? Caius Julius Cæsar, had he not been so inordinately great, they say that Brutus, Cassius, Antony, and the rest, had been greater. My chimney, were it not so mighty in its magnitude, my chambers had been larger. How often has my wife ruefully told me, that my chimney, like the English aristocracy, casts a contracting shade all round it. She avers that endless domestic inconveniences arise—more particularly from the chimney's stubborn central locality. The grand objection with her is, that it stands midway in the place where a fine entrance hall ought to be. In truth, there is no hall whatever to the house—nothing but a sort of square landing-place, as you enter from the wide front door. A roomy enough landing-place, I admit, but not attaining to the dignity of a hall. Now, as the front door is precisely in the middle of the front of the house, inwards it faces the chimney. In fact, the opposite wall of the landing-place is formed solely by the chimney; and hence—owing to the gradual tapering of the chimney—is a little less than twelve feet in width. Climbing the chimney in this part, is the principal stair-case—which, by three abrupt turns, and three minor landing-places, mounts to the second floor, where, over the front door, runs a sort of narrow gallery, something less than twelve feet long, leading to chambers on either hand. This gallery, of course, is railed; and so, looking down upon the stairs, and all those landing-places together, with the main one at bottom, resembles not a little a balcony for musicians, in some jolly old abode, in times Elizabethan. Shall I tell a weakness? I cherish the cobwebs there, and many a time arrest Biddy in the act of brushing them with her broom, and have many a quarrel with my wife and daughters about it.

Now the ceiling, so to speak, of the place where you enter the house, that ceiling is, in fact, the ceiling of the second floor, not the first. The two floors are made one here; so that ascending this turning stairs, you seem going up into a kind of soaring tower, or light-house. At the second landing, midway up the chimney, is a mysterious door, entering to a mysterious closet; and here I keep mysterious cordials, of a choice, mysterious flavor, made so by the constant nurturing and subtle ripening of the chimney's gentle heat, distilled through that warm mass of masonry. Better for wines is it than voyages to the Indies; my chimney itself a tropic. A chair by my chimney in a November day is as good for an invalid as a long season spent in Cuba. Often I think how grapes might ripen against my chimney. How my wife's geraniums bud there! Bud in December. Her eggs, too—can't keep them near the chimney, on account of hatching. Ah, a warm heart has my chimney.

How often my wife was at me about that projected grand entrance-hall of hers, which was to be knocked clean through the chimney, from one end of the house to the other, and astonish all guests by its generous amplitude. "But, wife," said I, "the chimney—consider the chimney: if you demolish the foundation, what is to support the superstructure?" "Oh, that will rest on the second floor." The truth is, women know next to nothing about the realities of architecture. However, my wife still talked of running her entries and partitions. She spent many long nights elaborating her plans; in imagination building her boasted hall through the chimney, as though its high mightiness were a mere spear of sorrel-top. At last, I gently reminded her that, little as she might fancy it, the chimney was a fact—a sober, substantial fact, which, in all her plannings, it would be well to take into full consideration. But this was not of much avail.

And here, respectfully craving her permission, I must say a few words about this enterprising wife of mine. Though in years nearly old as myself, in spirit she is young as my little sorrel mare, Trigger, that threw me last fall. What is extraordinary, though she comes of a rheumatic family, she is straight as a pine, never has any aches; while for me with the sciatica, I am sometimes as crippled up as any old apple tree. But she has not so much as a toothache. As for her hearing—let me enter the house in my dusty boots, and she away up in the attic. And for her sight—Biddy, the housemaid, tells other people's housemaids, that her mistress will spy a spot on the dresser straight through the pewter platter, put up on purpose to hide it. Her faculties are alert as her limbs and her senses. No danger of my spouse dying of torpor. The longest night in the year I've known her lie awake, planning her campaign for the morrow. She is a natural projector. The maxim, "Whatever is, is right," is not hers. Her maxim is, Whatever is, is wrong; and what is more, must be altered; and what is still more, must be altered right away. Dreadful maxim for the wife of a dozy old dreamer like me, who dote on seventh days as days of rest, and out of a sabbatical horror of industry, will, on a week day, go out of my road a quarter of a mile, to avoid the sight of a man at work.

That matches are made in heaven, may be, but my wife would have been just the wife for Peter the Great, or Peter the Piper. How she would have set in order that huge littered empire of the one, and with indefatigable painstaking picked the peck of pickled peppers for the other.

But the most wonderful thing is, my wife never thinks of her end. Her youthful incredulity, as to the plain theory, and still plainer fact of death, hardly seems Christian. Advanced in years, as she knows she must be, my wife seems to think that she is to teem on, and be inexhaustible forever. She doesn't believe in old age. At that strange promise in the plain of Mamre, my old wife, unlike old Abraham's, would not have jeeringly laughed within herself.

Judge how to me, who, sitting in the comfortable shadow of my chimney, smoking my comfortable pipe, with ashes not unwelcome at my feet, and ashes not unwelcome all but in my mouth; and who am thus in a comfortable sort of not unwelcome, though, indeed, ashy enough way, reminded of the ultimate exhaustion even of the most fiery life; judge how to me this unwarrantable vitality in my wife must come, sometimes, it is true, with a moral and a calm, but oftener with a breeze and a ruffle.

If the doctrine be true, that in wedlock contraries attract, by how cogent a fatality must I have been drawn to my wife! While spicily impatient of present and past, like a glass of ginger-beer she overflows with her schemes; and, with like energy as she puts down her foot, puts down her preserves and her pickles, and lives with them in a continual future; or ever full of expectations both from time and space, is ever restless for newspapers, and ravenous for letters. Content with the years that are gone, taking no thought for the morrow, and looking for no new thing from any person or quarter whatever, I have not a single scheme or expectation on earth, save in unequal resistance of the undue encroachment of hers.

Old myself, I take to oldness in things; for that cause mainly loving old Montaigne, and old cheese, and old wine; and eschewing young people, hot rolls, new books, and early potatoes, and very fond of my old claw-footed chair, and old club-footed Deacon White, my neighbor, and that still nigher old neighbor, my betwisted old grape-vine, that of a summer evening leans in his elbow for cosy company at my window-sill, while I, within doors, lean over mine to meet his; and above all, high above all, am fond of my high-mantled old chimney. But she, out of that infatuate juvenility of hers, takes to nothing but newness; for that cause mainly, loving new cider in autumn, and in spring, as if she were own daughter of Nebuchadnezzar, fairly raving after all sorts of salads and spinages, and more particularly green cucumbers (though all the time nature rebukes such unsuitable young hankerings in so elderly a person, by never permitting such things to agree with her), and has an itch after recently-discovered fine prospects (so no grave-yard be in the background), and also after Swedenborgianism, and the Spirit Rapping philosophy, with other new views, alike in things natural and unnatural; and immortally hopeful, is forever making new flower-beds even on the north side of the house, where the bleak mountain wind would scarce allow the wiry weed called hard-hack to gain a thorough footing; and on the road-side sets out mere pipe-stems of young elms; though there is no hope of any shade from them, except over the ruins of her great granddaughters' grave-stones; and won't wear caps, but plaits her gray hair; and takes the Ladies' Magazine for the fashions; and always buys her new almanac a month before the new year; and rises at dawn; and to the warmest sunset turns a cold shoulder; and still goes on at odd hours with her new course of history, and her French, and her music; and likes young company; and offers to ride young colts; and sets out young suckers in the orchard; and has a spite against my elbowed old grape-vine, and my club-footed old neighbor, and my claw-footed old chair, and above all, high above all, would fain persecute, unto death, my high-mantled old chimney. By what perverse magic, I a thousand times think, does such a very autumnal old lady have such a very vernal young soul? When I would remonstrate at times, she spins round on me with, "Oh, don't you grumble, old man (she always calls me old man), it's I, young I, that keep you from stagnating." Well, I suppose it is so. Yea, after all, these things are well ordered. My wife, as one of her poor relations, good soul, intimates, is the salt of the earth, and none the less the salt of my sea, which otherwise were unwholesome. She is its monsoon, too, blowing a brisk gale over it, in the one steady direction of my chimney.

Not insensible of her superior energies, my wife has frequently made me propositions to take upon herself all the responsibilities of my affairs. She is desirous that, domestically, I should abdicate; that, renouncing further rule, like the venerable Charles V., I should retire into some sort of monastery. But indeed, the chimney excepted, I have little authority to lay down. By my wife's ingenious application of the principle that certain things belong of right to female jurisdiction, I find myself, through my easy compliances, insensibly stripped by degrees of one masculine prerogative after another. In a dream I go about my fields, a sort of lazy, happy-go-lucky, good-for-nothing, loafing, old Lear. Only by some sudden revelation am I reminded who is over me; as year before last, one day seeing in one corner of the premises fresh deposits of mysterious boards and timbers, the oddity of the incident at length begat serious meditation. "Wife," said I, "whose boards and timbers are those I see near the orchard there? Do you know any thing about them, wife? Who put them there? You know I do not like the neighbors to use my land that way; they should ask permission first."

She regarded me with a pitying smile.

"Why, old man, don't you know I am building a new barn? Didn't you know that, old man?"

This is the poor old lady that was accusing me of tyrannizing over her.

To return now to the chimney. Upon being assured of the futility of her proposed hall, so long as the obstacle remained, for a time my wife was for a modified project. But I could never exactly comprehend it. As far as I could see through it, it seemed to involve the general idea of a sort of irregular archway, or elbowed tunnel, which was to penetrate the chimney at some convenient point under the staircase, and carefully avoiding dangerous contact with the fire-places, and particularly steering clear of the great interior flue, was to conduct the enterprising traveler from the front door all the way into the dining-room in the remote rear of the mansion. Doubtless it was a bold stroke of genius, that plan of hers, and so was Nero's when he schemed his grand canal through the Isthmus of Corinth. Nor will I take oath, that, had her project been accomplished, then, by help of lights hung at judicious intervals through the tunnel, some Belzoni or other might not have succeeded in future ages in penetrating through the masonry, and actually emerging into the dining-room, and once there, it would have been inhospitable treatment of such a traveler to have denied him a recruiting meal.

But my bustling wife did not restrict her objections, nor in the end confine her proposed alterations to the first floor. Her ambition was of the mounting order. She ascended with her schemes to the second floor, and so to the attic. Perhaps there was some small ground for her discontent with things as they were. The truth is, there was no regular passage-way up stairs or down, unless we again except that little orchestra-gallery before mentioned. And all this was owing to the chimney, which my gamesome spouse seemed despitefully to regard as the bully of the house. On all its four sides, nearly all the chambers sidled up to the chimney for the benefit of a fire-place. The chimney would not go to them; they must needs go to it. The consequence was, almost every room, like a philosophical system, was in itself an entry, or passage-way to other rooms, and systems of rooms—a whole suite of entries, in fact. Going through the house, you seem to be forever going somewhere, and getting nowhere. It is like losing one's self in the woods; round and round the chimney you go, and if you arrive at all, it is just where you started, and so you begin again, and again get nowhere. Indeed—though I say it not in the way of fault-finding at all—never was there so labyrinthine an abode. Guests will tarry with me several weeks and every now and then, be anew astonished at some unforeseen apartment.

The puzzling nature of the mansion, resulting from the chimney, is peculiarly noticeable in the dining-room, which has no less than nine doors, opening in all directions, and into all sorts of places. A stranger for the first time entering this dining-room, and naturally taking no special heed at what door he entered, will, upon rising to depart, commit the strangest blunders. Such, for instance, as opening the first door that comes handy, and finding himself stealing up stairs by the back passage. Shutting that door, he will proceed to another, and be aghast at the cellar yawning at his feet. Trying a third, he surprises the housemaid at her work. In the end, no more relying on his own unaided efforts, he procures a trusty guide in some passing person, and in good time successfully emerges. Perhaps as curious a blunder as any, was that of a certain stylish young gentleman, a great exquisite, in whose judicious eyes my daughter Anna had found especial favor. He called upon the young lady one evening, and found her alone in the dining-room at her needle-work. He stayed rather late; and after abundance of superfine discourse, all the while retaining his hat and cane, made his profuse adieus, and with repeated graceful bows proceeded to depart, after the fashion of courtiers from the Queen, and by so doing, opening a door at random, with one hand placed behind, very effectually succeeded in backing himself into a dark pantry, where he carefully shut himself up, wondering there was no light in the entry. After several strange noises as of a cat among the crockery, he reappeared through the same door, looking uncommonly crest-fallen, and, with a deeply embarrassed air, requested my daughter to designate at which of the nine he should find exit. When the mischievous Anna told me the story, she said it was surprising how unaffected and matter-of-fact the young gentleman's manner was after his reappearance. He was more candid than ever, to be sure; having inadvertently thrust his white kids into an open drawer of Havana sugar, under the impression, probably, that being what they call "a sweet fellow," his route might possibly lie in that direction.

Another inconvenience resulting from the chimney is, the bewilderment of a guest in gaining his chamber, many strange doors lying between him and it. To direct him by finger-posts would look rather queer; and just as queer in him to be knocking at every door on his route, like London's city guest, the king, at Temple Bar.

Now, of all these things and many, many more, my family continually complained. At last my wife came out with her sweeping proposition—in toto to abolish the chimney.

"What!" said I, "abolish the chimney? To take out the back-bone of anything, wife, is a hazardous affair. Spines out of backs, and chimneys out of houses, are not to be taken like frosted lead-pipes from the ground. Besides," added I, "the chimney is the one grand permanence of this abode. If undisturbed by innovators, then in future ages, when all the house shall have crumbled from it, this chimney will still survive—a Bunker Hill monument. No, no, wife, I can't abolish my back-bone."

So said I then. But who is sure of himself, especially an old man, with both wife and daughters ever at his elbow and ear? In time, I was persuaded to think a little better of it; in short, to take the matter into preliminary consideration. At length it came to pass that a master-mason—a rough sort of architect—one Mr. Scribe, was summoned to a conference. I formally introduced him to my chimney. A previous introduction from my wife had introduced him to myself. He had been not a little employed by that lady, in preparing plans and estimates for some of her extensive operations in drainage. Having, with much ado, extorted from my spouse the promise that she would leave us to an unmolested survey, I began by leading Mr. Scribe down to the root of the matter, in the cellar. Lamp in hand, I descended; for though up stairs it was noon, below it was night.

We seemed in the pyramids; and I, with one hand holding my lamp over head, and with the other pointing out, in the obscurity, the hoar mass of the chimney, seemed some Arab guide, showing the cobwebbed mausoleum of the great god Apis.

"This is a most remarkable structure, sir," said the master-mason, after long contemplating it in silence, "a most remarkable structure, sir."

"Yes," said I complacently, "every one says so."

"But large as it appears above the roof, I would not have inferred the magnitude of this foundation, sir," eyeing it critically.

Then taking out his rule, he measured it.

"Twelve feet square; one hundred and forty-four square feet! sir, this house would appear to have been built simply for the accommodation of your chimney."

"Yes, my chimney and me. Tell me candidly, now," I added, "would you have such a famous chimney abolished?"

"I wouldn't have it in a house of mine, sir, for a gift," was the reply. "It's a losing affair altogether, sir. Do you know, sir, that in retaining this chimney, you are losing, not only one hundred and forty-four square feet of good ground, but likewise a considerable interest upon a considerable principal?"

"How?"

"Look, sir," said he, taking a bit of red chalk from his pocket, and figuring against a whitewashed wall, "twenty times eight is so and so; then forty-two times thirty-nine is so and so—aint it, sir? Well, add those together, and subtract this here, then that makes so and so," still chalking away.

To be brief, after no small ciphering, Mr. Scribe informed me that my chimney contained, I am ashamed to say how many thousand and odd valuable bricks.

"No more," said I fidgeting. "Pray now, let us have a look above."

In that upper zone we made two more circumnavigations for the first and second floors. That done, we stood together at the foot of the stairway by the front door; my hand upon the knob, and Mr. Scribe hat in hand.

"Well, sir," said he, a sort of feeling his way, and, to help himself, fumbling with his hat, "well, sir, I think it can be done."

"What, pray, Mr. Scribe; *what* can be done?"

"Your chimney, sir; it can without rashness be removed, I think."

"*I* will think of it, too, Mr. Scribe," said I, turning the knob, and bowing him towards the open space without, "I will *think* of it, sir; it demands consideration; much obliged to ye; good morning, Mr. Scribe."

"It is all arranged, then," cried my wife with great glee, bursting from the nighest room.

"When will they begin?" demanded my daughter Julia.

"To-morrow?" asked Anna.

"Patience, patience, my dears," said I, "such a big chimney is not to be abolished in a minute."

Next morning it began again.

"You remember the chimney," said my wife.

"Wife," said I, "it is never out of my house, and never out of my mind."

"But when is Mr. Scribe to begin to pull it down?" asked Anna.

"Not to-day, Anna," said I.

"*When*, then?" demanded Julia, in alarm.

Now, if this chimney of mine was, for size, a sort of belfry, for ding-donging at me about it, my wife and daughters were a sort of bells, always chiming together, or taking up each other's melodies at every pause, my wife the key-clapper of all. A very sweet ringing, and pealing, and chiming, I confess; but then, the most silvery of bells may, sometimes, dismally toll, as well as merrily play. And as touching the subject in question, it became so now. Perceiving a strange relapse of opposition in me, wife and daughters began a soft and dirge-like, melancholy tolling over it.

At length my wife, getting much excited, declared to me, with pointed finger, that so long as that chimney stood, she should regard it as the monument of what she called my broken pledge. But finding this did not answer, the next day, she gave me to understand that either she or the chimney must quit the house.

Finding matters coming to such a pass, I and my pipe philosophized over them awhile, and finally concluded between us, that little as our hearts went with the plan, yet for peace' sake, I might write out the chimney's death-warrant, and, while my hand was in, scratch a note to Mr. Scribe.

Considering that I, and my chimney, and my pipe, from having been so much together, were three great cronies, the facility with which my pipe consented to a project so fatal to the goodliest of our trio; or rather, the way in which I and my pipe, in secret, conspired together, as it were, against our unsuspicious old comrade—this may seem rather strange, if not suggestive of sad reflections upon us two. But, indeed, we, sons of clay, that is my pipe and I, are no whit better than the rest. Far from us, indeed, to have volunteered the betrayal of our crony. We are of a peaceable nature, too. But that love of peace it was which made us false to a mutual friend, as soon as his cause demanded a vigorous vindication. But I rejoice to add, that better and braver thoughts soon returned, as will now briefly be set forth.

To my note, Mr. Scribe replied in person.

Once more we made a survey, mainly now with a view to a pecuniary estimate.

"I will do it for five hundred dollars," said Mr. Scribe at last, again hat in hand.

"Very well, Mr. Scribe, I will think of it," replied I, again bowing him to the door.

Not unvexed by this, for the second time, unexpected response, again he withdrew, and from my wife and daughters again burst the old exclamations.

The truth is, resolve how I would, at the last pinch I and my chimney could not be parted.

"So Holofernes will have his way, never mind whose heart breaks for it," said my wife next morning, at breakfast, in that half-didactic, half-reproachful way of hers, which is harder to bear than her most energetic assault. Holofernes, too, is with her a pet name for any fell domestic despot. So, whenever, against her most ambitious innovations, those which saw me quite across the grain, I, as in the present instance, stand with however little steadfastness on the defence, she is sure to call me Holofernes, and ten to one takes the first opportunity to read aloud, with a suppressed emphasis, of an evening, the first newspaper paragraph about some tyrannic day-laborer, who, after being for many years the

Caligula of his family, ends by beating his long-suffering spouse to death, with a garret door wrenched off its hinges, and then, pitching his little innocents out of the window, suicidally turns inward towards the broken wall scored with the butcher's and baker's bills, and so rushes headlong to his dreadful account.

Nevertheless, for a few days, not a little to my surprise, I heard no further reproaches. An intense calm pervaded my wife, but beneath which, as in the sea, there was no knowing what portentous movements might be going on. She frequently went abroad, and in a direction which I thought not unsuspicious; namely, in the direction of New Petra, a griffin-like house of wood and stucco, in the highest style of ornamental art, graced with four chimneys in the form of erect dragons spouting smoke from their nostrils; the elegant modern residence of Mr. Scribe, which he had built for the purpose of a standing advertisement, not more of his taste as an architect, than his solidity as a master-mason.

At last, smoking my pipe one morning, I heard a rap at the door, and my wife, with an air unusually quiet for her, brought me a note. As I have no correspondents except Solomon, with whom, in his sentiments, at least, I entirely correspond, the note occasioned me some little surprise, which was not diminished upon reading the following:—

"NEW PETRA, April 1st.

"SIR:—During my last examination of your chimney, possibly you may have noted that I frequently applied my rule to it in a manner apparently unnecessary. Possibly also, at the same time, you might have observed in me more or less of perplexity, to which, however, I refrained from giving any verbal expression.

"I now feel it obligatory upon me to inform you of what was then but a dim suspicion, and as such would have been unwise to give utterance to, but which now, from various subsequent calculations assuming no little probability, it may be important that you should not remain in further ignorance of.

"It is my solemn duty to warn you, sir, that there is architectural cause to conjecture that somewhere concealed in your chimney is a reserved space, hermetically closed, in short, a secret chamber, or rather closet. How long it has been there, it is for me impossible to say. What it contains is hid, with itself, in darkness. But probably a secret closet would not have been contrived except for some extraordinary object, whether for the concealment of treasure, or what other purpose, may be left to those better acquainted with the history of the house to guess.

"But enough: in making this disclosure, sir, my conscience is eased. Whatever step you choose to take upon it, is of course a matter of indifference to me; though, I confess, as respects the character of the closet, I cannot but share in a natural curiosity.

"Trusting that you may be guided aright, in determining whether it is Christian-like knowingly to reside in a house, hidden in which is a secret closet,

"I remain,

"With much respect,

"Yours very humbly,

"HIRAM SCRIBE."

My first thought upon reading this note was, not of the alleged mystery of manner to which, at the outset, it alluded—for none such had I at all observed in the master mason during his surveys—but of my late kinsman, Captain Julian Dacres, long a ship-master and merchant in the Indian trade, who, about thirty years ago, and at the ripe age of ninety, died a bachelor, and in this very house, which he had built. He was supposed to have retired into this country with a large fortune. But to the general surprise, after being at great cost in building himself this mansion, he settled down into a sedate, reserved, and inexpensive old age, which by the neighbors was thought all the better for his heirs: but lo! upon opening the will, his property was found to consist but of the house and grounds, and some ten thousand dollars in stocks; but the place, being found heavily mortgaged, was in consequence sold. Gossip had its day, and left the grass quietly to creep over the captain's grave, where he still slumbers in a privacy as unmolested as if the billows of the Indian Ocean, instead of the billows of inland verdure, rolled over him. Still, I remembered long ago, hearing strange solutions whispered by the country people for the mystery involving his will, and, by reflex, himself; and that, too, as well in conscience as purse. But people who could circulate the report (which they did), that Captain Julian Dacres had, in his day, been a Borneo pirate, surely were not worthy of credence in their collateral notions. It is queer what wild whimsies of rumors will, like toadstools, spring up about any eccentric stranger, who, settling down among a rustic population, keeps quietly to himself. With some, inoffensiveness would seem a prime cause of offense. But what chiefly had led me to scout at these rumors, particularly as referring to concealed treasure, was the circumstance, that the stranger (the same who razeed the roof and the chimney) into whose hands the estate had passed on my kinsman's death, was of that sort of character, that had there been the least ground for those reports, he would speedily have tested them, by tearing down and rummaging the walls.

Nevertheless, the note of Mr. Scribe, so strangely recalling the memory of my kinsman, very naturally chimed in with what had been mysterious, or at least unexplained, about him; vague flashings of ingots united in my mind with vague gleamings of skulls. But the first cool thought soon dismissed such chimeras; and, with a calm smile, I turned towards my wife, who, meantime, had been sitting near by, impatient enough, I dare say, to know who could have taken it into his head to write me a letter.

"Well, old man," said she, "who is it from, and what is it about?"

"Read it, wife," said I, handing it.

Read it she did, and then—such an explosion! I will not pretend to describe her emotions, or repeat her expressions. Enough that my daughters were quickly called in to share the excitement. Although they had never before dreamed of such a revelation as Mr. Scribe's; yet upon the first suggestion they instinctively saw the extreme likelihood of it. In corroboration, they cited first my kinsman, and second, my chimney; alleging that the profound mystery involving the former, and the equally profound masonry involving the latter, though both acknowledged facts, were alike preposterous on any other supposition than the secret closet.

But all this time I was quietly thinking to myself: Could it be hidden from me that my credulity in this instance would operate very favorably to a certain plan of theirs? How to get to the secret closet, or how to have any certainty about it at all, without making such fell work with the chimney as to render its set destruction superfluous? That my wife wished to get rid of the chimney, it needed no reflection to show; and that Mr. Scribe, for all his pretended disinterestedness, was not opposed to pocketing five hundred dollars by the operation, seemed equally evident. That my wife had, in secret, laid heads together with Mr. Scribe, I at present refrain from affirming. But when I consider her enmity against my chimney, and the steadiness with which at the last she is wont to carry out her schemes, if by hook or by crook she can, especially after having been once baffled, why, I scarcely knew at what step of hers to be surprised.

Of one thing only was I resolved, that I and my chimney should not budge.

In vain all protests. Next morning I went out into the road, where I had noticed a diabolical-looking old gander, that, for its doughty exploits in the way of scratching into forbidden inclosures, had been rewarded by its master with a portentous, four-pronged, wooden decoration, in the shape of a collar of the Order of the Garotte. This gander I cornered, and rummaging out its stiffest quill, plucked it, took it home, and making a stiff pen, inscribed the following stiff note:

"CHIMNEY SIDE, April 2.

"Mr. SCRIBE.

"Sir:—For your conjecture, we return you our joint thanks and compliments, and beg leave to assure you, that

"We shall remain,

"Very faithfully,

"The same,

"I and my Chimney."

Of course, for this epistle we had to endure some pretty sharp raps. But having at last explicitly understood from me that Mr. Scribe's note had not altered my mind one jot, my wife, to move me, among other things said, that if she remembered aright, there was a statute placing the keeping in private houses of secret closets on the same unlawful footing with the keeping of gunpowder. But it had no effect.

A few days after, my spouse changed her key.

It was nearly midnight, and all were in bed but ourselves, who sat up, one in each chimney-corner; she, needles in hand, indefatigably knitting a sock; I, pipe in mouth, indolently weaving my vapors.

It was one of the first of the chill nights in autumn. There was a fire on the hearth, burning low. The air without was torpid and heavy; the wood, by an oversight, of the sort called soggy.

"Do look at the chimney," she began; "can't you see that something must be in it?"

"Yes, wife. Truly there is smoke in the chimney, as in Mr. Scribe's note."

"Smoke? Yes, indeed, and in my eyes, too. How you two wicked old sinners do smoke!—this wicked old chimney and you."

"Wife," said I, "I and my chimney like to have a quiet smoke together, it is true, but we don't like to be called names."

"Now, dear old man," said she, softening down, and a little shifting the subject, "when you think of that old kinsman of yours, you *know* there must be a secret closet in this chimney."

"Secret ash-hole, wife, why don't you have it? Yes, I dare say there is a secret ash-hole in the chimney; for where do all the ashes go to that we drop down the queer hole yonder?"

"I know where they go to; I've been there almost as many times as the cat."

"What devil, wife, prompted you to crawl into the ash-hole! Don't you know that St. Dunstan's devil emerged from the ash-hole? You will get your death one of these days, exploring all about as you do. But supposing there be a secret closet, what then?"

"What, then? why what should be in a secret closet but——"

"Dry bones, wife," broke in I with a puff, while the sociable old chimney broke in with another.

"There again! Oh, how this wretched old chimney smokes," wiping her eyes with her handkerchief. "I've no doubt the reason it smokes so is, because that secret closet interferes with the flue. Do see, too, how the jams here keep settling; and it's down hill all the way from the door to this hearth. This horrid old chimney will fall on our heads yet; depend upon it, old man."

"Yes, wife, I do depend on it; yes, indeed, I place every dependence on my chimney. As for its settling, I like it. I, too, am settling, you know, in my gait. I and my chimney are settling together, and shall keep settling, too, till, as in a great feather-bed, we shall both have settled away clean out of sight. But this secret oven; I mean, secret closet of yours, wife; where exactly do you suppose that secret closet is?"

"That is for Mr. Scribe to say."

"But suppose he cannot say exactly; what, then?"

"Why then he can prove, I am sure, that it must be somewhere or other in this horrid old chimney."

"And if he can't prove that; what, then?"

"Why then, old man," with a stately air, "I shall say little more about it."

"Agreed, wife," returned I, knocking my pipe-bowl against the jam, "and now, to-morrow, I will a third time send for Mr. Scribe. Wife, the sciatica takes me; be so good as to put this pipe on the mantel."

"If you get the step-ladder for me, I will. This shocking old chimney, this abominable old-fashioned old chimney's mantels are so high, I can't reach them."

No opportunity, however trivial, was overlooked for a subordinate fling at the pile.

Here, by way of introduction, it should be mentioned, that besides the fire-places all round it, the chimney was, in the most hap-hazard way, excavated on each floor for certain curious out-of-the-way cupboards and closets, of all sorts and sizes, clinging here and there, like nests in the crotches of some old oak. On the second floor these closets were by far the most irregular and numerous. And yet this should hardly have been so, since the theory of the chimney was, that it pyramidically diminished as it ascended. The abridgment of its square on the roof was obvious enough; and it was supposed that the reduction must be methodically graduated from bottom to top.

"Mr. Scribe," said I when, the next day, with an eager aspect, that individual again came, "my object in sending for you this morning is, not to arrange for the demolition of my chimney, nor to have any particular conversation about it, but simply to allow you every reasonable facility for verifying, if you can, the conjecture communicated in your note."

Though in secret not a little crestfallen, it may be, by my phlegmatic reception, so different from what he had looked for; with much apparent alacrity he commenced the survey; throwing open the cupboards on the first floor, and peering into the closets on the second; measuring one within, and then comparing that measurement with the measurement without. Removing the fire-boards, he would gaze up the flues. But no sign of the hidden work yet.

Now, on the second floor the rooms were the most rambling conceivable. They, as it were, dovetailed into each other. They were of all shapes; not one mathematically square room among them all—a peculiarity which by the master-mason had not been unobserved. With a significant, not to say portentous expression, he took a circuit of the chimney, measuring the area of each room around it; then going down stairs, and out of doors, he measured the entire ground area; then compared the sum total of all the areas of all the rooms on the second floor with the ground area;

then, returning to me in no small excitement, announced that there was a difference of no less than two hundred and odd square feet—room enough, in all conscience, for a secret closet.

"But, Mr. Scribe," said I stroking my chin, "have you allowed for the walls, both main and sectional? They take up some space, you know."

"Ah, I had forgotten that," tapping his forehead; "but," still ciphering on his paper, "that will not make up the deficiency."

"But, Mr. Scribe, have you allowed for the recesses of so many fire-places on a floor, and for the fire-walls, and the flues; in short, Mr. Scribe, have you allowed for the legitimate chimney itself—some one hundred and forty-four square feet or thereabouts, Mr. Scribe?"

"How unaccountable. That slipped my mind, too."

"Did it, indeed, Mr. Scribe?"

He faltered a little, and burst forth with, "But we must not allow one hundred and forty-four square feet for the legitimate chimney. My position is, that within those undue limits the secret closet is contained."

I eyed him in silence a moment; then spoke:

"Your survey is concluded, Mr. Scribe; be so good now as to lay your finger upon the exact part of the chimney wall where you believe this secret closet to be; or would a witch-hazel wand assist you, Mr Scribe?"

"No, sir, but a crow-bar would," he, with temper, rejoined.

Here, now, thought I to myself, the cat leaps out of the bag. I looked at him with a calm glance, under which he seemed somewhat uneasy. More than ever now I suspected a plot. I remembered what my wife had said about abiding by the decision of Mr. Scribe. In a bland way, I resolved to buy up the decision of Mr. Scribe.

"Sir," said I, "really, I am much obliged to you for this survey. It has quite set my mind at rest. And no doubt you, too, Mr. Scribe, must feel much relieved. Sir," I added, "you have made three visits to the chimney. With a business man, time is money. Here are fifty dollars, Mr. Scribe. Nay, take it. You have earned it. Your opinion is worth it. And by the way,"—as he modestly received the money—"have you any objections to give me a—a—little certificate—something, say, like a steam-boat certificate, certifying that you, a competent surveyor, have surveyed my chimney, and found no reason to believe any unsoundness; in short, any—any secret closet in it. Would you be so kind, Mr. Scribe?"

"But, but, sir," stammered he with honest hesitation.

"Here, here are pen and paper," said I, with entire assurance.

Enough.

That evening I had the certificate framed and hung over the dining-room fire-place, trusting that the continual sight of it would forever put at rest at once the dreams and stratagems of my household.

But, no. Inveterately bent upon the extirpation of that noble old chimney, still to this day my wife goes about it, with my daughter Anna's geological hammer, tapping the wall all over, and then holding her ear against it, as I have seen the physicians of life insurance companies tap a man's chest, and then incline over for the echo. Sometimes of nights she almost frightens one, going about on this phantom errand, and still following the sepulchral response of the chimney, round and round, as if it were leading her to the threshold of the secret closet.

"How hollow it sounds," she will hollowly cry. "Yes, I declare," with an emphatic tap, "there is a secret closet here. Here, in this very spot. Hark! How hollow!"

"Psha! wife, of course it is hollow. Who ever heard of a solid chimney?"

But nothing avails. And my daughters take after, not me, but their mother.

Sometimes all three abandon the theory of the secret closet, and return to the genuine ground of attack—the unsightliness of so cumbrous a pile, with comments upon the great addition of room to be gained by its demolition, and the fine effect of the projected grand hall, and the convenience resulting from the collateral running in one direction and another of their various partitions. Not more ruthlessly did the Three Powers partition away poor Poland, than my wife and daughters would fain partition away my chimney.

But seeing that, despite all, I and my chimney still smoke our pipes, my wife reoccupies the ground of the secret closet, enlarging upon what wonders are there, and what a shame it is, not to seek it out and explore it.

"Wife," said I, upon one of these occasions, "why speak more of that secret closet, when there before you hangs contrary testimony of a master mason, elected by yourself to decide. Besides, even if there were a secret closet, secret it should remain, and secret it shall. Yes, wife, here for once I must say my say. Infinite sad mischief has resulted from the profane bursting open of secret recesses. Though standing in the heart of this house, though hitherto we have all nestled about it, unsuspicious of aught hidden within, this chimney may or may not have a secret closet.

But if it have, it is my kinsman's. To break into that wall, would be to break into his breast. And that wall-breaking wish of Momus I account the wish of a church-robbing gossip and knave. Yes, wife, a vile eaves-dropping varlet was Momus."

"Moses?—Mumps? Stuff with your mumps and your Moses!"

The truth is, my wife, like all the rest of the world, cares not a fig for my philosophical jabber. In dearth of other philosophical companionship, I and my chimney have to smoke and philosophize together. And sitting up so late as we do at it, a mighty smoke it is that we two smoky old philosophers make.

But my spouse, who likes the smoke of my tobacco as little as she does that of the soot, carries on her war against both. I live in continual dread lest, like the golden bowl, the pipes of me and my chimney shall yet be broken. To stay that mad project of my wife's, naught answers. Or, rather, she herself is incessantly answering, incessantly besetting me with her terrible alacrity for improvement, which is a softer name for destruction. Scarce a day I do not find her with her tape-measure, measuring for her grand hall, while Anna holds a yard-stick on one side, and Julia looks approvingly on from the other. Mysterious intimations appear in the nearest village paper, signed "Claude," to the effect that a certain structure, standing on a certain hill, is a sad blemish to an otherwise lovely landscape. Anonymous letters arrive, threatening me with I know not what, unless I remove my chimney. Is it my wife, too, or who, that sets up the neighbors to badgering me on the same subject, and hinting to me that my chimney, like a huge elm, absorbs all moisture from my garden? At night, also, my wife will start from sleep, professing to hear ghostly noises from the secret closet. Assailed on all sides, and in all ways, small peace have I and my chimney.

Were it not for the baggage, we would together pack up, and remove from the country.

What narrow escapes have been ours! Once I found in a drawer a whole portfolio of plans and estimates. Another time, upon returning after a day's absence, I discovered my wife standing before the chimney in earnest conversation with a person whom I at once recognized as a meddlesome architectural reformer, who, because he had no gift for putting up anything, was ever intent upon pulling down; in various parts of the country having prevailed upon half-witted old folks to destroy their old-fashioned houses, particularly the chimneys.

But worst of all was, that time I unexpectedly returned at early morning from a visit to the city, and upon approaching the house, narrowly escaped three brickbats which fell, from high aloft, at my feet. Glancing up, what was my horror to see three savages, in blue jean overalls, in the very act of commencing the long-threatened attack. Aye, indeed, thinking of those three brickbats, I and my chimney have had narrow escapes.

It is now some seven years since I have stirred from home. My city friends all wonder why I don't come to see them, as in former times. They think I am getting sour and unsocial. Some say that I have become a sort of mossy old misanthrope, while all the time the fact is, I am simply standing guard over my mossy old chimney; for it is resolved between me and my chimney, that I and my chimney will never surrender.

1856

THE PIAZZA

"With fairest flowers,
Whilst summer lasts, and I live here, Fidele—"

When I removed into the country, it was to occupy an old-fashioned farm-house, which had no piazza—a deficiency the more regretted, because not only did I like piazzas as somehow combining the coziness of in-doors with the freedom of out doors, and it is so pleasant to inspect your thermometer there, but the country round about was such a picture, that in berry time no boy climbs hill or crosses vale without coming upon easels planted in every nook, and sun-burnt painters painting there. A very paradise of painters. The circle of the stars cut by the circle of the mountains. At least, so looks it from the house; though, once upon the mountains, no circle of them can you see. Had the site been chosen five rods off, this charmed ring would not have been.

The house is old. Seventy years since, from the heart of the Hearth Stone Hills, they quarried the Kaaba, or Holy Stone, to which, each Thanksgiving, the social pilgrims used to come. So long ago, that, in digging for the foundation, the workmen used both spade and axe, fighting the Troglodytes of those subterranean parts—sturdy roots of a sturdy wood, encamped upon what is now a long land-slide of sleeping meadow, sloping away off from my poppy-bed. Of that knit wood, but one survivor stands—an elm, lonely through steadfastness.

Whoever built the house, he builded better than he knew; or else Orion in the zenith flashed down his Damocles' sword to him some starry night, and said, "Build there." For how, otherwise, could it have entered the builder's mind, that, upon the clearing being made, such a purple prospect would be his?—nothing less than Greylock, with all his hills about him, like Charlemagne among his peers.

Now, for a house, so situated in such a country, to have no piazza for the convenience of those who might desire to feast upon the view, and take their time and ease about it, seemed as much of an omission as if a picture-gallery should have no bench; for what but picture-galleries are the marble halls of these same limestone hills?—galleries hung, month after month anew, with pictures ever fading into pictures ever fresh. And beauty is like piety—you cannot run and read it; tranquillity and constancy, with, now-a-days, an easy chair, are needed. For though, of old, when reverence was in vogue, and indolence was not, the devotees of Nature, doubtless, used to stand and adore—just as, in the cathedrals of those ages, the worshipers of a higher Power did—yet, in these times of failing faith and feeble knees, we have the piazza and the pew.

During the first year of my residence, the more leisurely to witness the coronation of Charlemagne (weather permitting, they crown him every sunrise and sunset), I chose me, on the hill-side bank near by, a royal lounge of turf—a green velvet lounge, with long, moss-padded back; while at the head, strangely enough, there grew (but, I suppose, for heraldry) three tufts of blue violets in a field-argent of wild strawberries; and a trellis, with honey-suckle, I set for canopy. Very majestical lounge, indeed. So much so, that here, as with the reclining majesty of Denmark in his orchard, a sly ear-ache invaded me. But, if damps abound at times in Westminster Abbey, because it is so old, why not within this monastery of mountains, which is older?

A piazza must be had.

The house was wide—my fortune narrow; so that, to build a panoramic piazza, one round and round, it could not be—although, indeed, considering the matter by rule and square, the carpenters, in the kindest way, were anxious to gratify my furthest wishes, at I've forgotten how much a foot.

Upon but one of the four sides would prudence grant me what I wanted. Now, which side?

To the east, that long camp of the Hearth Stone Hills, fading far away towards Quito; and every fall, a small white flake of something peering suddenly, of a coolish morning, from the topmost cliff—the season's new-dropped lamb, its earliest fleece; and then the Christmas dawn, draping those dun highlands with red-barred plaids and tartans—goodly sight from your piazza, that. Goodly sight; but, to the north is Charlemagne—can't have the Hearth Stone Hills with Charlemagne.

Well, the south side. Apple-trees are there. Pleasant, of a balmy morning, in the month of May, to sit and see that orchard, white-budded, as for a bridal; and, in October, one green arsenal yard; such piles of ruddy shot. Very fine, I grant; but, to the north is Charlemagne.

The west side, look. An upland pasture, alleying away into a maple wood at top. Sweet, in opening spring, to trace upon the hill-side, otherwise gray and bare—to trace, I say, the oldest paths by their streaks of earliest green. Sweet, indeed, I can't deny; but, to the north is Charlemagne.

So Charlemagne, he carried it. It was not long after 1848; and, somehow, about that time, all round the world, these kings, they had the casting vote, and voted for themselves.

No sooner was ground broken, than all the neighborhood, neighbor Dives, in particular, broke, too—into a laugh. Piazza to the north! Winter piazza! Wants, of winter midnights, to watch the Aurora Borealis, I suppose; hope he's laid in good store of Polar muffs and mittens.

That was in the lion month of March. Not forgotten are the blue noses of the carpenters, and how they scouted at the greenness of the cit, who would build his sole piazza to the north. But March don't last forever; patience, and August comes. And then, in the cool elysium of my northern bower, I, Lazarus in Abraham's bosom, cast down the hill a pitying glance on poor old Dives, tormented in the purgatory of his piazza to the south.

But, even in December, this northern piazza does not repel—nipping cold and gusty though it be, and the north wind, like any miller, bolting by the snow, in finest flour—for then, once more, with frosted beard, I pace the sleety deck, weathering Cape Horn.

In summer, too, Canute-like, sitting here, one is often reminded of the sea. For not only do long ground-swells roll the slanting grain, and little wavelets of the grass ripple over upon the low piazza, as their beach, and the blown down of dandelions is wafted like the spray, and the purple of the mountains is just the purple of the billows, and a still August noon broods upon the deep meadows, as a calm upon the Line; but the vastness and the lonesomeness are so oceanic, and the silence and the sameness, too, that the first peep of a strange house, rising beyond the trees, is for all the world like spying, on the Barbary coast, an unknown sail.

And this recalls my inland voyage to fairy-land. A true voyage; but, take it all in all, interesting as if invented.

From the piazza, some uncertain object I had caught, mysteriously snugged away, to all appearance, in a sort of purpled breast-pocket, high up in a hopper-like hollow, or sunken angle, among the northwestern mountains—yet, whether, really, it was on a mountain-side, or a mountain-top, could not be determined; because, though, viewed from favorable points, a blue summit, peering up away behind the rest, will, as it were, talk to you over their heads, and plainly tell you, that, though he (the blue summit) seems among them, he is not of them (God forbid!), and, indeed, would have you know that he considers himself—as, to say truth, he has good right—by several cubits their superior, nevertheless, certain ranges, here and there double-filed, as in platoons, so shoulder and follow up upon one another, with their irregular shapes and heights, that, from the piazza, a nigher and lower mountain will, in most states of the atmosphere, effacingly shade itself away into a higher and further one; that an object, bleak on the former's crest, will, for all that, appear nested in the latter's flank. These mountains, somehow, they play at hide-and-seek, and all before one's eyes.

But, be that as it may, the spot in question was, at all events, so situated as to be only visible, and then but vaguely, under certain witching conditions of light and shadow.

Indeed, for a year or more, I knew not there was such a spot, and might, perhaps, have never known, had it not been for a wizard afternoon in autumn—late in autumn—a mad poet's afternoon; when the turned maple woods in the broad basin below me, having lost their first vermilion tint, dully smoked, like smouldering towns, when flames expire upon their prey; and rumor had it, that this smokiness in the general air was not all Indian summer—which was not used to be so sick a thing, however mild—but, in great part, was blown from far-off forests, for weeks on fire, in Vermont; so that no wonder the sky was ominous as Hecate's cauldron—and two sportsmen, crossing a red stubble buck-wheat field, seemed guilty Macbeth and foreboding Banquo; and the hermit-sun, hutted in an Adullam cave, well towards the south, according to his season, did little else but, by indirect reflection of narrow rays shot down a Sim-

plon pass among the clouds, just steadily paint one small, round, straw-
berry mole upon the wan cheek of northwestern hills. Signal as a candle.
One spot of radiance, where all else was shade.

Fairies there, thought I; some haunted ring where fairies dance.

Time passed; and the following May, after a gentle shower upon the
mountains—a little shower islanded in misty seas of sunshine; such a distant shower—and sometimes two, and three, and four of them, all visible
together in different parts—as I love to watch from the piazza, instead of
thunder storms, as I used to, which wrap old Greylock, like a Sinai, till
one thinks swart Moses must be climbing among scathed hemlocks there;
after, I say, that gentle shower, I saw a rainbow, resting its further end just
where, in autumn, I had marked the mole. Fairies there, thought I; remembering that rainbows bring out the blooms, and that, if one can but
get to the rainbow's end, his fortune is made in a bag of gold. Yon rainbow's end, would I were there, thought I. And none the less I wished it, for
now first noticing what seemed some sort of glen, or grotto, in the mountain side; at least, whatever it was, viewed through the rainbow's medium,
it glowed like the Potosi mine. But a work-a-day neighbor said, no doubt
it was but some old barn—an abandoned one, its broadside beaten in, the
acclivity its back-ground. But I, though I had never been there, I knew
better.

A few days after, a cheery sunrise kindled a golden sparkle in the same
spot as before. The sparkle was of that vividness, it seemed as if it could
only come from glass. The building, then—if building, after all, it was—
could, at least, not be a barn, much less an abandoned one; stale hay ten
years musting in it. No; if aught built by mortal, it must be a cottage; perhaps long vacant and dismantled, but this very spring magically fitted up
and glazed.

Again, one noon, in the same direction, I marked, over dimmed tops of
terraced foliage, a broader gleam, as of a silver buckler, held sunwards
over some croucher's head; which gleam, experience in like cases taught,
must come from a roof newly shingled. This, to me, made pretty sure the
recent occupancy of that far cot in fairy land.

Day after day, now, full of interest in my discovery, what time I could
spare from reading the Midsummer Night's Dream, and all about Titania, wishfully I gazed off towards the hills; but in vain. Either troops of
shadows, an imperial guard, with slow pace and solemn, defiled along the
steeps; or, routed by pursuing light, fled broadcast from east to west—old

wars of Lucifer and Michael; or the mountains, though unvexed by these mirrored sham fights in the sky, had an atmosphere otherwise unfavorable for fairy views. I was sorry; the more so, because I had to keep my chamber for some time after—which chamber did not face those hills.

At length, when pretty well again, and sitting out, in the September morning, upon the piazza, and thinking to myself, when, just after a little flock of sheep, the farmers' banded children passed, a-nutting, and said, "How sweet a day"—it was, after all, but what their fathers call a weather-breeder—and, indeed, was become so sensitive through my illness, as that I could not bear to look upon a Chinese creeper of my adoption, and which, to my delight, climbing a post of the piazza, had burst out in starry bloom, but now, if you removed the leaves a little, showed millions of strange, cankerous worms, which, feeding upon those blossoms, so shared their blessed hue, as to make it unblessed evermore—worms, whose germs had doubtless lurked in the very bulb which, so hopefully, I had planted: in this ingrate peevishness of my weary convalescence, was I sitting there; when, suddenly looking off, I saw the golden mountain-window, dazzling like a deep-sea dolphin. Fairies there, thought I, once more; the queen of fairies at her fairy-window; at any rate, some glad mountain-girl; it will do me good, it will cure this weariness, to look on her. No more; I'll launch my yawl—ho, cheerly, heart! and push away for fairy-land—for rainbow's end, in fairy-land.

How to get to fairy-land, by what road, I did not know; nor could any one inform me; not even one Edmund Spenser, who had been there—so he wrote me—further than that to reach fairy-land, it must be voyaged to, and with faith. I took the fairy-mountain's bearings, and the first fine day, when strength permitted, got into my yawl—high-pommeled, leather one—cast off the fast, and away I sailed, free voyager as an autumn leaf. Early dawn; and, sallying westward, I sowed the morning before me.

Some miles brought me nigh the hills; but out of present sight of them. I was not lost; for road-side golden-rods, as guide-posts, pointed, I doubted not, the way to the golden window. Following them, I came to a lone and languid region, where the grass-grown ways were traveled but by drowsy cattle, that, less waked than stirred by day, seemed to walk in sleep. Browse, they did not—the enchanted never eat. At least, so says Don Quixote, that sagest sage that ever lived.

On I went, and gained at last the fairy mountain's base, but saw yet no fairy ring. A pasture rose before me. Letting down five mouldering bars—

so moistly green, they seemed fished up from some sunken wreck—a wigged old Aries, long-visaged, and with crumpled horn, came snuffing up; and then, retreating, decorously led on along a milky-way of white-weed, past dim-clustering Pleiades and Hyades, of small forget-me-nots; and would have led me further still his astral path, but for golden flights of yellow-birds—pilots, surely, to the golden window, to one side flying before me, from bush to bush, towards deep woods—which woods themselves were luring—and, somehow, lured, too, by their fence, banning a dark road, which, however dark, led up. I pushed through; when Aries, re-nouncing me now for some lost soul, wheeled, and went his wiser way. Forbidding and forbidden ground—to him.

A winter wood road, matted all along with winter-green. By the side of pebbly waters—waters the cheerier for their solitude; beneath swaying fir-boughs, petted by no season, but still green in all, on I journeyed—my horse and I; on, by an old saw-mill, bound down and hushed with vines, that his grating voice no more was heard; on, by a deep flume clove through snowy marble, vernal-tinted, where freshet eddies had, on each side, spun out empty chapels in the living rock; on, where Jacks-in-the-pulpit, like their Baptist namesake, preached but to the wilderness, on, where a huge, cross-grain block, fern-bedded, showed where, in forgotten times, man after man had tried to split it, but lost his wedges for his pains—which wedges yet rusted in their holes; on, where, ages past, in step like ledges of a cascade, skull-hollow pots had been churned out by ceaseless whirling of a flint-stone—ever wearing, but itself unworn; on, by wild rapids pouring into a secret pool, but soothed by circling there awhile, issued forth serenely; on, to less broken ground, and by a little ring, where, truly, fairies must have danced, or else some wheel-tire been heated—for all was bare; still on, and up, and out into a hanging orchard, where maidenly looked down upon me a crescent moon, from morning.

My horse hitched low his head. Red apples rolled before him; Eve's apples; seek-no-furthers. He tasted one, I another; it tasted of the ground. Fairy land not yet, thought I, flinging my bridle to a humped old tree, that crooked out an arm to catch it. For the way now lay where path was none, and none might go but by himself, and only go by daring. Through black-berry brakes that tried to pluck me back, though I but strained towards fruitless growths of mountain-laurel; up slippery steeps to barren heights, where stood none to welcome. Fairy land not yet, thought I, though the morning is here before me.

Foot-sore enough and weary, I gained not then my journey's end, but came ere long to a craggy pass, dipping towards growing regions still beyond. A zigzag road, half overgrown with blueberry bushes, here turned among the cliffs. A rent was in their ragged sides; through it a little track branched off, which, upwards threading that short defile, came breezily out above, to where the mountain-top, part sheltered northward, by a taller brother, sloped gently off a space, ere darkly plunging; and here, among fantastic rocks, reposing in a herd, the foot-track wound, half beaten, up to a little, low-storied, grayish cottage, capped, nun-like, with a peaked roof.

On one slope, the roof was deeply weather-stained, and, nigh the turfy eaves-trough, all velvet-napped; no doubt the snail-monks founded mossy priories there. The other slope was newly shingled. On the north side, doorless and windowless, the clap-boards, innocent of paint, were yet green as the north side of lichened pines, or copperless hulls of Japanese junks, becalmed. The whole base, like those of the neighboring rocks, was rimmed about with shaded streaks of richest sod; for, with hearth-stones in fairy land, the natural rock, though housed, preserves to the last, just as in open fields, its fertilizing charm; only, by necessity, working now at a remove, to the sward without. So, at least, says Oberon, grave authority in fairy lore. Though setting Oberon aside, certain it is, that, even in the common world, the soil, close up to farm-houses, as close up to pasture rocks, is, even though untended, ever richer than it is a few rods off—such gentle, nurturing heat is radiated there.

But with this cottage, the shaded streaks were richest in its front and about its entrance, where the ground-sill, and especially the door-sill had, through long eld, quietly settled down.

No fence was seen, no inclosure. Near by—ferns, ferns, ferns; further—woods, woods, woods; beyond—mountains, mountains, mountains; then—sky, sky, sky. Turned out in æriel commons, pasture for the mountain moon. Nature, and but nature, house and all; even a low cross-pile of silver birch, piled openly, to season; up among whose silvery sticks, as through the fencing of some sequestered grave, sprang vagrant raspberry bushes—willful assertors of their right of way.

The foot-track, so dainty narrow, just like a sheep-track, led through long ferns that lodged. Fairy land at last, thought I; Una and her lamb dwell here. Truly, a small abode—mere palanquin, set down on the summit, in a pass between two worlds, participant of neither.

A sultry hour, and I wore a light hat, of yellow sinnet, with white duck trowsers—both relics of my tropic sea-going. Clogged in the muffling ferns, I softly stumbled, staining the knees a sea-green.

Pausing at the threshold, or rather where threshold once had been, I saw, through the open door-way, a lonely girl, sewing at a lonely window. A pale-cheeked girl, and fly-specked window, with wasps about the mended upper panes. I spoke. She shyly started, like some Tahiti girl, secreted for a sacrifice, first catching sight, through palms, of Captain Cook. Recovering, she bade me enter; with her apron brushed off a stool; then silently resumed her own. With thanks I took the stool; but now, for a space, I, too, was mute. This, then, is the fairy-mountain house, and here, the fairy queen sitting at her fairy window.

I went up to it. Downwards, directed by the tunneled pass, as through a leveled telescope, I caught sight of a far-off, soft, azure world. I hardly knew it, though I came from it.

"You must find this view very pleasant," said I, at last.

"Oh, sir," tears starting in her eyes, "the first time I looked out of this window, I said 'never, never shall I weary of this.'"

"And what wearies you of it now?"

"I don't know," while a tear fell, "but it is not the view, it is Marianna."

Some months back, her brother, only seventeen, had come hither, a long way from the other side, to cut wood and burn coal, and she, elder sister, had accompanied him. Long had they been orphans, and now, sole inhabitants of the sole house upon the mountain. No guest came, no traveler passed. The zigzag, perilous road was only used at seasons by the coal wagons. The brother was absent the entire day, sometimes the entire night. When at evening, fagged out, he did come home, he soon left his bench, poor fellow, for his bed; just as one, at last, wearily quits that, too, for still deeper rest. The bench, the bed, the grave.

Silent I stood by the fairy window, while these things were being told.

"Do you know," said she at last, as stealing from her story, "do you know who lives yonder? —I have never been down into that country— away off there, I mean; that house, that marble one," pointing far across the lower landscape; "have you not caught it? there, on the long hill-side: the field before, the woods behind; the white shines out against their blue; don't you mark it? the only house in sight."

I looked; and after a time, to my surprise, recognized, more by its position than its aspect, or Marianna's description, my own abode, glimmering much like this mountain one from the piazza. The mirage haze made it appear less a farm-house than King Charming's palace.

"I have often wondered who lives there; but it must be some happy one; again this morning was I thinking so."

"Some happy one," returned I, starting; "and why do you think that? You judge some rich one lives there?"

"Rich or not, I never thought; but it looks so happy, I can't tell how; and it is so far away. Sometimes I think I do but dream it is there. You should see it in a sunset."

"No doubt the sunset gilds it finely; but not more than the sunrise does this house, perhaps."

"This house? The sun is a good sun, but it never gilds this house. Why should it? This old house is rotting. That makes it so mossy. In the morning, the sun comes in at this old window, to be sure—boarded up, when first we came; a window I can't keep clean, do what I may—and half burns, and nearly blinds me at my sewing, besides setting the flies and wasps astir—such flies and wasps as only lone mountain houses know. See, here is the curtain—this apron—I try to shut it out with then. It fades it, you see. Sun gild this house? not that ever Marianna saw."

"Because when this roof is gilded most, then you stay here within."

"The hottest, weariest hour of day, you mean? Sir, the sun gilds not this roof. It leaked so, brother newly shingled all one side. Did you not see it? The north side, where the sun strikes most on what the rain has wetted. The sun is a good sun; but this roof, it first scorches, and then rots. An old house. They went West, and are long dead, they say, who built it. A mountain house. In winter no fox could den in it. That chimney-place has been blocked up with snow, just like a hollow stump."

"Yours are strange fancies, Marianna."

"They but reflect the things."

"Then I should have said, 'These are strange things,' rather than, 'Yours are strange fancies.' "

"As you will;" and took up her sewing.

Something in those quiet words, or in that quiet act, it made me mute again; while, noting, through the fairy window, a broad shadow stealing on, as cast by some gigantic condor, floating at brooding poise on outstretched wings, I marked how, by its deeper and inclusive dusk, it wiped away into itself all lesser shades of rock or fern.

"You watch the cloud," said Marianna.

"No, a shadow; a cloud's, no doubt—though that I cannot see. How did you know it? Your eyes are on your work."

"It dusked my work. There, now the cloud is gone, Tray comes back."

"How?"

"The dog, the shaggy dog. At noon, he steals off, of himself, to change his shape—returns, and lies down awhile, nigh the door. Don't you see him? His head is turned round at you; though, when you came, he looked before him."

"Your eyes rest but on your work; what do you speak of?"

"By the window, crossing."

"You mean this shaggy shadow—the nigh one? And, yes, now that I mark it, it is not unlike a large, black Newfoundland dog. The invading shadow gone, the invaded one returns. But I do not see what casts it."

"For that, you must go without."

"One of those grassy rocks, no doubt."

"You see his head, his face?"

"The shadow's? You speak as if *you* saw it, and all the time your eyes are on your work."

"Tray looks at you," still without glancing up; "this is his hour; I see him."

"Have you, then, so long sat at this mountain-window, where but clouds and vapors pass, that, to you, shadows are as things, though you speak of them as of phantoms; that, by familiar knowledge, working like a second sight, you can, without looking for them, tell just where they are, though, as having mice-like feet, they creep about, and come and go; that, to you, these lifeless shadows are as living friends, who, though out of sight, are not out of mind, even in their faces—is it so?"

"That way I never thought of it. But the friendliest one, that used to soothe my weariness so much, coolly quivering on the ferns, it was taken from me, never to return, as Tray did just now. The shadow of a birch. The tree was struck by lightning, and brother cut it up. You saw the cross-pile out-doors—the buried root lies under it; but not the shadow. That is flown, and never will come back, nor ever anywhere stir again."

Another cloud here stole along, once more blotting out the dog, and blackening all the mountain; while the stillness was so still, deafness might have forgot itself, or else believed that noiseless shadow spoke.

"Birds, Marianna, singing-birds, I hear none; I hear nothing. Boys and bob-o-links, do they never come a-berrying up here?"

"Birds, I seldom hear; boys, never. The berries mostly ripe and fall—few, but me, the wiser."

"But yellow-birds showed me the way—part way, at least."

"And then flew back. I guess they play about the mountain-side, but don't make the top their home. And no doubt you think that, living so lonesome here, knowing nothing, hearing nothing—little, at least, but sound of thunder and the fall of trees—never reading, seldom speaking, yet ever wakeful, this is what gives me my strange thoughts—for so you call them—this weariness and wakefulness together. Brother, who stands and works in open air, would I could rest like him; but mine is mostly but dull woman's work—sitting, sitting, restless sitting."

"But, do you not go walk at times? These woods are wide."

"And lonesome; lonesome, because so wide. Sometimes, 'tis true, of afternoons, I go a little way; but soon come back again. Better feel lone by hearth, than rock. The shadows hereabouts I know—those in the woods are strangers."

"But the night?"

"Just like the day. Thinking, thinking—a wheel I cannot stop; pure want of sleep it is that turns it."

"I have heard that, for this wakeful weariness, to say one's prayers, and then lay one's head upon a fresh hop pillow——"

"Look!"

Through the fairy window, she pointed down the steep to a small garden patch near by—mere pot of rifled loam, half rounded in by sheltering rocks—where, side by side, some feet apart, nipped and puny, two hop-vines climbed two poles, and, gaining their tip-ends, would have then joined over in an upward clasp, but the baffled shoots, groping awhile in empty air, trailed back whence they sprung.

"You have tried the pillow, then?"

"Yes."

"And prayer?"

"Prayer and pillow."

"Is there no other cure, or charm?"

"Oh, if I could but once get to yonder house, and but look upon whoever the happy being is that lives there! A foolish thought: why do I think it? Is it that I live so lonesome, and know nothing?"

"I, too, know nothing; and, therefore, cannot answer; but, for your sake, Marianna, well could wish that I were that happy one of the happy house you dream you see; for then you would behold him now, and, as you say, this weariness might leave you."

—Enough. Launching my yawl no more for fairy-land, I stick to the piazza. It is my box-royal; and this amphitheatre, my theatre of San Carlo. Yes, the scenery is magical—the illusion so complete. And Madam Meadow Lark, my prima donna, plays her grand engagement here; and, drinking in her sunrise note, which, Memnon-like, seems struck from the golden window, how far from me the weary face behind it.

But, every night, when the curtain falls, truth comes in with darkness. No light shows from the mountain. To and fro I walk the piazza deck, haunted by Marianna's face, and many as real a story.

1856

PART FOUR

STATUES IN ROME *AND* POEMS BY
HERMAN MELVILLE

Melville's tour of the Mediterranean and Holy Land in 1856–57 was a turning point. He left home an exhausted writer of prose and returned a poet. The transition, however, was not instantaneous. Following family advice, he lectured for three years speaking on familiar topics such as "The South Seas" and "Travel," but also something new: "Statues in Rome." No scripts for Melville's lectures survive. However, reconstructions have been assembled from accounts of the lectures reported in the local newspapers of the cities Melville visited throughout the eastern states and Canada.

The lecture on Roman statuary matched Melville's growing interest in art—he would become an avid collector of engravings and prints—and in the history, politics, and spirituality of western culture. These incipient thoughts would culminate in the ambitious modern epic *Clarel* (1876) and *Timoleon* (1891). But as Melville lectured, and brought in three crops on his farm Arrowhead, he worked steadily on his craft, and by 1860 he had enough poems to make a book.

Unfortunately, the book failed to materialize for want of a publisher. Entitled *Poems by Herman Melville*, its contents remain a matter of speculation. Later on, Melville may have placed some of these poems in *Timoleon* or *Weeds and Wildings*. He probably filed the rest with other pieces written over the years. But among this file of miscellaneous poems is a set of manuscripts whose distinctive blue ink on yellow paper may date them as earlier than the rest. A selection of these yellow-paper poems can be used to show the range of Melville's early poetic vision and skill. In a comic vein are the withering "Madam Mirror" and post-Darwinian "Man of the Cave of Engihoul." Tighter poems, such as "Fruit and Flower Painter" and "Immolated," examine art and the marketplace. The haunting "Pontoosuce," set in Wordsworthian woods, confronts death. This sampler of Melville's early verse provides a benchmark of the poet's promise, and a clear indication of the distance he would have to travel before arriving at his next book of poems.

Since these poems were not published in Melville's lifetime and exist in revised manuscript form only, each poem has been printed here in its earliest version with the later penciled revisions noted in the margin. But with the more heavily revised diptych of poems on the poet Camões, complete early and late versions of each poem are placed side by side, and are accompanied by explanatory revision narratives.

Statues in Rome

It might be supposed that the only proper judge of statues would be a sculptor, but it may be believed that others than the artist can appreciate and see the beauty of the marble art of Rome. If what is best in nature and knowledge cannot be claimed for the privileged profession of any order of men, it would be a wonder if, in that region called Art, there were, as to what is best there, any essential exclusiveness. True, the dilettante may employ his technical terms; but ignorance of these prevents not due feeling for Art, in any mind naturally alive to beauty or grandeur. Just as the productions of nature may be both appreciated by those who know nothing of Botany, or who have no inclination for it, so the creations of Art may be, by those ignorant of its critical science, or indifferent to it. Art strikes a chord in the lowest as well as in the highest; the rude and uncultivated feel its influence as well as the polite and polished. It is a spirit that pervades all classes. Nay, as it is doubtful whether to the scientific Linnaeus flowers yielded so much satisfaction as to the unscientific Burns, or struck so deep a chord in his bosom; so may it be a question whether the terms of Art may not inspire in artistic but still susceptible minds, thoughts, or emotions, not lower than those raised in the most accomplished of critics.

Yet, we find that many thus naturally susceptible to such impressions refrain from their utterance, out of fear lest in their ignorance of technicalities their unaffected terms might betray them, and that after all, feel as they may, they know little or nothing, and hence keep silence, not wishing to become presumptuous. There are many examples on record to show this, and not only this, but that the uneducated are very often more susceptible to this influence than the learned. May it not possibly be, that as Burns perhaps understood flowers as well as Linnaeus, and the Scotch peasant's poetical description of the daisy, "wee, modest, crimson-tipped flower," is rightly set above the technical definition of the Swedish professor, so in Art, just as in nature, it may not be the accredited wise man alone who, in all respects, is qualified to comprehend or describe.

With this explanation, I, who am neither critic nor connoisseur, thought fit to introduce some familiar remarks upon the sculptures in Rome, a subject which otherwise might be thought to lie peculiarly within the province of persons of a kind of cultivation to which I make no pretension. The topic is one of great extent, as Rome contains more objects of interest than perhaps any other place in the world. I shall speak of the impressions produced upon my mind as one who looks upon a work of art as he would upon a violet or a cloud, and admires or condemns as he finds an answering sentiment awakened in his soul. My object is to paint the appearance of Roman statuary objectively and afterward to speculate upon the emotions and pleasure that appearance is apt to excite in the human breast.

As you pass through the gate of St. John, on the approach to Rome from Naples, the first object of attraction is the group of colossal figures in stone surmounting, like storks, the lofty pediment of the church of St. John Lateran. Standing in every grand or animated attitude, they seem not only to attest that this is the Eternal City, but likewise, at its portal, to offer greeting in the name of that great company of statues which, amid the fluctuations of the human census, abides the true and undying population of Rome. It is, indeed, among these mute citizens that the stranger forms his most pleasing and cherished associations, to be remembered when other things in the Imperial City are forgotten.

On entering Rome itself, the visitor is greeted by thousands of statues, who, as representatives of the mighty past, hold out their hands to the present, and make the connecting link of centuries. Wherever you go in Rome, in streets, dwellings, churches, its gardens, its walks, its public squares, or its private grounds, on every hand statues abound, but by far the greatest assemblage of them is to be found in the Vatican. In that grand hall you will not only make new acquaintances, but will likewise revive many long before introduced by the historian. These are all well known by repute; they have been often described in the traveler's record and on the historic page; but the knowledge thus gained, however perfect the description may be, is poor and meager when compared with that gained by personal acquaintance. Here are ancient personages, the worthies of the glorious old days of the Empire and Republic. Histories and memoirs tell us of their achievements, whether on the field or in the forum, in public action or in the private walks of life; but here we find how they looked, and we learn them as we do living men. Here we find many deficiencies of the historian supplied by the sculptor, who has effected, in part, for the celebrities of old what the memoir writer of the present day does for modern ones; for to the sculptor belongs a task which was considered beneath the dignity of the historian.

In the expressive marble, Demosthenes, who is better known by statuary than by history, thus becomes a present existence. Standing face to face with the marble, one must say to himself, "This is he," so true has been the sculptor to his task. The strong arm, the muscular form, the large sinews, all bespeak the thunderer of Athens who hurled his powerful denunciations at Philip of Macedon; yet he resembles a modern advocate, face thin and haggard and his body lean. The arm that had gesticulated and swayed with its movement the souls of the Athenians has become small and shrunken. He looks as if a glorious course of idleness would be beneficial. Just so in the statue of Titus Vespasian, of whom we read a dim outline in Tacitus, stands mildly before us Titus himself. As the historian says, this Emperor was frank in his nature, and generous in his disposition. He has a short, thick figure and a round face, expressive of cheerfulness, good-humor, and joviality; and yet all know how different was his character from this outward seeming.

In the bust of Socrates is a kind of anomaly, for we see a countenance more like that of a bacchanal or the debauchee of a carnival than of a sober and decorous philosopher. At a first glance it reminds one much of the broad and rubicund phiz of an Irish comedian. It possesses in many respects the characteristics peculiar to the modern Hibernian. But a closer observer would see the simple-hearted, yet cool, sarcastic, ironical cast indicative of his true character.

The head of Julius Caesar fancy would paint as robust, grand, and noble; something that is elevated and commanding, typical of the warrior and statesman. But the statue gives a countenance of a businesslike cast that the present practical age would regard as a good representation of the President of the New York and Erie Railroad, or any other magnificent corporation. And such was the character of the man—practical, sound, grappling with the obstacles of the world like a giant.

In the bust of Seneca, whose philosophy would be Christianity itself save its authenticity, whose utterances so amazed one of the early fathers that he thought he must have corresponded with St. Paul, we see a face more like that of a disappointed pawnbroker, pinched and grieved. His semblance is just, according to the character of the *man,* though not of his *books.* For it was well known that he was avaricious and grasping, and dealt largely in mortgages and loans, and drove hard bargains even at that day. It is ironlike and inflexible, and would be no disgrace to a Wall Street broker.

Seeing the statue of Seneca's apostate pupil Nero at Naples, done in bronze, we can scarce realize that we are looking upon the face of the latter without finding something repulsive, half-demoniac in the expression. And yet the delicate features are only those of a genteelly dissipated youth, a fast and pleasant young man such as those we see in our own day, whom daily experience finds driving spanking teams and abounding on race-courses, with instincts and habits of his class, who would scarce be guilty of excessive cruelties.

The first view of Plato surprises one, being that of a Greek Grammont or Chesterfield. Engaged in the deep researches of philosophy as he was, we certainly should expect no fastidiousness in his appearance, neither a carefully adjusted toga or pomatumed hair. Yet such is the fact, for the long flowing locks of that aristocratic transcendentalist were as carefully parted as a modern belle's and his beard would have graced a Venetian exquisite. If this bust were true, he might have composed his works as if meditating on the destinies of the world under the hand of a hair-dresser or a modern *valet-de-chambre,* as Louis XIV mused over documents while he smelled his Cologne bottle.

Thus these statues confess and, as it were, prattle to us of much that does not appear in history and the written works of those they represent. This subject has been illustrated by instances taken from modern times with which we are all acquainted because in this way we best obtain a true knowledge of the appearance of the statues. They seem familiar and natural to us because the aspect of the human countenance is the same in all ages. If five thousand ancient Romans were mingled with a crowd of moderns in the Corso it would be difficult to distinguish the one from the other unless it were by a difference in dress. The same features—the same aspects—belong to us as belonged to them; the component parts of human character are the same now as then. And yet there was about all the Romans a heroic tone peculiar to ancient life. Their virtues were great and noble, and these virtues made them great and noble. They possessed a natural majesty that was not put on and taken off at pleasure, as was that of certain eastern monarchs when they put on or took off their garments of Tyrian dye. It is to be hoped that this is not wholly lost from the world, although the sense of earthly vanity inculcated by Christianity may have swallowed it up in humility.

Christianity has disenchanted many of the vague old rumors in reference to the ancients, so that we can now easily compare them with the moderns. The appearance of the statues, however, is often deceptive, and a true knowledge of their character is lost unless they are closely scrutinized. The arch dissembler Tiberius was handsome, refined, and even pensive in expression. "That Tiberius?" exclaimed a lady in our hearing. "He does not look so bad." Madam, thought I, if he had *looked* bad, he could not have been Tiberius. His statue has such a sad and musing air, so like Jerome in his cell, musing on the vanities of the world, that to some, not knowing for whom the statue was meant, it might convey the impression of a man broken by great afflictions, of so pathetic a cast is it. Yet a close analysis brings out all his sinister features, and a close study of the statue will develop the monster portrayed by the historian. For Tiberius was melancholy without pity, and sensitive without affection. He was, perhaps, the most wicked of men.

The statue which most of all in the Vatican excites the admiration of all visitors is the Apollo, the crowning glory, which stands alone in a little chapel, in the Belvidere court of the Vatican. Every visitor to Rome, immediately on his arrival, rushes to the chapel to behold the statue, and on his quitting the Eternal City, whether after a few weeks or many years, always makes a farewell visit to this same loadstone. Its very presence is overawing. Few speak, or even whisper, when they enter the cabinet where it stands. It is not a mere work of art that one gazes on, for there is a kind of divinity in it that lifts the imagination of the beholder above "things rank and gross in nature," and makes ordinary criticism impossible. If one were to try to convey some adequate notion, other than artistic, of a statue which so signally lifts the imaginations of men, he might hint that it gives a kind of visible response to that class of human aspirations of beauty and perfection that, according to Faith, cannot be truly gratified except in another world.

The statue seems to embody the attributes, physical and intellectual, which Milton bestowed on one of his angels, "Severe in youthful beauty." Milton's description of Zephon makes the angel an exact counterpart of the Apollo. He must have been inspired to a great degree by his recollections of this statue, once the idol of religion and now the idol of art; and the circumstance of his having passed a year in Italy might not be deemed unfortunate for England's great epic. In fact, the whole of that immortal poem, "Paradise Lost," is but a great Vatican done into verse. Milton must have gleaned from these representations of the great men or the gods of ancient Rome high ideas of the grand in form and bearing. Many of those ideas from heathen personages he afterwards appropriated to his celestials, just as the Pope's artist converted the old heathen Pantheon into a Christian church. Lucifer and his angels cast down from Heaven are thus taken from a group in a private palace at Padua, among the most wonderful works of statuary. This was sculptured out of a single solid block, five feet in height, by one of the later Italian artists. Three-score of the fallen lie wound together writhing and tortured, while, proud and sullen in the midst, is the nobler form of Satan, unbroken and defiant, his whole body breathing revenge and his attitude one never to submit or yield. The variety and power of the group cannot be surpassed.

Speaking of the Apollo reminds one of the Venus de Medici, although the one is at Rome and the other is at Florence. She is lovely, beautiful, but far less great than the Apollo, for her chief beauty is that of attitude. In the Venus the ideal and actual are blended, yet only representing nature in her perfection, a fair woman startled by some intrusion when leaving the bath. She is exceedingly refined, delicious in everything—no prude but a child of nature modest and unpretending. I have some authority for this statement, as one day from my mat in the Typee valley I saw a native maiden, in the precise attitude of the Venus, retreating with the grace of nature to a friendly covert. But still the Venus is of the earth, and the Apollo is divine. Should a match be made between them, the union would be like that of the sons of God with the daughters of men.

In a niche of the Vatican stands the Laocoön, the very semblance of a great and powerful man writhing with the inevitable destiny which he cannot throw off. Throes and pangs and struggles are given with a meaning that is not withheld. The hideous monsters embrace him in their mighty folds, and torture him with agonizing embraces. The Laocoön is grand and impressive, gaining half its significance from its symbolism— the fable that it represents; otherwise it would be no more than Paul Potter's "Bear Hunt" at Amsterdam. Thus the ideal statuary of Rome expresses the doubt and the dark groping of speculation in that age when the old mythology was passing away and men's minds had not yet reposed in the new faith. If the Apollo gives the perfect, and the Venus equally shows the beautiful, the Laocoön represents the tragic side of humanity and is the symbol of human misfortune.

Elsewhere in the Vatican is the Hall of Animals. In all the ancient statues representing animals there is a marked resemblance to those described in the book of Revelations. This class of Roman statuary and the pictures of the Apocalypse are nearly identical. But the ferocity in the appearance of some of these statues, such as the wolf and the slaughtered lamb, is compensated by the nature of others, like that of the goats at play around the sleeping shepherd. The quiet, gentle, and peaceful scenes of pastoral life are represented in some of the later of Roman statuary just as we find them described by that best of all pastoral poets, Wordsworth. The thought of many of these beautiful figures having been pleasing to the Romans at least persuades us that their violence as a conquering people did not engross them, and that the flame of kindness kindled in most men by nature was at no time in Roman breasts entirely stamped out. If we image the life that is in the statues and look at their more human aspects, we shall not find that the old Roman, stern and hard-hearted as we generally imagine him, was entirely destitute of tenderness and compassion, for though the ancients were ignorant of the principles of Christianity there were in them the germs of its spirit.

Thus, when I stood in the Coliseum, its mountain-chains of ruins waving with foliage girdling me round, the solitude was great and vast like that of savage nature, just such as one experiences when shut up in some great green hollow of the Appenine range, hemmed in by towering cliffs on every side. But the imagination must rebuild it as it was of old; it must be repeopled with the terrific games of the gladiators, with the frantic leaps and dismal howls of the wild, bounding beasts, with the shrieks and cries of the excited spectators. Unless this is done, how can we appreciate the Gladiator? It was such a feeling of the artist that created it, and there must be such a feeling on the part of the visitor to view it and view it aright. And so, restoring the shattered arches and terraces, I repeopled them with all the statues from the Vatican, and in the turfy glen of the arena below I placed the Fighting Gladiator from the Louvre, confronting him with the dying one from the Capitol. And as in fancy I heard the ruffian huzzas for the first rebounded from the pitiless hiss for the last, I felt that more than one in that host I had evoked shared not its passions, and looked not coldly on the dying gladiator whose eyes gazed far away to

> "where his rude hut by the Danube lay,
> *There* were his young barbarians all at play."

Some hearts were there that felt the horror as keenly as any of us would have felt it. None but a gentle heart could have conceived the idea of the Dying Gladiator, and he was Christian in all but the name.

It is with varied feelings that one travels through the sepulchral vaults of the Vatican. The sculptured monuments of the early Christians show the change that had come over the Roman people with the joyous triumph of the new religion—quite unlike the somber mementoes of modern times. The statues are of various character: Hope faces Despair; Joy comes to the relief of Sorrow. The marbles alternate. On one side Rachel weeps for her children and will not be comforted while Job curses his maker; and then Rachel is seen drying her tears as Job rises above his afflictions and rejoices. But just as a guide hurries us through these scenes with his torch-light, bringing out one statue in bold relief while a hundred or more are hidden in the gloom, so must I do to keep within the limits of an hour.

In passing from the inside of the Vatican to the square in front, we find ourselves surrounded by the mighty colonnades with their statues, which overshadow the area like the wings of an army of Titans, and the great pile of confused architecture which is the outside of the Vatican. If one stands a hundred feet in front of St. Peter's and looks up, a vast and towering pile meets his view. High, high above are the beetling crags and precipices of masonry, and yet higher still above all this, up against the heaven, like a balloon, is the dome. The mind is carried away with the very vastness. But throughout the Vatican it is different. The mind, instead of being bewildered within itself, is drawn out by the symmetry and beauty of the forms it beholds.

But nearly the whole of Rome is itself a Vatican on a large scale—everywhere are fallen columns and sculptured fragments. These are of different and varied character. Remarkable, however, among all are the sculptured horses of Monte Cavallo, riderless and rearing, seeming like those of Elijah to soar to heaven. The most of these, it is true, were works of Greek artists, and yet the grand spirit of Roman life inspired them, for the marble horses seem to represent the fiery audaciousness of Roman power. The equestrian group of Castor and Pollux reining in their horses illustrates the expression of untamed docility, rather than conquered obedience, which ancient artists have given to the horse. From this can be deduced the enlarged humanity of that elder day, when man gave himself none of those upstart airs of superiority over the brute creation which he now assumes. A modern inscription attributes these famous animals to the chisels of Phidias and Praxiteles. There is no doubt that they are works of Grecian art, brought to Rome when the land in which they were sculptured had been conquered. The horse was idealized by the ancient artists as majestic next to man, and they loved to sculpture them as they did heroes and gods. To the Greeks nature had no brute. Everything was a being with a soul, and the horse idealized the second order of animals just as man did the first. This ideal and magnificent conception of the horse, which had raised that animal into a sort of divinity, is unrivaled in its sublime loftiness of attitude and force of execution. In truth, nothing even in the statues of gods could be more noble than the appearance of these horses. We see other instances of this same profound appreciation of the form of the horse in the sculpture on the frieze of the Parthenon, now in the British Museum.

Of other statues of large size much might be said. The Moses by Michelangelo appears like a stern, bullying genius of druidical superstition; that of Perseus at Florence would form a theme by itself. This statue, by Benvenuto Cellini, is another astonishing conception, conceived in the fiery brain of the intense artist and brought to perfection as a bronze cast in the midst of flames which had indeed overshot their aim. Another noble statue, conceived in a very different spirit, is the Farnese Hercules, leaning on his club, which in its simplicity and bovine good nature reminds us of cheerful and humane things and makes our hearts incline towards him. This statue is not of that quick, smart, energetic strength that we should suppose would appertain to the powerful Samson or the mighty Hercules; but rather of a character like that of the lazy ox, confident of his own strength but loth to use it. No trifles would call it forth; it is reserved only for great occasions. To rightfully appreciate this, or, in fact, any other statue, one must consider where they came from and under what circumstances they were formed. In other respects they reveal their own history.

Thus to understand the statues of the Vatican it is necessary to visit often the scenes where they once stood—the Coliseum, which throws its shade like a mighty thunder cloud, the gardens, the Forum, the aqueducts, the ruined temples—and remember all that has there taken place. I regret that the time will not allow me to speak more fully of these surroundings. But Roman statuary is by no means confined to the Vatican, or even to Rome itself. The villas around the city are filled with it, and, in those quiet retreats, we catch some of the last and best glimpses of the art. Here, where nature has been raised by culture and refinement into an almost human character, are found many of those trophies which have challenged the admiration of the world; here, where once exhaled sweets like the airs of Verona, now comes the deadly malaria, repelling from these ancient myrtles and orange groves. This reminds us that in a garden originated the dread sentence, Death—that it was amidst such perfumed grottoes, bowers, and walks that the guests of a Lucretia Borgia were welcomed to a feast, but received with a pall.

Many of these villas were built long years ago by men of the heathen school, for the express purpose of preserving these ancient works of art. The villas which were to shield and protect them have now crumbled, while most of the statues which were to be thus preserved still live on. Notable is the Villa Albani, built as it was by one who had made art and antiquity the study of his life, as a place to preserve the splendid works he had collected. Here are the remains of antiquity from Pompeii, and we might bring back the guests to the rooms where they sat at the feast on the eve of the fatal eruption of Vesuvius. It was not unusual for them at their feasts to talk upon the subject of death and other like mournful themes forbidden to modern ears at such scenes. Such topics were not considered irrelevant to the occasion, and instead of destroying the interest of the feast by their ill-timed intrusion, they rather added to it a temperate zest. One of the finest of the statues to be found in this villa is the Minerva, a creature as purely and serenely sublime as it is possible

for human hands to form. Here also is to be found a medallion of Antinous with his eye reposing on a lotus of admirable design which he
holds in his hand. In this villa is a bust of Æsop, the dwarfed and deformed, whose countenance is irradiated by a lambent gleam of irony
such as plays round the pages of Goldsmith.

In conclusion, since we cannot mention all the different works, let us
bring them together and speak of them as a whole. It will be noticed that
statues, as a general thing, do not present the startling features and atti-
tudes of men, but are rather of a tranquil, subdued air such as men have
when under the influence of no passion. Not the least, perhaps, among
those causes which make the Roman museums so impressive is this same
air of tranquility. In chambers befitting stand the images of gods, while in
the statues of men, even the vilest, what was corruptible in their originals
here in pure marble puts on incorruption. They appeal to that portion of
our being which is highest and noblest. To some they are a complete
house of philosophy; to others they appeal only to the tenderer feelings
and affections. All who behold the Apollo confess its glory; yet we know
not to whom to attribute the glory of creating it. The chiseling them
shows the genius of the creator—the preserving them shows the bounty
of the good and the policy of the wise.

These marbles, the works of the dreamers and idealists of old, live on,
leading and pointing to good. They are the works of visionaries and
dreamers, but they are realizations of soul, the representations of the
ideal. They are grand, beautiful, and true, and they speak with a voice
that echoes through the ages. Governments have changed; empires have
fallen; nations have passed away; but these mute marbles remain—the
oracles of time, the perfection of art. They were formed by those who had
yearnings for something better, and strove to attain it by embodiments in
cold stone. We can ourselves judge with what success they have worked.
How well in the Apollo is expressed the idea of the perfect man. Who
could better it? Can art, not life, make the ideal?

Here, in statuary, was the Utopia of the ancients expressed. The Vatican itself is the index of the ancient world, just as the Washington Patent
Office is of the modern. But how is it possible to compare the one with
the other, when things that are so totally unlike cannot be brought together? What comparison could be instituted between a locomotive and
the Apollo? Is it as grand an object as the Laocoön? To undervalue art is

perhaps somewhat the custom now. The world has taken a practical turn, and we boast much of our progress, of our energy, of our scientific achievements—though science is beneath art, just as the instinct is beneath the reason. Do all our modern triumphs equal those of the heroes and divinities that stand there silent, the incarnation of grandeur and of beauty?

We moderns pride ourselves upon our superiority, but the claim can be questioned. We did invent the printing press, but from the ancients have we not all the best thought which it circulates, whether it be law, physics, or philosophy? As the Roman arch enters into and sustains our best architecture, does not the Roman spirit still animate and support whatever is soundest in societies and states? Or shall the scheme of Fourier supplant the code of Justinian? Only when the novels of Dickens shall silence the satires of Juvenal. The ancients of the ideal description, instead of trying to turn their impracticable chimeras, as does the modern dreamer, into social and political prodigies, deposited them in great works of art, which still live while states and constitutions have perished, bequeathing to posterity not shameful defects but triumphant successes. All the merchants in modern London have not enough in their coffers to reproduce the Apollo. If the Coliseum expresses the durability of Roman ideas, what does their Crystal Palace express? These buildings are exponents of the respective characters of ancients and moderns. But will the glass of the one bide the hail storms of eighteen centuries as well as the travertine of the other?

The deeds of the ancients were noble, and so are their arts; and as the one is kept alive in the memory of man by the glowing words of their own historians and poets, so should the memory of the other be kept green in the minds of men by the careful preservation of their noble statuary. The ancients live while these statues endure, and seem to breathe inspiration through the world, giving purpose, shape, and impetus to what was created high, or grand, or beautiful. Like the pillars of Rome itself, they are enduring illustrations of the perfection of ancient art.

> "While stands the Coliseum, Rome shall stand;
> When falls the Coliseum, Rome shall fall;
> And when Rome falls, the world."

1857

Poems by Herman Melville

Madam Mirror

With wrecks in a garret I'm stranded,
Where, no longer returning a face,
I take to reflections the deeper
On memories far to retrace.

In me have all people confided,
The maiden her charms has displayed,
And truths unrevealed and unuttered
To me have been freely betrayed.

Some truths* I might tell of the toilet   *tales
Did not tenderness make me forget;
But the glance of proud beauty slow fading
It dies not away from me yet;
Nor the eyes too long forgetting* to shine,—   *ceasing
Soliciting, shunning, well knowing that mine
Were too candid to flatter when met.

O* pledged unto trueness forever,   *But
My confessional close as the friar's,
How sacred to me are the trustful,*   *trusting

Here nothing for scandal transpires.
But ah, what of all that is perished,
Nor less shall again be, again!
What pangs after parties of pleasure,
What smiles but disclosures of pain!
O, the tears of the hopeless unloved,
O, the start at old age drawing near,

*more tragical far
   O, what shadows of thoughts unexpressed*
Like clouds on a lake have been here!
Tho' lone in a loft I must languish

*closet
   Far from chamber* and parlor at strife,

*anguish
   Content I escape from the discord*
Of the Real and the Seeming in life.

Fruit and Flower Painter

*She dens
   I den* in a garret
      As void as a drum;
In lieu of plum-pudding—

*She paints
      I paint* the plum!

*my
      No use in one's* grieving,

*I
        The shops you* must suit:
Broken hearts are but potsherds—
      Paint flowers and fruit!

*her
   How whistles my* garret,
      A seine for the snows:

*She hums *Si*
   I hum O* fortuna,

*paints
      And—paint* the rose!

      December is howling,
        But feign it a flute:
      Help on the deceiving—
        Paint flowers and fruit!

THE NEW ANCIENT OF DAYS,
or THE MAN OF THE CAVE OF ENGIHOUL
(See Lyell's *Antiquity of Man* and
Darwin's *Descent of Species*)

The man of bone confirms his throne
  In cave where fossils be;
Outdating every mummy known,
Not older Cuvier's mastadon,
   Nor older much the sea:
  Old as the Glacial Period, he;
And claims he calls to mind the day
When Thule's king, by reindeer drawn,
His sleigh-bells jingling in icy morn,
Slid clean from the Pole to the Wetterhorn
Over frozen waters in May!
   Oh, the man of the cave of Engihoul,
   With Eld doth he dote and drule?

A wizzard one, his lore is none
  Ye spell with A. B. C.;
But *do-do* tracks, all up and down
That slate he poreth much upon,
   His algebra may be:—
Yea, there he cyphers and sums it free;
To ages ere Indus met ocean's swell
Addeth aeons ere Satan or Saturn fell.
His totals of time make an awful schism,
Old Chronos he pitches adown the abysm,
Like a pebble down Carrisbrook well.
   Yea, the man of the cave of Engihoul
   From Moses knocks under the stool.

Touched up in stone, he keeps on loan*
  A monstrous* show, agree—
Megalosaurus, iguanadon,
Palaeotherium—Glypthaecon,
  And wooly old horses three;*

*In *bas relief* he late
has shown
*horrible

*A Barnum-show raree;

The vomit of slimy and sludgey sea:
Purposeless creatures, odd inchoate things
Which splashed thro' morasses on fleshly wings;
The cubs of Chaos, with eyes askance,
Preposterous griffins that squint at Chance
cracked   And Anarch's crazed decree!
         Oh the showman who dens in Engihoul,
         Would he fright us, or quiz us, or fool?

But, needs to own, he takes a tone,
nobs   Satiric on Adam, pardee!
        "Though in ages whose terms is yet to run,
Old Adam a seraph   A seraph your gran'son may have for son,
crab   Your gran'ther's a sponge, d'y'see!
kinsman   And why cut your uncle the ape?" adds he:
"Your trick of scratching is borrowed from him,
Grimace and cunning, with many a whim,
Your fidgets and hypoes, and each megrim—
All's traced in the family tree!"
         Ha, the wag of the cave of Engihoul:
         Buss me, gorilla and ghoul!

Obstreperous grown he'd fain dethrone
         Joe Smith, and e'en Jones Three;
Against even Jos and great Mahone
He flings his fossiliffer's stone
         And rattles his shanks for glee.
I'll settle these parvenu fellows, he-he!
Diluvian Jove of Ducalion's day—
A parting take to the Phocene clay!
He swears no Ens that takes a name
Commensurate is with the vasty claim
Of the protoplastic Fegee.
         O, the spook of the cave of Engihoul
         He flogs us and sends us to school.

Hyena of bone! Ah, beat him down,
    Great Pope, with Peter's key,
Ere the Grand Pan-Jam be overthrown
With Joe and Jos and great Mahone,
    And the firmament mix with the sea;
And then, my masters, where should we be?
But the ogre of bone he snickers alone,
He grins for his godless fee*:
"I have flung my stone, my fossil stone,   *glee
And your giant is dished,"* saith he.
    Imp! imp of the cave of Engihoul,   *gods, how they scamper
    Shall he grin like the Gorgon and rule?

To ——.

Ah, wherefore, lonely, to and fro
Flittest like the shades that go
Pale wandering by the weedy stream?
We, like these, are but a dream:
Then dreams, and less, our passions* be;   *miseries
Yea, fear and sorrow, and* despair   *pain,
Be* but phantoms. But what plea   *Are
Avails here? phantoms having power
To make the heart quake and the spirit cower.

VERSIONS OF "CAMOËNS"

Although some consider "Camoëns (Before)" and "Camoëns in the Hospital (After)" to be late poems, manuscript evidence suggests that they may have been composed early enough for Melville's projected 1860 volume of poems, and that the poet revised them considerably some years later. They were never published in Melville's life, and have appeared, since 1924, in different versions varying with each editor's reading of the manuscript revisions.

From the beginning, Melville's plan seems to have been to offer a pair of poems, similar in strategy to the short story diptychs (e.g. "The Paradise of Bachelors and the Tartarus of Maids") which present different perspectives on a single subject. In the earliest recorded conceptions of this poetic diptych (with its "Before" and "After" snapshots of the writing process), no author was specified. Later, Melville penciled first "Camoëns" and then "Tasso" as tentative titles. Melville admired both poets, who died neglected and institutionalized, although the Portuguese epic poet Luis de Camões (1524–80) was finally the richer, lifelong source for Melville.

Like the poem "Art" in *Timoleon*, these truncated sonnets devoted to the writing process are also dramatic monologues, first of the fiery necessities of creativity, and then of the failure of art in the marketplace. In revising both poems, Melville switched from first person (I) to third person (thy), thus muting Melville's own identification with Camões. His revisions to both "Camoëns" poems are so extensive, and in some cases inconclusive, that the poems are best understood by placing Melville's first and final versions of each poem side-by-side. The Revision Narratives for each set of poems explain specific changes.

———

CAMOËNS (BEFORE)
Version 1

[UNTITLED]

And ever must I fan this fire?
Thus ever in flame on flame aspire?
Ah, restless, restless, craving rest—
The Imperfect toward Perfection pressed.
5   Amen! The God demands thy best.
The earth with endless beauty teems
And Fancy yields new worlds of dreams:
Then hunt the flying herds of themes!
And fan, yet fan thy fervid fire,
10   Until some faultless thing may show
That fire can purge, as well as glow.
In ordered ardor, nobly strong
Flame to the height of epic song.

REVISION NARRATIVE

Melville tinkered with, then revised each of the opening couplets, finally canceling each couplet in succession. The following revisions may have occurred in any order. Melville revised "Amen! The God" to "Yea, for God" (line 5); "earth" to "world" (line 6), and "Fancy yields" to "thought provokes" (line 7). Line 10 is more heavily revised. Here, Melville considered variations on "faultless art" and "drossless art" before settling on "thy → the crucibled gold." In the last line, Melville considered "knight's song" or perhaps "knight's command" to be followed by a new final line: "and sing the undying song," all before canceling that line and settling on simply revising "epic song" to "ancient song."

CAMOËNS (BEFORE)
Version 2

1

Yea, for the God demands thy best.
The world with endless beauty teems,
And thought evokes new worlds of dreams:
Hunt then the flying herds of themes!
And fan, yet fan thy fervid fire,
Until the crucibled gold shall show
That fire can purge, as well as glow:
In ordered ardor, nobly strong,
Flame to the height of ancient song.

CAMOËNS (AFTER)
Version 1

[UNTITLED]

Ah, what avails the pageant verse,
Trophies and arms with music borne?
'Tis a base world; and some rehearse
How noblest meet ignoble scorn.
5   Vain now thy ardor, vain thy fire,
Delirium proved, though gods inspire:
A knife hath ripped thy chorded lyre.
Exhausted by the devouring lay,
Thou dost but fall a surer prey
10   To wiles and snares ill understood;
While they who work them, fair in face,
Still keep their strength in prudent place,
And claim they worthier run life's race,
Serving high God with useful good.

REVISION NARRATIVE

Melville first entitled the untitled poem "On a bust of Camoëns," then revised it to "Camoëns / 2. Suggested by a bust of that poet / (After)." Down the right side of the manuscript, Melville added "Camoëns in the hospital." As with "Camoëns (Before)," the name "Tasso" is also inscribed as an alternative title. Putting aside the minor tinkering in lines 1 and 3, one major pattern of revision is the vacillation between first and second person voice. In line 5 Melville changes "Vain now thy ardor" to "Vain all my ardor," but restores the original before settling on "the ardor." Similar corresponding revisions of "thy," "my" and "the" result in "the fire." And in line 9, Melville cancels both "Thou dost" and "I do" without restoring

CAMOËNS (AFTER)
Version 2

CAMOËNS (AFTER)

2. SUGGESTED BY A BUST OF THAT POET

What now avails the pageant verse,
Trophies and arms with music borne?
Base is the world; and some rehearse
How noblest meet ignoble scorn.
Vain now the ardor, vain the fire,   5
Delirium mere, unsound desire:
Fate's knife hath ripped the chorded lyre.
Exhausted by the exacting lay,
Thou dost but fall a surer prey
To wile and guile ill understood;   10
While they who work them, fair in face,
Still keep their strength in prudent place,
And claim they worthier run life's race,
Serving high God with useful good.

either. A second pattern of revision occurring in line 6, deals with madness, perhaps a reference to Tasso's unjust incarceration. Here, Melville alters "Delirium proved" to "Delirium mere." He also considered several alternatives to "though gods inspired": they are (in the following order) "and mad desire" then "insane desire" then back to "and mad desire," then finally "unsound desire." The shifts from "A knife" to "Fate's knife" (line 7) and from "wiles and snares" to "wile and guile" (line 10), as well as the vacillation from "with useful good" to "in practical mood" and back (line 14) seem pedestrian; whereas the shift from "devouring lay" to "exacting lay" tightens the line's sound quality

IMMOLATED

*happier

*mother

*flowers and,

*future

*Unanimous

Children of my Tempe* prime,
When One yet lived with me, and threw
Her rainbow over life and time,
Even Hope, my bride, and dame* to you!
O, nurtured in sweet pastoral air,
And fed on daisies,* light, and dew
Of morning meadows—spare, Ah, spare
Reproach; spare, and upbraid me not
That, yielding scarce to reckless mood
But jealous of your probable* lot,
I sealed you in a fate subdued.
Have I not saved you from the drear
Theft and ignoring which need be
The triumph of the insincere
Elect of* Mediocrity?
Rest therefore, free from all despite,
Snugged in the arms of comfortable night.

PONTOOSUCE

Crowning a bank* where gleams the lake below,   *bluff
Some pillared pines in well-spaced order stand
And like an open temple show.
And here in best of periods* bland,   *seasons
Autumnal noon-tide, I look forth*   *out
From dusk arcades upon a sun-lit North.*   *on sunshine all about.

Beyond the wave,* in upland cheer   *Lake
Fields, pastoral herds* and barns appear,   *fields
They skirt the hills where lonely roads
Revealed in links thro' tiers of woods
Wind up to indistinct abodes
And faery-peopled neighborhoods;   *further fainter
While far the faint blue mountains sleep*   mountains keep
In hazed repose of trances deep.*   *Hazed in romance
    impenetrably deep.

Look, corn in stacks, which keep the calm,*   *on many a farm
And orchards ripe in languorous charm,
As dreamy Nature, feeling sure
Of all her genial labor done,
And the last mellow fruitage won,
Would idle out her term mature;
Reposing like a thing reclined
In kinship with the* meditative mind.   *man's

For me, within the still* arcade—   *brown
Rich life, methought; sweet here in shade
And pleasant abroad in air!—But, nay,
A counter thought intrusive strayed,*   *played
A thought as old as thought itself,
Yet* who shall lay it on the shelf!—   *And

I felt the beauty bless the day
I knew the* opulence of autumn's dower;   *In
But evanescence will not stay!
A year ago was such bland* hour,   *an

As this, which but foreruns the blast

leaves   Shall sweep these live leaves to the dead ones past.

All dies!—

I stood in revery long.

ancient   Then, to forget death's cruel wrong,
I turned me in the deep arcade,
And there by chance in lateral glade
I saw low tawny mounds in lines
Relics of trunks of stately pines
Ranked erst in colonnades where, lo!
Erect succeeding pillars show!

Relapse! my former thoughts anew
Returned; and deeper stirring, green

*canceled lines   *And green.**—All dies! and not alone
The aspiring trees and men and grass;

The poet's   But glorious forms of beauty pass,
deeds they are   And noblest doings are at last undone
Even truth itself decays, and lo,

two added lines   From truth's sad ashes fraud and falsehood grow.

All dies!
The workman dies, and after him, the work;
Like to these pines whose graves I trace,
Statue and statuary fall upon their face:
In very amaranths the worm doth lurk,
Even stars, Chaldaeans say, have left their place.
Andes and Apalachee tell
Of havoc ere our Adam fell,
And present Nature as a moss doth show
On the ruins of the Nature of the aeons of long ago.

But look—and hark!

Adown the glade,
Where light and shadow sport at will,
Who cometh vocal, and arrayed
As in the first pale tints of morn—

So pure, rose-clear, and fresh and chill!
Some ground-pine sprigs her brow adorn,
The earthy rootlets tangled clinging.
Over tufts of moss which dead things made,
Under vital twigs which danced or swayed,
Along she floats, and lightly singing:

"Dies, all dies!
The grass it dies, but in vernal rain
Up it springs and it lives again;
Over and over, again and again
It lives, it dies and it lives again.
Who sighs that all dies?
Summer and winter, and pleasure and pain
And everything everywhere in God's reign,
They end, and anon they begin again:
Wane and wax, wax and wane:
Over and over and over amain
End, ever end, and begin again—
End, ever end, and forever and ever begin again!"

She ceased, and nearer slid, and hung
In dewy guise; then softlier sung:
"Since light and shade are equal set
And all revolves, nor more ye know,
Ah, why should tears the pale cheek fret
For aught that waneth here below.
Let go, let go!"

With that, her warm lips thrilled me through,
She kissed me, while her chaplet cold
Its rootlets brushed against my brow,
With all their humid clinging mould.
She vanished, leaving fragrant breath
And warmth and chill of mingled* life and death.   *wedded

PART FIVE
FROM BATTLE-PIECES

In 1860, Melville was in San Francisco planning to circumnavigate the globe on his brother Tom's ship, *The Meteor,* when he got news of the failure of his projected book of poems to attract a publisher. He cut short the tour and steamed home to a nation readying for civil war. For years Melville had lobbied government officials for a post abroad to support his writing career, but Lincoln's administration was no more interested than the others. Fortunately, his wife's recent inheritance enabled them to enjoy some degree of financial freedom. With the war on, Melville turned away from the witty and self-involved poems of former days, sold his "doggeral" verse for scrap, and began to read such moderns as Heine, Tennyson, and Arnold. Leaving his farm Arrowhead in Massachusetts for New York City, he followed the war in the dailies, and even visited the front, riding along as an observer for a few days with a scouting detail on the lookout for guerillas in Virginia's wilderness.

The Civil War gave Melville a new vision. As a national poet, he would sing both sides of the unfolding tragedy, and he would do so in many voices, but as the war progressed he attempted only a few poems, the full measure of his inspiration coming only with the fall of Richmond in April 1865. In the following year, he composed over seventy poems for *Battle-Pieces* (1866), from prophetic little lyrics like "The Portent" (about John Brown) to powerful polyphonic narratives like "Armies of the Wilderness," as well as an essay, "Supplement," arguing for tolerance and reconciliation.

Melville favored democracy ("the world's fairest hope") over slavery ("man's foulest crime"), and yet the union over abolition, but as a poet he sought "pathos" over "the glory of war." These are not poems of righteousness and patriotism but of the enthusiasms of fighting youths from both the North and the South, and bullets that "undeceive." These poems—haunting, gritty, remarkably tight—depict the mechanics of war ("pivot, and screw"), faces pressed in sod, and "the Atheist roar of riot." If nature's elms of Malvern Hill grow green again despite the volcanic rage of war, then America, too, "with empire in her eyes," must convert the pain of war to forgiveness and human understanding.

THE PORTENT
(1859)

Hanging from the beam,
  Slowly swaying (such the law),
Gaunt the shadow on your green,
  Shenandoah!
The cut is on the crown   5
(Lo, John Brown),
And the stabs shall heal no more.

Hidden in the cap
  Is the anguish none can draw;
So your future veils its face,   10
  Shenandoah!
But the streaming beard is shown
(Weird John Brown),
The meteor of the war.

MISGIVINGS
(1860)

When ocean-clouds over inland hills
  Sweep storming in late autumn brown,
And horror the sodden valley fills,
  And the spire falls crashing in the town,
I muse upon my country's ills—   5
The tempest bursting from the waste of Time
On the world's fairest hope linked with man's foulest crime.

Nature's dark side is heeded now—
  (Ah! optimist-cheer disheartened flown)—
A child may read the moody brow   10
  Of yon black mountain lone.
With shouts the torrents down the gorges go,
And storms are formed behind the storm we feel:
The hemlock shakes in the rafter, the oak in the driving keel.

THE CONFLICT OF CONVICTIONS
(1860–1)

On starry heights
   A bugle wails the long recall;
Derision stirs the deep abyss,
   Heaven's ominous silence over all.
Return, return, O eager Hope,   5
   And face man's latter fall.
Events, they make the dreamers quail;
Satan's old age is strong and hale,
A disciplined captain, gray in skill,
And Raphael a white enthusiast still;   10
Dashed aims, whereat Christ's martyrs pale,
Shall Mammon's slaves fulfill?

     (Dismantle the fort,
     Cut down the fleet—
     Battle no more shall be!   15
     While the fields for fight in æons to come
     Congeal beneath the sea.)

The terrors of truth and dart of death
   To faith alike are vain;
Though comets, gone a thousand years,   20
       Return again,
Patient she stands—she can no more—
And waits, nor heeds she waxes hoar.

     (At a stony gate,
     A statue of stone,   25
     Weed overgrown—
     Long 'twill wait!)

But God his former mind retains,
   Confirms his old decree;
The generations are inured to pains,   30
   And strong Necessity

Surges, and heaps Time's strand with wrecks.
   The People spread like a weedy grass,
   The thing they will they bring to pass,
And prosper to the apoplex.   35
The rout it herds around the heart,
   The ghost is yielded in the gloom;
Kings wag their heads—Now save thyself
   Who wouldst rebuild the world in bloom.

    (Tide-mark   40
    And top of the ages' strife,
    Verge where they called the world to come,
    The last advance of life—
    Ha ha, the rust on the Iron Dome!)

Nay, but revere the hid event;   45
   In the cloud a sword is girded on,
I mark a twinkling in the tent
   Of Michael the warrior one.
Senior wisdom suits not now,
The light is on the youthful brow.   50

    (Ay, in caves the miner see:
    His forehead bears a taper dim;
    Darkness so he feebly braves
    which foldeth him!)

But He who rules is old—is old;   55
Ah! faith is warm, but heaven with age is cold.

    (Ho ho, ho ho,
    The cloistered doubt
    Of olden times
    Is blurted out!)   60

The Ancient of Days forever is young,
   Forever the scheme of Nature thrives;
I know a wind in purpose strong—

It spins *against* the way it drives.
What if the gulfs their slimed foundations bare?   65
So deep must the stones be hurled
Whereon the throes of ages rear
The final empire and the happier world.

    (The poor old Past,
    The Future's slave,   70
    She drudged through pain and crime
    To bring about the blissful Prime,
    Then—perished. There's *a grave!)*

Power unanointed may come—
Dominion (unsought by the free)   75
    And the Iron Dome,
Stronger for stress and strain,
Fling her huge shadow athwart the main;
But the Founders' dream shall flee.
Age after age shall be   80
As age after age has been,
(From man's changeless heart their way they win);
And death be busy with all who strive—
Death, with silent negative.

    Yea and Nay—   85
    Each hath his say;
    But God He keeps the middle way.
    None was by
    When He spread the sky;
    Wisdom is vain, and prophesy   90

THE MARCH INTO VIRGINIA,
Ending in the First Manassas
(July, 1861)

Did all the lets and bars appear
   To every just or larger end,
Whence should come the trust and cheer?
   Youth must its ignorant impulse lend—
Age finds place in the rear.   5
   All wars are boyish, and are fought by boys,
The champions and enthusiasts of the state:
   Turbid ardors and vain joys
      Not barrenly abate—
Stimulants to the power mature,   10
   Preparatives of fate.

Who here forecasteth the event?
What heart but spurns at precedent
And warnings of the wise,
Contemned foreclosures of surprise?   15
The banners play, the bugles call,
The air is blue and prodigal.
   No berrying party, pleasure-wooed,
No picnic party in the May,
Ever went less loth than they   20
   Into that leafy neighborhood.
In Bacchic glee they file toward Fate,
Moloch's uninitiate;
Expectancy, and glad surmise
Of battle's unknown mysteries.   25
All they feel is this: 'tis glory,
A rapture sharp, though transitory,
Yet lasting in belaureled story.
So they gayly go to fight,
Chatting left and laughing right.   30

But some who this blithe mood present,
   As on in lightsome files they fare,

Shall die experienced ere three days are spent—
  Perish, enlightened by the vollied glare;
Or shame survive, and, like to adamant,   35
  Thy after shock, Manassas, share.

DUPONT'S ROUND FIGHT
(November, 1861)

In time and measure perfect moves
  All Art whose aim is sure;
Evolving rhyme and stars divine
  Have rules, and they endure.

Nor less the Fleet that warred for Right,   5
  And, warring so, prevailed,
In geometric beauty curved,
  And in an orbit sailed.

The rebel at Port Royal felt
  The Unity overawe,   10
And rued the spell. A type was here,
  And victory of LAW.

A Utilitarian View of the Monitor's Fight

Plain be the phrase, yet apt the verse,
   More ponderous than nimble;
For since grimed War here laid aside
His Orient pomp, 'twould ill befit
      Overmuch to ply   5
   The rhyme's barbaric cymbal.

Hail to victory without the gaud
   Of glory; zeal that needs no fans
Of banners; plain mechanic power
Plied cogently in War now placed—   10
      Where War belongs—
   Among the trades and artisans.

Yet this was battle, and intense—
   Beyond the strife of fleets heroic;
Deadlier, closer, calm 'mid storm;   15
No passion; all went on by crank,
      Pivot, and screw,
   And calculations of caloric.

Needless to dwell; the story's known.
   The ringing of those plates on plates   20
Still ringeth round the world—
The clangor of that blacksmiths' fray.
      The anvil-din
   Resounds this message from the Fates:

War shall yet be, and to the end;   25
   But war-paint shows the streaks of weather;
War yet shall be, but warriors
Are now but operatives; War's made
      Less grand than Peace,
   And a singe runs through lace and feather.   30

SHILOH
A Requiem
(April, 1862)

Skimming lightly, wheeling still,
    The swallows fly low
Over the field in clouded days,
    The forest-field of Shiloh—
Over the field where April rain   5
Solaced the parched ones stretched in pain
    Through the pause of night
    That followed the Sunday fight
        Around the church of Shiloh—
The church so lone, the log-built one,   10
That echoed to many a parting groan
        And natural prayer
    Of dying foemen mingled there—
Foemen at morn, but friends at eve—
    Fame or country least their care: 15
(What like a bullet can undeceive!)
    But now they lie low,
While over them the swallows skim,
    And all is hushed at Shiloh.

MALVERN HILL
(July, 1862)

Ye elms that wave on Malvern Hill
    In prime of morn and May,
Recall ye how McClellan's men
        Here stood at bay?
While deep within yon forest dim   5
    Our rigid comrades lay—
Some with the cartridge in their mouth,
Others with fixed arms lifted South—
        Invoking so
The cypress glades? Ah wilds of woe!   10

The spires of Richmond, late beheld
  Through rifts in musket-haze,
Were closed from view in clouds of dust
  On leaf-walled ways,
Where streamed our wagons in caravan;   15
  And the Seven Nights and Days
Of march and fast, retreat and fight,
Pinched our grimed faces to ghastly plight—
  Does the elm wood
Recall the haggard beards of blood?   20

The battle-smoked flag, with stars eclipsed,
  We followed (it never fell!)—
In silence husbanded our strength—
  Received their yell;
Till on this slope we patient turned   25
  With cannon ordered well;
Reverse we proved was not defeat;
But ah, the sod what thousands meet!—
  Does Malvern Wood
Bethink itself, and muse and brood?   30

    We elms of Malvern Hill
     Remember every thing;
    But sap the twig will fill:
    Wag the world how it will,
     Leaves must be green in Spring.   35

THE HOUSE-TOP
A Night Piece
(July, 1863)

No sleep. The sultriness pervades the air
And binds the brain—a dense oppression, such
As tawny tigers feel in matted shades,
Vexing their blood and making apt for ravage.
Beneath the stars the roofy desert spreads   5
Vacant as Libya. All is hushed near by.
Yet fitfully from far breaks a mixed surf
Of muffled sound, the Atheist roar of riot.
Yonder, where parching Sirius set in drought,
Balefully glares red Arson—there—and there.   10
The Town is taken by its rats—ship-rats
And rats of the wharves. All civil charms
And priestly spells which late held hearts in awe—
Fear-bound, subjected to a better sway
Than sway of self; these like a dream dissolve,   15
And man rebounds whole æons back in nature.
Hail to the low dull rumble, dull and dead,
And ponderous drag that shakes the wall.
Wise Draco comes, deep in the midnight roll
Of black artillery; he comes, though late;   20
In code corroborating Calvin's creed
And cynic tyrannies of honest kings;
He comes, nor parlies; and the Town, redeemed,
Gives thanks devout; nor, being thankful, heeds
The grimy slur on the Republic's faith implied,   25
Which holds that Man is naturally good,
And—more—is Nature's Roman, never to be scourged.

THE ARMIES OF THE WILDERNESS
(1863–4)

I

Like snows the camps on Southern hills
    Lay all the winter long,
Our levies there in patience stood—
    They stood in patience strong.
On fronting slopes gleamed other camps   5
    Where faith as firmly clung:
Ah, froward kin! so brave amiss—
    The zealots of the Wrong.

        In this strife of brothers
           (God, hear their country call),   10
        However it be, whatever betide,
           Let not the just one fall.

Through the pointed glass our soldiers saw
    The base-ball bounding sent,
They could have joined them in their sport   15
    But for the vale's deep rent.
And others turned the reddish soil,
    Like diggers of graves they bent:
The reddish soil and trenching toil
    Begat presentiment.   20

        Did the Fathers feel mistrust?
           Can no final good be wrought?
        Over and over, again and again
           Must the fight for the Right be fought?

They lead a Gray-back to the crag: 25
    "Your earth-works yonder—tell us, man!"
"A prisoner—no deserter, I,
    Nor one of the tell-tale clan."
His rags they mark: "True-blue like you
    Should wear the color—your Country's, man!"   30

He grinds his teeth: "However that be,
    Yon earth-works have their plan."

> *Such brave ones, foully snared*
>   *By Belial's wily plea,*
> *Were faithful unto the evil end—*   35
>   *Feudal fidelity.*

"Well, then, your camps—come, tell the names!"
    Freely he leveled his finger then:
"Yonder—see—are our Georgians; on the crest,
    The Carolinians; lower, past the glen,   40
Virginians—Alabamians—Mississippians—Kentuckians
    (Follow my finger)—Tennesseeans; and the ten
Camps *there*—ask your grave-pits; they'll tell.
    Halloa! I see the picket-hut, the den
Where I last night lay." "Where's Lee?"   45
    "In the hearts and bayonets of all yon men!"

> *The tribes swarm up to war*
>   *As in ages long ago,*
> *Ere the palm of promise leaved*
>   *And the lily of Christ did blow.*   50

Their mounted pickets for miles are spied
    Dotting the lowland plain,
The nearer ones in their veteran-rags—
    Loutish they loll in lazy disdain.
But ours in perilous places bide   55
    With rifles ready and eyes that strain
Deep through the dim suspected wood
    Where the Rapidan rolls amain.

> *The Indian has passed away,*
>   *But creeping comes another—*   60
> *Deadlier far. Picket,*
>   *Take heed—take heed of thy brother!*

From a wood-hung height, an outpost lone,
    Crowned with a woodman's fort,
The sentinel looks on a land of dole,   65
    Like Paran, all amort.
Black chimneys, gigantic in moor-like wastes,
    The scowl of the clouded sky retort;
The hearth is a houseless stone again—
    Ah! where shall the people be sought?   70

> *Since the venom such blastment deals,*
>   *The South should have paused, and thrice,*
> *Ere with heat of her hate she hatched*
>   *The egg with the cockatrice.*

A path down the mountain winds to the glade   75
    Where the dead of the Moonlight Fight lie low;
A hand reaches out of the thin-laid mould
    As begging help which none can bestow.
But the field-mouse small and busy ant
    Heap their hillocks, to hide if they may the woe: 80
By the bubbling spring lies the rusted canteen,
    And the drum which the drummer-boy dying let go.

> *Dust to dust, and blood for blood—*
>   *Passion and pangs! Has Time*
> *Gone back? or is this the Age*   85
>   *Of the world's great Prime?*

The wagon mired and cannon dragged
    Have trenched their scar; the plain
Tramped like the cindery beach of the damned—
    A site for the city of Cain.   90
And stumps of forests for dreary leagues
    Like a massacre show. The armies have lain
By fires where gums and balms did burn,
    And the seeds of Summer's reign.

> *Where are the birds and boys?*   95
> *Who shall go chestnutting when*
> *October returns? The nuts—*
> *O, long ere they grow again.*

They snug their huts with the chapel-pews,
    In court-houses stable their steeds—   100
Kindle their fires with indentures and bonds,
    And old Lord Fairfax's parchment deeds;
And Virginian gentlemen's libraries old—
    Books which only the scholar heeds—
Are flung to his kennel. It is ravage and range,   105
    And gardens are left to weeds.

> *Turned adrift into war*
> *Man runs wild on the plain,*
> *Like the jennets let loose*
> *On the Pampas—zebras again.*   110

Like the Pleiads dim, see the tents through the storm—
    Aloft by the hill-side hamlet's graves,
On a head-stone used for a hearth-stone there
    The water is bubbling for punch for our braves.
What if the night be drear, and the blast   115
    Ghostly shrieks? their rollicking staves
Make frolic the heart; beating time with their swords,
    What care they if Winter raves?

> *Is life but a dream? and so,*
> *In the dream do men laugh aloud?*   120
> *So strange seems mirth in a camp,*
> *So like a white tent to a shroud.*

II

The May-weed springs; and comes a Man
    And mounts our Signal Hill;
A quiet Man, and plain in garb—   125
    Briefly he looks his fill,

Then drops his gray eye on the ground,
   Like a loaded mortar he is still:
Meekness and grimness meet in him—
   The silent General.   130

> *Were men but strong and wise,*
>   *Honest as Grant, and calm,*
> *War would be left to the red and black ants,*
>   *And the happy world disarm.*

That eve a stir was in the camps,   135
   Forerunning quiet soon to come
Among the streets of beechen huts
   No more to know the drum.
The weed shall choke the lowly door,
   And foxes peer within the gloom,   140
Till scared perchance by Mosby's prowling men,
   Who ride in the rear of doom.

> *Far West, and further South,*
>   *Wherever the sword has been,*
> *Deserted camps are met,*   145
>   *And desert graves are seen.*

The livelong night they ford the flood;
   With guns held high they silent press,
Till shimmers the grass in their bayonets' sheen—
   On Morning's banks their ranks they dress;   150
Then by the forests lightly wind,
   Whose waving boughs the pennons seem to bless,
Borne by the cavalry scouting on—
   Sounding the Wilderness.

> *Like shoals of fish in spring*   155
>   *That visit Crusoe's isle,*
> *The host in the lonesome place—*
>   *The hundred thousand file.*

The foe that held his guarded hills
    Must speed to woods afar;   160
For the scheme that was nursed by the Culpepper hearth
    With the slowly-smoked cigar—
The scheme that smouldered through winter long
    Now bursts into act—into war—
The resolute scheme of a heart as calm   165
    As the Cyclone's core.

> *The fight for the city is fought*
> *In Nature's old domain;*
> *Man goes out to the wilds,*
> *And Orpheus' charm is vain.*   170

In glades they meet skull after skull
    Where pine-cones lay—the rusted gun,
Green shoes full of bones, the mouldering coat
    And cuddled-up skeleton;
And scores of such. Some start as in dreams,   175
    And comrades lost bemoan:
By the edge of those wilds Stonewall had charged—
    But the Year and the Man were gone.

> *At the height of their madness*
> *The night winds pause,*   180
> *Recollecting themselves;*
> *But no lull in these wars.*

A gleam!—a volley! And who shall go
    Storming the swarmers in jungles dread?
No cannon-ball answers, no proxies are sent—   185
    They rush in the shrapnel's stead.
Plume and sash are vanities now—
    Let them deck the pall of the dead;
They go where the shade is, perhaps into Hades,
    Where the brave of all times have led.   190

> *There's a dust of hurrying feet,*
> *Bitten lips and bated breath,*
> *And drums that challenge to the grave,*
> *And faces fixed, forefeeling death.*

What husky huzzahs in the hazy groves—   195
  What flying encounters fell;
Pursuer and pursued like ghosts disappear
  In gloomed shade—their end who shall tell?
The crippled, a ragged-barked stick for a crutch,
  Limp to some elfin dell—   200
Hobble from the sight of dead faces—white
  As pebbles in a well.

> *Few burial rites shall be;*
> *No priest with book and band*
> *Shall come to the secret place*   205
> *Of the corpse in the foeman's land.*

Watch and fast, march and fight—clutch your gun!
  Day-fights and night-fights; sore is the stress;
Look, through the pines what line comes on?
  Longstreet slants through the hauntedness!   210
'Tis charge for charge, and shout for yell:
  Such battles on battles oppress—
But Heaven lent strength, the Right strove well,
  And emerged from the Wilderness.

> *Emerged, for the way was won;*   215
> *But the Pillar of Smoke that led*
> *Was brand-like with ghosts that went up*
> *Ashy and red.*

None can narrate that strife in the pines,
  A seal is on it—Sabæan lore!   220
Obscure as the wood, the entangled rhyme
  But hints at the maze of war—

Vivid glimpses or livid through peopled gloom,
    And fires which creep and char—
A riddle of death, of which the slain   225
    Sole solvers are.

    Long they withhold the roll
      Of the shroudless dead. It is right;
    Not yet can we bear the flare
      Of the funeral light.   230

THE SWAMP ANGEL

There is a coal-black Angel
    With a thick Afric lip,
And he dwells (like the hunted and harried)
    In a swamp where the green frogs dip.
But his face is against a City   5
    Which is over a bay of the sea,
And he breathes with a breath that is blastment,
    And dooms by a far decree.

By night there is fear in the City,
    Through the darkness a star soareth on;   10
There's a scream that screams up to the zenith,
    Then the poise of a meteor lone—
Lighting far the pale fright of the faces,
    And downward the coming is seen;
Then the rush, and the burst, and the havoc,   15
    And wails and shrieks between.

It comes like the thief in the gloaming;
    It comes, and none may foretell
The place of the coming—the glaring;
    They live in a sleepless spell   20
That wizens, and withers, and whitens;
    It ages the young, and the bloom

Of the maiden is ashes of roses—
   The Swamp Angel broods in his gloom.

Swift is his messengers' going,   25
   But slowly he saps their halls,
As if by delay deluding.
   They move from their crumbling walls
Farther and farther away;
   But the Angel sends after and after,   30
By night with the flame of his ray—
   By night with the voice of his screaming—
Sends after them, stone by stone,
   And farther walls fall, farther portals,
And weed follows weed through the Town.   35

Is this the proud City? the scorner
   Which never would yield the ground?
Which mocked at the coal-black Angel?
   The cup of despair goes round.
Vainly she calls upon Michael   40
   ('The white man's seraph was he),
For Michael has fled from his tower
   To the Angel over the sea.

Who weeps for the woeful City
   Let him weep for our guilty kind;   45
Who joys at her wild despairing—
   Christ, the Forgiver, convert his mind.

THE COLLEGE COLONEL

He rides at their head;
　A crutch by his saddle just slants in view,
One slung arm is in splints, you see,
　Yet he guides his strong steed—how coldly too.

He brings his regiment home—　　　　　　　　　5
　Not as they filed two years before,
But a remnant half-tattered, and battered, and worn,
Like castaway sailors, who—stunned
　　By the surf's loud roar,
　Their mates dragged back and seen no more—　　10
Again and again breast the surge,
　And at last crawl, spent, to shore.

A still rigidity and pale—
　An Indian aloofness lones his brow;
He has lived a thousand years　　　　　　　　　15
Compressed in battle's pains and prayers,
　Marches and watches slow.

There are welcoming shouts, and flags;
　Old men off hat to the Boy,
Wreaths from gay balconies fall at his feet,　　20
　But to *him*—there comes alloy.

It is not that a leg is lost,
　It is not that an arm is maimed,
It is not that the fever has racked—
　Self he has long disclaimed.　　　　　　　　　25

But all through the Seven Days' Fight,
　And deep in the Wilderness grim,
And in the field-hospital tent,
　And Petersburg crater, and dim
Lean brooding in Libby, there came—　　　　　30
　Ah heaven!—what *truth* to him.

"THE COMING STORM"
A Picture by S. R. Gifford, and owned by E. B.
Included in the N. A. Exhibition, April, 1865

All feeling hearts must feel for him
   Who felt this picture. Presage dim—
Dim inklings from the shadowy sphere
   Fixed him and fascinated here.

A demon-cloud like the mountain one   5
   Burst on a spirit as mild
As this urned lake, the home of shades.
   But Shakspeare's pensive child

Never the lines had lightly scanned,
   Steeped in fable, steeped in fate;   10
The Hamlet in his heart was 'ware,
   Such hearts can antedate.

No utter surprise can come to him
   Who reaches Shakspeare's core;
That which we seek and shun is there—   15
   Man's final lore.

"FORMERLY A SLAVE"
An idealized Portrait, by E. Vedder,
in the Spring Exhibition of the National Academy, 1865

The sufferance of her race is shown,
   And retrospect of life,
Which now too late deliverance dawns upon;
   Yet is she not at strife.

Her children's children they shall know   5
   The good withheld from her;
And so her reverie takes prophetic cheer—
   In spirit she sees the stir

Far down the depth of thousand years,
    And marks the revel shine;   10
Her dusky face is lit with sober light,
    Sibylline, yet benign.

THE APPARITION
(A Retrospect)

Convulsions came; and, where the field
    Long slept in pastoral green,
A goblin-mountain was upheaved
(Sure the scared sense was all deceived),
    Marl-glen and slag-ravine.   5

The unreserve of Ill was there,
    The clinkers in her last retreat;
But, ere the eye could take it in,
Or mind could comprehension win,
    It sunk!—and at our feet.   10

So, then, Solidity's a crust—
    The core of fire below;
All may go well for many a year,
But who can think without a fear
    Of horrors that happen so?   15

ON THE SLAIN COLLEGIANS

Youth is the time when hearts are large,
    And stirring wars
Appeal to the spirit which appeals in turn
    To the blade it draws.
If woman incite, and duty show   5
    (Though made the mask of Cain),
Or whether it be Truth's sacred cause,
    Who can aloof remain

That shares youth's ardor, uncooled by the snow
Of wisdom or sordid gain?   10

The liberal arts and nurture sweet
Which give his gentleness to man—
    Train him to honor, lend him grace
Through bright examples meet—
That culture which makes never wan   15
With underminings deep, but holds
    The surface still, its fitting place,
    And so gives sunniness to the face
And bravery to the heart; what troops
    Of generous boys in happiness thus bred—   20
    Saturnians through life's Tempe led,
Went from the North and came from the South,
With golden mottoes in the mouth,
    To lie down midway on a bloody bed.

Woe for the homes of the North,   25
And woe for the seats of the South:
All who felt life's spring in prime,
And were swept by the wind of their place and time—
    All lavish hearts, on whichever side,
Of birth urbane or courage high,   30
Armed them for the stirring wars—
Armed them—some to die.
    Apollo-like in pride,
Each would slay his Python—caught
The maxims in his temple taught—   35
    Aflame with sympathies whose blaze
Perforce enwrapped him—social laws,
    Friendship and kin, and by-gone days—
Vows, kisses—every heart unmoors,
And launches into the seas of wars.   40
What could they else—North or South?
Each went forth with blessings given
By priests and mothers in the name of Heaven;

And honor in both was chief.
Warred one for Right, and one for Wrong?   45
So put it; but they both were young—
Each grape to his cluster clung,
All their elegies are sung.

The anguish of maternal hearts
    Must search for balm divine;   50
But well the striplings bore their fated parts
    (The heavens all parts assign)—
Never felt life's care or cloy.
Each bloomed and died an unabated Boy;
Nor dreamed what death was—thought it mere   55
Sliding into some vernal sphere.
They knew the joy, but leaped the grief,
Like plants that flower ere comes the leaf—
Which storms lay low in kindly doom,
And kill them in their flush of bloom.   60

AMERICA

I

Where the wings of a sunny Dome expand
I saw a Banner in gladsome air—
Starry, like Berenice's Hair—
Afloat in broadened bravery there;
With undulating long-drawn flow,⁣   5
As rolled Brazilian billows go
Voluminously o'er the Line.
The Land reposed in peace below;
   The children in their glee
Were folded to the exulting heart   10
   Of young Maternity.

II

Later, and it streamed in fight
   When tempest mingled with the fray,
And over the spear-point of the shaft
   I saw the ambiguous lightning play.   15
Valor with Valor strove, and died:
Fierce was Despair, and cruel was Pride;
And the lorn Mother speechless stood,
Pale at the fury of her brood.

III

Yet later, and the silk did wind   20
   Her fair cold form;
Little availed the shining shroud,
   Though ruddy in hue, to cheer or warm.
A watcher looked upon her low, and said—
She sleeps, but sleeps, she is not dead.   25
   But in that sleep contortion showed
The terror of the vision there—
   A silent vision unavowed,
Revealing earth's foundation bare,
   And Gorgon in her hidden place.   30
It was a thing of fear to see

So foul a dream upon so fair a face,
And the dreamer lying in that starry shroud.

IV

But from the trance she sudden broke—
    The trance, or death into promoted life;   35
At her feet a shivered yoke,
And in her aspect turned to heaven
    No trace of passion or of strife—
A clear calm look. It spake of pain,
But such as purifies from stain—   40
Sharp pangs that never come again—
    And triumph repressed by knowledge meet,
Power dedicate, and hope grown wise,
    And youth matured for age's seat—
Law on her brow and empire in her eyes.   45
    So she, with graver air and lifted flag;
While the shadow, chased by light,
Fled along the far-drawn height,
    And left her on the crag.

COMMEMORATIVE OF A NAVAL VICTORY

Sailors there are of gentlest breed,
　Yet strong, like every goodly thing;
The discipline of arms refines,
　And the wave gives tempering.
　The damasked blade its beam can fling;　　　　　5
It lends the last grave grace:
The hawk, the hound, and sworded nobleman
　In Titian's picture for a king,
Are of hunter or warrior race.

In social halls a favored guest　　　　　10
　In years that follow victory won,
How sweet to feel your festal fame
　In woman's glance instinctive thrown:
　Repose is yours— your deed is known,
It musks the amber wine;　　　　　15
It lives, and sheds a light from storied days
　Rich as October sunsets brown,
Which make the barren place to shine.

But seldom the laurel wreath is seen
　Unmixed with pensive pansies dark;　　　　　20
There's a light and a shadow on every man
　Who at last attains his lifted mark—
　Nursing through night the ethereal spark.
Elate he never can be;
He feels that spirits which glad had hailed his worth,　　　　　25
　Sleep in oblivion.—The shark
Glides white through the phosphorus sea.

SUPPLEMENT

Were I fastidiously anxious for the symmetry of this book, it would close with the notes. But the times are such that patriotism—not free from solicitude—urges a claim overriding all literary scruples.

It is more than a year since the memorable surrender, but events have not yet rounded themselves into completion. Not justly can we complain of this. There has been an upheaval affecting the basis of things; to altered circumstances complicated adaptations are to be made; there are difficulties great and novel. But is Reason still waiting for Passion to spend itself? We have sung of the soldiers and sailors, but who shall hymn the politicians?

In view of the infinite desirableness of Re-establishment, and considering that, so far as feeling is concerned, it depends not mainly on the temper in which the South regards the North, but rather conversely; one who never was a blind adherent feels constrained to submit some thoughts, counting on the indulgence of his countrymen.

And, first, it may be said that, if among the feelings and opinions growing immediately out of a great civil convulsion, there are any which time shall modify or do away, they are presumably those of a less temperate and charitable cast.

There seems no reason why patriotism and narrowness should go together, or why intellectual fairmindedness should be confounded with political trimming, or why serviceable truth should keep cloistered because not partisan. Yet the work of Reconstruction, if admitted to be feasible at all, demands little but common sense and Christian charity. Little but these? These are much.

Some of us are concerned because as yet the South shows no penitence. But what exactly do we mean by this? Since down to the close of the war she never confessed any for braving it, the only penitence now left her is that which springs solely from the sense of discomfiture; and since this evidently would be a contrition hypocritical, it would be unworthy in us to demand it. Certain it is that penitence, in the sense of voluntary humiliation, will never be displayed. Nor does this afford just ground for unreserved condemnation. It is enough, for all practical purposes, if the South have been taught by the terrors of civil war to feel that Secession, like Slavery, is against Destiny; that both now lie buried in one grave; that her fate is linked with ours; and that together we comprise the Nation.

The clouds of heroes who battled for the Union it is needless to eulogize here. But how of the soldiers on the other side? And when of a free community we name the soldiers, we thereby name the people. It was in subserviency to the slave-interest that Secession was plotted; but it was under the plea, plausibly urged, that certain inestimable rights guaranteed by the Constitution were directly menaced, that the people of the South were cajoled into revolution. Through the arts of the conspirators and the perversity of fortune, the most sensitive love of liberty was entrapped into the support of a war whose implied end was the erecting in our advanced century of an Anglo-American empire based upon the systematic degradation of man.

Spite this clinging reproach, however, signal military virtues and achievements have conferred upon the Confederate arms historic fame, and upon certain of the commanders a renown extending beyond the sea—a renown which we of the North could not suppress, even if we would. In personal character, also, not a few of the military leaders of the South enforce forbearance; the memory of others the North refrains from disparaging; and some, with more or less of reluctance, she can respect. Posterity, sympathizing with our convictions, but removed from our passions, may perhaps go farther here. If George IV. could, [out of the graceful instinct of a gentleman,] raise an honorable monument in the great fane of Christendom over the remains of the enemy of his dynasty,

Charles Edward, the invader of England and victor in the rout at Preston Pans—upon whose head the king's ancestor but one reign removed had set a price—is it probable that the grandchildren of General Grant will pursue with rancor, or slur by sour neglect, the memory of Stonewall Jackson?

But the South herself is not wanting in recent histories and biographies which record the deeds of her chieftains—writings freely published at the North by loyal houses, widely read here, and with a deep though saddened interest. By students of the war such works are hailed as welcome accessories, and tending to the completeness of the record.

Supposing a happy issue out of present perplexities, then, in the generation next to come, Southerners there will be yielding allegiance to the Union, feeling all their interests bound up in it, and yet cherishing unrebuked that kind of feeling for the memory of the soldiers of the fallen Confederacy that Burns, Scott, and the Ettrick Shepherd felt for the memory of the gallant clansmen ruined through their fidelity to the Stuarts—a feeling whose passion was tempered by the poetry imbuing it, and which in no wise affected their loyalty to the Georges, and which, it may be added, indirectly contributed excellent things to literature. But, setting this view aside, dishonorable would it be in the South were she willing to abandon to shame the memory of brave men who with signal personal disinterestedness warred in her behalf, though from motives, as we believe, so deplorably astray.

Patriotism is not baseness, neither is it inhumanity. The mourners who this summer bear flowers to the mounds of the Virginian and Georgian dead are, in their domestic bereavement and proud affection, as sacred in the eye of Heaven as are those who go with similar offerings of tender grief and love into the cemeteries of our Northern martyrs. And yet, in one aspect, how needless to point the contrast.

Cherishing such sentiments, it will hardly occasion surprise that, in looking over the battle-pieces in the foregoing collection, I have been tempted to withdraw or modify some of them, fearful lest in presenting, though but dramatically and by way of a poetic record, the passions and epithets of civil war, I might be contributing to a bitterness which every sensible American must wish at an end. So, too, with the emotion of victory as reproduced on some pages, and particularly toward the close. It should not be construed into an exultation misapplied—an exultation as ungenerous as unwise, and made to minister, however indirectly, to that kind of censoriousness too apt to be produced in certain natures by success after trying reverses. Zeal is not of necessity religion, neither is it always of the same essence with poetry or patriotism.

There were excesses which marked the conflict, most of which are perhaps inseparable from a civil strife so intense and prolonged, and involving warfare in some border countries new and imperfectly civilized. Barbarities also there were, for which the Southern people collectively can hardly be held responsible, though perpetrated by ruffians in their name. But surely other qualities—exalted ones—courage and fortitude matchless, were likewise displayed, and largely; and justly may these be held the characteristic traits, and not the former.

In this view, what Northern writer, however patriotic, but must revolt from acting on paper a part any way akin to that of the live dog to the dead lion; and yet it is right to rejoice for our triumph, so far as it may justly imply an advance for our whole country and for humanity.

Let it be held no reproach to any one that he pleads for reasonable consideration for our late enemies, now stricken down and unavoidably debarred, for the time, from speaking through authorized agencies for themselves. Nothing has been urged here in the foolish hope of conciliating those men—few in number, we trust—who have resolved never to be reconciled to the Union. On such hearts every thing is thrown away except it be religious commiseration, and the sincerest. Yet let them call to mind that unhappy Secessionist, not a military man, who with impious alacrity fired the first shot of the Civil War at Sumter, and a little more than four years afterward fired the last one into his own heart at Richmond.

Noble was the gesture into which patriotic passion surprised the people in a utilitarian time and country; yet the glory of the war falls short of its pathos—a pathos which now at last ought to disarm all animosity.

How many and earnest thoughts still rise, and how hard to repress them. We feel what past years have been, and years, unretarded years, shall come. May we all have moderation; may we all show candor. Though, perhaps, nothing could ultimately have averted the strife, and though to treat of human actions is to deal wholly with second causes, nevertheless, let us not cover up or try to extenuate what, humanly speaking, is the truth—namely, that those unfraternal denunciations, continued through years, and which at last inflamed to deeds that ended in bloodshed, were reciprocal; and that, had the preponderating strength and the prospect of its unlimited increase lain on the other side, on ours might have lain those actions which now in our late opponents we stigmatize under the name of Rebellion. As frankly let us own—what it would be unbecoming to parade were foreigners concerned—that our triumph was won not more by skill and bravery than by superior resources and crushing numbers; that it was a triumph, too, over a people for years politically misled by designing men, and also by some honestly-erring men, who from their position could not have been otherwise than broadly influential; a people who, though, indeed, they sought to perpetuate the curse of slavery, and even extend it, were not the authors of it, but (less fortunate, not less righteous than we) were the fated inheritors; a people who, having a like origin with ourselves, share essentially in whatever worthy qualities we may possess. No one can add to the lasting reproach which hopeless defeat has now cast upon Secession by withholding the recognition of these verities.

Surely we ought to take it to heart that that kind of pacification, based upon principles operating equally all over the land, which lovers of their country yearn for, and which our arms, though signally triumphant, did not bring about, and which law-making, however anxious, or energetic, or repressive, never by itself can achieve, may yet be largely aided by generosity of sentiment public and private. Some revisionary legislation and adaptive is indispensable; but with this should harmoniously work another kind of prudence, not unallied with entire magnanimity. Benevolence and policy—Christianity and Machiavelli—dissuade from penal severities toward the subdued. Abstinence here is as obligatory as considerate care for our unfortunate fellow-men late in bonds, and, if observed, would equally prove to be wise forecast. The great qualities of the South, those attested in the War, we can perilously alienate, or we may make them nationally available at need.

The blacks, in their infant pupilage to freedom, appeal to the sympathies of every humane mind. The paternal guardianship which for the interval government exercises over them was prompted equally by duty and benevolence. Yet such kindliness should not be allowed to exclude kindliness to communities who stand nearer to us in nature. For the future of the freed slaves we may well be concerned; but the future of the whole country, involving the future of the blacks, urges a paramount claim upon our anxiety. Effective benignity, like the Nile, is not narrow in its bounty, and true policy is always broad. To be sure, it is vain to seek to glide, with moulded words, over the difficulties of the situation. And for them who are neither partisans, nor enthusiasts, nor theorists, nor cynics, there are some doubts not readily to be solved. And there are fears. Why is not the cessation of war now at length attended with the settled calm of peace? Wherefore in a clear sky do we still turn our eyes toward the South, as the Neapolitan, months after the eruption, turns his toward Vesuvius? Do we dread lest the repose may be deceptive? In the recent convulsion has the crater but shifted? Let us revere that sacred uncertainty which forever impends over men and nations. Those of us who always abhorred slavery as an atheistical iniquity, gladly we join in the exulting chorus of humanity over its downfall. But we should remember that emancipation was accomplished not by deliberate legislation; only through agonized violence could so mighty a result be effected. In our natural solicitude to confirm the benefit of liberty to the blacks, let us forbear from measures of dubious constitutional rightfulness toward our white countrymen— measures of a nature to provoke, among other of the last evils, exterminating hatred of race toward race. In imagination let us place ourselves in the unprecedented position of the Southerners—their position as regards the millions of ignorant manumitted slaves in their midst, for whom some of us now claim the suffrage. Let us be Christians toward our fellow-whites, as well as philanthropists toward the blacks, our fellow-men. In all things, and toward all, we are enjoined to do as we would be done by. Nor should we forget that benevolent desires, after passing a certain point, can not undertake their own fulfillment without incurring the risk of evils beyond those sought to be remedied. Something may well be left to the graduated care of future legislation, and to heaven. In one point of view the co-existence of the two races in the South—whether the negro be bond or free—seems (even as it did to Abraham Lincoln) a grave evil. Emancipation has ridded the country of the reproach, but not wholly of the calamity. Especially in the present transition period for both races in the South, more or less of trouble may not unreasonably be anticipated; but let us not hereafter be too swift to charge the blame exclusively in any one quarter. With certain evils men must be more or less patient. Our institutions have a potent digestion, and may in time convert and assimilate to good all elements thrown in, however originally alien.

But, so far as immediate measures looking toward permanent Re-establishment are concerned, no consideration should tempt us to pervert the national victory into oppression for the vanquished. Should plausible promise of eventual good, or a deceptive or spurious sense of duty, lead us to essay this, count we must on serious consequences, not the least of which would be divisions among the Northern adherents of the Union. Assuredly, if any honest Catos there be who thus far have gone with us, no longer will they do so, but oppose us, and as resolutely as hitherto they have supported. But this path of thought leads toward those waters of bitterness from which one can only turn aside and be silent.

But supposing Re-establishment so far advanced that the Southern seats in Congress are occupied, and by men qualified in accordance with those cardinal principles of representative government which hitherto have prevailed in the land—what then? Why, the Congressmen elected by the people of the South will—represent the people of the South. This may seem a flat conclusion; but, in view of the last five years, may there not be latent significance in it? What will be the temper of those Southern members? and, confronted by them, what will be the mood of our own representatives? In private life true reconciliation seldom follows a violent quarrel; but, if subsequent intercourse be unavoidable, nice observances and mutual are indispensable to the prevention of a new rupture. Amity itself can only be maintained by reciprocal respect, and true friends are punctilious equals. On the floor of Congress North and South are to come together after a passionate duel, in which the South, though proving her valor, has been made to bite the dust. Upon differences in debate shall acrimonious recriminations be exchanged? shall censorious superiority assumed by one section provoke defiant self-assertion on the other? shall Manassas and Chickamauga be retorted for Chattanooga and Richmond? Under the supposition that the full Congress will be composed of gentlemen, all this is impossible. Yet, if otherwise, it needs no prophet of Israel to foretell the end. The maintenance of Congressional decency in the future will rest mainly with the North. Rightly will more forbearance be required from the North than the South, for the North is victor.

But some there are who may deem these latter thoughts inapplicable, and for this reason: Since the test-oath operatively excludes from Congress all who in any way participated in Secession, therefore none but Southerners wholly in harmony with the North are eligible to seats. This is true for the time being. But the oath is alterable; and in the wonted fluctuations of parties not improbably it will undergo alteration, assuming such a form, perhaps, as not to bar the admission into the National Legislature of men who represent the populations lately in revolt. Such a result would involve no violation of the principles of democratic government. Not readily can one perceive how the political existence of the millions of late Secessionists can permanently be ignored by this Republic. The years of the war tried our devotion to the Union; the time of peace may test the sincerity of our faith in democracy.

In no spirit of opposition, not by way of challenge, is any thing here thrown out. These thoughts are sincere ones; they seem natural—inevitable. Here and there they must have suggested themselves to many thoughtful patriots. And, if they be just thoughts, ere long they must have that weight with the public which already they have had with individuals.

For that heroic band—those children of the furnace who, in regions like Texas and Tennessee, maintained their fidelity through terrible trials—we of the North felt for them, and profoundly we honor them. Yet passionate sympathy, with resentments so close as to be almost domestic in their bitterness, would hardly in the present juncture tend to discreet legislation. Were the Unionists and Secessionists but as Guelphs and Ghibellines? If not, then far be it from a great nation now to act in the spirit that animated a triumphant town-faction in the Middle Ages. But crowding thoughts must at last be checked; and, in times like the present, one who desires to be impartially just in the expression of his views, moves as among sword-points presented on every side.

Let us pray that the great historic tragedy of our time may not have been enacted without instructing our whole beloved country through terror and pity; and may fulfillment verify in the end those expectations which kindle the bards of Progress and Humanity.

T H E   E N D.

PART SIX

FROM CLAREL: A POEM AND
PILGRIMAGE IN THE HOLY LAND

The years following the Civil War were the darkest for Melville. His career and family would suffer life-altering breakdowns, commensurate with the war itself. *Battle-Pieces* was (by modern measure) a startling debut for a poet, far superior to Melville's abandoned volume of 1860, but despite (or perhaps because of) its conciliatory vision, it did not sell. Deeply disappointed in this failure, Melville abandoned professional writing and settled into a patronage job in the U.S. Customs House. Deeper miseries were to come. In May 1867, Melville's wife of twenty years threatened a separation, and that fall, their son Malcolm committed suicide.

His life in shambles, Melville, nevertheless, continued to write. By 1870, he began work on *Clarel: A Poem and Pilgrimage in the Holy Land* (1876). Based on his 1857 tour of the Mideast, the epic (longer than *Paradise Lost*) is about a young American divinity student (Clarel) in Jerusalem, embroiled in a crisis of faith, who falls in love with a Jewish girl (Ruth), whose father is murdered. He journeys with various other wanderers to the Dead Sea, speaks with them of religion, science, and modern philosophy, regains some small sense of purpose, and returns to Jerusalem, only to find Ruth dead from grief.

No excerpt from *Clarel* can possibly render the scope and depth of the work, which is arguably America's most ambitious intellectual and emotional excursion in poetic form. The selected cantos represent only one thread in the poem's fabric of interwoven issues. Here, the problems of faith and sexuality speak directly to Clarel's alienated condition, and may reflect indirectly upon the condition of uncertainty that can plague young men in general, those like Melville in his youth who survive and those like Melville's youthful son who did not.

Throughout the poem, Clarel has been attracted to the reserved and withdrawn Vine (most likely based on Hawthorne), sensing in him a fraternal, intellectual, and homosocial bond, and in "Vine and Clarel" the two have their longest sustained interaction by the banks of the Jordan. Later, in Bethlehem, Clarel meets an attractive and worldly "prodigal" whose songs and merry indifference to the gloomy matters of doubt send Clarel back to his love.

VINE AND CLAREL
Book II, Canto 27

While now, to serve the pilgrim train,
The Arabs willow branches hew,
(For palms they serve in dearth of true),
Or, kneeling by the margin, stoop
To brim memorial bottles up;   5
And the Greek's wine entices two:
Apart see Clarel here incline,
Perplexed by that Dominican,
Nor less by Rolfe—capricious man:
"I cannot penetrate him.—Vine?"   10
    As were Venetian slats between
He espied him through a leafy screen,
Luxurious there in umbrage thrown,
Light sprays above his temples blown—
The river through the green retreat   15
Hurrying, reveling by his feet.
    Vine looked an overture, but said
Nothing, till Clarel leaned   half laid—
Beside him: then "We dream, or be
In sylvan John's baptistery.   20
May Pisa's equal beauty keep?—
But how bad habits persevere!
I have been moralizing here
Like any imbecile: as thus:
Look how these willows over-weep   25
The waves, and plain: 'Fleet so from us?
And wherefore? whitherward away?
Your best is here where wildings sway
And the light shadow's blown about;
Ah, tarry, for at hand's a sea   30
Whence ye shall never issue out
Once in.' They sing back: 'So let be!
We mad-caps hymn it as we flow—
Short life and merry! be it so!'"

Surprised at such a fluent turn,   35
The student did but listen—learn.

Putting aside the twigs which screened,
Again Vine spake, and lightly leaned
"Look; in yon vault so leafy dark,
At deep end lit by gemmy spark   40
Of mellowed sunbeam in a snare;
Over the stream—ay, just through there—
The sheik on that celestial mare
Shot, fading.—Clan of outcast Hagar,
Well do ye come by spear and dagger!   45
Yet in your bearing ye outvie
Our western Red Men, chiefs that stalk
In mud paint—whirl the tomahawk.—
But in these Nimrods noted you
The natural language of the eye,   50
Burning or liquid, flame or dew,
As still the changeable quick mood
Made transit in the wayward blood?
Methought therein one might espy,
For all the wildness, thoughts refined   55
By the old Asia's dreamful mind;
But hark—a bird?"
                                    Pure as the rain
Which diamondeth with lucid grain,
The white swan in the April hours
Floating between two sunny showers   60
Upon the lake, while buds unroll;
So pure, so virginal in shrine
Of true unworldliness looked Vine.
Ah, clear sweet ether of the soul
(Mused Clarel), holding him in view.   65
Prior advances unreturned
Not here he recked of, while he yearned—
O, now but for communion true
And close; let go each alien theme;
Give me thyself!

But Vine, at will   70
Dwelling upon his wayward dream,
Nor as suspecting Clarel's thrill
Of personal longing, rambled still;
"Methinks they show a lingering trace
Of some quite unrecorded race   75
Such as the Book of Job implies.
What ages of refinings wise
Must have forerun what there is writ—
More ages than have followed it.
At Lydda late, as chance would have,   80
Some tribesmen from the south I saw,
Their tents pitched in the Gothic nave,
The ruined one. Disowning law,
Not lawless lived they; no, indeed;
Their chief—why, one of Sydney's clan,   85
A slayer, but chivalric man;
And chivalry, with all that breed
Was Arabic or Saracen
In source, they tell. But, as men stray
Further from Ararat away   90
Pity it were did they recede
In carriage, manners, and the rest;
But no, for ours the palm indeed
In bland amenities far West!
Come now, for pastime let's complain;   95
Grudged thanks, Columbus, for thy main!
Put back, as 'twere—assigned by fate
To fight crude Nature o'er again,
By slow degrees we re-create.
But then, alas, in Arab camps   100
No lack, they say, no lack of scamps."
    Divided mind knew Clarel here;
The heart's desire did interfere.
Thought he, How pleasant in another
Such sallies, or in thee, if said   105
After confidings that should wed
Our souls in one:—Ah, call me brother!—

So feminine his passionate mood
Which, long as hungering unfed,
All else rejected or withstood.   110
   Some inklings he let fall. But no:
Here over Vine there slid a change—
A shadow, such as thin may show
Gliding along the mountain-range
And deepening in the gorge below.   115
   Does Vine's rebukeful dusking say—
Why, on this vernal bank to-day,
Why bring oblations of thy pain
To one who hath his share? here fain
Would lap him in a chance reprieve?   120
Lives none can help ye; that believe.
Art thou the first soul tried by doubt?
Shalt prove the last? Go, live it out.
But for thy fonder dream of love
In man toward man—the soul's caress—   125
The negatives of flesh should prove
Analogies of non-cordialness
In spirit.—E'en such conceits could cling
To Clarel's dream of vain surmise
And imputation full of sting.   130
But, glancing up, unwarned he saw
What serious softness in those eyes
Bent on him. Shyly they withdraw.
Enslaver, wouldst thou but fool me
With bitter-sweet, sly sorcery,   135
Pride's pastime? or wouldst thou indeed,
Since things unspoken may impede,
Let flow thy nature but for bar?—
Nay, dizzard, sick these feelings are;
How findest place within thy heart   140
For such solicitudes apart
From Ruth?—Self-taxings.
                  But a sign
Came here indicative from Vine,
Who with a reverent hushed air

His view directed toward the glade   145
Beyond, wherein a niche was made
Of leafage, and a kneeler there,
The meek one, on whom, as he prayed,
A golden shaft of mellow light,
Oblique through vernal cleft above,   150
And making his pale forehead bright,
Scintillant fell. By such a beam
From heaven descended erst the dove
On Christ emerging from the stream.
It faded; 'twas a transient ray;   155
And, quite unconscious of its sheen,
The suppliant rose and moved away,
Not dreaming that he had been seen.

When next they saw that innocent,
From prayer such cordial had he won   160
That all his aspect of content
As with the oil of gladness shone.
Less aged looked he. And his cheer
Took language in an action here·
The train now mustering in line,   165
Each pilgrim with a river-palm
In hand (except indeed the Jew),
The saint the head-stall need entwine
With wreathage of the same. When new
They issued from the wood, no charm   170
The ass found in such idle gear
Superfluous: with her long ear
She flapped it off, and the next thrust
Of hoof imprinted it in dust.
Meek hands (mused Vine), vainly ye twist   175
Fair garland for the realist.
    The Hebrew, noting whither bent
Vine's glance, a word in passing lent:
"Ho, tell us how it comes to be
That thou who rank'st not with beginners   180
Regard have for yon chief of sinners."

"Yon chief of sinners?"
                    "So names he
Himself. For one I'll not express
How I do loathe such lowliness."

THE PRODIGAL
Book IV, Canto 26

In adolescence thrilled by hope
Which fain would verify the gleam
And find if destiny concur,
How dwells upon life's horoscope
Youth, always an astrologer,   5
Forecasting happiness the dream!

   Slumber interred them; but not all,
For so it chanced that Clarel's cell
Was shared by one who did repel
The poppy. 'Twas a prodigal,   10
Yet pilgrim too in casual way,
And seen within the grots that day,
But only seen, no more than that.
In years he might be Clarel's mate.
Not talkative, he half reclined   15
In revery of dreamful kind;
Or might the fable, the romance
Be tempered by experience?
For ruling under spell serene,
A light precocity is seen.   20
That mobile face, voluptuous air
No Northern origin declare,
But Southern—where the nations bright,
The costumed nations, circled be
In garland round a tideless sea   25
Eternal in its fresh delight.
Nor less he owned the common day;
His avocation naught, in sooth—
A toy of Mammon; but the ray

And fair aureola of youth   30
Deific makes the prosiest clay.
From revery now by Clarel won
He brief his story entered on:
A native of the banks *of Rhone*
He traveled for a Lyons house   35
Which dealt in bales luxurious;
Detained by chance at Jaffa gray,
Rather than let ripe hours decay,
He'd run o'er, in a freak of fun,
Green Sharon to Jerusalem,   40
And thence, not far, to Bethlehem.
    Thy silvery voice, irreverent one!
'Twas musical; and Clarel said:
"Greatly I err, or thou art he
Who singing along the hill-side sped   45
At fall of night."
              "And heard you me?
'Twas sentimental, to be sure:
A little Spanish overture,
A Tombez air, which months ago
A young Peruvian let flow.   50
Locked friends we were; he's gone home now."
    To Clarel 'twas a novel style
And novel nature; and awhile
Mutely he dwelt upon him here.
Earnest to know how the most drear   55
Solemnity of Judah's glade
Affect might such a mind, he said
Something to purpose; but he shied.
One essay more; whereat he cried:
"*Amigo!* favored lads there are,   60
Born under such a lucky star,
They weigh not things too curious, see,
Albeit conforming to their time
And usages thereof, and clime:
Well, mine's that happy family."   65
    The student faltered—felt annoy:

Absorbed in problems ill-defined,
Am I too curious in my mind;
And, baffled in the vain employ,
Foregoing many an easy joy? 70
That thought he hurried from; and so
Unmindful in perturbed estate
Of that light intimation late,
He said: "On hills of dead Judæa
Wherever one may faring go, 75
He dreams—Fit place to set the bier
Of Jacob, brought from Egypt's mead:
Here's Atad's threshing-floor."
                                                    "Indeed?"
Scarce audible was that in tone;
Nor Clarel heard it, but went on: 80
" 'Tis Jephthah's daughter holds the hight;
She, she's the muse here.—But, I pray,
Confess to Judah's mournful sway."
He held his peace. "You grant the blight?"
"No Boulevards." "Do other lands 85
Show equal ravage you've beheld?"
"Oh, yes," and eyed his emerald
In ring. "But here a God commands,
A judgment dooms: you that gainsay?"
Up looked he quick, then turned away, 90
And with a shrug that gave mute sign
That here the theme he would decline.
But Clarel urged. As in despair
The other turned—invoked the air:
"Was it in such talk, Don Rovenna, 95
We dealt in Seville, I and you?
No! chat of love-wile and duenna
And *saya-manto* in Peru.
Ah, good Limeno, dear *amigo,*
What times were ours, the holidays flew; 100
Life, life a revel and clear *allegro;*
But home thou'rt gone; pity, but true!"
    At burst so lyrical, yet given

Not all without some mock in leaven,
Once more did Clarel puzzled sit;   105
But rallying in spite of it,
Continued: "Surely now, 'tis clear
That in the aspect of Judæa—"
    "My friend, it is just naught to me!
Why, why so pertinacious be?   110
Refrain!" Here, turning light away,
As quitting so the theme: "How gay
Damascus! orchard of a town:
Not yet she's heard the tidings though."
"Tidings?"
            "Tidings of long ago: 115
Isaiah's dark burden, malison:
Of course, to be perpetual fate:
Bat, serpent, screech-owl, and all that.
But truth is, grace and pleasure there,
In Abana and Pharpar's streams   120
(O shady haunts! O sherbert-air!)
So twine the place in odorous dreams,
How may she think to mope and moan,
The news not yet being got to town
That she's a ruin! Oh, 'tis pity,   125
For she, she is earth's senior city!—
Pray, who was he, that man of state
Whose footman at Elisha's gate
Loud rapped? The name has slipped. Howe'er,
That Damascene maintained it well: 130
'We've better streams than Israel,
Yea, fairer waters.'" Weetless here
Clarel betrayed half cleric tone:
"Naaman, you mean. Poor leper one,
'Twas Jordan healed him."
                        "As you please."   135
And hereupon the Lyonese—
(Capricious, or inferring late
That he had yielded up his state
To priggish inroad) gave mute sign

'Twere well to end.
         "But Palestine,"   140
Insisted Clarel, "do you not
Concede some strangeness to her lot?"
   "*Amigo*, how you persecute!
You all but tempt one to refute
These stale megrims. You of the West,   145
What devil has your hearts possessed,
You can't enjoy?—Ah, dear Rovenna,
With talk of donna and duenna,
You came too from that hemisphere,
But freighted with quite other cheer: 150
No pedant, no!" Then, changing free,
Laughed with a light audacity:
"Well, me for one, dame Judah here
Don't much depress: she's not austere—
Nature has lodged her in good zone—   155
The true wine-zone of Noah: the Cape
Yields no such bounty of the grape.
Hence took King Herod festal tone;
Else why the tavern-cluster gilt
Hang out before that fane he built,   160
The second temple?" Catching thus
A buoyant frolic impetus,
He bowled along: "Herewith agrees
The ducat of the Maccabees,
Graved with the vine. Methinks I see   165
The spies from Eshcol, full of glee
Trip back to camp with clusters swung
From jolting pole on shoulders hung:
'Cheer up, 'twill do; it needs befit;
Lo ye, behold the fruit of it!'   170
And, tell me, does not Solomon's harp
(Oh, that it should have taken warp
In end!) confirm the festa? Hear:
'Thy white neck is like ivory;
I feed among thy lilies, dear: 175
Stay me with flagons, comfort me

With apples; thee would I enclose!
Thy twin breasts are as two young roes.' "

   Clarel protested, yet as one
Part lamed in candor; and took tone   180
In formal wise: "Nay, pardon me,
But you misdeem it: Solomon's Song
Is allegoric—needs must be."
    "Proof, proof, pray, if 'tis not too long."
"Why, Saint Bernard——"
                  "Who? *Sir* Bernard?   185
Never that knight for me left caul!"
    "No, *Saint* Bernard, 'twas he of old
The Song's hid import first unrolled—
Confirmed in every after age:
The chapter-headings on the page   190
Of modern Bibles (in that Song)
Attest his rendering, and prolong:
A mystic burden."
              "Eh? so too
The Bonzes Hafiz' rhyme construe
Which lauds the grape of Shiraz. See,   195
They cant that in his frolic fire
Some bed-rid fakir would aspire
In foggy symbols. Me, oh me!—
What stuff of Levite and Divine!
Come, look at straight things more in line,   200
Blue eyes or black, which like you best?
Your Bella Donna, how's she dressed?"
    'Twas very plain this sprightly youth
Little suspected the grave truth
That he, with whom he thus made free,   205
A student was, a student late
Of reverend theology:
Nor Clarel was displeased thereat.
    The other now: "There is no tress
Can thrall one like a Jewess's.   210
A Hebrew husband, Hebrew-wed,

Is wondrous faithful, it is said;
Which needs be true; for, I suppose,
As bees are loyal to the rose,
So men to beauty. Of his girls,   215
On which did the brown Indian king,
Ahasuerus, shower his pearls?
Why, Esther: Judah wore the ring.
And Nero, captain of the world,
His arm about a Jewess curled—   220
Bright spouse, Poppæa. And with good will
Some Christian monarchs share the thrill,
In palace kneeling low before
Crowned Judah, like those nobs of yore.
These Hebrew witches! well-a-day,   225
Of Jeremiah what reck they?"

Clarel looked down: was he depressed?
The prodigal resumed: "Earth's best,
Earth's loveliest portrait, daintiest,
Reveals Judæan grace and form: 230
Urbino's ducal mistress fair—
Ay, Titian's Venus, golden-warm.
Her lineage languishes in air
Mysterious as the unfathomed sea:
That grave, deep Hebrew coquetry!   235
Thereby Bathsheba David won;
In bath a purposed bait!—Have done!—
Blushing? The cuticle's but thin!
Blushing? yet you my mind would win.
Priests make a goblin of the Jew: 240
Shares he not flesh with me—with you?"
    What wind was this? And yet it swayed
Even Clarel's cypress. He delayed
All comment, gazing at him there.
Then first he marked the clustering hair   245
Which on the bright and shapely brow
At middle part grew slantly low:
Rich, tumbled, chestnut hood of curls,

Like to a Polynesian girl's,
Who, inland eloping with her lover,   250
The deacon-magistrates recover—
With sermon and black bread reprove
Who fed on berries and on love.
    So young (thought Clarel) yet so knowing;
With much of dubious at the heart,   255
Yet winsome in the outward showing;
With whom, with what, hast thou thy part?
In flaw upon the student's dream
A wafture of suspicion stirred:
He spake: "The Hebrew, it would seem,   260
You study much; you have averred
More than most Gentiles well may glean
In voyaging mere from scene to scene
Of shifting traffic." Irksomeness
Here vexed the other's light address;   265
But, ease assuming, gay he said:
"Oh, in my wanderings, why, I've met,
Among all kinds, Hebrews well-read,
And some nor dull nor bigot-bred;
Yes, I pick up, nor all forget."   270
    So saying, and as to be rid
Of further prosing, he undid
His vesture, turned him, smoothed his cot:
"Late, late; needs sleep, though sleep's a sot."
    "A word," cried Clarel: "bear with me: 275
Just nothing strange at all you see
Touching the Hebrews and their lot?"
    Recumbent here: "Why, yes, they share
That oddity the Gypsies heir:
About *them* why not make ado?   280
The Parsees are an odd tribe too;
Dispersed, no country, and yet hold
By immemorial rites, we're told.
Amigo, do not scourge me on;
Put up, put up your monkish thong!   285
Pray, pardon now; by peep of sun

Take horse I must. Good night, with song:

> "Lights of Shushan, if your urn
>   Mellow shed the opal ray,
> To delude one—damsels, turn,   290
>   Wherefore tarry? why betray?
>   Drop your garlands and away!
> Leave me, phantoms that but feign;
> Sting me not with inklings vain!
>
> "But, if magic none prevail,   295
>   Mocking in untrue romance;
> Let your Paradise exhale
>   Odors; and enlink the dance;
>   And, ye rosy feet, advance
> Till ye meet morn's ruddy Hours   300
> Unabashed in Shushan's bowers!"

No more: they slept. A spell came down;
And Clarel dreamed, and seemed to stand
Betwixt a Shushan and a sand;
The Lyonese was lord of one,   305
The desert did the Tuscan own,
The pale pure monk. A zephyr fanned;
It vanished, and he felt the strain
Of clasping arms which would detain
His heart from such ascetic range.   310
He woke; 'twas day; he was alone,
The Lyonese being up and gone:
Vital he knew organic change,
Or felt, at least, that change was working—
A subtle innovator lurking.   315
   He rose, arrayed himself, and won
The roof to take the dawn's fresh air,
And heard a ditty, and looked down.
Who singing rode so debonair?
His cell-mate, flexible young blade,   320
Mounted in rear of cavalcade

Just from the gate, in rythmic way
Switching a light malacca gay:

    "Rules, who rules?
  Fools the wise, makes wise the fools—   325
    Every ruling overrules?
  Who the dame that keeps the house,
    Provides the diet, and oh, so quiet,
  Brings all to pass, the slyest mouse?
      Tell, tell it me: 330
  Signora Nature, who but she!"

EPILOGUE
Book IV, Canto 35

If Luther's day expand to Darwin's year,
Shall that exclude the hope—foreclose the fear?

  Unmoved by all the claims our times avow,
The ancient Sphinx still keeps the porch of shade;
And comes Despair, whom not her calm may cow,   5
And coldly on that adamantine brow
Scrawls undeterred his bitter pasquinade.
But Faith (who from the scrawl indignant turns)
With blood warm oozing from her wounded trust,
Inscribes even on her shards of broken urns   10
The sign o' the cross—*the spirit above the dust!*

  Yea, ape and angel, strife and old debate—
The harps of heaven and dreary gongs of hell;
Science the feud can only aggravate—
No umpire she betwixt the chimes and knell: 15
The running battle of the star and clod
Shall run forever—if there be no God.

  Degrees we know, unknown in days before;
The light is greater, hence the shadow more;
And tantalized and apprehensive Man   20

Appealing—Wherefore ripen us to pain?
Seems there the spokesman of dumb Nature's train.
   But through such strange illusions have they passed
Who in life's pilgrimage have baffled striven—
Even death may prove unreal at the last,   25
And stoics be astounded into heaven.

   Then keep thy heart, though yet but ill-resigned—
Clarel, thy heart, the issues there but mind;
That like the crocus budding through the snow—
That like a swimmer rising from the deep—   30
That like a burning secret which doth go
Even from the bosom that would hoard and keep;
Emerge thou mayst from the last whelming sea,
And prove that death but routs life into victory.

                                  1876

PART SEVEN

PROSE & POEM: *JOHN MARR,*
AND OTHERS

In the nine years following *Clarel* (1876), Melville continued to work for the U.S. Customs House in New York City. Advancing in age and all but forgotten, he nevertheless continued writing. Retirement in 1885 allowed him to reassemble some of his poems into clusters and issue them as books in highly limited numbers. But the books were only a sample of his work in progress.

John Marr and Other Sailors with Some Sea-Pieces (1888) gathers several elegiac character studies of seamen, reminiscent of the joy and death of past exploits. The book's title piece is a "prose & poem" portrait of the alienated artist who fantasizes about lost friends. Also included are over a dozen "Sea-Pieces," such as Melville's chilling "The Maldive Shark," the equally unsettling images of shipwreck in "The Berg" and "The Aeolian Harp," and the seemingly innocuous "Pebbles," seven concluding epigrams that crystallize Melville's lifelong obsession with the "inhuman sea."

Melville created other prose & poem works similar to "John Marr," which pair off genres and voices as an innovative means of narrative indirection. The most ambitious of these innovations was an intended book now referred to as *The Burgundy Club*, begun as early as 1859 and revised from the mid-1870s on, but never completed. In its introduction ("House of the Tragic Poet"), an unnamed editor reflects on poetry, origination, and publishing, then provides a prose sketch of and brief dedication to the genial Marquis de Grandvin whose tale, "At the Hostelry," he has "methodized" into verse. The poem, a "Symposium" of thirty artists on painting, is Melville's treatise on his aesthetic of the picturesque.

Equally compelling in narrative framing are the rarely printed "Rammon" and "Under the Rose." The poem portion of "Rammon," entitled "The Enviable Isles," appeared in *John Marr* without its prose introduction, which concerns a young prince's fascination with Buddhism. Here both prose and poem portions are reunited in their original format. "Under the Rose" is the comic palavering of a servant whose English master covets a vase but must settle for a Persian poem inspired by it. The train of associations from art object to poem to its translation is a shaggy-dog story with a devastating punch.

FROM JOHN MARR AND OTHER SAILORS WITH SOME SEA-PIECES

JOHN MARR

John Marr, toward the close of the last century born in America of a mother unknown, and from boyhood up to maturity a sailor under divers flags, disabled at last from further maritime life by a crippling wound received at close quarters with pirates of the Keys, eventually betakes himself for a livelihood to less active employment ashore. There, too, he transfers his rambling disposition acquired as a seafarer.

After a variety of removals, at first as a sail-maker from sea-port to sea-port, then adventurously inland as a rough bench-carpenter, he, finally, in the last-named capacity, settles down about the year 1838 upon what was then a frontier-prairie sparsely sprinkled with small oak-groves and yet fewer log-houses of a little colony but recently from one of our elder inland States. Here, putting a period to his rovings, he marries.

Ere long a fever, the bane of new settlements on teeming loam, and whose sallow livery was certain to show itself, after an interval, in the complexions of too many of these people, carries off his young wife and infant child. In one coffin put together by his own hands they are committed with meagre rites to the earth:—another mound, though a small one, in the wide prairie, nor far from where the Mound-Builders of a race only conjecturable had left their pottery and bones, one common clay, under a strange terrace serpentine in form.

With an honest stillness in his general mien; swarthy, and black-browed; with eyes that could soften or flash, but never harden, yet disclosing at times a melancholy depth, this kinless man had affections which, once placed, not readily could be dislodged, or resigned to a substituted object. Being now arrived at middle life he resolves never to quit the soil that holds the only beings ever connected with him by love in the family-tie. His log-house he lets to a new-comer, one glad enough to get it, and dwells with the household.

While the acuter sense of his bereavement becomes mollified by time, the void at heart abides. Fain, if possible, would he fill that void by cultivating social relations yet nearer than before, with a people whose lot he purposes sharing to the end—relations superadded to that mere work-a-day bond arising from participation in the same outward hardships making reciprocal helpfulness a matter of course. But here, and nobody to blame, he is obstructed.

More familiarly to consort, men of a practical turn must sympathetically converse, and upon topics of real life. But, whether as to persons or events, one can not always be talking about the present; much less, speculating about the future; one must needs recur to the past; which, with the mass of men, where the past is in any personal way a common inheritance, supplies, to most practical natures, the basis of sympathetic communion.

But the past of John Marr was not the past of these pioneers. Their hands had rested on the plough-tail; his upon the ship's helm. They knew but their own kind and their own usages; to him had been revealed something of the checkered globe. So limited unavoidably was the mental reach, and by consequence the range of sympathy, in this particular band of domestic emigrants, hereditary tillers of the soil, that the ocean, but a hearsay to their fathers, had now, through yet deeper inland removal, become to themselves little more than a rumor traditional and vague.

They were a staid people; staid through habituation to monotonous hardship; ascetics by necessity not less than through moral bias; nearly all of them sincerely, however narrowly, religious. They were kindly at need, after their fashion. But to a man wonted—as John Marr in his previous homeless sojournings could not but have been—to the free-and-easy tavern-clubs affording cheap recreation of an evening in certain old and comfortable sea-port towns of that time, and yet more familiar with the companionship afloat of the sailors of the same period, something was lacking. That something was geniality, the flower of life springing from some sense of joy in it, more or less. This their lot could not give to these hard-working endurers of the dispiriting malaria, men to whom a holiday never came; and they had too much of uprightness and no art at all or desire to affect what they did not really feel. At a corn-husking, their least grave of gatherings, did the lone-hearted mariner seek to divert his own thoughts from sadness, and in some degree interest theirs, by adverting to aught removed from the crosses and trials of their personal surroundings, naturally enough he would slide into some marine story or picture; but would soon recoil upon himself, and be silent; finding no encouragement to proceed. Upon one such occasion an elderly man—a blacksmith, and at Sunday gatherings an earnest exhorter, honestly said to him, "Friend, we know nothing of that here."

Such unresponsiveness in one's fellow creatures set apart from factitious life, and by their vocation—in those days little helped by machinery—standing, as it were, next of kin to Nature; this, to John Marr, seemed of a piece with the apathy of Nature herself as envisaged to him here on a prairie where none but the perished Mound-Builders had as yet left a durable mark.

The remnant of Indians thereabout—all but exterminated in their recent and final war with regular white troops, a war waged by the Red Men for their native soil and natural rights, had been coerced into the occupancy of wilds not very far beyond the Mississippi;—wilds *then*, but now the seats of municipalities and states. Prior to that, the bisons, once streaming countless in processional herds, or browsing as in an endless battle-line over these vast aboriginal pastures, had retreated, dwindled in number, before the hunters, in main a race distinct from the agricultural pioneers, though generally their advance-guard. Such a double exodus of man and beast left the plain a desert, green or blossoming indeed, but almost as forsaken as the Siberian Obi. Save the prairie-hen, sometimes startled from its lurking-place in the rank grass; and, in their migratory season, pigeons, high overhead on the wing, in dense multitudes eclipsing the day like a passing storm-cloud; save these—there being no wide woods with their underwood—birds were strangely few.

Blank stillness would for hours reign unbroken on this prairie. "It is the bed of a dried-up sea," said the companionless sailor—no geologist—to himself, musing at twilight upon the fixed undulations of that immense alluvial expanse bounded only by the horizon, and missing there the stir that, to alert eyes and ears, animates at all times the apparent solitudes of the deep.

But a scene quite at variance with one's antecedents may yet prove suggestive of them. Hooped round by a level rim, the prairie was to John Marr a reminder of ocean.

With some of his former shipmates, *chums* on certain cruises, he had contrived, prior to this last and more remote removal, to keep up a little correspondence at odd intervals. But from tidings of anybody or any sort, he, in common with the other settlers, was now cut off; quite cut off except from such news as might be conveyed over the grassy billows by the last-arrived prairie-schooner; the vernacular term in those parts and times for the emigrant-wagon arched high over with sail-cloth, and voyaging across the vast champaign. There was no reachable post-office; as yet, not even the rude little receptive box with lid and leathern hinges set up at convenient intervals, on a stout stake along some solitary green way, affording a perch for birds; and which, later in the unintermitting advance of the frontier, would perhaps decay into a mossy monument, attesting yet another successive overleaped limit of civilized life; a life which in America can to-day hardly be said to have any western bound but the ocean that washes Asia. Throughout these plains, now in places overpopulous with towns over-opulent; sweeping plains, elsewhere fenced off in every direction into flourishing farms—pale townsmen and hale farmers alike, in part, the descendants of the first sallow settlers; a region that half a century ago produced little for the sustenance of man, but to-day launching its superabundant wheat-harvest on the world; of this prairie, now everywhere intersected with wire and rail, hardly can it be said that at the period here written of there was so much as a traceable road. To the long-distance traveller, the oak groves, wide apart and varying in compass and form; these, with recent settlements, yet more widely separate, offered some landmarks; but otherwise he steered by the sun. In early midsummer, even going but from one log-encampment to the next—a journey, it might be, of hours or good part of a day—travel was much like navigation. In some more enriched depressions between the long green graduated swells, smooth as those of ocean becalmed receiving and subduing to its own tranquility the voluminous surge raised by some far-off hurricane of days previous; here one would catch the first indication of advancing strangers, either in the distance, as a far sail at sea, by the glistening white canvas of the wagon,—the wagon itself wading through the rank vegetation, and hidden by it,—or, failing that, when near to, in the ears of the team, peaking, if not above the tall tiger-lilies, yet above the yet taller grass.

Luxuriant this wilderness. But to its denizen, a friend left behind anywhere in the world, seemed not alone absent to sight, but an absentee from existence.

Though John Marr's shipmates could not all have departed life, yet as subjects of meditation they were like phantoms of the dead. As the growing sense of his environment threw him more and more upon retrospective musings, these phantoms, next to those of his wife and child, became spiritual companions, losing something of their first indistinctness and putting on at last a dim semblance of mute life. And they were lit by that aureola circling over any object of the affections in the past for reunion with which an imaginative heart passionately yearns.

He invokes these visionary ones, striving, as it were, to get into verbal communion with them; or, under yet stronger illusion, reproaching them for their silence:—

Since as in night's deck-watch ye show,
Why, lads, so silent here to me,
Your watchmate of times long ago?

Once, for all the darkling sea,
You your voices raised how clearly,   5
Striking in when tempest sung;
Hoisting up the storm-sail cheerly,
Life is storm—let storm! you rung.
Taking things as fated merely,
Child-like though the world ye spanned;   10
Nor holding unto life too dearly,
Ye who held your lives in hand:
Skimmers, who on oceans four
Petrels were, and larks ashore.

O, not from memory lightly flung,   15
Forgot, like strains no more availing,
The heart to music haughtier strung;

Nay, frequent near me, never staling,
Whose good feeling kept ye young.
Like tides that enter creek or stream,   20
Ye come, ye visit me; or seem
Swimming out from seas of faces,
Alien myriads memory traces,
To enfold me in a dream!

I yearn as ye. But rafts that strain,   25
Parted, shall they lock again?
Twined we were, entwined, then riven,
Ever to new embracements driven,
Shifting gulf-weed of the main!
And how if one here shift no more,   30
Lodged by the flinging surge ashore?

Nor less, as now, in eve's decline,
Your shadowy fellowship is mine.
Ye float around me, form and feature:—
Tattooings, ear-rings, love-locks curled;   35
Barbarians of man's simpler nature,
Unworldly servers of the world.
Yea, present all, and dear to me,
Though shades, or scouring China's sea.

Whither, whither, merchant-sailors,   40
Whitherward now in roaring gales?
Competing still, ye huntsman-whalers,
In leviathan's wake what boat prevails?
And man-of-war's men, whereaway?
If now no dinned drum beat to quarters   45
On the wilds of midnight waters—
Foemen looming through the spray;
Do yet your gangway lanterns, streaming,
Vainly strive to pierce below,
When, tilted from the slant plank gleaming,   50
A brother you see to darkness go?

But, gunmates lashed in shotted canvas,
If where long watch-below ye keep,
Never the shrill *"All hands up hammocks!"*
Breaks the spell that charms your sleep;   55
And summoning trumps might vainly call,
And booming guns implore—
A beat, a heart-beat musters all,
One heart-beat at heart-core.
It musters. But to clasp, retain;   60
To see you at the halyards main—
To hear your chorus once again!

THE ÆOLIAN HARP
AT THE SURF INN

List the harp in window wailing
  Stirred by fitful gales from sea:
Shrieking up in mad crescendo—
  Dying down in plaintive key!

Listen: less a strain ideal   5
  Than Ariel's rendering of the Real.
What that Real is, let hint
  A picture stamped in memory's mint.—

Braced well up, with beams aslant,
Betwixt the continents sails the *Phocion*   10
For Baltimore bound from Alicant.
Blue breezy skies white fleeces fleck
Over the chill blue white-capped ocean:
From yard-arm comes— "Wreck ho, a wreck!"

  Dismasted and adrift,   15
  Long time a thing forsaken;
  Overwashed by every wave
  Like the slumbering kraken;

Heedless if the billow roar,
Oblivious of the lull,   20

Leagues and leagues from shoal or shore,
It swims—a levelled hull:
Bulwarks gone—a shaven wreck,
Nameless, and a grass-green deck.
A lumberman: perchance, in hold   25
Prostrate pines with hemlocks rolled.

It has drifted, waterlogged,
Till by trailing weeds beclogged:
   Drifted, drifted, day by day,
   Pilotless on pathless way.   30
It has drifted till each plank
Is oozy as the oyster-bank:
   Drifted, drifted, night by night,
   Craft that never shows a light;
Nor ever, to prevent worse knell,   35
Tolls in fog the warning bell.
From collision never shrinking,
Drive what may through darksome smother;
Saturate, but never sinking,
Fatal only to the *other*!   40
   Deadlier than the sunken reef
Since still the snare it shifteth,
   Torpid in dumb ambuscade
Waylayingly it drifteth.

   O the sailors—O the sails!   45
   O the lost crews never heard of!
   Well the harp of Ariel wails
   Thoughts that tongue can tell no word of!

THE TUFT OF KELP

All dripping in tangles green,
　Cast up by a lonely sea,
If purer for that, O Weed,
　Bitterer, too, are ye?

THE MALDIVE SHARK

About the Shark, phlegmatical one,
Pale sot of the Maldive sea,
The sleek little pilot-fish, azure and slim,
How alert in attendance be.
From his saw-pit of mouth, from his charnel of maw　　5
They have nothing of harm to dread,
But liquidly glide on his ghastly flank
Or before his Gorgonian head;
Or lurk in the port of serrated teeth
In white triple tiers of glittering gates,　　　　10
And there find a haven when peril's abroad,
An asylum in jaws of the Fates!

They are friends; and friendly they guide him to prey,
Yet never partake of the treat—
Eyes and brains to the dotard lethargic and dull,　　15
Pale ravener of horrible meat.

THE BERG
(A DREAM)

I saw a Ship of martial build
(Her standards set, her brave apparel on)
Directed as by madness mere
Against a stolid Iceberg steer,
Nor budge it, though the infatuate Ship went down.　　5
The impact made huge ice-cubes fall
Sullen, in tons that crashed the deck;

But that one avalanche was all—
No other movement save the foundering wreck.

Along the spurs of ridges pale   10
Not any slenderest shaft and frail,
A prism over glass-green gorges lone,
Toppled; nor lace of traceries fine,
Nor pendant drops in grot or mine
Were jarred, when the stunned Ship went down.   15

Nor sole the gulls in cloud that wheeled
Circling one snow-flanked peak afar,
But nearer fowl the floes that skimmed
And crystal beaches, felt no jar.
No thrill transmitted stirred the lock   20
Of jack-straw needle-ice at base;
Towers undermined by waves—the block

Atilt impending—kept their place.
Seals, dozing sleek on sliddery ledges
Slipt never, when by loftier edges,   25
Through very inertia overthrown,
The impetuous Ship in bafflement went down.

Hard Berg (methought) so cold, so vast,
With mortal damps self-overcast;
Exhaling still thy dankish breath—   30
Adrift dissolving, bound for death;
Though lumpish thou, a lumbering one—
A lumbering lubbard loitering slow,
Impingers rue thee and go down,
Sounding thy precipice below,   35
Nor stir the slimy slug that sprawls
Along thy dense stolidity of walls.

PEBBLES

I

Though the Clerk of the Weather insist,
  And lay down the weather-law,
Pintado and gannet they wist
That the winds blow whither they list
  In tempest or flaw.

II

Old are the creeds, but stale the schools
  Revamped as the mode may veer.
But Orm from the schools to the beaches strays,
And, finding a Conch hoar with time, he delays
  And reverent lifts it to ear.
That Voice, pitched in far monotone,
  Shall it swerve? shall it deviate ever?
The Seas have inspired it, and Truth—
  Truth, varying from sameness never.

III

In hollows of the liquid hills
  Where the long Blue Ridges run,
The flattery of no echo thrills,
  For echo the seas have none;
Nor aught that gives man back man's strain—
The hope of his heart, the dream in his brain.

IV

On ocean where the embattled fleets repair,
Man, suffering inflictor, sails on sufferance there.

V

Implacable I, the old implacable Sea:
  Implacable most when most I smile serene—
Pleased, not appeased, by myriad wrecks in me.

VI

Curled in the comb of yon billow Andean,
　　Is it the Dragon's heaven-challenging crest?
Elemental mad ramping of ravening waters—
　　Yet Christ on the Mount, and the dove in her nest!

VII

Healed of my hurt, I laud the inhuman Sea—
Yea, bless the Angels Four that there convene;
For healed I am even by their pitiless breath
Distilled in wholesome dew named rosmarine.

From The Burgundy Club

House of the Tragic Poet

Upon entering the vestibule of one of the disinterred houses of Pompeii the visitor starts at a large black dog, his chain attached to a spiked collar, in act apparently of fiercely springing upon him. It is a life-like mosaic worked into the pavement. Under it appears the words

CAVE CANEM.

To moderns this abode is known as "The House of the Tragic Poet"; a hypothetical name bestowed by the antiquarians, and probably, because of the gravely dramatic character of certain frescoes on the walls within. But do these pictures justify the name? Originally, this abode was doubtless one of the most elegant in that ancient town. But in no age and nowhere have poets as a class luxuriated in sumptuous lodgement. Moreover, a poet, Pagan or Christian, even the most tragical of his tribe, by nature inclines, in things social, to all the amenities. And would a lover of the social amenities be guilty of so inhospitable a discourtesy as to set Cave Canem in his door-way?

No. I am disposed to think that this Pompeiian mansion, instead of being the residence of a poet was the house of some well-to-do publisher; who, in the device of the dog and motto, was but intent upon scaring away from his premises the unfortunate nuisance of the poetical tyro—with his unsaleable wares. And a very shrewd fellow was that publisher, well knowing the timid and nervous soul of the tyro, and more particularly his trepidation in act of crossing a publisher's threshold for the first time, and wisely inferring that an abrupt encounter there with a fierce black dog, even though a sham dog ferociously straining at him to the extremity of his chain, would so upset the tyro's feeble nervous system, that incontinently he would take to his heels. Why a publisher should have a well-grounded aversion to the tyro, is evident enough, but not equally plain, at least to everybody, is the reason for the poetical tyro's fantastic terror as to publisher, even when the latter refrains from adopting his Pompeiian brother's ingenious device.

But consider. Without the *afflatus* it is in vain to undertake poetry. The afflatus is simply intoxication, more or less. The poem completed, the debauch comes to an end; and the bard's Blue Monday begins. The nerves of the poet are in a shattered condition. And it is in this debilitated state, that in natural sequence to composition the thought of publication comes up, a thought formidable in his dire xxxxx. The shattered tyro is in the predicament of the rural actor who even previous to facing the foot-light is struck with stage fright. The Public, to whom the Publisher is the immediate pilot looms ahead like an unknown island at the ends of the earth to the navigator in darkness seeking a hospitable harbor. Who inhabits yon shore? Best stand boldly in for it. Ah, the temerarious Captain Cook was cooked and served up in his own cocked hat at a clam-bake of the tattooed savages!

Alas, I am merry enough here, but it is the grim merriment of the man who knows how it is himself. Yes, such, as I have attempted to describe, such or similar was the panic that set in upon me, when, in mature life as I am, I, after completing the transcribing and editing of the Pieces contained in this volume, whereof while assuming the responsibility I lay no claim to the authorship, for the first time in my life began to bethink me of publication. Doubtless my fears were heightened by the abrupt contrast between the studious shadowy solitude long habitual to me, and the projected glare of publicity.

You see, good reader, I am making a confidant of you, and that too in matters that another tyro-editor more discreet would very likely keep to himself, seeking to pass himself off as a veteran. But I desire to make a friend of you, and without frankness how accomplish it?

In that anxious uncertainty in which I found myself, I felt the imperative need of some one to inform and council me, and especially some private and not unfriendly eye to look at my manuscript before I ventured upon aught ulterior. For, the worst of it was that I began to suspect my manuscript of not being the thing it had flattered me with being.

"You must hire *somebody*," thought Moliere when he, distrustful of cultivated friends, resolved to try his comedy on his cook, and learn what *she* thought of it. Tho' for me, in my emergency, I had no dame of the spit to appeal to, being a bachelor and in lodgings, I was resolved upon seeking out somebody who should at least possess the presumable candor of the Frenchman's humble critic, even in preference to anybody having nothing but literary qualifications to recommend him. I cast about for such a prodigy and luckily succeeded better than Diogenes in his quest for the Honest Man. He was a mature individual, whom I had known in quite a friendly way as a boy Younker, poor and penniless, a petty shopkeeper's lad, but who, in the end, by dint of pluck and capacity, and alike educated by books and active contact with his fellows had step by step risen to an influential position as a member of the metropolitan press.

He knew all about Popular Opinion and the popular taste. Alike upon his judgement and good-will I thought I could implicitly rely. Nevertheless his first response to my petition was not encouraging. Said he, "It is a ticklish thing, believe me, to decide upon a book in manuscript. Print it and after I have seen what Old Bellwhether thinks of it, then will I give you my discreet opinion in the journal of which I have the honor to be the literary editor."

"Old Bellwhether!" exclaimed I, bewildered and in despair. But he only looked sagacious and said nothing. What is the loneliness of Crusoe, to that horrible solitude in which the literary tyro is thrown, whom the wariness of the wise, throws upon the resource of his own inexperienced judgement.

Whether it was that the expression of my face with some association of old lang syne touched him a little, one can not say, but he presently relented, and said, "O, fish up your heart again, my sweet fellow. I'll make an exception in your case. Let's have it, yes, I'll look it over and tell you about it in a couple of weeks or so."

But before the expiration of that term, chancing to come upon him at the crossing near the statue of the Illustrious Printer which adorns the triangular space in New York, ineptly enough christened by some Anglophilist Printing House Square, I hailed him, notwithstanding my mature years, with the nervous eagerness of a youthful tyro—"Well what think you of it?"

Halted by so sunny a challenge he gathered his thoughts together and after a pause during which he seemed adjusting his rejoinder to an exactitude of conscientious accuracy, sententiously he replied:

"Were I a publisher, I should decline it with thanks."

"Why, what's the matter?" I cried, alarmed at a blunt declaration so little foreseen.

"Well, for one thing, and the main thing, it is not in the current,—as, by the way, we here happen to be. Let us edge out of this crowd."

"But something that is not in the current," I exclaimed, at the same time slipping with him into an open stair-way near by; "something not in the current, something original, is exactly what all publishers clamor for, I am told."

"Exactly. But come to the pinch and they are as shy of it as you would be of a panther that, escaping from a menagerie, should come fawning up to you in the public highway. Besides, my friend, as regards your manuscript, the originality, let me frankly say, is mostly of the negative kind. You tell nothing new. Everybody in these days of minute travel knows all about Naples. Nor is that favorable to a romancer. In the treatment too, as in the theme, there is nothing American. Your very metre is as old as the hills. The time of your main piece, your *piece de resistance,* is laid more than a score of years back, an aeon to the popular mind. Yes, and your method is not that of the photographer—you paint. But worst of all I fail to see that anywhere you have laid an anchor to windward by conciliating the suffrages of the ladies, and in marked preference to those of the men."

Overwhelmed by all this, I could but interrogatingly exclaim—"The ladies?"

"The ladies," he echoed with [the] imperturbable self-possession of a proficient; "what women have always been in the gay world, the arbiters of the social success of men, this have they lately become in the literary sphere, as to every book, the design of which is at all to please."

"Well, well, well," I bitterly exclaimed, "there's Jack Gentian, good fellow as ever lived; there's Monsieur de Marquis, the best friend of man! I must give up the idea of introducing these genial gentlemen to their kind.—But tell me, now that I think of it, you have but advised me as to how a publisher having his eye on the Public might regard the manuscript. But did [it] at all please you yourself, as a private man?"

"Ah, that's quite another thing. Yes, parts of it are pretty good—gave me pleasure—amused me. But my knowledge of literature, not wholly restricted to the saleable books of the day—books of the mode—was a preparitive to the relish. It is otherwise with that peculiar aggregate known in contradistinction to the People as the Public."

"The People, God bless them, always and everywhere have a certain animal good sense and honesty. Feeling themselves to be ignorant as to most matters lying outside of their practical interests, they lay no claim to universal culture. But the Public, on the contrary, thinks itself highly cultivated, yes, and as to everything, nor has it any inkling of suspicions that possibly it may be a bit mistaken here."

"Profound philosophy perhaps," exclaimed I, "but what profit? Ah, you pronounce the death-warrant of the Marquis de Grandvin."

"Stay!" he cried, perhaps anew touched and by something new in my xxxxx pleasantry; "I don't mislike your Marquis. And—and—well I said just now that I as a private man was happily furnished with a fit preparative to the perusal of the stories you edit. Now a thought strikes me. Could people in general be prepared for it, educated up to it—and by some short and easy process, and could the preparative be one with the book itself, bound up with it; why, in that case some moderate success might come, tho mark me I will not guarantee it. But, come. A year or two ago a man in my set, Professor McQuick, benevolently composed a little Primer of first principles for private distribution among the Aristarchi of the pastoral press. But upon reconsideration thinking that in good part it was a shot rather fired over their heads than otherwise, he withheld the printing and distribution, and tossed the manuscript to me. Tho I do not endorse his principles in-toto, nevertheless some of them apply to your manuscript. Others are not so directly applicable. These last, however, can be weeded perhaps, and leave undisturbed the general effect. Pray, you have no preface I think?"

"None—as yet."

"Capital! This same Primer shall be the preface, an entire course of education, the preparative. I will get the Professor's assent and send it to you. Transcribe it just as it is, page it with the rest, and hey! for the publisher. But—" and here he assumed an earnestly admonitory air— "should the verdict be disastrous to you, don't try to find out who the publisher's reader is; and, if you *should* find out, don't go for him, don't assassinate him. I know all about that; it is insufferable."

To close. In all particulars I followed the excellent counsel of my excellent friend; and the present publication, prefaced by the Primer of Professor McQuick, is, thanks to the graciousness of the publisher, the humble result.

THE MARQUIS DE GRANDVIN

A countryman of Lafayette and Bartholdi, this gentleman is not unknown to some Americans, more especially perhaps, to some of us New-Yorkers. He is an honorary member of most of the Fifth Avenue clubs; anything but unwelcome at their chance gatherings, while, at their premeditated banquets his appearance—and he always happily times it—is commonly hailed by a plausive clapping of hands simultaneous with the vocal salutation. But a person of genial temper is not only very likely to be a popular man's man, but also, and beyond that, a favorite with the ladies. For it is something less venial than mere error in the old philosopher penally branded with a horrible name—misogynist, I think—and a soggy soul he must have been; it was something less venial than error in him to say, as he did, that women however apt to that grand passion which makes the one divine rapture of life, have nevertheless a constitutional incapacity for good-fellowship, that is, in the masculine acceptation of the term. Assuredly, Hymen knows, no few of them practically demonstrate their capacity for it. Some musky dew-drops from the Garden, expelled Eve unweetingly carried away quivering in her hair. More than man, she partakes of the paradisiac-spirit, the festal spirit. Under favorable conditions evincing a quicker aptitude to pleasure than man. How alert to twine the garland for the holiday! How instinctively prompt for that faint semblance of Eden, the picnic in the greenwood!

Now there is something in the fine open cheery aspect of the Marquis de Grandvin that conveys a thrill to these frames so exquisitely strung to happiness. Not invariably running the risk of incurring dark looks from their lords, the dames and sisters of the Benedicts of the clubs, at their balls and parties, cast upon the Marquis that kindled merry glance, which, according to the old French Epic whose theme is Roncesvalles the ladies bestowed upon Roland; not alone smitten by the fame and taken with the person of that noble accredited nephew of Charlemagne, but rightly inferring him to be not more a David against the Saracen than a champion against still more flagitious infidels, impugners of the sex. Yes, it is by instinct that all superior women recognize in this gentleman a cordial friend. Nor do they approve him the less for his friendly alliance with his charming sphere. This is a verity not out of keeping with another, namely, this feminine appreciation of the Marquis, gracious though it be, hardly extends to such of his qualities as partake of the *Grand Style*, as one may say, the highly elevated style; a style apparently demanding for its due appreciation, a robust habit, in short the masculine habit. For the most part, it is for his less exalted qualities, that the ladies approve De Grandvin. They approve him for the way in which he contributes to those amenities and gaieties in which the sexes upon common ground participate, and wherein, thanks to their gallantry of good nature, the countrymen of the Marquis de Grandvin have always excelled.

The foregoing hints as to what is the standing in America, or at least among some of us Americans, of the genial foreigner here ushered into a regard less exclusive; *that,* by patriotic intention goes before the recital that not alone in his own *Sweet France* are the blended suavity and power of his genius estimated at their just rate, but that in the high circles of every European capital he is received with even more than good-will.

Though the subject of this sketch, De Grandvin, be a patrician of hereditary mark, he was not consulted in the matter of his progenitors. At any rate, his cosmopolitan sympathies, transcending his class, go out to mankind. Under auspicious circumstances make his acquaintance, and whatever your degree in the social scale, you will find him friendly company, cordial and frank; without condescension, a solemn popery he never was guilty of.

As to his title, if here he be introduced as *The Marquis,* it is only because his troops of friends on both sides of the water, not excluding even the Levellers among them, insist upon retaining for him an inherited prefix which he himself long ago renounced; and doubtless for the reason that any appellative at all savoring of arbitrary rank is unsuitable to a man of liberal catholic mind.

In defence of their insistent employment of the title, a caprice hardly compatible with their political principles, the Levellers of his acquaintance, candid in inconsistency, freely admit that somehow there is something in it felicitously befitting the innately noble character of De Grandvin.

Though not so plentiful as our peaches in a good year, there are men of that noble quality that for being in their company enriches and mellows one. The wisdom they by contact give out is not celibate and sterile like Solomon's, but wedded to enjoyment, and hence productive. They would seem to be a confirmation of the otherwise disputable maxim of Spinoza, that every advance in joy implies an ascent in the scale of intelligence and capability. The influence of such a man insensibly disposes one to gentle charities, brave conceptions, heroic virtues. They are a suggestion of the potentialities in the unvitiated Adam, a creature, according to hallowed authority originally created but a little lower than the angels. Almost invariably these men have physical beauty; and the moral charm is in keeping with that, apparently, a spontaneous emanation from it. It is as golden wine down in a golden chalice, where, seen through the lustre suffusing the shadow the delicious fluid looks to be the exuded gathered sap of the precious metal.

It was of the Marquis de Grandvin that the landscape painter, B. Hobbema Brown, an inoffensive sort of theoretical misanthrope, with a treacherous flaw of lovingkindness in him—to borrow one of his own eccentric phrases; the same B. Hobbema who, returning in moonlight from a choice assemblage where he had been introduced to him and undergone the inevitable fascination of the contact; it was of him that Brown enthusiastically exclaimed to his companions, "What a god-send to meet such a man! He is a set-off against the battalions of his contraries. Between you and me, mankind taken in the lump, are the gods' job-lot. But, by heaven, the race that can produce a Marquis de Grandvin is not promiscuously to be contemned."

See there how the talismanic something in the sort of nature here indicated can operate upon another nature though of a temper not favorably disposed to receive its benign influence.

In the casual outcome of such a character gay fancies, and suggestions without stint, sallies of wit and *bon-homme*, all sharing more or less in a certain lyric glow; herein the spiritual bounty to us would seem to be an unconsciousness in the almoner, involving too an indifference or unconcern as to who may appropriate, or as to what purpose the appropriation may be applied. In this particular, what recks the Marquis de Grandvin, for example? He is the ripe peach-tree shedding its abundance, careless of the garner; he is the Prince of Golconda at the ball, some of whose innumerable diamond-buttons drop off from his raiment unheeded by him in the chance fleeting rubs and collisions of the dance. But how transitory these prodigal improvident ones can prove! And, once gone, how soon all but good as forgotten!

True, were an example here demanded, one adapted for popular illustration, not readily could it be supplied. Literature will not furnish it, since these natures never directly expressing themselves in literature, have no memorial place in its records. Neither are they Alexanders and Napoleons that the fame which is all but independent of literature should trumpet them. Nevertheless, in local tradition and comparatively recent I do find a citeable instance which tho' below the grade say of a De Grandvin, and but in a minor way to the purpose may perhaps for those reasons serve the better to actualize the general truth, in a measure bring it home.

Rufus Choate the Boston advocate when inspired to his best before an audience, how he exhilarated and elevated, and transported! But he is gone, and all those fine fire-works of elfish passion and wit, where are they? Vainly in the hushed Ceramicus of the libraries will you seek any enduring monument of that oratorical pyrotechnist. As well ransack the museums of Natural History for the bottled-up tail of Encke's comet. What shall we say then? Are there natures strong to draw and enthrall yet whose influence is like that of the magnet, only operative as a bodily presence? Yes, withdraw the magnet, and all is over. And holds this true as to the Marquis de Grandvin?

Yea, and shall he also at last vanish, sailing into the boundless Nil, leaving no phosphorescent wake or magic moon-glade behind? Shall naught remain of his cherub-sparkle and spirit? nothing of all those ineffable qualities that make him what Raphael, Milton's affable archangel, would be seen to be were he commissioned hither to dissuade mankind from ever perpetrating an inhumanity or a pun? And O, thou Admirable Crichton, nay, a thousand fold more admirable than he, for art thou not kindly as wise? of all thy more sustained sallies of bright fantasy and humor, let alone thy erratic coruscations, shall nothing be chrystalized into permanence? Nothing at last remain of our Lord Bountiful but the empty larder and void dusty bin. When we laud thee departed, shall the infidel twit us with—What were his assets? If the very plenitude and variety of thy shining gifts, and the preoccupation of thy social charm, if these indispose thee to drudge it as an "author," or operate as disqualifications; will no painstaking aspirant for the literary fame, essay the task of methodizing thee, or some little segment of thee, into the literary form? But even thy foremost disciple, Jack Gentian, though out of humble emulation he strive to follow thy devious footing; yet thy brow is among the stars; he ventures not to lift his head to thy height.

But I—ah, brimmed with thy genial flood—I, here, in the small hours, not long returned from a richer than Plato's "Banquet," where thou didst pour from thy cornucopia with a hand redundant as that of Millet's seed-sower, the profusion of thy good things; I, audacious that I am, resolved upon an emprise.

The Marquis, methought, tho' glorious, is not of the gods, the more reproach to their synod; but I will make them yield a place for him on their golden benches; I will make him an Immortal! How? Monumentalize him to the remotest posterity in a book fragrant as violets, yet lasting as the Pyramid!

Yes, and as the prophets of old, announcing the mind of their deity, in some instances dramatically put on his personality, even so will I assume that of De Grandvin. How otherwise indeed? since he it is that kindles me, inspires me, usurps me. I will snatch at those themes,—New Italy and the Old Masters,—whereon this very night we heard him so sportively romance; I will render the fine festivity of his tone; as well as the loftier touch; catch the rhythm of the waves of his seas of invention; swim out there; in short, I did by implication, say to myself an insane thing—I will imitate the inimitable!

The issue of the temerarious resolve, how humiliating! And no wonder. The inordinate aim, and the inadequate achievement! The soaring ambition of the balloon, and its abrupt drop at a fatal puncture!

Ye who have basked in the vital beams of the Marquis, place not in contrast his own radiant aspect side by side with the dim delineation of him in the preceding sketch. And, for the attempted rendering of his thought and style in the Piece to follow, take charitable example from the Persian, who in his comment upon the Icelandic version of the fervid orientalisms of Sadi and Hafiz, made humane allowances for the inherent difficulties and presumably numb fingers of the translator in penning it.

To M. DE GRANDVIN

Pardon me, Monsieur, if in the following sally I have endeavored, to methodize into literary form, and make consecutive, upon one of your favorite themes, something at least of that desultory wit, gaiety, knowledge and invention, so singularly yours; qualities evinced at their happiest upon convivial occasions, among company wholly congenial, more especially the worshipful guild of poets and artists, the confraternity of Asaph the Singer and the brethren of the Guild of St. Luke, of which worshipful order, as you are aware, I am an acolyte member.

It was not till the afflatus had left me, and I was calmly reviewing the inspired sheets that to my no small astonishment I perceived that so completely had your spirit possessed me that this possession in effect amounted to an impersonation of you. But since, peradventure, this may serve to vivify the work, you will let it pass, nor demur at my maintaining the fable in certain captions to the Parts.

Adieu, Monsieur. I would not longer detain to myself a guest who being the life of every company he enters, is so largely in social demand on these shores; a signal instance of that cordial good-will which every American entertains for the countrymen of Lafayette and Bartholdi.

Vive la France!

AT THE HOSTELRY

Be Borgia Pope, be Bomba King
The roses blow, the song-birds sing.

I

Not wanting in the traditional suavity of his countrymen, the Marquis makes his salutation. Thereafter, with an ulterior design, entering upon a running retrospect touching Italian affairs.

> Candid eyes in open faces
> Clear, not keen, no narrowing line;
> Hither turn your favoring graces
> Now the cloth is drawn for wine.

> In best of worlds if all's not bright,
> Allow, the shadow's chaced by light,

5

Though rest for neither yet may be.
And beauty's charm, where Nature reigns,
Nor crimes nor codes may quite subdue,
As witness Naples long in chains   10
Exposed dishevelled by the sea—
Ah, so much more her beauty drew,
Till Savoy's red-shirt Perseus flew
And cut that fair Andromeda free.

Then Fancy flies. Nor less the trite   15
Matter-of-fact transcends her flight:
A rail-way train took Naples' town;
But Garibaldi sped thereon:
This movement's rush sufficing there
To rout King Fanny, Bomba's heir,   20
Already stuffing trunks and hampers,
At news that from Sicilia passed—
The banished Bullock from the Pampas
Trampling the royal levies massed.
And, later: *He has swum the Strait,*   25
And in Calabria making head,
Cheered by the peasants garlanded,
Pushes for Naples' nearest gate.
From that red Taurus plunging on
With lowered horns and forehead dun,   30
Shall matadors save Bomba's son?
He fled. And her Redeemer's banners
Glad Naples greeted with strown flowers
Hurrahs and secular hosannas
That fidgety made all tyrant Powers.   35

Ye halls of history, arched by time,
Founded in fate, enlarged by crime,
Now shines like phosphorus scratched in dark
'Gainst your grimed walls the luminous mark
Of one who in no paladin age   40
Was knightly—him who lends a page
Now signal in time's recent story

Where scarce in vogue are "Plutarch's men,"
And jobbers deal in popular glory.—
But he the hero was a sword   45
Whereto at whiles Cavour was guard.
The point described a fiery arc,
A swerve of wrist ordained the mark.
Wise statesmanship, a ruling star
Made peace itself subserve the war.   50

In forging into fact a dream—
For dream it was, a dream for long—
Italia disenthralled and one,
Above her but the Alps—no thong
High flourished, held by Don or Hun;   55
Italia, how cut up, divided
Nigh paralysed, by cowls misguided;
Locked as in Chancery's numbing hand,
Fattening the predatory band
Of shyster-princes, whose ill sway   60
Still kept her a calamitous land;
In ending this, spite cruel delay,
And making, in the People's name,
Of Italy's disunited frame,
A unit and a telling State   65
Participant in the world's debate;
Few deeds of arms, in fruitful end,
The statecraft of Cavour transcend.
What towns with alien guards that teemed
Attest Art's Holy Land redeemed.   70

Slipt from the Grand Duke's gouty tread,
Florence, fair flower up-lifts the head.
Ancona, plucked from Peter's Chair,
With all the Papal fiefs in band,
Her Arch Imperial now may wear   75
For popular triumph and command.
And Venice: there the Croatian horde
Swagger no more with clattering sword

Ruffling the doves that dot the Square.
In Rome no furtive cloaked one now   80
Scribbles his gibe on Pasquin's brow,
Since wag his tongue at Popes who may
The Popedom needs endure his say.
But (happier) feuds with princelings cease,
The *People* federate a peace.   85
Cremona fiddles, blithe to see
Contentious cities comrades free.
Sicilia—Umbria—muster in
Their towns in squads, and hail Turin.
One state, one flag, one sword, one crown,   90
Till time build higher or Cade pull down.

Counts this for much? Well, more is won.
Brave public works are schemed or done.
Swart Tiber, dredged, may rich repay—
The Pontine Marsh, too, drained away.   95
And, far along the Tuscan shore
The weird Maremma reassume
Her ancient tilth and wheaten plume.
Ay, to reclaim Ansonia's land
The Spirit o' the Age he'll take a hand.   100
He means to dust each bric-a-brac city,
Pluck the feathers from all banditti;
The Pope he'll hat, and, yea or nay ye,
Modernize even poor old Pompeii!
Concede, accomplished aims unite   105
With many a promise hopeful and as bright.

II

Effecting a counterturn, the Marquis evokes—and from the Shades, as would seem—an inconclusive debate as to the exact import of a current term significant of that one of the manifold aspects of life and nature which under various forms all artists strive to transmit to canvas. A term, be it added, whereof the lexicons give definitions more lexicographical than satisfactory.

Ay, but the *Picturesque,* I wonder—
The *Picturesque* and *Old Romance!*
May these conform and share advance
With Italy and the world's career?
At little suppers, where I'm one,   5
My artist-friends this question ponder
When ale goes round; but, in brave cheer
The vineyards yield, they'll beading run
Like Arethusa burst from ground.
Ay, and in lateral freaks of gamesome wit   10
Moribund Old Romance irreverent twit.
"Adieu, rosettes!" sighs Steen in way
Of fun convivial, frankly gay,
"Adieu, rosettes and *point-de-vise!*—
All garnish strenuous time refuse;   15
In peacocks' tails put out the eyes!
Utility reigns—Ah, well-a-way!—
And bustles along in Bentham's shoes.
For the Picturesque—suffice, suffice
The picture that fetches a picturesque price!"   20

Less jovial ones propound at start,
"Your Picturesque in what inheres?
In nature point, in life, in art
Where the essential thing appears.
First settle that, we'll then take up   25
Your prior question."
                "Well, so be,"
Says Frater Lippi, who but he—
Exchanging late in changeable weather
The cowl for the cap, a cap and feather;   30
With wicked eye then twinkling fun,
Suppressed in friendly decorous tone,
"Here's Spagnoletto. He, I trow
Can best avail here, and bestead.—
Come then, hidalgo, what sayst thou?   35
The *Picturesque*—an example yield."
The man invoked, a man of brawn

Tho' stumpt in stature, raised his head
From sombre musings, and revealed
A brow by no blest angel sealed,   40
And mouth at corners droopt and drawn;
And, catching but the last words, said
"The Picturesque?—Have ye not seen
My Flaying of St. Bartholomew—
My Laurence on the gridiron lean?   45
There's Picturesque; and done as well
As old Giotto's *Damned in Hell*
At Pisa in the Campo Santa."
They turn hereat. In merriment
Ironic jeers the juniors vent,   50
"That's modest now, one hates a vaunter."
But Lippi: "Why not Guido cite
In *Herod's Massacre?*" weening well
The *Little Spaniard's* envious spite
Guido against, as gossips tell.   55
The sombrous one igniting here
And piercing Lippi's mannered mien
Flared up volcanic.—Ah, too clear,
At odds are furious and serene.

Misliking Lippi's mischievous eye   60
As much as Spagnoletto's mood,
And thinking to put unpleasantness by,
Swanvelt spake, that Dutchman good:
"Friends, but the Don errs not so wide.
Like beauty strange with horror allied,—   65
As shown in great Leonardo's head
Of snaky Medusa,—so as well
Grace and the Picturesque may dwell
With Terror. Vain here to divide—
The Picturesque has many a side.   70
For me, I take to Nature's scene
Some scene select, set off serene
With any tranquil thing you please—
A crumbling tower, a shepherd piping.

My master, sure, with this agrees,"   75
His turned appeal on Claude here lighting.
But he, the mildest tempered swain
And eke discreetest too, may be,
That ever came out from Lorraine
To lose himself in Arcady   80
(Sweet there to be lost, as some have been,
And find oneself in losing e'en)
To Claude no pastime, none, nor gain
Wavering in theory's wildering maze;
Better he likes, though sunny he,   85
To haunt the Arcadian woods in haze,
Intent shy charms to win or ensnare,
Beauty his Daphne, he the pursuer there.

So naught he said, whate'er he felt,
Yet friendly nodded to Swanevelt.   90

III

With all the ease of a Prince of the Blood gallantly testifying in behalf
of an indiscreet lady the Marquis incontinently fibs, laying the cornerstone of a Munchausen fable—

But you, ye pleasant faces wise
Saluted late, your candid eyes
Methinks ye rub them in surprise:
"What's this? Jan Steen and Lippi? Claude?
Long since they embarked for Far Abroad!   5
Have met them, you?"
                    "Indeed have I!
Ma foi! The immortals never die;
They are not so weak, they are not so craven;
They keep time's sea and skip the haven.—   10
Well, letting minor memories go:
With other illustrious ones in row
I met them once at that brave tavern
Founded by the first Delmonico,
Forefather of a flourishing line!   15

'Twas all in off-hand easy way—
Pour passer le temps, as loungers say.
In upper chamber did we sit
The dolts below never dreaming it.
The cloth was drawn—we left alone,   20
No solemn lackeys looking on.
In wine's meridian, halcyon noon,
Beatitude excludes elation.

Thus for a while. Anon ensues
All round their horizon, ruddying it,   25
Such Lights Auroral, mirth and wit—
Thy flashes, O Falernian Muse!

IV

After a little bye-scene between Van Dyke, and Franz Hals of Mech-
lin, an old topic is by the company, here and there, discussed anew. In
which rambling talk Adrian Brouwer, tickled undesignedly by two
chance-words from a certain grandee of artists, and more waggish than
polite in addressing Carlo Dolce and Rembrandt, whimsically delivers his
mind.

'Twas Hals began. He to Vandyck,
In whose well-polished gentle mien
The practiced courtier of Kings was seen:
"Van, how, pray, do these revels strike?
Once you'd have me to England—there   5
Riches to get at St. James's. Nay—
Patronage! 'Gainst that flattering snare,
The more if it lure from hearth away,
Old friends—old vintages carry the day!"
Whereto Vandyck, in silken dress   10
Not smoother than his courteousness
Smiled back, "Well, Franz, go then thy ways;
Thy pencil anywhere earns thee praise,
If not heapt gold.—But hark the chat!"
" 'Tis gay," said Hals, not deaf to that,   15
"And witty should be. O' the cup,

Wit rises in exhalation up!"
And sympathetic viewed the scene.
Then, turning, with yet livelier mien,
"More candid than kings, less coy than the Graces,   20
The pleasantness, Van, of these festival faces!—
But what's the theme?"
      The theme was bent—
Be sure, in no dry argument—
On the Picturesque, what 'tis,—its essence,   25
Fibre and root, bud, efflorescence,
Congenial soil, and where at best;
Till, drawing attention from the rest,
Some syllables dropt from Tintoretto,
Negligent dropt; with limp lax air   30
One long arm lolling over chair,
Nor less evincing latent nerve
Potential lazing in reserve.
For strong he was—the dyer's son,
A leonine strength, no strained falsetto—   35
The *Little Tinto*, Tintoretto,
Yes, Titan work by him was done.
And now as one in Art's degree
Superior to his topic—he:

"This *Picturesque* is scarce my care,   40
But note it now in Nature's work—
A thatched hut settling, rotting trees
Mossed over. Some decay must lurk:
In florid things but small its share.
You'll find it in Rome's squalid Ghetto,   45
In Algiers at the lazaretto,
In many a grimy slimy lair."

"Well put!" cried Brouwer with ruddled face,
His wine-stained vesture,—hardly new,—
Buttoned with silver florins true;   50
"*Grime* mark and *slime!*—Squirm not, *Sweet Charles,*"
Slyly, in tone mellifluous

Addressing Carlo Dolce thus,
Fidgety in shy fellowship,
Fastidious even to finger-tip,   55
And dainty prim; "In Art the stye
Is quite inodorous. Here am I:
I don't paint *smells,* no no, no no,
No more than Huysum here, whose touch
In pinks and tulips takes us so;   60
But haunts that reek may harbor much;
Hey, Teniers? Give us boors at inns,
Mud floor—dark settles—jugs—old bins,
Under rafters foul with fume that blinks
From logs too soggy much to blaze   65
Which yet diffuse an umberish haze
That beautifies the grime, methinks."
To Rembrandt then: "Your sooty stroke!
'Tis you, old sweep, believe in smoke."
But he, reserved in self-control,   70
Jostled by that convivial droll,
Seemed not to hear, nor silence broke.

V

One of the greater Dutchman dirges the departed three-deckers of De
Ruyter and Van Tromp. To divert from which monody, a Lesser Master
verbally hits off a kitchen-dresser, and in such sort as to evoke commen-
dation from one of the Grand Masters, who nevertheless proposes a certain transmuting enhancement in the spirit of the latter's own florid and
allegoric style.

Here Van der Velde, who dreamy heard
Familiar Brouwer's unanswered word,
Started from thoughts leagues off at sea:
"Believe in smoke? Why, ay, such smoke
As the swart old *Dunderberg* erst did fold—   5
When, like the cloud-voice from the mountain rolled,
Van Tromp through the bolts of her broadside spoke—
Bolts heard by me!" And lapsed in thought
Of yet other frays himself had seen

When, fired by adventurous love of Art,   10
With De Ruyter he'd cruised, yea, a tar had been.
Reminiscent he sat. Some lion-heart old,
Austerely aside, on latter days cast,
So muses on glories engulfed in the Past,
And laurelled ones stranded or overrolled   15
By eventful Time.—He awoke anon,
Or, rather, his dream took audible tone.—
Then filling his cup: "On Zealand's strand
I saw morn's rays slant 'twixt the bones
Of the oaken *Dunderberg* broken up;   20
Saw her ribbed shadow on the sand.
Ay— picturesque! But naught atones
For heroic navies, Pan's own ribs and knees,
But a story now that storied made the seas!"
There the gray master-hand marine   25
Fell back with desolated mien
Leaving the rest in fluttered mood
Disturbed by such an interlude
Scarce genial in over earnest tone,
Nor quite harmonious with their own.   30
To meet and turn the tide-wave there,
"For me, friends," Gerard Douw here said,
Twirling a glass with sprightly air,
"I too revere forefather Eld,
Just feeling's mine too for old oak,   35
One here am I with Van der Velde;
But take thereto in grade that's lesser:
I like old oak in kitchen-dresser,
The same set out with Delf ware olden
And well scoured copper sauce-pans—golden   40
In aureate rays that on the hearth
Flit like fairies or frisk in mirth.
Oak buffet too; and, flung thereon,
As just from evening-market won,
Pigeons and prawns, bunched carrots bright,   45
Gilled fish, clean radish red and white,
And greens and cauliflowers, and things

The good wife's good provider brings;
All these too touched with fire-side light.
On settle there, a Phillis pleasant   50
Plucking a delicate fat pheasant.
Agree, the picture's *picturesque.*"

"Ay, hollow beats all Arabesque!
But Phillis? Make her Venus, man,
Peachy and plump; and for the pheasant,   55
No fowl but will prove acquiescent
Promoted into Venus' swan;
Then in suffused warm rosy weather
Sublime them in sun-cloud together."
The Knight, Sir Peter Paul, 'twas he,   60
Hatted in rich felt, spick and span,
Right comely in equipment free
With court-air of Lord Chamberlain:
"So! 'twere a canvas meet for donor.
What say you, Paölo of Verona?"   65
Appealing here.
                    "Namesake, 'tis good!"
Laughed the frank master, gorgeous fellow,
Whose raiment matched his artist-mood:
Gold chain over russet velvet mellow—   70
A chain of honor; silver-gilt,
Gleamed at his side a jewelled hilt.
In feather high, in fortune free,
Like to a Golden Pheasant, he.
"By Paul, 'tis good, Sir Peter! Yet   75
Our Hollander here his picture set
In flushful light much like your own,
Tho' but from kitchen-ingle thrown.—
But come to Venice, Gerard,—do,"
Round turning genial on him there,   80
"Her sunsets,—there's hearth-light for you;
And matter for you on the Square.
To Venice, Gerard!"
                    "O, we Dutch

Signor, know Venice, like her much.   85
Our unction thence we got, some say,
Tho' scarce our subjects, nor your touch."—
"To Saint Mark's again, Mynheer, and stay!
We're Cyprus wine.—But, Monsieur," turning
To Watteau nigh; "You vow in France,   90
This *Pittoresque* our friends advance,
How seems it to your ripe discerning?"
"If by a sketch it best were shown,
A hand I'll try, yes, venture one:—
A chamber on the Grand Canal   95
In season, say, of Carnival.
A revel reigns; and, look, the host
Handsome as Caesar Borgia sits —"

"Then Borgia be it, bless your wits!"
Snapped Spagnoletto, late engrossed   100
In splenetic mood, now riling up;
"I'll lend you hints; and let His Grace
Be launching, ay, the loving-cup
Among the princes in the hall
At Sinigaglia: You recall?   105
I mean those gudgeons whom his smile
Flattered to sup, ere yet awhile,
In Hades with Domitian's lords.
Let sunny frankness charm his air,
His raiment lace with silver cords,   110
Trick forth the *'Christian statesman'* there.
And, mind ye, don't forget the pall;
Suggest it—how politeness ended:
Let lurk in shade of rearward wall
Three bravoes by the arras splendid."   115

VI

    The superb gentleman from Verona, pleasantly parrying the not-so-pleasant little man from Spain, resumes his off-hand sketch.—Toward Jan Steen, sapient spendthrift in shabby raiment, smoking his tavern-pipe and whiffing out his unconventional philosophy, Watteau, habited like one of his own holiday-courtiers in the Park of Fontainebleau, proves himself, tho' but in a minor incident, not lacking in considerate courtesy humane.

"O, O, too picturesque by half!"
Was Veronese's turning laugh;
"Nay, nay: but see, on ample round
Of marble table silver-bound
Prince Comus, in mosaic, crowned;   5
Vin d'oro there in chrystal flutes—
Shapley as those, good host of mine,
You summoned ere our *Sillery* fine
We popped to Bacchus in salutes;—
Well, cavaliers in manhood's flower   10
Fanning the flight o' the fleeing hour;
Dames, too, like sportful dolphins free:—
Silks iridescent, wit and glee.
Midmost, a Maltese knight of honor
Toasting and clasping his Bella Donna;   15
One arm round waist with pressure soft,
Returned in throbbed transporting rhyme;
A hand with minaret-glass aloft,
Pinnacle of the jovial prime!
What think? I daub, but daub it, true;   20
And yet some dashes there may do."

The Frank assented. But Jan Steen,
With fellowly yet thoughtful mien,
Puffing at skull-bowl pipe serene,
"Come, a brave sketch, no mincing one!   25
And yet, adzooks, to this I hold,
Be it cloth of frieze or cloth of gold,
All's picturesque beneath the sun;
I mean, all's picture; death and life
Pictures and pendants, nor at strife—   30
No, never to hearts that muse thereon.
For me, 'tis life, plain life, I limn—
Not satin-glossed and flossy-fine

(Our Turburg's forte here, good for him)
No, but the life that's *wine and brine,*   35
The mingled brew; the thing as spanned
By Jan who kept the Leyden tavern
And every rollicker fellowly scanned—
And, under his vineyard, lo, a cavern!
But jolly is Jan, and never in picture   40
Sins against sinners by Pharisee stricture.
Jan o' the Inn, 'tis he, for ruth
Dashes with fun art's canvas of truth."

Here Veronese swerved him round
With glance well-bred of ruled surprise   45
To mark a prodigal so profound,
Nor too good-natured to be wise.

Watteau, first complimenting Steen,
Ignoring there his thriftless guise,
Took up the fallen thread between.   50
Tho' unto Veronese bowing—
Much pleasure at his sketch avowing;
Yet fain he would in brief convey
Some added words—perchance, in way
To vindicate his own renown,   55
Modest and true in pictures done:
"Ay, Signor; but—your leave—admit,
Besides such scenes as well you've hit,
Your *Pittoresco* too abounds
In life of old patrician grounds   60
For centuries kept for luxury mere:
Ladies and lords in mimic dress
Playing at shepherd and shepherdess
By founts that sing *The sweet o' the year!*
But, Signor—how! what's this? you seem   65
Drugged off in miserable dream.
How? what impends?"
                    "Barbaric doom!
Worse than the Constable's sack of Rome!"

"*Ceil, ceil!* the matter? tell us, do."   70
"This cabbage *Utility, parbleu!*
What shall insure the Carnival—
The gondola—the Grand Canal?
That palaced duct they'll yet deplete,
Improve it to a huckster's street.   75
And why? forsooth, *malarial!*"
There ending, with odd grimace,
Reflected from the Frenchman's face.

VII

Brouwer inurbanely applauds Veronèse, and is convivially disrespect-
ful in covert remark on M. Angelo across the table.—Raphael's concern
for the melancholy estate of Albert Durer. And so forth.

At such a sally, half grotesque,
That indirectly seemed to favor
His *own* view of the Picturesque,
Suggesting Dutch canals in savor;
Pleased Brouwer gave a porpoise-snort,   5
A trunk-hose Triton trumping glee.
Claude was but moved to smile in thought;
The while Velazquez, seldom free,
Kept council with himself sedate,
Isled in his ruffed Castilian state,   10
Viewing as from aloft the mien
Of Hals hilarious, Lippi, Steen,
In chorus frolicking back the mirth
Of Brouwer, careless child of earth;
Salvator Rosa posing nigh   15
With sombre-proud satiric eye.

But Poussin, he, with antique air,
Complexioned like a marble old,
Unconscious kept in merit there
Art's pure Acropolis in hold.   20

For Durer, piteous good fellow—
(His Agnes seldom let him mellow)
His Sampson locks, dense curling brown,
Sideways umbrageously fell down,
Enshrining so the Calvary face.   25
Hals says, Angelico sighed to Durer,
Taking to heart his desperate case,
"Would, friend, that Paradise might allure her!"
If Fra Angelico so could wish
(That fleece that fed on lilies fine)   30
Ah, saints! the head in Durer's dish,
And how may hen-pecked seraph pine!

For Leonardo, lost in dream,
His eye absorbed the effect of light
Rayed thro' red wine in glass—a gleam   35
Pink on the polished table bright;
The subtle brain, convolved in snare,
Inferring and over-refining there.
But Michael Angelo, brief his stay,
And, even while present, sat withdrawn.   40
Irreverent Brouwer in sly way
To Lippi whispered, "Brother good,
How to be free and hob-nob with
Yon broken-nosed old monolith
Kin to the battered colossi-brood?   45
Challenged by rays of sunny wine
Not Memnon's stone in olden years
Ere magic fled, had grudged a sign!
Water he drinks, he munches bread.
And on pale lymph of fame may dine.   50
Cheaply is this Archangel fed!"

VIII

Herein, after noting certain topics glanced at by the company, the Marquis concludes the entertainment by rallying the Old Guard of Greybeards upon the somnolent tendency of their years. This, with polite considerateness he does under the fellowly form of the plural pronoun. Finally he recommends them to give audience, by way of pastime, to the "Afternoon in Naples" of his friend and disciple Jack Gentian. And so the genial Frenchman takes French leave, a judicious way of parting as best sparing the feelings on both sides.

So Brouwer, the droll. But others sit
Flinting at whiles scintillant wit
On themes whose tinder takes the spark,
Igniting some less light perchance—
The *romanesque* in men of mark;   5
And this, Shall coming time enhance
Through favoring influence, or abate
Character picturesquely great—
That rumored age whose scouts advance?
And costume too they touch upon: 10
The Cid, his net-work shirt of mail,
And Garibaldi's woolen one:
In higher art would each avail
So just expression nobly grace—
Declare the hero in the face?   15

On themes that under orchards old
The chapleted Greek would frank unfold,
And Socrates, a spirit divine,
Not alien held to cheerful wine,
That reassurer of the soul—   20
On these they chat.

But more, when they,
Even at the Inn of Inns do meet—
The Inn with greens above the door:
There the mahogany's waxed how bright,   25
And under chins such napkins white.

Never comes the mart's intrusive roar,
Nor heard the shriek that starts the train,
Nor teasing telegraph clicks again,
No news is cried and hurry is no more—
For us, whose lagging cobs delay
To win that tavern free from cumber,
Old lads, in saddle shall we slumber?
Here's Jack, whose genial sigh-and-laugh
Where youth and years yblend in sway,
Is like the alewife's half-and-half;
Jack Gentian, in whose beard of gray
Persistent threads of auburn tarry
Like streaks of amber after day
Down in the west; you'll not miscarry
Attending here his bright-and-sombre
Companion good to while the way
With Naples in the Times of Bomba.

30

35

40

END

A SEQUEL

Touching the Grand Canal's depletion
If Veronese did but feign,
Grave frolic of a gay Venetian
Masking in Jeremy his vein;
Believe, that others too may gambol
In syllables as light—yea, ramble
All over each esthetic park,
Playing, as on the violin,
One random theme our dames to win—
The Picturesque in Men of Mark
Nor here some lateral points they shun,
And pirouette on this, for one:

5

10

That rumored Age, whose scouts advance,
Musters it one chivalric lance?
Or shall it foster or abate
Qualities picturesquely great?

15

There's Garibaldi, off-hand hero,
A very Cid Campeadór,
Lion-Nemesis of Naples' Nero—
But, tut, why tell that story o'er!   20
A natural knight-errant, truly,
Nor priding him in parrying fence,
But charging at the helm-piece—hence
By statesmen deemed a lord unruly.
Well now, in days the gods decree,   25
Toward which the levellers scything move
(The Sibyl's page consult, and see)
Could this our Cid a hero prove?
What meet emprise? What plumed career?
No challenges from crime flagitious   30
When all is uniform in cheer;
For Tarquins—none would be extant.
Or, if they were, would hardly daunt,
Ferruling brats, like Dionysius;
And Mulciber's sultans, overawed,   35
In dumps and mumps, how far from menace,
Tippling some claret about deal board
Like Voltaire's kings at inn in Venice.
In fine, the dragons penned or slain,
What for St. George would then remain!   40

A don of rich erratic tone,
By jaunty junior club-men known
As one, who buckram in demur,
Applies then the Johnsonian *Sir;*
'Twas he that rollicked thus of late   45
Filliped by turn of chance debate.
Repeat he did, or vary more
The same conceit, in devious way
Of grandees with dyed whiskers hoar
Tho' virile yet: "Assume, and say   50
The Red Shirt Champion's natal day
Is yet to fall in promised time,
Millennium of the busy bee;

How would he fare in such a Prime?
By Jove, sir, not so bravely, see!   55
Never he'd quit his trading trips,
Perchance, would fag in trade at desk,
Or, slopped in slimy slippery sludge,
Lifelong on Staten Island drudge,
Melting his tallow, Sir, dipping his dips,   60
Scarce savoring much of the Picturesque!"
"Pardon," here purled a cultured wight
Lucid with transcendental light;
"Pardon, but tallow none nor trade
When, thro' this Iron Age's reign   65
The Golden one comes in again;
That's on the card."
           "She plays the spade!
Delving days, Sir, heave in sight—
Digging days, Sir; and, sweet youth,   70
They'll set on edge the sugary tooth:
A treadmill—Paradise they plight."

Let be, and curb this rhyming race!—

Angel O' the Age! Advance, God speed.
Harvest us all good grain in seed;   75
But sprinkle, do, some drops of grace
Nor polish us into commonplace.

RAMMON
AND "THE ENVIABLE ISLES"

In touching upon historical matters the romancer and poet have generously been accorded a certain license, elastic in proportion to the remoteness of the period embraced and consequent incompleteness and incertitude of our knowledge as to events, personages, and dates. It is upon this privilege, assumed for granted, that I here venture to proceed.

Rammon, not mentioned in canonic Scripture, the unrobust child of Solomon's old age and inheriting its despondent philosophy, was immoderately influenced thereby. Vanity of vanities—such is this life. As to a translated life in some world hereafter—far be that thought! A primary law binds the universe. The worlds are like apples on the tree; in flavor and tint one apple perchance may somewhat differ from another, but all partake of the same sap. One of the worlds we know. And what find we here? Much good, a preponderance of good; that is, good it would be could it be winnowed from the associate evil that taints it. But evil is no accident. Like good it is an irremovable element. Bale out your individual boat, if you can, but the sea abides.

To Rammon then cessation of being was the desirable event. But desired or not, an end or what would seem to be an end, does come. There he would have rested—rested but for Buddha.

Solomon a very lax Hebrew did not altogether repell foreign ideas. It was in his time that reports of Buddha and the Buddhistic belief had, along with the recorded spices and pearls, been conveyed into Palestine by that travelled and learned Indian dame, not less communicative than inquisitive, the Princess of Sheba. Through her it was that the doctrine of the successive transmigration of souls came to circulate, along with legends of Ashtaroth and Chemosh, among a people whose theocratic lawgiver was silent as to any life to come. A significant abstention; and serving the more to invest with speculative novelty Buddha's affirmative scheme. But profound doctrines not directly imparted by miracle, but through many removes and in the end through the sprightly chat of a clever queen, though naturally enough they might supply a passing topic for the amateur of thought, yet in any vital way they would scarcely affect but the exceptionally few This applies to Rammon. But the wonderful conceptions of Prince Rhanes were backed by something equally marvellous, his personality and life. These singularly appealed to Rammon also born a Prince, and conscious, too, that rank had not hardened his heart as to the mass of mankind, toilers and sufferers, nor in any wise intercepted a just view of the immense spectacle of things.

But, in large, his thought of Buddha partook of that tender awe with which long after Rammon's time, the earlier unconventional Christians were impressed by the story and character of Christ. It was not possible for him therefore to deem unworthy of regard any doctrine however repugnant to his understanding and desire, authentically ascribed to so transcendent a nature. Besides: If Buddha's estimate of this present life confirms, and more than confirms, Solomon my wise father's view, so much the more then should a son of his attend to what Buddha reveals or alleges touching an unescapable life indefinitely continuous after death.

Rammon was young; his precocious mind eagerly receptive; in practical matters the honesty of his intellect in part compensated for his lack of experience and acquired knowledge. Nevertheless he had no grounding in axiomatic matters of the first consequence in passing judgment upon those vast claims, sometimes made as from heaven itself, upon the credence of man. Moreover, in connection with Buddha it had never occurred to him as a conjecture, much less as a verity that the more spiritual, wide-seeing, conscientious and sympathetic the nature, so much the more is it spiritually isolated, and isolation is the mother of illusion.

Lost between reverential love for Buddha's person, and alarm at his confused teaching (like all transcendent teaching alike unprovable and irrefutable) and with none to befriend and enlighten him, there was no end to the sensitive Prince's reveries and misgivings.

He was left the more a prey to these disquietudes inasmuch as he took no part in public affairs. And for this reason.

Upon the accession of Rehoboam his half-brother, troubles began, ending in the permanent disruption of the kingdom, a calamity directly traceable to the young king's disdain of the advice of his father's councillors, and leaning to flatterers of his own age and arrogance of ignorance.

The depressing event confirmed Rammon in his natural bias for a life within. "What avails it now that Solomon my father was wise? Rehoboam succeeds. Such oscillations are not of a day. Why strive? Rehoboam is my brother."

"When the oil of coronation was not yet dry upon him and repentant Jeroboam proffered his allegiance, only imploring that the king would not make his yoke grievous, and while the king had not yet determined the matter, I said to him, 'It is not wisdom to repulse a penitent. Jeroboam is valorous, a mighty man. If you make him hopeless of lenity, he will stir up mischief, perchance a rebellion.' When I said this much to the king my brother, without a word he turned on his heel. Then I foresaw what would come, and now I see it. But now as then he holds me for an imbecile. He surrounds himself with those who he calls practical men."

"Why strive?" And he withdrew to his meditations and abstractions.

But an interruption not unwelcome occurred. Though as a people the Hebrews were not disposed to superfluous intercourse with the Gentile races, yet in one instance they would seem to have made exception. The commercial alliance between Solomon and Hiram partook something of personal good feeling which radiating out, resulted in an international amity that for a period survived both monarchs.

And so it came to pass that Zardi an improvisator of the coast, a versatile man, in repute for gifts other than the one popularly characterizing him, made a visit to the court in Jerusalem, a court still retaining something of the magnificence and luxury introduced by the Son of Jethro the shepherd. News of the Tyrian's arrival reaches Rammon's retreat. It interests him.

With a view of eliciting something bearing on those questions that never cease agitating his heart, he effects a privy interview with the newcomer; thinking beforehand, "My countrymen are stay-at-homes; whatever is earnest in their thought is as constricted as their territory; but here comes an urbane stranger, travelled intellectual,—Well, we shall see!"

For Zardi he was struck with the pure-minded ingenuousness of Rammon born to a station not favorable to candor. He was interested, perhaps entertained, by his youth and ardor entangled in problems which he for his own part had never seriously considered, holding them not more abstruse than profitless: But humoring a Prince so amiable, affably he lends himself to Rammon's purpose. But it is not long before Rammon divines that Zardi, exempt from popular errors though he was, endowed with knowledge far beyond his own, ready and fluent, so bright too and prepossessing, was in essential character little more than a highly agreeable man-of-the-world, and as such, unconsciously pledged to avert himself in a light hearted way, from entire segments of life and thought. A fair urn, beautifully sculptured, but opaque and clay. True, among other things he is a poet; if a sensuous relish for the harmonious as to numbers and the thoughts they embody and a magic facility in improvising that double harmony, makes a poet, then Zardi is such, and it is not necessary for a poet to be a seer. With a passionate exclamation he breaks off the conference, and for diversion from his disappointment solicits a trial of the accomplished stranger's improvising gift.

Let us attend the Prince and Zardi at that point in their interview when after some general discussion as to the strange doctrines troubling the former, he takes up the one mainly disturbing him, and makes a heartfelt appeal.

> "Who, friend, that have lived, taking ampler view,
> Running life's chances, would life renew?"

> "Ay, Prince, but why fear? no visions dismay
> When turning to enter death's chamber of spell
> One waves back to life a good-natured farewell,   5
> 'Bye-Bye, I must sleep.' That's our Tyrian way."

> "Nor hereabouts very new.
> But, piercing our Sadducees' comfortable word,
> Buddha, benign yet terrible, is heard:
> It is Buddha, I rue.—   10
> From Ever-and-a-Day, friend, ravish me away!

Fable me something that may solace or repay—
Something of your art."

                    "Well,—for a theme?"

"A Phoenician are you. And your voyagers of Tyre   15
From Ophir's far strand they return full of dream
That leaps to the heart of the nearby desire.
Fable me, then, those Enviable Isles
Whereof King Hiram's tars used to tell;
How looms the dim shore when the land is ahead;   20
And what the strange charm the tarrier beguiles
Time without end content there to dwell.
Ay, fable me, do, those enviable isles."

The Enviable Isles

Through storms you reach them and from storms are free.
    Afar descried, the foremost drear in hue,
But, nearer, green; and, on the marge, the sea
    Makes thunder low and mist of rainbowed dew.

But, inland, where the sleep that folds the hills   5
A dreamier sleep, the trance of God, instills—
    On uplands hazed, in wandering airs aswoon,
Slow-swaying palms salute love's cypress tree
    Adown in vale where pebbly runlets croon
A song to lull all sorrow and all glee.

Sweet-fern and moss in many a glade are here,   10
    Where, strown in flocks, what cheek-flushed myriads lie
Dimpling in dream—unconscious slumberers mere,
    While billows endless round the beaches die.

Under the Rose

*(Being an extract from an old MS entitled Travels in Persia
By a servant to My Lord the Ambassador.)*

These roses of divers hues, red, yellow, pink and white, the black slave, a
clean-limbed adolescent comely for all his flat nose; he, before offering
them to my Lord to refresh him with their color and scent, did, at the
Azem's bidding, drop into a delicate vase of amber; and so cunningly
withal, that they fell as of themselves into the attitude of young damsels
leaning over the balustrade of a dome and gazing downward; so that the
vase itself was all but hidden from view, at least much of the upper part
thereof, where I noted that certain *releivos* were, though truly, I could get
but a peep thereof at that time.

On the next day but one, repairing to the same villa where the Azem
made abode for that month, and there waiting to convey a reply to a missive from my Lord; I saw by chance on a marble buffet the same vase then
empty; and going up to it, curiously observed the *releivos* before hidden by
the flowers. They were of a mystical type, methought, something like certain pictures in the great Dutch Bible in a library at Oxon setting forth
the enigmas of the Song of the Wise Man, to wit, King Solomon. I hardly
knew what to make of them; and so would as lief have seen the roses in
their stead. Yet for the grace of it, if not the import whichever that might
be, was I pleased with a round device of sculpture on one side, about the
bigness of my Lord's seal to a parchment, showing the figure of an angel
with a spade under arm like a vineyarder, and bearing roses in a pot; and

a like angel-figure clad like a cellerer, and with a wine-jar on his shoulder; and these two angels side by side pacing toward a meagre wight very doleful and Job-like, squatted hard by a sepulchre, as meditating thereon; and all done very lively in small.

But the thing that meseems ever most strange was the amber where this device and sundry other inventions were cut; for in parts it held marvelously congealed within its substance certain little relics of perished insects as of the members of flies in a frozen syrup or marmalade. Never had I seen the like thereof before; and my Lord to whom that night I spoke of it as he was drinking his posset about the time of his retiring, he instructed me that that sort of amber was of the rarest and esteemed exceeding precious, and spake of a famous piece in the Great Duke's museum at Florence; and much wished that the Azem had given him that vase in place of the jeweled scimitar you wot of.

"And Geoffrey" quoth my Lord somewhat eagerly, "did'st thou note if the vessel was of one whole piece or in two parts, the bowl-part and the standard?"

But verily I could not answer to purpose here, for I did in no wise handle the vase; and I doubt had the jealousy of the attendants permitted it; so that, was there any junction of two or more parts, right deftly was the same hidden by the craft of the artificer.

It befell that at the next coming together of my Lord and the Azem which was about that stale affair of the two factors at Aleppo; my Lord after that business and when their black drink, coffee, had been offered us in little cups of filigree fine as my lady's Flanders lace, and great jasmine-stem'd pipes two yards long, likewise, as is ceremonious custom; my Lord, I say, holding the amber mouth-piece before him, shaped somewhat like a lemon and of a wondrous clear tint much the same, and of a diameter not behind, for among these people the higher the rank or the longer the purse, the greater the costly mouth-piece, the same being but gently pressed against the lips at the orifice of the inhaled vapor; my Lord I say, holding this fair oval of clear amber before him, turned, through the interpreter, the discourse to considerations of the occult nature of this substance whereof it was fashioned; declaring, among other items, his incredulity touching the strange allegement that amber was sometimes found with bees glued up therein as in their own crystallized honey, or, if not bees, then fleas and flies.

With the wondrous sedate courtesy of all the grandees in these parts, the Azem with his silvery spade-beard sitting cross-legged on the green silken cushions; he, though never understanding a word of my Lord's English, yet very gravely and attentively as before, heard him out; him, my Lord, first, I mean, leaning over toward him, his hand to his ear, for, certes, he was somewhat deaf, being in years; leaning over towards him, I say, and thereafter relaxing and falling back somewhat on the cushions, and so giving another sort of heed to the interpreter; who having delivered his burden, the Azem did nothing but give a little clap with his hands, whereupon, as it were one of the painted manikins in the great clock at Strasbourg, a pretty little page issued from a sort of draped closet nearby; to whom his master made a sign; whereat the page brought to my Lord the aforesaid amber vase, empty, and put it into his two hands; who made as if surprised; and after scrutinizing it, and turning it round and round, and discovering the imbedded relics, affected great admiration at being so promptly and in that tacit manner confuted in his misbelief; and much did he laud the beauty of the vase, as well; insomuch that the interpreter, a precise clerk in his careful vocation, verily he seemed as sore put to it to render my Lord.

But if herein, and all along, my Lord's purpose was so to work on the Azem as that he, seeing his great pleasure in the vase, might be drawn to make a gift of it; I say, if this were my Lord's intent, it prospered not to the fulfillment, for as much as it was now the Azem's turn to say how much he himself esteemed the vase, declaring that at such rate did he prize it, he would not barter it, no, not for a certain villa he spoke of, though mightily he coveted the same. For besides the beauty of the vessel and the rare sculpture on it, and its being incomparably the biggest piece of amber known in those parts; besides all this, it was the very vase, he avouched—and with a kind of ardor strange to note in one so much upon his turbaned dignity—the very vase, in sooth, that being on a bridal festival filled with roses on the palace of the old Shar Gold-Beak at Shiraz, had tempted their great poet, one Sugar-Lips, to a closer inspection, when tenderly dividing the flowers one from another, and noting the little anatomies congealed in the amber, he was incontrovertibly prompted to the inditing of certain verses; for which cause the vase thenceforth forever was inestimable.

To which extravagances my Lord listened with his wonted civility, nay, and with a special graciousness, but for all that a bit sadly too, meseemed, and would now again have swerved the discourse; but the Azem was beforehand, and bade the page bring him something from a silver-bound chest nearby in an alcove. It was a vellum book, about the bigness of a prayer-book for church-going, but very rich, with jeweled clasps, and writ by some famous scribe in the fair Persian text, and illuminated withal like unto the great Popish parchment folios I have seen. And this book, surely of great cost, the Azem with his own hands right noble did present to my Lord, putting his finger on a certain page whereon were traced those verses aforesaid.

But, shortly after, some sherbert and sweetmeats being served, and the Azem's own mules being at the garden gate, and, the more to honor us, with gorgeous new trappings; our train withdrew in the same state as when we entered, that is, the one great captain-soldier leading, with a mighty truncheon in his hand, and his troop making a lane through which we proceeded to the saddles, they the while salaaming and paying extreme obeisance to my Lord, which indeed was but their bounden duty, for he was an Englishman and my noble master.

Now a Greek renegado, one long dwelling in Persia, a scholar, and at whiles employed by my Lord, he being expert in divers tongues of both continents and learned in the chirography of the Persian and Arabic; this polyglot infidel—the more shame to him for turning his back on his Savior—he being at the embassy one day, which was I know not what kind of strange holiday with these folk; my Lord for his recreation and by way of challenge, being a little merry as was his wont sometimes for a brief space after dinner; he commanded the Greek to put those verses into English rhyme if he could, and on the instant, or as soon soever as might be.

Upon which the Greek said, "My Lord, I will try; but, I pray thee, give me wine," glancing at the table where remained certain wicker flasks of the choice vintages both of Persia and Cyprus; "Yes, wine, my Lord," he repeated.

"Now," demanded my master severely, "Bethink thee now, my Lord," quoth he, saluting; "This same Sugar Lips' verses being all grapes, or veritably saturated with the ripe juice thereof, there is no properly rendering them without a cup or two of the same; and, behold, my Lord, I am sober."

My master after a moment seeming to debate in his mind whether this proceeded from a strange familiar impudence in the varlet, or from an honest superstition however silly, for he delivered himself very soberly and discreetly, commanded wine to be served him; when the renegado, quaffing like a good fellow his cup or two, which were indeed five, for I took the tally; he, I say, quaffing at whiles, and all the time holding the vellum book in one hand,—and, sooth, but one hand he had, the other having been smitten off by a scimitar, whether in honorable fray or by the executioner, I wot not; he, ever and anon scanning the page, humming and hooing to himself and swaying his body like the dervishes hereabouts, at last after thus mighty ado, sang—he scarce said it—the interpreted verses; which were these:

> Specks, tiny specks, in this translucent amber:
> Your leave, bride-roses, may one pry and see?
> How odd! a dainty little skeleton-chamber;
> And—odder yet—sealed walls but windows be!
> Death's open secret.—Well, we *are;*
> And here the jolly angel with the jar!

Wherein, in the ultimate verse, Sugar-Lips did particularize, doubtless, one of the twain in the releivo of the little medallion on one side of the vase, of which cunning piece I have in the foregoing made account.

"And is that all?" said my Lord composedly, but scarce cheerfully, when the renegado had made an end; "And is that all? And call you that a crushing from the grape? The black grape, I wis"; there checking himself, as a wise man will do catching himself tripping in an indiscreet sincerity; which to cover, peradventure, he, suddenly rising, retired to his chamber, and though commanding his visage somewhat, yet in pace and figure, showing the spirit within sadly distraught; for sooth, the last Michaelmas his birthday he was three score and three years old, and in privy fear, as I know who long was near him, of a certain sudden malady whereof his father and grandfather before him had died about that age.

But for my part I always esteemed this a mighty weakness in so great a man to let the ribald wit of a vain ballader, and he a heathen, make heavy his heart. For me who am but a small one, I was in secret pleased with the lax pleasantry of this Sugar-Lips but in such sort as one is tickled with the profane capering of a mountebank at Bartholemew's fair by Thames. However, had I been, God knows, of equal reverend years with my master and subject by probable inheritance to the like sudden malady with him, peradventure I myself in that case might have waxed sorrowful, doubting whether the grape were not under the black grape as he phrased it whereupon that vain balladry had been distilled.

But now no more hereof, nor of the amber vase, which like unto some little man in great place hath been made overmuch of, as the judicious reader hereof may opine.

PART EIGHT
BILLY BUDD

The novella we know as *Billy Budd* is actually one of Melville's most striking and enduring prose & poem works. He began writing it around 1885, first as a poem about the final thoughts of a handsome sailor, who, in this case, is guilty of mutiny and condemned to hang. (See "Versions of Billy.") Like the dramatic monologues in *John Marr*, the poem "Billy in the Darbies" was to be prefaced with a headnote briefly explaining Billy's situation. But as Melville revised both poem and prose, the headnote grew in size with the successive addition of materials concerning, first, the inexplicably iniquitous Claggart, who falsely accuses an innocent Billy of conspiracy, and then the intellectual Captain Vere, who executes the boy. Eventually, the little poem & prose work grew into the novella we know today, a devastating tragedy that ends with a poem.

But *Billy Budd* was never fully completed and remained unpublished at the time of Melville's death in 1891. The manuscript was rediscovered in 1919, and its publication in 1924 helped trigger the Melville Revival and seal Melville's international reputation. More textually fluid than any other Melville work, it has been edited from manuscript three times, and adapted for stage, opera, and film. Part of its appeal resides in the considerable critical debate over who the story's principal tragic figure may be: the Christ-like Billy who accepts death as his duty, or Vere, whose adherence to reason and law outweighs his heart, or even Claggart, whose envy and violence are a "mystery of iniquity" linked to some inherent evil, or homophobic self-loathing. Readers debate its message, too. Is Melville advocating a martyred acceptance of authority, or ironically resisting against the "forms, measured forms" that require men absurdly and knowingly to sentence innocents to death? Melville's distant narrator (like the narrator of "Benito Cereno") plays a role by strategically playing no role at all, for his preference not to moralize throws judgment in our laps, making the reader, too, a victim of this tragedy.

Following the text of *Billy Budd*, we offer fragments of the early prose & poem version to convey some sense of the "Ur–*Billy Budd*" from which the larger work we now know evolved.

BILLY BUDD, SAILOR: AN INSIDE NARRATIVE

DEDICATED TO
JACK CHASE
ENGLISHMAN

*Wherever that great heart may now be Here on Earth or harbored in
Paradise Captain of the Main top in the year 1843
in the U.S. Frigate* United States

———

1

In the time before steamships, or then more frequently than now, a
stroller along the docks of any considerable seaport would occasionally
have his attention arrested by a group of bronzed mariners, man-of-war's
men or merchant sailors in holiday attire, ashore on liberty. In certain instances they would flank, or like a bodyguard quite surround, some superior figure of their own class, moving along with them like Aldebaran
among the lesser lights of his constellation. That signal object was the
"Handsome Sailor" of the less prosaic time alike of the military and merchant navies. With no perceptible trace of the vain-glorious about him,
rather with the offhand unaffectedness of natural regality, he seemed to
accept the spontaneous homage of his shipmates.

A somewhat remarkable instance recurs to me. In Liverpool, now half
a century ago, I saw under the shadow of the great dingy street-wall of
Prince's Dock (an obstruction long since removed) a common sailor so

intensely black that he must needs have been a native African of the unadulterate blood of Ham—a symmetric figure much above the average height. The two ends of a gay silk handkerchief thrown loose about the neck danced upon the displayed ebony of his chest, in his ears were big hoops of gold, and a Highland bonnet with a tartan band set off his shapely head. It was a hot noon in July; and his face, lustrous with perspiration, beamed with barbaric good humor. In jovial sallies right and left, his white teeth flashing into view, he rollicked along, the center of a company of his shipmates. These were made up of such an assortment of tribes and complexions as would have well fitted them to be marched up by Anacharsis Cloots before the bar of the first French Assembly as Representatives of the Human Race. At each spontaneous tribute rendered by the wayfarers to this black pagod of a fellow—the tribute of a pause and stare, and less frequently an exclamation—the motley retinue showed that they took that sort of pride in the evoker of it which the Assyrian priests doubtless showed for their grand sculptured Bull when the faithful prostrated themselves.

To return. If in some cases a bit of a nautical Murat in setting forth his person ashore, the Handsome Sailor of the period in question evinced nothing of the dandified Billy-be-Dam, an amusing character all but extinct now, but occasionally to be encountered, and in a form yet more amusing than the original, at the tiller of the boats on the tempestuous Erie Canal or, more likely, vaporing in the groggeries along the towpath. Invariably a proficient in his perilous calling, he was also more or less of a mighty boxer or wrestler. It was strength and beauty. Tales of his prowess were recited. Ashore he was the champion; afloat the spokesman; on every suitable occasion always foremost. Close-reefing topsails in a gale, there he was, astride the weather yardarm-end, foot in the Flemish horse as stirrup, both hands tugging at the earing as at a bridle, in very much the attitude of young Alexander curbing the fiery Bucephalus. A superb figure, tossed up as by the horns of Taurus against the thunderous sky, cheerily hallooing to the strenuous file along the spar.

The moral nature was seldom out of keeping with the physical make. Indeed, except as toned by the former, the comeliness and power, always attractive in masculine conjunction, hardly could have drawn the sort of honest homage the Handsome Sailor in some examples received from his less gifted associates.

Such a cynosure, at least in aspect, and something such too in nature, though with important variations made apparent as the story proceeds, was welkin-eyed Billy Budd—or Baby Budd, as more familiarly, under circumstances hereafter to be given, he at last came to be called—aged twenty-one, a foretopman of the British fleet toward the close of the last decade of the eighteenth century. It was not very long prior to the time of the narration that follows that he had entered the King's service, having been impressed on the Narrow Seas from a homeward-bound English merchantman into a seventy-four outward bound, H.M.S. *Bellipotent;* which ship, as was not unusual in those hurried days, having been obliged to put to sea short of her proper complement of men. Plump upon Billy at first sight in the gangway the boarding officer, Lieutenant Ratcliffe, pounced, even before the merchantman's crew was formally mustered on the quarter deck for his deliberate inspection. And him only he elected. For whether it was because the other men when ranged before him showed to ill advantage after Billy, or whether he had some scruples in view of the merchantman's being rather short-handed, however it might be, the officer contented himself with his first spontaneous choice. To the surprise of the ship's company, though much to the lieutenant's satisfaction, Billy made no demur. But, indeed, any demur would have been as idle as the protest of a goldfinch popped into a cage.

Noting this uncomplaining acquiescence, all but cheerful, one might say, the shipmaster turned a surprised glance of silent reproach at the sailor. The shipmaster was one of those worthy mortals found in every vocation, even the humbler ones—the sort of person whom everybody agrees in calling "a respectable man." And— nor so strange to report as it may appear to be—though a ploughman of the troubled waters, lifelong contending with the intractable elements, there was nothing this honest soul at heart loved better than simple peace and quiet. For the rest, he was fifty or thereabouts, a little inclined to corpulence, a prepossessing face, unwhiskered, and of an agreeable color—a rather full face, humanely intelligent in expression. On a fair day with a fair wind and all going well, a certain musical chime in his voice seemed to be the veritable unobstructed outcome of the innermost man. He had much prudence, much conscientiousness, and there were occasions when these virtues were the cause of overmuch disquietude in him. On a passage, so long as his craft was in any proximity to land, no sleep for Captain Graveling. He took to heart those serious responsibilities not so heavily borne by some shipmasters.

Now while Billy Budd was down in the forecastle getting his kit together, the *Bellipotent*'s lieutenant, burly and bluff, nowise disconcerted by Captain Graveling's omitting to proffer the customary hospitalities on an occasion so unwelcome to him, an omission simply caused by preoccupation of thought, unceremoniously invited himself into the cabin, and also to a flask from the spirit locker, a receptacle which his experienced eye instantly discovered. In fact he was one of those sea dogs in whom all the hardship and peril of naval life in the great prolonged wars of his time never impaired the natural instinct for sensuous enjoyment. His duty he always faithfully did; but duty is sometimes a dry obligation, and he was for irrigating its aridity, whensoever possible, with a fertilizing decoction of strong waters. For the cabin's proprietor there was nothing left but to play the part of the enforced host with whatever grace and alacrity were practicable. As necessary adjuncts to the flask, he silently placed tumbler and water jug before the irrepressible guest. But excusing himself from partaking just then, he dismally watched the unembarrassed officer deliberately diluting his grog a little, then tossing it off in three swallows, pushing the empty tumbler away, yet not so far as to be beyond easy reach, at the same time settling himself in his seat and smacking his lips with high satisfaction, looking straight at the host.

These proceedings over, the master broke the silence; and there lurked a rueful reproach in the tone of his voice: "Lieutenant, you are going to take my best man from me, the jewel of 'em."

"Yes, I know," rejoined the other, immediately drawing back the tumbler preliminary to a replenishing. "Yes, I know. Sorry."

"Beg pardon, but you don't understand, Lieutenant. See here, now. Before I shipped that young fellow, my forecastle was a rat-pit of quarrels. It was black times, I tell you, aboard the *Rights* here. I was worried to that degree my pipe had no comfort for me. But Billy came; and it was like a Catholic priest striking peace in an Irish shindy. Not that he preached to them or said or did anything in particular; but a virtue went out of him, sugaring the sour ones. They took to him like hornets to treacle; all but the buffer of the gang, the big shaggy chap with the fire-red whiskers. He indeed, out of envy, perhaps, of the newcomer, and thinking such a "sweet and pleasant fellow," as he mockingly designated him to the others, could hardly have the spirit of a gamecock, must needs bestir himself in trying to get up an ugly row with him. Billy forebore with him and reasoned with him in a pleasant way—he is something like myself, Lieutenant, to whom aught like a quarrel is hateful—but nothing served. So, in the second dogwatch one day, the Red Whiskers in presence of the others, under pretense of showing Billy just whence a sirloin steak was cut—for the fellow had once been a butcher—insultingly gave him a dig under the ribs. Quick as lightning Billy let fly his arm. I dare say he never meant to do quite as much as he did, but anyhow he gave the burly fool a terrible drubbing. It took about half a minute, I should think. And, lord bless you, the lubber was astonished at the celerity. And will you believe it, Lieutenant, the Red Whiskers now really loves Billy—loves him, or is the biggest hypocrite that ever I heard of. But they all love him. Some of 'em do his washing, darn his old trousers for him; the carpenter is at odd times making a pretty little chest of drawers for him. Anybody will do anything for Billy Budd; and it's the happy family here. But now, Lieutenant, if that young fellow goes—I know how it will be aboard the *Rights*. Not again very soon shall I, coming up from dinner, lean over the capstan smoking a quiet pipe—no, not very soon again, I think. Ay, Lieutenant, you are going to take away the jewel of 'em; you are going to take away my peacemaker!" And with that the good soul had really some ado in checking a rising sob.

"Well," said the lieutenant, who had listened with amused interest to all this and now was waxing merry with his tipple; "well, blessed are the peacemakers, especially the fighting peacemakers. And such are the seventy-four beauties some of which you see poking their noses out of the portholes of yonder warship lying to for me," pointing through the cabin window at the *Bellipotent*. "But courage! Don't look so downhearted, man. Why, I pledge you in advance the royal approbation. Rest assured that His Majesty will be delighted to know that in a time when his hardtack is not sought for by sailors with such avidity as should be, a time also when some shipmasters privily resent the borrowing from them a tar or two for the service; His Majesty, I say, will be delighted to learn that *one* shipmaster at least cheerfully surrenders to the King the flower of his flock, a sailor who with equal loyalty makes no dissent.—But where's my beauty? Ah," looking through the cabin's open door, "here he comes; and, by Jove, lugging along his chest—Apollo with his portmanteau!— My man," stepping out to him, "you can't take that big box aboard a warship. The boxes there are mostly shot boxes. Put your duds in a bag, lad. Boot and saddle for the cavalryman, bag and hammock for the man-of-war's man."

The transfer from chest to bag was made. And, after seeing his man into the cutter and then following him down, the lieutenant pushed off from the *Rights-of-Man*. That was the merchant ship's name, though by her master and crew abbreviated in sailor fashion into the *Rights*. The hardheaded Dundee owner was a staunch admirer of Thomas Paine, whose book in rejoinder to Burke's arraignment of the French Revolution had then been published for some time and had gone everywhere. In christening his vessel after the title of Paine's volume the man of Dundee was something like his contemporary shipowner, Stephen Girard of Philadelphia, whose sympathies, alike with his native land and its liberal philosophers, he evinced by naming his ships after Voltaire, Diderot, and so forth.

But now, when the boat swept under the merchantman's stern, and officer and oarsmen were noting—some bitterly and others with a grin—the name emblazoned there; just then it was that the new recruit jumped up from the bow where the coxswain had directed him to sit, and waving hat to his silent shipmates sorrowfully looking over at him from the taffrail, bade the lads a genial good-bye. Then, making a salutation as to the ship herself, "And good-bye to you too, old *Rights-of-Man*."

"Down, sir!" roared the lieutenant, instantly assuming all the rigor of his rank, though with difficulty repressing a smile.

To be sure, Billy's action was a terrible breach of naval decorum. But in that decorum he had never been instructed; in consideration of which the lieutenant would hardly have been so energetic in reproof but for the concluding farewell to the ship. This he rather took as meant to convey a covert sally on the new recruit's part, a sly slur at impressment in general, and that of himself in especial. And yet, more likely, if satire it was in effect, it was hardly so by intention, for Billy, though happily endowed with the gaiety of high health, youth, and a free heart, was yet by no means of a satirical turn. The will to it and the sinister dexterity were alike wanting. To deal in double meanings and insinuations of any sort was quite foreign to his nature.

As to his enforced enlistment, that he seemed to take pretty much as he was wont to take any vicissitude of weather. Like the animals, though no philosopher, he was, without knowing it, practically a fatalist. And it may be that he rather liked this adventurous turn in his affairs, which promised an opening into novel scenes and martial excitements.

Aboard the *Bellipotent* our merchant sailor was forthwith rated as an able seaman and assigned to the starboard watch of the foretop. He was soon at home in the service, not at all disliked for his unpretentious good looks and a sort of genial happy-go-lucky air. No merrier man in his mess: in marked contrast to certain other individuals included like himself among the impressed portion of the ship's company; for these when not actively employed were sometimes, and more particularly in the last dog-watch when the drawing near of twilight induced revery, apt to fall into a saddish mood which in some partook of sullenness. But they were not so young as our foretopman, and no few of them must have known a hearth of some sort, others may have had wives and children left, too probably, in uncertain circumstances, and hardly any but must have had acknowledged kith and kin, while for Billy, as will shortly be seen, his entire family was practically invested in himself.

2

Though our new-made foretopman was well received in the top and on the gun decks, hardly here was he that cynosure he had previously been among those minor ship's companies of the merchant marine, with which companies only had he hitherto consorted.

He was young; and despite his all but fully developed frame, in aspect looked even younger than he really was, owing to a lingering adolescent expression in the as yet smooth face all but feminine in purity of natural complexion but where, thanks to his seagoing, the lily was quite suppressed and the rose had some ado visibly to flush through the tan.

To one essentially such a novice in the complexities of factitious life, the abrupt transition from his former and simpler sphere to the ampler and more knowing world of a great warship; this might well have abashed him had there been any conceit or vanity in his composition. Among her miscellaneous multitude, the *Bellipotent* mustered several individuals who however inferior in grade were of no common natural stamp, sailors more signally susceptive of that air which continuous martial discipline and repeated presence in battle can in some degree impart even to the average man. As the Handsome Sailor, Billy Budd's position aboard the seventy-four was something analogous to that of a rustic beauty transplanted from the provinces and brought into competition with the highborn dames of the court. But this change of circumstances he scarce noted. As little did he observe that something about him provoked an ambiguous smile in one or two harder faces among the bluejackets. Nor less unaware was he of the peculiar favorable effect his person and demeanor had upon the more intelligent gentlemen of the quarter-deck. Nor could this well have been otherwise. Cast in a mold peculiar to the finest physical examples of those Englishmen in whom the Saxon strain would seem not at all to partake of any Norman or other admixture, he showed in face that humane look of reposeful good nature which the Greek sculptor in some instances gave to his heroic strong man, Hercules. But this again was subtly modified by another and pervasive quality. The ear, small and shapely, the arch of the foot, the curve in mouth and nostril, even the indurated hand dyed to the orange-tawny of the toucan's bill, a hand telling alike of the halyards and tar bucket; but, above all, something in the mobile expression, and every chance attitude and movement, something suggestive of a mother eminently favored by Love and the Graces; all this strangely indicated a lineage in direct contradiction to his lot. The mysteriousness here became less mysterious through a matter of fact elicited when Billy at the capstan was being formally mustered into the service. Asked by the officer, a small, brisk little gentleman as it chanced, among other questions, his place of birth, he replied, "Please, sir, I don't know."

"Don't know where you were born? Who was your father?"

"God knows, sir."

Struck by the straightforward simplicity of these replies, the officer next asked, "Do you know anything about your beginning?"

"No, sir. But I have heard that I was found in a pretty silk-lined basket hanging one morning from the knocker of a good man's door in Bristol."

"*Found,* say you? Well," throwing back his head and looking up and down the new recruit; "well, it turns out to have been a pretty good find. Hope they'll find some more like you, my man; the fleet sadly needs them."

Yes, Billy Budd was a foundling, a presumable by-blow, and, evidently, no ignoble one. Noble descent was as evident in him as in a blood horse.

For the rest, with little or no sharpness of faculty or any trace of the wisdom of the serpent, nor yet quite a dove, he possessed that kind and degree of intelligence going along with the unconventional rectitude of a sound human creature, one to whom not yet has been proffered the questionable apple of knowledge. He was illiterate; he could not read, but he could sing, and like the illiterate nightingale was sometimes the composer of his own song.

Of self-consciousness he seemed to have little or none, or about as much as we may reasonably impute to a dog of Saint Bernard's breed.

Habitually living with the elements and knowing little more of the land than as a beach, or, rather, that portion of the terraqueous globe providentially set apart for dance-houses, doxies, and tapsters, in short what sailors call a "fiddler's green," his simple nature remained unsophisticated by those moral obliquities which are not in every case incompatible with that manufacturable thing known as respectability. But are sailors, frequenters of fiddlers' greens, without vices? No; but less often than with landsmen do their vices, so called, partake of crookedness of heart, seeming less to proceed from viciousness than exuberance of vitality after long constraint: frank manifestations in accordance with natural law. By his original constitution aided by the co-operating influences of his lot, Billy in many respects was little more than a sort of upright barbarian, much such perhaps as Adam presumably might have been ere the urbane Serpent wriggled himself into his company.

And here be it submitted that apparently going to corroborate the doctrine of man's Fall, a doctrine now popularly ignored, it is observable that where certain virtues pristine and unadulterate peculiarly characterize anybody in the external uniform of civilization, they will upon scrutiny seem not to be derived from custom or convention, but rather to be out of keeping with these, as if indeed exceptionally transmitted from a period prior to Cain's city and citified man. The character marked by such qualities has to an unvitiated taste an untampered-with flavor like that of berries, while the man thoroughly civilized, even in a fair specimen of the breed, has to the same moral palate a questionable smack as of a compounded wine. To any stray inheritor of these primitive qualities found, like Caspar Hauser, wandering dazed in any Christian capital of our time, the good-natured poet's famous invocation, near two thousand years ago, of the good rustic out of his latitude in the Rome of the Caesars, still appropriately holds:

> Honest and poor, faithful in word and thought,
> What hath thee, Fabian, to the city brought?

Though our Handsome Sailor had as much of masculine beauty as one can expect anywhere to see; nevertheless, like the beautiful woman in one of Hawthorne's minor tales, there was just one thing amiss in him. No visible blemish indeed, as with the lady; no, but an occasional liability to a vocal defect. Though in the hour of elemental uproar or peril he was everything that a sailor should be, yet under sudden provocation of strong heart-feeling his voice, otherwise singularly musical, as if expressive of the harmony within, was apt to develop an organic hesitancy, in fact more or less of a stutter or even worse. In this particular Billy was a striking instance that the arch interferer, the envious marplot of Eden, still has more or less to do with every human consignment to this planet of Earth. In every case, one way or another he is sure to slip in his little card, as much as to remind us—I too have a hand here.

The avowal of such an imperfection in the Handsome Sailor should be evidence not alone that he is not presented as a conventional hero, but also that the story in which he is the main figure is no romance.

3

At the time of Billy Budd's arbitrary enlistment into the *Bellipotent* that ship was on her way to join the Mediterranean fleet. No long time elapsed before the junction was effected. As one of that fleet the seventy-four participated in its movements, though at times on account of her superior sailing qualities, in the absence of frigates, dispatched on separate duty as a scout and at times on less temporary service. But with all this the story has little concernment, restricted as it is to the inner life of one particular ship and the career of an individual sailor.

It was the summer of 1797. In the April of that year had occurred the commotion at Spithead followed in May by a second and yet more serious outbreak in the fleet at the Nore. The latter is known, and without exaggeration in the epithet, as "the Great Mutiny." It was indeed a demonstration more menacing to England than the contemporary manifestoes and conquering and proselyting armies of the French Directory. To the British Empire the Nore Mutiny was what a strike in the fire brigade would be to London threatened by general arson. In a crisis when the kingdom might well have anticipated the famous signal that some years later published along the naval line of battle what it was that upon occasion England expected of Englishmen; *that* was the time when at the mastheads of the three-deckers and seventy-fours moored in her own roadstead—a fleet the right arm of a Power then all but the sole free conservative one of the Old World—the bluejackets, to be numbered by thousands, ran up with huzzas the British colors with the union and cross wiped out; by that cancellation transmuting the flag of founded law and freedom defined, into the enemy's red meteor of unbridled and unbounded revolt. Reasonable discontent growing out of practical grievances in the fleet had been ignited into irrational combustion as by live cinders blown across the Channel from France in flames.

The event converted into irony for a time those spirited strains of Dibdin—as a song-writer no mean auxiliary to the English government at that European conjuncture—strains celebrating, among other things, the patriotic devotion of the British tar: "And as for my life, 'tis the King's!"

Such an episode in the Island's grand naval story her naval historians naturally abridge, one of them (William James) candidly acknowledging that fain would he pass it over did not "impartiality forbid fastidiousness." And yet his mention is less a narration than a reference, having to do hardly at all with details. Nor are these readily to be found in the libraries. Like some other events in every age befalling states everywhere, including America, the Great Mutiny was of such character that national pride along with views of policy would fain shade it off into the historical background. Such events cannot be ignored, but there is a considerate way of historically treating them. If a well-constituted individual refrains from blazoning aught amiss or calamitous in his family, a nation in the like circumstance may without reproach be equally discreet.

Though after parleyings between government and the ringleaders, and concessions by the former as to some glaring abuses, the first uprising—that at Spithead—with difficulty was put down, or matters for the time pacified; yet at the Nore the unforeseen renewal of insurrection on a yet larger scale, and emphasized in the conferences that ensued by demands deemed by the authorities not only inadmissible but aggressively insolent, indicated—if the Red Flag did not sufficiently do so—what was the spirit animating the men. Final suppression, however, there was; but only made possible perhaps by the unswerving loyalty of the marine corps and a voluntary resumption of loyalty among influential sections of the crews.

To some extent the Nore Mutiny may be regarded as analogous to the distempering irruption of contagious fever in a frame constitutionally sound, and which anon throws it off.

At all events, of these thousands of mutineers were some of the tars who not so very long afterwards—whether wholly prompted thereto by patriotism, or pugnacious instinct, or by both—helped to win a coronet for Nelson at the Nile, and the naval crown of crowns for him at Trafalgar. To the mutineers, those battles and especially Trafalgar were a plenary absolution and a grand one. For all that goes to make up scenic naval display and heroic magnificence in arms, those battles, especially Trafalgar, stand unmatched in human annals.

4

In this matter of writing, resolve as one may to keep to the main road, some bypaths have an enticement not readily to be withstood. I am going to err into such a bypath. If the reader will keep me company I shall be glad. At the least, we can promise ourselves that pleasure which is wickedly said to be in sinning, for a literary sin the divergence will be.

Very likely it is no new remark that the inventions of our time have at last brought about a change in sea warfare in degree corresponding to the revolution in all warfare effected by the original introduction from China into Europe of gunpowder. The first European firearm, a clumsy contrivance, was, as is well known, scouted by no few of the knights as a base implement, good enough peradventure for weavers too craven to stand up crossing steel with steel in frank fight. But as ashore knightly valor, though shorn of its blazonry, did not cease with the knights, neither on the seas—though nowadays in encounters there a certain kind of displayed gallantry be fallen out of date as hardly applicable under changed circumstances—did the nobler qualities of such naval magnates as Don John of Austria, Doria, Van Tromp, Jean Bart, the long line of British admirals, and the American Decaturs of 1812 become obsolete with their wooden walls.

Nevertheless, to anybody who can hold the Present at its worth without being inappreciative of the Past, it may be forgiven, if to such an one the solitary old hulk at Portsmouth, Nelson's *Victory*, seems to float there, not alone as the decaying monument of a fame incorruptible, but also as a poetic reproach, softened by its picturesqueness, to the *Monitors* and yet mightier hulls of the European ironclads. And this not altogether because such craft are unsightly, unavoidably lacking the symmetry and grand lines of the old battleships, but equally for other reasons.

There are some, perhaps, who while not altogether inaccessible to that poetic reproach just alluded to, may yet on behalf of the new order be disposed to parry it; and this to the extent of iconoclasm, if need be. For example, prompted by the sight of the star inserted in the *Victory*'s quarter-deck designating the spot where the Great Sailor fell, these martial utilitarians may suggest considerations implying that Nelson's ornate publication of his person in battle was not only unnecessary, but not military, nay, savored of foolhardiness and vanity. They may add, too, that at Trafalgar it was in effect nothing less than a challenge to death; and death came; and that but for his bravado the victorious admiral might possibly have survived the battle, and so, instead of having his sagacious dying injunctions overruled by his immediate successor in command, he himself when the contest was decided might have brought his shattered fleet to anchor, a proceeding which might have averted the deplorable loss of life by shipwreck in the elemental tempest that followed the martial one.

Well, should we set aside the more than disputable point whether for various reasons it was possible to anchor the fleet, then plausibly enough the Benthamites of war may urge the above. But the *might-have-been* is but boggy ground to build on. And, certainly, in foresight as to the larger issue of an encounter, and anxious preparations for it—buoying the deadly way and mapping it out, as at Copenhagen—few commanders have been so painstakingly circumspect as this same reckless declarer of his person in fight.

Personal prudence, even when dictated by quite other than selfish considerations, surely is no special virtue in a military man; while an excessive love of glory, impassioning a less burning impulse, the honest sense of duty, is the first. If the name *Wellington* is not so much of a trumpet to the blood as the simpler name *Nelson,* the reason for this may perhaps be inferred from the above. Alfred in his funeral ode on the victor of Waterloo ventures not to call him the greatest soldier of all time, though in the same ode he invokes Nelson as "the greatest sailor since our world began."

At Trafalgar Nelson on the brink of opening the fight sat down and wrote his last brief will and testament. If under the presentiment of the most magnificent of all victories to be crowned by his own glorious death, a sort of priestly motive led him to dress his person in the jewelled vouchers of his own shining deeds; if thus to have adorned himself for the altar and the sacrifice were indeed vainglory, then affectation and fustian is each more heroic line in the great epics and dramas, since in such lines the poet but embodies in verse those exaltations of sentiment that a nature like Nelson, the opportunity being given, vitalizes into acts.

5

Yes, the outbreak at the Nore was put down. But not every grievance was redressed. If the contractors, for example, were no longer permitted to ply some practices peculiar to their tribe everywhere, such as providing shoddy cloth, rations not sound, or false in the measure; not the less impressment, for one thing, went on. By custom sanctioned for centuries, and judicially maintained by a Lord Chancellor as late as Mansfield, that mode of manning the fleet, a mode now fallen into a sort of abeyance but never formally renounced, it was not practicable to give up in those years. Its abrogation would have crippled the indispensable fleet, one wholly under canvas, no steam power, its innumerable sails and thousands of cannon, everything in short, worked by muscle alone; a fleet the more insatiate in demand for men, because then multiplying its ships of all grades against contingencies present and to come of the convulsed Continent.

Discontent foreran the Two Mutinies, and more or less it lurkingly survived them. Hence it was not unreasonable to apprehend some return of trouble sporadic or general. One instance of such apprehensions: In the same year with this story, Nelson, then Rear Admiral Sir Horatio, being with the fleet off the Spanish coast, was directed by the admiral in command to shift his pennant from the *Captain* to the *Theseus;* and for this reason: that the latter ship having newly arrived on the station from home, where it had taken part in the Great Mutiny, danger was apprehended from the temper of the men; and it was thought that an officer like Nelson was the one, not indeed to terrorize the crew into base subjection, but to win them, by force of his mere presence and heroic personality, back to an allegiance if not as enthusiastic as his own yet as true.

So it was that for a time, on more than one quarter-deck, anxiety did exist. At sea, precautionary vigilance was strained against relapse. At short notice an engagement might come on. When it did, the lieutenants assigned to batteries felt it incumbent on them, in some instances, to stand with drawn swords behind the men working the guns.

6

But on board the seventy-four in which Billy now swung his hammock, very little in the manner of the men and nothing obvious in the demeanor of the officers would have suggested to an ordinary observer that the Great Mutiny was a recent event. In their general bearing and conduct the commissioned officers of a warship naturally take their tone from the commander, that is if he have that ascendancy of character that ought to be his.

Captain the Honorable Edward Fairfax Vere, to give his full title, was a bachelor of forty or thereabouts, a sailor of distinction even in a time prolific of renowned seamen. Though allied to the higher nobility, his advancement had not been altogether owing to influences connected with that circumstance. He had seen much service, been in various engagements, always acquitting himself as an officer mindful of the welfare of his men, but never tolerating an infraction of discipline; thoroughly versed in the science of his profession, and intrepid to the verge of temerity, though never injudiciously so. For his gallantry in the West Indian waters as flag lieutenant under Rodney in that admiral's crowning victory over De Grasse, he was made a post captain.

Ashore, in the garb of a civilian, scarce anyone would have taken him for a sailor, more especially that he never garnished unprofessional talk with nautical terms, and grave in his bearing, evinced little appreciation of mere humor. It was not out of keeping with these traits that on a passage when nothing demanded his paramount action, he was the most undemonstrative of men. Any landsman observing this gentleman not conspicuous by his stature and wearing no pronounced insignia, emerging from his cabin to the open deck, and noting the silent deference of the officers retiring to leeward, might have taken him for the King's guest, a civilian aboard the King's ship, some highly honorable discreet envoy on his way to an important post. But in fact this unobtrusiveness of demeanor may have proceeded from a certain unaffected modesty of manhood sometimes accompanying a resolute nature, a modesty evinced at all times not calling for pronounced action, which shown in any rank of life suggests a virtue aristocratic in kind. As with some others engaged in various departments of the world's more heroic activities, Captain Vere though practical enough upon occasion would at times betray a certain dreaminess of mood. Standing alone on the weather side of the quarter-deck, one hand holding by the rigging, he would absently gaze off at the blank sea. At the presentation to him then of some minor matter inter-rupting the current of his thoughts, he would show more or less irascibili-ty; but instantly he would control it.

In the navy he was popularly known by the appellation "Starry Vere." How such a designation happened to fall upon one who whatever his sterling qualities was without any brilliant ones, was in this wise: A fa-vorite kinsman, Lord Denton, a freehearted fellow, had been the first to meet and congratulate him upon his return to England from his West In-dian cruise; and but the day previous turning over a copy of Andrew Marvell's poems had lighted, not for the first time, however, upon the lines entitled "Appleton House," the name of one of the seats of their common ancestor, a hero in the German wars of the seventeenth century, in which poem occur the lines:

> This 'tis to have been from the first
> In a domestic heaven nursed,
> Under the discipline severe
> Of Fairfax and the starry Vere.

And so, upon embracing his cousin fresh from Rodney's great victory wherein he had played so gallant a part, brimming over with just family pride in the sailor of their house, he exuberantly exclaimed, "Give ye joy, Ed; give ye joy, my starry Vere!" This got currency, and the novel prefix serving in familiar parlance readily to distinguish the *Bellipotent*'s captain from another Vere his senior, a distant relative, an officer of like rank in the navy, it remained permanently attached to the surname.

7

In view of the part that the commander of the *Bellipotent* plays in scenes shortly to follow, it may be well to fill out that sketch of him outlined in the previous chapter.

Aside from his qualities as a sea officer Captain Vere was an excep-tional character. Unlike no few of England's renowned sailors, long and arduous service with signal devotion to it had not resulted in absorbing and *salting* the entire man. He had a marked leaning toward everything intellectual. He loved books, never going to sea without a newly replenished library, compact but of the best. The isolated leisure, in some cases so wearisome, falling at intervals to commanders even during a war cruise, never was tedious to Captain Vere. With nothing of that literary taste which less heeds the thing conveyed than the vehicle, his bias was toward those books to which every serious mind of superior order occupying any active post of authority in the world naturally inclines: books treating of actual men and events no matter of what era—history, biography, and unconventional writers like Montaigne, who, free from cant and convention, honestly and in the spirit of common sense philosophize upon realities. In this line of reading he found confirmation of his own more reserved thoughts—confirmation which he had vainly sought in social converse, so that as touching most fundamental topics, there had got to be established in him some positive convictions which he forefelt would abide in him essentially unmodified so long as his intelligent part remained unimpaired. In view of the troubled period in which his lot was cast, this was well for him. His settled convictions were as a dike against those invading waters of novel opinion social, political, and otherwise, which carried away as in a torrent no few minds in those days, minds by nature not inferior to his own. While other members of that aristocracy to which by birth he belonged were incensed at the innovators mainly because their theories were inimical to the privileged classes, Captain Vere disinterestedly opposed them not alone because they seemed to him insusceptible of embodiment in lasting institutions, but at war with the peace of the world and the true welfare of mankind.

With minds less stored than his and less earnest, some officers of his rank, with whom at times he would necessarily consort, found him lacking in the companionable quality, a dry and bookish gentleman, as they deemed. Upon any chance withdrawal from their company one would be apt to say to another something like this: "Vere is a noble fellow, Starry Vere. 'Spite the gazettes, Sir Horatio" (meaning him who became Lord Nelson) "is at bottom scarce a better seaman or fighter. But between you and me now, don't you think there is a queer streak of the pedantic running through him? Yes, like the King's yarn in a coil of navy rope?"

Some apparent ground there was for this sort of confidential criticism; since not only did the captain's discourse never fall into the jocosely familiar, but in illustrating of any point touching the stirring personages and events of the time he would be as apt to cite some historic character or incident of antiquity as he would be to cite from the moderns. He seemed unmindful of the circumstance that to his bluff company such remote allusions, however pertinent they might really be, were altogether alien to men whose reading was mainly confined to the journals. But considerateness in such matters is not easy to natures constituted like Captain Vere's. Their honesty prescribes to them directness, sometimes far-reaching like that of a migratory fowl that in its flight never heeds when it crosses a frontier.

8

The lieutenants and other commissioned gentlemen forming Captain Vere's staff it is not necessary here to particularize, nor needs it to make any mention of any of the warrant officers. But among the petty officers was one who, having much to do with the story, may as well be forthwith introduced. His portrait I essay, but shall never hit it. This was John Claggart, the master-at-arms. But that sea title may to landsmen seem somewhat equivocal. Originally, doubtless, that petty officer's function was the instruction of the men in the use of arms, sword or cutlass. But very long ago, owing to the advance in gunnery making hand-to-hand encounters less frequent and giving to niter and sulphur the pre-eminence over steel, that function ceased; the master-at-arms of a great warship becoming a sort of chief of police charged among other matters with the duty of preserving order on the populous lower gun decks.

Claggart was a man about five-and-thirty, somewhat spare and tall, yet of no ill figure upon the whole. His hand was too small and shapely to have been accustomed to hard toil. The face was a notable one, the features all except the chin cleanly cut as those on a Greek medallion; yet the chin, beardless as Tecumseh's, had something of strange protuberant broadness in its make that recalled the prints of the Reverend Dr. Titus Oates, the historic deponent with the clerical drawl in the time of Charles II and the fraud of the alleged Popish Plot. It served Claggart in his office that his eye could cast a tutoring glance. His brow was of the sort phrenologically associated with more than average intellect; silken jet curls partly clustering over it, making a foil to the pallor below, a pallor tinged with a faint shade of amber akin to the hue of time-tinted marbles of old. This complexion, singularly contrasting with the red or deeply bronzed visages of the sailors, and in part the result of his official seclusion from the sunlight, though it was not exactly displeasing, nevertheless seemed to hint of something defective or abnormal in the constitution and blood. But his general aspect and manner were so suggestive of an education and career incongruous with his naval function that when not actively engaged in it he looked like a man of high quality, social and moral, who for reasons of his own was keeping incog. Nothing was known of his former life. It might be that he was an Englishman; and yet there lurked a bit of accent in his speech suggesting that possibly he was not such by birth, but through naturalization in early childhood. Among certain grizzled sea gossips of the gun decks and forecastle went a rumor perdue that the master-at-arms was a *chevalier* who had volunteered into the King's navy by way of compounding for some mysterious swindle whereof he had been arraigned at the King's Bench. The fact that nobody could substantiate this report was, of course, nothing against its secret currency. Such a rumor once started on the gun decks in reference to almost anyone below the rank of a commissioned officer would, during the period assigned to this narrative, have seemed not altogether wanting in credibility to the tarry old wiseacres of a man-of-war crew. And indeed a man of Claggart's accomplishments, without prior nautical experience entering the navy at mature life, as he did, and necessarily allotted at the start to the lowest grade in it; a man too who never made allusion to his previous life ashore; these were circumstances which in the dearth of exact knowledge as to his true antecedents opened to the invidious a vague field for unfavorable surmise.

But the sailors' dogwatch gossip concerning him derived a vague plausibility from the fact that now for some period the British navy could so little afford to be squeamish in the matter of keeping up the muster rolls, that not only were press gangs notoriously abroad both afloat and ashore, but there was little or no secret about another matter, namely, that the London police were at liberty to capture any able-bodied suspect, any questionable fellow at large, and summarily ship him to the dockyard or fleet. Furthermore, even among voluntary enlistments there were instances where the motive thereto partook neither of patriotic impulse nor yet of a random desire to experience a bit of sea life and martial adventure. Insolvent debtors of minor grade, together with the promiscuous lame ducks of morality, found in the navy a convenient and secure refuge, secure because, once enlisted aboard a King's ship, they were as much in sanctuary as the transgressor of the Middle Ages harboring himself under the shadow of the altar. Such sanctioned irregularities, which for obvious reasons the government would hardly think to parade at the time and which consequently, and as affecting the least influential class of mankind, have all but dropped into oblivion, lend color to something for the truth whereof I do not vouch, and hence have some scruple in stating; something I remember having seen in print though the book I cannot recall; but the same thing was personally communicated to me now more than forty years ago by an old pensioner in a cocked hat with whom I had a most interesting talk on the terrace at Greenwich, a Baltimore Negro, a Trafalgar man. It was to this effect: In the case of a warship short of hands whose speedy sailing was imperative, the deficient quota, in lack of any other way of making it good, would be eked out by drafts culled direct from the jails. For reasons previously suggested it would not perhaps be easy at the present day directly to prove or disprove the allegation. But allowed as a verity, how significant would it be of England's straits at the time confronted by those wars which like a flight of harpies rose shrieking from the din and dust of the fallen Bastille. That era appears measurably clear to us who look back at it, and but read of it. But to the grandfathers of us graybeards, the more thoughtful of them, the genius of it presented an aspect like that of Camoëns' Spirit of the Cape, an eclipsing menace mysterious and prodigious. Not America was exempt from apprehension. At the height of Napoleon's unexampled conquests, there were Americans who had fought at Bunker Hill who looked forward to the possibility that the Atlantic might prove no barrier against the ultimate schemes of this French portentous upstart from the revolutionary chaos who seemed in act of fulfilling judgment prefigured in the Apocalypse.

But the less credence was to be given to the gun-deck talk touching Claggart, seeing that no man holding his office in a man-of-war can ever hope to be popular with the crew. Besides, in derogatory comments upon anyone against whom they have a grudge, or for any reason or no reason mislike, sailors are much like landsmen: they are apt to exaggerate or romance it.

About as much was really known to the *Bellipotent*'s tars of the master-at-arms' career before entering the service as an astronomer knows about a comet's travels prior to its first observable appearance in the sky. The verdict of the sea quidnuncs has been cited only by way of showing what sort of moral impression the man made upon rude uncultivated natures whose conceptions of human wickedness were necessarily of the narrowest, limited to ideas of vulgar rascality—a thief among the swinging hammocks during a night watch, or the man-brokers and land-sharks of the seaports.

It was no gossip, however, but fact that though, as before hinted, Claggart upon his entrance into the navy was, as a novice, assigned to the least honorable section of a man-of-war's crew, embracing the drudgery, he did not long remain there. The superior capacity he immediately evinced, his constitutional sobriety, an ingratiating deference to superiors, together with a peculiar ferreting genius manifested on a singular occasion; all this, capped by a certain austere patriotism, abruptly advanced him to the position of master-at-arms.

Of this maritime chief of police the ship's corporals, so called, were the immediate subordinates, and compliant ones; and this, as is to be noted in some business departments ashore, almost to a degree inconsistent with entire moral volition. His place put various converging wires of underground influence under the chief's control, capable when astutely worked through his understrappers of operating to the mysterious discomfort, if nothing worse, of any of the sea commonalty.

9

Life in the foretop well agreed with Billy Budd. There, when not actually engaged on the yards yet higher aloft, the topmen, who as such had been picked out for youth and activity, constituted an aerial club lounging at ease against the smaller stun'sails rolled up into cushions, spinning yarns like the lazy gods, and frequently amused with what was going on in the busy world of the decks below. No wonder then that a young fellow of Billy's disposition was well content in such society. Giving no cause of offense to anybody, he was always alert at a call. So in the merchant service it had been with him. But now such a punctiliousness in duty was shown that his topmates would sometimes good-naturedly laugh at him for it. This heightened alacrity had its cause, namely, the impression made upon him by the first formal gangway-punishment he had ever witnessed, which befell the day following his impressment. It had been incurred by a little fellow, young, a novice afterguardsman absent from his assigned post when the ship was being put about; a dereliction resulting in a rather serious hitch to that maneuver, one demanding instantaneous promptitude in letting go and making fast. When Billy saw the culprit's naked back under the scourge, gridironed with red welts and worse, when he marked the dire expression in the liberated man's face as with his woolen shirt flung over him by the executioner he rushed forward from the spot to bury himself in the crowd, Billy was horrified. He resolved that never through remissness would he make himself liable to such a visitation or do or omit aught that might merit even verbal reproof. What then was his surprise and concern when ultimately he found himself getting into petty trouble occasionally about such matters as the stowage of his bag or something amiss in his hammock, matters under the police oversight of the ship's corporals of the lower decks, and which brought down on him a vague threat from one of them.

So heedful in all things as he was, how could this be? He could not understand it, and it more than vexed him. When he spoke to his young topmates about it they were either lightly incredulous or found something comical in his unconcealed anxiety. "Is it your bag, Billy?" said one. "Well, sew yourself up in it, bully boy, and then you'll be sure to know if anybody meddles with it."

Now there was a veteran aboard who because his years began to disqualify him for more active work had been recently assigned duty as mainmastman in his watch, looking to the gear belayed at the rail roundabout that great spar near the deck. At off-times the foretopman had picked up some acquaintance with him, and now in his trouble it occurred to him that he might be the sort of person to go to for wise counsel. He was an old Dansker long anglicized in the service, of few words, many wrinkles, and some honorable scars. His wizened face, time-tinted and weather-stained to the complexion of an antique parchment, was here and there peppered blue by the chance explosion of a gun cartridge in action.

He was an *Agamemnon* man, some two years prior to the time of this story having served under Nelson when still captain in that ship immortal in naval memory, which dismantled and in part broken up to her bare ribs is seen a grand skeleton in Haden's etching. As one of a boarding party from the *Agamemnon* he had received a cut slantwise along one temple and cheek leaving a long pale scar like a streak of dawn's light falling athwart the dark visage. It was on account of that scar and the affair in which it was known that he had received it, as well as from his blue-peppered complexion, that the Dansker went among the *Bellipotent*'s crew by the name of "Board Her-in-the-Smoke."

Now the first time that his small weasel eyes happened to light on Billy Budd, a certain grim internal merriment set all his ancient wrinkles into antic play. Was it that his eccentric unsentimental old sapience, primitive in its kind, saw or thought it saw something which in contrast with the warship's environment looked oddly incongruous in the Handsome Sailor? But after slyly studying him at intervals, the old Merlin's equivocal merriment was modified; for now when the twain would meet, it would start in his face a quizzing sort of look, but it would be but momentary and sometimes replaced by an expression of speculative query as to what might eventually befall a nature like that, dropped into a world not without some mantraps and against whose subtleties simple courage lacking experience and address, and without any touch of defensive ugliness, is of little avail; and where such innocence as man is capable of does yet in a moral emergency not always sharpen the faculties or enlighten the will.

However it was, the Dansker in his ascetic way rather took to Billy. Nor was this only because of a certain philosophic interest in such a character. There was another cause. While the old man's eccentricities, sometimes bordering on the ursine, repelled the juniors, Billy, undeterred thereby, revering him as a salt hero, would make advances, never passing the old *Agamemnon* man without a salutation marked by that respect which is seldom lost on the aged, however crabbed at times or whatever their station in life.

There was a vein of dry humor, or what not, in the mastman; and, whether in freak of patriarchal irony touching Billy's youth and athletic frame, or for some other and more recondite reason, from the first in addressing him he always substituted *Baby* for Billy, the Dansker in fact being the originator of the name by which the foretopman eventually became known aboard ship.

Well then, in his mysterious little difficulty going in quest of the wrinkled one, Billy found him off duty in a dogwatch ruminating by himself, seated on a shot box of the upper gun deck, now and then surveying with a somewhat cynical regard certain of the more swaggering promenaders there. Billy recounted his trouble, again wondering how it all happened.

The salt seer attentively listened, accompanying the foretopman's recital with queer twitchings of his wrinkles and problematical little sparkles of his small ferret eyes. Making an end of his story, the foretopman asked, "And now, Dansker, do tell me what you think of it."

The old man, shoving up the front of his tarpaulin and deliberately rubbing the long slant scar at the point where it entered the thin hair, laconically said, "Baby Budd, *Jemmy Legs*" (meaning the master-at-arms) "is down on you."

"*Jemmy Legs!*" ejaculated Billy, his welkin eyes expanding. "What for? Why, he calls me 'the sweet and pleasant young fellow,' they tell me."

"Does he so?" grinned the grizzled one; then said, "Ay, Baby lad, a sweet voice has Jemmy Legs."

"No, not always. But to me he has. I seldom pass him but there comes a pleasant word."

"And that's because he's down upon you, Baby Budd."

Such reiteration, along with the manner of it, incomprehensible to a novice, disturbed Billy almost as much as the mystery for which he had sought explanation. Something less unpleasingly oracular he tried to extract; but the old sea Chiron, thinking perhaps that for the nonce he had sufficiently instructed his young Achilles, pursed his lips, gathered all his wrinkles together, and would commit himself to nothing further.

Years, and those experiences which befall certain shrewder men subordinated lifelong to the will of superiors, all this had developed in the Dansker the pithy guarded cynicism that was his leading characteristic.

10

The next day an incident served to confirm Billy Budd in his incredulity as to the Dansker's strange summing up of the case submitted. The ship at noon, going large before the wind, was rolling on her course, and he below at dinner and engaged in some sportful talk with the members of his mess, chanced in a sudden lurch to spill the entire contents of his soup pan upon the new-scrubbed deck. Claggart, the master-at-arms, official rattan in hand, happened to be passing along the battery in a bay of which the mess was lodged, and the greasy liquid streamed just across his path. Stepping over it, he was proceeding on his way without comment, since the matter was nothing to take notice of under the circumstances, when he happened to observe who it was that had done the spilling. His countenance changed. Pausing, he was about to ejaculate something hasty at the sailor, but checked himself, and pointing down to the streaming soup, playfully tapped him from behind with his rattan, saying in a low musical voice peculiar to him at times, "Handsomely done, my lad! And handsome is as handsome did it, too!" And with that passed on. Not noted by Billy as not coming within his view was the involuntary smile, or rather grimace, that accompanied Claggart's equivocal words. Aridly it drew down the thin corners of his shapely mouth. But everybody taking his remark as meant for humorous, and at which therefore as coming from a superior they were bound to laugh "with counterfeited glee," acted accordingly; and Billy, tickled, it may be, by the allusion to his being the Handsome Sailor, merrily joined in; then addressing his messmates exclaimed, "There now, who says that Jemmy Legs is down on me!"

"And who said he was, Beauty?" demanded one Donald with some surprise. Whereat the foretopman looked a little foolish, recalling that it was only one person, Board-Her-in-the-Smoke, who had suggested what to him was the smoky idea that this master-at-arms was in any peculiar way hostile to him. Meantime that functionary, resuming his path, must have momentarily worn some expression less guarded than that of the bitter smile, usurping the face from the heart—some distorting expression perhaps, for a drummer-boy heedlessly frolicking along from the opposite direction and chancing to come into light collision with his person was strangely disconcerted by his aspect. Nor was the impression lessened when the official, impetuously giving him a sharp cut with the rattan, vehemently exclaimed, "Look where you go!"

11

What was the matter with the master-at-arms? And, be the matter what it might, how could it have direct relation to Billy Budd, with whom prior to the affair of the spilled soup he had never come into any special contact official or otherwise? What indeed could the trouble have to do with one so little inclined to give offense as the merchant-ship's "peacemaker," even him who in Claggart's own phrase was "the sweet and pleasant young fellow"? Yes, why should Jemmy Legs, to borrow the Dansker's expression, be "down" on the Handsome Sailor? But, at heart and not for nothing, as the late chance encounter may indicate to the discerning, down on him, secretly down on him, he assuredly was.

Now to invent something touching the more private career of Claggart, something involving Billy Budd, of which something the latter should be wholly ignorant, some romantic incident implying that Claggart's knowledge of the young bluejacket began at some period anterior to catching sight of him on board the seventy-four—all this, not so difficult to do, might avail in a way more or less interesting to account for whatever of enigma may appear to lurk in the case. But in fact there was nothing of the sort. And yet the cause necessarily to be assumed as the sole one assignable is in its very realism as much charged with that prime element of Radcliffian romance, the mysterious, as any that the ingenuity of the author of *The Mysteries of Udolpho* could devise. For what can more partake of the mysterious than an antipathy spontaneous and profound such as is evoked in certain exceptional mortals by the mere aspect of some other mortal, however harmless he may be, if not called forth by this very harmlessness itself?

Now there can exist no irritating juxtaposition of dissimilar personalities comparable to that which is possible aboard a great warship fully manned and at sea. There, every day among all ranks, almost every man comes into more or less of contact with almost every other man. Wholly there to avoid even the sight of an aggravating object one must needs give it Jonah's toss or jump overboard himself. Imagine how all this might eventually operate on some peculiar human creature the direct reverse of a saint!

But for the adequate comprehending of Claggart by a normal nature these hints are insufficient. To pass from a normal nature to him one must cross "the deadly space between." And this is best done by indirection.

Long ago an honest scholar, my senior, said to me in reference to one who like himself is now no more, a man so unimpeachably respectable that against him nothing was ever openly said though among the few something was whispered, "Yes, X—— is a nut not to be cracked by the tap of a lady's fan. You are aware that I am the adherent of no organized religion, much less of any philosophy built into a system. Well, for all that, I think that to try and get into X——, enter his labyrinth and get out again, without a clue derived from some source other than what is known as 'knowledge of the world'—that were hardly possible, at least for me."

"Why," said I, "X——, however singular a study to some, is yet human, and knowledge of the world assuredly implies the knowledge of human nature, and in most of its varieties."

"Yes, but a superficial knowledge of it, serving ordinary purposes. But for anything deeper, I am not certain whether to know the world and to know human nature be not two distinct branches of knowledge, which while they may coexist in the same heart, yet either may exist with little or nothing of the other. Nay, in an average man of the world, his constant rubbing with it blunts that finer spiritual insight indispensable to the understanding of the essential in certain exceptional characters, whether evil ones or good. In a matter of some importance I have seen a girl wind an old lawyer about her little finger. Nor was it the dotage of senile love. Nothing of the sort. But he knew law better than he knew the girl's heart. Coke and Blackstone hardly shed so much light into obscure spiritual places as the Hebrew prophets. And who were they? Mostly recluses."

At the time, my inexperience was such that I did not quite see the drift of all this. It may be that I see it now. And, indeed, if that lexicon which is based on Holy Writ were any longer popular, one might with less difficulty define and denominate certain phenomenal men. As it is, one must turn to some authority not liable to the charge of being tinctured with the biblical element.

In a list of definitions included in the authentic translation of Plato, a list attributed to him, occurs this: "Natural Depravity: a depravity according to nature," a definition which, though savoring of Calvinism, by no means involves Calvin's dogma as to total mankind. Evidently its intent makes it applicable but to individuals. Not many are the examples of this depravity which the gallows and jail supply. At any rate, for notable instances, since these have no vulgar alloy of the brute in them, but invariably are dominated by intellectuality, one must go elsewhere. Civilization, especially if of the austerer sort, is auspicious to it. It folds itself in the mantle of respectability. It has its certain negative virtues serving as silent auxiliaries. It never allows wine to get within its guard. It is not going too far to say that it is without vices or small sins. There is a phenomenal pride in it that excludes them. It is never mercenary or avaricious. In short, the depravity here meant partakes nothing of the sordid or sensual. It is serious, but free from acerbity. Though no flatterer of mankind it never speaks ill of it.

But the thing which in eminent instances signalizes so exceptional a nature is this: Though the man's even temper and discreet bearing would seem to intimate a mind peculiarly subject to the law of reason, not the less in heart he would seem to riot in complete exemption from that law, having apparently little to do with reason further than to employ it as an ambidexter implement for effecting the irrational. That is to say: Toward the accomplishment of an aim which in wantonness of atrocity would seem to partake of the insane, he will direct a cool judgment sagacious and sound. These men are madmen, and of the most dangerous sort, for their lunacy is not continuous, but occasional, evoked by some special object; it is protectively secretive, which is as much as to say it is self-contained, so that when, moreover, most active it is to the average mind not distinguishable from sanity, and for the reason above suggested: that whatever its aims may be—and the aim is never declared—the method and the outward proceeding are always perfectly rational.

Now something such an one was Claggart, in whom was the mania of an evil nature, not engendered by vicious training or corrupting books or licentious living, but born with him and innate, in short "a depravity according to nature."

Dark sayings are these, some will say. But why? Is it because they somewhat savor of Holy Writ in its phrase "mystery of iniquity"? If they do, such savor was far enough from being intended, for little will it commend these pages to many a reader of today.

The point of the present story turning on the hidden nature of the master-at-arms has necessitated this chapter. With an added hint or two in connection with the incident at the mess, the resumed narrative must be left to vindicate, as it may, its own credibility.

12

That Claggart's figure was not amiss, and his face, save the chin, well molded, has already been said. Of these favorable points he seemed not insensible, for he was not only neat but careful in his dress. But the form of Billy Budd was heroic; and if his face was without the intellectual look of the pallid Claggart's, not the less was it lit, like his, from within, though from a different source. The bonfire in his heart made luminous the rose-tan in his cheek.

In view of the marked contrast between the persons of the twain, it is more than probable that when the master-at-arms in the scene last given applied to the sailor the proverb "Handsome is as handsome does," he there let escape an ironic inkling, not caught by the young sailors who heard it, as to what it was that had first moved him against Billy, namely, his significant personal beauty.

Now envy and antipathy, passions irreconcilable in reason, nevertheless in fact may spring conjoined like Chang and Eng in one birth. Is Envy then such a monster? Well, though many an arraigned mortal has in hopes of mitigated penalty pleaded guilty to horrible actions, did ever anybody seriously confess to envy? Something there is in it universally felt to be more shameful than even felonious crime. And not only does everybody disown it, but the better sort are inclined to incredulity when it is in earnest imputed to an intelligent man. But since its lodgment is in the heart not the brain, no degree of intellect supplies a guarantee against it. But Claggart's was no vulgar form of the passion. Nor, as directed toward Billy Budd, did it partake of that streak of apprehensive jealousy that marred Saul's visage perturbedly brooding on the comely young David. Claggart's envy struck deeper. If askance he eyed the good looks, cheery health, and frank enjoyment of young life in Billy Budd, it was because these went along with a nature that, as Claggart magnetically felt, had in its simplicity never willed malice or experienced the reactionary bite of that serpent. To him, the spirit lodged within Billy, and looking out from his welkin eyes as from windows, that ineffability it was which made the dimple in his dyed cheek, suppled his joints, and dancing in his yellow curls made him pre eminently the Handsome Sailor. One person excepted, the master-at-arms was perhaps the only man in the ship intellectually capable of adequately appreciating the moral phenomenon presented in Billy Budd. And the insight but intensified his passion, which assuming various secret forms within him, at times assumed that of cynic disdain, disdain of innocence—to be nothing more than innocent! Yet in an aesthetic way he saw the charm of it, the courageous free-and-easy temper of it, and fain would have shared it, but he despaired of it.

With no power to annul the elemental evil in him, though readily enough he could hide it; apprehending the good, but powerless to be it; a nature like Claggart's, surcharged with energy as such natures almost invariably are, what recourse is left to it but to recoil upon itself and, like the scorpion for which the Creator alone is responsible, act out to the end the part allotted it.

13

Passion, and passion in its profoundest, is not a thing demanding a pala-tial stage whereon to play its part. Down among the groundlings, among the beggars and rakers of the garbage, profound passion is enacted. And the circumstances that provoke it, however trivial or mean, are no mea-sure of its power. In the present instance the stage is a scrubbed gun deck, and one of the external provocations a man-of-war's man's spilled soup.

Now when the master-at-arms noticed whence came that greasy fluid streaming before his feet, he must have taken it—to some extent wilfully, perhaps—not for the mere accident it assuredly was, but for the sly es-cape of a spontaneous feeling on Billy's part more or less answering to the antipathy on his own. In effect a foolish demonstration, he must have thought, and very harmless, like the futile kick of a heifer, which yet were the heifer a shod stallion would not be so harmless. Even so was it that into the gall of Claggart's envy he infused the vitriol of his contempt. But the incident confirmed to him certain telltale reports purveyed to his ear by "Squeak," one of his more cunning corporals, a grizzled little man, so nicknamed by the sailors on account of his squeaky voice and sharp vis-age ferreting about the dark corners of the lower decks after interlopers, satirically suggesting to them the idea of a rat in a cellar.

From his chief's employing him as an implicit tool in laying little traps for the worriment of the foretopman—for it was from the master-at-arms that the petty persecutions heretofore adverted to had proceeded—the corporal, having naturally enough concluded that his master could have no love for the sailor, made it his business, faithful understrapper that he was, to foment the ill blood by perverting to his chief certain innocent frolics of the good-natured foretopman, besides inventing for his mouth sundry contumelious epithets he claimed to have overheard him let fall. The master-at-arms never suspected the veracity of these reports, more especially as to the epithets, for he well knew how secretly unpopular may become a master-at-arms, at least a master-at-arms of those days, zealous in his function, and how the bluejackets shoot at him in private their raillery and wit; the nickname by which he goes among them (Jemmy Legs) implying under the form of merriment their cherished disrespect and dislike. But in view of the greediness of hate for pabulum it hardly needed a purveyor to feed Claggart's passion.

An uncommon prudence is habitual with the subtler depravity, for it has everything to hide. And in case of an injury but suspected, its secretiveness voluntarily cuts it off from enlightenment or disillusion; and, not unreluctantly, action is taken upon surmise as upon certainty. And the retaliation is apt to be in monstrous disproportion to the supposed offense; for when in anybody was revenge in its exactions aught else but an inordinate usurer? But how with Claggart's conscience? For though consciences are unlike as foreheads, every intelligence, not excluding the scriptural devils who "believe and tremble," has one. But Claggart's conscience being but the lawyer to his will, made ogres of trifles, probably arguing that the motive imputed to Billy in spilling the soup just when he did, together with the epithets alleged, these, if nothing more, made a strong case against him; nay, justified animosity into a sort of retributive righteousness. The Pharisee is the Guy Fawkes prowling in the hid chambers underlying some natures like Claggart's. And they can really form no conception of an unreciprocated malice. Probably the master-at-arms' clandestine persecution of Billy was started to try the temper of the man; but it had not developed any quality in him that enmity could make official use of or even pervert into plausible self-justification; so that the occurrence at the mess, petty if it were, was a welcome one to that peculiar conscience assigned to be the private mentor of Claggart; and, for the rest, not improbably it put him upon new experiments.

14

Not many days after the last incident narrated, something befell Billy Budd that more graveled him than aught that had previously occurred.

It was a warm night for the latitude; and the foretopman, whose watch at the time was properly below, was dozing on the uppermost deck whither he had ascended from his hot hammock, one of hundreds suspended so closely wedged together over a lower gun deck that there was little or no swing to them. He lay as in the shadow of a hillside, stretched under the lee of the booms, a piled ridge of spare spars amidships between foremast and mainmast among which the ship's largest boat, the launch, was stowed. Alongside of three other slumberers from below, he lay near that end of the booms which approaches the foremast; his station aloft on duty as a foretopman being just over the deck-station of the forecastlemen, entitling him according to usage to make himself more or less at home in that neighborhood.

Presently he was stirred into semiconsciousness by somebody, who must have previously sounded the sleep of the others, touching his shoulder, and then, as the foretopman raised his head, breathing into his ear in a quick whisper, "Slip into the lee forechains, Billy; there is something in the wind. Don't speak. Quick, I will meet you there," and disappearing.

Now Billy, like sundry other essentially good-natured ones, had some of the weaknesses inseparable from essential good nature; and among these was a reluctance, almost an incapacity of plumply saying *no* to an abrupt proposition not obviously absurd on the face of it, nor obviously unfriendly, nor iniquitous. And being of warm blood, he had not the phlegm tacitly to negative any proposition by unresponsive inaction. Like his sense of fear, his apprehension as to aught outside of the honest and natural was seldom very quick. Besides, upon the present occasion, the drowse from his sleep still hung upon him.

However it was, he mechanically rose and, sleepily wondering what could be in the wind, betook himself to the designated place, a narrow platform, one of six, outside of the high bulwarks and screened by the great deadeyes and multiple columned lanyards of the shrouds and backstays; and, in a great warship of that time, of dimensions commensurate to the hull's magnitude; a tarry balcony in short, overhanging the sea, and so secluded that one mariner of the *Bellipotent*, a Nonconformist old tar of a serious turn, made it even in daytime his private oratory.

In this retired nook the stranger soon joined Billy Budd. There was no moon as yet; a haze obscured the starlight. He could not distinctly see the stranger's face. Yet from something in the outline and carriage, Billy took him, and correctly, for one of the afterguard.

"Hist! Billy," said the man, in the same quick cautionary whisper as before. "You were impressed, weren't you? Well, so was I"; and he paused, as to mark the effect. But Billy, not knowing exactly what to make of this, said nothing. Then the other: "We are not the only impressed ones, Billy. There's a gang of us.—Couldn't you—help—at a pinch?"

"What do you mean?" demanded Billy, here thoroughly shaking off his drowse.

"Hist, hist!" the hurried whisper now growing husky. "See here," and the man held up two small objects faintly twinkling in the night-light; "see, they are yours, Billy, if you'll only——"

But Billy broke in, and in his resentful eagerness to deliver himself his vocal infirmity somewhat intruded. "D—d—damme, I don't know what you are d—d—driving at, or what you mean, but you had better g—g—go where you belong!" For the moment the fellow, as confounded, did not stir; and Billy, springing to his feet, said, "If you d—don't start, I'll t—t—toss you back over the r—rail!" There was no mistaking this, and the mysterious emissary decamped, disappearing in the direction of the mainmast in the shadow of the booms.

"Hallo, what's the matter?" here came growling from a forecastleman awakened from his deck-doze by Billy's raised voice. And as the foretopman reappeared and was recognized by him: "Ah, Beauty, is it you? Well, something must have been the matter, for you st—st—stuttered."

"Oh," rejoined Billy, now mastering the impediment, "I found an afterguardsman in our part of the ship here, and I bid him be off where he belongs."

"And is that all you did about it, Foretopman?" gruffly demanded another, an irascible old fellow of brick-colored visage and hair who was known to his associate forecastlemen as "Red Pepper." "Such sneaks I should like to marry to the gunner's daughter!"—by that expression meaning that he would like to subject them to disciplinary castigation over a gun.

However, Billy's rendering of the matter satisfactorily accounted to these inquirers for the brief commotion, since of all the sections of a ship's company the forecastlemen, veterans for the most part and bigoted in their sea prejudices, are the most jealous in resenting territorial encroachments, especially on the part of any of the afterguard, of whom they have but a sorry opinion—chiefly landsmen, never going aloft except to reef or furl the mainsail, and in no wise competent to handle a marlinspike or turn in a deadeye, say.

15

This incident sorely puzzled Billy Budd. It was an entirely new experience, the first time in his life that he had ever been personally approached in underhand intriguing fashion. Prior to this encounter he had known nothing of the afterguardsman, the two men being stationed wide apart, one forward and aloft during his watch, the other on deck and aft.

What could it mean? And could they really be guineas, those two glittering objects the interloper had held up to his (Billy's) eyes? Where could the fellow get guineas? Why, even spare buttons are not so plentiful at sea. The more he turned the matter over, the more he was nonplussed, and made uneasy and discomfited. In his disgustful recoil from an overture which, though he but ill comprehended, he instinctively knew must involve evil of some sort, Billy Budd was like a young horse fresh from the pasture suddenly inhaling a vile whiff from some chemical factory, and by repeated snortings trying to get it out of his nostrils and lungs. This frame of mind barred all desire of holding further parley with the fellow, even were it but for the purpose of gaining some enlightenment as to his design in approaching him. And yet he was not without natural curiosity to see how such a visitor in the dark would look in broad day.

He espied him the following afternoon in his first dogwatch below, one of the smokers on that forward part of the upper gun deck allotted to the pipe. He recognized him by his general cut and build more than by his round freckled face and glassy eyes of pale blue, veiled with lashes all but white. And yet Billy was a bit uncertain whether indeed it were he—yonder chap about his own age chatting and laughing in freehearted way, leaning against a gun; a genial young fellow enough to look at, and something of a rattlebrain, to all appearance. Rather chubby too for a sailor, even an afterguardsman. In short, the last man in the world, one would think, to be overburdened with thoughts, especially those perilous thoughts that must needs belong to a conspirator in any serious project, or even to the underling of such a conspirator.

Although Billy was not aware of it, the fellow, with a side long watchful glance, had perceived Billy first, and then noting that Billy was looking at him, thereupon nodded a familiar sort of friendly recognition as to an old acquaintance, without interrupting the talk he was engaged in with the group of smokers. A day or two afterwards, chancing in the evening promenade on a gun deck to pass Billy, he offered a flying word of goodfellowship, as it were, which by its unexpectedness, and equivocalness under the circumstances, so embarrassed Billy that he knew not how to respond to it, and let it go unnoticed.

Billy was now left more at a loss than before. The ineffectual speculations into which he was led were so disturbingly alien to him that he did his best to smother them. It never entered his mind that here was a matter which, from its extreme questionableness, it was his duty as a loyal bluejacket to report in the proper quarter. And, probably, had such a step been suggested to him, he would have been deterred from taking it by the thought, one of novice magnanimity, that it would savor overmuch of the dirty work of a telltale. He kept the thing to himself. Yet upon one occasion he could not forbear a little disburdening himself to the old Dansker, tempted thereto perhaps by the influence of a balmy night when the ship lay becalmed; the twain, silent for the most part, sitting together on deck, their heads propped against the bulwarks. But it was only a partial and anonymous account that Billy gave, the unfounded scruples above referred to preventing full disclosure to anybody. Upon hearing Billy's version, the sage Dansker seemed to divine more than he was told; and after a little meditation, during which his wrinkles were pursed as into a point, quite effacing for the time that quizzing expression his face sometimes wore: "Didn't I say so, Baby Budd?"

"Say what?" demanded Billy.

"Why, *Jemmy Legs* is *down* on you."

"And what," rejoined Billy in amazement, "has *Jemmy Legs* to do with that cracked afterguardsman?"

"Ho, it was an afterguardsman, then. A cat's-paw, a cat's-paw!" And with that exclamation, whether it had reference to a light puff of air just then coming over the calm sea, or a subtler relation to the afterguardsman, there is no telling, the old Merlin gave a twisting wrench with his black teeth at his plug of tobacco, vouchsafing no reply to Billy's impetuous question, though now repeated, for it was his wont to relapse into grim silence when interrogated in skeptical sort as to any of his sententious oracles, not always very clear ones, rather partaking of that obscurity which invests most Delphic deliverances from any quarter.

Long experience had very likely brought this old man to that bitter prudence which never interferes in aught and never gives advice.

16

Yes, despite the Dansker's pithy insistence as to the master-at-arms being at the bottom of these strange experiences of Billy on board the *Bellipotent*, the young sailor was ready to ascribe them to almost anybody but the man who, to use Billy's own expression, "always had a pleasant word for him." This is to be wondered at. Yet not so much to be wondered at. In certain matters, some sailors even in mature life remain unsophisticated enough. But a young seafarer of the disposition of our athletic foretopman is much of a child-man. And yet a child's utter innocence is but its blank ignorance, and the innocence more or less wanes as intelligence waxes. But in Billy Budd intelligence, such as it was, had advanced while yet his simple-mindedness remained for the most part unaffected. Experience is a teacher indeed; yet did Billy's years make his experience small. Besides, he had none of that intuitive knowledge of the bad which in natures not good or incompletely so foreruns experience, and therefore may pertain, as in some instances it too clearly does pertain, even to youth.

And what could Billy know of man except of man as a mere sailor? And the old-fashioned sailor, the veritable man before the mast, the sailor from boyhood up, he, though indeed of the same species as a landsman, is in some respects singularly distinct from him. The sailor is frankness, the landsman is finesse. Life is not a game with the sailor, demanding the long head—no intricate game of chess where few moves are made in straightforwardness and ends are attained by indirection, an oblique, tedious, barren game hardly worth that poor candle burnt out in playing it.

Yes, as a class, sailors are in character a juvenile race. Even their deviations are marked by juvenility, this more especially holding true with the sailors of Billy's time. Then too, certain things which apply to all sailors do more pointedly operate here and there upon the junior one. Every sailor, too, is accustomed to obey orders without debating them; his life afloat is externally ruled for him; he is not brought into that promiscuous commerce with mankind where unobstructed free agency on equal terms—equal superficially, at least—soon teaches one that unless upon occasion he exercise a distrust keen in proportion to the fairness of the appearance, some foul turn may be served him. A ruled undemonstrative distrustfulness is so habitual, not with businessmen so much as with men who know their kind in less shallow relations than business, namely, certain men of the world, that they come at last to employ it all but unconsciously; and some of them would very likely feel real surprise at being charged with it as one of their general characteristics.

17

But after the little matter at the mess Billy Budd no more found himself in strange trouble at times about his hammock or his clothes bag or what not. As to that smile that occasionally sunned him, and the pleasant passing word, these were, if not more frequent, yet if anything more pronounced than before.

But for all that, there were certain other demonstrations now. When

Claggart's unobserved glance happened to light on belted Billy rolling along the upper gun deck in the leisure of the second dogwatch, exchanging passing broadsides of fun with other young promenaders in the crowd, that glance would follow the cheerful sea Hyperion with a settled meditative and melancholy expression, his eyes strangely suffused with incipient feverish tears. Then would Claggart look like the man of sorrows. Yes, and sometimes the melancholy expression would have in it a touch of soft yearning, as if Claggart could even have loved Billy but for fate and ban. But this was an evanescence, and quickly repented of, as it were, by an immitigable look, pinching and shriveling the visage into the momentary semblance of a wrinkled walnut. But sometimes catching sight in advance of the foretopman coming in his direction, he would, upon their nearing, step aside a little to let him pass, dwelling upon Billy for the moment with the glittering dental satire of a Guise. But upon any abrupt unforeseen encounter a red light would flash forth from his eye like a spark from an anvil in a dusk smithy. That quick, fierce light was a strange one, darted from orbs which in repose were of a color nearest approaching a deeper violet, the softest of shades.

Though some of these caprices of the pit could not but be observed by their object, yet were they beyond the construing of such a nature. And the thews of Billy were hardly compatible with that sort of sensitive spiritual organization which in some cases instinctively conveys to ignorant innocence an admonition of the proximity of the malign. He thought the master-at-arms acted in a manner rather queer at times. That was all. But the occasional frank air and pleasant word went for what they purported to be, the young sailor never having heard as yet of the "too fair-spoken man."

Had the foretopman been conscious of having done or said anything to provoke the ill will of the official, it would have been different with him, and his sight might have been purged if not sharpened. As it was, innocence was his blinder.

So was it with him in yet another matter. Two minor officers, the armorer and captain of the hold, with whom he had never exchanged a word, his position in the ship not bringing him into contact with them, these men now for the first began to cast upon Billy, when they chanced to encounter him, that peculiar glance which evidences that the man from whom it comes has been some way tampered with, and to the prejudice of him upon whom the glance lights. Never did it occur to Billy as a thing to be noted or a thing suspicious, though he well knew the fact, that the armorer and captain of the hold, with the ship's yeoman, apothecary, and others of that grade, were by naval usage messmates of the master-at-arms, men with ears convenient to his confidential tongue.

But the general popularity that came from our Handsome Sailor's manly forwardness upon occasion and irresistible good nature, indicating no mental superiority tending to excite an invidious feeling, this good will on the part of most of his shipmates made him the less to concern himself about such mute aspects toward him as those whereto allusion has just been made, aspects he could not so fathom as to infer their whole import.

As to the afterguardsman, though Billy for reasons already given necessarily saw little of him, yet when the two did happen to meet, invariably came the fellow's offhand cheerful recognition, sometimes accompanied by a passing pleasant word or two. Whatever that equivocal young person's original design may really have been, or the design of which he might have been the deputy, certain it was from his manner upon these occasions that he had wholly dropped it.

It was as if his precocity of crookedness (and every vulgar villain is precocious) had for once deceived him, and the man he had sought to entrap as a simpleton had through his very simplicity ignominiously baffled him.

But shrewd ones may opine that it was hardly possible for Billy to refrain from going up to the afterguardsman and bluntly demanding to know his purpose in the initial interview so abruptly closed in the forechains. Shrewd ones may also think it but natural in Billy to set about sounding some of the other impressed men of the ship in order to discover what basis, if any, there was for the emissary's obscure suggestions as to plotting disaffection aboard. Yes, shrewd ones may so think. But something more, or rather something else than mere shrewdness is perhaps needful for the due understanding of such a character as Billy Budd's.

As to Claggart, the monomania in the man—if that indeed it were—as involuntarily disclosed by starts in the manifestations detailed, yet in general covered over by his self-contained and rational demeanor; this, like a subterranean fire, was eating its way deeper and deeper in him. Something decisive must come of it.

18

After the mysterious interview in the forechains, the one so abruptly ended there by Billy, nothing especially germane to the story occurred until the events now about to be narrated.

Elsewhere it has been said that in the lack of frigates (of course better sailers than line-of-battle ships) in the English squadron up the Straits at that period, the *Bellipotent* 74 was occasionally employed not only as an available substitute for a scout, but at times on detached service of more important kind. This was not alone because of her sailing qualities, not common in a ship of her rate, but quite as much, probably, that the character of her commander, it was thought, specially adapted him for any duty where under unforeseen difficulties a prompt initiative might have to be taken in some matter demanding knowledge and ability in addition to those qualities implied in good seamanship. It was on an expedition of the latter sort, a somewhat distant one, and when the *Bellipotent* was almost at her furthest remove from the fleet, that in the latter part of an afternoon watch she unexpectedly came in sight of a ship of the enemy. It proved to be a frigate. The latter, perceiving through the glass that the weight of men and metal would be heavily against her, invoking her light heels crowded sail to get away. After a chase urged almost against hope and lasting until about the middle of the first dogwatch, she signally succeeded in effecting her escape.

Not long after the pursuit had been given up, and ere the excitement incident thereto had altogether waned away, the master-at-arms, ascending from his cavernous sphere, made his appearance cap in hand by the mainmast respectfully waiting the notice of Captain Vere, then solitary walking the weather side of the quarter-deck, doubtless somewhat chafed at the failure of the pursuit. The spot where Claggart stood was the place allotted to men of lesser grades seeking some more particular interview either with the officer of the deck or the captain himself. But from the latter it was not often that a sailor or petty officer of those days would seek a hearing; only some exceptional cause would, according to established custom, have warranted that.

Presently, just as the commander, absorbed in his reflections, was on the point of turning aft in his promenade, he became sensible of Claggart's presence, and saw the doffed cap held in deferential expectancy.

Here be it said that Captain Vere's personal knowledge of this petty officer had only begun at the time of the ship's last sailing from home, Claggart then for the first, in transfer from a ship detained for repairs, supplying on board the *Bellipotent* the place of a previous master-at-arms disabled and ashore.

No sooner did the commander observe who it was that now deferentially stood awaiting his notice than a peculiar expression came over him. It was not unlike that which uncontrollably will flit across the countenance of one at unawares encountering a person who, though known to him indeed, has hardly been long enough known for thorough knowledge, but something in whose aspect nevertheless now for the first provokes a vaguely repellent distaste. But coming to a stand and resuming much of his wonted official manner, save that a sort of impatience lurked in the intonation of the opening word, he said "Well? What is it, Master-at-arms?"

With the air of a subordinate grieved at the necessity of being a messenger of ill tidings, and while conscientiously determined to be frank yet equally resolved upon shunning overstatement, Claggart at this invitation, or rather summons to disburden, spoke up. What he said, conveyed in the language of no uneducated man, was to the effect following, if not altogether in these words, namely, that during the chase and preparations for the possible encounter he had seen enough to convince him that at least one sailor aboard was a dangerous character in a ship mustering some who not only had taken a guilty part in the late serious troubles, but others also who, like the man in question, had entered His Majesty's service under another form than enlistment.

At this point Captain Vere with some impatience interrupted him: "Be direct, man; say *impressed men.*"

Claggart made a gesture of subservience, and proceeded. Quite lately he (Claggart) had begun to suspect that on the gun decks some sort of movement prompted by the sailor in question was covertly going on, but he had not thought himself warranted in reporting the suspicion so long as it remained indistinct. But from what he had that afternoon observed in the man referred to, the suspicion of something clandestine going on had advanced to a point less removed from certainty. He deeply felt, he added, the serious responsibility assumed in making a report involving such possible consequences to the individual mainly concerned, besides tending to augment those natural anxieties which every naval commander must feel in view of extraordinary outbreaks so recent as those which, he sorrowfully said it, it needed not to name.

Now at the first broaching of the matter Captain Vere, taken by surprise, could not wholly dissemble his disquietude. But as Claggart went on, the former's aspect changed into restiveness under something in the testifier's manner in giving his testimony. However, he refrained from interrupting him. And Claggart, continuing, concluded with this: "God forbid, your honor, that the *Bellipotent*'s should be the experience of the——"

"Never mind that!" here peremptorily broke in the superior, his face altering with anger, instinctively divining the ship that the other was about to name, one in which the Nore Mutiny had assumed a singularly tragical character that for a time jeopardized the life of its commander. Under the circumstances he was indignant at the purposed allusion. When the commissioned officers themselves were on all occasions very heedful how they referred to the recent events in the fleet, for a petty officer unnecessarily to allude to them in the presence of his captain, this struck him as a most immodest presumption. Besides, to his quick sense of self-respect it even looked under the circumstances something like an attempt to alarm him. Nor at first was he without some surprise that one who so far as he had hitherto come under his notice had shown considerable tact in his function should in this particular evince such lack of it.

But these thoughts and kindred dubious ones flitting across his mind were suddenly replaced by an intuitional surmise which, though as yet obscure in form, served practically to affect his reception of the ill tidings. Certain it is that, long versed in everything pertaining to the complicated gun-deck life, which like every other form of life has its secret mines and dubious side, the side popularly disclaimed, Captain Vere did not permit himself to be unduly disturbed by the general tenor of his subordinate's report.

Furthermore, if in view of recent events prompt action should be taken at the first palpable sign of recurring insubordination, for all that, not judicious would it be, he thought, to keep the idea of lingering disaffection alive by undue forwardness in crediting an informer, even if his own subordinate and charged among other things with police surveillance of the crew. This feeling would not perhaps have so prevailed with him were it not that upon a prior occasion the patriotic zeal officially evinced by Claggart had somewhat irritated him as appearing rather supersensible and strained. Furthermore, something even in the official's self-possessed and somewhat ostentatious manner in making his specifications strangely reminded him of a bandsman, a perjurous witness in a capital case before a court-martial ashore of which when a lieutenant he (Captain Vere) had been a member.

Now the peremptory check given to Claggart in the matter of the arrested allusion was quickly followed up by this: "You say that there is at least one dangerous man aboard. Name him."

"William Budd, a foretopman, your honor."

"William Budd!" repeated Captain Vere with unfeigned astonishment. "And mean you the man that Lieutenant Ratcliffe took from the merchantman not very long ago, the young fellow who seems to be so popular with the men—Billy, the Handsome Sailor, as they call him?"

"The same, your honor; but for all his youth and good looks, a deep one. Not for nothing does he insinuate himself into the good will of his shipmates, since at the least they will at a pinch say—all hands will—a good word for him, and at all hazards. Did Lieutenant Ratcliffe happen to tell your honor of that adroit fling of Budd's, jumping up in the cutter's bow under the merchantman's stern when he was being taken off? It is even masked by that sort of good-humored air that at heart he resents his impressment. You have but noted his fair cheek. A mantrap may be under the ruddy-tipped daisies."

Now the Handsome Sailor as a signal figure among the crew had naturally enough attracted the captain's attention from the first. Though in general not very demonstrative to his officers, he had congratulated Lieutenant Ratcliffe upon his good fortune in lighting on such a fine specimen of the *genus homo,* who in the nude might have posed for a statute of young Adam before the Fall. As to Billy's adieu to the ship *Rights-of-Man,* which the boarding lieutenant had indeed reported to him, but, in a deferential way, more as a good story than aught else, Captain Vere, though mistakenly understanding it as a satiric sally, had but thought so much the better of the impressed man for it; as a military sailor, admiring the spirit that could take an arbitrary enlistment so merrily and sensibly. The foretopman's conduct, too, so far as it had fallen under the captain's notice, had confirmed the first happy augury, while the new recruit's qualities as a "sailor-man" seemed to be such that he had thought of recommending him to the executive officer for promotion to a place that would more frequently bring him under his own observation, namely, the captaincy of the mizzentop, replacing there in the starboard watch a man not so young whom partly for that reason he deemed less fitted for the post. Be it parenthesized here that since the mizzentopmen have not to handle such breadths of heavy canvas as the lower sails on the mainmast and foremast, a young man if of the right stuff not only seems best adapted to duty there, but in fact is generally selected for the captaincy of that top, and the company under him are light hands and often but striplings. In sum, Captain Vere had from the beginning deemed Billy Budd to be what in the naval parlance of the time was called a "King's bargain": that is to say, for His Britannic Majesty's navy a capital investment at small outlay or none at all.

After a brief pause, during which the reminiscences above mentioned passed vividly through his mind and he weighed the import of Claggart's last suggestion conveyed in the phrase "mantrap under the daisies," and the more he weighed it the less reliance he felt in the informer's good faith, suddenly he turned upon him and in a low voice demanded: "Do you come to me, Master-at-arms, with so foggy a tale? As to Budd, cite me an act or spoken word of his confirmatory of what you in general charge against him. Stay," drawing nearer to him; "heed what you speak. Just now, and in a case like this, there is a yardarm-end for the false witness."

"Ah, your honor!" sighed Claggart, mildly shaking his shapely head as in sad deprecation of such unmerited severity of tone. Then, bridling—erecting himself as in virtuous self-assertion—he circumstantially alleged certain words and acts which collectively, if credited, led to presumptions mortally inculpating Budd. And for some of these averments, he added, substantiating proof was not far.

With gray eyes impatient and distrustful essaying to fathom to the bottom Claggart's calm violet ones, Captain Vere again heard him out; then for the moment stood ruminating. The mood he evinced, Claggart—himself for the time liberated from the other's scrutiny—steadily regarded with a look difficult to render: a look curious of the operation of his tactics, a look such as might have been that of the spokesman of the envious children of Jacob deceptively imposing upon the troubled patriarch the blood-dyed coat of young Joseph.

Though something exceptional in the moral quality of Captain Vere made him, in earnest encounter with a fellow man, a veritable touchstone of that man's essential nature, yet now as to Claggart and what was really going on in him his feeling partook less of intuitional conviction than of strong suspicion clogged by strange dubieties. The perplexity he evinced proceeded less from aught touching the man informed against—as Claggart doubtless opined—than from considerations how best to act in regard to the informer. At first, indeed, he was naturally for summoning that substantiation of his allegations which Claggart said was at hand. But such a proceeding would result in the matter at once getting abroad, which in the present stage of it, he thought, might undesirably affect the ship's company. If Claggart was a false witness—that closed the affair. And therefore, before trying the accusation, he would first practically test the accuser; and he thought this could be done in a quiet, undemonstrative way.

The measure he determined upon involved a shifting of the scene, a transfer to a place less exposed to observation than the broad quarterdeck. For although the few gun-room officers there at the time had, in due observance of naval etiquette, withdrawn to leeward the moment Captain Vere had begun his promenade on the deck's weather side; and though during the colloquy with Claggart they of course ventured not to diminish the distance; and though throughout the interview Captain Vere's voice was far from high, and Claggart's silvery and low; and the wind in the cordage and the wash of the sea helped the more to put them beyond earshot; nevertheless, the interview's continuance already had attracted observation from some topmen aloft and other sailors in the waist or further forward.

Having determined upon his measures, Captain Vere forthwith took action. Abruptly turning to Claggart, he asked, "Master-at-arms, is it now Budd's watch aloft?"

"No, your honor."

Whereupon, "Mr. Wilkes!" summoning the nearest midshipman. "Tell Albert to come to me." Albert was the captain's hammock-boy, a sort of sea valet in whose discretion and fidelity his master had much confidence. The lad appeared.

"You know Budd, the foretopman?"

"I do, sir."

"Go find him. It is his watch off. Manage to tell him out of earshot that he is wanted aft. Contrive it that he speaks to nobody. Keep him in talk yourself. And not till you get well aft here, not till then let him know that the place where he is wanted is my cabin. You understand. Go.— Master-at-arms, show yourself on the decks below, and when you think it time for Albert to be coming with his man, stand by quietly to follow the sailor in."

19

Now when the foretopman found himself in the cabin, closeted there, as it were, with the captain and Claggart, he was surprised enough. But it was a surprise unaccompanied by apprehension or distrust. To an immature nature essentially honest and humane, forewarning intimations of subtler danger from one's kind come tardily if at all. The only thing that took shape in the young sailor's mind was this: Yes, the captain, I have always thought, looks kindly upon me. Wonder if he's going to make me his coxswain. I should like that. And may be now he is going to ask the master-at-arms about me.

"Shut the door there, sentry," said the commander; "stand without, and let nobody come in.—Now, Master-at-arms, tell this man to his face what you told of him to me," and stood prepared to scrutinize the mutually confronting visages.

With the measured step and calm collected air of an asylum physician approaching in the public hall some patient beginning to show indications of a coming paroxysm, Claggart deliberately advanced within short range of Billy and, mesmerically looking him in the eye, briefly recapitulated the accusation.

Not at first did Billy take it in. When he did, the rose-tan of his cheek looked struck as by white leprosy. He stood like one impaled and gagged. Meanwhile the accuser's eyes, removing not as yet from the blue dilated ones, underwent a phenomenal change, their wonted rich violet color blurring into a muddy purple. Those lights of human intelligence, losing human expression, were gelidly protruding like the alien eyes of certain uncatalogued creatures of the deep. The first mesmeristic glance was one of serpent fascination; the last was as the paralyzing lurch of the torpedo fish.

"Speak, man!" said Captain Vere to the transfixed one, struck by his aspect even more than by Claggart's. "Speak! Defend yourself!" Which appeal caused but a strange dumb gesturing and gurgling in Billy; amazement at such an accusation so suddenly sprung on inexperienced nonage; this, and, it may be, horror of the accuser's eyes, serving to bring out his lurking defect and in this instance for the time intensifying it into a convulsed tongue-tie; while the intent head and entire form straining forward in an agony of ineffectual eagerness to obey the injunction to speak and defend himself, gave an expression to the face like that of a condemned vestal priestess in the moment of being buried alive, and in the first struggle against suffocation.

Though at the time Captain Vere was quite ignorant of Billy's liability to vocal impediment, he now immediately divined it, since vividly Billy's aspect recalled to him that of a bright young schoolmate of his whom he had once seen struck by much the same startling impotence in the act of eagerly rising in the class to be foremost in response to a testing question put to it by the master. Going close up to the young sailor, and laying a soothing hand on his shoulder, he said, "There is no hurry, my boy. Take your time, take your time." Contrary to the effect intended, these words so fatherly in tone, doubtless touching Billy's heart to the quick, prompted yet more violent efforts at utterance—efforts soon ending for the time in confirming the paralysis, and bringing to his face an expression which was as a crucifixion to behold. The next instant, quick as the flame from a discharged cannon at night, his right arm shot out, and Claggart dropped to the deck. Whether intentionally or but owing to the young athlete's superior height, the blow had taken effect full upon the forehead, so shapely and intellectual-looking a feature in the master-at-arms; so that the body fell over lengthwise, like a heavy plank tilted from erectness. A gasp or two, and he lay motionless.

"Fated boy," breathed Captain Vere in tone so low as to be almost a whisper, "what have you done! But here, help me."

The twain raised the felled one from the loins up into a sitting position. The spare form flexibly acquiesced, but inertly. It was like handling a dead snake. They lowered it back. Regaining erectness, Captain Vere with one hand covering his face stood to all appearance as impassive as the object at his feet. Was he absorbed in taking in all the bearings of the event and what was best not only now at once to be done, but also in the sequel? Slowly he uncovered his face; and the effect was as if the moon emerging from eclipse should reappear with quite another aspect than that which had gone into hiding. The father in him, manifested towards Billy thus far in the scene, was replaced by the military disciplinarian. In his official tone he bade the foretopman retire to a stateroom aft (pointing it out), and there remain till thence summoned. This order Billy in silence mechanically obeyed. Then going to the cabin door where it opened on the quarter-deck, Captain Vere said to the sentry without, "Tell somebody to send Albert here." When the lad appeared, his master so contrived it that he should not catch sight of the prone one. "Albert," he said to him, "tell the surgeon I wish to see him. You need not come back till called."

When the surgeon entered—a self-poised character of that grave sense and experience that hardly anything could take him aback— Captain Vere advanced to meet him, thus unconsciously intercepting his view of Claggart, and, interrupting the other's wonted ceremonious salutation, said, "Nay. Tell me how it is with yonder man," directing his attention to the prostrate one.

The surgeon looked, and for all his self-command somewhat started at the abrupt revelation. On Claggart's always pallid complexion, thick black blood was now oozing from nostril and ear. To the gazer's professional eye it was unmistakably no living man that he saw.

"Is it so, then?" said Captain Vere, intently watching him. "I thought it. But verify it." Whereupon the customary tests confirmed the surgeon's first glance, who now, looking up in unfeigned concern, cast a look of intense inquisitiveness upon his superior. But Captain Vere, with one hand to his brow, was standing motionless. Suddenly, catching the surgeon's arm convulsively, he exclaimed, pointing down to the body, "It is the divine judgment on Ananias! Look!"

Disturbed by the excited manner he had never before observed in the *Bellipotent*'s captain, and as yet wholly ignorant of the affair, the prudent surgeon nevertheless held his peace, only again looking an earnest interrogatory as to what it was that had resulted in such a tragedy.

But Captain Vere was now again motionless, standing absorbed in thought. Again starting, he vehemently exclaimed, "Struck dead by an angel of God! Yet the angel must hang!"

At these passionate interjections, mere incoherences to the listener as yet unapprised of the antecedents, the surgeon was profoundly discomposed. But now, as recollecting himself, Captain Vere in less passionate tone briefly related the circumstances leading up to the event. "But come; we must dispatch," he added. "Help me to remove him" (meaning the body) "to yonder compartment," designating one opposite that where the foretopman remained immured. Anew disturbed by a request that, as implying a desire for secrecy, seemed unaccountably strange to him, there was nothing for the subordinate to do but comply.

"Go now," said Captain Vere with something of his wonted manner. "Go now. I presently shall call a drumhead court. Tell the lieutenants what has happened, and tell Mr. Mordant" (meaning the captain of marines), "and charge them to keep the matter to themselves."

20

Full of disquietude and misgiving, the surgeon left the cabin. Was Captain Vere suddenly affected in his mind, or was it but a transient excitement, brought about by so strange and extraordinary a tragedy? As to the drumhead court, it struck the surgeon as impolitic, if nothing more. The thing to do, he thought, was to place Billy Budd in confinement, and in a way dictated by usage, and postpone further action in so extraordinary a case to such time as they should rejoin the squadron, and then refer it to the admiral. He recalled the unwonted agitation of Captain Vere and his excited exclamations, so at variance with his normal manner. Was he unhinged?

But assuming that he is, it is not so susceptible of proof. What then can the surgeon do? No more trying situation is conceivable than that of an officer subordinate under a captain whom he suspects to be not mad, indeed, but yet not quite unaffected in his intellects. To argue his order to him would be insolence. To resist him would be mutiny.

In obedience to Captain Vere, he communicated what had happened to the lieutenants and captain of marines, saying nothing as to the captain's state. They fully shared his own surprise and concern. Like him too, they seemed to think that such a matter should be referred to the admiral.

21

Who in the rainbow can draw the line where the violet tint ends and the orange tint begins? Distinctly we see the difference of the colors, but where exactly does the one first blendingly enter into the other? So with sanity and insanity. In pronounced cases there is no question about them.

But in some supposed cases, in various degrees supposedly less pronounced, to draw the exact line of demarcation few will undertake, though for a fee becoming considerate some professional experts will. There is nothing namable but that some men will, or undertake to, do it for pay.

Whether Captain Vere, as the surgeon professionally and privately surmised, was really the sudden victim of any degree of aberration, every one must determine for himself by such light as this narrative may afford.

That the unhappy event which has been narrated could not have happened at a worse juncture was but too true. For it was close on the heel of the suppressed insurrections, an aftertime very critical to naval authority, demanding from every English sea commander two qualities not readily interfusable—prudence and rigor. Moreover, there was something crucial in the case.

In the jugglery of circumstances preceding and attending the event on board the *Bellipotent,* and in the light of that martial code whereby it was formally to be judged, innocence and guilt personified in Claggart and Budd in effect changed places. In a legal view the apparent victim of the tragedy was he who had sought to victimize a man blameless; and the indisputable deed of the latter, navally regarded, constituted the most heinous of military crimes. Yet more. The essential right and wrong involved in the matter, the clearer that might be, so much the worse for the responsibility of a loyal sea commander, inasmuch as he was not authorized to determine the matter on that primitive basis.

Small wonder then that the *Bellipotent*'s captain, though in general a man of rapid decision, felt that circumspectness not less than promptitude was necessary. Until he could decide upon his course, and in each detail; and not only so, but until the concluding measure was upon the point of being enacted, he deemed it advisable, in view of all the circumstances, to guard as much as possible against publicity. Here he may or may not have erred. Certain it is, however, that subsequently in the confidential talk of more than one or two gun rooms and cabins he was not a little criticized by some officers, a fact imputed by his friends and vehemently by his cousin Jack Denton to professional jealousy of Starry Vere. Some imaginative ground for invidious comment there was. The maintenance of secrecy in the matter, the confining all knowledge of it for a time to the place where the homicide occurred, the quarter-deck cabin; in these particulars lurked some resemblance to the policy adopted in those tragedies of the palace which have occurred more than once in the capital founded by Peter the Barbarian.

The case indeed was such that fain would the *Bellipotent*'s captain have deferred taking any action whatever respecting it further than to keep the foretopman a close prisoner till the ship rejoined the squadron and then submitting the matter to the judgment of his admiral.

But a true military officer is in one particular like a true monk. Not with more of self-abnegation will the latter keep his vows of monastic obedience than the former his vows of allegiance to martial duty.

Feeling that unless quick action was taken on it, the deed of the foretopman, so soon as it should be known on the gun decks, would tend to awaken any slumbering embers of the Nore among the crew, a sense of the urgency of the case overruled in Captain Vere every other consideration. But though a conscientious disciplinarian, he was no lover of authority for mere authority's sake. Very far was he from embracing opportunities for monopolizing to himself the perils of moral responsibility, none at least that could properly be referred to an official superior or shared with him by his official equals or even subordinates. So thinking, he was glad it would not be at variance with usage to turn the matter over to a summary court of his own officers, reserving to himself, as the one on whom the ultimate accountability would rest, the right of maintaining a supervision of it, or formally or informally interposing at need. Accordingly a drumhead court was summarily convened, he electing the individuals composing it: the first lieutenant, the captain of marines, and the sailing master.

In associating an officer of marines with the sea lieutenant and the sailing master in a case having to do with a sailor, the commander perhaps deviated from general custom. He was prompted thereto by the circumstance that he took that soldier to be a judicious person, thoughtful, and not altogether incapable of grappling with a difficult case unprecedented in his prior experience. Yet even as to him he was not without some latent misgiving, for withal he was an extremely good-natured man, an enjoyer of his dinner, a sound sleeper, and inclined to obesity—a man who though he would always maintain his manhood in battle might not prove altogether reliable in a moral dilemma involving aught of the tragic. As to the first lieutenant and the sailing master, Captain Vere could not but be aware that though honest natures, of approved gallantry upon occasion, their intelligence was mostly confined to the matter of active seamanship and the fighting demands of their profession.

The court was held in the same cabin where the unfortunate affair had taken place. This cabin, the commander's, embraced the entire area under the poop deck. Aft, and on either side, was a small stateroom, the one now temporarily a jail and the other a dead-house, and a yet smaller compartment, leaving a space between expanding forward into a goodly oblong of length coinciding with the ship's beam. A skylight of moderate dimension was overhead, and at each end of the oblong space were two sashed porthole windows easily convertible back into embrasures for short carronades.

All being quickly in readiness, Billy Budd was arraigned, Captain Vere necessarily appearing as the sole witness in the case, and as such temporarily sinking his rank, though singularly maintaining it in a matter apparently trivial, namely, that he testified from the ship's weather side, with that object having caused the court to sit on the lee side. Concisely he narrated all that had led up to the catastrophe, omitting nothing in Claggart's accusation and deposing as to the manner in which the prisoner had received it. At this testimony the three officers glanced with no little surprise at Billy Budd, the last man they would have suspected either of the mutinous design alleged by Claggart or the undeniable deed he himself had done. The first lieutenant, taking judicial primacy and turning toward the prisoner, said, "Captain Vere has spoken. Is it or is it not as Captain Vere says?"

In response came syllables not so much impeded in the utterance as might have been anticipated. They were these: "Captain Vere tells the truth. It is just as Captain Vere says, but it is not as the master-at-arms said. I have eaten the King's bread and I am true to the King."

"I believe you, my man," said the witness, his voice indicating a suppressed emotion not otherwise betrayed.

"God will bless you for that, your honor!" not without stammering said Billy, and all but broke down. But immediately he was recalled to self-control by another question, to which with the same emotional difficulty of utterance he said, "No, there was no malice between us. I never bore malice against the master-at-arms. I am sorry that he is dead. I did not mean to kill him. Could I have used my tongue I would not have struck him. But he foully lied to my face and in presence of my captain, and I had to say something, and I could only say it with a blow, God help me!"

In the impulsive aboveboard manner of the frank one the court saw confirmed all that was implied in words that just previously had perplexed them, coming as they did from the testifier to the tragedy and promptly following Billy's impassioned disclaimer of mutinous intent— Captain Vere's words, "I believe you, my man."

Next it was asked of him whether he knew of or suspected aught savoring of incipient trouble (meaning mutiny, though the explicit term was avoided) going on in any section of the ship's company.

The reply lingered. This was naturally imputed by the court to the same vocal embarrassment which had retarded or obstructed previous answers. But in main it was otherwise here, the question immediately recalling to Billy's mind the interview with the afterguardsman in the forechains. But an innate repugnance to playing a part at all approaching that of an informer against one's own shipmates—the same erring sense of uninstructed honor which had stood in the way of his reporting the matter at the time, though as a loyal man-of-war's man it was incumbent on him, and failure so to do, if charged against him and proven, would have subjected him to the heaviest of penalties; this, with the blind feeling now his that nothing really was being hatched, prevailed with him. When the answer came it was a negative.

"One question more," said the officer of marines, now first speaking and with a troubled earnestness. "You tell us that what the master-at-arms said against you was a lie. Now why should he have so lied, so maliciously lied, since you declare there was no malice between you?"

At that question, unintentionally touching on a spiritual sphere wholly obscure to Billy's thoughts, he was nonplussed, evincing a confusion indeed that some observers, such as can readily be imagined, would have construed into involuntary evidence of hidden guilt. Nevertheless, he strove some way to answer, but all at once relinquished the vain endeavor, at the same time turning an appealing glance towards Captain Vere as deeming him his best helper and friend. Captain Vere, who had been seated for a time, rose to his feet, addressing the interrogator. "The question you put to him comes naturally enough. But how can he rightly answer it?—or anybody else, unless indeed it be he who lies within there," designating the compartment where lay the corpse. "But the prone one there will not rise to our summons. In effect, though, as it seems to me, the point you make is hardly material. Quite aside from any conceivable motive actuating the master-at-arms, and irrespective of the provocation to the blow, a martial court must needs in the present case confine its attention to the blow's consequence, which consequence justly is to be deemed not otherwise than as the striker's deed."

This utterance, the full significance of which it was not at all likely that Billy took in, nevertheless caused him to turn a wistful interrogative look toward the speaker, a look in its dumb expressiveness not unlike that which a dog of generous breed might turn upon his master, seeking in his face some elucidation of a previous gesture ambiguous to the canine intelligence. Nor was the same utterance without marked effect upon the three officers, more especially the soldier. Couched in it seemed to them a meaning unanticipated, involving a prejudgment on the speaker's part. It served to augment a mental disturbance previously evident enough.

The soldier once more spoke, in a tone of suggestive dubiety addressing at once his associates and Captain Vere: "Nobody is present—none of the ship's company, I mean—who might shed lateral light, if any is to be had, upon what remains mysterious in this matter."

"That is thoughtfully put," said Captain Vere; "I see your drift. Ay, there is a mystery; but, to use a scriptural phrase, it is a 'mystery of iniquity,' a matter for psychologic theologians to discuss. But what has a military court to do with it? Not to add that for us any possible investigation of it is cut off by the lasting tongue-tie of—him—in yonder," again designating the mortuary stateroom. "The prisoner's deed—with that alone we have to do."

To this, and particularly the closing reiteration, the marine soldier, knowing not how aptly to reply, sadly abstained from saying aught. The first lieutenant, who at the outset had not unnaturally assumed primacy in the court, now overrulingly instructed by a glance from Captain Vere, a glance more effective than words, resumed that primacy. Turning to the prisoner, "Budd," he said, and scarce in equable tones, "Budd, if you have aught further to say for yourself, say it now."

Upon this the young sailor turned another quick glance toward Captain Vere; then, as taking a hint from that aspect, a hint confirming his own instinct that silence was now best, replied to the lieutenant, "I have said all, sir."

The marine—the same who had been the sentinel without the cabin door at the time that the foretopman, followed by the master-at-arms, entered it—he, standing by the sailor throughout these judicial proceedings, was now directed to take him back to the after compartment originally assigned to the prisoner and his custodian. As the twain disappeared from view, the three officers, as partially liberated from some inward constraint associated with Billy's mere presence, simultaneously stirred in their seats. They exchanged looks of troubled indecision, yet feeling that decide they must and without long delay. For Captain Vere, he for the time stood—unconsciously with his back toward them, apparently in one of his absent fits—gazing out from a sashed porthole to windward upon the monotonous blank of the twilight sea. But the court's silence continuing, broken only at moments by brief consultations, in low earnest tones, this served to arouse him and energize him. Turning, he to-and-fro paced the cabin athwart; in the returning ascent to windward climbing the slant deck in the ship's lee roll, without knowing it symbolizing thus in his action a mind resolute to surmount difficulties even if against primitive instincts strong as the wind and the sea. Presently he came to a stand before the three. After scanning their faces he stood less as mustering his thoughts for expression than as one inly deliberating how best to put them to well-meaning men not intellectually mature, men with whom it was necessary to demonstrate certain principles that were axioms to himself. Similar impatience as to talking is perhaps one reason that deters some minds from addressing any popular assemblies.

When speak he did, something, both in the substance of what he said and his manner of saying it, showed the influence of unshared studies modifying and tempering the practical training of an active career. This, along with his phraseology, now and then was suggestive of the grounds whereon rested that imputation of a certain pedantry socially alleged against him by certain naval men of wholly practical cast, captains who nevertheless would frankly concede that His Majesty's navy mustered no more efficient officer of their grade than Starry Vere.

What he said was to this effect: "Hitherto I have been but the witness, little more; and I should hardly think now to take another tone, that of your coadjutor for the time, did I not perceive in you—at the crisis too—a troubled hesitancy, proceeding, I doubt not, from the clash of military duty with moral scruple—scruple vitalized by compassion. For the compassion, how can I otherwise than share it? But, mindful of paramount obligations, I strive against scruples that may tend to enervate decision. Not, gentlemen, that I hide from myself that the case is an exceptional one. Speculatively regarded, it well might be referred to a jury of casuists. But for us here, acting not as casuists or moralists, it is a case practical, and under martial law practically to be dealt with.

"But your scruples: do they move as in a dusk? Challenge them. Make them advance and declare themselves. Come now; do they import something like this: If, mindless of palliating circumstances, we are bound to regard the death of the master-at-arms as the prisoner's deed, then does that deed constitute a capital crime whereof the penalty is a mortal one. But in natural justice is nothing but the prisoner's overt act to be considered? How can we adjudge to summary and shameful death a fellow creature innocent before God, and whom we feel to be so?—Does that state it aright? You sign sad assent. Well, I too feel that, the full force of that. It is Nature. But do these buttons that we wear attest that our allegiance is to Nature? No, to the King. Though the ocean, which is inviolate Nature primeval, though this be the element where we move and have our being as sailors, yet as the King's officers lies our duty in a sphere correspondingly natural? So little is that true, that in receiving our commissions we in the most important regards ceased to be natural free agents. When war is declared are we the commissioned fighters previously consulted? We fight at command. If our judgments approve the war, that is but coincidence. So in other particulars. So now. For suppose condemnation to follow these present proceedings. Would it be so much we ourselves that would condemn as it would be martial law operating through us? For that law and the rigor of it, we are not responsible. Our vowed responsibility is in this: That however pitilessly that law may operate in any instances, we nevertheless adhere to it and administer it.

"But the exceptional in the matter moves the hearts within you. Even so too is mine moved. But let not warm hearts betray heads that should be cool. Ashore in a criminal case, will an upright judge allow himself off the bench to be waylaid by some tender kinswoman of the accused seeking to touch him with her tearful plea? Well, the heart here, sometimes the feminine in man, is as that piteous woman, and hard though it be, she must here be ruled out."

He paused, earnestly studying them for a moment; then resumed.

"But something in your aspect seems to urge that it is not solely the heart that moves in you, but also the conscience, the private conscience. But tell me whether or not, occupying the position we do, private conscience should not yield to that imperial one formulated in the code under which alone we officially proceed?"

Here the three men moved in their seats, less convinced than agitated by the course of an argument troubling but the more the spontaneous conflict within.

Perceiving which, the speaker paused for a moment; then abruptly changing his tone, went on.

"To steady us a bit, let us recur to the facts.—In wartime at sea a man-of-war's man strikes his superior in grade, and the blow kills. Apart from its effect the blow itself is, according to the Articles of War, a capital crime. Furthermore——"

"Ay, sir," emotionally broke in the officer of marines, "in one sense it was. But surely Budd purposed neither mutiny nor homicide."

"Surely not, my good man. And before a court less arbitrary and more merciful than a martial one, that plea would largely extenuate. At the Last Assizes it shall acquit. But how here? We proceed under the law of the Mutiny Act. In feature no child can resemble his father more than that Act resembles in spirit the thing from which it derives—War. In His Majesty's service—in this ship, indeed—there are Englishmen forced to fight for the King against their will. Against their conscience, for aught we know. Though as their fellow creatures some of us may appreciate their position, yet as navy officers what reck we of it? Still less recks the enemy. Our impressed men he would fain cut down in the same swath with our volunteers. As regards the enemy's naval conscripts, some of whom may even share our own abhorrence of the regicidal French Directory, it is the same on our side. War looks but to the frontage, the appearance. And the Mutiny Act, War's child, takes after the father. Budd's intent or non-intent is nothing to the purpose.

"But while, put to it by those anxieties in you which I cannot but respect, I only repeat myself—while thus strangely we prolong proceedings that should be summary—the enemy may be sighted and an engagement result. We must do; and one of two things must we do—condemn or let go."

"Can we not convict and yet mitigate the penalty?" asked the sailing master, here speaking, and falteringly, for the first.

"Gentlemen, were that clearly lawful for us under the circumstances, consider the consequences of such clemency. The people" (meaning the ship's company) "have native sense; most of them are familiar with our naval usage and tradition; and how would they take it? Even could you explain to them—which our official position forbids—they, long molded by arbitrary discipline, have not that kind of intelligent responsiveness that might qualify them to comprehend and discriminate. No, to the people the foretopman's deed, however it be worded in the announcement, will be plain homicide committed in a flagrant act of mutiny. What penalty for that should follow, they know. But it does not follow. *Why?* they will ruminate. You know what sailors are. Will they not revert to the recent outbreak at the Nore? Ay. They know the well-founded alarm—the panic it struck throughout England. Your clement sentence they would account pusillanimous. They would think that we flinch, that we are afraid of them—afraid of practicing a lawful rigor singularly demanded at this juncture, lest it should provoke new troubles. What shame to us such a conjecture on their part, and how deadly to discipline. You see then, whither, prompted by duty and the law, I steadfastly drive. But I beseech you, my friends, do not take me amiss. I feel as you do for this unfortunate boy. But did he know our hearts, I take him to be of that generous nature that he would feel even for us on whom in this military necessity so heavy a compulsion is laid."

With that, crossing the deck he resumed his place by the sashed porthole, tacitly leaving the three to come to a decision. On the cabin's opposite side the troubled court sat silent. Loyal lieges, plain and practical, though at bottom they dissented from some points Captain Vere had put to them, they were without the faculty, hardly had the inclination, to gainsay one whom they felt to be an earnest man, one too not less their superior in mind than in naval rank. But it is not improbable that even such of his words as were not without influence over them, less came home to them than his closing appeal to their instinct as sea officers: in the forethought he threw out as to the practical consequences to discipline, considering the unconfirmed tone of the fleet at the time, should a man-of-war's man's violent killing at sea of a superior in grade be allowed to pass for aught else than a capital crime demanding prompt infliction of the penalty.

Not unlikely they were brought to something more or less akin to that harassed frame of mind which in the year 1842 actuated the commander of the U.S. brig-of-war *Somers* to resolve, under the so-called Articles of War, Articles modeled upon the English Mutiny Act, to resolve upon the execution at sea of a midshipman and two sailors as mutineers designing the seizure of the brig. Which resolution was carried out though in a time of peace and within not many days' sail of home. An act vindicated by a naval court of inquiry subsequently convened ashore. History, and here cited without comment. True, the circumstances on board the *Somers* were different from those on board the *Bellipotent*. But the urgency felt, well-warranted or otherwise, was much the same.

Says a writer whom few know, "Forty years after a battle it is easy for a noncombatant to reason about how it ought to have been fought. It is another thing personally and under fire to have to direct the fighting while involved in the obscuring smoke of it. Much so with respect to other emergencies involving considerations both practical and moral, and when it is imperative promptly to act. The greater the fog the more it imperils the steamer, and speed is put on though at the hazard of running somebody down. Little ween the snug card players in the cabin of the responsibilities of the sleepless man on the bridge."

In brief, Billy Budd was formally convicted and sentenced to be hung at the yardarm in the early morning watch, it being now night. Otherwise, as is customary in such cases, the sentence would forthwith have been carried out. In wartime on the field or in the fleet, a mortal punishment decreed by a drumhead court—on the field sometimes decreed by but a nod from the general—follows without delay on the heel of conviction, without appeal.

22

It was Captain Vere himself who of his own motion communicated the finding of the court to the prisoner, for that purpose going to the compartment where he was in custody and bidding the marine there to withdraw for the time.

Beyond the communication of the sentence, what took place at this interview was never known. But in view of the character of the twain briefly closeted in that stateroom, each radically sharing in the rarer qualities of our nature—so rare indeed as to be all but incredible to average minds however much cultivated—some conjectures may be ventured.

It would have been in consonance with the spirit of Captain Vere should he on this occasion have concealed nothing from the condemned one—should he indeed have frankly disclosed to him the part he himself had played in bringing about the decision, at the same time revealing his actuating motives. On Billy's side it is not improbable that such a confession would have been received in much the same spirit that prompted it. Not without a sort of joy, indeed, he might have appreciated the brave opinion of him implied in his captain's making such a confidant of him. Nor, as to the sentence itself, could he have been insensible that it was imparted to him as to one not afraid to die. Even more may have been. Captain Vere in end may have developed the passion sometimes latent under an exterior stoical or indifferent. He was old enough to have been Billy's father. The austere devotee of military duty, letting himself melt back into what remains primeval in our formalized humanity, may in end have caught Billy to his heart, even as Abraham may have caught young Isaac on the brink of resolutely offering him up in obedience to the exacting behest. But there is no telling the sacrament, seldom if in any case revealed to the gadding world, wherever under circumstances at all akin to those here attempted to be set forth two of great Nature's nobler order embrace. There is privacy at the time, inviolable to the survivor; and holy oblivion, the sequel to each diviner magnanimity, providentially covers all at last.

The first to encounter Captain Vere in act of leaving the compartment was the senior lieutenant. The face he beheld, for the moment one expressive of the agony of the strong, was to that officer, though a man of fifty, a startling revelation. That the condemned one suffered less than he who mainly had effected the condemnation was apparently indicated by the former's exclamation in the scene soon perforce to be touched upon.

23

Of a series of incidents within a brief term rapidly following each other, the adequate narration may take up a term less brief, especially if explanation or comment here and there seem requisite to the better understanding of such incidents. Between the entrance into the cabin of him who never left it alive, and him who when he did leave it left it as one condemned to die; between this and the closeted interview just given, less than an hour and a half had elapsed. It was an interval long enough, however, to awaken speculations among no few of the ship's company as to what it was that could be detaining in the cabin the master-at-arms and the sailor; for a rumor that both of them had been seen to enter it and neither of them had been seen to emerge, this rumor had got abroad upon the gun decks and in the tops, the people of a great warship being in one respect like villagers, taking microscopic note of every outward movement or non-movement going on. When therefore, in weather not at all tempestuous, all hands were called in the second dogwatch, a summons under such circumstances not usual in those hours, the crew were not wholly unprepared for some announcement extraordinary, one having connection too with the continued absence of the two men from their wonted haunts.

There was a moderate sea at the time; and the moon, newly risen and near to being at its full, silvered the white spar deck wherever not blotted by the clear-cut shadows horizontally thrown of fixtures and moving men. On either side the quarter-deck the marine guard under arms was drawn up; and Captain Vere, standing in his place surrounded by all the wardroom officers, addressed his men. In so doing, his manner showed neither more nor less than that properly pertaining to his supreme position aboard his own ship. In clear terms and concise he told them what had taken place in the cabin: that the master-at-arms was dead, that he who had killed him had been already tried by a summary court and condemned to death, and that the execution would take place in the early morning watch. The word *mutiny* was not named in what he said. He refrained too from making the occasion an opportunity for any preachment as to the maintenance of discipline, thinking perhaps that under existing circumstances in the navy the consequence of violating discipline should be made to speak for itself.

Their captain's announcement was listened to by the throng of standing sailors in a dumbness like that of a seated congregation of believers in hell listening to the clergyman's announcement of his Calvinistic text.

At the close, however, a confused murmur went up. It began to wax. All but instantly, then, at a sign, it was pierced and suppressed by shrill whistles of the boatswain and his mates. The word was given to about ship.

To be prepared for burial Claggart's body was delivered to certain petty officers of his mess. And here, not to clog the sequel with lateral matters, it may be added that at a suitable hour, the master-at-arms was committed to the sea with every funeral honor properly belonging to his naval grade.

In this proceeding as in every public one growing out of the tragedy strict adherence to usage was observed. Nor in any point could it have been at all deviated from, either with respect to Claggart or Billy Budd, without begetting undesirable speculations in the ship's company, sailors, and more particularly men-of-war's men, being of all men the greatest sticklers for usage. For similar cause, all communication between Captain Vere and the condemned one ended with the closeted interview already given, the latter being now surrendered to the ordinary routine preliminary to the end. His transfer under guard from the captain's quarters was effected without unusual precautions—at least no visible ones. If possible, not to let the men so much as surmise that their officers anticipate aught amiss from them is the tacit rule in a military ship. And the more that some sort of trouble should really be apprehended, the more do the officers keep that apprehension to themselves, though not the less unostentatious vigilance may be augmented. In the present instance, the sentry placed over the prisoner had strict orders to let no one have communication with him but the chaplain. And certain unobtrusive measures were taken absolutely to insure this point.

24

In a seventy-four of the old order the deck known as the upper gun deck was the one covered over by the spar deck, which last, though not without its armament, was for the most part exposed to the weather. In general it was at all hours free from hammocks; those of the crew swinging on the lower gun deck and berth deck, the latter being not only a dormitory but also the place for the stowing of the sailors' bags, and on both sides lined with the large chests or movable pantries of the many messes of the men.

On the starboard side of the *Bellipotent*'s upper gun deck, behold Billy Budd under sentry lying prone in irons in one of the bays formed by the regular spacing of the guns comprising the batteries on either side. All these pieces were of the heavier caliber of that period. Mounted on lumbering wooden carriages, they were hampered with cumbersome harness of breeching and strong side-tackles for running them out. Guns and carriages, together with the long rammers and shorter linstocks lodged in loops overhead—all these, as customary, were painted black; and the heavy hempen breechings, tarred to the same tint, wore the like livery of the undertakers. In contrast with the funereal hue of these surroundings, the prone sailor's exterior apparel, white jumper and white duck trousers, each more or less soiled, dimly glimmered in the obscure light of the bay like a patch of discolored snow in early April lingering at some upland cave's black mouth. In effect he is already in his shroud, or the garments that shall serve him in lieu of one. Over him but scarce illuminating him, two battle lanterns swing from two massive beams of the deck above. Fed with the oil supplied by the war contractors (whose gains, honest or otherwise, are in every land an anticipated portion of the harvest of death), with flickering splashes of dirty yellow light they pollute the pale moonshine all but ineffectually struggling in obstructed flecks through the open ports from which the tampioned cannon protrude. Other lanterns at intervals serve but to bring out somewhat the obscurer bays which, like small confessionals or side-chapels in a cathedral, branch from the long dim-vistaed broad aisle between the two batteries of that covered tier.

Such was the deck where now lay the Handsome Sailor. Through the rose-tan of his complexion no pallor could have shown. It would have taken days of sequestration from the winds and the sun to have brought about the effacement of that. But the skeleton in the cheekbone at the point of its angle was just beginning delicately to be defined under the warm-tinted skin. In fervid hearts self-contained, some brief experiences devour our human tissue as secret fire in a ship's hold consumes cotton in the bale.

But now lying between the two guns, as nipped in the vice of fate, Billy's agony, mainly proceeding from a generous young heart's virgin experience of the diabolical incarnate and effective in some men—the tension of that agony was over now. It survived not the something healing in the closeted interview with Captain Vere. Without movement, he lay as in a trance, that adolescent expression previously noted as his taking on something akin to the look of a slumbering child in the cradle when the warm hearth-glow of the still chamber at night plays on the dimples that at whiles mysteriously form in the cheek, silently coming and going there. For now and then in the gyved one's trance a serene happy light born of some wandering reminiscence or dream would diffuse itself over his face, and then wane away only anew to return.

The chaplain, coming to see him and finding him thus, and perceiving no sign that he was conscious of his presence, attentively regarded him for a space, then slipping aside, withdrew for the time, peradventure feeling that even he, the minister of Christ though receiving his stipend from Mars, had no consolation to proffer which could result in a peace transcending that which he beheld. But in the small hours he came again. And the prisoner, now awake to his surroundings, noticed his approach, and civilly, all but cheerfully, welcomed him. But it was to little purpose that in the interview following, the good man sought to bring Billy Budd to some godly understanding that he must die, and at dawn. True, Billy himself freely referred to his death as a thing close at hand; but it was something in the way that children will refer to death in general, who yet among their other sports will play a funeral with hearse and mourners.

Not that like children Billy was incapable of conceiving what death really is. No, but he was wholly without irrational fear of it, a fear more prevalent in highly civilized communities than those so-called barbarous ones which in all respects stand nearer to unadulterate Nature. And, as elsewhere said, a barbarian Billy radically was—as much so, for all the costume, as his countrymen the British captives, living trophies, made to march in the Roman triumph of Germanicus. Quite as much so as those later barbarians, young men probably, and picked specimens among the earlier British converts to Christianity, at least nominally such, taken to Rome (as today converts from lesser isles of the sea may be taken to London), of whom the Pope of that time, admiring the strangeness of their personal beauty so unlike the Italian stamp, their clear ruddy complexion and curled flaxen locks, exclaimed, "Angles" (meaning *English*, the modern derivative), "Angles, do you call them? And is it because they look so like angels?" Had it been later in time, one would think that the Pope had in mind Fra Angelico's seraphs, some of whom, plucking apples in gardens of the Hesperides, have the faint rosebud complexion of the more beautiful English girls.

If in vain the good chaplain sought to impress the young barbarian with ideas of death akin to those conveyed in the skull, dial, and crossbones on old tombstones, equally futile to all appearance were his efforts to bring home to him the thought of salvation and a Savior. Billy listened, but less out of awe or reverence, perhaps, than from a certain natural politeness, doubtless at bottom regarding all that in much the same way that most mariners of his class take any discourse abstract or out of the common tone of the workaday world. And this sailor way of taking clerical discourse is not wholly unlike the way in which the primer of Christianity, full of transcendent miracles, was received long ago on tropic isles by any superior *savage*, so called—a Tahitian, say, of Captain Cook's time or shortly after that time. Out of natural courtesy he received, but did not appropriate. It was like a gift placed in the palm of an outreached hand upon which the fingers do not close.

But the *Bellipotent*'s chaplain was a discreet man possessing the good sense of a good heart. So he insisted not in his vocation here. At the instance of Captain Vere, a lieutenant had apprised him of pretty much everything as to Billy; and since he felt that innocence was even a better thing than religion wherewith to go to Judgment, he reluctantly withdrew; but in his emotion not without first performing an act strange enough in an Englishman, and under the circumstances yet more so in any regular priest. Stooping over, he kissed on the fair cheek his fellow man, a felon in martial law, one whom though on the confines of death he felt he could never convert to a dogma; nor for all that did he fear for his future.

Marvel not that having been made acquainted with the young sailor's essential innocence the worthy man lifted not a finger to avert the doom of such a martyr to martial discipline. So to do would not only have been as idle as invoking the desert, but would also have been an audacious transgression of the bounds of his function, one as exactly prescribed to him by military law as that of the boatswain or any other naval officer. Bluntly put, a chaplain is the minister of the Prince of Peace serving in the host of the God of War—Mars. As such, he is as incongruous as a musket would be on the altar at Christmas. Why, then, is he there? Because he indirectly subserves the purpose attested by the cannon; because too he lends the sanction of the religion of the meek to that which practically is the abrogation of everything but brute Force.

25

The night so luminous on the spar deck, but otherwise on the cavernous ones below, levels so like the tiered galleries in a coal mine—the luminous night passed away. But like the prophet in the chariot disappearing in heaven and dropping his mantle to Elisha, the withdrawing night transferred its pale robe to the breaking day. A meek, shy light appeared in the East, where stretched a diaphanous fleece of white furrowed vapor. That light slowly waxed. Suddenly *eight bells* was struck aft, responded to by one louder metallic stroke from forward. It was four o'clock in the morning. Instantly the silver whistles were heard summoning all hands to witness punishment. Up through the great hatchways rimmed with racks of heavy shot the watch below came pouring, overspreading with the watch already on deck the space between the mainmast and foremast including that occupied by the capacious launch and the black booms tiered on either side of it, boat and booms making a summit of observation for the powder-boys and younger tars. A different group comprising one watch of topmen leaned over the rail of that sea balcony, no small one in a seventy-four, looking down on the crowd below. Man or boy, none spake but in whisper, and few spake at all. Captain Vere—as before, the central figure among the assembled commissioned officers—stood nigh the break of the poop deck facing forward. Just below him on the quarter-deck the marines in full equipment were drawn up much as at the scene of the promulgated sentence.

At sea in the old time, the execution by halter of a military sailor was generally from the foreyard. In the present instance, for special reasons the mainyard was assigned. Under an arm of that yard the prisoner was presently brought up, the chaplain attending him. It was noted at the time, and remarked upon afterwards, that in this final scene the good man evinced little or nothing of the perfunctory. Brief speech indeed he had with the condemned one, but the genuine Gospel was less on his tongue than in his aspect and manner towards him. The final preparations personal to the latter being speedily brought to an end by two boatswain's mates, the consummation impended. Billy stood facing aft. At the penultimate moment, his words, his only ones, words wholly unobstructed in the utterance, were these: "God bless Captain Vere!" Syllables so unanticipated coming from one with the ignominious hemp about his neck—a conventional felon's benediction directed aft towards the quarters of honor; syllables too delivered in the clear melody of a singing bird on the point of launching from the twig—had a phenomenal effect, not unenhanced by the rare personal beauty of the young sailor, spiritualized now through late experiences so poignantly profound.

Without volition, as it were, as if indeed the ship's populace were but the vehicles of some vocal current electric, with one voice from alow and aloft came a resonant sympathetic echo: "God bless Captain Vere!" And yet at that instant Billy alone must have been in their hearts, even as in their eyes.

At the pronounced words and the spontaneous echo that voluminously rebounded them, Captain Vere, either through stoic self-control or a sort of momentary paralysis induced by emotional shock, stood erectly rigid as a musket in the ship-armorer's rack.

The hull, deliberately recovering from the periodic roll to leeward, was just regaining an even keel when the last signal, a preconcerted dumb one, was given. At the same moment it chanced that the vapory fleece hanging low in the East was shot through with a soft glory as of the fleece of the Lamb of God seen in mystical vision, and simultaneously therewith, watched by the wedged mass of upturned faces, Billy ascended; and, ascending, took the full rose of the dawn.

In the pinioned figure arrived at the yard-end, to the wonder of all no motion was apparent, none save that created by the slow roll of the hull in moderate weather, so majestic in a great ship ponderously cannoned.

26

When some days afterwards, in reference to the singularity just mentioned, the purser, a rather ruddy, rotund person more accurate as an accountant than profound as a philosopher, said at mess to the surgeon, "What testimony to the force lodged in will power," the latter, saturnine, spare, and tall, one in whom a discreet causticity went along with a manner less genial than polite, replied, "Your pardon, Mr. Purser. In a hanging scientifically conducted—and under special orders I myself directed how Budd's was to be effected—any movement following the completed suspension and originating in the body suspended, such movement indicates mechanical spasm in the muscular system. Hence the absence of that is no more attributable to will power, as you call it, than to horsepower— begging your pardon."

"But this muscular spasm you speak of, is not that in a degree more or less invariable in these cases?"

"Assuredly so, Mr. Purser."

"How then, my good sir, do you account for its absence in this instance?"

"Mr. Purser, it is clear that your sense of the singularity in this matter equals not mine. You account for it by what you call will power—a term not yet included in the lexicon of science. For me, I do not, with my present knowledge, pretend to account for it at all. Even should we assume the hypothesis that at the first touch of the halyards the action of Budd's heart, intensified by extraordinary emotion at its climax, abruptly stopped—much like a watch when in carelessly winding it up you strain at the finish, thus snapping the chain—even under that hypothesis how account for the phenomenon that followed?"

"You admit, then, that the absence of spasmodic movement was phenomenal."

"It was phenomenal, Mr. Purser, in the sense that it was an appearance the cause of which is not immediately to be assigned."

"But tell me, my dear sir," pertinaciously continued the other, "was the man's death effected by the halter, or was it a species of euthanasia?"

"*Euthanasia,* Mr. Purser, is something like your *will power.* I doubt its authenticity as a scientific term—begging your pardon again. It is at once imaginative and metaphysical—in short, Greek.—But," abruptly changing his tone, "there is a case in the sick bay that I do not care to leave to my assistants. Beg your pardon, but excuse me." And rising from the mess he formally withdrew.

27

The silence at the moment of execution and for a moment or two continuing thereafter, a silence but emphasized by the regular wash of the sea against the hull or the flutter of a sail caused by the helmsman's eyes being tempted astray, this emphasized silence was gradually disturbed by a sound not easily to be verbally rendered. Whoever has heard the freshet-wave of a torrent suddenly swelled by pouring showers in tropical mountains, showers not shared by the plain; whoever has heard the first muffled murmur of its sloping advance through precipitous woods may form some conception of the sound now heard. The seeming remoteness of its source was because of its murmurous indistinctness, since it came from close by, even from the men massed on the ship's open deck. Being inarticulate, it was dubious in significance further than it seemed to indicate some capricious revulsion of thought or feeling such as mobs ashore are liable to, in the present instance possibly implying a sullen revocation on the men's part of their involuntary echoing of Billy's benediction. But ere the murmur had time to wax into clamor it was met by a strategic command, the more telling that it came with abrupt unexpectedness: "Pipe down the starboard watch, Boatswain, and see that they go."

Shrill as the shriek of the sea hawk, the silver whistles of the boatswain and his mates pierced that ominous low sound, dissipating it; and yielding to the mechanism of discipline the throng was thinned by one-half. For the remainder, most of them were set to temporary employments connected with trimming the yards and so forth, business readily to be got up to serve occasion by any officer of the deck.

Now each proceeding that follows a mortal sentence pronounced at sea by a drumhead court is characterized by promptitude not perceptibly merging into hurry, though bordering that. The hammock, the one which had been Billy's bed when alive, having already been ballasted with shot and otherwise prepared to serve for his canvas coffin, the last offices of the sea undertakers, the sailmaker's mates, were now speedily completed. When everything was in readiness a second call for all hands, made necessary by the strategic movement before mentioned, was sounded, now to witness burial.

The details of this closing formality it needs not to give. But when the tilted plank let slide its freight into the sea, a second strange human murmur was heard, blended now with another inarticulate sound proceeding from certain larger seafowl who, their attention having been attracted by the peculiar commotion in the water resulting from the heavy sloped dive of the shotted hammock into the sea, flew screaming to the spot. So near the hull did they come, that the stridor or bony creak of their gaunt double-jointed pinions was audible. As the ship under light airs passed on, leaving the burial spot astern, they still kept circling it low down with the moving shadow of their outstretched wings and the croaked requiem of their cries.

Upon sailors as superstitious as those of the age preceding ours, men-of-war's men too who had just beheld the prodigy of repose in the form suspended in air, and now foundering in the deeps; to such mariners the action of the seafowl, though dictated by mere animal greed for prey, was big with no prosaic significance. An uncertain movement began among them, in which some encroachment was made. It was tolerated but for a moment. For suddenly the drum beat to quarters, which familiar sound happening at least twice every day, had upon the present occasion a signal peremptoriness in it. True martial discipline long continued superinduces in average man a sort of impulse whose operation at the official word of command much resembles in its promptitude the effect of an instinct.

The drumbeat dissolved the multitude, distributing most of them along the batteries of the two covered gun decks. There, as wonted, the guns' crews stood by their respective cannon erect and silent. In due course the first officer, sword under arm and standing in his place on the quarter-deck, formally received the successive reports of the sworded lieutenants commanding the sections of batteries below; the last of which reports being made, the summed report he delivered with the customary salute to the commander. All this occupied time, which in the present case was the object in beating to quarters at an hour prior to the customary one. That such variance from usage was authorized by an officer like Captain Vere, a martinet as some deemed him, was evidence of the necessity for unusual action implied in what he deemed to be temporarily the mood of his men. "With mankind," he would say, "forms, measured forms, are everything; and that is the import couched in the story of Orpheus with his lyre spellbinding the wild denizens of the wood." And this he once applied to the disruption of forms going on across the Channel and the consequences thereof.

At this unwonted muster at quarters, all proceeded as at the regular hour. The band on the quarter-deck played a sacred air, after which the chaplain went through the customary morning service. That done, the drum beat the retreat; and toned by music and religious rites subserving the discipline and purposes of war, the men in their wonted orderly manner dispersed to the places allotted them when not at the guns.

And now it was full day. The fleece of low-hanging vapor had vanished, licked up by the sun that late had so glorified it. And the circumambient air in the clearness of its serenity was like smooth white marble in the polished block not yet removed from the marble-dealer's yard.

28

The symmetry of form attainable in pure fiction cannot so readily be achieved in a narration essentially having less to do with fable than with fact. Truth uncompromisingly told will always have its ragged edges; hence the conclusion of such a narration is apt to be less finished than an architectural finial.

How it fared with the Handsome Sailor during the year of the Great Mutiny has been faithfully given. But though properly the story ends with his life, something in way of sequel will not be amiss. Three brief chapters will suffice.

In the general rechristening under the Directory of the craft originally forming the navy of the French monarchy, the *St. Louis* line-of-battle ship was named the *Athée* (the *Atheist*). Such a name, like some other substituted ones in the Revolutionary fleet, while proclaiming the infidel audacity of the ruling power, was yet, though not so intended to be, the aptest name, if one consider it, ever given to a warship; far more so indeed than the *Devastation,* the *Erebus* (the *Hell*), and similar names bestowed upon fighting ships.

On the return passage to the English fleet from the detached cruise during which occurred the events already recorded, the *Bellipotent* fell in with the *Athée.* An engagement ensued, during which Captain Vere, in the act of putting his ship alongside the enemy with a view of throwing his boarders across her bulwarks, was hit by a musket ball from a porthole of the enemy's main cabin. More than disabled, he dropped to the deck and was carried below to the same cockpit where some of his men already lay. The senior lieutenant took command. Under him the enemy was finally captured, and though much crippled was by rare good fortune successfully taken into Gibraltar, an English port not very distant from the scene of the fight. There, Captain Vere with the rest of the wounded was put ashore. He lingered for some days, but the end came. Unhappily he was cut off too early for the Nile and Trafalgar. The spirit that 'spite its philosophic austerity may yet have indulged in the most secret of all passions, ambition, never attained to the fulness of fame.

Not long before death, while lying under the influence of that magical drug which, soothing the physical frame, mysteriously operates on the subtler element in man, he was heard to murmur words inexplicable to his attendant: "Billy Budd, Billy Budd." That these were not the accents of remorse would seem clear from what the attendant said to the *Bellipotent*'s senior officer of marines, who, as the most reluctant to condemn of the members of the drumhead court, too well knew, though here he kept the knowledge to himself, who Billy Budd was.

29

Some few weeks after the execution, among other matters under the head of "News from the Mediterranean," there appeared in a naval chronicle of the time, an authorized weekly publication, an account of the affair. It was doubtless for the most part written in good faith, though the medium, partly rumor, through which the facts must have reached the writer served to deflect and in part falsify them. The account was as follows:

"On the tenth of the last month a deplorable occurrence took place on board H.M.S. *Bellipotent.* John Claggart, the ship's master-at-arms, discovering that some sort of plot was incipient among an inferior section of the ship's company, and that the ringleader was one William Budd; he, Claggart, in the act of arraigning the man before the captain, was vindictively stabbed to the heart by the suddenly drawn sheath knife of Budd.

"The deed and the implement employed sufficiently suggest that though mustered into the service under an English name the assassin was no Englishman, but one of those aliens adopting English cognomens whom the present extraordinary necessities of the service have caused to be admitted into it in considerable numbers.

"The enormity of the crime and the extreme depravity of the criminal appear the greater in view of the character of the victim, a middle-aged man respectable and discreet, belonging to that minor official grade, the petty officers, upon whom, as none know better than the commissioned gentlemen, the efficiency of His Majesty's navy so largely depends. His function was a responsible one, at once onerous and thankless; and his fidelity in it the greater because of his strong patriotic impulse. In this instance as in so many other instances in these days, the character of this unfortunate man signally refutes, if refutation were needed, that peevish saying attributed to the late Dr. Johnson, that patriotism is the last refuge of a scoundrel.

"The criminal paid the penalty of his crime. The promptitude of the punishment has proved salutary. Nothing amiss is now apprehended aboard H.M.S. *Bellipotent.*"

The above, appearing in a publication now long ago superannuated and forgotten, is all that hitherto has stood in human record to attest what manner of men respectively were John Claggart and Billy Budd.

30

Everything is for a term venerated in navies. Any tangible object associated with some striking incident of the service is converted into a monument. The spar from which the foretopman was suspended was for some few years kept trace of by the bluejackets. Their knowledges followed it from ship to dockyard and again from dockyard to ship, still pursuing it even when at last reduced to a mere dockyard boom. To them a chip of it was as a piece of the Cross. Ignorant though they were of the secret facts of the tragedy, and not thinking but that the penalty was somehow unavoidably inflicted from the naval point of view, for all that, they instinctively felt that Billy was a sort of man as incapable of mutiny as of wilful murder. They recalled the fresh young image of the Handsome Sailor, that face never deformed by a sneer or subtler vile freak of the heart within. This impression of him was doubtless deepened by the fact that he was gone, and in a measure mysteriously gone. On the gun decks of the *Bellipotent* the general estimate of his nature and its unconscious simplicity eventually found rude utterance from another foretopman, one of his own watch, gifted, as some sailors are, with an artless *poetic* temperament. The tarry hand made some lines which, after circulating among the shipboard crews for a while, finally got rudely printed at Portsmouth as a ballad. The title given to it was the sailor's.

BILLY IN THE DARBIES

Good of the chaplain to enter Lone Bay
And down on his marrowbones here and pray
For the likes just o' me, Billy Budd.—But, look:
Through the port comes the moonshine astray!
It tips the guard's cutlass and silvers this nook;   5
But 'twill die in the dawning of Billy's last day.
A jewel-block they'll make of me tomorrow,
Pendant pearl from the yardarm-end
Like the eardrop I gave to Bristol Molly—
O, 'tis me, not the sentence they'll suspend.   10
Ay, ay, all is up; and I must up too,
Early in the morning, aloft from alow.
On an empty stomach now never it would do.
They'll give me a nibble—bit o' biscuit ere I go.
Sure, a messmate will reach me the last parting cup;   15
But, turning heads away from the hoist and the belay,
Heaven knows who will have the running of me up!

No pipe to those halyards.—But aren't it all sham?
A blur's in my eyes; it is dreaming that I am.
A hatchet to my hawser? All adrift to go?   20
The drum roll to grog, and Billy never know?
But Donald he has promised to stand by the plank;
So I'll shake a friendly hand ere I sink.
But—no! It is dead then I'll be, come to think.
I remember Taff the Welshman when he sank.   25
And his cheek it was like the budding pink.
But me they'll lash in hammock, drop me deep.
Fathoms down, fathoms down, how I'll dream fast asleep.
I feel it stealing now. Sentry, are you there?
Just ease these darbies at the wrist,   30
And roll me over fair!
I am sleepy, and the oozy weeds about me twist.

VERSIONS OF BILLY

The text of *Billy Budd,* based upon the writer's complete but unpolished manuscript, represents Melville's last intentions before death interrupted his lifelong affair with writing. In 1962, Harrison Hayford and Merton M. Sealts, Jr. determined that the novella we know as *Billy Budd* actually grew out of a brief prose headnote introducing the poem "Billy in the Darbies." (In the novella a version of this poem stands as the concluding ironic commentary.) Manuscript fragments of the original headnote and poem have survived. This "Ur–*Billy Budd*" represents Melville's early intentions and provides a distinct idea of how Melville envisioned Billy's character and the poem's structure at the beginning of the writing process.

The Billy of this early version is far less innocent, politically and sexually, than the Billy we have previously known, and far more revolutionary. He acknowledges his guilt ("My game is up") and implicitly absolves his presumed co-conspirators—the ship's cosmopolitan crew of "Moor & Swede"—for their coming role as his hangmen. His Christ-like martyrdom, carefully muted in the novella, is made explicit in the opening lines of this early version of the poem, which Melville eventually deleted.

The "Ur–*Billy Budd*" exists on four manuscript leaves, one prose and three poetry. As working drafts, both the prose headnote and poem are heavily revised and incomplete. The prose note fragment is the opening to what was probably only a single paragraph that stresses Billy's beauty and geniality but seems inconclusive as to his heritage and guilt. The three poetic leaves are successive rewrites of consecutively overlapping portions of a poem, some lines of which appear only slightly modified in the final version of "Billy in the Darbies," others of which exist as nothing more than single-word thematic abbreviations of the content Melville would eventually flesh out. The transcriptions here represent the final, revised text found on each manuscript leaf. The Revision Narrative relates Melville's earlier revisions to the italicized phrases in each text.

THE UR–*BILLY BUDD*

Prose Headnote

Billy Budd [1] sometimes known among his shipmates under the knicknames *"Beauty,"* and *The Jewel* [2], he being not only genial in temper, and sparklingly so; but in person also goodly to behold [3]; his features, ear, foot, and in a less degree even his sailor hands but more strikingly his frame and natural carriage indicating a lineage contradicting his lot [4]. He, in war time, captain of a gun's crew in a seventy-four, is summarily condemned at sea to be hung as the ringleader of an incipient mutiny the spred of which was apprehended, a mutiny projected under the [end of leaf]

Poem [Leaf 1]

1 Very good of him, Ay, so long to stay
2 And on his marrow bone here to pray
3 For the likes of me. I bless his story
4 The Good Being hung and gone to glory.—
5 What's this? Only the sun taking leave
6 Crimson through the gun-port. My last eve.

REVISION NARRATIVE

Prose Headnote: Melville originally followed Billy's name [1] with the epithet "a rollicking seaman." Other "knicknames" he considered for Billy were "Handsome" and "Handsome Jewel" [2]. In all surviving versions of the adjoining poem, Billy imagines himself a "jewel-block" hanging from the yardarm, like a "pendant pearl" or "eardrop" he once gave to "Bristol Molly." [3] Melville at first called Billy "a brilliant object" then "not only sparklingly pleasant but a goodly object to behold" before settling on "goodly to behold." [4] Initially, Melville seemed undecided whether to stress "some ignoble lineage" or Billy's "exceptional" or "superior and noble stock." *Poem [Leaf 1]:* Here and in Leaf 2, Melville ceaselessly revised line 3 from "Nor bad his story" to "I like his story" to "I bless his story." "His" may refer to Jesus or the chaplain ("him" in line 1) who tells Billy about Jesus. For "Crimson" in line 6, Melville originally inscribed "Raying."

Poem [Leaf 2]

1 Very good of him ay, to enter Lone Bay
2 And down on his marrowbones here & pray
3 For the likes of me. And good his story—
4 Of The good boy hung and gone to glory,
5 Hung for the likes of me. But, look,
6 Plays on the cannon, the sun's last leave
7 Burning thru the port here—Billy's last eve.—
8 And there goes Tidds our mess's privy cook
9 A jewel block——
10 A pearl——
11 O, its me.
12 Messmates
13 Shipmates
14 No song to those halyard, they'll hoist away
15 Sorry for ye, boys, but ye needs obey

Poem [Leaf 3]

A All's up and I must up too.
B Early in the morning the deed they will do
15 Our little game's up they needs must obey.
16 And to these and many another crew
17 Since who was my mammy I never could say
18 In my last queer dream here I bid adieu—
19 For most part a dream of ships no more—
20 A muster of men from every shore—
21 Hail to ye, fellows, and is it you?
22 Country men, yes, and Moor & Swede,
23 Christian Pagan Cannibal breed

REVISION NARRATIVE

Poem [Leaf 2]: As alternatives to "so long to say" in Leaf 1, Melville in line 1 here has "to come my way" then "ay, to sail my way" and finally "ay, to enter Lone Bay." Melville continued tinkering with line 3. Beginning with "I bless his story," he revises to "I hail his story" then "He told a story" and then finally "And good his story." Here, "The Good Being" in Leaf 1, line 4 appears as "The Good boy."

Poem [Leaf 3]: Lines A and 15 were originally a couplet: "So be, so be, no malice bear they / Since the game is up they needs must obey." Melville then inserted line B in between: "All in the morning the deed they will do." He then revised line A to "All's up and I must up to [sic]." Melville also revised "the game is up" in the original couplet to "The little game's up" to "My little game's up" and "Our little game's up." Melville canceled line 21.

PART NINE

FROM TIMOLEON, ETC.

Retirement in 1885 gave Melville only six years, and he did not waste them. He continued to read deeply. In philosophy, he took up Schopenhauer, but also his old friend Plato, and Aristotle as well; and in literature, he devoured Balzac and Whitman. He searched the galleries for new prints and engravings to add to a collection that already exceeded three hundred items. But most of his time went into assembling poems into books. Melville's fourth and final volume of poetry appeared in 1891, the year of his death. Unlike its predecessor *John Marr*, there is little of the sea in *Timoleon, Etc.*, but a great deal about art and sexuality.

In "After the Pleasure Party," one of Melville's more complex and daring poems, the poet assumes the voice of a female astronomer spurned in love and pondering the odd strictures of desire and heterosexuality. Other poems, like "In a Bye-Canal," comically address the issue of temptation and seduction, while Melville's most famous poem, "Art," compresses the "meeting and mating" of sexuality into the blendings and fusings of the creative process. *Timoleon*'s architectural poems, such as "Milan Cathedral," "The Parthenon," and "The Great Pyramid," attempt equally compelling fusions of ancient and modern sensibilities: neo-gothic aspiration,

Hellenistic repose (even in ruins), and the monumental inscrutability of Egypt's earliest imposition of itself upon the "dumb I AM" of God. But in the wistfully sardonic, easy flowing "Syra," modern life returns: Greeks and Turks with tasseled Phrygian caps mingle in marketplaces, and Proserpine lives, on the face of a coin.

Melville's well-known poem "Art" was heavily revised in manuscript, and its evolving revisions reveal Melville's creative process, even as the poem itself discusses that process. Offered here are six sequential versions of "Art" as it evolved to its final printed text.

AFTER THE PLEASURE PARTY

LINES TRACED
UNDER AN IMAGE OF
AMOR THREATENING

Fear me, virgin whosoever
Taking pride from love exempt,
Fear me, slighted. Never, never
Brave me, nor my fury tempt:
Downy wings, but wroth they beat
Tempest even in reason's seat.

Behind the house the upland falls
With many an odorous tree—
White marbles gleaming through green halls—
Terrace by terrace, down and down,
And meets the star-lit Mediterranean Sea.   5

'Tis Paradise. In such an hour
Some pangs that rend might take release.
Nor less perturbed who keeps this bower
Of balm, nor finds balsamic peace?
From whom the passionate words in vent   10
After long revery's discontent?

"Tired of the homeless deep,
Look how their flight yon hurrying billows urge
    Hitherward but to reap
Passive repulse from the iron-bound verge!   15
Insensate, can they never know
'Tis mad to wreck the impulsion so?

"An art of memory is, they tell:
But to forget! forget the glade
Wherein Fate sprung Love's ambuscade,   20
To flout pale years of cloistral life
And flush me in this sensuous strife.
'Tis Vesta struck with Sappho's smart.

No fable her delirious leap:
With more of cause in desperate heart,   25
Myself could take it—but to sleep!

"Now first I feel, what all may ween,
That soon or late, if faded e'en,
One's sex asserts itself. Desire,
The dear desire through love to sway,   30
Is like the Geysers that aspire—
Through cold obstruction win their fervid way.
But baffled here—to take disdain,
To feel rule's instinct, yet not reign;
To dote; to come to this drear shame—   35
Hence the winged blaze that sweeps my soul
Like prairie-fires that spurn control,
Where withering weeds incense the flame.

"And kept I long heaven's watch for this,
Contemning love, for this, even this?   40
O terrace chill in Northern air,
O reaching ranging tube I placed
Against yon skies, and fable chased
Till, fool, I hailed for sister there
Starred Cassiopea in Golden Chair.   45
In dream I throned me, nor I saw
In cell the idiot crowned with straw.

"And yet, ah yet, scarce ill I reigned,
Through self-illusion self-sustained,
When now—enlightened, undeceived—   50
What gain I, barrenly bereaved!
Than this can be yet lower decline—
Envy and spleen, can these be mine?

"The peasant-girl demure that trod
Beside our wheels that climbed the way,   55
And bore along a blossoming rod
That looked the sceptre of May-Day—

On her—to fire this petty hell,
His softened glance how moistly fell!
The cheat! on briers her buds were strung;   60
And wiles peeped forth from mien how meek.
The innocent bare-foot! young, so young!
To girls, strong man's a novice weak.
To tell such beads! And more remain,
Sad rosary of belittling pain.   65

  "When after lunch and sallies gay
Like the Decameron folk we lay
In sylvan groups; and I   let be!
O, dreams he, can he dream that one
Because not roseate feels no sun?   70
The plain lone bramble thrills with Spring
As much as vines that grapes shall bring.

  "Me now fair studies charm no more.
Shall great thoughts writ, or high themes sung
Damask wan cheeks—unlock his arm   75
About some radiant ninny flung?
How glad, with all my starry lore,
I'd buy the veriest wanton's rose
Would but my bee therein repose.

  "Could I remake me! or set free   80
This sexless bound in sex, then plunge
Deeper than Sappho, in a lunge
Piercing Pan's paramount mystery!
For, Nature, in no shallow surge
Against thee either sex may urge,   85
Why hast thou made us but in halves—
Co-relatives? This makes us slaves.
If these co-relatives never meet
Selfhood itself seems incomplete.
And such the dicing of blind fate   90
Few matching halves here meet and mate.
What Cosmic jest or Anarch blunder

The human integral clove asunder
And shied the fractions through life's gate?

"Ye stars that long your votary knew   95
Rapt in her vigil, see me here!
Whither is gone the spell ye threw
When rose before me Cassiopea?
Usurped on by love's stronger reign—
But, lo, your very selves do wane: 100
Light breaks—truth breaks! Silvered no more,
But chilled by dawn that brings the gale
Shivers yon bramble above the vale,
And disillusion opens all the shore."

One knows not if Urania yet   105
The pleasure-party may forget;
Or whether she lived down the strain
Of turbulent heart and rebel brain;
For Amor so resents a slight,
And hers had been such haught disdain,   110
He long may wreak his boyish spite,
And boy-like, little reck the pain.

One knows not, no. But late in Rome
(For queens discrowned a congruous home)
Entering Albani's porch she stood   115
Fixed by an antique pagan stone
Colossal carved. No anchorite seer,
Not Thomas à Kempis, monk austere,
Religious more are in their tone;
Yet far, how far from Christian heart   120
That form august of heathen Art.
Swayed by its influence, long she stood,
Till surged emotion seething down,
She rallied and this mood she won:

"Languid in frame for me,   125
To-day by Mary's convent-shrine,

Touched by her picture's moving plea
In that poor nerveless hour of mine,
I mused—A wanderer still must grieve.
Half I resolved to kneel and believe,   130
Believe and submit, the veil take on.
But thee, arm'd Virgin! less benign,
Thee now I invoke, thou mightier one.
Helmeted woman—if such term
Befit thee, far from strife   135
Of that which makes the sexual feud
And clogs the aspirant life—
O self-reliant, strong and free,
Thou in whom power and peace unite,
Transcender! raise me up to thee,   140
Raise me and arm me!"

          Fond appeal.
For never passion peace shall bring,
Nor Art inanimate for long
Inspire. Nothing may help or heal   145
While Amor incensed remembers wrong.
Vindictive, not himself he'll spare;
For scope to give his vengeance play
Himself he'll blaspheme and betray.

    Then for Urania, virgins everywhere,   150
O pray! Example take too, and have care.

THE RAVAGED VILLA

In shards the sylvan vases lie,
   Their links of dance undone,
And brambles wither by thy brim,
   Choked Fountain of the Sun!
The spider in the laurel spins,
   The weed exiles the flower:
And, flung to kiln, Apollo's bust
   Makes lime for Mammon's tower.

MAGIAN WINE

Amulets gemmed, to Miriam dear,
Adown in liquid mirage gleam;
Solomon's Syrian charms appear,
   Opal and ring supreme.
The rays that light this Magian Wine   5
Thrill up from semblances divine.

And, seething though the rapturous wave,
What low Elysian anthems rise:
Sybilline inklings blending rave,
   Then lap the verge with sighs.   10
Delirious here the oracles swim
Ambiguous in the beading hymn.

THE GARDEN OF METRODORUS

   The Athenians mark the moss-grown gate
And hedge untrimmed that hides the haven green:
   And who keeps here his quiet state?
   And shares he sad or happy fate
Where never foot-path to the gate is seen?   5

   Here none come forth, here none go in,
Here silence strange, and dumb seclusion dwell:
   Content from loneness who may win?

And is this stillness peace or sin
Which noteless thus apart can keep its dell?   10

IN A GARRET

Gems and jewels let them heap—
      Wax sumptuous as the Sophi:
For me, to grapple from Art's deep
      One dripping trophy!

MONODY

To have known him, to have loved him,
      After loneness long;
And then to be estranged in life,
      And neither in the wrong;
And now for death to set his seal—   5
      Ease me, a little ease, my song!

By wintry hills his hermit-mound
      The sheeted snow-drifts drape,
And houseless there the snow-bird flits
      Beneath the fir-tree's crape: 10
Glazed now with ice the cloistral vine
      That hid the shyest grape.

LONE FOUNTS

Though fast youth's glorious fable flies,
View not the world with worldling's eyes;
Nor turn with weather of the time.
Foreclose the coming of surprise:
Stand where Posterity shall stand;
Stand where the Ancients stood before,
And, dipping in lone founts thy hand,
Drink of the never-varying lore:
Wise once, and wise thence evermore.

VERSIONS OF "ART"

"Art" is Melville's most frequently anthologized poem. Along with "Dupont's Round Fight" and the posthumously published Camoëns poems, among others, "Art" examines the creative process, claiming for it here a fiery mating and mystic fusing of "unlike things," comparable to the mythic and sensual struggle between Jacob and Angel in the Old Testament. Readers know the poem almost exclusively in its printed version, but it also exists in manuscript, which bears evidence of at least six stages of revision, each constituting an early version of the poem. Thus, "Art" is not only *about* the making of a poem; its successive manuscript versions *enact* the making of a poem. By inspecting all versions of this fluid text, readers may determine to what degree Melville's writing practice corresponds to his vision of the creative process.

Melville may have begun "Art" in the 1870s, about the time he was composing *Clarel,* and bits of phrasing scattered throughout Melville's epic ("nervous energies," "thought's extremes agree," "brave schemes") are echoed in the poem. In content, "Art" resembles Washington Allston's sonnet "Art" with its fiery transcendentalism and final Hebraic imagery. But in structure, it is more of a "truncated sonnet" (see the Camoëns poems). Although its sound, development, and startling final couplet make it sonnet-like, its deliberately imperfect rhyme scheme and only eleven four-beat lines make it shorter in all dimensions than the traditional pentameter sonnet. Melville's strategic resistance to this poetic convention is also revealed in his incessant revision.

The surviving documents for "Art" consist of four working draft leaves (pinned to each other) and a fair copy. Each of the four draft leaves is a fragment of the poem representing a stage of development in the composition of the poem, but each fragment also bears considerable revision, suggesting additional substages. The six versions of "Art" reproduced here are a good guess at what Melville might have done as he revised his poem. The Revision Narratives explain each hypothetical step and the specific revisions italicized in each text.

Version 1: Epigram

—ɪɪ—

Hard to grapple and upsweep
One dripping trophy from the deep.

—ɪɪ—

In him who would evoke—create,
Contraries must meet and mate;
Flames that burn, and winds that freeze;

Version 2: Expansion

In him who would evoke—create,
Contraries must meet and mate;
Flames that burn, and winds that freeze;
Sad patience—joyous energies;
Humility, and pride, and scorn;
Reverence; love and hate twin-born;
Instinct and culture; era meet

REVISION NARRATIVE, VERSIONS 1 AND 2

The earliest surviving manuscript indicates that Melville first conceived of his poem as one of two epigrams of two to maybe four lines, defining creation as the meeting and mating of contraries. But the two epigrams grew into separate poems, the first with its "dripping trophy" becoming "In a Garret," and the second becoming "Art." In Version 1, Melville transcribes only three lines of his "meet and mate" epigram, waiting, it seems, for an inspired fourth line to be added later. But that line was not forthcoming. Perhaps because of some inadequacy of its abstract flame/wind image, Melville inevitably expanded his epigram by adding one set upon another of more concrete paired contraries to create Version 2.

VERSION 3: RESHAPING
Art
—‖—

In him who would evoke —create,
What extremes must meet and mate;
Flame that burns,—a wind to freeze;
Sad patience—joyous energies;
Humility, *yet* pride, and scorn;
Audacity—reverence; love and hate
Instinct and culture. *These must mate*
With more than Even Jacob's heart

REVISION NARRATIVE, VERSION 3

With the epigrammatic concision undermined by so many paired contraries, Melville worked in Version 3 toward a more shapely structure for his longer poem, giving it a title, pairing "Audacity" with "reverence," and inserting the first crystallization of the poem's concluding image of Jacob's heart. In line 2, Melville also vacillated between "contraries" and "extremes" (actually settling back to "contraries"). He was modulating on the mating of opposites, a notion of bipolarity he would eventually drop altogether in Version 5. Finally, by removing "twin-born" from "love and hate," Melville breaks his couplet's rhyme, thus consciously leaving "scorn" in line 6 the only unrhymed end-of-line word. Melville keeps this innovation throughout all subsequent versions, thus giving his "truncated sonnet," its unconventional "ragged edge."

VERSION 4: REVISED ENDING

In him who would evoke—create,
What extremes must meet and mate;
Flame that burns,—a wind to freeze;
Sad patience—joyous energies;
Humility, yet pride, and scorn;
Instinct and study; love and hate;
Audacity—reverence; these must mate—
With much of mystic Jacob's heart
To wrestle with that angel—Art.

VERSION 5: REVISED OPENING

In placid hours we easy dream
Of many a bright unbodied scheme.
But forms to give, true life create
What unlike things must meet and mate;
A flame to melt—a wind to freeze;
Sad patience,—joyous energies;
Humility, yet pride, and scorn;
Instinct and study; love and hate;
Audacity—reverence. These must mate—
And fuse with Jacob's mystic heart
To wrestle with *the* angel—Art.

REVISION NARRATIVE, VERSION 4

In line 6, Melville revises "culture" to "study" to give the paired contrary
"Instinct and study," which along with the removal of "era" in Version 3
eradicates an apparent reference to Matthew Arnold's *Culture and Anarchy.*
At the same time he repositions "Instinct and study" so that "Audacity—
reverence" becomes the dramatic culmination of his paired contraries. In
addition, Melville enhances the Hebraism of his final Jacob image by
adding the images of mysticism and angelic struggle.

VERSION 6: FAIR COPY

Art

In placid hours *well pleased we* dream
Of many a *brave* unbodied scheme.
But *form to lend, pulsed* life create,
What unlike things must meet and mate;
A flame to melt—a wind to freeze;
Sad patience—joyous energies;
Humility—yet pride and scorn;
Instinct and study; love and hate;
Audacity—reverence. These must mate,
And fuse with Jacob's mystic heart,
To wrestle with the angel—Art.

REVISION NARRATIVE, VERSIONS 5 AND 6

In Version 5, Melville develops a new opening. Because the startling leap of "angel—Art" introduced in the last line of Version 4 too closely mirrors "evoke—create" in line 1, he reconceives the opening altogether to establish a Wordsworthian placidity of inspiration, which intensifies the contrast to come of the more fiery, less transcendental, process of the actual creation of "true life" in art. In line 4, the conversion of "extremes" to "unlike things" unhinges the bipolar contraries from idealized antithesis and redefines them more concretely in terms of the natural dissimilitude of material objects, or for that matter gender and sexuality, which in the "meet and mate" phrasing, present in all versions, has been the poem's implied force of creativity. This hidden sensuality is augmented by the revision of "burns" to "melt" (line 5) and the insertion of "fuse" (line 10). In Version 6, the fair copy and final print text of "Art" add to this sensualizing process, especially with the revision of "true life" to "pulsed life" in line 3. By altering "easy" to "well pleased" and "bright" to "brave," Melville further heightens the contrast between the mental conception of an idea and the actual expression or embodiment of that idea in words.

BUDDHA

"For what is your life? It is
even a vapor that appeareth for a
little time and then vanisheth away."

Swooning swim to less and less,
    Aspirant to nothingness!
Sobs of the worlds, and dole of kinds
    That dumb endurers be—
Nirvana! absorb us in your skies,
    Annul us into Thee.

C———'s LAMENT

How lovely was the light of heaven,
What angels leaned from out the sky
In years when youth was more than wine
And man and nature seemed divine
Ere yet I felt that youth must die.   5

Ere yet I felt that youth must die
How insubstantial looked the earth,
Aladdin-land! in each advance,
Or here or there, a new romance;
I never dreamed would come a dearth.   10

And nothing then but had its worth,
Even pain. Yes, pleasure still and pain
In quick reaction made of life
A lovers' quarrel, happy strife
In youth that never comes again.   15

But will youth never come again?
Even to his grave-bed has he gone,
And left me lone, to wake by night
With heavy heart that erst was light?
O, lay it at his head—a stone!   20

SHELLEY'S VISION

Wandering late by morning seas
When my heart with pain was low—
Hate the censor pelted me—
Deject I saw my shadow go.

In elf-caprice of bitter tone   5
I too would pelt the pelted one:
At my shadow I cast a stone.

When lo, upon that sun-lit ground
I saw the quivering phantom take
The likeness of Saint Stephen crowned: 10
Then did self-reverence awake.

THE AGE OF THE ANTONINES

While faith forecasts Millennial years
Spite Europe's embattled lines,
Back to the Past one glance be cast—
    The Age of the Antonines!
O summit of fate, O zenith of time   5
When a pagan gentleman reigned,
And the olive was nailed to the inn of the world
Nor the peace of the just was feigned.
    A halcyon Age, afar it shines,
Solstice of Man and the Antonines.   10

Hymns to the nations' friendly gods
Went up from the fellowly shrines,
No demagogue beat the pulpit-drum
    In the Age of the Antonines!
The sting was not dreamed to be taken from death, 15
No Paradise pledged or sought,
But they reasoned of fate at the flowing feast
Nor stifled the fluent thought.

We sham, we shuffle while faith declines—
They were frank in the Age of the Antonines. 20

Orders and ranks they kept degree,
Few felt how the parvenu pines,
No lawmaker took the lawless one's fee
   In the Age of the Antonines!
Under law made will the world reposed 25
And the ruler's right confessed,
For the heavens elected the Emperor then,
The foremost of men the best.
   Ah, might we read in America's signs
The Age restored of the Antonines. 30

In a Bye-Canal

A swoon of noon, a trance of tide,
The hushed siesta brooding wide
   Like calms far off Peru;
No floating wayfarer in sight,
Dumb noon, and haunted like the night 5
   When Jael the wiled one slew.

A languid impulse from the oar
Plied by my indolent gondolier
Tinkles against a palace hoar,
   And, hark, response I hear! 10
A lattice clicks; and, lo, I see,
Between the slats, mute summoning me,
What loveliest eyes of scintillation,
What basilisk glance of conjuration!

   Fronted I have, part taken the span 15
Of portents in nature and peril in man.
I have swum—I have been
'Twixt the whale's black flukes and the white shark's fin;
The enemy's desert have wandered in,

And there have turned, have turned and scanned, 20
Following me how noiselessly,
Envy and Slander, lepers hand in hand.
All this. But at the latticed eye—
"Hey! Gondolier, you sleep, my man;
Wake up!" And, shooting by, we ran; 25
The while I mused, This, surely, now,
Confutes the Naturalists, allow!
Sirens, true sirens verily be,
Sirens, waylayers in the sea.

Well, wooed by these same deadly misses, 30
    Is it shame to run?
No! flee them did divine Ulysses,
    Brave, wise, and Venus' son.

MILAN CATHEDRAL

Through light green haze, a rolling sea
Over gardens where redundance flows,
    The fat old plain of Lombardy,
The White Cathedral shows.

    Of Art the miracles 5
    Its tribes of pinnacles
Gleam like to ice-peaks snowed; and higher,
    Erect upon each airy spire
    In concourse without end,
Statues of saints over saints ascend 10
Like multitudinous forks of fire.

What motive was the master-builder's here?
Why these synodic hierarchies given,
Sublimely ranked in marble sessions clear,
Except to signify the host of heaven. 15

THE PARTHENON

I
Seen aloft from afar

Estranged in site,
Aerial gleaming, warmly white,
You look a sun-cloud motionless
In noon of day divine;
Your beauty charmed enhancement takes   5
In Art's long after-shine.

II
Nearer viewed

Like Lais, fairest of her kind,
In subtlety your form's defined—
The cornice curved, each shaft inclined,
While yet, to eyes that do but revel   10
    And take the sweeping view,
Erect this seems, and that a level,
    To line and plummet true.

Spinoza gazes; and in mind
Dreams that one architect designed   15
    Lais—and you!

III
The Frieze

What happy musings genial went
With airiest touch the chisel lent
   To frisk and curvet light
Of horses gay—their riders grave—   20
Contrasting so in action brave
   With virgins meekly bright,
Clear filing on in even tone
With pitcher each, one after one
   Like water-fowl in flight.   25

IV
The Last Tile

When the last marble tile was laid
The winds died down on all the seas;
   Hushed were the birds, and swooned the glade;
   Ictinus sat; Aspasia said
"Hist!—Art's meridian, Pericles!"   30

OFF CAPE COLONNA

Aloof they crown the foreland lone,
   From aloft they loftier rise—
Fair columns, in the aureola rolled
   From sunned Greek seas and skies.
They wax, sublimed to fancy's view,   5
A god-like group against the blue.

Overmuch like gods! Serene they saw
   The wolf-waves board the deck,
And headlong hull of Falconer,
   And many a deadlier wreck.   10

THE ARCHIPELAGO

Sail before the morning breeze
The Sporads through and Cyclades,
They look like isles of absentees—
      Gone whither?

You bless Apollo's cheering ray,   5
But Delos, his own isle, to-day
Not e'en a Selkirk there to pray
      God friend me!

Scarce lone these groups, scarce lone and bare,
When Theseus roved a Raleigh there,   10
Each isle a small Virginia fair—
      Unravished.

Nor less, though havoc fell they rue,
They still retain, in outline true,
Their grace of form when earth was new   15
      And primal.

But beauty clear, the frame's as yet,
Never shall make one quite forget
Thy picture, Pan, therein once set—
      Life's revel!   20

'Tis Polynesia reft of palms,
Seaward no valley breathes her balms—
Not such as musk thy rings of calms,
      Marquesas!

SYRA
(A Transmitted Reminiscence)

Fleeing from Scio's smouldering vines
(Where when the sword its work had done
The Turk applied the torch) the Greek
Came here, a fugitive stript of goods,
Here to an all but tenantless isle,   5
Nor here in footing gained at first,
Felt safe. Still from the turbaned foe
Dreading the doom of shipwrecked men
Whom feline seas permit to land
Then pounce upon and drag them back,   10
For height they made, and prudent won
A cone-shaped fastness on whose flanks
With pains they pitched their eyrie camp,
Stone huts, whereto they wary clung;
But, reassured in end, come down—   15
Multiplied through compatriots now,
Refugees like themselves forlorn—
And building along the water's verge
Begin to thrive; and thriving more
When Greece at last flung off the Turk,   20
Make of the haven mere a mart.

I saw it in its earlier day—
Primitive, such an isled resort
As hearthless Homer might have known
Wandering about the Ægean here.   25
Sheds ribbed with wreck-stuff faced the sea
Where goods in transit shelter found.
And here and there a shanty-shop
Where Fez-caps, swords, tobacco, shawls,
Pistols, and orient finery, Eve's—   30
(The spangles dimmed by hands profane)
Like plunder on a pirate's deck
Lay orderless in such loose way
As to suggest things ravished or gone astray.

Above a tented inn with fluttering flag   35
A sunburnt board announced Greek wine
In selfsame text Anacreon knew,
Dispensed by one named "Pericles."
Got up as for the opera's scene,
Armed strangers, various, lounged or lazed,   40
Lithe fellows tall, with gold-shot eyes,
Sunning themselves as leopards may.

Off-shore lay xebecs trim and light,
And some but dubious in repute.
But on the strand, for docks were none,   45
What busy bees! no testy fry;
Frolickers, picturesquely odd,
With bales and oil-jars lading boats,
Lighters that served an anchored craft,
Each in his tasseled Phrygian cap,   50
Blue Eastern drawers and braided vest;
And some with features cleanly cut
As Proserpine's upon the coin.
Such chatterers all! like children gay
Who make believe to work, but play.   55

I saw, and how help musing too.
Here traffic's immature as yet:
Forever this juvenile fun hold out
And these light hearts? Their garb, their glee,
Alike profuse in flowing measure,   60
Alike inapt for serious work,
Blab of grandfather Saturn's prime
When trade was not, nor toil nor stress,
But life was leisure, merriment, peace,
And lucre none, and love was righteousness.   65

THE GREAT PYRAMID

Your masonry—and is it man's?
More like some Cosmic artizan's.
Your courses as in strata rise,
Beget you do a blind surmise
      Like Grampians.   5

Far slanting up your sweeping flank
Arabs with Alpine goats may rank,
And there they find a choice of passes
Even like to dwarfs that climb the masses
      Of glaciers blank.   10

Shall lichen in your crevice fit?
Nay, sterile all and granite-knit:
Weather nor weather-stain ye rue,
But aridly you cleave the blue
      As lording it.   15

Morn's vapor floats beneath your peak,
Kites skim your side with pinion weak;
To sand-storms, battering, blow on blow,
Raging to work your overthrow,
      You—turn the cheek.   20

All elements unmoved you stem,
Foursquare you stand and suffer them:
Time's future infinite you dare,
While, for the Past, 'tis you that wear
      Eld's diadem.   25

Slant from your inmost lead the caves
And labyrinths rumored. These who braves
And penetrates (old palmers said)
Comes out afar on deserts dead
      And, dying, raves.   30

Craftsmen, in dateless quarries dim,
Stones formless into form did trim,
Usurped on Nature's self with Art,
And bade this dumb I AM to start,
Imposing Him.   35

PART TEN

FROM WEEDS AND WILDINGS,
CHIEFLY: WITH A ROSE OR TWO

Melville lived long enough to witness a small but certain resurrec-tion of his reputation. But while publishers inquired about issuing new editions and abridgments of old works, Melville was privately issuing his poetry in runs of twenty-five copies. At his death in 1891 he left a box of manuscripts—his current works in progress—but it was not until their discovery in 1919 that these works began to see the light of day. The Melville Revival was begun.

While *Billy Budd* gained almost immediate popularity, other works, such as *The Burgundy Club*, "Rammon," and "Under the Rose," remained in obscurity. Among those neglected is *Weeds and Wildings Chiefly: With a Rose or Two*, a book of poems dedicated to Melville's wife. The first half of the book consists of a score of deceptively simple-minded ditties about flowers and woodland creatures, all reminiscent of Arrowhead days shared by husband and wife. The second half, featured here, includes the prose & poem piece "Rip Van Winkle's Lilac" and a set of highly sensual poems generally re-ferred to as Melville's "Rose Poems."

"Rip Van Winkle's Lilac," an innovative retelling of Washington Irving's famous tale, recasts Rip as an emblem of the artist whose legacy, a single sprig of lilac, has in time proliferated throughout the land. In addition, Melville introduces two new characters, a bohemian who sketches Rip's picturesque lilac and a puritanical villager who disparages all color but the sacred white of his church. As prose gives way to poem, Rip's widespread lilac foretells Melville's own resurrection.

Melville's brilliant but neglected Rose Poems are a set of devotionals in praise of physical and spiritual love. The opening wintry poems contrast barren virginity with hot love-making in the snow. In "The Vial of Attar," the problem of death and the promise of resurrection are compressed within the imagery of the rose and the complex interdependency of bloom and attar (rose oil). "Rose Window" hints of resolution in the transfiguring light from a church's stained glass. A love letter to his wife, Melville's Rose Poems articulate the writer's life-long quandary over faith and doubt in the wholly new terms of transcendence through physical love.

The Little Good Fellows

Make way, make way, give leave to rove
Your orchard under as above;
A yearly welcome if ye love!
　　And all who loved us alway throve.

Love for love. For ever we　　　　　　　　　　5
When some unfriended man we see
Lifeless under forest-eaves,
Cover him with buds and leaves;
And charge the chipmunk, mouse, and mole—
Molest not this poor human soul!　　　　　　　10

Then let us never on green floor
Where your paths wind roundabout,
Keep to the middle in misdoubt,
Shy and aloof, unsure of ye;
But come, like grass to stones on moor,　　　　15
Fearless wherever mortals be.

But toss your caps, O maids and men,
Snow-bound long in farm-house pen:
We chase Old Winter back to den.
See our red waistcoats! Alive be then—　　　　20
Alive to the bridal-favors when
They blossom your orchards every Spring,
And cock-robin curves on the bridegroom's wing!

The Chipmunk

Heart of autumn!
  Weather meet,
Like to sherbert
  Cool and sweet.

Stock-still I stand,   5
  And *him* I see
Prying, peeping
  From Beech Tree,
Crickling, crackling
  Gleefully!   10
But, affrighted
  By wee sound,
Presto! vanish—
  Whither bound?

So did Baby,   15
  Crowing mirth,
E'en as startled
By some inkling
  Touching Earth,
Flit (and whither?)   20
  From our hearth!

Rip Van Winkle's Lilac

Riverward emerging toward sunset in leafy June from a dark upper clove or gorge of the Kattskills, dazed with his long sleep in an innermost hollow of those mountains, the good-hearted good-for-nothing comes to an upland pasture. Hearing his limping footfall in the loneliness, the simpletons of young steers, there left to themselves for the summer, abruptly lifting their heads from the herbage, stand as stupefied with astonishment while he passes.

In further descent he comes to a few raggedly cultivated fields detached and apart; but no house as yet, and presently strikes a wood-chopper's winding road lonesomely skirting the pastoral uplands, a road for the most part unfenced, and in summer so little travelled that the faint wheel-tracks were traceable but as forming long parallel depressions in the natural turf. This slant descending way the dazed one dimly recalls as joining another less wild and leading homeward. Even so it proved. For anon he comes to the junction. There he pauses in startled recognition of a view only visible in perfection at that point; a view deeply stamped in his memory, he having been repeatedly arrested by it when going on his hunting or birding expeditions. It was where, seen at the far end of a long vistaed clove, the head of one distant blue summit peered over the shoulder of a range not so blue as less lofty and remote. To Rip's present frame of mind, by no means normal, that summit seemed like a inquisitive man standing on tiptoes in a crowd to get a better look at some extraordinary object. Inquisitively it seemed to scrutinise him across the green solitudes, as much as to say, "Who, I wonder, art thou? And where, pray, didst thou come from?" This freak of his disturbed imagination was not without pain to poor Rip. That mountain so well remembered, on his part, *him* had it forgotten? quite forgotten him, and in a day? But the evening now drawing on revives him with the sweet smells it draws from the grasses and shrubs. Proceeding on his path he after a little becomes sensible of a prevailing fragrance wholly new to him, at least in that vicinity, a wafted deliciousness growing more and more pronounced as he nears his house, one standing all by itself and remote from others. Suddenly, at a turn of the road it comes into view. Hereupon, something that he misses there, and quite another thing that he sees, bring him amazed to a stand. Where, according to his hazy reminiscences, all had been without floral embellishment of any kind save a small plot of pinks and hollyhocks in the sunny rear of the house—a little garden tended by the Dame herself—lo, a Lilac of unusual girth and height stands in full flower hard by the open door, usurping, as it were, all but the very spot which he could only recall as occupied by an immemorial willow.

Now Rip's humble abode, a frame one, though indeed, as he remembered it, quite habitable, had in some particulars never been carried to entire completion; the builder and original proprietor, a certain honest woodman, while about to give it the last touches having been summoned away to join his progenitors in that paternal house where the Good Book assures us are many mansions. This sudden arrest of the work left the structure in a condition rather slatternly as to externals. Though a safe shelter enough from the elements, ill fitted was it as a nuptial bower for the woodman's heir, none other than Rip, his next living kin; who, enheartened by his inheritance, boldly took the grand venture of practical life—matrimony. Yes, the first occupants were Rip and his dame, then the bride. A winsome bride it was too, with attractiveness all her own; her dowry consisting of little more than a chest of clothes, some cooking utensils, a bed and a spinning-wheel. A fair shape, cheeks of dawn, and black eyes were hers, eyes indeed with a roguish twinkle at times, but apparently as little capable of snapping as two soft sable violets.

Well, after a few days occupancy of the place, returning thereto at sunset from a romantic ramble among the low-whispering pines, Rip the while feelingly rehearsing to his beloved some memories of his indulgent mother now departed, she suddenly changed the subject. Pointing to the unfinished house, she amiably suggested to the bridegroom that he could readily do what was needful to putting it in trim; for was not her dear Rip a bit of a carpenter? But Rip, though rather taken at unawares, delicately pleaded something to the effect that the clattering hammer and rasping saw would be a rude disturbance to the serene charm of the honeymoon. Setting out a little orchard for future bearing, would suit the time better. And this he engaged shortly to do. "Sweetheart," he said in conclusion, with sly magnetism twining an arm round her jimp waist, "Sweetheart, I will take up the hammer and saw in good time." That good time proved very dilatory; in fact, it never came. But, good or bad, time has a persistent, never-halting way of running on, and by so doing brings about wonderful changes and transformations. Ere very long the bride developed into the dame; the bridegroom into that commonplace entity, the married man. Moreover, some of those pleasing qualities which in the lover had won the inexperienced virgin's affections, turned out to be the very points least desirable, as of least practical efficacy in a husband, one not born to fortune, and who therefore, to advance himself in the work-a-day world, must needs energetically elbow his way therein, quite regardless of the amenities while so doing; either this, or else resort to the sinuous wisdom of the serpent.

Enough. Alike with the unfinished house, and its tenants new to the complexities of the lock wedlock, things took their natural course. As to the house, never being treated to a protective coat of paint, since Rip's exchequer was always at low ebb, it soon contracted, signally upon its northern side, a gray weather-stain, supplying one topic for Dame Van Winkle's domestic reproaches; for these in end came, though, in the present instance, they did not wholly originate in any hard utilitarian view of matters.

Women, more than men, disrelishing the idea of old age, are sensitive, even the humblest of them, to aught in any way unpleasantly suggestive of it. And the gray weather-stain not only gave the house the aspect of age, but worse; for in association with palpable evidences of its recentness as an erection, it imparted a look forlornly human, even the look of one grown old before his time. The roof quite as much as the clapboards contributed to make notable in it the absence of that spirit of youth which the sex, however hard the individual lot, inheriting more of the instinct of Paradise than ourselves, would fain recognise in everything. The shingles there, with the supports for the shingler—which temporary affairs had through Rip's remissness been permanently left standing—these it took but a few autumns to veneer with thin mosses, especially in that portion where the betrayed purpose expressed by the uncompleted abode had been lamented over by a huge willow—the object now missing—a willow of the weeping variety, under whose shade the house had originally been built. Broken bits of rotted twigs and a litter of discolored leaves were the tears continually wept by this ancient Jeremiah upon the ever-greening roof of the house fatally arrested in course of completion.

No wonder that so untidy an old inhabitant had always been the object of Dame Van Winkle's dislike. And when Rip, no longer the bridegroom, in obedience to her imperative command, attacking it with an axe none of the sharpest, and finding the needful energetic blows sorely jarring to the natural quiescence of his brain-pan, ignominiously gave it up, the indignant dame herself assaulted it. But the wenned trunk was of inordinate diameter, and, under the wens, of an obtuse soft toughness all but invincible to the dulled axe. In brief the venerable tree long remained a monument of the negative victory of stubborn inertia over spasmodic activity and an ineffectual implement.

But the scythe that advances forever and never needs whetting, sweeping that way at last, brought the veteran to the sod. Yes, during Rip's sylvan slumbers the knobby old inhabitant had been gathered to his fathers. Falling prone, and luckily away from the house, in time it made its own lowly monument; an ever-crumbling one, to be sure, yet, all the more for that, tenderly dressed by the Spring: an umber-hued mound of mellow punk, mossed in spots, with wild violets springing from it here and there, attesting the place of the departed, even the same place where it fell. But, behold: shooting up above the low dilapidated eaves, the Lilac now laughed where the inconsolable willow had wept. Lightly it dropt upon the green roof the pink little bells from its bunched blossoms in place of the old willow's yellowed leaves. Seen from the wood, as Rip in his reappearance viewed it, in part it furnished a gay screen to the late abode, now a tenantless ruin, hog-backed at last by the settling of the ridge-pole in the middle, abandoned to leisurely decay, and to crown its lack of respectability, having a scandalous name as the nightly rendezvous of certain disreputable ghosts, including that of poor Rip himself. Nevertheless, for all this sad decay and disrepute, there must needs have been something of redeeming attractiveness in these deserted premises, as the following incident may show, the interest whereof may perchance serve to justify its insertion even at this critical point.

In the month of blossoms long after Rip's disappearance in the mountain forests, followed in time by the yet more mysterious evanishment of his dame under the sod of the lowlands, a certain meditative vagabondo, to wit, a young artist, in his summer wanderings after the Picturesque, was so taken by the pink Lilac relieved against the greenly ruinous house, that camping under his big umbrella before these admirable objects one fine afternoon he opened his box of colors, brushes, and so forth, and proceeded to make a study.

While thus quietly employed he arrested the attention of a gaunt, hatchet faced, stony-eyed individual, with a gray sort of salted complexion like that of dried cod-fish, jogging by on a lank white horse. The stranger alighted, and after satisfying his curiosity as to what the artist was about, expressed his surprise that such an object as a miserable old ruin should be thought worth painting. "Why," said he, "if you *must* idle it this way—can find nothing useful to do, paint something respectable, or, better, something godly; paint our new tabernacle—there it is," pointing right ahead to a rectangular edifice stark on a bare hill-side, with an aspiring wooden steeple whereon the distant blue peaks of the Kattskills placidly looked down, peradventure mildly wondering whether any rivalry with them was intended. "Yes, paint *that* now," he continued; "just the time for it; it got its last coat only the other day. Ain't it white, though!"

A cadaver! shuddered the artist to himself, glancing at it and instantly averting his eyes. More vividly than ever he felt the difference between dead planks or dead iron smeared over with white-lead; the difference between these and white marble, when new from the quarry sparkling with the minute mica in it, or mellowed by ages, taking on another and more genial tone endearing it to that Pantheistic antiquity, the sense whereof is felt or latent in every one of us. In visionary flash he saw in their prime the perfect temples of Attica flushed with Apollo's rays on the hill-tops, or on the plain at eve disclosed in glimpses through the sacred groves around them. For the moment, in this paganish dream he quite lost himself.

"Why don't you speak?" irritably demanded the other; "won't you paint it?"

"It is sufficiently painted already, heaven knows," said the artist coming to himself with a discharging sigh, and now resignedly setting himself again to his work.

"You will stick to this wretched old ruin then, will you?"

"Yes, and the Lilac."

"The Lilac? and black what-do-ye-call-it—lichen, on the trunk, so old is it. It is half-rotten, and its flowers spring from the rottenness under it, just as the moss on those eaves does from the rotting shingles."

"Yes, decay is often a gardener," assented the other.

"What's that gibberish? I tell you this beggarly ruin is no more a fit object for a picture than the disreputable vagabond who once lived in it."

"Ah!" now first pricking his ears; "who was he? Tell me."

And straightway the hatchet-faced individual rehearsed, and in a sort of covertly admonitory tone, Rip's unheroic story up to the time of his mysterious disappearance. This, by the way, he imputed to a Providential visitation overtaking a lazy reprobate whose chief occupation had been to loaf up and down the country with a gun and game-bag, much like some others with a big umbrella and a box.

"Thank you, friend," said the sedate one, never removing his eyes from his work, "Thank you; but what should we poor devils of Bohemians do for the Picturesque, if Nature was in all things a precisian, each building like that church, and every man made in your image.—But, bless me, what am I doing, I must tone down the green here!"

"Providence will take you in hand one of these days, young man," in high dudgeon exclaimed the other; "Yes, it will give you a *toning down*, as you call it. *Made in my image!* You wrest Holy Writ. I shake the dust off my feet and leave you for profane."

"Do," was the mildly acquiescent and somewhat saddish response; and the busy brush intermitted not, while the lean visitor, remounting his lank albino, went on his way.

But presently in an elevated turn of the hilly road man and horse, outlined against the vivid blue sky, obliquely crossed the Bohemian's sight, and the next moment as if swallowed by the grave disappeared in the descent.

"What is that verse in the Apocalypse," murmured the artist to himself, now suspending the brush, and ruminatingly turning his head sideways, "the verse that prompted Benjamin West to his big canvas?—*'And I looked, and behold a pale horse, and his name that sat on him was Death.'* Well, I won't allegorise and be mystical, and all that, nor even say that Death dwells not under the cemetery turf, since rather it is Sleep inhabits there; no, only this much will I say, that to-day have I seen him, even Death, seen him in the guise of a living man on a living horse; that he dismounted and had speech with me; and that though an unpleasant sort of person, and even a queer threatener withal, yet, if one meets him, one must get along with him as one can; for his ignorance is extreme. And what under heaven indeed should such a phantasm as Death know, for all that the Appearance tacitly claims to be a somebody that knows much?"

Luck is a good deal in this world. Had the Bohemian, instead of chancing that way when he did, come in the same season but a few years later, the period of the present recital, who knows but that the opportunity might have been furnished him of sketching tattered Rip himself in his picturesque resurrection bewildered and at a stand before his own door, even as erewhile we left him.

Ere sighting the premises, Rip's doddered faculties had been sufficiently nonplussed by various unaccountable appearances, such as branch-roads which he could not recall, and fields rustling with young grain where he seemed to remember waving woods; so that now the absence of the old willow and its replacement by the Lilac—a perfect stranger, standing sentry at his own door, and, as it were, challenging his right to further approach—these final phenomena quite confound him.

Recovering his senses a little, while yet with one hand against his wrinkled brow remaining bodily transfixed, in wandering sort half unconsciously he begins:

> "Ay,—no!—My brain is addled yet;
> With last night's flagons-full I forget.
> But, look.—Well, well, it so must be,
> For there it *is*, and, sure, I see.
> Yon Lilac is all right, no doubt,   5
> Though never before, Rip—spied him out!
> But where's the willow?—Dear, dear me!
> This is the hill-side,—sure; the stream
> Flows yon; and *that*, wife's house would seem
> But for the silence. Well, may be,   10
> For this one time—Ha! do I see
> Those burdocks going in at door?

They only loitered round before!
No,—ay!—Bless me, it is the same.
But yonder Lilac! how now came—   15
Rip, where does Rip Van Winkle live?
Lilac? a lilac? Why, just there,
If my cracked memory don't deceive,
'Twas *I* set out a Lilac fair,
Yesterday morning, seems to me.   20
Yea, sure, that it might thrive and come
To plead for me with wife, though dumb.
I found it—dear me—well, well, well,
Squirrels and angels they can tell!
My head!—whose head?—Ah, Rip (I'm Rip),   25
That Lilac was a little slip,
And yonder Lilac is a tree!"

But why rehearse in every section
The wildered good-fellow's resurrection,
Happily told by happiest Irving   30
Never from genial verity swerving;
And, more to make the story rife,
By Jefferson acted true to life.
Me here it but behooves to tell
Of things that posthumously fell.   35

It came to pass as years went on
(An Indian file in stealthy flight
With purpose never man has known)
A villa brave transformed the site
Of Rip's abode to nothing gone,   40
Himself remanded into night.
Each June the owner joyance found
In one prized tree that held its ground,
One tenant old where all was new,—
Rip's Lilac to its youth still true.   45
Despite its slant ungainly trunk
Atwist and black like strands in junk,
Annual yet it flowered aloft

In juvenile pink, complexion soft.
That owner hale, long past his May,   50
His children's children—every one
Like those Rip romped with in the sun—
Merrily plucked the clusters gay.
The place a stranger scented out
By Boniface told in vinous way—   55
"Follow the fragrance!" Truth to own
Such reaching wafture ne'er was blown
From common Lilac. Came about
That neighbors, unconcerned before
When bloomed the tree by lowly door,   60
Craved now one little slip to train;
Neighbor from neighbor begged again.
On every hand stem shot from slip,
Till, lo, that region now is dowered
Like the first Paradise embowered,   65
Thanks to poor good-for-nothing Rip!

Some think those parts should bear his name;
But, no,—the blossoms take the fame.
Slant finger-posts by horsemen scanned
Point the green miles—*To Lilac Land.*   70

Go ride there down one charmful lane,
O reader mine, when June's at best,
A dream of Rip shall slack the rein,
For there his heart flowers out confessed.
And there you'll say,—O, hard ones, truce!   75
See, where man finds in man no use,
Boon Nature finds one—Heaven be blest!

Nine Rose Poems

The Ambuscade

Meek crossing of the bosom's lawn,
Averted revery veil-like drawn,
Well beseem thee, nor obtrude
The cloister of thy virginhood.
And yet, white nun, that seemly dress   5
Of purity pale passionless,
A May-snow is; for fleeting term,
Custodian of love's slumbering germ—
Nay, nurtures it, till time disclose
How frost fed Amor's burning rose.   10

Under the Ground

Between a garden and old tomb
Disused, a foot-path threads the clover;
And there I met the gardener's boy
Bearing some dewy chaplets over.

I marvelled, for I just had passed   5
The charnel vault and shunned its gloom:

"Stay, whither wend you, laden thus?
Roses! You would not these inhume?"

"Yea, for against the bridal hour
My Master fain would keep their bloom;   10
A charm in the dank o' the vault there is,
Yea, we the rose entomb."

AMOROSO

Rosamond, my Rosamond
    Of roses is the rose;
Her bloom belongs to summer,
    Nor less in winter glows,
When, mossed in furs all cosey,   5
    We speed it o'er the snows
By ice-bound streams enchanted,
    While red Arcturus, he
A huntsman ever ruddy,
    Sees a ruddier star by me.   10

O Rosamond, Rose Rosamond,
    Is yonder Dian's reign?
Look, the icicles despond
    Chill drooping from the fane!
But Rosamond, Rose Rosamond,   15
    In us, a plighted pair,
Frost makes with flame a bond,—
    One purity they share.
To feel your cheek like ice,
    While snug the furs inclose—   20
This is spousal love's device,
This is Arctic Paradise,
    And wooing in the snows!
Rosamond, my Rosamond,
    Rose Rosamond, Moss-Rose!   25

THE NEW ROSICRUCIANS

To us, disciples of the Order
    Whose rose-vine twines the Cross,
Who have drained the rose's chalice
    Never heeding gain or loss;
For all the preacher's din   5
There is no mortal sin—
—No, none to us but Malice!

Exempt from that, in blest recline
    We let life's billows toss;
If sorrow come, anew we twine   10
    The Rose-Vine round the Cross.

THE VIAL OF ATTAR

    Lesbia's lover when bereaved
In pagan times of yore
    Ere the gladsome tidings ran
Of reunion evermore,
    He wended from the pyre   5
How hopeless in return—
    Ah, the vial hot with tears
For the ashes cold in urn!

    But I, the Rose's lover,
When *my* beloved goes   10
    Followed by the Asters
Toward the sepulchre of snows,
Then, solaced by the Vial,
    Less grieve I for the Tomb,
Not widowed of the fragrance   15
    If parted from the bloom—
Parted from the bloom
    That was but for a day;

Rose! I dally with thy doom:
The solace will not stay!   20
    There is nothing like the bloom;
    And the Attar poignant minds me
Of the bloom that's passed away.

HEARTH-ROSES

The Sugar-Maple embers in bed
Here fended in Garden of Fire,
Like the Roses yield musk,
Like the Roses are red,
Like the Roses expire   5
    Lamented when low;
But, excelling the flower,
    Are odorous in ashes
    As e'en in their glow.

Ah, Love, when life closes,   10
Dying the death of the just,
May we vie with Hearth-Roses,
Smelling sweet in our dust.

ROSE WINDOW

The preacher took from *Solomon's Song*
Four words for text with mystery rife—
The Rose of Sharon,—figuring Him
The Resurrection and the Life;
And, pointing many an urn in view,   5
How honied a homily he drew.

There, in the slumberous afternoon,
Through minster gray, in lullaby rolled
The hummed metheglin charged with swoon.
Drowsy, my decorous hands I fold   10
Till sleep overtakes with dream for boon.

I saw an Angel with a Rose
Come out of Morning's garden-gate,
And lamp-like hold the Rose aloft.
He entered a sepulchral Strait.   15
I followed. And I saw the Rose
Shed dappled dawn upon the dead;
The shrouds and mort-cloths all were lit
To plaids and chequered tartans red.

I woke. The great Rose-Window high,   20
A mullioned wheel in gable set,
Suffused with rich and soft in dye
Where Iris and Aurora met;
Aslant in sheaf of rays it threw
From all its foliate round of panes   25
Transfiguring light on dingy stains,
While danced the motes in dusty pew.

ROSARY BEADS

I.

The Accepted Time

Adore the Roses; nor delay
    Until the rose-fane fall,
Or ever their censers cease to sway:
    "To-day!" the rose-priests call.

II.

Without Price

Have the Roses. Needs no pelf
    The blooms to buy,
Nor any rose-bed to thyself
    Thy skill to try:
But live up to the Rose's light,
Thy meat shall turn to roses red,
    Thy bread to roses white.

III.

Grain by Grain

Grain by grain the Desert drifts
Against the Garden-Land;
Hedge well thy Roses, heed the stealth
Of ever-creeping Sand.

THE DEVOTION OF THE FLOWERS TO THEIR LADY

Attributed to Clement Drouon, monk, a Provençal of noble birth in the
11th century. In earlier life a troubadour, a devotee of Love and the Rose,
but eventually, like some others of his stamp in that age, for an unrevealed
cause retiring from the gay circles where he had long been a caressed favorite and ultimately disappearing from the world in a monastery.

O Queen, we are loyal: shall sad ones forget?
    We are natives of Eden—
Sharing its memory with you,
      and your handmaidens yet.

You bravely dissemble with looks that beguile   5
    Musing mortals to murmur
Reproachful, "So festal, O Flower,
      we but weary the while?

What nothing has happened? no event to make wan?
    Begetting things hateful—   10
Old age, decay, and the sorrows,
      devourers of man?"

They marvel and marvel how came you so bright,
    Whence the splendor, the joyance—
Florid revel of joyance,   15
      the Cypress in sight!

Scarce *you* would poor Adam upbraid that his fall
    Like a land-slide by waters

Rolled an out-spreading impulse
　　　　disordering all;　　　　　　　　　　　　　　20

That the Angel indignant, with eyes that foreran
　　　　The betrayed generations,
Cast out the flowers wherewith Eve
　　　　　decked her nuptials with man.

Ah, exile is exile though spiced be the sod,　　　　25
　　　　In Shushan we languish—
Languish with secret desire
　　　　　for the garden of God.

　　　　But all of us yet—
We the Lilies whose pallor is passion,　　　　　　30
　　We the Pansies that muse nor forget—
In harbinger airs how we freshen,
When, clad in the amice of gray silver-hemmed,
　　Meek coming in twilight and dew,
The Day-Spring, with pale priestly hand and begemmed,　　35
　　Touches, and coronates you:—
Breathing, O daughter of far descent,
Banished, yet blessed in banishment,
　　Whereto is appointed a term;
Flower, voucher of Paradise, visible pledge,　　　　40
　　Rose, attesting it spite of the Worm.

NOTES

PART ONE. STARTING OUT

Melville composed poetry in his adolescent years and published at least two "Fragments from a Writing Desk" before reaching twenty. During his major fiction-writing period (1846 to 1857), he published nine novels (including his first novel, *Typee*), over a dozen shorter works, and a collection of tales. A reliable critical edition of each has been established in the now-standard Northwestern-Newberry (NN) *Writings of Herman Melville*.

Fragments from a Writing Desk, No. 2. First appeared on May 4, 1839, in Melville's local newspaper, the *Democratic Press, and Lansingburgh Advertiser,* under the initials "L.A.V." The magazine text is from the NN *Piazza Tales, and Other Prose Writings, 1839–1860*.

Page 6, l. 5: In his "Reflections on the Revolution in France" (1790) *Edmund Burke* (1729–97) writes: "But the age of chivalry is gone. That of sophisters, economists, and calculators has succeeded." **Page 8, l. 34:** *Bob Acres* is the diffident rival to Captain Absolute's Lydia, in Richard Sheridan's *The Rivals* (1775), who feels his courage "oozing out at the palms of his hands."

Typee. Melville revised his working draft of *Typee* considerably, and then continued to revise as the book went into print; thus, the first edition varies considerably from the manuscript (located at the New York Public Library). The "fluid text edition" of Chapter 14 showcases selected revisions Melville made in both manuscript and print versions. The base text is John Murray's first British edition.

The bracketed words and boxed passages indicating Melville's original wordings are taken from the final reading text of the manuscript as transcribed by Bryant in *Melville Unfolding*. Further notes below provide more specific "revision narratives" explaining Melville's strategies. **Page 15, l. 11:** In manuscript, Melville would typically revise "savage" to one of two less offensive terms, either "native" or "islander," and the appearance of "islander" in print suggests that this is what he did. However, the manuscript also shows that Melville first revised "natives" to "savages" (thus pandering to the reader's expectation of savagery), and only later, before going to print, did he revise "savages" to "islanders." **Page 16, Box:** Melville may have deleted this musical image as being too sophisticated an observation for a "common sailor" like Tommo to make. **Page 18, l. 19:** For *goodly bunch of grapes* (see note to *Clarel*, Book 4, Canto 26, ll. 160–168, in Part Six). **Page 19, l. 1:** In manuscript, Fayaway's name is consistently rendered in Polynesian form as "Faaua." But in this instance, Faaua has been altered to Fayaway by the careful insertion of "y's" and the conversion of the "u" to a "w." This raises the question of when (and why) Melville westernized his Polynesian spellings. **Page 19, Box:** This paragraph-long expansion of Fayaway's character dramatizes rather than merely describes her "sweet manner." The revision augments Fayaway's "liveliest sympathy" for Tommo. Melville tinkered with the passage before inserting it, and he initially gave Fayaway an "expression," then a "glance of pity," which eventually evolved into the more wondrous "glistening eyes gazing into mine." **Page 20, Box:** "Hope deferred maketh the heart sick, but when the desire cometh, it is a tree of life" (Proverbs 13:12). **Pages 21 and 22, Box:** In these revision sites, Melville tones down his intense feelings of anger, bitterness, and remorse for Toby, whose whereabouts remained a mystery until the actual Richard Tobias Greene read *Typee* and made his presence known. **Page 21, ll. 16–32:** Contrary to his strategy of removing "savage" from the manuscript, Melville kept "these treacherous savages" (**21, ll. 16–17**). However, in the following paragraph he toned down "the conduct of the savages" to "the conduct of the islanders" (**21, l. 25**), and further on vacillated between "islanders" and "savages," finally settling on "natives" (**21, ll. 31–32**). The final sequence of references, as one reads from the tormented phrase "treacherous savages" to the more clinical "conduct of the islanders" to the finally less abrasive "natives," suggests a measured transformation of the Polynesians from aggressors to the more sympathetic family Tommo eventually (if only temporarily) joins. **Page 22, Box:** The *pleasing & popular religious tract* alluded to is Mary Martha Sherwood's 1814 missionary pamphlet *Little Henry and His Bearer*, which called upon white children to help convert Asia to Christianity; it appeared in over one hundred editions by 1884. Melville probably removed the passage because its saccharin sentiments ran counter to his newly evolved anti-imperialism. **Page 23, Box:** As Tommo's anxiety over Toby's absence abates, his sexual interest in Fayaway grows. His daily bath and rubdown sends him into "transport" and inspires the references to Macheath (the promiscuous thief in John Gay's 1728 *The Beggar's Opera*), doxies (prostitutes), sultans, houris in seraglios, and the sensual Sardanapalus. In manuscript, Melville's older brother Gansevoort furiously canceled Macheath, letting the steamy Oriental references pass, but later in print, these, too, were expunged. **Pages 23–24, Box:** The fire-lighting scene is a sublimation of some mode of male sexuality. This deleted manuscript passage referring to Kory-Kory's *particular gratification*, makes the masturbatory element all the more explicit. But by cutting this passage, Melville also removed "Promethean operation," an apt classical allusion to the Greek titan Prometheus, known as the light-bearer, and a representative of the creative sexual acts Kory-Kory is simulating. **Page 24, l. 32:** The Roman *Vestals* were virgins who guarded the eternal flame, a spiritual homage to Vesta, goddess of the hearth, and a practical source of fire. The point of Tommo's ribald joke is that, while the Typees would save themselves the labor of making fire if they had a college of Vestals to keep a flame going, they could never maintain such a college because there are no virgins in Typee.

PART TWO. THE ART OF TELLING THE TRUTH
Melville did not propound an integrated theory of his art in any one treatise. Instead, his aesthetics must be derived through several essayistic moments throughout his fiction and poetry, but also his letters, reviews, and lectures (see Part Four).
Melville's Correspondence. Compared to his relatives, Melville was not a devoted correspondent. Recently discovered collections of letters (located at the New York Public Library and the Berkshire Athenaeum in Pittsfield, Massachusetts) attest to an extensive practice of family correspondence, but only one or two letters from Melville were added to the three hundred letters already found. (His letters to his wife were probably destroyed.) Despite his reluctance to correspond, his letters shed light on his private character and creative practice. The texts of letters printed here are from the NN edition of *Correspondence*, edited by Lynn Horth.
Page 29, To John Murray, 15 July 1846. Toby, Tommo's companion in *Typee*, is based on Melville's shipmate Richard Tobias Greene, who, upon reading *Typee*, announced that he was alive. Here, Melville is forwarding newspaper accounts of Greene's escape to British publisher *John Murray*, who later added "The Story of Toby" to *Typee* but did not accept the expurgations Melville argues for in this letter.

Page 32, To Evert A. Duyckinck, 3 March 1849. Melville debates the merits of transcendentalist Ralph Waldo Emerson, whom Melville's editor and friend *Evert A. Duyckinck* had earlier disparaged. Melville distances himself enough from Emerson to sustain Duyckinck's good graces, but clearly admires the transcendentalist's ability to "dive." **L. 1:** Sealts links the *rainbow* reference to a newspaper depiction of Emerson riding an inverted rainbow, symbolic of his optimism ("Emerson's Rainbow"). **L. 6:** Melville had borrowed Duyckinck's copy of *Sir Thomas Browne*, the seventeenth-century physician and mystic, and later purchased his own copy. **L. 7:** In 1847, Melville had published in *Yankee Doodle* several brief satires on Mexican War hero and President-elect *Zachary Taylor*, entitled "Authentic Anecdotes of Old Zack."

Page 33, to Evert A. Duyckinck, 5 April 1849. **L. 9:** By invoking the *Art of … oldageifying youth in books*, Melville addresses the dilemma of how to be current but also relevant for the ages to come. **Page 34, L. 6:** *Charles Fenno Hoffman* (1806–84), an editor for Duyckinck's *Literary World*, was institutionalized for the rest of his life in 1849. **L. 22:** *"That affair of mine"* refers to *Mardi*. **L. 30:** *Pierre Bayle's Dictionnaire historique et critique* (1697–1702) responded to scientific and religious legends of the day.

Page 36, To Nathaniel Hawthorne, [16 April?] 1851. Melville's "review" of Hawthorne's *The House of the Seven Gables* (1851) eventually leads to *this* Being *of the matter* (37, l. 34), i.e. the condition of ontological awareness, or the problem of consciousness that plagues Ahab and inspires Ishmael to poetic heights.

Page 38, To Nathaniel Hawthorne, [1 June?] 1851. Written as he was "driving" *Moby-Dick* "through the press" (39, l. 24), Melville's most revealing letter ranges through issues of social reform, truth telling and writing in a democracy, literary reputation, creative unfolding, God, and Goethe's pantheistic "all feeling." **Page 38, l. 30:** German poet and dramatist *Johann Friedrich von Schiller* (1759–1805) was a central figure in the "sturm und drang" period. **Page 39, l. 3:** *John Howard* (1726–90) was a relentless and effective prison reformer. **L. 16:** Anthony Ashley Cooper, the third *Lord Shaftesbury* (1671–1713), felt that a sure test of a truth is that it can withstand laughter. **Page 41, l. 23:** Melville began his professional writing career composing *Typee* in the winter of 1845 at the age of twenty-five. **L. 30:** Poet and polymath of German romanticism, *Johan Wolfgang von Goethe* (1749–1832) promoted the notion of transcendental oneness, or " 'all' feeling."

Page 42, To Nathaniel Hawthorne [17?] November 1851. With *Moby-Dick* finally in print, Melville is already contemplating his next novel, *Pierre*, which he compares to a *Kraken* (43, l. 37), the mythical Norwegian sea beast. **Page 43, l. 3:** John and Sarah *Morewood* purchased the Melville family mansion, next to Melville's Arrowhead, and renamed it Broad Hall in 1850. **L. 30:** In Acts 26:25, Paul tells *Festus:* "I am not mad …; but speak forth the words of truth and soberness."

Page 44, To Sophia Peabody Hawthorne, 8 January 1852. Melville responds to an unlocated letter in which Hawthorne's wife, Sophia, constructed an allegorical interpretation of "The Spirit-Spout" (*Moby-Dick*, Ch. 51), wherein a whale's mysterious night-time spouting "seemed some plumed and glittering god uprising from the sea."

Melville's Reviews. Melville published five reviews, all in Duyckinck's *Literary World.* They are on J. Ross Browne's *Etchings of a Whaling Cruise* (6 March 1847), Francis Parkman's *The California and Oregon Trail* (31 March 1849), Cooper's *The Sea Lions* (28 April 1849) and *The Red Rover* (16 March 1850), and Hawthorne's *Mosses from an Old Manse* (17 and 24 August 1850). The latter not only praises Hawthorne's darker vision and "great intellect in repose" but is a manifesto of American literary nationalism. He wrote the essay in August 1850 as he was composing *Moby-Dick* and about to host a picnic for several literary friends (Duyckinck, Oliver Wendell Holmes, James T. Fields, Cornelius Mathews, and Hawthorne included). Revisions to the fair copy manuscript of the review (located at the New York Public Library) suggest that Duyckinck urged Melville to tone down some of his excesses. The text for "Hawthorne and His Mosses," based on the manuscript not Duyckinck's print version, is from the NN *Piazza Tales.*

Hawthorne and His Mosses. Page 47, l. 18: *Junius* is the pseudonym of an unidentified British letter writer of Whig sentiments in the 1760s and 1770s. **Page 48, l. 28:** The Calvinist and Federalist *Timothy Dwight* (1752–1817) was first among the Connecticut Wits. **Page 54, l. 12:** Melville originally wrote, "Shakespeares are this day being born on the banks of the Ohio." But at Duyckinck's urging, he revised it in manuscript to read: "men not very much inferior to Shakespeare are this day being born...." However, the NN editors of the text printed here have rejected that revision, assuming that it was coerced. **Page 55, ll. 1–5:** Melville originally wrote these two sentences as they appear here. However, in manuscript he toned down the nationalism by cutting the second sentence and revising the first sentence to read: "If Shakespeare has not been equalled, give the world time, & he is sure to be surpassed, in one hemisphere or the other." The NN editors assume Duyckinck coerced Melville to make this revision, and therefore do not accept it. **Ll. 21–24:** Melville's first list of authors was shorter and pluralized: "No Hawthornes Emersons Whittiers Danas Coopers." He later revised to the singular and included Irving, Bryant, and Nathaniel Parker Willis. Duyckinck then removed the particular names and revised the text to allude simply to "strong literary individualities among us, as there are some dozen at least." The NN editors restored Melville's longer list of "individualities." **L. 31:** Richard Emmons's *Fredoniad* is an epic poem of the War of 1812.

PART THREE. TALES AND SKETCHES
During his greatest productivity as a magazine writer (1853–1856), Melville published exclusively with *Harper's New Monthly Magazine* (H) and *Putnam's Monthly* (P). He may have shaped his tales to suit the variant editorial agendas of these two periodicals (Post-Lauria), but others argue that Melville submitted his work to one or the other journal indifferently. Melville wrote at least eighteen short works (counting each diptych as two), along with the serialization of *Israel Potter,* which appeared in nine installments in *Putnam's* from July 1854 to March 1855. Additional unlocated works—known only as titles such as "The Agatha Tale," "The Isle of the Cross," and "Tortoise Hunting"—may yet be found either in manuscripts or unattributed publications. In 1856, Melville composed an introductory sketch entitled "The Piazza" for his collection of five *Putnam's* pieces, entitled *The Piazza Tales,* and issued them through Dix & Edwards.

The tales and sketches were published (and probably composed) in the following order (with publisher and publication dates in parentheses): "Bartleby, the Scrivener" (P, Nov.–Dec. 1853), "Cock-A-Doodle-Doo!" (H, Dec. 1853), "The Encantadas" (P, Mar.–May 1854), "The Two Temples" (rejected May 1854; pub. 1924), "Poor Man's Pudding and Rich Man's Crumbs" (H, June 1854), "The Happy Failure" (H, July 1854), "The Lightning-Rod Man" (P, Aug. 1854), "The Fiddler" (H, Sept. 1854), *Israel Potter* installments (P, July 1854–Mar. 1855), "The Paradise of Bachelors and the Tartarus of Maids" (H, April 1855), "The Bell-Tower" (P, Aug. 1855), "Benito Cereno" (P, Oct.–Dec. 1855), "Jimmy Rose" (H, Nov. 1855), "The 'Gees" (H, Mar. 1856), "I and My Chimney" (P, Mar. 1856), "The Apple-Tree Table" (P, May 1856), "The Piazza" (pub. Feb. 1856 in *The Piazza Tales*).

The texts in this volume are taken from the NN *Piazza Tales.* Except for two works which did not appear in magazine format, these texts are based on each tale's first magazine printing. The text for "The Two Temples" derives from the fair-copy manuscript located at the Houghton Library, Harvard University; and that of "The Piazza" is based on its first published version in *The Piazza Tales.* Book versions of the tales vary considerably from the magazine versions. In preparing the texts for the tales that appeared in both magazine and book format, the NN editors altered the magazine texts slightly to reflect their understanding of Melville's late intentions in the book.

Bartleby. According to Leyda, a likely source for Bartleby is Eli James Fly (d. 1854), a boyhood friend whom Melville helped along during a final period of mental instability. Melville may have borrowed his notion of law offices and the *Dead Letter* from various contemporary reports and sketches (Bergmann, Parker). **Page 66, l. 8:** German fur trader *John Jacob Astor* (1763–1848) became the world's wealthiest man through shrewd Manhattan real estate dealings. **Page 80, l. 11:** The ancient city of *Petra,* carved into the red sandstone cliffs in Jordan's Edom Desert, was destroyed by an earthquake in A.D. 363 and rediscovered by Swiss archaeologist Johann Burckhardt in 1812. Melville never visited Petra but devotes a canto to it in *Clarel* (Book 2, Canto 30). **Page 80, l. 16:** Melville would have known of the violent Roman general *Marius* through Plutarch; however, according to Kelley, the more thoughtful Marius derives from John Vanderlyn's painting *Caius Marius Amidst the Ruins of Carthage* (1807). **Page 95, l. 21:** Built in 1837, the Manhattan House of Detention for Men, or *Tombs,* got its nickname from its architectural resemblance to an Egyptian tomb. A fragment from a fair-copy manuscript of "Bartleby" indicates that Melville's elaboration on the gloomy "Egyptian character of the masonry" (**97, l. 30**) was a late addition. **Page 98, l. 8:** Job laments, "I should have slept: then had I been at rest, With *kings and counsellors* of the earth, which built desolate places for themselves" (Job 3:13–14).

Cock-A-Doodle-Doo! Early admirers of Melville's seriocomic tale took it to be an attack on transcendentalists Emerson and Thoreau, even though Melville's admiration for both gave him little cause to satirize them. Melville's references to railroad accidents and roosters are based on contemporary reports of such disasters and the breed called Shanghai chicken. **Page 99, title:** According to Leyda, Melville heard Italian baritone *Ferdinand Beneventano* sing Donizetti's *Lucia di Lammermoor* twice in 1847. **Page 103, l. 13:** Melville rewrites stanza 7 of Wordsworth's "Resolution and Independence": "We Poets in our youth begin in gladness; / But thereof come in the end despondency and madness." **L. 19:** On November 15, 1849, Melville ascended London's *Primrose Hill* in Regent's Park. To the north were open fields, "but cityward it was like a view of hell." **Page 104, l. 5:** The narrator's reading of Laurence Stern's *Tristram Shandy* (1760–67) evokes the tradition of "amiable humorists" Charles Lamb and Washington Irving and its comic fusions of benevolism and misanthropy (Bryant, *Melville and Repose*). The "joke" about Uncle Toby concerns his inability to perform his marital function. **Page 111, l. 27:** Melville revered Robert Burton's *Anatomy of Melancholy* (1621), an early medical and philosophical treatise on depression. **Page 120, l. 10:** *Oh death, where is thy sting?* (1 Corinthians 15:55).

The Chola Widow. The tale of Hunilla is "Sketch Eighth," or "Norfolk Isle and the Chola Widow," of *The Encantadas, or Enchanted Isles.* In 1841, Melville spent two weeks in the Galápagos Islands, and sighted the islands on subsequent Pacific voyages (Parker, *Herman Melville,* 200). Using such sources as Darwin's *Voyage of the Beagle* (1839) and David Porter's *Journal of a Cruise* (1815), Melville may have also based "Sketch Eighth" on contemporary accounts of female desertion, including "The Agatha Story," concerning an abandoned Nantucket wife (NN *Cor-*

respondence, 241, 621–25), which, Parker argues, may have also been written up as "The Isle of the Cross," a composition Melville was "prevented" from publishing. Melville's pseudonym in *The Encantadas*, Salvator R. Tarnmoor, derives from his favorite Italian picturesque painter Salvator Rosa (1615–73), whose paintings Melville first viewed at the Dulwich Gallery in London. The epigraph to "The Chola Widow" is from three sources: Spenser's *The Faerie Queene* (II.XII.xxvii. 5–9), Thomas Chatterton's "The Mynstrelles Songe" from Ælla (I.82–83), and William Collins's "Dirge in Cymbeline." **Page 133, l. 22:** Melville's editor, Charles F. Briggs, omitted "a few words" which he felt did not harm the concluding image of "the beast's armorial cross," and which, he further reported, brought tears to poet James Russell Lowell.

The Two Temples. Melville's diptych comparing an American upper-class church and Britain's egalitarian theatre was rejected in May 1854 by Charles F. Briggs who worried that Melville's attack on New York's newly built Grace Church in "Temple First" might "sway against us the whole power of the pulpit" (NN *Piazza Tales* 702). Opened in 1846, the Gothic-style cathedral (still standing) was situated directly across the street from Melville's now-demolished townhouse. Both are in view of the Astor Place Opera House where the actor William Macready, featured in "Temple Second," performed *Macbeth* in May 1849, triggering the Astor Place Riot, killing over twenty people. **Page 134, dedication:** Irish playwright *James Sheridan Knowles* (1784–1862) was best known for *Virginius* (1820). According to Berthold, Melville's use of Bulwer-Lytton's monarchic play *Cardinal Richlieu* in "Temple Second" contrasts sharply with his dedication to the highly republican Knowles. **Page 139, l. 2:** *Edward Pusey* (1800–82) joined with John Cardinal Newman in the Oxford Movement to bring Anglicanism closer to its Roman origins. Melville's satiric barb is in the suggestion that the "low church" congregation is moving toward Pusey's "high church" doctrines. **Page 142, l. 13:** *William Macready* (1793–1873) was England's pre-eminent Shakespearean, whose intellectual style was in stark contrast to his blustery American rival Edwin Forrest (1806–72). Forrest heckled Macready; Macready snubbed Forrest; and when Macready appeared at Astor Place Opera House, the anglophobic Astor Place Riot ensued.

The Paradise of Bachelors and the Tartarus of Maids. Melville's most familiar "diptych" is based almost entirely upon personal experience. On December 19, 1849, Melville joined several publishers, painters, writers, and barristers for dinner at Elm Court at the Inns of Court in London's Temple district between Fleet Street and the Thames. Modeled on Jerusalem's Church of the Holy Sepulchre, the Temple was built in 1185 by the crusader Knights Templar. By the fourteenth century the environs became lodgings for lawyers and students. Melville declared his festive evening to be "The Paradise of Batchelors" (NN *Journal* 44). Back home, Melville took his mother, wife, and daughter to Dalton, Massachusetts, near Mt. Greylock to purchase "a sleigh-load" of paper (NN *Correspondence* 178), as in "The Tartarus of Maids." **Page 147, l. 5:** *Benedick* is a confirmed bachelor who, in Shakespeare's *Much Ado About Nothing*, nevertheless marries. **Page 150, l. 23:** A *Bencher* is an administrator for the Inns of Court; R.F.C. refers to Robert Francis Cooke, a relative of publisher John Murray, who hosted Melville in London. **Page 152, l. 25:** Paul writes in his first letter to *Timothy*, "Drink no longer water, but use a little wine for thy stomach's sake and thine often infirmities" (1 Timothy 5:23). **Page 155, l. 3:** Melville's allegorical description of *Woedolor Mountain* (Mt. Greylock just) with its Mad Maid's Bellows-pipe, Dantean gateway, Black Notch, Devil's Dungeon, and Blood River suggests the female reproductive system. **Page 160, l. 24:** *Actaeon* is a hunter of Greek legend, who upon seeing Artemis bathing is turned into a stag and eaten by his hounds. *Mumbling*, here, means chewing.

The Bell-Tower. With its allegorical manner and themes of art, ambition, anger, and the mechanical, "The Bell-Tower" is an homage to Hawthorne. Sweeney finds a source for Talus, Bannadonna's mechanical creation, in Hawthorne's retelling of the Theseus legend in "The Minotaur"; and Morsberger links the artist to Benvenuto Cellini. Castronovo argues that the tale reflects America's conflict over slavery. The tale also recalls Hawthorne's "The Artist of the Beautiful" as well as Poe's fascination with automata. Bannadonna's theory of art and duplication needs to be read in the context of "Hawthorne and His Mosses" and the poem "Art." **Page 169, l. 33:** Melville did not view the famous *Campanile* and *Torre dell'Orologio* (clock tower), situated on either side of the Cathedral of St. Mark in Venice, until April 1857. **Page 171, l. 17:** A *domino* is a long, hooded cloak with eye mask worn at masquerades or during Carnivale.

Benito Cereno. Melville's most complex tale is also his most controversial and perhaps his favorite, for he considered entitling his collection of tales *Benito Cereno & Other Sketches.* Melville's source is Chapter 18 of Amasa Delano's 1817 *Narrative of Voyages and Travels* (NN *Piazza Tales,* 809–47), which relates the real Delano's encounter with a slave revolt on board the Spanish ship *Tryal* in 1799. Melville borrowed heavily, but charges of plagiarism are easily dispelled when Melville's characterizations, plotting, inventions, and complicated narratorial restructuring are taken into consideration. Mid-twentieth-century readers found "Benito Cereno" embarrassing for its presumed racist treatment of the Africans; however, more recent admirers acknowledge Melville's naturalistic critique of racism and how one human horror (slavery) leads to counter-horrors (deception, terrorism, murder, and, it is implied, cannibalism). Composed in 1854–55 as tensions leading to Civil War were mounting, "Benito Cereno," if rightly read, was

Melville's reminder to America that "the negro" is human, and that slavery has its consequences. **Page 184, l. 14:** *Black Friars,* the order of St. Dominic, or Dominicans, wore black robes and established a monastery in London, which Henry VIII desacralized and converted into a theatre; hence the association between Black Friars and performance. **Page 186, l. 21:** The Africans are tearing apart pieces of old rope (*junk*) to create hemp caulking (*oakum*) for boat seams. **Page 226, l. 16:** The letters of diplomat Philip Stanhope, *Lord Chesterfield* (1693–1774), to his son served readers as a moral guide in the education of young gentlemen. While he always advanced solid Christian views, Chesterfield also noted that it is more important to maintain the strict appearance of ethical behavior than to be strictly ethical; thus, applying the term Chesterfieldian to the richly duplicitous Francesco is itself somewhat duplicitous.

The 'Gees. Melville's "memorandum" is his least known response to racism. Karcher argues that Melville is satirizing contemporary ethnology, which makes Africans out as inferior. **Page 259, l. 29:** *George Fox* (1624–91) founded the Society of Friends, or Quakers, in England in 1648. **Page 261, l. 29:** The son of Nebuchadnezzar and the last king of Babylon, *Belshazzar* sees his fate written on the wall in the Book of Daniel and suffers a shaking in his knees.

I and My Chimney. In *Moby-Dick,* Ishmael shifts his "conceit of attainable felicity" away from Ahabian intellect and toward "the heart, the bed ... the fire-side" (Ch. 94). Imagine Ishmael having attained such domesticity, and you have the genial speaker who battles to prevent wife and neighbors from taking down his revered chimney, symbol of his beset masculinity. The house is based on the Melville farmhouse Arrowhead, which in 1863, Melville sold to his brother Allan, who had various passages from "I and My Chimney" inscribed around the living room mantelpiece. According to Melville's editor, George William Curtis, the tale is "thoroughly magazinish," but more recent readers find deeper relevance in its bawdy sexual imagery (hinting at circumcision, castration, and something anal) and its insistence upon preserving one's secret inner self. **Page 266, l. 17:** Built by Louis XIV for his mistress, the Grand *Trianon* is one of two "small" palaces on the grounds of Versailles. **Page 267, l. 12:** *Louis Kossuth,* the Hungarian revolutionary of 1848, was warmly received in the U.S. in December 1851. Previously, the Taylor administration's support of the Hungarians drew the wrath of the Austrians, which led Daniel Webster to call the House of Hapsburg just a "patch on the earth's surface" compared to America's fertile region, and, Melville implies, the narrator's own patch of turf. **Page 273, l. 9:** *Whatever is, is right* is from Pope's "Essay on Man" (1732–34). **Page 274, l. 21:** Swedish scientist and mystic *Emmanuel Swedenborg* (1688–1772) proposed connections between nature and spirit as well as notions of human transcendence, which became the basis for the

Church of the New Jerusalem (1788). The bogus supernaturalism of "spirit rapping" came in vogue in the latter half of the nineteenth century. **Page 277, l. 35:** In 1825 Lafayette laid the cornerstone for the *Bunker Hill monument,* a massive granite obelisk on the site of the famous Revolutionary War battle. Melville's 1855 novel *Israel Potter* is ironically dedicated to the monument. **Page 280, l. 28:** The proud Assyrian general *Holofernes* nearly subdued the Hebrews; however, at the last minute, Judith made her way into the Assyrian camp and slayed him. **Page 285, l. 14:** The devil, in the form of a woman, confronted Archbishop of Canterbury *Dunstan* (924–88), who subdued the individual by pinching his nose with a pair of red-hot tongs. **Page 289, l. 4:** *Momus* is the persistent fault-finding god who complained that man should have been made with a see-through chest so that secrets of the heart might be seen.

The Piazza. Melville composed the last of his short works from this period as an introductory tale to frame the five other pieces included in *The Piazza Tales* (1856). In its final paragraphs, the piazza or porch becomes a "box-royal" from which the writer may observe the playing out of "many as real a story" of alienation as he has found with Marianna (see Tennyson's "Mariana" and "Mariana at the mooted grange" in *Measure for Measure*). Thus, the stage is set for Bartleby, Benito Cereno, Hunilla, and the speaker of "I and My Chimney." Melville's piazza at Arrowhead was replaced by a picture window in the early twentieth century, but restored in the 1970s. The epigraph is from *Cymbeline,* IV, ii. **Page 291, l. 13:** Melville seems to be confusing the name of the cubelike structure, or *Kaaba,* in Mecca with its sacred stone. **Page 292, l. 25:** The speaker's earache reminds him of Hamlet's father, who was murdered when Claudius poured poison in his ear while he slept. **Page 293, l. 19:** *Dives* is a rich man; *Lazarus* poor. In Luke 16, both die, but Lazarus abides with Abraham while Dives ends up in torment. **L. 32:** Danish king of England *Canute* (1016–35), weary of courtiers flattering his power, sat on the seashore and commanded the tide to come no further; when the waves did not oblige, his flatterers were reproved. **Page 295, l. 35:** *Titania* is the queen of fairies in Shakespeare's *A Midsummer Night's Dream;* Oberon (**p. 298, l. 21**) is her husband. **Page 298, l. 36:** In Edmund Spenser's *The Faerie Queen, Una* represents true religion who unites with the Red Crosse Knight (Anglican church); the *lamb* is Christ.

Part Four. Statues in Rome *and* Poems by Herman Melville
Melville's Lectures. Melville gave three one-hour lectures from 1857 to 1860. "Statues in Rome" was his first and most widely delivered, with "The South Seas" and "Travel" following in decreasing frequency of presentation. No scripts or working drafts of the lectures have been found; however, in 1957, Sealts constructed texts for each lecture based on newspaper accounts of their structure,

development, and wording. In 1987, the NN editors updated those "composite texts" for *The Piazza Tales and Other Prose Pieces, 1839–1860,* from which the text of "Statues in Rome" is here taken.

Statues in Rome. Drawing upon his visit to Italy in spring 1857, Melville's lecture on Roman statuary is the writer's earliest, direct statement on the fine arts, and should be read in the context of "Hawthorne and His Mosses," "The Bell-Tower," and such later poems as "Camoëns," "At the Hostelry," and "Art." The lecture also reveals Melville's habits as a collector, museum-goer, and interest in the hanging and placement of art objects.

Poems by Herman Melville. In 1860 Melville assembled a volume entitled *Poems by Herman Melville,* which failed to secure a publisher. No table of contents for this project survives, but several of the 1860 poems most certainly appear later in *Timoleon* and the unpublished *Weeds and Wildings.* At his death, Melville left twenty-five or so "miscellaneous" poems that do not fall into any project category. Among these are several neatly transcribed, fair-copy poems on high-quality yellow paper. According to Ryan, these works, here identified as "yellow-paper poems," predate Melville's other manuscripts, which are inscribed on less refined paper. Although we cannot date the yellow-paper poems more specifically, they may have originally been included among the *Poems* of 1860. With that possibility in mind, the editor of this volume has arranged a selection of yellow-paper poems to stimulate thinking about Melville's early poetic talent. (See also note on "Monody" in Part Nine.) The texts for these poems were established through direct inspection of the manuscripts located at the Houghton Library, Harvard University. Here, Melville's original wordings are taken as the base text and revisions are noted in the margins.

Madam Mirror. In "Hawthorne and His Mosses," Melville singled out Hawthorne's "Monsieur du Miroir" as having "mystical depth of meaning." Melville extends the comic trope of a mirror reflecting, as it were, on those who peer into it. The meter is generally anapestic and recalls the limerick, a popular form brought into print in 1846 by nonsense versifier Edward Lear. **Page 320, l. 4:** "What pangs after parties of pleasure" anticipates "After the Pleasure Party" in *Timoleon.*

Fruit and Flower Painter. Originally composed in the first person, the monologue concerns an artist (presumably male) who resorts to commercial painting to make a living and forget his "broken heart." In revision, Melville shifts from first- to third-person female point of view, thus making the deceived artist a woman. Melville was not happy with his original title and considered four others including "Ashes of Roses." The image, from Shakespeare's *Romeo and Juliet:* "The roses in thy lips and cheeks shall fade to paly ashes" (IV.i.99), recurs in "The Swamp Angel" (Part Five).

The New Ancient of Days, or The Man of the Cave of Engihoul. In this nose-thumbing rant, human fossils belie traditional Christian assumptions of creation. Melville could not choose one title over the other. "The New Ancient of Days" plays on the familiar Biblical phrase: "I beheld till the thrones were cast down, and the Ancient of days did sit, whose garment was white as snow" (Daniel 7:9). "The Cave of Engihoul," discussed in Charles Lyell's *Antiquity of Man* (1863), refers to the cavern of Engihoul on the Meuse River near Liège, where Neanderthal remains were discovered in the 1830s. Stanza five's "fossilifer's stone" is an egregious pun on the alchemical notion of the "philosopher's stone" and Lyell's oft-repeated term "fossiliferous." With "Descent of Species," it is not clear if Melville intended the comical conflation of Darwin's *Origin of the Species* and *Descent of Man,* but given the poem's full range of satiric targets, including the huckster *P.T. Barnum* and Mormon *Joseph Smith,* the humor seems likely.

To——. Melville considered including this poem among his Rose Poems, in *Weeds and Wildings,* but dropped it, no doubt because it lacks a rose or two. The poem echoes the "palely loitering" knight of Keats's "La Belle Dame Sans Merci." (See also "Pontoosuce.")

Camoëns (Before) and (After). Melville considered two couplets to open "Camoëns (Before)," and canceled both. This has created an editorial mare's nest. The 1924 Constable edition of Melville's works includes both; Vincent (1948) and Leyda (1952) selected three of the four lines as an opener. Cohen (1964) began with the second of the two couplets only. In the fluid text version, the reader may read all of the text Melville composed and consider as well a fourth editorial option, which is to eliminate the couplets altogether as Melville seems to have intended. Although Melville had been familiar early on with the work of Portuguese epic poet Luis de Camões (1524–80), Monteiro contends that Melville may have composed these poems around 1867 when Melville's marriage was faltering and soon after he purchased Strangford's translation of Camões for his wife.

Immolated. Scholars have wondered whether this poem refers to an actual bonfire of poetry. Leyda speculates that in cleaning house before leaving Arrowhead in 1862, Melville copied the poems he wished to keep (on yellow paper perhaps?) and burned the rest (*Log* 653). However, Howard does not mention the alleged event. Earlier that year, Melville had sold his "doggerel" for scrap, and yet this disposal for money does not accord with the salvatory act implied in the poem. Or, Melville may have based the poem on an imagined immolation.

Pontoosuce. Melville's four-beat meter finds a middle ground between Keats's ballad "La Belle Dame Sans Merci" and Wordsworth's "Prelude." The poem refers to one of Melville's favorite haunts, Lake Pontoosuc, situated just north of Pittsfield near the site of Balance Rock, the "Memnon Stone" featured in *Pierre.* Because Melville's revisions are not finalized, editors have offered slightly different versions of the poem. **Page 332, ll. 12–14 and 19–20:** Vincent (1948) and Warren (1970) include these lines ("Even truth itself decays ... fraud and falsehood grow"), but Cohen (1964) does not. However, no previous edition includes the three canceled lines ("Relapse!... and green") originally appearing after line 42, which may have been deleted at the time of the insertion of lines 48–49.

PART FIVE. *FROM* BATTLE-PIECES
Melville dedicated his first published poems to "the memory of the three hundred thousand" who died in the Civil War. Published in August 1866 by Harper & Brothers, it was poorly received (see Introduction) and after ten years had sold only 525 copies. The volume is divided into three sections: the Battle-Pieces proper, a section of "Verses Inscriptive and Memorial," and a prose "Supplement." References to the Bible, Shakespeare, and Milton's Michael and Raphael proliferate, but Melville also relied upon *The Rebellion Record,* a multivolume compendium of facts and literary responses to the war. Five of the battle-pieces appeared in *Harper's New Monthly Magazine* as prepublication releases. Melville altered these five slightly for the first edition of *Battle-Pieces;* he also supplied notes to about one third of the poems as well as the essay-length "Supplement" arguing for reconciliation. Melville revised certain poems in his own copy of the book. The texts, taken from NN's forthcoming *Published Poems,* are based on the first appearance (magazine or book) of a given poem and are then emended to reflect the editors' understanding of Melville's final intentions.
The Portent. On October 16, 1859, abolitionist *John Brown* (b. 1800) led twenty-one men on a raid of the Federal armory in Harpers Ferry, Virginia, in an attempt to trigger a slave revolt. He was convicted of treason and hanged on December 2, 1859. A fearsome fanatic and yet revered martyr, Brown is *Weird* (l. 13) both for his fateful anger and strange prophetic brilliance. *The cut is on the crown* (l. 5) echoes Shakespeare's *Henry V:* "it is no English treason to cut French crowns" (IV, i, 245). The *cap* (l. 8) refers to Brown's execution hood, which does not fully conceal his beard.
Misgivings. In moving from "The Portent" to "Misgivings," Melville signals his variable voice, unexpected imagery, metrical skill, and formal experimentation. **L. 7:** *Man's foulest crime* generally refers to slavery, but might also evoke the dissolution of the union.
The Conflict of Convictions. Melville's note: "The gloomy lull of the early part of the winter of 1860–1, seeming big with final disaster to our institutions, affected some minds that believed them to constitute one of the great hopes of mankind, much as the eclipse which came over the promise of the first French Revolution affected kindred natures, throwing them for the time into doubts and misgivings

universal." This poem is the first of several that use a responsive chorus (in italics), which allows Melville to create a dialogue between alternative voices. **L. 35:** The *Iron Dome* (also in "America") is the dome of the Capitol building in Washington, D.C., under construction during the war. **Ll. 52–54:** Melville tinkered with these lines in his copy of *Battle-Pieces:* in line 52 he originally printed "a blinking light" rather than "a taper dim," and in line 54 "A meagre wight!" rather than "Which foldeth him!"

The March into Virginia. Up until 1863, the Civil War went poorly for the North. In the first Battle of Bull Run (July 21, 1861) at *Manassas* Junction, Virginia, McDowell's green Northern troops arrived expecting a picnic but were routed by Beauregard's outnumbered Confederates. The humiliation was repeated a year later at the second battle of Manassas in August of 1862. In the first print edition, Melville's last line reads: "The throe of Second Manassas share"; however, in his copy of the book, he considered three alternatives, including "Thy after shock, Manassas, share," printed here. Cohen and Warren stay with the first printed version.

Dupont's Round Fight. *Samuel Dupont* defeated the Confederates in the naval Battle of Port Royal, off Hilton Head, South Carolina, on November 7, 1861. Two rebel forts were situated on either side of the Broad River. Dupont maneuvered his gunboats in an elliptical fashion in the channel between them so that his guns, always firing, were always pointed at one fort or the other.

A Utilitarian View of the Monitor's Fight. The legendary encounter between the two ironclads *Monitor* and *Merrimac* took place on May 9, 1862, in Hampton Roads, Virginia. The *Merrimac* had previously dealt a severe blow to the Union's wooden ships and was returning to finish the job when the *Monitor* steamed into view and stalemated the situation, thus preserving the Northern fleet. This metrical tour de force is a shrewd prophecy of mechanical warfare to come.

Shiloh. In his attempt to cut the Confederacy in two by commanding the Mississippi, Grant made his way south through the Tennessee Valley. However, on April 6, 1862, he was surprised near Pittsburgh Landing on the Tennessee by Johnston's rebel forces. On the second day, Grant pushed the Confederate lines to the nearby log cabin called Shiloh Church. **L. 16:** Melville tucks one of literature's best antiwar lines—"What like a bullet can undeceive!"—between parentheses.

Malvern Hill. Hoping to take Richmond in his Peninsular campaign and holding strong at Malvern Hill, Virginia, Union commander George McClellan nevertheless retreated, thus ending the Seven Days' Battle, on July 1, 1862. Melville visited the field on his trip behind enemy lines in April 1864 when Mosby, not Lee, was at issue.

The House-top. Melville had not yet relocated to New York City when in mid-July 1863 the city erupted in the bloodiest urban riot of the century. Lincoln's

Emancipation Proclamation in January had already set Irish immigrants on edge about the possibility of freed slaves glutting the Northern labor market, and when the Conscription Act drafted the poor but allowed rich men to buy their way out, New York workers went on a three-day rampage resulting in the lynching of black men, the burning of the Colored Orphanage Asylum, and the deaths of over one hundred people. So severe was the violence that five Union regiments were taken from the still smoldering Gettysburg battlefield to put the riot down. Melville's note to this poem quotes the chivalrous fourteenth-century courtier Jean Froissart: " 'I dare not write the horrible and inconceivable atrocities committed,' says Froissart, in alluding to the remarkable sedition in France during his time. The like may be hinted of some proceedings of the draft-rioters." The poem is, for Melville, a rare instance of blank verse. **L. 9:** *Parching Sirius,* the brightest star in the northern sky, is associated with summertime heat and drought. **L. 19:** *Wise Draco* is the Athenian law-giver.

The Armies of the Wilderness. The Wilderness, a densely wooded area along the Rapidan River in the Blue Ridge foothills of Spotsylvania County, Virginia, was the site of three battles; Melville also draws connections to the *Pillar of Smoke* (l. 217) that guided the Israelites in their wilderness wanderings. The poem is set after the first battle, at Chancellorsville (where Stonewall Jackson died, l. 177) on May 2, 1863, and before the second and third engagements: The Battle of the Wilderness and the Battle of Spotsylvania, both in May 1864. At this point, Grant ("The silent General," l. 130) had taken over the Union forces, and when Melville paid his visit in April to Culpepper, Virginia (l. 160), Grant was preparing for his first encounter with the under-equipped Lee, who, using the terrain to his advantage, was aided by the guerilla tactics of *John Mosby* (l. 141). Melville left before the fierce battles ensued, but his poem records the tensions preceding the fight and the grim spectacle of soldiers coming upon the skeletal remains from the previous year's engagement. **L. 14:** In his copy of the poem, Melville offered the tentative revision of "football" for *"base-ball,"* but only Vincent has printed that alternative; Warren allows that since a football is easier to see from a distance, the revision would be logical, yet he does not change the text. But since Melville does not cancel the word "base-ball," and since one cannot imagine him as anything other than a baseball fan, the word remains. **L. 34:** *Belial* is one of Milton's fallen angels and a personification of evil. **L. 66:** *Paran* is a desolate region of the Sinai. **L. 74:** the *cockatrice,* whose glance and breath can kill, is a fabled monster hatched by a serpent from a cock's egg. (See *basilisk* in "In a Bye-Canal," Part Nine.) **L. 76:** the *Moonlight Fight* refers to a night engagement near Rappahannock Station. **L. 220:** *Sabaean lore* refers to the riddles Sheba (or Saba) posed to Solomon.

The Swamp Angel. Melville's note borrows from *The Rebellion Record:* "The great

Parrott gun, planted in the marshes of James Island, and employed in the prolonged, though at time intermitted Charleston, was known among our soldiers as
the Swamp Angel." In their bombardment of Charleston in August 1863, Union
forces on marshy Morris (not James) Island aimed at its St. Michael's Church (**l.
40**). "The Swamp Angel" is Melville's most explicit statement on the plight of
African-Americans. **L. 23:** Melville considered the title "Ashes of Roses" for his
early poem "Fruit and Flower Painter" (see Part Four).

The College Colonel. In four successive commands, the wiry Harvard volunteer
William Francis Bartlett endured repeated physical torment: a lost leg, three
body wounds, and incarceration in the Confederacy's infamous Libby prison
camp. Melville observed him on parade in Pittsfield on August 22, 1863. **L. 29:**
The idea at the siege of *Petersburg* was to tunnel under the Confederate forces,
detonate four tons of explosives, and in the ensuing mayhem seize the day; instead, ill-advised Union soldiers charged into the resulting crater and were
slaughtered by bewildered Confederates. Grant called it a "stupendous failure."

"The Coming Storm" and "Formerly a Slave." Both poems are based on paintings
Melville viewed at New York's National Academy of Design in April 1865, soon
after Lincoln's death. *Edwin Booth,* the famous Shakespearean actor and brother of
assassin John Wilkes Booth, owned *Sanford Robinson Gifford's* landscape "The
Coming Storm." Artist *Elihu Vedder* painted former slave Jane Jackson, whom he
had found near his Broadway studio selling peanuts and praising her son in
the Union Army to passersby. He displayed the portrait, entitled "Jane Jackson,
formerly a Slave," in the same National Academy exhibition with Gifford's
"Coming Storm." Later, Vedder used the Jackson figure for his painting of "The
Cumaen Sibyl," the prophetess who led Aeneas back to his father and on to establish Roman culture. Sensing the same prophetic potential in Jackson's face,
Melville composed "Formerly a Slave" as a projection of future social redemption for the descendants of African-American slaves. Melville so admired Vedder,
whom he never met, that he dedicated *Timoleon* to him.

On the Slain Collegians. Melville's note: "The records of Northern colleges attest
what numbers of our noblest youth went from them to the battle-field. Southern
members of the same classes arrayed themselves on the side of Secession; while
southern seminaries contributed large quotas. Of all these, what numbers
marched who never returned except on the shield." Popular during the Vietnam
War, "On the Slain Collegians" is Melville's elegy for the "unabated Boy," the
youth cut off before life can turn to grief, as well as an elegy for elegies: the
mourning of a poetic form that simply cannot give solace when war kills "in
the flush of bloom." **Ll. 34 and 21:** After killing the monster *Python,* Apollo puri-
fied himself in the waters of *Tempe,* the Edenic valley of Roman myth.

America. Melville's conclusion to the principal section of *Battle-Pieces* evokes the image of an allegorized America presiding over the Capitol dome in Washington (see "The Conflict of Convictions").

Commemorative of a Naval Victory. Cohen associates this poem with Melville's cousin Guert Gansevoort, who served honorably on the *Somers* when it became the center of controversy over the execution of falsely accused mutineers. But there is little evidence to suggest that Melville is alluding to any particular naval episode or "Victory." Like "The College Colonel," the poem establishes a heroic character and concludes with haunting doubts.

Supplement. In a bid to establish himself as a national poet, Melville included this essay to underscore his theme of reconciliation and to guide his reader to a higher, more accepting form of republican patriotism. In fact, reviewers who had little patience for such reasoning (and less for the experimental poetry) derided *Battle-Pieces* for its meliorative politics, and Melville's volume might have fared better without the essay. In his copy of *Battle-Pieces*, Melville made three revisions. **Page 364, l. 21:** He altered "intellectual impartiality" to "intellectual fairmindedness." **Page 365, l. 36:** In reference to George IV, he deleted "out of the graceful instinct of a gentleman." **Page 371, l. 23:** And in the final paragraph he revised "terrible" to "great."

PART SIX. *FROM* CLAREL: A POEM AND PILGRIMAGE IN THE HOLY LAND

Melville's modern epic was inspired by his 1857 tour of the Holy Land, but he probably did not begin writing it until 1870. Around this time he assembled a number of source books, including Arthur Penrhyn Stanley's *Sinai and Palestine,* William Bartlett's *Forty Days in the Desert,* and William Thomson's *The Land and the Book.* He also purchased the posthumous American and Italian *Note-Books* of Hawthorne, the model for Vine. Melville was also familiar with books of travel in the Near East by Bayard Taylor, John Lloyd Stephens, and others, as well as studies of the Bible such as John Kitto's *Cyclopedia of Biblical Literature.*

The 18,000 lines of iambic tetrameter are divided into four books, relating the discourses of eight major characters and at least twenty others on a trip from Jerusalem to the Dead Sea and back via the monastery of Mar Saba and Bethlehem. The irregularly rhymed four-beat couplets can be taxing; however, readers can find similar approaches in poets as diverse as Byron and Whittier. Publication of the epic, in two volumes, by G. P. Putnam's Sons was achieved through a generous subvention by Melville's uncle Peter Gansevoort, to whom *Clarel* is dedicated. Only 350 copies were published, of which 220 were eventually destroyed to avoid storage costs. The few who reviewed it were not commendatory, and the "metrical affair," as Melville put it, lapsed into obscurity.

Clarel was reprinted in the 1924 Constable edition, but was not systematically edited until Bezanson produced his 1943 Yale dissertation, the basis for his 1960 Hendricks House edition. Melville revised his copy of *Clarel,* and drawing upon these revisions, Bezanson emended the poem in 283 places. His introduction and notes were augmented in the 1991 NN edition. Following Bezanson's editorial principles, the NN editors nevertheless emended the text in 193 places, some different from Bezanson's emendations. The cantos selected here are drawn from the NN edition.

Vine and Clarel (Book II, Canto 27). Having reached the Jordan, where *John the Baptist* (l. 20) preached, Clarel and his fellow pilgrims pause while Arab guides fetch souvenir vials of water and *willow branches* (l. 2), palm fronds having been taken by tourists. In the preceding cantos, Rolfe (an intellectual adventurer and model humanist) and Derwent (a facile but articulate Anglican priest) respond to an encounter with a Dominican monk, who has offered compelling arguments for Catholicism. But here, Clarel overhears the normally silent Vine soliloquize on Arab versus Western chivalry and hopes to draw the man out: "Give me thyself" (l. 70). Clarel, a divinity student plagued by religious doubt, is emotionally and sexually divided as well. His presumed soul mate, Vine, sparks his "feminine" mood (l. 108), and in a complex section (ll. 102–42) in which unspoken facial expressions seem to speak to one another, we seem to hear Vine rejecting Clarel's advance as if to say: You are not the only one to suffer doubt; "Go, live it out" (l. 123). Clarel's thoughts return to Ruth. The canto ends with an interaction between Vine and the scornful Jewish atheist *Margoth* (l. 167) over *Nehemiah,* the poem's harmless Christian innocent referred to as "the meek one" (l. 148) and "chief of sinners." Nehemiah has fashioned wreathes of palm leaves for the pilgrims and the ass he rides: Margoth is appalled at such simplicity. **Page 375, l. 11:** In "In a Bye Canal" (see Part Nine), a Venetian woman watches the speaker through the louvered slats of a shutter. **L. 20:** Melville observed the dome-like *St. John's Baptistery,* situated beside Pisa's Leaning Tower, on March 23, 1857. **L. 26:** *Plain* here means to lament; see also "complain" in line 95. The Jordan empties into the *Dead Sea* (l. 30), which has no further outlet. **Page 376, l. 44:** *Hagar* is Abraham's rejected wife and mother of the wanderer Ishmael, who is the legendary progenitor of all Arabs. **Page 377, l. 80:** Melville visited *Lydda,* this village site of a Crusader church just west of Jerusalem, on January 20, 1857. **L. 85:** The poet *Sir Phillip Sidney* (1554–86) died in battle and typified British renaissance chivalry. **Page 378, l. 139:** *Dizzard* is an easily flustered fool.

The Prodigal (Book IV, Canto 26). The prodigal (or Lyonese) is a young French merchant from Lyons, whose sensual songs we first hear in an earlier canto as Rolfe and Ungar (an embittered former Confederate) debate democracy. Clarel now rooms with the prodigal and cannot understand the youth's ability to find pleasure in Judaea's texts, women, and terrain, which, for Clarel, are gloomy reminders of his religious doubt. Clarel is drawn to the beautiful youth, who is likened to a Polynesian maiden eloping with her lover (l. 249). As with his encounter with Vine, Clarel's sexual ambivalence matches his religious doubt. The next morning Clarel wakens from a dream revitalized, but the prodigal has left. **Page 382, ll. 76–81:** Joseph brought the body of his father, Jacob, to *Atad* (Genesis 50:1–13). Before her sacrifice, *Jephthah's* daughter (in Judges 11:29–40) wanders the hills lamenting her virginity. Clarel's point is that the Judaean wilderness is filled with death and sorrow. **Ll. 95 and 98:** *Don Rovenna* is the prodigal's *Locked friend* (l. 51) and fellow carouser. The *saya-manto* is a South American veil. **Page 383, l. 114:** The prodigal's sarcasm is that the ancient city of Damascus continues to be happy because it has not gotten the news from Clarel that the Near East is such a gloomy place. **Ll. 129–34:** The prodigal cannot recall *Naaman,* but oblivious to the prodigal's point, Clarel (ever the divinity student) supplies the name. He is *weetless,* i.e. unknown or clueless. **Page 384, ll. 160–64:** A *fane* is a porch. In Numbers 13 Moses sends *spies* into Canaan (Eschol) to reconnoiter, and they return with a cluster of grapes hanging from a staff (see also *Typee,* page 18 l. 19). The *Maccabees* are Jewish patriots who resisted the Romans in the first century B.C.; their coins bear the emblem of the grape cluster. **Page 385, ll. 180–94:** Clarel is once again instructing the prodigal: the (love) Song of Solomon was construed spiritually by St. Bernard. But, according to Bezanson, the prodigal counters that Buddhist monks (Bonzes) have similarly (mis)interpreted the sensual works of Persian poet Hafiz. **L. 197:** A *fakir* is a Moslem mendicant and mystic. **Page 386, l. 226:** The prodigal's question is: What do these lovely Jewish girls know about the wild prophetic warnings of Jeremiah? **Page 388, ll. 288–301:** *Shushan* is both the palace of Ahasuerus (Xerxes) and capital of ancient Persia; it is also the setting for the Book of Esther in which *Ahasuerus* falls in love with the Jewess *Esther* (see also lines 217–18) and reverses a command to annihilate all Jews (hence the feast of Purim). Some versions of Esther begin with the dream of Mordecai that prophesies this reversal, and Clarel's dream, which has him torn between the sensuality of Shushan and the sandy asceticism of monastic life, also prefigures his own reversal and return to his love, the Jewess Ruth. **Page 388, l. 306:** The *Tuscan* refers to the austere monk Salvaterra appearing in Book IV, Cantos 13–16. **L. 310:** The NN editors have altered the original "each ascetic range" to "such ascetic range" presumably because "ascetic range" would refer only to the monk's sandy asceticism, the Lyonese being hardly ascetic at all (see also Milder, "Dearth").

Epilogue (Book IV, Canto 35). Clarel quickly returns to Jerusalem on Ash

Wednesday, only to discover that Ruth and her mother, Agar, have died of grief over the murder of her father, Nathan, the event that initiated Clarel's ten-day journey. Clarel wanders Jerusalem until Whitsunday (Pentecost), the seventh Sunday after Easter, which marks the holy spirit's descent upon the disciples.

PART SEVEN. PROSE & POEM: *JOHN MARR,* AND OTHERS
Melville wrote several prose & poem pieces (see Introduction), only two of which were published (in *John Marr*); the rest, including *The Burgundy Club,* "Rammon," "Under the Rose," *Billy Budd* (see Part Eight), and "Rip Van Winkle's Lilac" (see Part Ten), remained in his papers at his death. These manuscripts were casually edited in the 1924 Constable edition. Parts of each were re-edited by Vincent (1948), and selections also appeared in Cohen (1964) and Warren (1970). The NN texts are forthcoming in *Published Poems* and *Billy Budd and Other Late Manuscripts.*

John Marr and Other Sailors, with Some Sea-Pieces. Melville's shortest volume of poems was published anonymously by Theodore L. De Vinne & Co. in 1888 with a run of only twenty-five copies for distribution among friends. *John Marr* is dedicated to the maritime novelist W. Clark Russell, who in turn dedicated *An Ocean Tragedy* to Melville. Revisions in the fair copy, located at the Houghton Library, Harvard University, indicate that Melville was tinkering with the poems up to the last minute; his own copy of the volume has further alterations. The texts from *John Marr* included here are from the forthcoming NN edition of the *Published Poems.*

John Marr. This opening prose & poem piece combines familial and maritime associations. The prose setting recalls Melville's revered uncle Thomas, who in economic hard times relocated his family to Galena, Illinois, in the summer of 1838. Melville's vision of the oceanic prairie derives from his visit out West in 1840. Melville also maintained relations with old sea-faring associates throughout his life. He gave a copy of *Moby-Dick* to one of his *Acushnet* mates, Henry Hubbard, in 1853, and he corresponded with Richard Tobias Greene (Toby of *Typee*) until Toby's death. Melville's younger brother, Thomas, was the director of Staten Island's Snug Harbor, the seaman's retirement facility, and Melville's frequent visits there no doubt inspired his maritime reminiscences.

The Aeolian Harp. This stringed window device catches breezes and makes music. **L. 14:** See also "*Wreck,* ho! the wreck—Jerusalem!" (*Clarel,* Book IV, Canto 1, line 187).

The Maldive Shark. In fair copy, Melville revised "Pale mumbler" ("mumble" means to chew) in the last line to "Pale gorger" before settling on *Pale ravener of horrible meat.*

The Berg (A Dream). Melville revised his original concluding image, "thy dead indifference of walls," to *thy dense stolidity of walls* in his copy of *John Marr.*

Pebbles I–VII. Originally entitled "Epigrams," these bits of flotsam extract the suffering and natural indifference of previous poems in *John Marr* and build, one poem to the next, a response that celebrates emotional survival rather than any transcendence of "the inhuman Sea," and in such survival achieves a reverence for the alienated self. **II, l. 3:** *Orm* is the aged seaman Daniel Orme in a manuscript sketch by that name, perhaps a prose introduction to this pebble and probably also intended for inclusion in *John Marr.* Orme is an obsolete word for the husk of a flower. **III, l. 5:** *Man's strain* is humanity's outflow of impassioned language, as well as strife. **VII, l. 2:** The *Angels Four* are the four angels of the apocalypse sent to destroy earth and sea but are restrained by another angel until God's servants are made safe or "sealed" (Revelation 7:1–4). **L. 4:** *Rosmarine* is rosemary, but literally means "sea dew."

The Burgundy Club. The manuscripts collectively referred to as *The Burgundy Club* constitute Melville's most ambitious prose & poem project: a book consisting of two long poems, with several prose sketches designed to frame them. This study of "New Italy and the Old Masters," which culminates Melville's lifelong attempt to combine art and politics, has been studied either as prose or as poem but rarely with a sense of its integration of prose and poem. Melville's initial inspiration for this was his 1857 tour of the Mediterranean. Melville may have begun writing the two poems, "At the Hostelry" (on painting) and "Naples in the Time of Bomba" (on Italian politics), as early as 1862 when he purchased Vasari's *Lives of the Most Eminent Painters,* or even earlier in 1859 when he borrowed Duyckinck's copies of Vasari and Luigi Lanzi's *History of Painting.* References to Garibaldi's death in 1862 also date revisions of the poems to the mid-1860s. According to Sealts, Melville returned to the project soon after the publication of *Clarel* (1876), and then again in 1886, to work on the prose sketches. Melville may not have imagined his overall plan for the book from the start, but in later years, according to Sandberg, he developed an organizing principle through the device of an unnamed editor introduced in "House of the Tragic Poet," who provides introductory sketches of two figures, the Marquis de Grandvin and Jack Gentian. Each of these two members of the Burgundy Club, a gathering of genialists reminiscent of "The Paradise of Bachelors," is noted for a narrative (Grandvin on art; Gentian on politics), which the unnamed editor has "methodized" into verse. Melville's first title for the project was "Parthenope" (the Greek name for Naples); he also conceived of Grandvin's piece as "A Symposium of Old Masters at Delmonico's" (the famous New York restaurant). The sketches and poems were not reliably transcribed or assembled in a coherent ordering until Sandberg's 1989 Northwestern dissertation, which supplies the text of the selections in this volume. (Sandberg's text will appear in the forthcoming NN edition of *Billy Budd and Other Late Manuscripts*.) The present volume offers the first half of *The Burgundy Club*, including its general introduction ("House of the Tragic Poet"), the opening sketch of the Marquis de Grandvin, and its accompanying poem, "At the Hostelry."

House of the Tragic Poet. Melville frames *The Burgundy Club* by assuming the role of an unnamed poet-editor who beseeches an old friend and publisher to accept his verse renderings of Grandvin's and Gentian's narratives. In "House of the Tragic Poet," Melville tweaks the literary establishment, which he had sedulously avoided for decades. **Page 406, l. 22:** British explorer of the South Pacific, Captain *James Cook*, was killed in 1778 in an encounter with militant Hawaiians. Legends that Cook was cannibalized persisted throughout the century. **Page 407, l. 14:** A *Younker* is a Dutch youth. **Page 409, l. 22:** Aristarchus of the Library at Alexandria was the first to edit Homer; Melville's facetious *Aristarchi of the pastoral press* would be highly learned individuals, and yet McQuick's "primer" is over their heads.

The Marquis de Grandvin. The Marquis's name emphasizes his love of wine and Bacchic geniality. A bachelor, he nevertheless distinguishes himself from the misogynists of his clan (see "The Paradise of Bachelors and the Tartarus of Maids") by his ability to find "common ground" with both sexes and to inspire good fellowship among women as well as men. **Page 410, l. 5:** American Revolutionary hero *Marquis de Lafayette* (1757–1834) and sculptor of the Statue of Liberty *Frédéric Bartholdi* (1834–1904) are exemplary French liberals, hence fitting compatriots for Grandvin. **Ll. 19 and 29:** *Hymen* is the classical god of marriage, depicted as a young man with a torch and a veil; a *Benedict* is a bachelor who marries despite himself. **L. 31:** *Roncesvalle* is the site of *Charlemagne's* defeat and of the death of his champion, *Roland*. **Page 411, l. 21:** Grandvin's *cosmopolitan sympathies* put him in line with a range of figures whose multitalented open-mindedness mark them as either hucksters or heroes (see Bryant, *Melville and Repose*). **L. 28:** *Levellers* were seventeenth-century advocates of parliamentary democracy and universal male suffrage. **Page 413, l. 13:** Sandberg identifies *Rufus Choate* (1799–1859) as the skilled orator who replaced Daniel Webster in the Senate. **L. 29:** *James Crichton* was a sixteenth-century adventurer dubbed Admirable by his biographer Thomas Urquhart.

At the Hostelry. Melville's interest in painting and the picturesque grew steadily throughout his career, especially after his two trips to Europe (1849 and 1857). The term *picturesque* was contested among seventeenth- and eighteenth-century aestheticians. Uvedale Price argued that it was rooted in a feeling of curiosity achieved through a response to a subject's "roughness" and "irregularity"; however, the associationist Richard Payne Knight thought of it as a visual habit of framing a subject. As "Hawthorne and His Mosses" reveals, Melville was drawn to Price's perspective as well as Hawthorne's notion of the "moral picturesque," a view of the mind as blending light and dark moods, and of the *chiaroscuro* as a form of self-conscious self-restraint or "toning down" of personality (see Bryant, *Melville and Repose,* pp. 16–19). **Part I.** The opening references to the *Risorgimento,* or "resurrection" of the Italian nation from 1859 to 1870 orchestrated by *Camillo Cavour* (**l. 46**) and in part fulfilled by *red-shirted Giuseppe Garibaldi* (**ll. 13 and 18**), prefigures the second poem in *The Burgundy Club,* "Naples in the Time of Bomba." *Bomba* (**l. 31**) is Ferdinand II, the repressive Bourbon King of the Two Sicilies infamous for his bombardment of Messina in 1848 (hence his sobriquet). In that year Garibaldi returned from exile in the *Pampas* of South America (**l. 23**) and in 1859 led forces that in 1860 expelled Bomba's son *King Fanny* (**l. 20**), an event which set in motion the establishment of the Savoy King Victor Emmanuel of Turin. **L. 10:** According to Berthold, *Naples long in chains* refers to a political cartoon of the time. **L. 81:** In sixteenth-century Rome, lampoons and satires were posted on the brow of the statue of *Pasquin,* hence the term "pasquinade." **L. 91:** *Jack Cade* was a British revolutionary who led an insurrection against Henry VI. **Part II. L. 2:** *Old Romance* recalls the psychological plungings of Hawthorne's novels, which Melville emulated in *Moby-Dick* and *Pierre.* **L. 9:** *Arethusa* is a nymph who, in escaping the river god, was transformed into a fountain on an island in the harbor of Syracuse. **L. 12:** *Jan Steen* (1626–79), Dutch painter of comic tavern scenes. **L. 28:** *Frater Lippo Lippi* (1406–69), Florentine painter noted for his depictions of mischievous Christ childs and cherubs. **L. 33:** Giuseppe Ribera or *Spagnoletto* (1590–1652), Spanish court painter who specialized in chiaroscuro effects. **L. 47:** *Giotto* (1266–1337), first of the Florentine artists of the Italian Renaissance; Melville viewed his frescoes of the Campo Santa in Pisa on March 23, 1857, noting that "wags" had painted them. **L. 63:** *Herman van Swanevelt* (1600–55), Dutch landscape artist. **L. 76:** Noted practitioner of the picturesque landscape, *Claude Lorraine* (1600–88), like the greatest painters in the poem, Leonardo and Michael Angelo, says nothing; Melville viewed several of his paintings in Rome, on March 7, 1857, saying, "All their effect is of atmosphere. He paints the air." **Part III. L. 27:** *Falernian* is an ancient Roman wine. **Part IV. L. 1:** *Franz Hals* (1581–1666), Dutch genre painter; Melville viewed his "Portrait of a Painter and His Wife" and other "convivial scenes" in Amsterdam on April 24, 1857. **L. 1:** *Anthony Van Dyck* (1599–1641), Flemish court painter for England's Charles I; Melville viewed his portraits of children in Turin on April 10, 1857. **L. 36:** Jacopo Robusti (1518–94), or *Tintoretto* (the little son of a dyer), is the great

Venetian artist who excelled his mentor Titian (hence the pun in "Titan work" in line 37). Melville gives him one of the poem's better lines about the picturesque: "Some decay must lurk." **L. 48:** *Adriaen Brouwer* (1605–38), Flemish painter of drinking scenes. **L. 53:** According to Sandberg, Florentine painter *Carlo Dolci* (1616–86) is noted for his "finicky" style; Melville viewed his "Magdelen" in Rome on March 4, 1857. **L. 59:** *Huysum* is a seventeenth- and eighteenth-century Dutch family of still-life painters (a father and two sons) specializing in highly realistic renderings of flowers. **L. 62:** *David Teniers* the Younger (1610–90), Flemish genre painter; Melville viewed his works in Turin and Amsterdam on April 10 and 24, 1857. **Part V. L. 1:** *Willem Van der Velde* (1633–1707), Dutch painter of maritime scenes. **L. 32:** *Gerard Dou* (1613–75), Dutch genre painter. **L. 65:** *Paola Caliari,* or *Veronese* (1528–88), Venetian artist; Melville viewed his work in Rome on March 10, 1857. **L. 90:** *Antoine Watteau* (1684–1721), French painter of country festivals and comic characters in the rococo style. **L. 105:** *Sinigaglia,* city in which Cesare Borgia had several friends over for a poisonous repast. Melville viewed portraits of him and his sister Lucrezia, of whom he remarked, "no wicked look about her, good looking dame—rather fleshy" (NN *Journal,* p. 111). **Part VII. L. 8:** *Diego Velázquez* (1599–1660), Spanish court painter. **L. 15:** *Salvator Rosa* (see note to "The Encantadas" in Part Three). **L. 17:** *Nicholas Poussin* (1594–1665); Melville viewed the French artist's "Assumption of Mary," along with works by Salvator Rosa, at the Dulwich Gallery on November 17, 1849. Later, he collected and framed a "silvery" print of Poussin's "Landscape with a Man Washing His Feet at a Fountain," which hung in his New York City home (Wallace, "Melville's Prints"). **L. 21:** *Albrecht Dürer* (1471–1528), German painter known for his engravings; Guido di Pietro (1387–1455) joined the Dominican order as Fra Giovanni of Fiesole and became known as "Il Beato *Angelico.*" **A Sequel. L. 32:** *Tarquins,* legendary line of sixth-century Roman kings, whose crimes set in motion events leading to the founding of the Republic.

Rammon and "The Enviable Isles." Potentially Melville's most artfully integrated prose & poem work, "Rammon" is also textually problematic. Apparently, Melville first composed the poem "The Enviable Isles," and then wrote (but never polished) the sketch "Rammon" as a prose introduction. He probably intended the entire prose & poem piece for *John Marr,* but though the poem fit that volume's maritime themes, the biblical prose sketch would have been out of place. Melville separated the two and placed "The Enviable Isles" with the subtitle "(From 'Rammon')" just before "Pebbles" at the end of *John Marr.* The two parts remained textually separated for decades. Vincent printed "The Enviable Isles" (along with the rest of *John Marr*) but placed his inaccurate transcription of "Rammon" among the "Unpublished Poems." In 1959, Eleanor M. Tilton reunited the two, placing the poem in its proper location after the prose section. The text of her edited transcription has been reprinted here.

In its entirety, "Rammon" is a daring prose & poem piece; the sketch offers the oddly anachronistic but believable combination of Judaic and Buddhist teachings, the conflict between transcendence, commerce, and politics, and the gradual transition through verse dialogue from the prose section to the tight sonnet-like poem. Recasting the biblical events of I Kings 9–12, "Rammon" plays fast and loose with historical detail. Solomon never had a son Rammon; nor could Rammon in the tenth century B.C. know of Buddha of the fifth; nor was the Egyptian *Queen of Sheba* (**437, l. 3**) an Indian "dame" or "Princess." According to scripture, the wise (but in Melville's term "lax") King Solomon loved "strange women" (to the tune of 700 wives, 300 concubines), and one or two led him into worshipping the goddess *Ashtorath* (i.e. Astarte or Venus) and the god *Chemosh* (**437, l. 5**). Encouraged by prophecies, *Jeroboam* (**438, l. 15**) rose up against Solomon but is defeated and sent into exile. Upon Solomon's death, his son *Rehoboam* (the fictional Rammon's half brother [**438, l. 6**]) succeeds to the throne and is called upon by Jeroboam and the people of Israel to lighten the "yoke grievous" (**438, l. 16**) of his oppression. Ignoring the advice of older counselors (and of Rammon) and following his younger advisors, Rehoboam increases the restrictions. The fictional *Zardi* (**438, l. 30**), the *improvisator* (i.e. one who can compose or recite without preparation), comes from the Phoenician commercial port of *Tyre* (in present day Lebanon), once ruled by *Hiram* (**438, l. 27**), who supplied the cedars with which Solomon built his temple in Jerusalem. **Page 436, l. 17:** Originally, Melville wrote "death is the desirable ultimatum. But desired or not, death comes, or seems to come." His revision of the first and second "deaths" with *cessation of being* and *an end,* respectively, enhances Rammon's transcendental focus. **L. 20:** Melville first called Solomon "a large hearted & genial king," and then one "impatient" with the "religion of his fathers," before settling on *"lax."* Late in life, Solomon authored the world-weary "Ecclesiastes," one of Melville's favorite texts. **Page 437, l. 13:** It is not clear what the inscription *Rhanes* means here. Tilton speculates that Melville may have been trying to recall Buddha's son, Rahula; but the context calls for Buddha's own name, "Siddharta." Melville's late interest in Buddha is articulated in his short *Timoleon* poem by that name. **Page 438, l. 33:** Melville seems to be referring to Solomon, who indeed introduced magnificence and luxury to the throne, but he was not a shepherd nor the son of *Jethro.* The shepherd Jethro is the father-in-law of Moses. Melville may have been confusing Jethro with Jesse, the father of David (a shepherd) and Solomon's grandfather. **Page 439, verse l. 8:** The *Sadducees* were a Hebrew sect at the time of Christ who denied the resurrection of the dead and other traditional thinking. **Verse l. 16:** Hiram's navy brings gold to Solomon from *Ophir* (I Kings 10:11).

The Enviable Isles. With its fourteen lines of iambic pentameter, the poem is structurally the closest Melville came to writing a traditional sonnet (see also "Art"). Its drowsy images, "on the marge," or shoreline, recall Tennyson's "The Lotos-Eaters."

Under the Rose. Melville's most comic prose & poem piece, "Under the Rose" so thoroughly embeds its speck of a poem within its prose monologue that one is tempted to read it as a prose sketch only. However, the ramblings of the pretentious servant about his covetous diplomat master, the sly Persian Azem, and a one-handed alcoholic Greek translator are designed to direct our attention away from a careful progression of objects—vase, roses, and poem—that lead us to a vision of death. The piece is a literary version of the "In Arcadia Ego" (death in the garden) motif found in still-lifes in which dead flies (or worse) inhabit pictures of flowers in full bloom.

The fair-copy manuscript of "Under the Rose," located at Houghton Library, Harvard University, has clearly been prepared for submission to a publisher, although Melville revised it slightly. Its title suggests a link to the Rose Poems of *Weeds and Wildings,* but it is not listed in any of that volume's tables of contents. "Under the Rose" was transcribed (inaccurately) for the 1924 Constable edition; the new text here is based on direct inspections of the manuscript and edited by the editor of this volume. **Page 441, title.** Melville inscribed "Iran" next to "Persia" in the title without canceling either. **L. 16:** Solomon's love poems are known as *"The Song of Solomon"* or *"The Song of Songs."* **Page 441, l. 21–442, l. 1:** Melville originally wrote "gardener" then revised to *vineyarder,* which he also canceled. For *cellerer* (or "cellarer," one who fetches provisions for a monastery), Melville had originally written "porter." **Page 442, l. 10:** *Posset* is warm spicy wine or ale in milk. **L. 12:** Melville visited the Natural History Museum near the *Grand Ducal (Pitti) Palace* in Florence on March 27, 1857, and saw "Lapis lazuli—chrystal vessels, dragons, perfumers &c &c." as well as morbid displays of bodies and body parts, but amber is not mentioned. **L. 23:** A *factor* is a minor loan official; *Aleppo* (Syria) is one of the oldest, continuously inhabited commercial cities in the world. **Page 443, l. 9:** On April 21, 1857, Melville visited the *Cathedral at Strasbourg* and observed its clock, which at noon features a procession of animated figures (see also "The Bell-Tower"). **L. 33:** For *anatomies,* Melville originally wrote first "creatures" and then "corpses." **Page 444, l. 4:** Melville originally wrote "good clerk" for *famous scribe.* **Ll. 27–28:** Originally, Melville wrote "I must have wine" for *I pray thee, give me wine;* the revision enhances the speaker's archaic diction. **Page 445, l. 26:** *Michaelmas* (September 29) is the day for hiring servants and renewing leases. **L. 33:** *Bartholomew Fair* was held annually at St. Bartholomew's church in London until 1855.

PART EIGHT. BILLY BUDD

Billy Budd exists as a manuscript of over 350 leaves, and since Melville did not publish the work in his lifetime, nor complete a final draft, print versions have varied considerably. Raymond Weaver was the first to transcribe the manuscript in his 1924 Constable edition. F. Barron Freeman's more scholarly 1948 Harvard University Press edition included Melville's manuscript revisions but proved textually problematic. Harrison Hayford and Merton M. Sealts, Jr.'s 1962 University of Chicago Press edition demonstrated the novella's genesis from a modest prose & poem piece featuring the poem "Billy in the Darbies" (see Introduction). Their text, reprinted here, has become the most widely adopted version of Melville's manuscript. (A slightly modified version of the Hayford-Sealts text prepared for the NN edition is forthcoming.)

Page 449, dedication: Melville met *John J. Chase* on the U.S. frigate *United States* on his return home from the Pacific and included him as a central figure in *White-Jacket.* **Page 450, l. 11:** One of Melville's favorite images of democratic cosmopolitanism is of the Prussian *Jean-Baptiste Clootz,* who led a deputation of men of all nationalities to address the National Assembly during the French Revolution. He took the name *Anacharsis* from the wise Scythian who came to Solon's Athens in sixth century B.C. **L. 30:** *Bucephalus* is the conqueror Alexander's horse. **L. 31:** The constellation *Taurus* is the bull, and red Aldebaran is its main star. **Page 451, l. 2:** *"Baby" Budd* may be a concealed reference to Melville's suicide son, Malcolm (see "The Chipmunk," Part Ten). **Page 453, l. 34:** A *portmanteau* is a utilitarian travel trunk with drawers. Melville's arrangement of words slyly defines "man" as a fusion of beauty (*Apollo*) and practicality. **Page 455, l. 22:** Melville's association of Billy's youthful beauty with the *rose* continues to the scene of his hanging when he ascends to meet "the full rose of the dawn" (p. 514). **Page 456, l. 8:** Melville viewed the *Farnese Hercules* alongside a grouping of sculpted bulls in Naples on February 21, 1857, and commented on its "gravely benevolent face." He later elaborated on the "bovine good nature" and ox-like self-confident strength of the sculpture in "Statues in Rome." **L. 30:** A *by-blow* is an illegitimate child. **L. 33:** In speaking to his disciples on their future life, Jesus advised, "be ye therefore *wise as serpents,* and harmless as doves" (Matthew 10:16). **Page 457, l. 28:** A teenage youth who emerged from the woods near Nuremberg in 1829, *Caspar Hauser* had no recollection of his past or identity. **L. 36:** In *Hawthorne's* "The Birthmark," a scientist attempts to remove a hand-like mark from his wife's cheek, but kills her in the process. **Pages 458, l. 2:** Billy's *vocal de-*

fect recalls the "deaf and dumb" lover in "Fragments from a Writing Desk, No. 2." **Page 459, l. 8:** British dramatist *Charles Dibdin* (1745–1814) was also noted for his nautical songs. **Page 460, l. 31:** The Union ironclad *Monitor* symbolizes modern mechanized warfare in "A Utilitarian View of the Monitor's Fight" and here stands as a contrast to the more human but no less tragic dimension of war in "the time before steamships." **Page 461, l. 18:** *Jeremy Bentham* (1748–1832) based his political philosophy on the pragmatic principle of "utility." In questioning whether Nelson's heroic self-endangerment was practical, Melville necessarily calls Vere into question as well. **Page 464, l. 12:** Melville annotated his 1857 edition of the *Poetical Works of Andrew Marvell* (1621–78) just as he was preparing his never published 1860 volume of poems. **Page 465, l. 9:** Melville's description of the "unconventional" sixteenth-century French essayist *Michel de Montaigne* as being "free from cant" resonates with a prose note on Shakespeare Melville composed on a single manuscript leaf: "Shakespeare was so phenomenal a modern that not yet have we come up to him—utterly without secular hypocrisy superstition or secular cant." **Page 466, ll. 28–29:** *Titus Oates* (1649–1705) contrived the Popish Plot of 1678 alleging that traitors were planning to assassinate Charles II and put the Catholic James on the throne. **Page 467, l. 13:** A *chevalier* is a confidence man. **Page 474, l. 12:** In the popular gothic novels of *Ann Radcliffe* (1764–1823), apparently supernatural events always prove to be explicable, but the mystery of Claggart's hatred has no easy "Radcliffean" explanation. **Page 476, l. 21:** The phrase the *mystery of iniquity,* repeated later by Vere, is from Paul's second letter to the Thessalonians 2:7. **Page 477, l. 7:** *Chang and Eng* were the original Siamese (or conjoined) twins displayed by P. T. Barnum in the mid-nineteenth century. **Page 479, l. 13:** The *Pharisees* were a sect of Hebrews paying strict adherence to laws, and came to be equated with self-righteous hypocrisy. *Guy Fawkes* conspired in the Gunpowder Plot (1605) to blow up Parliament. Melville's point is that Claggart's depravity leads him to self-delusions which lead to self-destruction. **Page 485, ll. 4–6:** *Hyperion* is Apollo the sun god. The *man of sorrows* is Christ. **L. 14:** The *Guise* were an aristocratic sixteenth-century French family noted for their intrigues against the Huguenots. **Page 495, l. 24:** In Acts 4:1–5, Peter catches *Ananias* trying to withhold a portion of his offering to God, and Ananias immediately "gives up the ghost." **Page 498, l. 3:** *Peter the Barbarian* is Czar Peter the Great, founder of St. Petersburg. **Page 515, l. 12:** Hayford and Sealts cite Sutton's attribution of Schopenhauer to Melville's nonstandard use of *euthanasia.* Here, the word suggests a self-willed self-annihilation like the annulment of self Melville mentions in his poem "Buddha." **Page 518, l. 1:** The *Directory* was the French Revolutionary government of 1795–99 (supplanted by Napoleon's Consulate), which, in this case, gave secular names to ships of the monarchy. **Page 521, l. 32:** Melville's final image of *oozy weeds* is taken from Jonah 2:5: "The depth closed me round about, the weeds were wrapped about my head."

The Ur–Billy Budd. Evidence of Melville's initial prose & poem piece, or "Ur–*Billy Budd*," is located on four discarded manuscript leaves. They were preserved because Melville used the backs of those sheets to compose part of his sketch "Daniel Orme." In creating the text for the "Ur–*Billy Budd*," the present editor prepared a transcription based on a direct inspection of the manuscript leaves and edited the transcription to represent Melville's final revision stage for each leaf. The edited transcription is accompanied by revision narratives that explain selected revisions on each manuscript leaf.

PART NINE. *FROM* TIMOLEON, ETC.

Timoleon and Other Ventures in Minor Verse, or *Timoleon, Etc.,* was published on May 15, 1891, four months before Melville's death. The Caxton Press printed only twenty-five copies, and it does not seem to have been reviewed. The volume is dedicated to artist Elihu Vedder, whom Melville had never met but whose paintings he admired (see "Formerly a Slave" in Part Five). *Timoleon* begins with two major works, the title poem and "After the Pleasure Party," with ancient and modern settings respectively, but political and sexual themes that transcend both cultures. The remaining "minor verse" ranges from epigrams and sonnet-like poems dealing with art to various travel pieces entitled "Fruit of Travel of Long Ago," which draw upon Melville's 1857 tour of the Mediterranean. Two sets of manuscripts survive; one in Melville's hand and a second fair copy in Elizabeth Shaw Melville's hand, both with revisions by Melville. The selections reprinted here are from the forthcoming NN edition of the *Published Poems.*

After the Pleasure Party. The poem weaves several voices: "Amor [i.e. Cupid] Threatening" of the opening italicized stanza, the poet who sets the scene and responds to Urania's condition, and Urania herself (in quotation). *Urania* (l. 105), an astronomer—her *reaching ranging tube* (l. 42) is her telescope—takes her name from the muse of Astronomy but also the Uranian Aphrodite, or goddess of heavenly (i.e., Platonic) love. Plato's discourse on love in the *Symposium* (alluded to in ll. 84–94) is based on the creation myth in which human souls are originally attached in pairs (of all sexual combinations) but then cataclysmically separated at birth so that the split halves spend their earthly lives hoping to match up again with their former soul mates. Uranian love (in the form of "Greek love" or boy-love) was also invoked by British homosexual poets of the 1880s (Smith). However, Melville's Urania has been spurned by a male friend for a younger female "ninny" (l. 76); Urania's distress is that her envy shall distract her from a higher love. According to Howard, Urania is based on Maria Mitchell, the Nantucket astronomer whom Melville met in 1852, but her plight might also reflect upon his own marriage to Elizabeth Shaw Melville, a fine life-companion, perhaps, but not a soul mate. However, Melville's Rose Poems (Part Ten), dedicated to Elizabeth, suggest otherwise. The NN text restores quotation marks which Melville included in manuscript but deleted in print. **L. 23:** *Vesta* is the Roman goddess of the hearth; *Sappho* is the seventh-century Greek poet who, legend has it, was spurned in love and threw herself off a cliff. **L. 67:** In Boccaccio's *Decameron* (ca. 1350) several Florentines gathering in the countryside to escape the plague tell each other a hundred tales. **L. 83:** *Pan* is the god of shepherds but also a symbol of pastoral sensuality. The death of Pan is supposed to have coincided with the birth of Christ. **L. 91:** Melville repeats the phrase *meet and mate* in "Art." **L. 115:** On his visit to the *Villa Albani* in Rome on February 28, 1857, Melville may have seen that museum's statue of Athena (the *arm'd Virgin* of l. 132) but his journal entry focuses on the bas-relief of the beautiful young man Antinous ("head like moss-rose with curls & buds"). **L. 118:** In his "Imitation of Christ" the mystic, Augustinian monk *Thomas à Kempis* (1380–1471) writes of the soul's progression to a universalized state of Christian perfection.

Magian Wine. A Magi is a prophet or seer; however, Melville originally entitled the poem "Magic wine" and featured "Merlin" in line 1, not *Miriam,* the sister of Moses. *Elysium* is a land of peace for virtuous souls in Greek mythology.

The Garden of Metrodorus. Metrodorus was a Greek skeptic and friend of Epicurus.

In a Garret. As with "Pebbles" in *John Marr,* the epigram crystallizes a moment in the creative process. The last two lines first appeared as one of two epigrams in Version 1 of "Art" (see Versions of "Art"). Melville visited the ornate cathedral of *St. Sophia* in Constantinople on December 13, 1856.

Monody. Originally a solo choral song in Greek performances, a *monody* is a dirge in stanzas of equal length. Since Mumford, Melville's poem has been read as a lament for Hawthorne, who died in 1864; however, Hayford finds no convincing evidence for this, aside from the image of the "cloistral vine" which evokes the shy Hawthornesque "Vine" in *Clarel.* The manuscript reveals that the poem's second stanza, which resonates with "The Chipmunk," began as a yellow-paper poem (see Introduction and Part Four). Melville scissored away the original opening lines and clipped the remaining yellow-paper stanza onto the present opening stanza, composed on different paper. Like Emerson's "Threnody," the poem may be about the death of a son, in this case Melville's Malcolm.

C———'s Lament. Manuscript inscriptions indicate that "C" stands for British romantic *Samuel Taylor Coleridge* (1772–1834).

Shelley's Vision. St. Stephen, the first Christian martyr, was stoned to death.
The Age of the Antonines. Melville sent a copy of this poem in a March 31, 1877, letter to his brother-in-law John Hoadley. Edward Gibbon, whose *Decline and Fall of the Roman Empire* Melville cites in the letter, praised the reign of the two second-century A.D. Antonines, Hadrian and Marcus Aurelius, for their integrity and wise administration. By 1877, Melville was in his tenth year as a customs inspector working, with integrity, for one of the nation's most corrupt government offices.
In a Bye-Canal. Melville visited Venice on April 1–6, 1857, and commented on the beauty of the women he encountered while taking moonlit walks along the Grand Canal: "The clear rich, golden brown [complexion]. The clear cut features, like a cameo.—The vision from the window at end of long, narrow passage." L. 6: Heber's wife, *Jael,* killed the escaping Sisera by letting him sleep in her tent and driving a tent nail through his temples (Judges 4:17–22). L. 14: The *basilisk,* or cockatrice, is a legendary reptile whose look and breath can kill.
Milan Cathedral. Melville visited Milan cathedral on April 7, 1857, and marveled at its "wonderful grandure" and "groups of angels on points of pinnacles & everywhere."
The Parthenon. Melville toured Athens February 7–10, 1857. In each of the four vignettes Melville brings us closer to the temple, and further back in time. In II Melville notes the optical effect of straight lines achieved through subtle bulgings in each column, and in III he describes the sculpted horses which once decorated the *frieze,* or triangular area above the columns. The sculptures themselves (the so-called Elgin Marbles) had already been shipped to England, and Melville may have viewed them on his November 1849 trip to London. L. 7: *Lais* was a kept woman of high rank. L. 14: Seventeenth-century Jewish philosopher *Spinoza* saw all matter as finite extensions of an infinite spirit. Ll. 29–30: *Ictinus* is the reputed architect of the Parthenon, commissioned by *Pericles* during the Golden Age of Athens in fifth century B.C. *Aspasia* was Pericles's mistress.
Off Cape Colonna. The temple of Poseidon at Sunium, on the eastern tip of the Attic peninsula, overlooks Cape Colonna. *William Falconer* (l. 9) was shipwrecked there and based his famous poem, *The Shipwreck* (1762), on the experience.
Syra. Melville visited Syra, the main port of the Cyclades, an archipelago encircling the island of Delos in the Aegean, three times and was fascinated by the "decayed picturesque" of its colorfully costumed people. L. 1: In 1821 Greeks escaped to Syra from the Turkish massacres of *Scio* and Mytelene (NN *Journal,* p. 71). L. 37: *Anacreon* was a sixth-century B.C. poet of love and wine. Ll. 37–39: On Christmas 1856 Melville noted that the old men of Syra looked like *Pericles* and likened the bustling port scene to a London *opera.* L. 53: Pluto absconded to

Hades with *Proserpine* (Persephone), daughter of Demeter, but allowed her to return in spring and summer each year. The irony is that in Syra's lively community this symbol of fertility is co-opted for coinage.

The Great Pyramid. Melville toured the Pyramids in January 1857: "It was in these pyramids that was conceived the idea of Jehovah. Terrible mixture of the cunning and awful."

PART TEN. *FROM* WEEDS AND WILDINGS, CHIEFLY: WITH A ROSE OR TWO
The manuscript of *Weeds and Wildings* was among Melville's literary remains. Opening with a lengthy dedicatory reminiscence to "Winnefred" (his wife Elizabeth), it consists of a cycle of short poems in seasonal progression entitled "The Year" (generally set at Arrowhead), seven other pastoral poems entitled "This, That, and the Other," the central prose & poem piece "Rip Van Winkle's Lilac," and a two-part concluding section of Rose Poems entitled "A Rose or Two" with nine poems called "As They Fell" and two others, "The Rose Farmer" and "L'envoi." In the mid-1880s, Melville had conceived of a book of poems entitled "Meadows and Seas" consisting of most of these and the *John Marr* poems. Melville disassembled this omnibus to publish *John Marr* on its own in 1888, and in the remaining years of his life he reconfigured the remaining "Meadows" poems into *Weeds and Wildings,* relentlessly rearranging their order in various tables of contents. Like *Timoleon,* the manuscript has little to do with the sea; its deceptively light pastorals treat the problem of extracting "joyance" out of death, youth out of aging, and the picturesque out of decay. In their tight rhythms and restrained moments, each floral poem builds to the volume's final pieces—"Rip" and the Rose Poems—in which art and sexuality become a sensual paradise, and the artist (a gardener of lilacs and roses) outlives us all. The poems took Melville in new directions, beyond the classical restraint of Greek form in *Timoleon* to the sensuality of the Persian poets and medieval troubadours. The text printed here is from Robert C. Ryan's 1967 Northwestern University dissertation, and will appear in the forthcoming NN edition of *Billy Budd and Other Late Manuscripts.*

The Little Good Fellows. L. 6: In manuscript Melville revised "self-slayer sad" to the present "unfriended man." This may be a "toning down" of a reference to Melville's son Malcolm, who committed suicide in 1867 (Bryant, "Melville's Rose Poems"). The revision also brings the poem more closely in line with Melville's source, the dirge in John Webster's *The White Devil* (Act V, scene 4), which features "The friendlesse bodies of unburied men."

The Chipmunk. Ll. 15–16: Originally, Melville made no mention of *Baby,* simply writing "So crowing mirth," so that it is the Chipmunk that flits away. Later, he revised by adding "did Baby," thus creating a comparison between the chipmunk and "Baby." Melville's revision in line 21 of "the hearth" to "our hearth" makes the connection to Malcolm almost certain.

Rip Van Winkle's Lilac. Melville's appreciation for Washington Irving's geniality and picturesque vision was longstanding (Bryant, *Melville & Repose*). In a brief dedication "To a Happy Shade," Melville apologizes to Irving for "poaching" on his famous story about the idle Rip who sleeps through the American Revolution. According to Ryan, the prose note grew from a brief description of Rip and the Dame into the expanded sketch with the painter of the picturesque. The sketch supplies two self-portraits, Rip and the painter, who witness the same Lilac but never meet. The poem converts Irving's Rip into an artist-gardener who (like Melville) awaits a resurrection through the proliferation of his Lilac, a flowery emblem of his refusal to do anything "useful." **Page 558, l. 6:** Like Irving's Rip, Melville's Rip thinks he has slept only one night. **L. 16:** Unlike Irving's termagent Dame Van Winkle, Melville's *Dame* is a "winsome bride." **L. 25:** "In my Father's house are many mansions" (John 14:2). **Page 562, l. 21:** *Precisian* is a sixteenth-century term for Puritan, or strict follower of religious codes. **L. 36:** American-born British artist *Benjamin West* (1738–1820) was noted for his "ten-acre" canvases on Biblical topics. Ryan identifies the painting as "Death on a Pale Horse" (see Revelation 6:8). **Page 564, l. 33:** *Joseph Jefferson* (1809–1905) toured the nation playing the lead in Dion Boucicault's stage adaptation of "Rip Van Winkle." **L. 45:** Melville posted a motto by his desk: "Keep true to the dreams of your youth."

Amoroso. **L. 8:** *Arcturus* is the brightest star in the constellation Boötes, the plow-man. **L. 23:** Melville's original word "sparking" was revised to *wooing.*

The New Rosicrucians. The Rosicrucians are a mystic organization founded in 1614 that traces its roots to the legendary Christian Rosenkreuz of the fifteenth century. Their symbol is the cross entwined with a rose. Melville's "new" Rosi-crucians also recalls the Oriental mysticism of the Theosophist movement formed in 1875.

The Vial of Attar. The central image (line 7) is the lachrymatory used by ancient Romans to preserve the tears of the bereaved as a remembrance of the departed. The parallel modern practice of collecting attar (or the oil extracted from pressed rose petals), however, provides only temporary solace in the absence of the bloom itself. **L. 1:** *Lesbia* is the name that first-century B.C. poet Catullus gave to his lover (Clodia).

Rose Window. The preacher's sermon—from Song of Solomon 2:1, "I am the rose of Sharon, and the lily of the valleys"—no doubt interprets Solomon's sensual love poem into a Christian allegory; and, like the honey brew *metheglin* (l. 9), or mead, it puts the poet to sleep. **L. 12:** The *Angel with a Rose* recalls the angel bearing a pot of roses in "Under the Rose" (Part Seven). Finkelstein connects both to Islamic traditions. **L. 23:** *Iris* is the goddess of the rainbow, and *Aurora* of the dawn.

The Devotion of the Flowers. Melville's annotations of Thomas Warton's *History of English Poetry* suggest that he may have patterned the fictional monk, Clement Drouon, on French Protestant poet Clément Marot (1496–1544), who was criticized for his playful translation of the Psalms. **L. 26:** For *Shushan,* see note on "Prodigal" (l. 228) in *Clarel.* **L. 33:** An *amice* is a scarf-like religious vestment.

BIBLIOGRAPHY

EDITIONS

Bryant, John. *Melville Unfolding: Typee and the Fluid Text, with a Transcription of the Typee Manuscript*. Ann Arbor: University of Michigan Press.

Cohen, Hennig, ed. *Selected Poems of Herman Melville*. New York: Anchor Books, 1964; Carbondale: Southern Illinois University Press, 1964.

———, ed. *The Battle-Pieces of Herman Melville*. New York: Thomas Yoseloff, 1964.

Hayford, Harrison, Hershel Parker, and G. Thomas Tanselle, eds. *The Writings of Herman Melville*. 16 Vols. Evanston and Chicago: Northwestern University Press and The Newberry Library, 1968–.

Clarel: A Poem and Pilgrimage in the Holy Land (with notes by Walter E. Bezanson), 1991.

Correspondence (ed. Lynn Horth), 1993.

Journals (ed. Howard C. Horsford, and Lynn Horth), 1989.

The Piazza Tales and Other Prose Pieces, 1839–1860 (with notes by Merton M. Sealts, Jr. and Alma MacDougall), 1987.

Hayford, Harrison, and Merton M. Sealts, Jr., eds. *Billy Budd, Sailor: An Inside Narrative By Herman Melville*. Chicago: University of Chicago Press, 1962.

Leyda, Jay. *The Portable Melville*. New York: Viking Press, 1952.

Matthiessen, F. O., ed. *Herman Melville: Selected Poems*. Norfolk, Conn.: New Directions, 1944.

Robillard, Douglas, ed. *The Poems of Herman Melville*. Kent, Ohio: Kent State University Press, 2000.

Ryan, Robert C. " 'Weeds and Wildings Chiefly: With a Rose or Two,' by Herman Melville; Reading Text and Genetic Text, Edited from the Manuscripts, with Introductions and Notes." Ph.D. Dissertation, Northwestern University, 1967. (Mel. Diss., #167.)

Sandberg, Robert Allen. "Melville's Unfinished 'Burgundy Club' Book: A Reading Edition Edited from the Manuscripts with Introduction and Notes." Ph.D. Dissertation. Northwestern University, 1989.

Sealts, Merton M., Jr. *Melville as Lecturer.* Cambridge, Mass.: Harvard University Press, 1957.

Thorp, Willard. *Herman Melville: Representative Selections.* New York: American Book Company, 1938.

Tilton, Eleanor M. "Melville's 'Rammon': A Text and Commentary." *Harvard Library Bulletin* 13 (Winter 1959): 50–91.

Vincent, Howard P., ed. *Collected Poems of Herman Melville.* Chicago: Hendricks House, 1947.

Warren, Robert Penn. *Selected Poems of Herman Melville.* New York: Random House, 1970.

BIBLIOGRAPHY AND GUIDES

Boswell, Jeanetta. *Herman Melville and the Critics: A Checklist of Criticism, 1900–1978.* Scarecrow Author Bibliographies 53. Metuchen, N.J.: Scarecrow Press, 1981.

Bryant, John, ed. *A Companion to Melville Studies.* Westport, Conn.: Greenwood Press, 1986.

Bryant, John. *Melville Dissertations, 1924–1980: An Annotated Bibliography and Subject Index.* Westport, Conn.: Greenwood Press, 1983.

Cowen, Wilson Walker. "Melville's Marginalia." Ph.D. Dissertation, Harvard University, 1965.

Higgins, Brian, and Hershel Parker, eds. *Herman Melville: The Contemporary Reviews.* New York: Cambridge University Press, 1995.

Higgins, Brian. *Herman Melville: An Annotated Bibliography, 1846–1930.* Boston: G.K. Hall, 1979.

———. *Herman Melville: A Reference Guide, 1931–1960.* Reference Guide to Literature. Boston: G. K. Hall, 1987.

Leyda, Jay. *The Melville Log.* 2 vols. New York: Harcourt, Brace, 1951, Rpt. with supplement: New York: Gordian Press, 1969.

Madison, Mary K. *Melville's Sources.* Evanston, Ill.: Northwestern University Press, 1987.

Melville Society. Melville Society Extracts (1969–). *Leviathan: A Journal of Melville Studies* (1999–).

Newman, Lea Bertani Vozar. *A Reader's Guide to the Short Stories of Herman Melville.* Boston: G. K. Hall, 1986.

Sealts, Merton M., Jr. *Melville's Reading.* Columbia: University of South Carolina Press, 1988.

BIOGRAPHICAL STUDIES

Arvin, Newton. *Herman Melville.* New York: William Sloan Associates, 1950.

Cohen, Hennig, and Donald Yannella. *Herman Melville's Malcolm Letter: "Man's Final Lore."* New York: Fordham University Press and The New York Public Library, 1991.

Garner, Stanton. *The Civil War World of Herman Melville.* Lawrence: University Press of Kansas, 1993.

Howard, Leon. *Herman Melville: A Biography.* Berkeley: University of California Press, 1951.

Kring, Walter D., and Jonathan S. Carey. "Two Discoveries Concerning Herman Melville." *Proceedings of the Massachusetts Historical Society* 87 (1975): 137–41.

Metcalf, Eleanor Melville. *Herman Melville: Cycle and Epicycle.* Cambridge, Mass.: Harvard University Press, 1953.

Miller, Edwin Haviland. *Herman Melville: A Biography.* New York: Braziller, 1975.

Mumford, Lewis. *Herman Melville.* New York: Harcourt, Brace, 1929.

Parker, Hershel. *Herman Melville: A Biography.* Baltimore: Johns Hopkins University Press, 1996.

Robertson-Lorant, Laurie. *Melville: A Biography.* New York: Clarkson Potter Publishers, 1996.

Sealts, Merton M., Jr. *The Early Lives of Melville: Nineteenth-Century Biographical Sketches and Their Authors.* Madison: University of Wisconsin Press, 1974.

Weaver, Raymond M. *Herman Melville: Mariner and Mystic.* New York: George H. Doran, 1921.

CRITICISM

Adler, Joyce Sparer. *War in Melville's Imagination.* New York: New York University Press, 1981.

Anderson, Charles R. *Melville in the South Seas.* New York: Columbia University, 1939.

Bergmann, Johannes Dietrich. " 'Bartleby' and The Lawyer's Story." *American Literature* 47 (November 1975): 432–36.

Berthoff, Warner. *The Example of Melville.* Princeton, N.J.: Princeton University Press, 1962.

Berthold, Dennis. "Melville, Garibaldi, and the Medusa of Revolution," *American Literary History* 9.3 (Fall 1997): 425–59.

———. "Class Acts: The Astor Place Riots and Melville's 'The Two Temples,' " *American Literature* 71 (September 1999): 429–61.

Bickley, R. Bruce, Jr. *The Method of Melville's Short Fiction.* Durham, N.C.: Duke University Press, 1975.

Bryant, John. *Melville and Repose: The Rhetoric of Humor in the American Renaissance.* New York: Oxford, 1993.

——. "Melville's Rose Poems: As They Fell," *Arizona Quarterly* 52.4 (Winter 1996): 49–84.

——. "Toning Down the Green: Melville's Picturesque." In Sten, *Savage Eye,* pp. 145–61.

Bryant, John, and Robert Milder, eds. *Melville's Evermoving Dawn: Centennial Essays.* Kent, Ohio: Kent State University Press, 1997.

Buell, Lawrence. "Melville the Poet." In Levine, *Cambridge Companion,* pp. 135–56.

Charvat, William. "Melville and the Common Reader." In *The Profession of Authorship in America,* ed. Matthew Bruccoli. (Columbus: Ohio State University Press, 1968), pp. 262–82.

Coffler, Gail. "Classical Iconography in the Aesthetics of *Billy Budd, Sailor,*" in Sten, *Savage Eye,* pp. 257–76.

Delbanco, Andrew. "Melville's Sacramental Style." *Raritan* 12 (1993): 69–91.

Dillingham, William B. *Melville's Short Fiction 1853–1856.* Athens: University of Georgia Press, 1977.

Eby, E. H. "Herman Melville's 'Tartarus of Maids.'" *Modern Language Quarterly* 1 (March 1940): 95–100.

Finkelstein, Dorothee Metlitsky. *Melville's Orienda.* New Haven, Conn.: Yale University Press, 1961.

Fisher, Marvin. *Going Under: Melville's Short Fiction and the American 1850s.* Baton Rouge: Louisiana State University Press, 1977.

Franklin, H. Bruce. "The Island Worlds of Darwin and Melville." *The Centennial Review* 11 (Summer 1967): 353–70.

——. "Slavery and Empire: Melville's 'Benito Cereno,'" In Bryant and Miller, *Melville's Evermoving Dawn,* pp. 147–61.

Hayford, Harrison. "The Significance of Melville's 'Agatha' Letters." *ELH: A Journal of English Literary History* 13 (December 1946): 299–310.

——. "Melville's 'Monody': For Hawthorne?" In NN *Clarel,* pp. 883–93.

Inge, M. Thomas, ed. *Bartleby the Inscrutable: A Collection of Commentary on Herman Melville's Tale "Bartleby the Scrivener."* Hamden, Conn.: Archon Books, 1979.

Karcher, Carolyn L. *Shadow Over the Promised Land: Slavery, Race and Violence in Melville's America.* Baton Rouge: Louisiana State University Press, 1980.

Kelley, Wyn. "Melville and John Vanderlyn: Ruin and Historical Fate from 'Bartleby' to *Israel Potter.*" In Sten, *Savage Eye,* pp. 117–26.

Levine, Robert S. *A Cambridge Companion to Herman Melville.* New York: Cambridge University Press, 1998.

Martin, Robert K. *Hero, Captain, and Stranger: Male Friendship, Social Critique and Literary Form in the Sea Novels of Herman Melville.* Chapel Hill: University of North Carolina Press, 1986.

Marx, Leo. "Melville's Parable of the Walls." *Sewanee Review* 61 (Autumn 1953): 602–27.

Milder, Robert. "In Behalf of 'Dearth.' " *Leviathan: A Journal of Melville Studies* 1.2 (October 1999): 63–69.

———. "The Rhetoric of Melville's *Battle-Pieces,*" *Nineteenth-Century Literature* 44 (1989): 173–200.

Miller, James E., Jr. *A Reader's Guide to Herman Melville.* New York: Farrar, Straus, 1962.

Monteiro, George. *The Presence of Camões: Influences on the Literature of England, American and South Africa.* Lexington: University Press of Kentucky, 1996.

Morsberger, Robert E. "Melville's 'The Bell-Tower' and Benvenuto Cellini." *American Literature* (November, 1972): 459–62.

Moss, Sidney P. " 'Cock-A-Doodle-Doo!' and Some Legends in Melville Scholarship." *American Literature* (May 1968): 192–210.

Parker, Hershel. *Reading Billy Budd.* Evanston, Ill.: Northwestern University Press, 1990.

———. "Dead Letters and Melville's Bartleby." *Resources for American Literary Study* 4 (1974): 90–99.

———. "Herman Melville's *The Isle of the Cross:* A Survey and Chronology." *American Literature* 62 (March 1990): 1–16.

———. "The Lost Poems (1860) and Melville's First Urge to Write an Epic Poem." In Bryant and Miller, *Melville's Evermoving Dawn,* pp. 260–75.

Post-Lauria, Sheila. *Correspondent Colorings: Melville in the Marketplace.* Amherst: University of Massachusetts Press, 1996.

Robert K. Wallace, "Melville's Prints: The E. Barton Chapin, Jr., Family Collection." *Leviathan: A Journal of Melville Studies* 2.1 (March 2000): 5–66.

Rogin, Michael Paul. *Subversive Genealogy: The Politics and Art of Herman Melville.* New York: Alfred A. Knopf, 1983.

Ryan, Robert C. "Melville Revises 'Art.' " In Bryant and Miller, *Melville's Evermoving Dawn,* pp. 307–320.

Sealts, Merton M., Jr. "Herman Melville's 'I and My Chimney,' " in his *Pursuing Melville,* pp. 11–22.

———. "Melville and Emerson's Rainbow," in his *Pursuing Melville,* pp. 250–77.

———. "Melville's Burgundy Club Sketches," in his *Pursuing Melville,* pp. 78–90.

———. *Pursuing Melville, 1940–1980.* Madison: University of Wisconsin, 1982.

Shurr, William H. *The Mystery of Iniquity: Melville as Poet, 1857–1891.* Lexington: University Press of Kentucky, 1972.

Smith, Timothy d'Arch. *Love in Earnest.* London: Routledge & Kegan Paul, 1970.

Stafford, William T. *Melville's Billy Budd and the Critics.* San Francisco: Wadsworth, 1961.

Stein, William Bysshe. *The Poetry of Melville's Later Years: Time, History, Myth, and Religion.* Albany: State University of New York Press, 1970.

Sten, Christopher, ed. *Savage Eye: Melville and the Visual Arts.* Kent, Ohio: Kent State University Press, 1991.

Sutton, Walter. "Melville and the Great God Budd," *Prairie Schooner* 34 (Summer 1960): 128–33.

Sweeney, Gerard M. "Melville's Hawthornian Bell-Tower: A Fairy-Tale Source." *American Literature* 45 (May 1973): 279–85.

INDEX OF POETRY TITLES

Index of Poetry First Lines

ABOUT THE EDITOR

JOHN BRYANT is a professor of English at Hofstra University. One of the foremost Melville scholars in the United States, he is editor of *Leviathan: A Journal of Melville Studies,* and has been editor of the Melville Society, one of the oldest and largest single-author societies in America, since 1990. Bryant's many books include *Melville and Repose* (1993), *Melville's Evermoving Dawn* (with Robert Milder, 1997), *A Companion to Melville Studies* (1986), and two forthcoming works, *The Fluid Text* and *Melville Unfolding.* He is also editor of the Penguin American Classics edition of *Typee,* and the forthcoming Modern Library Paperback Classics edition of *The Confidence-Man.*

A Note on the Type

The principal text of this Modern Library edition was set in a digitized
version of Janson, a typeface that dates from about 1690 and was cut by
Nicholas Kis, a Hungarian working in Amsterdam. The original matrices
have survived and are held by the Stempel foundry in Germany. Hermann
Zapf redesigned some of the weights and sizes for Stempel, basing his
revisions on the original design.